# DEAN KOONTZ

## THREE COMPLETE NOVELS

*Also by Dean Koontz*

DRAGON TEARS

HIDEAWAY

COLD FIRE

THE BAD PLACE

MIDNIGHT

WATCHERS

STRANGERS

TWILIGHT EYES

DARKFALL

PHANTOMS

WHISPERS

THE MASK

NIGHT CHILLS

SHATTERED

THE VOICE OF THE NIGHT

THE SERVANTS OF TWILIGHT

THE HOUSE OF THUNDER

SHADOWFIRES

# DEAN KOONTZ

## THREE COMPLETE NOVELS

◆◆◆

### LIGHTNING
### THE FACE OF FEAR
### THE VISION

G. P. PUTNAM'S SONS    NEW YORK

G. P. Putnam's Sons
*Publishers Since 1838*
200 Madison Avenue
New York, NY 10016

Library of Congress Cataloging-in-Publication Data

Koontz, Dean R. (Dean Ray), date.
[Novels.   Selections]
Three complete novels / Dean Koontz.
p.   cm.
Contents: Lightning—The face of fear—The vision.
ISBN 0-399-13843-9
I. Title.
PS3561.O55A6   1993          92-35322 CIP
813'.54—dc20

*Printed in the United States of America*
2   3   4   5   6   7   8   9   10

# CONTENTS

# LIGHTNING

◆ ◆ ◆

*To Greg and Joan Benford.*
*Sometimes I think that you're*
*the most interesting people*
*we know. Then I always take*
*two aspirin and lie down.*
*But the thought persists.*

*The wailing of the newborn infant*
*is mingled with the dirge for the dead.*

—LUCRETIUS


*I'm not afraid to die.*
*I just don't want to be there when it happens.*

—WOODY ALLEN


*Roller coaster:*
*1) a small gravity railroad . . . with steep inclines*
*that produce sudden, speedy plunges*
*for thrill-seeking passengers.*

—THE RANDOM HOUSE DICTIONARY

# PART ONE

# LAURA

◆ ◆ ◆

*Being deeply loved by someone*
*gives you strength;*
*while loving someone deeply*
*gives you courage.*
—LAO-TZU

# 1
### ◆ ◆ ◆
# A Candle in the Wind

## ONE

A storm struck on the night Laura Shane was born, and there was a strangeness about the weather that people would remember for years.

Wednesday, January 12, 1955, was frigid, gray, and somber. At twilight thick, fluffy snowflakes spiraled out of the low sky, and the people of Denver huddled in expectation of a Rocky Mountain blizzard. By ten o'clock that night, a bitterly cold gale blew in from the west, howling out of the mountain passes and shrieking down those rugged, wooded slopes. The snowflakes grew smaller, until they were as fine as sand, and they sounded as abrasive as sand, too, when the wind blew them across the windows of Dr. Paul Markwell's book-lined study.

Markwell slumped in the chair behind his desk, drinking Scotch to keep warm. The persistent chill that troubled him was not caused by a winter draft but by an internal frigidity of the mind and heart.

In the four years since his only child, Lenny, had died of polio, Markwell's drinking had gotten steadily worse. Now, though on call for emergencies at County Medical, he picked up the bottle and poured more Chivas Regal.

In the enlightened year of 1955, children were being inoculated with Dr. Jonas Salk's vaccine, and the day was near when no child would be paralyzed or die from poliomyelitis. But Lenny had been afflicted in 1951, a year before Salk tested the vaccine. The boy's respiratory muscles had been paralyzed, too, and the case had been complicated by bronchopneumonia. Lenny never had a chance.

From the mountains to the west, a low rumble echoed across the winter night, but at first Markwell thought nothing of it. He was so involved with his own enduring, bile-black grief that sometimes he was only subliminally aware of events that transpired around him.

A photograph of Lenny stood on his desk. Even after four years he was tortured by his son's smiling face. He should have put the photo away but instead left it in view because unceasing self-flagellation was his method of attempting to atone for his guilt.

None of Paul Markwell's colleagues was aware of his drinking problem. He never appeared to be drunk. The errors he made in the treatment of some patients had resulted in complications that might have arisen naturally and were not attributed to malpractice. But *he* knew that he had blundered, and self-loathing only induced him to drink more.

The rumbling came again. This time he recognized the thunder, but he still did not wonder about it.

The phone rang. The Scotch had left him numb and slow to react, so he did not pick up the receiver until the third ring. "Hello?"

"Dr. Markwell? Henry Yamatta." Yamatta, an intern at County Medical, sounded nervous. "One of your patients, Janet Shane, was just brought in by her husband. She's in labor. Fact is, they were delayed by the storm, so she was well along when they got here."

Markwell drank Scotch while he listened. Then, pleased to hear that his voice was not slurred, he asked, "She still in first stage?"

"Yes, but her labor pains are intense and unusually protracted for this point in the process. There's blood-tinged vaginal mucus—"

"That's to be expected."

Impatiently Yamatta said, "No, no. This isn't ordinary show."

*Show*, or blood-tainted vaginal mucus, was a reliable sign that labor was impending. However Yamatta had said Mrs. Shane was already well into labor. Markwell had blundered by suggesting that the intern was reporting ordinary show.

Yamatta said, "Not enough blood for hemorrhage, but something's wrong. Uterine inertia, obstruction of the pelvis, systemic disease—"

"I'd have noticed any physiological irregularity that would've made pregnancy dangerous," Markwell said sharply. But he knew that he might *not* have noticed . . . if he had been drunk. "Dr. Carlson's on duty tonight. If something goes wrong before I get there, he—"

"We've just had four accident victims brought in, two in bad shape. Carlson's hands are full. We need you, Dr. Markwell."

"I'm on my way. Twenty minutes."

Markwell hung up, finished his Scotch, and took a peppermint lozenge from his pocket. Since becoming a heavy drinker, he always carried mints. As he unwrapped the lozenge and popped it into his mouth, he left the study and went along the hall to the foyer closet.

He was drunk, and he was going to deliver a baby, and maybe he was going to botch it, which would mean the end of his career, the destruction of his reputation, but he did not care. In fact he anticipated that catastrophe with a perverse longing.

He was pulling on his overcoat when a peal of thunder rocked the night. The house reverberated with it.

He frowned and looked at the window beside the front door. Fine, dry snow swirled against the glass, briefly hung suspended as the wind held its breath, then swirled again. On a couple of other occasions over the years, he had heard thunder in a snowstorm, though always at the beginning, always soft and far away, nothing as menacing as this.

Lightning flashed, then again. Falling snow flickered queerly in the inconstant light, and the window was briefly transformed into a mirror in which Markwell saw his own haunted face. The subsequent crash of thunder was the loudest yet.

He opened the door and peered curiously at the turbulent night. The hard-driving wind hurled snow under the porch roof, drifting it against the front wall of the house. A fresh, two- or three-inch white mantle covered the lawn, and the windward boughs of the pine trees were flocked as well.

Lightning flared bright enough to sting Markwell's eyes. The thunderclap was so tremendous that it seemed to come not only from the sky but from the ground, too, as if heaven and earth were splitting open, announcing Armageddon. Two extended, overlapping, brilliant bolts seared the darkness. On all sides eerie silhouettes leaped, writhed, throbbed. The shadows of porch railings, balusters, trees, barren shrubs, and streetlamps were so weirdly distorted by every flash that Markwell's familiar world acquired the characteristics of a surrealistic painting: the unearthly light illuminated common objects in such a way as to give them mutant forms, altering them disturbingly.

Disoriented by the blazing sky, thunder, wind, and billowing white curtains of the storm, Markwell abruptly *felt* drunk for the first time that night. He wondered how much of the bizarre electrical phenomenon was real and how much was alcohol-induced hallucination. He edged cautiously across the slippery porch to the head of the steps that led to the snow-covered front walk, and he leaned against a porch post, craning his head out to look up at the light-shattered heavens.

A chain of thunderbolts made the front lawn and street appear to jump repeatedly as if that scene were a length of motion picture film stuttering in a jammed projector. All color was burned out of the night, leaving only the dazzling white of the lightning, the starless sky, the sparkling white of snow, and ink-black shuddering shadows.

As he stared in awe and fear at the freakish celestial display, another jagged crack opened in the heavens. The earth-seeking tip of the hot bolt touched an iron streetlamp only sixty feet away, and Markwell cried out in fear. At the moment of contact the night became incandescent, and the glass panes in the lamp exploded. The clap of thunder vibrated in Markwell's teeth; the porch floor rattled. The cold air instantly reeked of ozone and hot iron.

Silence, stillness, and darkness returned.

Markwell had swallowed the peppermint.

Astonished neighbors appeared on their porches along the street. Or perhaps they were present throughout the tumult, and perhaps he saw them only when the comparative calm of an ordinary blizzard was restored. A few trudged through the snow to have a closer look at the stricken streetlamp, the iron crown of which appeared half melted. They called to one another and to Markwell, but he did not respond.

He had not been sobered by the terrifying exhibition. Afraid that neighbors would detect his drunkenness, he turned away from the porch steps and went into the house.

Besides, he had no time to chat about the weather. He had a pregnant woman to treat, a baby to deliver.

Striving to regain control of himself, he took a wool scarf from the foyer closet, wound it around his neck, and crossed the ends over his chest. His hands were trembling, and his fingers were slightly stiff, but he managed to button his overcoat. Fighting dizziness, he pulled on a pair of galoshes.

He was gripped by the conviction that the incongruous lightning had some special meaning for him. A sign, an omen. Nonsense. Just the whiskey confusing him. Yet the feeling remained as he went into the garage, put up the door, and backed the car into the driveway, the chain-wrapped winter tires crunching and clinking softly in the snow.

As he shifted the car into park, intending to get out and close the garage, someone rapped hard on the window beside him. Startled, Markwell turned his head and saw a man bending down and peering at him through the glass.

The stranger was approximately thirty-five. His features were bold, well-formed. Even through the partly fogged window he was a striking man. He was wearing a navy peacoat with the collar turned up. In the arctic air his nostrils smoked, and when he spoke, the words were dressed in pale puffs of breath. ''Dr. Markwell?''

Markwell rolled down the window. "Yes?"

"Dr. Paul Markwell?"

"Yes, yes. Didn't I just say so? But I've no office hours here tonight, and I'm on my way to see a patient at the hospital."

The stranger had unusually blue eyes that conjured in Markwell the image of a clear winter sky reflected in the millimeter-thin ice of a just-freezing pond. They were arresting, quite beautiful, but he knew at once that they were also the eyes of a dangerous man.

Before Markwell could throw the car into gear and reverse toward the street where help might be found, the man in the peacoat thrust a pistol through the open window. "Don't do anything stupid."

When the muzzle pressed into the tender flesh under his chin, the physician realized with some surprise that he did not want to die. He had long nursed the idea that he was ready to embrace death. Yet now, instead of welcoming the realization of his will to live, he was guilt-stricken. To embrace life seemed a betrayal of the son with whom he could be joined only in death.

"Kill the headlights, Doctor. Good. Now switch off the engine."

Markwell withdrew the key from the ignition. "Who are you?"

"That's not important."

"It is to me. What do you want? What're you going to do to me?"

"Cooperate, and you won't be hurt. But try to get away, and I'll blow your damn head off, then empty the gun into your dead body just for the hell of it." His voice was soft, inaptly pleasant, but full of conviction. "Give me the keys."

Markwell passed them through the open window.

"Now come out of there."

Slowly sobering, Markwell got out of the car. The vicious wind bit his face. He had to squint to keep the fine snow out of his eyes.

"Before you close the door, roll up the window." The stranger crowded him, allowing no avenue of escape. "Okay, very good. Now, Doctor, walk with me to the garage."

"This is crazy. What—"

"*Move.*"

The stranger stayed at Markwell's side, holding him by the left arm. If someone was watching from a neighboring house or from the street, the gloom and falling snow would conceal the gun.

In the garage, at the stranger's direction, Markwell pulled the big door shut. The cold, unoiled hinges squealed.

"If you want money—"

"Shut up and get in the house."

"Listen, a patient of mine is in labor at the county—"

"If you don't shut up, I'll use the butt of this pistol to smash every tooth in your head, and you won't be *able* to talk."

Markwell believed him. Six feet tall, about a hundred and eighty pounds, the man was Markwell's size but was intimidating. His blond hair was frosted with melting snow, and as the droplets trickled down his brow and temples, he appeared to be as devoid of humanity as an ice statue at a winter carnival. Markwell had no doubt that in a physical confrontation the stranger in the peacoat would win handily against most adversaries, especially against one middle-aged, out-of-shape, drunken physician.

Bob Shane felt claustrophobic in the cramped maternity-ward lounge provided for expectant fathers. The room had a low acoustic-tile ceiling, drab green walls, and a single window rimed with frost. The air was too warm. The six chairs and two end tables were too much furniture for the narrow space. He had an urge to push through the double swinging doors into the corridor, race to the other end of the hospital, cross the main public lounge, and break out into the cold night, where there was no stink of antiseptics or illness.

He remained in the maternity lounge, however, to be near to Janet if she needed him. Something was wrong. Labor was supposed to be painful but not as agonizing as the brutal, extended contractions that Janet had endured for so long. The physicians would not admit that serious complications had arisen, but their concern was apparent.

Bob understood the source of his claustrophobia. He was not actually afraid that the walls were closing in. What was closing in was death, perhaps that of his wife or of his unborn child—or both.

The swinging doors opened inward, and Dr. Yamatta entered.

As he rose from his chair, Bob bumped the end table, scattering half a dozen magazines across the floor. "How is she, Doc?"

"No worse." Yamatta was a short, slender man with a kind face and large, sad eyes. "Dr. Markwell will be here shortly."

"You're not delaying her treatment until he arrives, are you?"

"No, no, of course not. She's getting good care. I just thought you'd be relieved to know that your own doctor is on his way."

"Oh. Well, yeah . . . thank you. Listen, can I see her, Doc?"

"Not yet," Yamatta said.

"When?"

"When she's . . . in less distress."

"What kind of answer's that? When will she *be* in less distress? When the hell will she come out of this?" He instantly regretted the outburst. "I . . . I'm sorry, Doc. It's just . . . I'm afraid."

"I know. I know."

\* \* \*

An inside door connected Markwell's garage to the house. They crossed the kitchen and followed the first-floor hallway, switching on lights as they went. Clumps of melting snow fell off their boots.

The gunman looked into the dining room, living room, study, medical office, and the patients' waiting room, then said, "Upstairs."

In the master bedroom the stranger snapped on one of the lamps. He moved a straight-backed, needlepoint chair away from the vanity and stood it in the middle of the room.

"Doctor, please take off your gloves, coat, and scarf."

Markwell obeyed, dropping the garments on the floor, and at the gunman's direction he sat in the chair.

The stranger put the pistol on the dresser and produced a coiled length of sturdy rope from one pocket. He reached beneath his coat and withdrew a short, wide-bladed knife that was evidently kept in a sheath attached to his belt. He cut the rope into pieces with which, no doubt, to bind Markwell to the chair.

The doctor stared at the pistol on the dresser, calculating his chances of reaching the weapon before the gunman could get it. Then he met the stranger's winter-blue eyes and realized that his scheming was as transparent to his adversary as a child's simple cunning was apparent to an adult.

The blond man smiled as if to say, Go ahead, go for it.

Paul Markwell wanted to live. He remained docile and compliant, as the intruder tied him, hand and foot, to the needlepoint chair.

Making the knots tight but not painfully so, the stranger seemed oddly concerned about his captive. "I don't want to have to gag you. You're drunk, and with a rag jammed in your mouth, you might vomit, choke to death. So to some extent I'm going to trust you. But if you cry out for help at any time, I'll kill you on the spot. Understand?"

"Yes."

When the gunman spoke more than a few words, he revealed a vague accent, so mild that Markwell could not place it. He clipped the ends of some words, and occasionally his pronunciation had a guttural note that was barely perceptible.

The stranger sat on the edge of the bed and put one hand on the telephone. "What's the number of the county hospital?"

Markwell blinked. "Why?"

"Damn it, I asked you the number. If you won't give it to me, I'd rather beat it out of you than look it up in the directory."

Chastened, Markwell gave him the number.

"Who's on duty there tonight?"

"Dr. Carlson. Herb Carlson."

"Is he a good man?"

"What do you mean?"

"Is he a better doctor than you—or is he a lush too?"

"I'm not a lush. I have—"

"You're an irresponsible, self-pitying, alcoholic wreck, and you know it. Answer my question, Doctor. Is Carlson reliable?"

Markwell's sudden nausea resulted only partly from overindulgence in Scotch; the other cause was revulsion at the truth of what the intruder had said. "Yeah, Herb Carlson's good. A very good doctor."

"Who's the supervising nurse tonight?"

Markwell had to ponder that for a moment. "Ella Hanlow, I think. I'm not sure. If it isn't Ella, it's Virginia Keene."

The stranger called the county hospital and said he was speaking on behalf of Dr. Paul Markwell. He asked for Ella Hanlow.

A blast of wind slammed into the house, rattling a loose window, whistling in the eaves, and Markwell was reminded of the storm. As he watched the fast-falling snow at the window, he felt another gust of disorientation blow through him. The night was so eventful—the lightning, the inexplicable intruder—that suddenly it did not seem real. He pulled at the ropes that bound him to the chair, certain that they were fragments of a whiskey dream and would dissolve like gossamer, but they held him fast, and the effort made him dizzy again.

At the phone the stranger said, "Nurse Hanlow? Dr. Markwell won't be able to come to the hospital tonight. One of his patients there, Janet Shane, is having a difficult labor. Hmmmm? Yes, of course. He wants Dr. Carlson to handle the delivery. No, no, I'm afraid he can't possibly make it. No, not the weather. He's drunk. That's right. He'd be a danger to the patient. No . . . he's so drunk, there's no point putting him on the line. Sorry. He's been drinking a lot lately, trying to cover it, but tonight he's worse than usual. Hmmmm? I'm a neighbor. Okay. Thank you, Nurse Hanlow. Goodbye."

Markwell was angry but also surprisingly relieved to have his secret revealed. "You bastard, you've ruined me."

"No, Doctor. You've ruined yourself. Self-hatred is destroying your career. And it drove your wife away from you. The marriage was already troubled, sure, but it might've been saved if Lenny had lived, and it might even have been saved after he died if you hadn't withdrawn into yourself so completely."

Markwell was astonished. "How the hell do you know what it was like with me and Anna? And how do you know about Lenny? I've never met you before. How can you know anything about me?"

Ignoring the questions, the stranger piled two pillows against the padded headboard of the bed. He swung his wet, dirty, booted feet onto the covers and stretched out. "No matter how you feel about it, losing your son wasn't your fault. You're just a physician, not a miracle worker. But losing Anna *was* your fault. And what you've become—an extreme danger to your patients—that's your fault too.''

Markwell started to object, then sighed and let his head drop forward until his chin was on his chest.

"You know what your trouble is, Doctor?"

"I suppose you'll tell me."

"Your trouble is you never had to struggle for anything, never knew adversity. Your father was well-to-do, so you got everything you wanted, went to the finest schools. And though you were successful in your practice, you never needed the money—you had your inheritance. So when Lenny got polio, you didn't know how to deal with adversity because you'd never had any practice. You hadn't been *inoculated,* so you had no resistance, and you got a bad case of despair.''

Lifting his head, blinking until his vision cleared, Markwell said, "I can't figure this."

"Through all this suffering, you've learned something, Markwell, and if you'll sober up long enough to think straight, you might get back on track. You've still got a slim chance to redeem yourself."

"Maybe I don't want to redeem myself."

"I'm afraid that could be true. I think you're scared to die, but I don't know if you have the guts to go on living."

The doctor's breath was sour with stale peppermint and whiskey. His mouth was dry, and his tongue swollen. He longed for a drink.

He halfheartedly tested the ropes that bound his hands to the chair. Finally, disgusted by the self-pitying whine in his own voice but unable to regain his dignity, he said, "What do you want from me?"

"I want to prevent you from going to the hospital tonight. I want to be damn sure you don't deliver Janet Shane's baby. You've become a butcher, a potential killer, and you have to be stopped this time."

Markwell licked his dry lips. "I still don't know who you are."

"And you never will, Doctor. You never will."

Bob Shane had never been so scared. He repressed his tears, for he had the superstitious feeling that revealing his fear so openly would tempt the fates and insure Janet's and the baby's deaths.

He leaned forward in the waiting-room chair, bowed his head, and prayed silently: Lord, Janet could've done better than me. She's so pretty, and I'm as homely as a rag rug. I'm just a grocer, and my corner store isn't ever going to turn big profits, but she loves me. Lord, she's good, honest, humble . . . she doesn't deserve to die. Maybe You want to take her 'cause she's already good enough for heaven. But *I'm* not good enough yet, and I need her to help me be a better man.

One of the lounge doors opened.

Bob looked up.

Doctors Carlson and Yamatta entered in their hospital greens.

The sight of them frightened Bob, and he rose slowly from his chair.

Yamatta's eyes were sadder than ever.

Dr. Carlson was a tall, portly man who managed to look dignified even in his baggy hospital uniform. "Mr. Shane . . . I'm sorry. I'm so sorry, but your wife died in childbirth."

Bob stood rock-still, as if the dreadful news had transformed his flesh to stone. He heard only part of what Carlson said:

" . . . major uterine obstruction . . . one of those women not really designed to have children. She should never have gotten pregnant. I'm sorry . . . so sorry . . . everything we could . . . massive hemorrhaging . . . but the baby . . . "

The word "baby" broke Bob's paralysis. He took a halting step toward Carlson. "What did you say about the baby?"

"It's a girl," Carlson said. "A healthy little girl."

Bob had thought everything was lost. Now he stared at Carlson, cautiously hopeful that a part of Janet had not died and that he was not, after all, entirely alone in the world. "Really? A girl?"

"Yes," Carlson said. "She's an exceptionally beautiful baby. Born with a full head of dark brown hair."

Looking at Yamatta, Bob said, "My baby lived."

"Yes," Yamatta said. His poignant smile flickered briefly. "And you've got Dr. Carlson to thank. I'm afraid Mrs. Shane never had a chance. In less experienced hands the baby might've been lost too."

Bob turned to Carlson, still afraid to believe. "The . . . the baby lived, and that's something to be thankful for, anyway, isn't it?"

The physicians stood in awkward silence. Then Yamatta put one hand on Bob Shane's shoulder, perhaps sensing that the contact would comfort him.

Though Bob was five inches taller and forty pounds heavier than the diminutive doctor, he leaned against Yamatta. Overcome with grief he wept, and Yamatta held him.

The stranger stayed with Markwell for another hour, though he spoke no more and would respond to none of Markwell's questions. He lay on the bed, staring at the ceiling, so intent on his thoughts that he seldom moved.

As the doctor sobered, a throbbing headache began to torment him. As usual his hangover was an excuse for even greater self-pity than that which had driven him to drink.

Eventually the intruder looked at his wristwatch. "Eleven-thirty. I'll be going now." He got off the bed, came to the chair, and again drew the knife from beneath his coat.

Markwell tensed.

"I'm going to saw partway through your ropes, Doctor. If you struggle with them for half an hour or so, you'll be able to free yourself. Which gives me time enough to get out of here."

As the man stooped behind the chair and set to work, Markwell expected to feel the blade slip between his ribs.

But in less than a minute the stranger put the knife away and went to the bedroom door. "You do have a chance to redeem yourself, Doctor. I think you're too weak to do it, but I hope I'm wrong."

Then he walked out.

For ten minutes, as Markwell struggled to free himself, he heard occasional noises downstairs. Evidently the intruder was searching for valuables. Although he had seemed mysterious, perhaps he was nothing but a burglar with a singularly odd modus operandi.

Markwell finally broke loose at twenty-five past midnight. His wrists were severely abraded, bleeding.

Though he had not heard a sound from the first floor in half an hour, he took his pistol from the nightstand drawer and descended the stairs with caution. He went to his office in the professional wing, where he expected to find drugs missing from his medical supplies; neither of the two tall, white cabinets had been touched.

He hurried into his study, convinced that the flimsy wall safe had been opened. The safe was unbreached.

Baffled, turning to leave, he saw empty whiskey, gin, tequila, and vodka bottles piled in the bar sink. The intruder had paused only to locate the liquor supply and pour it down the drain.

A note was taped to the bar mirror. The intruder had printed his message in neat block letters:

IF YOU DON'T STOP DRINKING, IF YOU DON'T LEARN TO ACCEPT LENNY'S DEATH, YOU WILL PUT A GUN IN YOUR MOUTH AND BLOW YOUR BRAINS OUT WITHIN ONE YEAR. THIS IS NOT A PREDICTION. THIS IS A FACT.

Clutching the note and the gun, Markwell looked around the empty room, as if the stranger was still there, unseen, a ghost that could choose at will between visibility and invisibility. "Who are you?" he demanded. "Who the *hell* are you?"

Only the wind at the window answered him, and its mournful moan had no meaning that he could discern.

\* \* \*

At eleven o'clock the next morning, after an early meeting with the funeral director regarding Janet's body, Bob Shane returned to the county hospital to see his newborn daughter. After he donned a cotton gown, a cap, and a surgical mask, and after thoroughly scrubbing his hands under a nurse's direction, he was permitted into the nursery, where he gently lifted Laura from her cradle.

Nine other newborns shared the room. All of them were cute in one way or another, but Bob did not believe he was unduly prejudiced in his judgment that Laura Jean was the cutest of the crop. Although the popular image of an angel required blue eyes and blond hair, and though Laura had brown eyes and hair, she was nevertheless angelic in appearance. During the ten minutes that he held her, she did not cry; she blinked, squinted, rolled her eyes, yawned. She looked pensive, too, as if perhaps she knew that she was motherless and that she and her father had only each other in a cold, difficult world.

A viewing window, through which relatives could see the newborns, filled one wall. Five people were gathered at the glass. Four were smiling, pointing, and making funny faces to entertain the babies.

The fifth was a blond man wearing a navy peacoat and standing with his hands in his pockets. He did not smile or point or make faces. He was staring at Laura.

After a few minutes during which the stranger's gaze did not shift from the child, Bob became concerned. The guy was good looking and clean-cut, but there was a hardness in his face, too, and some quality that could not be put into words but that made Bob think this was a man who had seen and done terrible things.

He began to remember sensational tabloid stories of kidnappers, babies being sold on the black market. He told himself that he was paranoid, imagining a danger where none existed because, having lost Janet, he was now worried about losing his daughter as well. But the longer the blond man studied Laura, the more uneasy Bob became.

As if sensing that uneasiness, the man looked up. They stared at each other. The stranger's blue eyes were unusually bright, intense. Bob's fear deepened. He held his daughter closer, as if the stranger might smash through the nursery window to seize her. He considered calling one of the creche nurses and suggesting that she speak to the man, make inquiries about him.

Then the stranger smiled. His was a broad, warm, genuine smile that transformed his face. In an instant he no longer looked sinister but friendly. He winked at Bob and mouthed one word through the thick glass: "Beautiful."

Bob relaxed, smiled, realized his smile could not be seen behind his mask, and nodded a thank you.

The stranger looked once more at Laura, winked at Bob again, and walked away from the window.

Later, after Bob Shane had gone home for the day, a tall man in dark clothing approached the creche window. His name was Kokoschka. He studied the infants; then his field of vision shifted, and he became aware of his colorless reflection in the polished glass. He had a broad, flat face with sharp-edged features, lips so thin and hard that they seemed to be made of horn. A two-inch dueling scar marked his left cheek. His dark eyes had no depth, as if they were painted ceramic spheres, much like the cold eyes of a shark cruising in shadowy ocean trenches. He was amused to realize how starkly his face contrasted to the innocent visages of the cradled babies beyond the window; he smiled, a rare expression for him, which imparted no warmth to his face but actually made him appear more threatening.

He looked beyond his reflection again. He had no trouble finding Laura Shane among the swaddled infants, for the surname of each child was printed on a card and affixed to the back of his or her cradle.

Why is there such interest in you, Laura? he wondered. Why is your life so important? Why all this energy expended to see that you are brought safely into the world? Should I kill you now and put an end to the traitor's scheme?

He'd be able to murder her without compunction. He had killed children before, though none quite so young as this. No crime was too terrible if it furthered the cause to which he had devoted his life.

The babe was sleeping. Now and then her mouth worked, and her tiny face briefly wrinkled, as perhaps she dreamed of the womb with regret and longing.

At last he decided not to kill her. Not yet.

"I can always eliminate you later, little one," he murmured. "When I understand what part you play in the traitor's plans, *then* I can kill you."

Kokoschka walked away from the window. He knew he would not see the girl again for more than eight years.

# TWO

In southern California rain falls rarely in the spring, summer, and autumn. The true rainy season usually begins in December and ends in March. But on Saturday the second of April, 1963, the sky was overcast, and humidity was high. Holding open the front door of his

small, neighborhood grocery in Santa Ana, Bob Shane decided that
the prospects were good for one last big downpour of the season.

The ficus trees in the yard of the house across the street and the date
palm on the corner were motionless in the dead air and seemed to
droop as if with the weight of the oncoming storm.

By the cash register, the radio was turned low. The Beach Boys
were singing their new hit "Surfin' U.S.A." Considering the weather,
their tune was as appropriate as "White Christmas" sung in July.

Bob looked at his watch: three-fifteen.

There'll be rain by three-thirty, he thought, and a lot of it.

Business had been good during the morning, but the afternoon had
been slow. At the moment no shoppers were in the store.

The family-owned grocery faced new, deadly competition from con-
venience-store chains like 7-Eleven. He was planning to shift to a deli-
style operation, offering more fresh foods, but was delaying as long
as possible because a deli required considerably more work.

If the oncoming storm was bad he would have few customers the
rest of the day. He might close early and take Laura to a movie.

Turning from the door, he said, "Better get the boat, doll."

Laura was kneeling at the head of the first aisle, across from the
cash register, absorbed in her work. Bob had carried four cartons of
canned soup from the stockroom, then Laura had taken over. She was
only eight years old, but she was a reliable kid, and she liked to help
out around the store. After stamping the correct price on each of the
cans, she stacked them on the shelves, remembering to cycle the
merchandise, putting the new soup behind the old.

She looked up reluctantly. "Boat? What boat?"

"Upstairs in the apartment. The boat in the closet. From the look
of the sky, we're going to need it to get around later today."

"Silly," she said. "We don't have a boat in the closet."

He walked behind the checkout counter. "Nice little blue boat."

"Yeah? In a closet? Which closet?"

He began to clip packages of Slim Jims to the metal display rack
beside the snack pack crackers. "The library closet, of course."

"We don't have a library."

"We don't? Oh. Well, now that you mention it, the boat isn't in
the library. It's in the closet in the toad's room."

She giggled. "What toad?"

"Why, you mean to tell me that you don't know about the
toad?"

Grinning, she shook her head.

"As of today we are renting a room to a fine, upstanding toad from
England. A gentleman toad who's here on the queen's business."

Lightning flared and thunder rumbled through the April sky. On the radio, static crackled through The Cascades' "Rhythm of the Rain."

Laura paid no attention to the storm. She was not frightened of things that scared most kids. She was so self-confident and self-contained that sometimes she seemed to be an old lady masquerading as a child. "Why would the queen let a toad handle her business?"

"Toads are excellent businessmen," he said, opening one of the Slim Jims and taking a bite. Since Janet's death, since moving to California to start over, he had put on fifty pounds. He had never been a handsome man. Now at thirty-eight he was pleasantly round, with little chance of turning a woman's head. He was not a great success, either; no one got rich operating a corner grocery. But he didn't care. He had Laura, and he was a good father, and she loved him with all her heart, as he loved her, so what the rest of the world might think of him was of no consequence. "Yes, toads are excellent businessmen indeed. And this toad's family has served the crown for hundreds of years. In fact he's been knighted. Sir Thomas Toad."

Lightning crackled brighter than before. The thunder was louder as well.

Having finished stocking the soup shelves, Laura rose from her knees and wiped her hands on the white apron that she was wearing over T-shirt and jeans. She was lovely; with her thick, brown hair and large, brown eyes, she bore more than a passing resemblance to her mother. "And how much rent is Sir Thomas Toad paying?"

"Six pence a week."

"Is he in the room next to mine?"

"Yes, the room with the boat in the closet."

She giggled again. "Well, he better not snore."

"He said the same of you."

A battered, rusted Buick pulled up in front of the store, and as the driver's door opened, a third thunderbolt blasted a hole in the darkening sky. The day was filled with molten light that appeared to flow liquidly along the street outside, sprayed lavalike over the parked Buick and the passing cars. The accompanying thunder shook the building from roof to foundation, as though the stormy heavens were reflected in the land below, precipitating an earthquake.

"Wow!" Laura said, moving fearlessly toward the windows.

Though no rain had fallen yet, wind suddenly swept in from the west, harrying leaves and litter before it.

The man who got out of the decrepit, blue Buick was looking at the sky in astonishment.

Bolt after bolt of lightning pierced the clouds, seared the air, cast their blazing images in windows and automobile chrome, and with each flash came thunder that struck the day with god-size fists.

The lightning spooked Bob. When he called to Laura—"Honey, get away from the windows"—she rushed behind the counter and let him put an arm around her, probably more for his comfort than hers.

The man from the Buick hurried into the store. Looking out at the fulminous sky, he said, "You see that, man? Whew!"

The thunder faded; silence returned.

Rain fell. Fat droplets at first struck the windows without much force then came in blinding torrents that blurred the world beyond the small shop.

The customer turned and smiled. "Some show, huh?"

Bob started to respond but fell silent when he took a closer look at the man, sensing trouble as a deer might sense a stalking wolf. The guy was wearing scuffed engineer boots, dirty jeans, and a stained windbreaker half zipped over a soiled white T-shirt. His windblown hair was oily, and his face was shaded with beard stubble. He had bloodshot, fevered eyes. A junkie. Approaching the counter, he drew a revolver from his windbreaker, and the gun was no surprise.

"Gimme what's in the register, asshole."

"Sure."

"Make it quick."

"Just take it easy."

The junkie licked his pale, cracked lips. "Don't hold out on me, asshole."

"Okay, okay, sure. You got it," Bob said, trying to push Laura behind him with one hand.

"Leave the girl so I can see her! I want to *see* her. Now, right now, get her the fuck out from behind you!"

"Okay, just cool off."

The guy was strung out as taut as a dead man's grin, and his entire body vibrated visibly. "Right where I can see her. And don't you reach for nothin' but the cash register, don't you go reachin' for no gun, or I'll blow your fuckin' head off."

"I don't have a gun," Bob assured him. He glanced at the rain-washed windows, hoping that no other customers would arrive while the holdup was in progress. The junkie seemed so unstable that he might shoot anyone who walked through the door.

Laura tried to ease behind her father, but the junkie said, "Hey, don't move!"

Bob said, "She's only eight—"

"She's a bitch, they're all fuckin' bitches no matter how big or little." His shrill voice cracked repeatedly. He sounded even more frightened than Bob was, which scared Bob more than anything else.

Though he was focused intently on the junkie and the revolver, Bob was also crazily aware that the radio was playing Skeeter Davis singing "The End of the World," which struck him as uncomfortably prophetic. With the excusable superstition of a man being held at gunpoint, he wished fervently that the song would conclude before it magically precipitated the end of his and Laura's world.

"Here's the money, here's all of it, take it."

Scooping the cash off the counter and stuffing it into a pocket of his dirty windbreaker, the man said, "You got a storeroom in back?"

"Why?"

With one arm the junkie angrily swept the Slim Jims, Life Savers, crackers, and chewing gum off the counter onto the floor. He thrust the gun at Bob. "You got a storeroom, asshole, I know you do. We're gonna go back there in the storeroom."

Bob's mouth was suddenly dry. "Listen, take the money and go. You got what you want. Just go. Please."

Grinning, more confident now that he had the money, emboldened by Bob's fear but still visibly trembling, the gunman said, "Don't worry, I ain't gonna kill no one. I'm a lover not a killer. All I want's a piece of that little bitch, and then I'm out of here."

Bob cursed himself for not having a gun. Laura was clinging to him, trusting in him, but he could do nothing to save her. On the way to the storeroom, he'd lunge at the junkie, try to grab the revolver. He was overweight, out of shape. Unable to move fast enough, he would be shot in the gut and left to die on the floor, while the filthy bastard took Laura into the back room and raped her.

"Move," the junkie said impatiently. "*Now!*"

A gun fired, Laura screamed, and Bob pulled her tight against him, sheltering her, but it was the junkie who had been shot. The bullet struck his left temple, blowing out part of his skull, and he went down hard atop the Slim Jims and crackers and chewing gum that he had knocked off the counter, dead so instantaneously that he did not even reflexively pull the trigger of his own revolver.

Stunned, Bob looked to his right and saw a tall, blond man with a pistol. Evidently he had entered the building through the rear service door and had crept silently through the storage room. Upon entering the grocery he had shot the junkie without warning. As he stared at the dead body, he looked cool, dispassionate, as if he were an experienced executioner.

"Thank God," Bob said, "police."

"I'm not the police." The man wore gray slacks, a white shirt, and a dark gray jacket under which a shoulder holster was visible.

Bob was confused, wondering if their rescuer was *another* thief about to take over where the junkie had been violently interrupted.

The stranger looked up from the corpse. His eyes were pure blue, intense, and direct.

Bob was sure that he had seen the guy before, but he could not remember where or when.

The stranger looked at Laura. "You all right, sweetheart?"

"Yes," she said, but she clung to her father.

The pungent odor of urine rose from the dead man, for he had lost control of his bladder at the moment of death.

The stranger crossed the room, stepping around the corpse, and engaged the dead-bolt lock on the front door. He pulled down the shade. He looked worriedly at the big display windows over which flowed a continuous film of rain, distorting the stormy afternoon beyond. "No way to cover those, I guess. We'll just have to hope nobody comes along and looks in."

"What're you going to do to us?" Bob asked.

"Me? Nothing. I'm not like that creep. I don't want anything from you. I just locked the door so we could work out the story you're going to have to tell the police. We have to get it straight before anyone walks in here and sees the body."

"Why do I need a story?"

Stooping beside the corpse, the stranger took a set of car keys and the wad of money from the pockets of the bloodstained windbreaker. Rising again, he said, "Okay, what you have to tell them is that there were *two* gunmen. This one wanted Laura, but the other was sickened by the idea of raping a little girl, and he just wanted to get out. So they argued, it got nasty, the other one shot this bastard and skipped with the money. Can you make that sound right?"

Bob was reluctant to believe that he and Laura had been spared. With one arm he held his daughter tightly against him. "I . . . I don't understand. You weren't really with him. You're not in trouble for killing him—after all, he was going to kill us. So why don't we just tell them the truth?"

Stepping to the end of the checkout counter, returning the money to Bob, the man said, "And what is the truth?"

"Well . . . you happened along and saw the robbery in progress—"

"I didn't just *happen* along, Bob. I've been watching over you and Laura." Slipping his pistol into his shoulder holster, the man looked down at Laura. She stared at him wide-eyed. He smiled and whispered, "Guardian angel."

Not believing in guardian angels, Bob said, "Watching over us? From where, how long, why?"

In a voice colored by urgency and by a vague, unplaceable accent that Bob heard for the first time, the stranger said, "Can't tell you that." He glanced at the rain-washed windows. "And I can't afford to be questioned by police. So you've got to get this story straight."

Bob said, "Where do I know you from?"

"You don't know me."

"But I'm sure I've seen you before."

"You haven't. You don't need to know. Now for God's sake, hide that money and leave the register empty; it'll seem odd if the second man left without what he came for. I'll take his Buick, abandon it in a few blocks, so you can give the cops a description of it. Give them a description of me, too. It won't matter."

Thunder rumbled outside, but it was low and distant, not like the explosions with which the storm had begun.

The humid air thickened as the slower-spreading, coppery scent of blood mixed with the stench of urine.

Queasy, leaning on the counter but still holding Laura at his side, Bob said, "Why can't I just tell them how you interrupted the robbery, shot the guy, and didn't want publicity, so you left?"

Impatient, the stranger raised his voice. "An armed man just happens to stroll by while the robbery's in progress and decides to be a hero? The cops won't believe a cockeyed story like that."

"That's what happened—"

"But they won't buy it! Listen, they'll start thinking maybe *you* shot the junkie. Since you don't own a gun, at least not according to public record, they'll wonder if maybe it was an illegal weapon and if you disposed of it after you shot this guy, then cooked up a crazy story about some Lone Ranger type walking in and saving your ass."

"I'm a respectable businessman with a good reputation."

In the stranger's eyes a peculiar sadness arose, a haunted look. "Bob, you're a nice man . . . but you're a little naive sometimes."

"What're you—"

The stranger held up a hand to silence him. "In a crunch a man's reputation never counts for as much as it ought to. Most people are good-hearted and willing to give a man the benefit of the doubt, but the poisonous few are eager to see others brought down, ruined." His voice had fallen to a whisper, and although he continued to look at Bob, he seemed to be seeing other places, other people. "Envy, Bob. Envy eats them alive. If you had money, they'd envy you that. But since you don't, they envy you for having such a good, bright, loving daughter. They envy you for just being a happy man. They envy you for *not* envying them. One of the greatest sorrows of human existence is that some people aren't happy merely to be alive but find their happiness only in the misery of others."

The charge of naiveté was one that Bob could not refute, and he knew the stranger spoke the truth. He shivered.

After a moment of silence, the man's haunted expression gave way to a look of urgency again. "And when the cops decide you're lying about the Lone Ranger who saved you, then they'll begin to wonder if maybe the junkie wasn't here to rob you at all, if maybe you knew him, had a falling out with him over something, even *planned* his murder and tried to make it look like a robbery. That's how cops think, Bob. Even if they can't pin this on you, they'll try so hard that they'll make a mess of your life. Do you want to put Laura through that?"

"No."

"Then do it my way."

Bob nodded. "I will. Your way. But who the hell are you?"

"That doesn't matter. We don't have time for it anyway." He stepped behind the counter and stooped in front of Laura, face to face with her. "Did you understand what I told your father? If the police ask you what happened—"

"You were with that man," she said, pointing in the general direction of the corpse.

"That's right."

"You were his friend," she said, "but then you started arguing about me, though I'm not sure why,'cause I didn't do anything—"

"It doesn't matter why, honey," the stranger said.

Laura nodded. "And the next thing you shot him and ran out with all our money and drove away, and I was very scared."

The man looked up at Bob. "Eight years old, huh?"

"She's a smart girl."

"But it'd still be best if the cops didn't question her much."

"I won't let them."

"If they do," Laura said, "I'll just cry and cry till they stop."

The stranger smiled. He stared at Laura so lovingly that he made Bob uneasy. His manner was not that of the pervert who had wanted to take her into the storeroom; his expression was tender, affectionate. He touched her cheek. Astonishingly, tears shimmered in his eyes. He blinked, stood. "Bob, put that money away. Remember, *I* left with it."

Bob realized the wad of cash was still in his hand. He jammed it into his pants pocket, and his loose apron concealed the bulge.

The stranger unlocked the door and put up the shade. "Take care of her, Bob. She's special." Then he dashed into the rain, letting the door stand open behind him, and got into the Buick. The tires squealed as he pulled out of the parking lot.

The radio was on, but Bob heard it for the first time since "The End of the World" had been playing, before the junkie had been shot. Now Shelley Fabares was singing "Johnny Angel."

Suddenly he heard the rain again, not just as a dull background hiss and patter but really *heard* it, beating furiously on the windows and on the roof of the apartment above. In spite of the wind rushing through the open door, the stink of blood and urine was abruptly far worse than it had been a moment ago, and just as precipitously, as if coming out of a trance of terror and regaining his full senses, he realized how close his precious Laura had come to dying. He scooped her into his arms, lifted her off the floor, and held her, repeating her name, smoothing her hair. He buried his face against her neck and smelled the sweet freshness of her skin, felt the pulse of the artery in her throat, and thanked God that she was alive.

"I love you, Laura."

"I love you, too, Daddy. I love you because of Sir Tommy Toad and a million other reasons. But we've got to call the police now."

"Yes, of course," he said, reluctantly putting her down.

His eyes were full of tears. He was so unnerved that he could not recall where the telephone was.

Laura had already taken the handset off the hook. She held it out to him. "Or I can call them, Daddy. The number's right here on the phone. Do you want me to call them?"

"No. I'll do it, baby." Blinking back tears, he took the phone from her and sat on the old wooden stool behind the cash register.

She put one hand on his arm, as if she knew he needed her touch.

Janet had been emotionally strong. But Laura's strength and self-possession were unusual for her age, and Bob Shane was not sure where they came from. Maybe being motherless made her self-reliant.

"Daddy?" Laura said, tapping the phone with one finger. "The police, remember?"

"Oh, yeah," he said. Trying not to gag on the odor of death that permeated the store, he dialed the police emergency number.

Kokoschka sat in a car across the street from Bob Shane's small grocery, thoughtfully fingering the scar on his cheek.

The rain had stopped. The police had gone. Neon shop signs and lampposts lit at nightfall, but the macadam streets glistened darkly in spite of that illumination, as if the pavement absorbed the light instead of reflecting it.

Kokoschka had arrived in the neighborhood simultaneously with Stefan, the blond and blue-eyed traitor. He had heard the shooting, had seen Stefan flee in the dead man's car, had joined the crowd of onlookers when the police arrived, and had learned most of the details of what had happened in the store.

He had, of course, seen through Bob Shane's preposterous story about Stefan having been merely a second thief. Stefan was not their assailant but their self-appointed guardian, and he had no doubt lied to cover his true identity.

Laura had been saved again.

But why?

Kokoschka tried to imagine what part the girl could possibly play in the traitor's plans, but he was stumped. He knew nothing would be gained by interrogating the girl, for she was too young to have been told anything useful. The reason for her rescue would be as much a mystery to her as it was to Kokoschka.

He was sure that her father knew nothing, either. The girl was obviously the one who interested Stefan, not the father, so Bob Shane would not have been made privy to Stefan's origins or intentions.

Finally Kokoschka drove several blocks to a restaurant, had dinner, then returned to the grocery well after nightfall. He parked on the side street, in the shadows under the expansive fronds of a date palm. The store was dark, but lights shone at the windows of the second-floor apartment.

From a deep pocket of his raincoat, he withdrew a revolver. It was a snub-nosed Colt Agent .38, compact but powerful. Kokoschka admired well-designed and well-made weapons, and he especially liked the feel of this gun in his hand: this was Death himself imprisoned in steel.

Kokoschka could cut the Shanes' phone wires, quietly force entry, kill the girl and her father, and slip away before police responded to the shots. He had a talent and affinity for that kind of work.

But if he killed them without knowing *why* he was killing them, without understanding what role they played in Stefan's schemes, he might later discover that eliminating them was a mistake. He had to know Stefan's purpose before acting.

Reluctantly he put the revolver in his pocket.

# THREE

In the windless night, rain fell straight down on the city, as if every droplet was enormously heavy. It drummed noisily on the roof and windshield of the small, black car.

At one o'clock in the morning on that Tuesday in late March, the rainswept streets, flooded at some intersections, were generally deserted but for military vehicles. Stefan chose an indirect route to the institute to avoid known inspection stations, but he was afraid of encountering an impromptu checkpoint. His papers were in order, and his security clearance exempted him from the new curfew. Nevertheless he preferred not to come under the scrutiny of military police. He could not afford to have the car searched, for the suitcase on the back seat contained copper wire, detonators, and plastic explosives not legally in his possession.

Because his breath fogged the windshield, because rain obscured the eerily dark city, because the car's wipers were worn, and because the hooded headlights illuminated a limited field of vision, he almost missed the narrow, cobblestone street that led behind the institute. He braked, turned the wheel sharply. The sedan took the corner with a shudder and a squeal of tires, sliding slightly on the slick cobbles.

He parked in darkness near the rear entrance, got out of the car, and took the suitcase from the back seat. The institute was a drab, four-story brick building with heavily barred windows. An air of menace hung about the place, though it did not look as if it harbored secrets that would radically change the world. The metal door had concealed hinges and was painted black. He pushed the button, heard the buzzer ring inside, and waited nervously for a response.

He was wearing rubber boots and a trenchcoat with the collar turned up, but he had neither a hat nor an umbrella. The cold rain pasted his hair to his skull and drizzled down the nape of his neck.

Shivering, he looked at a slit window that was set in the wall beside the door. It was six inches wide, a foot high, with glass that was mirrored from outside, transparent from inside.

He patiently listened to the rain beating on the car, splashing in puddles, and gurgling in a nearby downspout. With a cold sizzle it struck the leaves of plane trees at the curb.

A light came on above the door. It was in a cone-shaped shade, the yellow glow tightly contained and directed straight down on him.

Stefan smiled at the mirrored observation window, at the guard he could not see.

The light went out, the lock bolts clattered open, and the door swung inward. He knew the guard: Viktor something, a stout, fiftyish man with close-cropped gray hair and steel-rimmed spectacles, who was more pleasant-tempered than he looked and was in fact a mother hen who worried about the health of friends and acquaintances.

"Sir, what are you doing out at this hour, in this downpour?"

"Couldn't sleep."

"Dreadful weather. Come in, in! You'll catch cold for sure."

"Kept worrying about work I'd left undone, so I thought I might as well come in and *do* it."

"You'll work yourself into an early grave, sir. Truly you will."

As Stefan stepped into the antechamber and watched the guard close the door, he searched his memory for a scrap of knowledge about Viktor's personal life. "From the look of you, I guess your wife still makes those incredible noodle dishes you've told me about."

Turning from the door, Viktor laughed softly, patted his belly. "I swear, she's employed by the devil to lead me into sin, primarily gluttony. What's that, sir, a suitcase? Are you moving in?"

Wiping rain from his face with one hand, Stefan said, "Research data. Took it home weeks ago, been working on it evenings."

"Have you no private life at all?"

"I get twenty minutes for myself every second Thursday."

Viktor clucked his tongue disapprovingly. He stepped to the desk that occupied a third of the floor space in the small room, picked up the phone, and called the other night guard, who was stationed in a similar antechamber at the front entrance to the institute. When anyone was let in after hours, the admitting guard always alerted his colleague at the other end of the building, in part to avoid false alarms and perhaps the accidental shooting of an innocent visitor.

Dripping rain on the worn carpet runner, fishing a set of keys from his trenchcoat pocket, Stefan went to the inner door. Like the outer portal, it was made of steel with concealed hinges. However, it could be unlocked only with two keys turned in tandem—one belonging to an authorized employee, the other carried by the guard on duty. The work being conducted at the institute was so extraordinary and secret that even the night watchmen could not be trusted to have access to the labs and file rooms.

Viktor put down the phone. "How long are you staying, sir?"

"A couple of hours. Is anyone else working tonight?"

"No. You're the only martyr. And no one truly appreciates martyrs, sir. You'll work yourself to death, I swear, and for what? Who'll care?"

"Eliot wrote: 'Saints and martyrs rule from the tomb.' "

"Eliot? He a poet or something?"

"T. S. Eliot, a poet, yes."

" 'Saints and martyrs rule from the tomb'? I don't know about this fellow. Doesn't sound like an *approved* poet. Sounds subversive." Viktor laughed warmly, apparently amused by the ridiculous notion that his hard-working friend could be a traitor.

Together they opened the inner door.

Stefan lugged the suitcase of explosives into the institute's ground floor hallway, where he switched on the lights.

"If you're going to make a habit of working in the middle of the night," Viktor said, "I'll bring you one of my wife's cakes to give you energy."

"Thank you, Viktor, but I hope not to make a habit of this."

The guard closed the metal door. The lock bolt clanked shut automatically.

Alone in the hallway Stefan thought, not for the first time, that he was fortunate in his appearance: blond, strong-featured, blue-eyed. His looks partly explained why he could brazenly carry explosives into the institute without expecting to be searched. Nothing about him was dark, sly, or suspect; he was the ideal, angelic when he smiled, and his devotion to country would never be questioned by men like Viktor, men whose blind obedience to the state and whose beery, sentimental patriotism prevented them from thinking clearly about a lot of things. A lot of things.

He rode the elevator to the third floor and went directly to his office where he turned on a brass, gooseneck lamp. After removing his rubber boots and trenchcoat, he selected a manila folder from the file cabinet and arranged its contents across the desk to create a convincing impression that work was underway. In the unlikely event that another staff member decided to put in an appearance in the heart of the night, as much as possible must be done to allay suspicion.

Carrying the suitcase and a flashlight that he had taken from an inner pocket of his trenchcoat, he climbed the stairs past the fourth floor and ascended all the way to the attic. The flashlight revealed huge timbers from which a few misdriven nails bristled here and there. Though the attic had a rough wood floor, it was not used for storage and was empty of all but a film of gray dust and spiderwebs. The space under the highly pitched slate roof was sufficient to allow him to stand erect along the center of the building, though he would have to drop to his hands and knees when he worked closer to the eaves.

With the roof only inches away, the steady roar of the rain was as thunderous as the flight of an endless fleet of bombers crossing low overhead. That image came to mind perhaps because he believed that exactly such ruination would be the inevitable fate of his city.

He opened the suitcase. Working with the speed and confidence of a demolitions expert, he placed the bricks of plastic explosives and shaped each charge to direct the power of the explosion downward and inward. The blast must not merely blow the roof off but pulverize the middle floors and bring the heavy roof slates and timbers crashing down through the debris to cause further destruction. He secreted the plastique among the rafters and in the corners of the long room, even pried up a couple of floorboards and left explosives under them.

Outside, the storm briefly abated. But soon more ominous peals of thunder rolled across the night, and the rain returned, falling harder than before. The long-delayed wind arrived, too, keening along the gutters and moaning under the eaves; its strange, hollow voice seemed simultaneously to threaten and mourn the city.

Chilled by the unheated attic air, he conducted his delicate work with increasingly tremulous hands. Though shivering, he broke out in a sweat.

He inserted a detonator in every charge and strung wire from all the charges to the northwest corner of the attic. He braided them to a single copper line and dropped it down a ventilation chase that went all the way to the basement.

The charges and wire were as well concealed as possible and would not be spotted by someone who merely opened the attic door for a quick look. But on closer inspection or if the space was needed for storage, the wires and molded plastique surely would be noticed.

He needed twenty-four hours during which no one would go into the attic. That wasn't much to ask, considering that he was the only one who had visited the institute's garret in months.

Tomorrow night he would return with a second suitcase and plant charges in the basement. Crushing the building between simultaneous explosions above and below was the only way to be certain of reducing it—and its contents—to splinters, gravel, and twisted scraps. After the blast and accompanying fire, no files must remain to rekindle the dangerous research now conducted there.

The great quantity of explosives, although carefully placed and shaped, would damage structures on all sides of the institute, and he was afraid that other people, some of them no doubt innocent, would be killed in the blast. Those deaths could not be avoided. He dared not use less plastique, for if every file and every duplicate of every file throughout the institute were not utterly destroyed, the project might be quickly relaunched. And this was a project that must be brought to an end swiftly, for the hope of all mankind hinged on its destruction. If innocent people perished, he would just have to live with the guilt.

In two hours, at a few minutes past three o'clock, he finished his work in the attic.

He returned to his office on the third floor and sat for a while behind his desk. He did not want to leave until his sweat-soaked hair had dried and he had stopped trembling, for Viktor might notice.

He closed his eyes. In his mind he summoned Laura's face. He could always calm himself with thoughts of her. The mere fact of her existence brought him peace and greater courage.

# FOUR

Bob Shane's friends did not want Laura to attend her father's funeral. They believed that a twelve-year-old girl ought to be spared such a grim ordeal. She insisted, however, and when she wanted anything as badly as she wanted to say one last goodbye to her father, no one could thwart her.

That Thursday, July 24, 1967, was the worst day of her life, even more distressing than the preceding Tuesday when her father had died. Some of the anesthetizing shock had worn off, and Laura no longer felt numb; her emotions were closer to the surface and less easily controlled. She was beginning to realize fully how much she had lost.

She chose a dark blue dress because she did not own a black one. She wore black shoes and dark blue socks, and she worried about the socks because they made her feel childish, frivolous. Having never worn nylons, however, she didn't think it a good idea to don them for the first time at the funeral. She expected her father to look down from heaven during the service, and she intended to be just the way he remembered her. If he saw her in nylons, a changeling striving awkwardly to be grown up, he might be embarrassed for her.

At the funeral home she sat in the front row between Cora Lance, who owned a beauty shop half a block from Shane's Grocery, and Anita Passadopolis, who had done charity work with Bob at St. Andrew's Presbyterian Church. Both were in their late fifties, grandmotherly types who touched Laura reassuringly and watched her with concern.

They did not need to worry about her. She would not cry, become hysterical, or tear out her hair. She understood death. Everyone had to die. People died, dogs died, cats died, birds died, flowers died. Even the ancient redwood trees died sooner or later, though they lived twenty or thirty times longer than a person, which didn't seem right. On the other hand, living a thousand years as a tree would be a lot duller than living just forty-two years as a happy human being. Her father had been forty-two when his heart failed—bang, a sudden attack—which was too young. But that was the way of the world, and crying about it was pointless. Laura prided herself on her sensibleness.

Besides, death was not the end of a person. Death was actually only the beginning. Another and better life followed. She knew that must be true because her father had told her so, and her father never lied. Her father was the most truthful man, and kind, and sweet.

As the minister approached the lectern to the left of the casket, Cora Lance leaned close to Laura. "Are you okay, dear?"

"Yes. I'm fine," she said, but she did not look at Cora. She dared not meet anyone's eyes, so she studied inanimate things with great interest.

This was the first funeral home she had ever entered, and she did not like it. The burgundy carpet was ridiculously thick. The drapes and upholstered chairs were burgundy, too, with only minimal gold trim, and the lamps had burgundy shades, so all the rooms appeared to have been decorated by an obsessed interior designer with a burgundy fetish.

Fetish was a new word for her. She used it too much, just as she always overused a new word, but in this case it was appropriate.

Last month, when she'd first heard the lovely word "sequestered," meaning "secluded or isolated," she had used it at every opportunity, until her father had begun to tease her with silly variations: "Hey, how's my little sequestrian this morning?" he would say, or "Potato chips are a high turnover item, so we'll shift them into the first aisle, closer to the register,'cause the corner they're in now is sort of sequesteriacious." He enjoyed making her giggle, as with his tales of Sir Tommy Toad, a British amphibian he had invented when she was eight years old and whose comic biography he embellished nearly every day. In some ways her father had been more of a child than she was, and she had loved him for that.

Her lower lip trembled. She bit it. Hard. If she cried, she'd be doubting what her father had always told her about the next life, the better life. By crying she would be pronouncing him dead, dead for once and all, forever, *finito*.

She longed to be sequestered in her room above the grocery, in bed, the covers pulled over her head. That idea was so appealing, she figured she could easily develop a fetish for sequestering herself.

From the funeral home they went to the cemetery.

The graveyard had no headstones. The plots were marked by bronze plaques on marble bases set flush with the ground. The rolling green lawns, shaded by huge Indian laurels and smaller magnolias, might have been mistaken for a park, a place to play games and run and laugh—if not for the open grave over which Bob Shane's casket was suspended.

Last night she'd awakened twice to the sound of distant thunder, and though half asleep she had thought she'd seen lightning flickering at the windows, but if unseasonal storms had passed through during the darkness, there was no sign of them now. The day was blue, cloudless.

Laura stood between Cora and Anita, who touched her and murmured reassurances, but she was not comforted by anything they did or said. The bleak chill in her deepened with each word of the minister's final prayer, until she felt as if she were standing unclothed in an arctic winter instead of in the shade of a tree on a hot, windless July morning.

The funeral director activated the motorized sling on which the casket was suspended. Bob Shane's body was lowered into the earth.

Unable to watch the slow descent of the casket, having difficulty drawing breath, Laura turned away, slipped out from under the caring hands of her two honorary grandmothers, and took a few steps across the cemetery. She was as cold as marble; she needed to escape the shade. She stopped as soon as she reached sunlight, which felt warm on her skin but which failed to relieve her chills.

She stared down the long, gentle hill for perhaps a minute before she saw the man standing at the far end of the cemetery in shadows at the edge of a large grove of laurels. He was wearing light tan slacks and a white shirt that appeared faintly luminous in that gloom, as if he were a ghost who had forsaken his usual night haunts for daylight. He was watching her and the other mourners around Bob Shane's grave near the top of the slope. At that distance Laura could not see his face clearly, but she could discern that he was tall and strong and blond— and disturbingly familiar.

The observer intrigued her, though she did not know why. As if spellbound, she descended the hill, stepping between and across the graves. The nearer she drew to the blond, the more familiar he looked. At first he did not react to her approach, but she knew he was studying her intently; she could feel the weight of his gaze.

Cora and Anita called to her, but she ignored them. Seized by an inexplicable excitement, she walked faster, now only a hundred feet from the stranger.

The man retreated into the false twilight among the trees.

Afraid that he would slip away before she had gotten a good look at him—yet not certain why seeing him more clearly was so important—Laura ran. The soles of her new black shoes were slippery, and several times she nearly fell. At the place where he had been standing, the grass was trampled flat, so he was no ghost.

Laura saw a flicker of movement among the trees, the spectral white of his shirt. She hurried after him. Only sparse, pale grass grew under the laurels, beyond the reach of the sun. However, surface roots and treacherous shadows sprouted everywhere. She stumbled, grabbed the trunk of a tree to avoid a bad fall, regained her balance, looked up— and discovered that the man had vanished.

The grove was comprised of perhaps a hundred trees. The branches were densely interlaced, allowing sunlight through only in thin golden threads, as if the fabric of the sky had begun unraveling into the woods. She hurried forward, squinting at the darkness. Half a dozen times she thought she saw him, but it was always phantom movement, a trick of light or of her own mind. When a breeze sprang up, she was certain she heard his furtive footsteps in the masking rustle of the leaves, but when she pursued the crisp sound, its source eluded her.

After a couple of minutes she came out of the trees to a road that served another section of the sprawling cemetery. Cars were parked along the verge, sparkling in the brightness, and a hundred yards away was a group of mourners at another graveside service.

Laura stood at the edge of the lane, breathing hard, wondering where the man in the white shirt had gone and why she had been compelled to chase him.

The blazing sun, the cessation of the short-lived breeze, and the return of perfect silence to the cemetery made her uneasy. The sun seemed to pass through her as if she was transparent, and she was strangely light, almost weightless, and mildly dizzy too: She felt as if she were in a dream, floating an inch above an unreal landscape.

I'm going to pass out, she thought.

She put one hand against the front fender of a parked car and gritted her teeth, struggling to hold on to consciousness.

Though she was only twelve she did not often think or act like a child, and she never *felt* like a child—not until that moment in the cemetery when suddenly she felt very young, weak, and helpless.

A tan Ford came slowly along the road, slowing even further as it drew near her. Behind the wheel was the man in the white shirt.

The moment she saw him, she knew why he'd seemed familiar. Four years ago. The robbery. Her guardian angel. Although she had been just eight years old at the time, she would never forget his face.

He brought the Ford almost to a halt and drifted by her slowly, scrutinizing her as he passed. They were just a few feet apart.

Through the open window of his car, every detail of his handsome face was as clear as on that terrible day when she had first seen him in the store. His eyes were as brilliantly blue and riveting as she had remembered. When their gazes locked, she shuddered.

He said nothing, did not smile, but studied her intently, as if trying to fix every detail of her appearance in his mind. He stared at her the way a man might stare at a tall glass of cool water after crossing a desert. His silence and unwavering gaze frightened Laura but also filled her with an inexplicable sense of security.

The car was rolling past her. She shouted, "Wait!"

She pushed away from the car against which she had been leaning, dashed toward the tan Ford. The stranger accelerated and sped out of the graveyard, leaving her alone in the sun until a moment later she heard a man speak behind her, "Laura?"

When she turned she could not see him at first. He called her name again, softly, and she spotted him fifteen feet away at the edge of the trees, standing in the purple shadows under an Indian laurel. He wore black slacks, a black shirt, and seemed out of place in this summer day.

Curious, perplexed, wondering if somehow this man was connected with her guardian angel, Laura started forward. She closed to within two steps of the new stranger before she realized that the disharmony between him and the bright, warm summer day was not solely a result of his black clothing; wintry darkness was an integral part of the man himself; a coldness seemed to come from within him, as if he had been born to dwell in polar regions or in the high caves of ice-bound mountains.

She stopped less than five feet from him.

He said no more but stared at her intently, with a look that seemed as much puzzlement as anything.

She saw a scar on his left cheek.

"Why you?" the wintry man asked, and he took a step forward, reaching for her.

Laura stumbled backward, suddenly too scared to cry out.

From the middle of the copse of trees, Cora Lance called, "Laura? Are you all right, Laura?"

The stranger reacted to the nearness of Cora's voice, turned, and moved away through the laurels, his black-clad body disappearing quickly in the shadows, as if he had not been a real man at all but a bit of darkness briefly come to life.

Five days after the funeral, on Tuesday the twenty-ninth of July, Laura was back in her own room above the grocery store for the first time in a week. She was packing and saying goodbye to the place that had been home to her for as long as she could recall.

Pausing to rest, she sat on the edge of the rumpled bed, trying to remember how secure and happy she had been in that room only days ago. A hundred paperback books, mostly dog and horse stories, were shelved in one corner. Fifty miniature dogs and cats—glass, brass, porcelain, pewter—filled the shelves above the headboard of her bed.

She had no pets, for the health code prohibited animals in an apartment above a grocery. Some day she hoped to have a dog, perhaps even a horse. But more importantly she might be a veterinarian when she grew up, a healer of sick and injured animals.

Her father had said she could be anything: a vet, a lawyer, a movie star, anything. "You can be a moose herder if you want, or a ballerina on a pogo stick. Nothing can stop you."

Laura smiled, remembering how her father had imitated a ballerina on a pogo stick. But she also remembered he was gone, and a dreadful emptiness opened in her.

She cleaned out the closet, carefully folded her clothes, and filled two large suitcases. She had a steamer trunk as well, into which she packed her favorite books, a few games, a teddy bear.

Cora and Tom Lance were taking an inventory of the contents of the rest of the small apartment and of the grocery store downstairs. Laura was going to stay with them, though she was not yet clear as to whether the arrangement was permanent or temporary.

Made nervous and fretful by thoughts of her uncertain future, Laura returned to her packing. She pulled open the drawer in the nearest of the two nightstands and froze at the sight of the elfin boots, tiny umbrella, and four-inch-long neck scarf that her father had acquired as proof that Sir Tommy Toad indeed rented quarters from them.

He had persuaded one of his friends, a skilled leatherworker, to make the boots, which were wide and shaped to accommodate webbed feet. He had obtained the umbrella from a shop that sold miniatures, and he had made the green-plaid scarf himself, laboriously fashioning fringe for the ends of it. On her ninth birthday, when she came home from school, the boots and umbrella were standing against the wall just inside the apartment door, and the scrap of scarf was hung carefully on the coatrack. "Sssshh," her father whispered dramatically. "Sir Tommy has just returned from an arduous trip to Ecuador on the queen's business—she owns a diamond farm there, you know—and he's exhausted. I'm sure he'll sleep for *days*. However, he told me to wish you a very happy birthday, and he left a gift in the yard out back." The gift had been a new Schwinn bicycle.

Now, staring at the three items in the nightstand drawer, Laura realized that her father had not died alone. With him had gone Sir Tommy Toad, the many other characters he had created, and the silly but wonderful fantasies with which he'd entertained her. The webbed-foot boots, the tiny umbrella, and the little scarf looked so sweet and pathetic; she could almost believe that Sir Tommy, in fact, had been real and that he was now gone to a better world of his own. A low, miserable groan escaped her. She fell onto the bed and buried her face in the pillows, muffling her agonized sobs, and for the first time since her father's death she finally let her grief overwhelm her.

She did not want to live without him, yet she must not only live but prosper because every day of her life would be a testament to him.

Even as young as she was, she understood that by living well and being a good person, she would make it possible for her father to go on living in some small way through her.

But facing the future with optimism and finding happiness was going to be hard. She now knew that life was frighteningly subject to tragedy and change, blue and warm one moment, cold and stormy the next, so you never knew when a bolt of lightning might strike someone you cared about. Nothing lasts forever. Life is a candle in the wind. That was a hard lesson for a girl her age, and it made her feel old, very old, ancient.

When the flood of warm tears abated, she did not take long to collect herself, for she did not want the Lances to discover that she had been crying. If the world was hard and cruel and unpredictable, then it did not seem wise to show the slightest weakness.

She carefully wrapped the webbed-foot boots, umbrella, and little scarf in tissue paper. She tucked them away in the steamer trunk.

When she had disposed of the contents of both nightstands, she went to her desk to clean that out as well, and on the felt blotter she found a folded sheet of tablet paper with a message for her in clear, elegant, almost machine-neat handwriting.

*Dear Laura,*
*Some things are meant to be, and no one can prevent them. Not even your special guardian. Be content with the knowledge that your father loved you with all his heart in a way that few people are ever lucky enough to be loved. Though you think now that you will never be happy again, you are wrong. In time happiness will come to you. This is not an empty promise. This is a fact.*

The note was unsigned, but she knew who must have written it: the man who had been at the cemetery, who had studied her from the passing car, who years ago saved her and her father from being shot. No one else could call himself her special guardian. A tremor swept through her not because she was afraid but because the strangeness and the mystery of her guardian filled her with curiosity and wonder.

She hurried to the bedroom window and pushed aside the sheer curtain that hung between the drapes, certain that she would see him standing in the street, watching the store, but he was not there.

The man in dark clothing was not there, either, but she had not expected to see him. She had half convinced herself that the other stranger was unrelated to her guardian, that he had been in the cemetery for some other reason. He had known her name . . . but perhaps he had heard Cora calling her earlier, from the top of the graveyard hill. She was able to put him out of her mind because she did not *want* him to be part of her life, not as she so desperately wanted to have a special guardian.

She read the message again.

Although she did not understand who the blond man was or why he had taken an interest in her, Laura was reassured by the note he had left. Understanding wasn't always necessary, as long as you *believed*.

# FIVE

The following night, after he had planted explosives in the attic of the institute, Stefan returned with the same suitcase, claiming he had insomnia again. Anticipating the post-midnight visit, Viktor had brought half of one of his wife's cakes as a gift.

Stefan nibbled at the cake while he shaped and placed the plastic explosives. The enormous basement was divided into two rooms, and unlike the attic it was used daily by employees. He would have to conceal the charges and wires with considerable care.

The first chamber contained research files and a pair of long, oak worktables. The file cabinets were six feet tall and stood in banks along two of the walls. He was able to place the explosives atop the cabinets, tucking them toward the back, against the walls, where not even the tallest man on the staff could see them.

He strung the wires behind the cabinets, though he was forced to drill a small hole in the partition between halves of the cellar in order to continue that detonation line into the next chamber. He managed to put the hole in an inconspicuous place, and the wires were visible only for a couple of inches on either side of the partition.

The second room was used for storage of office and lab supplies and to cage the score of animals—several hamsters, a few white rats, two dogs, one energetic monkey in a big cage with three bars to swing on—that had participated in (and survived) the institute's early experiments. Though the animals were of no more use, they were kept in order to learn if over the long term they developed unforeseen medical problems that could be related to their singular adventures.

Stefan molded powerful charges of plastique into hollow spaces toward the back of the stacked supplies and brought all of the wires to the screened ventilation chase down which he had dropped the attic wires the previous night, and, as he worked, he felt the animals watching with unusual intensity, as if they knew they had less than twenty-four hours to live. His cheeks flushed with guilt, which strangely he had failed to feel when contemplating the deaths of the men who worked in the institute, perhaps because the animals were innocent and the men were not.

By four o'clock in the morning, Stefan had finished both the job in the basement and the work he had to do in his office on the third floor. Before leaving the institute, he went to the main lab on the ground floor and for a minute stared at the gate.

The gate.

The scores of dials and gauges and graphs in the gate's support machinery all glowed softly orange, yellow, or green, for the power to it was never turned off. The thing was cylindrical, twelve feet long and eight feet in diameter, barely visible in the dim light; its stainless-steel outer skin gleamed with faint reflections of the spots of light in the machinery that lined three of the room's walls.

He had used the gate scores of times, but he was still in awe of it— not so much because it was an astonishing scientific breakthrough but because its potential for evil was unlimited. It was not a gate to hell, but in the hands of the wrong men, it might as well have been just that. And it was indeed in the hands of the wrong men.

After thanking Viktor for the cake and claiming to have eaten all that he had been given—though in fact he fed the larger part of it to the animals—Stefan drove back to his apartment.

For the second night in a row, a storm raged. Rain slashed out of the northwest. Water foamed out of downspouts into nearby drains, drizzled off roofs, puddled in the streets, and overflowed gutters, and because the city was almost entirely dark, the pools and streams looked more like oil than water. Only a few military personnel were out, and they all wore dark slickers that made them look as if they were creatures from an old Gothic novel by Bram Stoker.

Stefan took a direct route home, making no effort to skirt the known police inspection stations. His papers were in order; his exemption from curfew was current; and he was no longer transporting illegally obtained explosives.

In his apartment he set the alarm on the large bedside clock and fell almost immediately to sleep. He desperately needed his rest because, in the afternoon to come, there would be two arduous journeys and much killing. If he was not fully alert, he might find himself on the wrong end of a bullet.

His dreams were of Laura, which he interpreted as a good omen.

# 2
### ◆◆◆
# The Enduring Flame

## ONE

Laura Shane was swept from her twelfth through her seventeenth years as if she were a tumbleweed blown across the California deserts, coming to rest briefly here and there in becalmed moments, torn loose and sent rolling again as soon as the wind gusted.

She had no relatives, and she could not stay with her father's best friends, the Lances. Tom was sixty-two, and Cora was fifty-seven, and though married thirty-five years, they had no children. The prospect of raising a young girl daunted them.

Laura understood and bore no grudge against them. On the day in August when she left the Lance house in the company of a woman from the Orange County Child Welfare Agency, Laura kissed both Cora and Tom and assured them that she would be fine. Riding away in the social worker's car, she waved gaily, hoping they felt absolved.

Absolved. That word was a recent acquisition. Absolved: freed from the consequences of one's actions; to set free or release from some duty, obligation, or responsibility. She wished that she could grant herself absolution from the obligation to make her way in the world without the guidance of a loving father, absolution from the responsibility to live and carry on his memory.

From the Lances' house she was conveyed to a child shelter—the McIlroy Home—an old, rambling, twenty-seven-room Victorian mansion built by a produce magnate in the days of Orange County's agricultural glory. Later it had been converted to a dormitory where children in public custody were housed temporarily between foster homes.

That institution was unlike any she had read about in fiction. For one thing, it lacked kindly nuns in flowing black habits.

And there was Willy Sheener.

Laura first noticed him shortly after arriving at the home, while a social worker, Mrs. Bowmaine, was showing her to the room she would share with—she had been told—the Ackerson twins and a girl named Tammy. Sheener was sweeping a tile-floored hallway with a pushbroom.

He was strong, wiry, pale, freckled, about thirty, with hair the color of a new copper penny and green eyes. He smiled and whistled softly while he worked. "How're you this morning, Mrs. Bowmaine?"

"Right as rain, Willy." She clearly liked Sheener. "This is Laura Shane, a new girl. Laura, this is Mr. Sheener."

Sheener stared at Laura with a creepy intensity. When he managed to speak, the words were thick, "Uhhh . . . welcome to McIlroy."

Following the social worker, Laura glanced back at Sheener. With no one but Laura to see, he lowered one hand to his crotch and lazily massaged himself.

Laura did not look at him again.

Later, as she was unpacking her meager belongings, trying to make her quarter of the third-floor bedroom more like home, she turned and saw Sheener in the doorway. She was alone, for the other kids were at play in the backyard or the game room. His smile was different from the one with which he'd favored Mrs. Bowmaine: predatory, cold. Light from one of the two small windows fell across the doorway and met his eyes at such an angle as to make them appear silver instead of green, like the cataract-filmed eyes of a dead man.

Laura tried to speak but could not. She edged backward until she came up against the wall beside her bed.

He stood with his arms at his sides, motionless, hands fisted.

The McIlroy Home was not air conditioned. The bedroom windows were open, but the place was tropically hot. Yet Laura had not been sweating until she turned and saw Sheener. Now her T-shirt was damp.

Outside, children at play shouted and laughed. They were nearby, but they sounded far away.

The hard, rhythmic rasp of Sheener's breathing seemed to grow louder, gradually drowning out the voices of the children.

For a long time neither of them moved or spoke. Then abruptly he turned and walked away.

Weak-kneed, sweat-soaked, Laura moved to her bed and sat on the edge of it. The mushy mattress sagged, and the springs creaked.

As her thudding heartbeat decelerated, she surveyed the gray-walled room and despaired of her circumstances. In the four corners were narrow, iron-framed beds with tattered chenille spreads and lumpy pillows. Each bed had a battered, Formica-topped nightstand, and on each was a metal reading lamp. The scarred dresser had eight drawers, two of which were hers. There were two closets, and she was allotted half of one. The ancient curtains were faded, stained; they hung limp and greasy from rust-spotted rods. The entire house was moldering and haunted; the air had a vaguely unpleasant odor; and Willy Sheener roamed the rooms and halls as if he were a malevolent spirit waiting for the full moon and the blood games attendant thereon.

That night after dinner the Ackerson twins closed the door to the room and encouraged Laura to join them on the threadbare maroon carpet where they could sit in a circle and share secrets.

Their other roomie—a strange, quiet, frail blonde named Tammy— had no interest in joining them. Propped up by pillows, she sat in bed and read a book, nibbling her nails continuously, mouselike.

Laura liked Thelma and Ruth Ackerson immediately. Having just turned twelve, they were only months younger than Laura and were wise for their age. They had been orphaned when they were nine and had lived at the shelter for almost three years. Finding adoptive parents for children their age was difficult, especially for twins who were determined not to be split up.

Not pretty girls, they were astonishingly identical in their plainness: lusterless brown hair, myopic brown eyes, broad faces, blunt chins, wide mouths. Although lacking in good looks, they were abundantly intelligent, energetic, and good-natured.

Ruth was wearing blue pajamas with dark green piping on the cuffs and collar, blue slippers; her hair was tied in a ponytail. Thelma wore raspberry-red pajamas and furry yellow slippers, each with two buttons painted to represent eyes, and her hair was unfettered.

With darkfall the insufferable heat of the day had passed. They were less than ten miles from the Pacific, so the night breezes made comfortable sleep possible. Now, with the windows open, currents of mild air stirred the aged curtains and circulated through the room.

"Summer's a bore here," Ruth told Laura as they sat in a circle on the floor. "We're not allowed off the property, and it's just not big enough. And in the summer all the do-gooders are busy with their own vacations, their own trips to the beach, so they forget about us."

"Christmas is great, though," Thelma said.

"All of November and December are great," Ruth said.

"Yeah," Thelma said. "Holidays are fine because the do-gooders start feeling guilty about having so much when we poor, drab, homeless waifs have to wear newspaper coats, cardboard shoes, and eat last year's gruel. So they send us baskets of goodies, take us on shopping sprees and to the movies, though never the *good* movies."

"Oh, I like some of them," Ruth said.

"The kind of movies where no one ever, ever gets blown up. And *never* any feelies. They'll never take us to a movie in which some guy puts his hand on a girl's boob. Family films. Dull, dull, dull."

"You'll have to forgive my sister," Ruth told Laura. "She thinks she's on the trembling edge of puberty—"

"I *am* on the trembling edge of puberty! I feel my sap rising!" Thelma said, thrusting one thin arm into the air above her head.

Ruth said, "The lack of parental guidance has taken a toll on her, I'm afraid. She hasn't adapted well to being an orphan."

"You'll have to forgive *my* sister," Thelma said. "She's decided to skip puberty and go directly from childhood to senility."

Laura said, "What about Willy Sheener?"

The Ackerson twins glanced knowingly at each other and spoke with such synchronization that not a fraction of a second was lost between their statements: "Oh, a disturbed man," Ruth said, and Thelma said, "He's scum," and Ruth said, "He needs therapy," and Thelma said, "No, what he needs is a hit over the head with a baseball bat maybe a dozen times, maybe two dozen, then locked away for the rest of his life."

Laura told them about encountering Sheener in her doorway.

"He didn't say anything?" Ruth asked. "That's creepy. Usually he says 'You're a very pretty little girl' or—"

"—he offers you candy." Thelma grimaced. "Can you *imagine?* Candy? How trite! It's as if he learned to be a scumbag by reading those booklets the police hand out to warn kids about perverts."

"No candy," Laura said, shivering as she remembered Sheener's sun-silvered eyes and heavy, rhythmic breathing.

Thelma leaned forward, lowering her voice to a stage whisper. "Sounds like the White Eel was tongue-tied, too hot even to *think* of his usual lines. Maybe he has a special lech for you, Laura."

"White Eel?"

"That's Sheener," Ruth said. "Or just the Eel for short."

"Pale and slick as he is," Thelma said, "the name fits. I'll bet the Eel has a special lech for you. I mean, kid, you *are* a knockout."

"Not me," Laura said.

"Are you kidding?" Ruth said. "That dark hair, those big eyes."

Laura blushed and started to protest, and Thelma said, "Listen, Shane, the Dazzling Ackerson Duo—Ruth and moi—cannot abide false modesty any more than we can tolerate bragging. We're straight-from-the-shoulder types. We know what *our* strengths are, and we're proud of them. God knows, neither of us will win the Miss America contest, but we're intelligent, very intelligent, and we're not reluctant to admit to brains. And *you* are gorgeous, so stop being coy."

"My sister is sometimes too blunt and too colorful in the way she expresses herself," Ruth said apologetically.

"And *my* sister," Thelma told Laura, "is trying out for the part of Melanie in *Gone With the Wind*." She put on a thick Southern accent and spoke with exaggerated sympathy: "Oh, Scarlett doesn't mean any harm. Scarlett's a lovely girl, really she is. Rhett is so lovely at heart, too, and even the Yankees are lovely, even those who sacked Tara, burned our crops, and made boots out of the skin of our babies."

Laura began to giggle halfway through Thelma's performance.

"So drop the modest maiden act, Shane! You're gorgeous."

"Okay, okay. I know I'm . . . pretty."

"Kiddo, when the White Eel saw you, a fuse blew in his brain."

"Yes," Ruth agreed, "you stunned him. That's why he couldn't even think to reach in his pocket for the candy he always carries."

"Candy!" Thelma said. "Little bags of M&Ms, Tootsie Rolls!"

"Laura, be real careful," Ruth warned. "He's a sick man—"

"He's a geek!" Thelma said. "A sewer rat!"

From the far corner of the room, Tammy said softly, "He's not as bad as you say."

The blond girl was so quiet, so thin and colorless, so adept at fading into the background that Laura had forgotten her. Now she saw that Tammy had put her book aside and was sitting up in bed; she had drawn her bony knees against her chest and wrapped her arms around her legs. She was ten, two years younger than her roommates, small for her age. In a white nightgown and socks Tammy looked more like an apparition than like a real person.

"He wouldn't hurt anyone," Tammy said hesitantly, tremulously, as though stating her opinion about Sheener—about anything, anyone—was like walking on a tightrope without a net.

"He *would* hurt someone if he could get away with it," Ruth said.

"He's just . . ." Tammy bit her lip. "He's . . . lonely."

"No, honey," Thelma said, "he's not lonely. He's so much in love with himself that he'll never be lonely."

Tammy looked away from them. She got up, slipped her feet into floppy slippers, and mumbled. "Almost bedtime." She took her toiletry kit from her nightstand and shuffled out of the room, closing the door behind her, heading for one of the baths at the end of the hall.

"She takes the candy," Ruth explained.

An icy wave of revulsion washed through Laura. "Ah, no."

"Yes," Thelma said. "Not because she wants the candy. She's . . . messed up. She needs the kind of approval she gets from the Eel."

"But why?" Laura asked.

Ruth and Thelma exchanged another of their looks, through which they seemed to debate an issue and reach a decision in a second or two, without words. Sighing, Ruth said, "Well, see, Tammy needs that kind of approval because . . . her father taught her to need it."

Laura was jolted. "Her own *father?*"

"Not all the kids at McIlroy are orphans," Thelma said. "Some are here because their parents committed crimes and went to jail. And others were abused by their folks physically or . . . sexually."

The freshening air coming through the open windows was probably only a degree or two colder than when they had sat down in a circle on the floor, but it seemed to Laura like a chilly late-autumn wind that had mysteriously leaped the months and infiltrated the August night.

Laura said, "But Tammy doesn't really *like* it?"

"No, I don't think she does," Ruth said. "But she's—"

"—compelled," Thelma said, "can't help herself. Twisted."

They were all silent, thinking the unthinkable, and finally Laura said, "Strange and . . . so sad. Can't we stop it? Can't we tell Mrs. Bowmaine or one of the other social workers about Sheener?"

"It wouldn't do any good," Thelma said. "The Eel would deny it, and *Tammy* would deny it, too, and we don't have any proof."

"But if she's not the only kid he's abused, one of the others—"

Ruth shook her head. "Most have gone to foster homes, adoptive parents, or back to their own families. Those two or three still here . . . well, they're either like Tammy, or they're just scared to death of the Eel, too scared ever to rat on him."

"Besides," Thelma said, "the adults don't want to know, don't want to deal with it. Bad publicity for the home. And it makes them look stupid to have this going on under their noses. Besides, who can believe children?" Thelma imitated Mrs. Bowmaine, catching the note of phoniness so perfectly that Laura recognized it at once: "Oh, my dear, they're horrible, lying little creatures. Noisy, rambunctious, bothersome little beasts, capable of destroying Mr. Sheener's fine reputation for the fun of it. If only they could be drugged, hung on wall hooks, and fed intravenously, how much more efficient that system would be, my dear—and really so much better for them, too."

"Then the Eel would be cleared," Ruth said, "and he'd come back to work, and he'd find ways to make us pay for speaking against him. It happened that way before with another perv who used to work here, a guy we called Ferret Fogel. Poor Denny Jenkins . . . "

"Denny ratted on Ferret Fogel; he told Bowmaine the Ferret molested him and two other boys. Fogel was suspended. But the two other boys wouldn't support Denny's story. They were afraid of the Ferret . . . but they also had this sick need for his approval. When Bowmaine and her staff interrogated Denny—"

"They hammered at him," Ruth said angrily, "with trick questions, trying to trip him up. He got confused, contradicted himself, so they said he was making it all up."

"And Fogel came back to work," Thelma said.

"He bided his time," Ruth said, "and then he found ways to make Denny miserable. He tormented the boy relentlessly until one day . . . Denny just started screaming and couldn't stop. The doctor had to give him a shot, and then they took him away. Emotionally disturbed, they said." She was on the brink of tears. "We never saw him again."

Thelma put one hand on her sister's shoulder. To Laura, she said, "Ruth was fond of Denny. He was a nice boy. Small, shy, sweet . . . he never had a chance. That's why you've got to be tough with the White Eel. You can't let him see that you're afraid of him. If he tries anything, scream. And kick him in the crotch."

Tammy returned from the bathroom. She did not look at them but stepped out of her slippers and got under the covers.

Although Laura was repulsed by the thought of Tammy submitting to Sheener, she regarded the frail blonde with less disgust than sympathy. No sight could be more pitiful than that small, lonely, defeated girl lying on her narrow, sagging bed.

That night Laura dreamed of Sheener. He had his own human head, but his body was that of a white eel, and wherever Laura ran, Sheener slithered after her, wriggling under closed doors and other obstacles.

# TWO

Sickened by what he'd just seen, Stefan returned from the institute's main lab to his third-floor office. He sat at his desk with his head in his hands, shaking with horror and anger and fear.

That red-haired bastard, Willy Sheener, was going to rape Laura repeatedly, beat her half to death, and leave her so traumatized that she would never recover. That was not just a possibility; it would come to pass if Stefan did not move to prevent it. He had *seen* the aftermath: Laura's bruised face, broken mouth. Her eyes had been the worst of it, so flat looking and half-dead, the eyes of a child who no longer had the capacity for joy or hope.

Cold rain tapped on the office windows, and that hollow sound seemed to reverberate within him, as if the terrible things he had seen had left him burnt out, an empty shell.

He had saved Laura from the junkie in her father's grocery, but here was another pedophile already. One of the things he had learned from the experiments in the institute was that reshaping fate was not always easy. Destiny struggled to reassert the pattern that was meant to be. Perhaps being molested and psychologically destroyed was such an immutable part of Laura's fate that Stefan could not prevent it from happening sooner or later. Perhaps he could not save her from Willy Sheener, or perhaps if he thwarted Sheener, *another* rapist would enter the girl's life. But he had to try.

Those half-dead, joyless eyes . . .

## THREE

Seventy-six children resided at the McIlroy Home, all twelve or younger; upon turning thirteen, they were transferred to Caswell Hall in Anaheim. Since the oak-paneled dining hall would hold only forty, meals were served in two shifts. Laura was on the second shift, as were the Ackerson twins.

Standing in the cafeteria line between Thelma and Ruth on her first morning at the shelter, Laura saw that Willy Sheener was one of the four attendants serving from behind the counter. He monitored the milk supply and dispensed sweet rolls with a pair of tongs.

As Laura moved along the line, the Eel spent more time looking at her than at the kids he was serving.

"Don't let him intimidate you," Thelma whispered.

Laura tried to meet Sheener's gaze—and his challenge—boldly. But she was the one who always broke the staring match.

When she reached his station, he said, "Good morning, Laura," and put a sweet roll on her tray, a particular pastry he had saved for her. It was twice as large as the others, with more cherries and icing.

On Thursday, Laura's third full day at the shelter, she endured a how-are-we-adjusting meeting with Mrs. Bowmaine in the social worker's first-floor office. Etta Bowmaine was stout, with an unflattering wardrobe of flower-print dresses. She spoke in clichés and platitudes with that gushy insincerity that Thelma had imitated perfectly, and she asked a lot of questions to which she actually did not want honest answers. Laura lied about how happy she was at McIlroy, and the lies pleased Mrs. Bowmaine enormously.

Returning to her room on the third floor, Laura encountered the Eel on the north stairs. She turned at the second landing, and he was on the next flight, wiping the oak handrail with a rag. An unopened bottle of furniture polish stood on the step below him.

She froze, and her heart began to pound double time, for she knew he had been lying in wait for her. He'd have known about her summons to Mrs. Bowmaine's office and would have counted on her using the nearest stairs to return to her room.

They were alone. At any time another child or staff member might come along, but for the moment they were alone.

Her first impulse was to retreat and use the south stairs, but she remembered what Thelma had said about standing up to the Eel and about how his type preyed only on weaklings. She told herself that the best thing to do was walk past him without saying a word, but her feet seemed to have been nailed to the step; she could not move.

Looking down at her from half a flight up, the Eel smiled. It was a horrible smile: His skin was white, and his lips were colorless, but his crooked teeth were as yellow and mottled with brownish spots as the skin of a ripe banana. Under his unruly copper-red hair, his face resembled a clown's countenance—not the kind of clown you'd see in a circus but the kind you might run into on Halloween night, the kind that might carry a chainsaw instead of a seltzer bottle.

"You're a very pretty little girl, Laura."

She tried to tell him to go to hell. She couldn't speak.

"I'd like to be your friend," he said.

Somehow she found the strength to start up the steps toward him.

He smiled even more broadly, perhaps because he thought she was responding to his offer of friendship. He reached into a pocket of his khaki pants and withdrew a couple of Tootsie Rolls.

Laura recalled Thelma's comical assessment of the Eel's stupidly unimaginative gambits, and suddenly he did not look as scary to her as he had before. Offering Tootsie Rolls, leering at her, Sheener was a ridiculous figure, a caricature of evil, and she would have laughed at him if she had not known what he had done to Tammy and other girls. Though she could not quite laugh, the Eel's ludicrous appearance and manner gave her the courage to move swiftly around him.

When he realized she was not going to take the candy or respond to his offer of friendship, he put a hand on her shoulder to stop her.

She angrily took hold of his hand and threw it off. "Don't you ever touch me, you geek."

She hurried up the stairs, struggling against a desire to run. If she ran he would know that her fear of him had not been entirely banished. He must see absolutely no weakness in her, for weakness would encourage him to continue harassing her.

By the time she was only two steps from the next landing, she allowed herself to hope that she had won, that her toughness had impressed him. Then she heard the unmistakable sound of a zipper. Behind her, in a loud whisper he said, "Hey, Laura, look at this. Look at what I have for you." There was a demented, hateful tone in his voice. "Look, look at what's in my hand now, Laura."

She did not glance back.

She reached the landing and started up the next flight, thinking: There's no reason to run; you don't *dare* run, don't run, don't run.

From one flight below, the Eel said, "Look at the big Tootsie Roll I have in my hand now, Laura. It's lots bigger than those others."

On the third floor Laura hurried directly to the bathroom where she vigorously scrubbed her hands. She felt filthy after taking hold of Sheener's hand in order to remove it from her shoulder.

Later, when she and the Ackerson twins convened their nightly powwow on the floor of their room, Thelma howled with laughter when she heard about the Eel wanting Laura to look at his "big Tootsie Roll." She said, "He's priceless, isn't he? Where do you think he gets these lines of his? Does Doubleday publish the *Perverts' Book of Classic Come-ons* or something?"

"The point is," Ruth said worriedly, "he wasn't turned off when Laura stood up to him. I don't think he's going to give up on her as quickly as he gives up on other girls who resist him."

That night Laura had difficulty sleeping. She thought about her special guardian, and she wondered if he would appear as miraculously as before and if he would deal with Willy Sheener. Somehow she didn't think she could count on him this time.

During the following ten days, as August waned, the Eel shadowed Laura as reliably as the moon shadowed the earth. When she and the Ackerson twins went to the game room to play cards or Monopoly, Sheener arrived within ten minutes and set to work ostensibly washing windows or polishing furniture or repairing a drapery rod, though in fact his attention was primarily focused on Laura. If the girls sought refuge in a corner of the playground behind the mansion, either to talk or play a game of their own devising, Sheener entered the yard shortly thereafter, having suddenly found shrubbery that had to be pruned or fertilized. And although the third floor was for girls only, it was open to male staff members for the purpose of maintenance between ten in the morning and four in the afternoon on weekdays, so Laura could not escape to her room during those hours with any degree of safety.

Worse than the Eel's diligence was the frightening rate at which his dark passion for her grew, a sick need revealed by the steadily increasing intensity of his gaze and the sour sweat that burst from him when he was in the same room with her for more than a few minutes.

Laura, Ruth, and Thelma tried to convince themselves that the threat from the Eel lessened with every day he did not act, that his hesitation revealed his awareness of Laura as unsuitable prey. At heart they knew they were hoping to slay the dragon with a wish, but they were unable to face the full extent of the danger till a Saturday afternoon late in

August, when they returned to their room and found Tammy destroying Laura's book collection in a fit of twisted jealousy.

The library of fifty paperbacks—her favorite books, which she had brought with her from the apartment above the grocery—were kept under Laura's bed. Tammy had brought them out into the middle of the room and in a hateful frenzy had ripped apart two-thirds of them.

Laura was too shocked to act, but Ruth and Thelma pulled the girl away from the books and restrained her.

Because those were her favorite books, because her father bought them for her and they were therefore a link to him, but most of all because she owned so little, Laura was pained by the destruction. Her possessions were so meager, of no value, but she suddenly realized that they formed ramparts against the worst cruelties of life.

Tammy lost interest in the books now that the true object of her rage stood before her. "I hate you, I hate you!" Her pale, drawn face was alive for the first time since Laura had known her, flushed and contorted with emotion. The bruiselike circles around her eyes hadn't vanished, but they no longer made her appear weak or broken; instead she looked wild, savage. "I hate you, Laura, I hate you!"

"Tammy, honey," Thelma said, struggling to hold on to the girl, "Laura's never done anything to you."

Breathing hard but no longer thrashing to break free of Ruth and Thelma, Tammy shrieked at Laura: "You're all he talks about, he isn't interested in me any more, just you, he can't stop talking about you, I hate you, why did you have to come here, I hate you!"

No one had to ask her to whom she was referring. The Eel.

"He doesn't want me anymore, nobody wants me now, he only wants me so I can help him get to you. Laura, Laura, Laura. He wants me to trick you into a place where he can get you alone, where it'll be safe for him, but I won't do it, I won't! 'Cause then what would I have once he's got you? Nothing." Her face was a furious red. Worse than her rage was the awful desperation that lay behind it.

Laura ran out of the room, down the long hall into the lavatory. Sick with disgust and fear, she fell to her knees on the cracked yellow tiles before one of the toilets and threw up. Once her stomach was purged she went to one of the sinks, rinsed her mouth repeatedly, then splashed cold water on her face. When she raised her head and looked in the mirror, the tears came at last.

It was not her own loneliness or fear that brought her to tears. She was crying for Tammy. The world was an unthinkably mean place if it would allow a ten-year-old girl's life to be devalued to such an extent that the only words of approval she ever heard from an adult were those spoken by the demented man who abused her, that the only possession in which she could take pride was the underdeveloped sexual aspect of her own thin, prepubescent body.

Laura realized that Tammy's situation was infinitely worse than her own. Even stripped of her books, Laura had good memories of a loving, kind, gentle father, which Tammy did not. If what few things she owned were taken from her, Laura would still be whole of mind, but Tammy was psychologically damaged, perhaps beyond repair.

# FOUR

Sheener lived in a bungalow on a quiet street in Santa Ana. It was one of those neighborhoods built after World War II: small, neat houses with interesting architectural details. In this summer of 1967, the various types of ficus trees had reached maturity, spreading their limbs protectively over the homes; Sheener's place was further cloaked by overgrown shrubbery—azaleas, eugenias, and red-flowering hibiscus.

Near midnight, using a plastic loid, Stefan popped the lock on the back door and let himself into the house. As he inspected the bungalow, he boldly turned on lights and did not bother to draw the drapes at the windows.

The kitchen was immaculate. The blue Formica counters glistened. The chrome handles on the appliances, the faucet in the sink, and the metal frames of the kitchen chairs all gleamed, unmarred by a single fingerprint.

He opened the refrigerator, not sure what he expected to find there. Perhaps an indication of Willy Sheener's abnormal psychology; a former victim of his molestations, murdered and frozen to preserve the memories of twisted passion? Nothing that dramatic. However, the man's fetish for neatness was obvious: All the food was stored in matching Tupperware containers.

Otherwise, the only thing odd about the contents of both the refrigerator and cupboards was the preponderance of sweets: ice cream, cookies, cakes, candies, pies, doughnuts, even animal crackers. There were a great many novelty foods, too, like Spaghetti-Os and cans of vegetable soup in which the noodles were shaped like popular cartoon characters. Sheener's larder looked as if it had been stocked by a child with a checkbook but no adult supervision.

Stefan moved deeper into the house.

# FIVE

The confrontation over the shredded books was sufficient to drain what little spirit Tammy possessed. She said no more about Sheener and seemed no longer to harbor any animosity toward Laura. Retreating further into herself day by day, she averted her eyes from everyone, hung her head lower; her voice grew softer.

Laura wasn't sure which was less tolerable—the constant threat posed by the White Eel or watching Tammy's already wispy personality fading further as she slid toward a state hardly more active than catatonia. But on Thursday, August 31, those two burdens were lifted unexpectedly from Laura's shoulders when she learned that she would be transferred to a foster home in Costa Mesa the following day, Friday.

However, she regretted leaving the Ackersons. Though she'd known them only a few weeks, friendships forged in extremity solidified faster and felt more enduring than those made in more ordinary times.

That night, as the three of them sat on the floor of their room, Thelma said, "Shane, if you wind up with a good family, a happy home, just settle down snug and *enjoy*. If you're in a good place, forget us, make new friends, get on with your life. *But* the legendary Ackerson sisters—Ruth and moi—have been through the foster-family mill, three bad ones, so let me assure you that if you wind up in a *rotten* place, you don't have to stay there."

Ruth said, "Just weep a lot and let everyone know how unhappy you are. If you can't weep, pretend to."

"Sulk," Thelma advised. "Be clumsy. Accidentally break a dish each time you've got to wash them. Make a nuisance of yourself."

Laura was surprised. "You did all that to get back into McIlroy?"

"That and more," Ruth said.

"But didn't you feel terrible—breaking their things?"

"It was harder for Ruth than me," Thelma said. "I've got the devil in me, while Ruth is the reincarnation of an obscure, treacly, fourteenth-century nun whose name we've not yet ascertained."

Within one day Laura knew she did not want to remain in the care of the Teagel family, but she tried to make it work because at first she thought their company was preferable to returning to McIlroy.

Real life was just a misty backdrop to Flora Teagel, for whom only crossword puzzles were of interest. She spent days and evenings at the table in her yellow kitchen, wrapped in a cardigan regardless of the weather, working through books of crossword puzzles one after another with a dedication both astonishing and idiotic.

She usually spoke to Laura only to give her lists of chores and to seek help with knotty crossword clues. As Laura stood at the sink, washing dishes Flora might say, "What's a seven-letter word for cat?"

Laura's answer was always the same: "I don't know."

" 'I don't know, I don't know, I don't know,' " Mrs. Teagel mocked. "You don't seem to know anything, girl. Aren't you paying attention in school? Don't you care about language, about words?"

Laura, of course, was *fascinated* with words. To her, words were things of beauty, each like a magical powder or potion that could be combined with other words to create powerful spells. But to Flora Teagel, words were game chips needed to fill blank puzzle squares, annoyingly elusive clusters of letters that frustrated her.

Flora's husband, Mike, was a squat, baby-faced truck driver. He spent evenings in an armchair, poring over the *National Enquirer* and its clones, absorbing useless facts from dubious stories about alien contact and devil-worshiping movie stars. His taste for what he called "exotic news" would have been harmless if he'd been as self-absorbed as his wife, but he often popped in on Laura when she was doing chores or in those rare moments when she was given time for homework, and he insisted on reading aloud the more bizarre articles.

She thought these stories were stupid, illogical, pointless, but she could not tell him so. She had learned that he would not be offended if she said his newspapers were rubbish. Instead he'd regard her pityingly; then with maddening patience, with an infuriating know-it-all manner found only in the overeducated and totally ignorant, he would proceed to explain how the world worked. At length. Repeatedly. "Laura, you've got a lot to learn. The big shots who run things in Washington, *they* know about the aliens and the secrets of Atlantis . . . "

As different as Flora was from Mike, they shared one belief: that the purpose of sheltering a foster child was to obtain a free servant. Laura was expected to clean, do laundry, iron clothes, and cook.

Their own daughter—Hazel, an only child—was two years older than Laura and thoroughly spoiled. Hazel never cooked, washed dishes, did laundry, or cleaned house. Though she was just fourteen, she had perfectly manicured, painted fingernails and toenails. If you had deducted from her age the number of hours she had spent primping in front of a mirror, she would have been only five years old.

"On laundry day," she explained on Laura's first day in the Teagel house, "you must press *my* clothes first. And always be sure that you hang them in my closet arranged according to color."

I've read this book and seen this movie, Laura thought. Gad, I've got the lead in *Cinderella!*

"I'm going to be a major movie star or a model," Hazel said. "So my face, hands, and body are my future. I've got to protect them."

When Mrs. Ince—the wire-thin, whippet-faced child-welfare worker assigned to the case—paid a scheduled visit to the Teagel house on Saturday morning, September 16, Laura intended to demand to be returned to McIlroy Home. The threat posed by Willy Sheener had come to seem less of a problem than everyday life with the Teagels.

Mrs. Ince arrived on schedule to find Flora washing the first dishes she had washed in two weeks. Laura was sitting at the kitchen table, apparently working a crossword puzzle that in fact had been shoved into her hands only when the doorbell had rung.

In that portion of the visit devoted to a private interview with Laura in her bedroom, Mrs. Ince refused to believe what she was told about Laura's load of housework. "But dear, Mr. and Mrs. Teagel are exemplary foster parents. You don't look to me as if you've been worked to the bone. You've even gained a few pounds."

"I didn't accuse them of starving me," Laura said. "But I never have time for schoolwork. I go to bed every night exhausted—"

"Besides," Mrs. Ince interrupted, "foster parents are expected not merely to house children but to *raise* them, which means teaching manners and deportment, instilling good values and good work habits."

Mrs. Ince was hopeless.

Laura resorted to the Ackersons' plan for shedding an unwanted foster family. She began to clean haphazardly. When she was done with the dishes, they were spotted and streaked. She ironed wrinkles *into* Hazel's clothes.

Because the destruction of most of her book collection had taught her a profound respect for property, Laura could not break dishes or anything else that belonged to the Teagels, but for that part of the Ackerson Plan she substituted scorn and disrespect. Working a puzzle, Flora asked for a six-letter word meaning "a species of ox," and Laura said, "Teagel." When Mike began to recount a flying-saucer story he had read in the *Enquirer*, she interrupted to spin a tale about mutated mole men living secretly in the local supermarket. To Hazel, Laura suggested that her big break in show business might best be achieved by applying to serve as Ernest Borgnine's stand-in: "You're a dead-ringer for him, Hazel. They've *got* to hire you!"

Her scorn led swiftly to a spanking. With his big, callused hands Mike had no need of a paddle. He thumped her across the bottom, but she bit her lip and refused to give him the satisfaction of her tears. Watching from the kitchen doorway, Flora said, "Mike, that's enough. Don't mark her." He quit reluctantly only when his wife entered the room and stayed his hand.

That night Laura had difficulty sleeping. For the first time she had employed her love of words, the power of language, to achieve a desired effect, and the Teagels' reactions were proof that she could use words well. Even more exciting was the half-formed thought, still too new to be fully understood, that she might possess the ability not only to defend herself with words but to earn her way in the world with them, perhaps even as an author of the kind of books she so much enjoyed. With her father she'd talked of being a doctor, ballerina, veterinarian, but that had been just talk. None of those dreams had filled her with as much excitement as the prospect of being a writer.

The next morning, when she went down to the kitchen and found the three Teagels at breakfast, she said, "Hey, Mike, I've just discovered there's an intelligent squid from Mars living in the toilet tank."

"What *is* this?" Mike demanded.

Laura smiled and said, "Exotic news."

Two days later Laura was returned to McIlroy Home.

# SIX

Willy Sheener's living room and den were furnished as if an ordinary man lived there. Stefan was not sure what he had expected. Evidence of dementia, perhaps, but not this neat, orderly home.

One of the bedrooms was empty, and the other was decidedly odd. The only bed was a narrow mattress on the floor. The pillowcases and sheets were for a child's room, emblazoned with the colorful, antic figures of cartoon rabbits. The nightstand and dresser were scaled to a child's dimensions, pale blue, with stenciled animals on the sides and drawers: giraffes, rabbits, squirrels. Sheener owned a collection of Little Golden Books, as well, and other children's picture books, stuffed animals, and toys suitable for a six- or seven-year-old.

At first Stefan thought that room was designed for the seduction of neighborhood children, that Sheener was unstable enough to seek out prey even on his home ground, where the risk was greatest. But there was no other bed in the house, and the closet and dresser drawers were filled with a man's clothing. On the walls were a dozen framed photos of the same red-headed boy, some as an infant, some when he was seven or eight, and the face was identifiably that of a younger Sheener. Gradually Stefan realized the decor was for Willy Sheener's benefit alone. The creep slept here. At bedtime Sheener evidently retreated into a fantasy of childhood, no doubt finding a desperately needed peace in his eerie, nightly regression.

Standing in the middle of that strange room, Stefan felt both saddened and repelled. It seemed that Sheener molested children not solely or even primarily for the sexual thrill of it but to absorb their youth, to become young again like them; through perversion he seemed to be trying to descend not into moral squalor so much as into a lost innocence. He was equally pathetic and despicable, inadequate to the challenges of adult life but nonetheless dangerous for his inadequacies.

Stefan shivered.

# SEVEN

Her bed in the Ackerson twins' room was now occupied by another kid. Laura was assigned to a small, two-bed room at the north end of the third floor near the stairs. Her bunkmate was nine-year-old Eloise Fischer, who had pigtails, freckles, and a demeanor too serious for a child. "I'm going to be an accountant when I grow up," she told Laura. "I like numbers a lot. You can add up a column of numbers and get the same answer every time. There're no surprises with numbers; they're not at all like people." Eloise's parents had been convicted of drug dealing and sent to prison, and she was in McIlroy while the court decided which relative would be given custody of her.

As soon as Laura had unpacked, she hurried to the Ackersons' room. Bursting in on them, she cried, "I is free, I is free!"

Tammy and the new girl looked at her blankly, but Ruth and Thelma ran to her and hugged her, and it was like coming home to real family.

"Your foster family didn't like you?" Ruth asked.

Thelma said, "Ah ha! You used the Ackerson Plan."

"No, I killed them all while they slept."

"That'll work," Thelma agreed.

The new girl, Rebecca Bogner, was about eleven. She and the Ackersons obviously were not sympatico. Listening to Laura and the twins, Rebecca kept saying "you're weird" and "too weird" and "jeez, what weirdos," with such an air of superiority and disdain that she poisoned the atmosphere as effectively as a nuclear detonation.

Laura and the twins went outside to a corner of the playground where they could share five weeks of news without Rebecca's snotty commentary. It was early October, and the days were still warm, though at a quarter till five the air was cooling. They wore jackets and sat on the lower branches of the jungle gym, which was abandoned now that the younger children were washing up for the early dinner.

They had not been in the yard five minutes before Willy Sheener arrived with an electric shrub trimmer. He set to work on a eugenia hedge about thirty feet from them, but his attention was on Laura.

At dinner the Eel was at his serving station on the cafeteria line, passing out cartons of milk and pieces of cherry pie. He had saved the largest slice for Laura.

* * *

On Monday she entered a new school where the other kids already had four weeks to make friends. Ruth and Thelma were in a couple of her classes, which made it easier to adjust, but she was reminded that the primary condition of an orphan's life was instability.

Tuesday afternoon, when Laura returned from school, Mrs. Bowmaine stopped her in the hall. "Laura, may I see you in my office?"

Mrs. Bowmaine was wearing a purple floral-pattern dress that clashed with the rose and peach floral patterns of her office drapes and wallpaper. Laura sat in a rose-patterned chair. Mrs. Bowmaine stood at her desk, intending to deal with Laura quickly and move on to other tasks. Mrs. Bowmaine was a bustler, a busy-busy type.

"Eloise Fischer left our charge today," Mrs. Bowmaine said.

"Who got custody?" Laura asked. "She liked her grandmother."

"It was her grandmother," Mrs. Bowmaine confirmed.

Good for Eloise. Laura hoped the pigtailed, freckled, future accountant would find something to trust besides cold numbers.

"Now you've no roommate," Mrs. Bowmaine said briskly, "and we've no vacant bed elsewhere, so you can't just move in with—"

"May I make a suggestion?"

Mrs. Bowmaine frowned with impatience and consulted her watch.

Laura said quickly, "Ruth and Thelma are my best friends, and their roomies are Tammy Hinsen and Rebecca Bogner. But I don't think Tammy and Rebecca get along well with Ruth and Thelma, so—"

"We want you children to learn how to live with people different from you. Bunking with girls you already like won't build character. Anyway, the point is, I can't make new arrangements until tomorrow; I'm busy today. So I want to know if I can trust you to spend the night alone in your current room."

"Trust me?" Laura asked in confusion.

"Tell me the truth, young lady. Can I trust you alone tonight?"

Laura could not figure what trouble the social worker anticipated from a child left alone for one night. Perhaps she expected Laura to barricade herself in the room so effectively that police would have to blast the door, disable her with tear gas, and drag her out in chains.

Laura was as insulted as she was confused. "Sure, I'll be okay. I'm not a baby. I'll be fine."

"Well . . . all right. You'll sleep by yourself tonight, but we'll make other arrangements tomorrow."

After leaving Mrs. Bowmaine's colorful office for the drab hallways, climbing the stairs to the third floor, Laura suddenly thought: *the White Eel!* Sheener would know she was going to be alone tonight. He knew everything that went on at McIlroy, and he had keys, so he could return in the night. Her room was next to the north stairs, so he could slip out of the stairwell into her room, overpower her in seconds. He'd club her or drug her, stuff her in a burlap sack, take her away, lock her in a cellar, and no one would know what had happened to her.

She turned at the second-floor landing, descended the stairs two at a time, and rushed back toward Mrs. Bowmaine's office, but when she turned the corner into the front hall, she nearly collided with the Eel. He had a mop and a wringer-equipped bucket on wheels, which was filled with water reeking of pine-scented cleanser.

He grinned at her. Maybe it was only her imagination, but she was certain that he already knew she would be alone that night.

She should have stepped by him, gone to Mrs. Bowmaine, and begged for a change in the night's sleeping arrangements. She could not make accusations about Sheener, or she would wind up like Denny Jenkins—disbelieved by the staff, tormented relentlessly by her ne-mesis—but she could have found an acceptable excuse for her change of mind.

She also considered rushing at him, shoving him into his bucket, knocking him on his butt, and telling him that she was tougher than him, that he had better not mess with her. But he was different from the Teagels. Mike, Flora, and Hazel were small-minded, obnoxious, ignorant, but comparatively sane. The Eel was insane, and there was no way of knowing how he would react to being knocked flat.

As she hesitated, his crooked, yellow grin widened.

A flush touched his pale cheeks, and Laura realized it might be a flush of desire, which made her nauseous.

She walked away, dared not run until she had climbed the stairs and was out of his sight. Then she sprinted for the Ackersons' room.

"You'll sleep here tonight," Ruth said.

"Of course," Thelma said, "you'll have to stay in your room until they finish the bed check, then sneak down here."

From her corner where she was sitting in bed doing math homework, Rebecca Bogner said, "We've only got four beds."

"I'll sleep on the floor," Laura said.

"This is against the rules," Rebecca said.

Thelma made a fist and glowered at her.

"Okay, all right," Rebecca agreed. "I never said *I* didn't want her to stay. I just pointed out that it's against the rules."

Laura expected Tammy to object, but the girl lay on her back in bed, atop the covers, staring at the ceiling, apparently lost in her own thoughts and uninterested in their plans.

In the oak-paneled dining room, over an inedible dinner of pork chops, gluey mashed potatoes, and leathery green beans—and under the watchful eyes of the Eel—Thelma said, "As for why Bowmaine wanted to know if she could trust you alone . . . she's afraid you'll try suicide."

Laura was incredulous.

"Kids have done it here," Ruth said sadly. "Which is why they stuff at least two of us into even very small rooms. Being alone too much . . . that's one of the things that seems to trigger the impulse."

Thelma said, "They won't let Ruth and me share one of the small rooms because, since we're identical twins, they think we're really like *one* person. They think they'd no sooner close the door on us than we'd hang ourselves."

"That's ridiculous," Laura said.

"Of course it's ridiculous," Thelma agreed. "Hanging isn't flamboyant enough. The amazing Ackerson sisters—Ruth and moi—have a flair for the dramatic. We'd commit hara-kiri with stolen kitchen knives, or if we could get hold of a chainsaw . . ."

Throughout the room conversations were conducted in moderate voices, for adult monitors patrolled the dining hall. The third-floor Resident Advisor, Miss Keist, passed behind the table where Laura sat with the Ackersons, and Thelma whispered, "Gestapo."

When Miss Keist passed, Ruth said, "Mrs. Bowmaine means well, but she just isn't good at what she does. If she took time to learn what kind of person you are, Laura, she'd never worry about you committing suicide. You're a survivor."

As she pushed her inedible food around her plate, Thelma said, "Tammy Hinsen was once caught in the bathroom with a packet of razor blades, trying to get up the nerve to slash her wrists."

Laura was suddenly impressed by the mix of humor and tragedy, absurdity and bleak realism, that formed the peculiar pattern of their lives at McIlroy. One moment they were bantering amusingly with one another; a moment later they were discussing the suicidal tendencies of girls they knew. She realized that such an insight was beyond her years, and as soon as she returned to her room, she would write it down in the notebook of observations she had recently begun to keep.

Ruth had managed to choke down the food on her plate. She said, "A month after the razor-blade incident, they held a surprise search of our rooms, looking for dangerous objects. They found Tammy had a can of lighter fluid and matches. She'd intended to go into the showers, cover herself with lighter fluid, and set herself on fire."

"Oh, God." Laura thought of the thin, blond girl with the ashen complexion and the sooty rings around her eyes, and it seemed that her plan to immolate herself was only a desire to speed up the slow fire that for a long time had been consuming her from within.

"They sent her away two months for intense therapy," Ruth said.

"When she came back," Thelma said, "the adults talked about how much better she was, but she seemed the same to Ruth and me."

Ten minutes after Miss Keist's nightly room check, Laura left her bed. The deserted, third-floor hall was lit only by three safety lamps. Dressed in pajamas, carrying a pillow and blanket, she hurried barefoot to the Ackersons' room.

Only Ruth's bedside lamp was aglow. She whispered, "Laura, you sleep on my bed. I've made a place for myself on the floor."

"Well, unmake it and get back in your bed," Laura said.

She folded her blanket several times to make a pad on the floor, near the foot of Ruth's bed, and she lay on it with her pillow.

From her own bed Rebecca Bogner said, "We're all going to get in trouble over this."

"What're you afraid they'll do to us?" Thelma asked. "Stake us in the backyard, smear us with honey, and leave us for the ants?"

Tammy was sleeping or pretending to sleep.

Ruth turned out her light, and they settled down in darkness.

The door flew open, and the overhead light snapped on. Dressed in a red robe, scowling fiercely, Miss Keist entered the room. "So! Laura, what're you doing here?"

Rebecca Bogner groaned. "I *told* you we'd get in trouble."

"Come back to your room right this minute, young lady."

The swiftness with which Miss Keist appeared was suspicious, and Laura looked at Tammy Hinsen. The blonde was no longer feigning sleep. She was leaning on one elbow, smiling thinly. Evidently she had decided to assist the Eel in his quest for Laura, perhaps with the hope of regaining her status as his favorite.

Miss Keist escorted Laura to her room. Laura got into bed, and Miss Keist stared at her for a moment. "It's warm. I'll open the window." Returning to the bed, she studied Laura thoughtfully. "Is there anything you want to tell me? Is anything wrong?"

Laura considered telling her about the Eel. But what if Miss Keist waited to catch the Eel as he crept into her room, and what if he didn't show? Laura would never be able to accuse the Eel again because she'd have a *history* of accusing him; no one would take her seriously. Then even if Sheener raped her, he'd get away with it.

"No, nothing's wrong," she said.

Miss Keist said, "Thelma's too sure of herself for a girl her age, full of false sophistication. If you're foolish enough to break the rules again just to have an all-night gabfest, develop some friends worth taking the risk for.''

''Yes, ma'am,'' Laura said just to get rid of her, sorry that she had even considered responding to the woman's moment of concern.

After Miss Keist left, Laura did not get out of bed and flee. She lay in darkness, certain there would be another bed check in half an hour. Surely the Eel would not slither around until midnight, and it was only ten, so between Miss Keist's next visit and the Eel's arrival, she'd have plenty of time to get to a safe place.

Far, far away in the night, thunder grumbled. She sat up in bed. Her guardian! She threw back the covers and ran to the window. She saw no lightning. The distant rumble faded. Perhaps it had not been thunder after all. She waited ten minutes or more, but nothing else happened. Disappointed, she returned to bed.

Shortly after ten-thirty the doorknob creaked. Laura closed her eyes, let her mouth fall open, and feigned sleep.

Someone stepped quietly across the room, stood beside the bed.

Laura breathed slowly, evenly, deeply, but her heart was racing.

It was Sheener. She *knew* it was him. Oh, God, she had forgotten he was insane, that he was unpredictable, and now he was here earlier than she'd expected, and he was preparing the hypodermic. He'd jam her into a burlap sack and carry her away as if he was a brain-damaged Santa Claus come to steal children rather than leave gifts.

The clock ticked. The cool breeze rustled the curtains.

At last the person beside the bed retreated. The door closed.

It had been Miss Keist, after all.

Trembling violently, Laura got out of bed and pulled on her robe. She folded the blanket over her arm and left the room without slippers because she would make less noise if she was barefoot.

She could not return to the Ackersons' room. Instead she went to the north stairs, cautiously opened the door, and stepped onto the dimly lit landing. She listened for the sound of the Eel's footsteps below. She descended warily, expecting to encounter Sheener, but she reached the ground floor safely.

Shivering as the cool tile floor imparted its chill to her bare feet, she took refuge in the game room. She didn't turn on the lights but relied on the ghostly glow of the streetlamps that penetrated the windows and silvered the edges of the furniture. She eased past chairs and game tables, bedding down on her folded blanket behind the sofa.

She dozed fitfully, waking repeatedly from nightmares. The old mansion was filled with stealthy sounds in the night: the creaking of floorboards overhead, the hollow popping of ancient plumbing.

# EIGHT

Stefan turned out all the lights and waited in the bedroom that was furnished for a child. At three-thirty in the morning, he heard Sheener returning. Stefan moved silently behind the bedroom door. A few minutes later Willy Sheener entered, switched on the light, and started toward the mattress. He made a queer sound as he crossed the room, partly a sigh and partly the whimper of an animal escaping from a hostile world into its burrow.

Stefan closed the door, and Sheener spun around at the sound of movement, shocked that his nest had been invaded. "Who . . . who are you? What the hell are you doing here?"

From a Chevy parked in the shadows across the street, Kokoschka watched Stefan depart Willy Sheener's house. He waited ten minutes, got out of the car, walked around to the back of the bungalow, found the door ajar, and cautiously went inside.

He located Sheener in a child's bedroom, battered and bloody and still. The air reeked of urine, for the man had lost control of his bladder.

Someday, Kokoschka thought with grim determination and a thrill of sadism, I'm going to hurt Stefan even worse than this. Him and that damned girl. As soon as I understand what part she plays in his plans and why he's jumping across decades to reshape her life, I'll put both of them through the kind of pain that no one knows this side of hell.

He left Sheener's house. In the backyard he stared up at the star-spattered sky for a moment, then returned to the institute.

# NINE

Shortly after dawn, before the first of the shelter's residents had arisen but when Laura felt the danger from Sheener had passed, she left her bed in the game room and returned to the third floor. Everything in her room was as she had left it. There was no sign that she'd had an intruder during the night.

Exhausted, bleary-eyed, she wondered if she had given the Eel too much credit for boldness and daring. She felt somewhat foolish.

She made her bed—a housekeeping chore every McIlroy child was expected to perform—and when she lifted her pillow she was paralyzed by the sight of what lay under it. A single Tootsie Roll.

\* \* \*

That day the White Eel did not come to work. He had been awake all night preparing to abduct Laura and no doubt needed his sleep.

"How does a man like that sleep at all?" Ruth wondered as they gathered in a corner of McIlroy's playground after school. "I mean, doesn't his conscience keep him awake?"

"Ruthie," Thelma said, "he doesn't have a conscience."

"Everyone does, even the worst of us. That's how God made us."

"Shane," Thelma said, "prepare to assist me in an exorcism. Our Ruth is once again possessed by the moronic spirit of Gidget."

In an uncharacteristic stroke of compassion, Mrs. Bowmaine moved Tammy and Rebecca to another room and allowed Laura to bunk with Ruth and Thelma. For the time being the fourth bed was vacant.

"It'll be Paul McCartney's bed," Thelma said, as she and Ruth helped Laura settle in. "Anytime the Beatles are in town, Paul can come use it. And *I'll* use Paul!"

"Sometimes," Ruth said, "you're embarrassing."

"Hey, I'm only expressing healthy sexual desire."

"Thelma, you're only twelve!" Ruth said exasperatedly.

"Thirteen's next. Going to have my first period any day now. We'll wake up one morning, and there'll be so much blood this place will look like there's been a massacre."

*"Thelma!"*

Sheener did not come to work on Thursday, either. His days off that week were Friday and Saturday, so by Saturday evening, Laura and the twins speculated excitedly that the Eel would never show up again, that he had been run down by a truck or had contracted beriberi.

But at Sunday morning breakfast, Sheener was at the buffet. He had two black eyes, a bandaged right ear, a swollen upper lip, a six-inch scrape along his left jaw, and he was missing two front teeth.

"Maybe he *was* hit by a truck," Ruth whispered as they moved forward in the cafeteria line.

Other kids were commenting on Sheener's injuries, and some were giggling. But they either feared and despised him or scorned him, so none cared to speak to him directly about his condition.

Laura, Ruth, and Thelma fell silent as they reached the buffet. The closer they drew to him, the more battered he appeared. His black eyes were not new but a few days old, yet the flesh was still horribly discolored and puffy; initially both eyes must have been nearly swollen shut. His split lip looked raw. Where his face was not bruised or abraded, his usually milk-pale skin was gray. Under his mop of frizzy, copper-red hair, he was a ludicrous figure—a circus clown who had taken a pratfall down a set of stairs without knowing how to land properly and avoid injury.

He did not look up at any of the kids as he served them but kept his eyes on the milk and breakfast pastries. He seemed to tense when Laura came before him, but he did not raise his eyes.

At their table Laura and the twins arranged their chairs so they could watch the Eel, a turn of events they would not have contemplated an hour ago. But he was now less fearful than intriguing. Instead of avoiding him, they spent the day following him on his chores, trying to be casual about it, as if they just happened to wind up in the same places he did, watching him surreptitiously. Gradually it became clear that he was aware of Laura but was avoiding even glancing at her. He looked at other kids, paused in the game room to speak softly to Tammy Hinsen on one occasion, but seemed as loath to meet Laura's eyes as he would have been to stick his fingers in an electric socket.

By late morning Ruth said, "Laura, he's afraid of you."

"Damned if he isn't," Thelma said. "Was it *you* who beat him up, Shane? Have you been hiding the fact that you're a karate expert?"

"It *is* strange, isn't it? Why's he afraid of me?"

But she knew. Her special guardian. Though she had thought she would have to deal with Sheener herself, her guardian had come through again, warning Sheener to stay away from her.

She was not sure why she was reluctant to share the story of her mysterious protector with the Ackersons. They were her best friends. She trusted them. Yet intuitively she felt that the secret of her guardian was meant to remain a secret, that what little she knew of him was sacred knowledge, and that she had no right to prattle on about him to other people, reducing sacred knowledge to mere gossip.

During the following two weeks the Eel's bruises faded, and the bandage came off his ear to reveal angry red stitches where that flap of flesh nearly had been torn off. He continued to keep his distance from Laura. When he served her in the dining hall, he no longer saved the best dessert for her, and he continued to refuse to meet her eyes.

Occasionally, however, she caught him glaring at her from across a room. Each time he quickly turned away, but in his fiery green eyes she now saw something worse than his previous twisted hunger: rage. Obviously he blamed her for the beating he had suffered.

On Friday, October 27, she learned from Mrs. Bowmaine that she was going to be transferred to another foster home the following day. A couple in Newport Beach, Mr. and Mrs. Dockweiler, were new to the foster-child program and eager to have her.

"I'm sure this will be a more compatible arrangement," Mrs. Bowmaine said, standing at her desk in a blazing yellow floral-print dress that made her look like a sun-porch sofa. "The trouble you caused at the Teagels' better not be repeated with the Dockweilers."

That night in their room, Laura and the twins tried to put on brave faces and discuss the approaching separation in the equanimous spirit with which they had faced her departure for the Teagels'. But they were closer now than a month ago, so close that Ruth and Thelma had begun to speak of Laura as if she were their sister. Thelma even once had said, "The amazing Ackerson sisters—Ruth, Laura, and moi," and Laura had felt more wanted, more loved, more *alive* than at any time in the three months since her father died.

"I love you guys," Laura said.

Ruth said, "Oh, Laura," and burst into tears.

Thelma scowled. "You'll be back in no time. These Dockweilers will be horrid people. They'll make you sleep in the garage."

"I hope so," Laura said.

"They'll beat you with rubber hoses—"

"That would be good."

This time the lightning that struck her life was *good* lightning, or at least that was how it seemed at first.

The Dockweilers lived in a huge house in an expensive section of Newport Beach. Laura had her own bedroom with an ocean view. It was decorated in earth tones, mostly beige.

Showing her the room for the first time, Carl Dockweiler said, "We didn't know what your favorite colors were, so we left it like this, but we can repaint the whole thing, however you want it." He was fortyish, big as a bear, barrel-chested, with a broad, rubbery face that reminded her of John Wayne if John Wayne had been a bit amusing looking. "Maybe a girl your age wants a pink room."

"Oh, no, I like it just the way it is!" Laura said. Still in a state of shock over the sudden opulence into which she had been plunged, she moved to the window and looked out at the splendid view of Newport Harbor, where yachts bobbed on sun-spangled water.

Nina Dockweiler joined Laura and put one hand on her shoulder. She was lovely, with smoky coloring, dark hair, and violet eyes, a china doll of a woman. "Laura, the child-welfare file said you loved books, but we didn't know what kind of books, so we're going straight to the bookstore and buy whatever you'd like."

At Waldenbooks Laura chose five paperbacks, and the Dockweilers urged her to buy more, but she felt guilty about spending their money. Carl and Nina scouted the shelves, plucking off volumes and reading cover copy to her, adding them to her pile if she showed the slightest interest. At one point Carl was crawling on his hands and knees in the young-adult section, scanning titles on the bottom shelf—"Hey, here's one about a dog. You like animal stories? Here's a spy story!"—and he was such a comical sight that Laura giggled. By the time they left the store, they'd bought one hundred books, *bagsful* of books.

Their first dinner together was at a pizza parlor, where Nina exhibited a surprising talent for magic by plucking a pepperoni ring from behind Laura's ear, then making it vanish.

"That's amazing," Laura said. "Where'd you learn that?"

"I owned an interior design firm, but I had to give it up eight years ago. Health reasons. Too stressful. I wasn't used to sitting at home like a lump, so I did all the things I'd dreamed of when I was a businesswoman with no spare time. Like learning magic."

"Health reasons?" Laura said.

Security was a treacherous rug that people kept pulling out from under her, and now someone was getting ready to jerk the rug again.

Her fear must have been evident, for Carl Dockweiler said, "Don't worry. Nina was born with a bum heart, a structural defect, but she'll live as long as you or me if she avoids stress."

"Can't they operate?" Laura asked, putting down the slice of pizza she had just picked up, her appetite having suddenly fled.

"Cardiovascular surgery's advancing rapidly," Nina said. "In a couple years maybe. But, honey, it's nothing to worry about. I'll take care of myself, especially now I've got a daughter to spoil!"

"More than anything," Carl said, "we wanted kids, but couldn't have them. By the time we decided to adopt, we discovered Nina's heart condition, so then the adoption agencies wouldn't approve us."

"But we qualify as foster parents," Nina said, "so if you like living with us, you can stay forever, just as if you were adopted."

That night in her big bedroom with its view of the sea—now an almost scary, vast expanse of darkness—Laura told herself that she must not like the Dockweilers too much, that Nina's heart condition foreclosed any possibility of real security.

The following day, Sunday, they took her shopping for clothes and would have spent fortunes if she had not finally begged them to stop. With their Mercedes crammed full of her new clothes, they went to a Peter Sellers comedy, and after the movie they had dinner at a hamburger restaurant where the milkshakes were humongous.

Pouring catsup on her french fries, Laura said, "You guys are lucky that child-welfare sent me to you instead of some other kid."

Carl raised his eyebrows. "Oh?"

"Well, you're nice, *too* nice—and a lot more vulnerable than you realize. Any kid would see how vulnerable you really are, and a lot would take advantage of you. Mercilessly. But you can relax with me. I'll never take advantage of you or make you sorry you took me in."

They stared at her in amazement.

At last Carl looked at Nina. "They've tricked us. She's not twelve. They've palmed off a dwarf on us."

That night in bed, as she waited for sleep, Laura repeated her litany of self-protection: "Don't like them too much, don't like them too much . . ." But already she liked them enormously.

The Dockweilers sent her to a private academy where the teachers were more demanding than those in the public schools she had attended, but she relished the challenge and performed well. Slowly she made new friends. She missed Thelma and Ruth, but she took some comfort from knowing they would be pleased that she had found happiness.

She even began to think that she could have faith in the future and could dare to *be* happy. After all, she had a special guardian, didn't she? Perhaps even a guardian angel. Surely any girl blessed with a guardian angel was destined for love, happiness, and security.

But would a guardian angel actually shoot a man in the head? Beat another man to a bloody pulp? Never mind. She had a handsome guardian, angel or not, and foster parents who loved her, and she could not refuse happiness when it showered on her by the bucketful.

On Tuesday, December 5, Nina had her monthly appointment with her cardiologist, so no one was at home when Laura returned from school that afternoon. She let herself in with her key and put her textbooks on the Louis XIV table in the foyer near the foot of the stairs.

The enormous living room was decorated in shades of cream, peach, and pale green, which made it cozy in spite of its size. As she paused at the windows to enjoy the view, she thought of how much better it would be if Ruth and Thelma could enjoy it with her—and suddenly it seemed the most natural thing that they should be there.

Why not? Carl and Nina loved kids. They had enough love for a houseful of kids, for a thousand kids.

"Shane," she said aloud, "you're a genius."

She went to the kitchen and prepared a snack to take to her room. She poured a glass of milk, heated a chocolate croissant in the oven, and got an apple from the refrigerator, as she mulled over the ways in which she might broach the subject of the twins with the Dockweilers. The plan was such a natural that by the time she carried her snack to the swinging door that separated kitchen and dining room and pushed it open with her shoulder, she had been unable to think of a single approach that would fail.

The Eel was waiting in the dining room, and he grabbed her and slammed her up against the wall so hard that he knocked the wind out of her. The apple and chocolate croissant flew off the plate, the plate flew out of her hand, he knocked the glass of milk out of her other hand, and it struck the dining-room table, shattering noisily. He pulled her away from the wall but slammed her into it again, pain flashed down her back, her vision clouded, she knew she dared not black out, so she held on to consciousness, held on tenaciously though she was wracked with pain, breathless, and half concussed.

Where was her guardian? Where?

Sheener shoved his face close to hers, and terror seemed to sharpen her senses, for she was acutely aware of every detail of his rage-wrenched countenance: the still-red suture marks where his torn ear had been reattached to his head, the blackheads in the creases around his nose, the acne scars in his mealy skin. His green eyes were too strange to be human, as alien and fierce as those of a cat.

Her guardian would pull the Eel off her at any second now, pull him off her and kill him. Any second now.

"I got you," he said, his voice shrill, manic, "now you're mine, honey, and you're gonna tell me who that son of a bitch was, the one who beat on me, I'll blow his head off."

He was holding her by her upper arms, his fingers digging into her flesh. He lifted her off the floor, raised her to his eye level, and pinned her against the wall. Her feet dangled in the air.

"Who is the bastard?" He was so strong for his size. He lifted her away from the wall, slammed her against it again, keeping her at eye level. "Tell me, honey, or I'll tear *your* ear off."

Any second now. Any second.

Pain still throbbed through her back, but she was able to draw breath, although what she drew in was *his* breath, sour and nauseating.

"Answer me, honey."

She could die waiting for a guardian angel to intervene.

She kicked him in the crotch. It was a perfect shot. His legs were planted wide, and he was so unaccustomed to girls who fought back that he never saw it coming. His eyes widened—they actually looked like human eyes for an instant—and he made a low, strangled sound. His hands dropped away from her. Laura collapsed to the floor, and Sheener staggered backward, lost his balance, fell against the dining-room table, folded to his side on the Chinese carpet.

Nearly immobilized by pain, shock, and fear, Laura could not get to her feet. Rag legs. Limp. So crawl. She could crawl. Away from him. Frantically. Toward the dining-room archway. Hoping to be able to stand by the time she reached the living room. He grabbed her left ankle. She tried to kick loose. No good. Rag legs. Sheener held on. Cold fingers. Corpse-cold. He made a thin, shrieking sound. Weird. She put her hand in a milk-soaked patch of carpet. Saw the broken glass. The top of the tumbler had shattered. The heavy base was intact, crowned with sharp spears. Drops of milk clinging to it. Still winded, half paralyzed by pain, the Eel seized her other ankle. Hitched-twitched-dragged himself toward her. He was still shrieking. Like a bird. Going to throw himself on top of her. Pin her. She seized the broken glass. Cut her thumb. Didn't feel a thing. He let go of her ankles to grab at her thighs. She flipped-writhed onto her back. As if *she* were an eel. Thrust the jagged end of the broken tumbler at him, not intending to stab him, hoping only to ward him off. But he was heaving himself onto her, falling onto her, and the three glass points speared into his throat. He tried to pull away. Twisted the tumbler. The points broke off in his flesh. Choking, gagging, he nailed her to the floor with his body. Blood streamed from his nose. She squirmed. He clawed at her. His knee bore down hard on her hip. His mouth was at her throat. He bit her. Just nipped her skin. He'd get a bigger bite next time if she let him. She thrashed. Breath whistled and rattled in his ruined throat. She slithered free. He grabbed. She kicked. Her legs worked better now. The kick landed solidly. She crawled toward the living room. Gripped the frame of the dining-room archway. Pulled herself to her feet. Glanced back. The Eel was on his feet as well, a dining-room chair raised like a club. He swung it. She dodged. The chair hit the frame of the archway with a thunderous sound. She staggered into the living room, heading for the foyer, the door, escape. He threw the chair. It struck her shoulder. She went down. Rolled. Looked up. He towered over her, seized her left arm. Her strength faded. Darkness pulsed at the edges of her vision. He gripped her other arm. She was finished. Would have been finished, anyway, if the glass in his throat had not finally worked through one more artery. Blood suddenly *gushed* from his nose. He collapsed atop her, a great and terrible weight, dead.

She could not move, could barely breathe, and had to struggle to hold fast to consciousness. Above the eerie sound of her own strangled sobs, she heard a door open. Footsteps.

"Laura? I'm home." It was Nina's voice, light and cheery at first, then shrill with horror: "Laura? Oh, my God, *Laura!*"

Laura strove to push the dead man off her, but she was able to squirm only half free of the corpse, just far enough to see Nina standing in the foyer archway.

For a moment the woman was paralyzed by shock. She stared at her cream and peach and seafoam-green living room, the tasteful decor now liberally accented with crimson smears. Then her violet eyes returned to Laura, and she snapped out of her trance. "Laura, oh, dear God, Laura." She took three steps forward, halted abruptly, and bent over, hugging herself as if she had been hit in the stomach. She made an odd sound: "Uh, uh, uh, uh, uh." She tried to straighten up. Her face was contorted. She could not seem to stand erect, and finally she crumpled to the floor and made no sound at all.

It could not happen like this. This wasn't fair, damn it.

New strength, born of panic and of love for Nina, filled Laura. She wriggled free of Sheener and crawled quickly to her foster mother.

Nina was limp. Her beautiful eyes were open, sightless.

Laura put her bloody hand to Nina's neck, feeling for a pulse. She thought she found one. Weak, irregular, but a pulse.

She pulled a cushion off a chair and put it under Nina's head, then ran into the kitchen where the numbers of the police and fire departments were on the wall phone. Shakily, she reported Nina's heart attack and gave the fire department their address.

When she hung up, she knew everything was going to be all right because she had already lost one parent to a heart attack, her father, and it would be just too absurd to lose Nina the same way. Life had absurd moments, yes, but life *itself* wasn't absurd. Life was strange, difficult, miraculous, precious, tenuous, mysterious, but not flat-out absurd. So Nina would live because Nina dying made no sense.

Still scared and worried but feeling better, Laura hurried back to the living room and knelt beside her foster mother, held her.

Newport Beach had first-rate emergency services. The ambulance arrived no more than three or four minutes after Laura had called for it. The two paramedics were efficient and well equipped. Within just a few minutes, however, they pronounced Nina dead, and no doubt she had been dead from the moment she collapsed.

# TEN

One week after Laura returned to McIlroy and eight days before Christmas, Mrs. Bowmaine reassigned Tammy Hinsen to the fourth bed in the Ackersons' room. In an unusual private session with Laura, Ruth, and Thelma, the social worker explained the reasoning behind that reassignment: "I know you say Tammy isn't happy with you girls, but she seems to get along better there than anywhere else. We've had her in several rooms, but the other children can't tolerate her. I don't know what it is about the child that makes her an outcast, but her other roommates usually end up using her as a punching bag."

Back in their room, before Tammy arrived, Thelma settled into a basic yoga position on the floor, legs folded in a pretzel form, heels against hips. She had become interested in yoga when the Beatles endorsed Eastern meditation, and she had said that when she finally met Paul McCartney (which was her indisputable destiny), "it would be nice if we have something in common, which we will if I can talk with some authority about this yoga crap."

Now, instead of meditating she said, "What would that cow have done if I'd said, 'Mrs. Bowmaine, the kids don't like Tammy because she let herself be diddled by the Eel, and she helped him target other vulnerable girls, so as far as they're concerned, she's the enemy.' What would Bovine Bowmaine have done when I laid *that* on her?"

"She'd have called you a lying scuz," Laura said, flopping down on her sway-backed bed.

"No doubt. Then she'd have eaten me for lunch. Do you believe the size of that woman? She gets bigger by the week. Anyone that big is dangerous, a ravenous omnivore capable of eating the nearest child, bones and all, as casually as she'd consume a pint of fudge ripple."

At the window, looking down at the playground behind the mansion, Ruth said, "It's not fair the way the other kids treat Tammy."

"Life isn't fair," Laura said.

"Life isn't a weenie roast, either," Thelma said. "Jeez, Shane, don't wax philosophical if you're going to be trite. You know we hate triteness here only slightly less than we hate turning on the radio and hearing Bobbie Gentry singing *Ode to Billy Joe*."

When Tammy moved in an hour later, Laura was tense. She had killed Sheener, after all, and Tammy had been dependent on him. She expected Tammy to be bitter and angry, but in fact the girl greeted her only with a sincere, shy, and piercingly sad smile.

After Tammy had been with them two days, it became clear that she viewed the loss of the Eel's twisted affections with perverse regret but also with relief. The fiery temper she had revealed when she tore apart Laura's books was quenched. She was once again that drab, bony, washed-out girl who, on Laura's first day at McIlroy, had seemed more of an apparition than a real person, in danger of dissolving into smoky ectoplasm and, with the first good draft, dissipating entirely.

After the deaths of the Eel and Nina Dockweiler, Laura attended half-hour sessions with Dr. Boone, a psychotherapist, when he visited McIlroy every Tuesday and Saturday. Boone was unable to understand that Laura could absorb the shock of Willy Sheener's attack and Nina's tragic death without psychological damage. He was puzzled by her articulate discussions of her feelings and the adult vocabulary with which she expressed her adjustment to events in Newport Beach. Having been motherless, having lost her father, having endured many crises and much terror—but most of all, having benefited from her father's wondrous love—she was as resilient as a sponge, absorbing what life presented. However, though she could speak of Sheener with dispassion and of Nina with as much affection as sadness, the psychiatrist viewed her adjustment as merely apparent and not real.

"So you dream about Willy Sheener?" he asked as he sat beside her on the sofa in the small office reserved for him at McIlroy.

"I've only dreamed of him twice. Nightmares, of course. But all kids have nightmares."

"You dream about Nina, too. Are those nightmares?"

"Oh, no! Those are lovely dreams."

He looked surprised. "When you think of Nina, you feel sad?"

"Yes. But also . . . I remember the fun of shopping with her, trying on dresses and sweaters. I remember her smile and her laugh."

"And guilt? Do you feel guilty about what happened to Nina?"

"No. Maybe Nina wouldn't have died if I hadn't moved in with them and drawn Sheener after me, but I can't feel guilty about that. I tried hard to be a good foster daughter to them, and they were happy with me. What happened was that life dropped a big custard pie on us, and that's not my fault; you can never see the custard pies coming. It's not good slapstick if you see the pie coming."

"Custard pie?" he asked, perplexed. "You see life as slapstick comedy? Like the Three Stooges?"

"Partly."

"Life is just a joke then?"

"No. Life is serious *and* a joke at the same time."

"But how can that be?"

"If you don't know," she said, "maybe I should be the one asking the questions here."

She filled many pages of her current notebook with observations about Dr. Will Boone. Of her unknown guardian, however, she wrote nothing. She tried not to think of him, either. He had failed her. Laura had come to depend on him; his heroic efforts on her behalf had made her feel *special,* and feeling special had helped her cope since her father's death. Now she felt foolish for ever looking beyond herself for survival. She still had the note he had left on her desk after her father's funeral, but she no longer reread it. And day by day her guardian's previous efforts on her behalf seemed more like fantasies akin to those of Santa Claus, which must be outgrown.

On Christmas afternoon they returned to their room with the gifts they received from charities and do-gooders. They wound up in a sing-along of holiday songs, and both Laura and the twins were amazed when Tammy joined in. She sang in a low, tentative voice.

Over the next couple of weeks she nearly ceased biting her nails altogether. She was only slightly more outgoing than usual, but she seemed calmer, more content with herself than she had ever been.

"When there's no perv around to bother her," Thelma said, "maybe she gradually starts to feel clean again."

Friday, January 12, 1968, was Laura's thirteenth birthday, but she did not celebrate it. She could find no joy in the occasion.

On Monday, she was transferred from McIlroy to Caswell Hall, a shelter for older children in Anaheim, five miles away.

Ruth and Thelma helped her carry her belongings downstairs to the front foyer. Laura had never imagined that she would so intensely regret leaving McIlroy.

"We'll be coming in May," Thelma assured her. "We turn thirteen on May second, and then we're out of here. We'll be together again."

When the social worker from Caswell arrived, Laura was reluctant to go. But she went.

Caswell Hall was an old high school that had been converted to dormitories, recreational lounges, and offices for social workers. As a result the atmosphere was more institutional than at McIlroy.

Caswell was also more dangerous than McIlroy because the kids were older and because many were borderline juvenile delinquents. Marijuana and pills were available, and fights among the boys—and even among the girls—were not infrequent. Cliques formed, as they had at McIlroy, but at Caswell some of the cliques were perilously close in structure and function to street gangs. Thievery was common.

Within a few weeks Laura realized that there were two types of survivors in life: those, like her, who found the requisite strength in having once been loved with great intensity; and those who, having not been loved, learned to thrive on hatred, suspicion, and the meager rewards of revenge. They were at once scornful of the need for human feeling and envious of the capacity for it.

She lived with great caution at Caswell but never allowed fear to diminish her. The thugs were frightening but also pathetic and, in their posturing and rituals of violence, even funny. She found no one like the Ackersons with whom to share the black humor, so she filled her notebooks with it. In those neatly written monologues, she turned inward while she waited for the Ackersons to be thirteen; that was an intensely rich time of self-discovery and increasing understanding of the slapstick, tragic world into which she had been born.

On Saturday, March 30, she was in her room at Caswell, reading, when she heard one of her roomies—a whiny girl named Fran

Wickert—talking to another girl in the hall, discussing a fire in which kids had been killed. Laura was eavesdropping with only half an ear until she heard the word "McIlroy."

A chill pierced her, freezing her heart, numbing her hands. She dropped the book and raced into the hallway, startling the girls. "When? When was this fire?"

"Yesterday," Fran said.

"How many were k-killed?"

"Not many, two kids I think, maybe only one, but I heard if you was there you could smell burnin' meat. Is that the grossest thing—"

Advancing on Fran, Laura said, "What were their names?"

"Hey, let me go."

"Tell me their names!"

"I don't know any names. Christ, what's the matter with you?"

Laura did not remember letting go of Fran, and she did not recall leaving the grounds of the shelter, but suddenly she found herself on Katella Avenue, blocks from Caswell Hall. Katella was a commercial street in that area, and in some places there was no sidewalk, so she ran on the shoulder of the road, heading east, with traffic whizzing by on her right side. Caswell was five miles from McIlroy, and she was not sure she knew the entire route, but trusting to instinct she ran until she was exhausted, then walked until she could run again.

The rational course would have been to go straight to one of the Caswell counselors and ask for the names of those kids killed in the fire at McIlroy. But Laura had the peculiar idea that the Ackerson twins' fate rested entirely upon her willingness to make the difficult trip to McIlroy to inquire about them, that if she asked about them by phone she would be told they were dead, that if instead she endured the physical punishment of the five-mile run, she'd find the Ackersons were safe. That was superstition, but she succumbed to it anyway.

Twilight descended. The late-March sky was filled with muddy-red and purple light, and the edges of the scattered clouds appeared to be aflame by the time Laura came within sight of the McIlroy Home. With relief she saw that the front of the old mansion was unmarked by fire.

Although she was soaked with sweat and shaking with exhaustion, though she had a throbbing headache, she did not slow when she saw the unscorched mansion but maintained her pace for the final block. She passed six kids in the ground-floor hallways and three more on the stairs, and two of them spoke to her by name. But she did not stop to ask them about the blaze. She had to *see*.

On the last flight of stairs she caught the scent of a fire's aftermath: the acrid, tarry stench of burnt things; the lingering, sour smell of smoke. When she went through the door at the top of the stairwell, she saw that the windows were open at each end of the third-floor hall and that electric fans had been set up in the middle of the corridor to blow the tainted air in both directions.

The Ackersons' room had a new, unpainted door frame and door, but the surrounding wall was scorched and smeared with black soot. A hand-printed sign warned of danger. Like all the doors in McIlroy, this one had no lock, so she ignored the sign and flung open the door and stepped across the threshold and saw what she had been so afraid of seeing: destruction.

The hall lights behind her and the purple glow of twilight at the windows did not adequately illuminate the room, but she saw that the remains of the furniture had been cleaned out; the place was empty but for the reeking ghost of the fire. The floor was blackened by soot and charred, though it looked structurally sound. The walls were smoke-damaged. The closet doors had been reduced to ashes but for a few burnt chunks of wood clinging to the hinges, which had partially melted. Both windows had blown out or been broken by those fleeing the flames; now those gaps were temporarily covered by sections of clear-plastic dropcloths stapled to the walls. Fortunately for the other kids at McIlroy, the fire had burned upward rather than outward, eating through the ceiling. She looked overhead into the mansion's attic where massive, blackened beams were dimly visible in the gloom. Apparently the flames had been stopped before they'd broken through to the roof, for she could not see the sky.

She was breathing laboriously, noisily, not only because of the exhausting trip from Caswell but because a vise of panic was squeezing her chest painfully, making it difficult to inhale. And every breath of the bitterly scented air brought the nauseating taste of carbon.

From that moment in her room at Caswell when she had heard of the fire at McIlroy, she had known the cause, though she had not wanted to admit to the knowledge. Tammy Hinsen once had been caught with a can of lighter fluid and matches with which she planned to set herself afire. On hearing of that intended self-immolation, Laura had known that Tammy had been serious about it because immolation seemed such a *right* form of suicide for her, an externalization of the inner fire that had been consuming her for years.

Please, God, she was alone in the room when she did it, please.

Gagging on the stink and taste of destruction, Laura turned away from the fire-blasted room and stepped into the third-floor corridor.

"Laura?"

She looked up and saw Rebecca Bogner. Laura's breath came and went in wrenching inhalations, shuddering exhalations, but somehow she croaked their names: "Ruth . . . Thelma?"

Rebecca's bleak expression denied the possibility that the twins had escaped unharmed, but Laura repeated the precious names, and in her ragged voice she heard a pathetic, beseeching note.

"Down there," Rebecca said, pointing toward the north end of the hall. "The next to the last room on the left."

With a sudden rush of hope, Laura ran to the indicated room. Three beds were empty, but in the fourth, revealed by the light of a reading lamp, was a girl lying on her side, facing the wall.

"Ruth? Thelma?"

The girl on the bed slowly rose—one of the Ackersons, unharmed. She wore a drab, badly wrinkled, gray dress; her hair was in disarray; her face was puffy, her eyes moist with tears. She took a step toward Laura but stopped as if the effort of walking was too great.

Laura rushed to her, hugged her.

With her head on Laura's shoulder, face against Laura's neck, she spoke at last in a tortured voice. "Oh, I wish it'd been me, Shane. If it had to be one of us, why couldn't it have been me?"

Until the girl spoke, Laura had assumed that she was Ruth.

Refusing to accept that horror, Laura said, "Where's Ruthie?"

"Gone. Ruthie's gone. I thought you knew, my Ruthie's dead."

Laura felt as if something deep within her had torn. Her grief was so powerful that it precluded tears; she was stunned, numb.

For the longest time they just held each other. Twilight faded toward night. They moved to the bed and sat on the edge.

A couple of kids appeared at the door. They evidently shared the room with Thelma, but Laura waved them away.

Looking at the floor, Thelma said, "I woke up to this shrieking, such a horrible shrieking . . . and all this *light* so bright it hurt my eyes. And then I realized the room was on fire. *Tammy* was on fire. Blazing like a torch. Thrashing in her bed, blazing and shrieking . . . "

Laura put an arm around her and waited.

" . . . The fire leaped off Tammy—*whoosh* up the wall, her bed was on fire, and fire was spreading across the floor, the rug was burning . . . "

Laura remembered how Tammy had sung with them on Christmas and had thereafter been calmer day by day, as if gradually finding inner peace. Now it was obvious that the peace she'd found had been based on the determination to end her torment.

"Tammy's bed was nearest the door, the door was on fire, so I broke the window over my bed. I called to Ruth, she . . . s-she said she was coming, there was smoke, I couldn't see, then Heather Dorning, who was bunking in your old bed, she came to the window, so I helped her get out, and the smoke was sucked out of the window, so the room cleared a little, which was when I saw Ruth was trying to throw her own blanket over Tammy to s-smother the flames, but that blanket caught f-fire, too, and I saw Ruth . . . Ruth . . . Ruth on fire . . . ''

Outside, the last purple light melted into darkness.

The shadows in the corners of the room deepened.

The lingering burnt odor seemed to grow stronger.      " . . . and I would've gone to her, I would've gone, but just then the f-fire *exploded,* it was everywhere in the room, and the smoke was black and so thick, and I couldn't see Ruth any more or anything . . . then I heard sirens, loud and close, sirens, so I tried to tell myself they'd get there in time to help Ruth, which was a l-l-lie, a lie I told myself and wanted to believe, and . . . I left her there, Shane. Oh, God, I went out the window and left Ruthie on f-f-fire, burning . . . ''

"You couldn't do anything else," Laura assured her.

"I left Ruthie burning."

"There was nothing you could do."

"I left Ruthie."

"There was no point in you dying too."

"I left Ruthie burning."

In May, after her thirteenth birthday, Thelma was transferred to Caswell and assigned to a room with Laura. The social workers agreed to that arrangement because Thelma was suffering from depression and was not responding to therapy. Maybe she would find the succor she needed in her friendship with Laura.

For months Laura despaired of reversing Thelma's decline. At night Thelma was plagued by dreams, and by day she stewed in self-recrimination. Eventually, time healed her, though her wounds never entirely closed. Her sense of humor gradually returned, and her wit became as sharp as ever, but there was a new melancholy in her.

They shared a room at Caswell Hall for five years, until they left the custody of the state and embarked on lives under no one's control but their own. They shared many laughs during those years. Life was good again but never the same as it had been before the fire.

# ELEVEN

In the main lab of the institute, the dominant object was the gate through which one could step into other ages. It was a huge, barrel-shaped device, twelve feet long and eight feet in diameter, of highly polished steel on the outside, lined with polished copper on the inside. It rested on copper blocks that held it eighteen inches off the floor. Thick electrical cables trailed from it, and within the barrel strange currents made the air shimmer as if it were water.

Kokoschka returned through time to the gate, materializing inside that enormous cylinder. He had made several trips that day, shadowing Stefan in far times and places, and at last he had learned why the traitor was obsessed with reshaping the life of Laura Shane. He hurried to the mouth of the gate and stepped down onto the lab floor, where two scientists and three of his own men were waiting for him.

"The girl has nothing to do with the bastard's plots against the government, nothing to do with his attempts to destroy the time-travel project," Kokoschka said. "She's an entirely separate matter, just a personal crusade of his."

"So now we know everything he's done and why," said one of the scientists, "and you can eliminate him."

"Yes," Kokoschka said, crossing the room to the main programming board. "Now that we've uncovered all the traitor's secrets, we can kill him."

As he sat down at the programming board, intending to reset the gate to deliver him to yet another time, where he could surprise the traitor, Kokoschka decided to kill Laura, too. It would be an easy job, something he could handle by himself, for he would have the element of surprise on his side; he preferred to work alone, anyway, whenever possible; he disliked sharing the pleasure. Laura Shane was no danger to the government or to its plans to reshape the future of the world, but he would kill her first and in front of Stefan, merely to break the traitor's heart before putting a bullet in it. Besides, Kokoschka liked to kill.

# 3

◆ ◆ ◆

# A Light in the Dark

## ONE

On Laura Shane's twenty-second birthday, January 12, 1977, she received a toad in the mail. The box in which it came bore no return address, and no note was enclosed. She opened it at the desk by the window in the living room of her apartment, and the clear sunlight of the unusually warm winter day glimmered pleasingly on the charming little figurine. The toad was ceramic, two inches tall, standing on a ceramic lily pad, wearing a top hat and holding a cane.

Two weeks earlier the campus literary magazine had published "Amphibian Epics," a short story of hers about a girl whose father spun fanciful tales of an imaginary toad, Sir Tommy of England. Only she knew that the piece was as much fact as fiction, though someone apparently intuited at least something of the true importance that the story had for her, because the grinning toad in the top hat was packed with extraordinary care. It was carefully wrapped in a swatch of soft cotton cloth tied with red ribbon, then further wrapped in tissue paper, nestled in a plain white box in a bed of cotton balls, and that box was packed in a nest of shredded newspaper inside a still larger box. No one would go to such trouble to protect a five-dollar, novelty figurine unless the packing was meant to signify the sender's perception of the depth of her emotional involvement with the events of "Amphibian Epics."

To afford the rent, she shared her off-campus apartment in Irvine with two juniors at the university, Meg Falcone and Julie Ishimina, and at first she thought perhaps one of them had sent the toad. They seemed unlikely candidates, for Laura was not close to either of them. They were busy with studies and interests of their own; and they had lived with her only since the previous September. They claimed to have no knowledge of the toad, and their denials seemed sincere.

She wondered if Dr. Matlin, the faculty adviser to the literary magazine at UCI, might have sent the figurine. Since her sophomore year, when she had taken Matlin's course in creative writing, he had encouraged her to pursue her talent and polish her craftsmanship. He had been particularly fond of "Amphibian Epics," so maybe he had sent the toad to say "well done." But why no return address, no card? Why the secrecy? No, that was out of character for Harry Matlin.

She had a few casual friends at the university, but she was not truly close to anyone because she had little time to make and sustain deep friendships. Between her studies, her job, and her writing, she used up all the hours of the day not devoted to sleeping or eating. She could think of no one who would have gone out of his way to buy the toad, package it, and mail it anonymously.

A mystery.

The following day her first class was at eight o'clock and her last at two. She returned to her nine-year-old Chevy in the campus parking lot at a quarter till four, unlocked the door, got behind the wheel—and was startled to see another toad on the dashboard.

It was two inches high and four inches long. This one was also ceramic, emerald green, reclining with one arm bent and its head propped on its hand. It was smiling dreamily.

She was sure she had left the car locked, and in fact it had been locked when she returned from class. The enigmatic giver of toads had evidently gone to considerable trouble to open the Chevy without a key—a loid of some kind or a coathanger worked through the top of the window to the lock button—and leave the toad in a dramatic fashion.

Later she put the reclining toad on her nightstand where the top hat-and-cane fellow already stood. She spent the evening in bed, reading. From time to time her attention drifted away from the page to the ceramic figures.

The next morning when she left the apartment, she found a small box on her doorstep. Inside was another meticulously wrapped toad. It was cast in pewter, sitting upon a log, holding a banjo.

The mystery deepened.

In the summer she put in a full shift as a waitress at Hamburger Hamlet in Costa Mesa, but during the school year her course load was so heavy that she could work only three evenings a week. The Hamlet was an upscale hamburger restaurant providing good food for reasonable prices in a moderately plush ambience—crossbeam ceiling, lots of wood paneling, hugely comfortable armchairs—so the customers were usually happier than those in other places where she had waited tables.

Even if the atmosphere had been seedy and the customers surly, she would have kept the job; she needed the money. On her eighteenth birthday, four years ago, she learned that her father had established a trust fund, consisting of the assets liquidated upon his death, and that the trust could not be touched by the state to pay for her care at McIlroy Home and Caswell Hall. At that time the funds had become hers to spend, and she had applied them toward living and college expenses. Her father hadn't been rich; there was only twelve thousand dollars even after six years of accrued interest, not nearly enough for four years of rent, food, clothing, and tuition, so she depended upon her income as a waitress to make up the difference.

On Sunday evening, January 16, she was halfway through her shift at the Hamlet when the host escorted an older couple, about sixty, to one of the booths in Laura's station. They asked for two Michelobs while they studied the menu. A few minutes later, when she returned from the bar with the beers and two frosted mugs on a tray, she saw a ceramic toad on their table. She nearly dropped the tray in surprise.

She looked at the man, at the woman, and they were grinning at her, but they weren't *saying* anything, so she said, "*You've* been giving me toads? But I don't even know you—do I?"

The man said, "Oh, you've gotten more of these, have you?"

"This is the fourth. You didn't bring this for me, did you? But it wasn't here a few minutes ago. Who put it on the table?"

He winked at his wife, and she said to Laura, "You've got a secret admirer, dear."

"Who?"

"Young fella was sitting at that table over there," the man said, pointing across the room to a station served by a waitress named Amy Heppleman. The table was now empty; the busboy had just finished clearing away the dirty dishes. "Soon as you left to get our beers, he comes over and asks if he can leave this here for you."

It was a Christmas toad in a Santa suit, without a beard, a sack of toys over its shoulder.

The woman said, "You don't really know who he is?"

"No. What'd he look like?"

"Tall," the man said. "Quite tall and husky. Brown hair."

"Brown eyes too," his wife said. "Soft-spoken."

Holding the toad, staring at it, Laura said, "There's something about this . . . something that makes me uneasy."

"Uneasy?" the woman said. "But it's just a young man who's smitten with you, dear."

"Is it?" she wondered.

Laura found Amy Heppleman at the salad preparation counter and sought a better description of the toad-giver.

"He had a mushroom omelet, whole-wheat toast, and a Coke," Amy said, using a pair of stainless-steel tongs to fill two bowls with salad greens. "Didn't you see him sitting there?"

"I didn't notice him, no."

"Biggish guy. Jeans. A blue-checkered shirt. His hair was cut too short, but he was kinda cute if you like the moose type. Didn't talk much. Seemed kinda shy."

"Did he pay with a credit card?"

"No. Cash."

"Damn," Laura said.

She took the Santa toad home and put it with the other figurines.

The following morning, Monday, as she left the apartment, she found yet another plain white box on the doorstep. She opened it reluctantly. It contained a clear glass toad.

When Laura returned from the UCI campus that same afternoon, Julie Ishimina was sitting at the dinette table, reading the daily paper and drinking a cup of coffee. "You got another one," she said, pointing to a box on the kitchen counter. "Came in the mail."

Laura tore open the elaborately wrapped package. The sixth toad was actually a pair of toads—salt and pepper shakers.

She put the shakers with the other figurines on her nightstand, and for a long while she sat on the edge of her bed, frowning at that growing collection.

At five o'clock that afternoon she called Thelma Ackerson in Los Angeles and told her about the toads.

Lacking a trust fund of any size, Thelma had not even considered college, but as she said, that was no tragedy because she was not interested in academics. Upon completing high school, she had gone straight from Caswell Hall to Los Angeles, intent upon breaking into show business as a stand-up comic.

Nearly every night, from about six o'clock until two in the morning, she hung around the comedy clubs—the Improv, the Comedy Store, and all their imitators—angling for a six-minute, unpaid shot on the stage, making contacts (or hoping to make them), competing with a horde of young comics for the coveted exposure.

She worked days to pay the rent, moving from job to job, some of them decidedly peculiar. Among other things she had worn a chicken suit and sung songs and waited tables in a weird "theme" pizza parlor, and she'd been a picket-line stand-in for a few Writers Guild West members who were required by their union to participate in a strike action but who preferred to pay someone a hundred bucks a day to carry a placard for them and sign their names on the duty roster.

Though they lived just ninety minutes apart, Laura and Thelma got together only two or three times a year, usually just for a long lunch or dinner, because they led busy lives. But regardless of the time between visits, they were instantly comfortable with each other and quick to share their most intimate thoughts and experiences. "The McIlroy-Caswell bond," Thelma once said, "is stronger than being blood brothers, stronger than the Mafia covenant, stronger than the bond between Fred Flintstone and Barney Rubble, and those two are *close*."

Now, after she listened to Laura's story, Thelma said, "So what's your problem, Shane? Sounds to me like some big, shy hunk of a guy has a crush on you. Lots of women would swoon over this."

"Is that what it is, though? An innocent crush?"

"What else?"

"I don't know. But it . . . makes me uneasy."

"Uneasy? These toads are all cute little things, aren't they? None of them is a snarling toad? None of them is holding a bloody little butcher knife? Or a little ceramic chainsaw?''

''No.''

''He hasn't sent you any *beheaded* toads, has he?''

''No, but—''

''Shane, the last few years have been calm, though of course you've had a pretty eventful life. It's understandable that you'd expect this guy to be Charles Manson's brother. But it's almost a sure bet he's just what he appears to be—a guy who admires you from afar, is maybe a little shy, and has a streak of romance in him about eighteen inches wide. How's your sex life?''

''I don't have any,'' Laura said.

''Why not? You're not a virgin. There was that guy last year—''

''Well, you know that didn't work out.''

''Nobody since?''

''No. What do you think—I'm promiscuous?''

''Sheesh! Kiddo, two lovers in twenty-two years would not make you promiscuous even by the pope's definition. Unbend a little. Relax. Stop being a worrier. Flow with this, see where it goes. He might just turn out to be Prince Charming.''

''Well . . . maybe I will. I guess you're right.''

''But, Shane?''

''Yeah?''

''Just for luck, from now on you better carry a .357 Magnum.''

''Very funny.''

''Funny is my business.''

During the following three days Laura received two more toads, and by Saturday morning, the twenty-second, she was equally confused, angry, and afraid. Surely no secret admirer would string the game out so long. Each new toad seemed to be mocking rather than honoring her. There was a quality of obsession in the giver's relentlessness.

She spent much of Friday night in a chair by the big living-room window, sitting in the dark. Through the half-open drapes, she had a view of the apartment building's covered veranda and the area in front of her own door. If he came during the night, she intended to confront him in the act. By three-thirty in the morning he had not arrived, and she dozed off. When she woke in the morning, no package was on the doorstep.

After she showered and ate a quick breakfast, she went down the outside stairs and around to the back of the building where she kept her car in the covered stall assigned to her. She intended to go to the library to do some research work, and it looked like a good day for being indoors. The winter sky was gray and low, and the air had a prestorm heaviness that filled her with foreboding—a feeling that intensified when she found another box on the dashboard of her locked Chevy. She wanted to scream in frustration.

Instead she sat behind the wheel and opened the package. The other figurines had been inexpensive, no more than ten or fifteen dollars each, some probably as cheap as three bucks, but the newest was an exquisite miniature porcelain that surely cost at least fifty dollars. However, she was less interested in the toad than in the box in which it had come. It was not plain, as before, but imprinted with the name of a gift shop—Collectibles—in the South Coast Plaza shopping mall.

Laura drove directly to the mall, arrived fifteen minutes before Collectibles opened, waited on a bench in the promenade, and was first through the shop's door when it was unlocked. The store's owner and manager was a petite, gray-haired woman named Eugenia Farvor. "Yes, we handle this line," she said after listening to Laura's succinct explanation and examining the porcelain toad, "and in fact I sold it myself just yesterday to the young man."

"Do you know his name?"

"I'm sorry, no."

"What did he look like?"

"I remember him well because of his size. Very tall. Six five, I'd say. And very broad in the shoulders. He was quite well dressed. A gray pinstripe suit, blue and gray striped tie. I admired the suit, in fact, and he said it wasn't easy finding clothes to fit him."

"Did he pay cash?"

"Mmmmm . . . no, I believe he used a credit card."

"Would you still have the charge slip?"

"Oh, yes, we usually run a day or two behind in organizing them and transferring them to the master ticket for deposit." Mrs. Farvor led Laura past glass display cases filled with porcelains, Lalique and Waterford crystal, Wedgwood plates, Hummel figurines, and other expensive items, to the cramped office at the back of the store. Then she suddenly had second thoughts about sharing her customer's identity. "If his intentions are innocent, if he's just an admirer of yours— and I must say there seemed no harm in him; he seemed quite nice— then I'll be spoiling everything for him. He'll want to be revealing himself to you according to his own plan."

Laura tried hard to charm the woman and win her sympathy. She could not recall ever having spoken more eloquently or with such feeling; usually she was not as good at vocalizing her feelings as she was at putting them down in print. Genuine tears sprang to her assistance, surprising her even more than they did Eugenia Farvor.

From the MasterCard charge slip, she obtained his name—Daniel Packard—and his telephone number. She went directly from the gift shop to a public telephone in the mall and looked him up. There were two Daniel Packards in the book, but the one with that number lived on Newport Avenue in Tustin.

When she returned to the mall parking lot, a cold drizzle was falling. She turned up her coat collar, but she had neither a hat nor an umbrella. By the time she got to her car, her hair was wet, and she was chilled. She shivered all the way from Costa Mesa to North Tustin.

She figured there was a good chance he would be at home. If he was a student, he would not be in class on Saturday. If he worked an ordinary nine-to-five job, he would probably not be at the office, either. And the weather ruled out many of the usual weekend pastimes for outdoor-oriented southern Californians.

His address was an apartment complex of two-story, Spanish-style buildings, eight of them, in a garden setting. For a few minutes she hurried from building to building on winding walkways under dripping palms and coral trees, looking for his apartment. By the time she found it—a first-floor, end unit in the building farthest from the street—her hair was soaked. Her chill had deepened. Discomfort dulled her fear and sharpened her anger, so she rang his bell without hesitation.

He evidently did not peek through the fisheye security lens, for when he opened the door and saw her, he looked stunned. He was maybe five years older than she, and he was a big man indeed, fully six feet five, two hundred and forty pounds, all muscle. He was wearing jeans and a pale-blue T-shirt smeared with grease and spotted with another oily substance; his well-developed arms were formidable. His face was shadowed by beard stubble and smudged with more grease, and his hands were black.

Carefully staying back from the door, beyond his reach, Laura simply said, "Why?"

"Because . . . " He shifted from one foot to the other, almost too big for the doorway in which he stood. "Because . . . "

"I'm waiting."

He wiped one grease-covered hand through his close-cropped hair and seemed oblivious of the resultant mess. His eyes shifted away from her; he looked out at the rain-lashed courtyard as he spoke. "How . . . how'd you find out it was me?"

"That's not important. What's important is that I don't know you, I've never seen you before, and yet I've got a toad menagerie that you've sent me, you come around in the middle of the night to leave them on my doorstep, you break into my car to leave them on the dashboard, and it's been going on for *weeks*, so don't you think it's time I knew what this is all about?''

Still not looking at her, he flushed and said, "Well, sure, but I didn't . . . wasn't ready . . . didn't think the time was right.''

"The time was right a week ago!''

"Ummmm.''

"So tell me. *Why?*''

Looking down at his greasy hands, he said quietly, "Well, see . . . ''

"Yes?''

"I love you.''

She stared at him, incredulous. He finally looked at her. She said, "You *love* me? But you don't even *know* me. How can you love a person you've never met?''

He looked away from her, rubbed his filthy hand through his hair again, and shrugged. "I don't know, but there it is, and I . . . uh . . . well, ummmm, I have this feeling, see, this feeling that I've got to spend the rest of my life with you.''

With cold rainwater trickling from her wet hair down the nape of her neck and along the curve of her spine, with her day at the library shot—how could she concentrate on research after this insane scene?—and with more than a little disappointment that her secret admirer had turned out to be this dirty, sweaty, inarticulate lummox, Laura said, "Listen, Mr. Packard, I don't want you sending me any more toads.''

"Well, see, I really want to send them.''

"But I don't want to receive them. And tomorrow I'll mail back the ones you've sent me. No, today. I'll mail them back today.''

He met her eyes again, blinked in surprise, and said, "I thought you liked toads.''

With growing anger, she said, "I *do* like toads. I love toads. I think toads are the cutest things in creation. Right now I even wish I *were* a toad, but I don't want *your* toads. Understand?''

"Ummmm.''

"Don't harass me, Packard. Maybe some women surrender to your weird mix of heavy-handed romance and sweaty macho charm, but I'm not one of them, and I can protect myself, don't think I can't. I'm a lot tougher than I look, and I've dealt with worse than you.''

She turned away from him, walked out from under the veranda into the rain, returned to her car, and drove back to Irvine. She shook all the way home, not only because she was wet and chilled but because she was in the grip of anger. The nerve of him!

At her apartment she undressed, bundled up in a quilted robe, and brewed a pot of coffee with which to ward off the chills.

She had just taken her first sip of coffee when the phone rang. She answered it in the kitchen. It was Packard.

Speaking so rapidly that he ran his sentences together in long gushes, he said, "Please don't hang up on me, you're right, I'm stupid about these things, an idiot, but give me just one minute to explain myself, I was fixing the dishwasher when you came, that's why I was such a mess, greasy and sweaty, had to pull it from under the counter myself, the landlord would have fixed it, but going through management takes a week, and I'm good with my hands, I can fix anything, it was a rainy day, nothing else to do, so why not fix it myself, I never figured you to show up. My name's Daniel Packard, but you know that already, I'm twenty-eight, I was in the army until '73, graduated from the University of California at Irvine with a degree in business just three years ago, work as a stockbroker now, but I take a couple night courses at the university, which is how I came across your story about the toad in the campus literary magazine, it was terrific, I loved it, a great story, really, so I went to the library and searched through back issues to find everything else you'd written, and I read it all, and a *lot* of it was good, damned good, not all of it, but a lot. I fell in love with you somewhere along the way, with the person I knew from her writing, because the writing was so beautiful and so real. One evening I was sitting there in the library reading one of your stories—they won't let anyone check out back issues of the literary magazine, they have them in binders, and you have to read them in the library—and this librarian was passing behind my chair, and she leaned over and asked if I liked the story, I said I did, and she said, 'Well, the author's right over there, if you want to tell her it's good,' and there you were just three tables away with a stack of books, doing research, scowling, making notes, and you were gorgeous. See, I knew you would be beautiful *inside* because your stories are beautiful, the sentiment in them is beautiful, but it never occurred to me that you'd be beautiful *outside*, too, and there was no way I could approach you because I've always been tongue-tied and stumble-footed around beautiful women, maybe because my mother was beautiful but cold and forbidding, so now maybe I think all beautiful women will reject me the way my mother did—a little half-baked analysis there—but it sure would've been a lot easier for me if you'd been ugly or at least plain looking. Because of your story I thought I'd use the toads, that whole secret admirer bit with the gifts, as a way to soften you up, and I planned to reveal myself after the third or fourth toad, I really did, but I kept delaying because I didn't want to be rejected, I guess, and I knew it was getting crazy, toad after toad after toad, but I just couldn't stop it and forget you, yet I wasn't able to face you, either, and that's it. I never meant you any harm, I sure didn't mean to upset you, can you forgive me, I hope you can."

He stopped at last, exhausted.

She said, "Well."

He said, "So will you go out with me?"

Surprised by her own response, she said, "Yes."

"Dinner and a movie?"

"All right."

"Tonight? Pick you up at six?"

"Okay."

After she hung up she stood for a while, staring at the phone. Finally she said aloud, "Shane, are you nuts?" Then she said, "But he told me my writing was 'so beautiful and so real.' "

She went into her bedroom and looked at the collection of toads on the nightstand. She said, "He's inarticulate and silent one time, a babbler the next. He could be a psycho killer, Shane." Then she said, "Yeah, he could be, but he's also a great literary critic."

Because he had suggested dinner and a movie, Laura dressed in a gray skirt, white blouse, and maroon sweater, but he showed up in a dark blue suit, white shirt with French cuffs, blue silk tie with tie chain, silk display handkerchief, and highly polished black wingtips, as if he were going to the season opener at the opera. He carried an umbrella and escorted her from her apartment to his car with one hand under her right arm, with such solemn concern that he seemed convinced that she would dissolve if touched by one drop of rain or shatter into a million pieces if she slipped and fell.

Considering the difference in their dress and the considerable difference in their size—at five-five, she was one foot shorter than he was; at a hundred fifteen pounds, she was less than half his weight—she felt almost as if she were going on a date with her father or an older brother. She was not a petite woman, but on his arm and under his umbrella she felt positively tiny.

He was uncommunicative again in the car, but he blamed it on the need to drive with special care in such rotten weather. They went to a small Italian restaurant in Costa Mesa, a place in which Laura had eaten a few good meals in the past. They sat down at their table and were given menus, but even before the waitress could ask if they would like a drink, Daniel said, "This is no good, this is all wrong, let's find another place."

Surprised, she said, "But why? This is fine. Their food's very good here."

"No, really, this is all wrong. No atmosphere, no style, I don't want you to think, ummmm," and now he was babbling as he'd done on the phone, blushing, "ummmm, well, anyway, this is no good, not right for our first date, I want this to be special," and he got up, "ummmm, I think I know just the place, I'm sorry, Miss"—this to the startled young waitress—"I hope we haven't inconvenienced you," and he was pulling back Laura's chair, helping her up, "I know just the place, you'll like it, I've never eaten there but I've heard it's really good, excellent." Other customers were staring, so Laura stopped protesting. "It's close, too, just a couple of blocks from here."

They returned to his car, drove two blocks, and parked in front of an unpretentious-looking restaurant in a strip shopping center.

By now Laura knew him well enough to realize that his sense of courtliness required her to wait for him to come around and open her car door, but when he opened it she saw he was standing in a ten-inch-deep puddle. "Oh, your shoes!" she said.

"They'll dry out. Here, you hold the umbrella over yourself, and I'll lift you across the puddle."

Nonplussed, she allowed herself to be plucked from the car and carried over the puddle as if she weighed no more than a feather pillow. He put her down on higher pavement and, without the umbrella, he sloshed back to the car to close the door.

The French restaurant had less atmosphere than the Italian place. They were shown to a corner table too near the kitchen, and Daniel's saturated shoes squished and squeaked all the way across the room.

"You'll catch pneumonia," she worried when they were seated and had ordered two Dry Sacks on the rocks.

"Not me. I've got a good immune system. Never get sick. One time in Nam, during an action, I was cut off from my unit, spent a week on my own in the jungle, rained every minute, I was *shriveled* by the time I found my way back to friendly territory, but I never even got the sniffles."

As they sipped their drinks and studied the menu and ordered, he was more relaxed than Laura had yet seen him, and he actually proved to be a coherent, pleasant, even amusing conversationalist. But when the appetizers were served—salmon in dill sauce for her, scallops in pastry for him—it swiftly became clear that the food was terrible, even though the prices were twice those at the Italian place that they had left, and course by course, as his embarrassment grew, his ability to sustain his end of the conversation declined drastically. Laura proclaimed everything delicious and choked down every bite, but it was no use; he was not fooled.

The kitchen staff and the waiter were also slow. By the time Daniel had paid the check and escorted her back to the car—lifting her across the puddle again as if she were a little girl—they were half an hour late for the movie they had intended to see.

"That's all right," she said, "we can go in late and stay to see the first half hour of the next showing."

"No, no," he said. "That's a terrible way to see a movie. It'll ruin it for you. I wanted this night to be perfect."

"Relax," she said. "I'm having fun."

He looked at her with disbelief, and she smiled, and he smiled, too, but his smile was sick.

"If you don't want to go to the movie now," she said, "that's all right, too. Wherever you want to go, I'm game."

He nodded, started the car, and drove out to the street. They had gone a few miles before she realized that he was taking her home.

All the way from his car to her door, he apologized for what a lousy evening it had been, and she repeatedly assured him that she was not in the least disappointed with a moment of it. At her apartment, the instant she inserted her key in the door, he turned and fled down the stairs from the second-floor veranda, neither asking for a goodnight kiss nor giving her a chance to invite him in.

She stepped to the head of the stairs and watched him descend, and he was halfway down when a gust of wind turned his umbrella inside out. He fought with it the rest of the way, twice almost losing his balance. When he reached the walk below, he finally got the umbrella corrected—and the wind immediately turned it inside out again. In frustration he threw it into some nearby shrubbery, then looked up at Laura. He was soaked from head to toe by then, and in the pale light from a lamppost she could see that his suit hung on him shapelessly. He was a *huge* man, strong as two bulls, but he had been done in by little things—puddles, a gust of wind—and there was something quite funny about that. She knew she should not laugh, *dared* not laugh, but a laugh burst from her anyway.

"You're too damned beautiful, Laura Shane!" he shouted from the walk below. "God help me, you're just too beautiful." Then he hurried away through the night.

Feeling bad about laughing but unable to stop, she went into the apartment and changed into pajamas. It was only twenty till nine.

He was either a hopeless basket case or the sweetest man she had known since her father died.

At nine-thirty the phone rang. He said, "Will you ever go out with me again?"

"I thought you'd never call."

"You will?"

"Sure."

"Dinner and a movie?" he asked.

"Sounds good."

"We won't go back to that horrible French place. I'm sorry about that, I really am."

"I don't care where we go," she said, "but once we sit down in the restaurant, promise me we'll *stay* there."

"I'm a bonehead about some things. And like I said . . . I never have been able to cope around beautiful women."

"Your mother."

"That's right. Rejected me. Rejected my father. Never felt *any* warmth from that woman. Walked out on us when I was eleven."

"Must've hurt."

"You're more beautiful than she was, and you scare me to death."

"How flattering."

"Well, sorry, but I meant it to be. The thing is, beautiful as you are, you're not *half* as beautiful as your writing, and that scares me even more. Because what could a genius like you ever see in a guy like me—except maybe comic relief?"

"Just one question, Daniel."

"Danny."

"Just one question, Danny. What the hell kind of stockbroker are you? Any good at all?"

"I'm first-rate," he said with such genuine pride that she knew he was telling the truth. "My clients swear by me, and I've got a nice little portfolio of my own that's outperformed the market three years running. As a stock analyst, broker, and investment adviser, I never give the wind a chance to turn my umbrella inside out."

# TWO

The afternoon following the placement of the explosives in the basement of the institute, Stefan took what he expected to be his next to last trip on the Lightning Road. It was an illicit jaunt to January 10, 1988, not on the official schedule and conducted without the knowledge of his colleagues.

Light snow was falling in the San Bernardino Mountains when he arrived, but he was dressed for the weather in rubber boots, leather gloves, and navy peacoat. He took cover under a dense copse of pines, intending to wait until the fierce lightning stopped flaring.

He checked his wristwatch in the flickering celestial light and was startled to see how late he had arrived. He had less than forty minutes to reach Laura before she was killed. If he screwed up and arrived too late, there would be no second chance.

Even while the last white flashes seared the overcast sky, while hard crashes of thunder still echoed back to him from distant peaks and ridges, he hurried away from the trees and down a sloping field where the snow was knee-deep from previous winter storms. There was a crust on the snow, through which he kept breaking with each step, and progress was as difficult as if he had been wading through deep water. He fell twice, and snow got down the tops of his boots, and the savage wind tore at him as if it possessed consciousness and the desire to destroy him. By the time he reached the end of the field and climbed over a snowbank onto the two-lane state highway that led to Arrowhead in one direction and Big Bear in the other, his pants and coat were crusted with frozen snow, his feet were freezing, and he had lost more than five minutes.

The recently plowed highway was clean except for the wispy snow snakes that slithered across the pavement on shifting currents of air. But already the tempo of the storm had increased. The flakes were much smaller than when he had arrived and were falling twice as fast as they had been minutes ago. Soon the road would be treacherous.

He noticed a sign by the side of the pavement—LAKE ARROW- HEAD 1 MILE—and was shocked to discover how much farther he was from Laura than he had expected to be.

Squinting into the wind, looking north, he saw a warm glimmer of electric lightning in the dreary, iron-gray afternoon: a single-story building and parked cars about three hundred yards away, on the right. He headed immediately in that direction, keeping his head tucked down to protect his face from the icy teeth of the wind.

He had to find a car. Laura had less than half an hour to live, and she was ten miles away.


## THREE

Five months after that first date, on Saturday, July 16, 1977, six weeks after graduating from UCI, Laura married Danny Packard in a civil ceremony before a judge in his chambers. The only guests in attendance, both of whom served as witnesses, were Danny's father, Sam Packard, and Thelma Ackerson.

Sam was a handsome, silver-haired man of about five ten, dwarfed by his son. Throughout the brief ceremony, he wept, and Danny kept turning around and saying, "You all right, Dad?" Sam nodded and blew his nose and told them to go on with it, but a moment later he was crying again, and Danny was asking him if he was all right, and Sam blew his nose as if imitating the mating calls of geese. The judge said, "Son, your father's tears are tears of joy, so if we could get on with this—I have three more ceremonies to perform."

Even if the groom's father had not been an emotional wreck, and even if the groom had not been a giant with the heart of a fawn, their wedding party would have been memorable because of Thelma. Her hair was cut in a strange, shaggy style, with a pompom-like spray in front that was tinted purple. In the middle of summer—and at a wedding, yet—she was wearing red high heels, tight black slacks, and tattered black blouse—carefully, purposefully tattered—gathered at the waist with a length of ordinary steel chain used as a belt. She was wearing exaggerated purple eye makeup, blood-red lipstick, and one earring that looked like a fishhook.

After the ceremony, as Danny was having a private word with his father, Thelma huddled with Laura in a corner of the courthouse lobby and explained her appearance. "It's called the punk look, the latest thing in Britain. No one's wearing it over here yet. In fact hardly anyone's wearing it in Britain, either, but in a few years everyone will dress like this. It's great for my act. I look freaky, so people want to laugh as soon as I step on the stage. It's also good for *me*. I mean, face it, Shane, I'm not exactly blossoming with age. Hell, if homely was a disease and had an organized charity, I'd be their poster child. But the two great things about punk style is you get to hide behind flamboyant makeup and hair, so no one can tell just how homely you are—and you're supposed to look weird, anyway. Jesus, Shane, Danny's a big guy. You've told me so much about him on the phone, but you never once said he was so huge. Put him in a Godzilla suit, turn him loose in New York, film the results, and you could make one of those movies without having to build expensive miniature sets. So you love him, huh?"

"I *adore* him," Laura said. "He's as gentle as he is big, maybe because of all the violence he saw and was a part of in Vietnam, or maybe because he's always been gentle at heart. He's sweet, Thelma, and he's thoughtful, and he thinks I'm one of the best writers he's ever read."

"And when he first started giving you toads, you thought he was a psychopath."

"A minor misjudgment."

Two uniformed police officers passed through the courthouse lobby, flanking a bearded young man in handcuffs, taking him to one of the courtrooms. The prisoner gave Thelma a looking over as he passed and said, "Hey, mama, let's get it on!"

"Ah, the Ackerson charm," Thelma said to Laura. "You get a guy who's a combination of a Greek god, a teddy bear, and Bennett Cerf, and I get crude propositions from the dregs of society. But come to think of it, I never even used to get that, so maybe my time is coming yet."

"You underrate yourself, Thelma. You always have. Some very special guy's going to see what a treasure you are—"

"Charles Manson when he's paroled."

"No. Someday you're going to be every bit as happy as I am. I know it. Destiny, Thelma."

"Good heavens, Shane, you've become a raging optimist! What about the lightning? All those deep conversations we had on the floor of our room at Caswell—you remember? We decided that life is just an absurdist comedy, and every once in a while it's suddenly interrupted with thunderbolts of tragedy to give the story balance, to make the slapstick seem funnier by comparison."

"Maybe it's struck for the last time in my life," Laura said.

Thelma stared hard at her. "Wow. I know you, Shane, and I know you realize what emotional risk you're putting yourself at by even just *wanting* to be this happy. I hope you're right, kid, and I bet you are. I bet there'll be no more lightning for you."

"Thank you, Thelma."

"And I think your Danny is a sweetheart, a jewel. But I'll tell you something that ought to mean a lot more than my opinion: Ruthie would have loved him too; Ruthie would have thought he was perfect."

They held each other tightly, and for a moment they were young girls again, defiant yet vulnerable, filled with both the cockeyed confidence and the terror of blind fate that had shaped their shared adolescence.

Sunday, July 24, when they returned from a week-long honeymoon in Santa Barbara, they went grocery shopping, then cooked dinner together—tossed salad, sourdough bread, microwave meatballs, and spaghetti—at the apartment in Tustin. She'd given up her own place and moved in with him a few days before the wedding. According to the plan that they had worked out, they would stay at the apartment for two years, maybe three. (They had talked about their future so often and in such detail that they now capitalized those two words in their minds—The Plan—as if they were referring to some cosmic owner's manual that had come with their marriage and that could be relied upon for an accurate picture of their destiny as husband and wife.) So after two years, maybe three, they would be able to afford the down payment on the right house without dipping into the tidy stock portfolio that Danny was building, and only then would they move.

They dined at the small table in the alcove off the kitchen, where they had a view of the king palms in the courtyard in the golden late-afternoon sun, and they discussed the key part of The Plan, which was for Danny to support them while Laura stayed home and wrote her first novel. "When you're wildly rich and famous," he said, twirling spaghetti on his fork, "then I'll leave the brokerage and spend my time managing our money."

"What if I'm never rich and famous?"

"You will be."

"What if I can't even get published?"

"Then I'll divorce you."

She threw a crust of bread at him. "Beast."

"Shrew."

"You want another meatball?"

"Not if you're going to throw it."

"My rage has passed. I make good meatballs, don't I?"

"Excellent," he agreed.

"That's worth celebrating, don't you think—that you have a wife who makes good meatballs?"

"Definitely worth celebrating."

"So let's make love."

Danny said, "In the middle of dinner?"

"No, in bed." She pushed back her chair and got up. "Come on. Dinner can always be reheated."

During that first year they made love frequently, and in their intimacies Laura found more than sexual release, something far more than she had expected. Being with Danny, holding him within her, she felt so close to him that at times it almost seemed as if they were one person—one body and one mind, one spirit, one dream. She loved him wholeheartedly, yes, but that feeling of oneness was more than love, or at least different from love. By their first Christmas together, she understood that what she felt was a sense of belonging not experienced in a long time, a sense of family; for this was her husband and she was his wife, and one day from their union would come children—after two or three years, according to The Plan—and within the shelter of the family was a peace not to be found elsewhere.

She would have thought that working and living in continuous happiness, harmony, and security day after day would lead to mental lethargy, that her writing would suffer from too much happiness, that she needed a balanced life with down days and miseries to keep the sharp edge on her work. But the idea that an artist needed to suffer to do her best work was a conceit of the young and inexperienced. The happier she grew, the better she wrote.

Six weeks before their first wedding anniversary, Laura finished a novel, *Jericho Nights*, and sent a copy to a New York literary agent, Spencer Keene, who had responded favorably to a query letter a month earlier. Two weeks later Keene called to say he would represent the book, expected a quick sale, and thought she had a splendid future as a novelist. With a swiftness that startled even the agent, he sold it to the first house to which it was submitted, Viking, for a modest but perfectly respectable advance of fifteen thousand dollars, and the deal was concluded on Friday, July 14, 1978, two days before Laura and Danny's anniversary.

# FOUR

The place he had seen from farther up the road was a restaurant and tavern in the shadows of enormous Ponderosa pines. The trees stood over two hundred feet tall, bedecked with clusters of six-inch cones, with beautifully fissured bark, some boughs bent low under the weight of snow from previous storms. The single-story building was made of logs; it was so sheltered by trees on three sides that its slate roof was covered with more pine needles than snow. The windows were either steamed over or frosted, and the light from within was pleasingly diffused by that translucent film on the glass.

In the parking lot in front of the building were two Jeep wagons, two pickup trucks, and a Thunderbird. Relieved that no one would be able to see him through the tavern windows, Stefan went directly to one of the Jeeps, tried the door, found it unlocked, and got in behind the steering wheel, closing the door after him.

He drew the Walther PPK/S .380 from the shoulder holster he was wearing inside his peacoat. He put it on the seat at his side.

His feet were painfully cold, and he wanted to pause and empty the snow out of his boots. But he had arrived late, and his original schedule was shot, so he dared not waste a minute. Besides, if his feet hurt, they weren't frozen; he wasn't in danger of frostbite yet.

The keys were not in the ignition. He slid the seat back, bent down, groped under the dashboard, located the ignition wires, and had the engine running in a minute.

Stefan sat up just as the owner of the Jeep, breath reeking of beer, pulled open the door. "Hey, what the hell you doing, pal?"

The rest of the snowswept parking lot was still deserted. They were alone.

Laura would be dead in twenty-five minutes.

The Jeep's owner reached for him, and he allowed himself to be dragged from behind the steering wheel, plucking his pistol off the seat as he went, and in fact he threw himself into the other man's grasp, using the momentum to send his adversary staggering backward on the slippery parking lot. They fell. As they hit the ground, he was on top, and he jammed the muzzle under the guy's chin.

"Jesus, mister! Don't kill me."

"We're getting up now. Easy, damn you, no sudden moves."

When they were on their feet Stefan moved behind the guy, quickly reversed his grip on the Walther, used it as a club, struck once, hard enough to knock the man unconscious without doing permanent damage. The owner of the Jeep went down again, stayed down, limp.

Stefan glanced at the tavern. No one else had come out.

He could hear no traffic approaching on the road, but then again the howling wind might mask the sound of an engine.

As the snow began to fall harder, he put the pistol in the deep pocket of his peacoat and dragged the unconscious man to the nearest other vehicle, the Thunderbird. It was unlocked, and he heaved the guy into the rear seat, closed the door, and hurried back to the Jeep.

The engine had died. He hot-wired it again.

As he put the Jeep in gear and swung it around toward the road, the wind shrieked at the window beside him. The falling snow grew denser, blizzard-thick, and clouds of yesterday's snow were whipped up from the ground and spun in sparkling columns. The giant, shadow-swaddled pines swayed and shuddered under winter's assault.

Laura had little more than twenty minutes to live.

# FIVE

They celebrated the publishing contract for *Jericho Nights* and the otherworldly harmony of their first year of marriage by spending their anniversary at a favorite place—Disneyland. The sky was blue, cloudless; the air was dry and hot. Virtually oblivious of the summer crowds, they rode the Pirates of the Caribbean, had their pictures taken with Mickey Mouse, got dizzy spinning in the Mad Hatter's teacups, had their portraits drawn by a caricaturist, ate hot dogs and ice cream and chocolate-covered frozen bananas on sticks, and danced that evening to a Dixieland band in New Orleans Square.

The park became even more magical after nightfall, and they rode the Mark Twain paddlewheel steamboat around Tom Sawyer's Island for the third time, standing at the railing on the top level, near the bow, with their arms around each other. Danny said, "You know why we like this place so much? 'Cause it's of the world yet untainted *by* the world. And that's our marriage."

Later, over strawberry sundaes at the Carnation Pavilion, at a table beneath trees strung with white Christmas lights, Laura said, "Fifteen thousand bucks for a year's work . . . not exactly a fortune."

"It isn't slave wages either." He pushed his sundae aside, leaned forward, slid her sundae aside, too, and took her hands across the table. "The money will come eventually because you're brilliant, but money isn't what I care about. What I care about is that you've got something special to share. No. That's not exactly what I mean. You don't just *have* something special, you *are* something special. In some way I understand but can't explain, I know that what you *are*, when shared, will bring as much hope and joy to people in far places as it brings to me here at your side."

Blinking away sudden tears, she said, "I love you."

*Jericho Nights* was published ten months later, in May of 1979. Danny insisted she use her maiden name because he knew that through all the bad years in McIlroy Home and Caswell Hall, she had endured in part because she wanted to grow up and make something of herself as a testament to her father and perhaps, as well, to the mother she had never known. The book sold few copies, was not chosen by any book clubs, and was licensed by Viking to a paperback publisher for a small advance.

"Doesn't matter," Danny told her. "It'll come in time. It'll all come in time. Because of what you *are*."

By then she was deep into her second novel, *Shadrach*. Working ten hours a day, six days a week, she finished it that July.

On a Friday she sent one copy to Spencer Keene in New York and gave the original script to Danny. He was the first to read it. He left work early and began reading at one o'clock Friday afternoon in his living-room armchair, then shifted to the bedroom, slept only four hours, and by ten o'clock Saturday morning he was back in the armchair and two-thirds of the way through the script. He would not talk about it, not a word. "Not until I'm done. It wouldn't be fair to you to start analyzing and reacting until I've finished, until I've grasped your entire pattern, and it wouldn't be fair to me, either, because in discussing it you're sure to give away some plot turn or other."

She kept peeking at him to see if he was frowning, smiling, or responding to the story in any way, and even when he was reacting she worried that it was the *wrong* reaction to whatever scene he might be reading. By ten-thirty Saturday, she couldn't bear to stay around the apartment any longer, so she drove to South Coast Plaza, browsed in bookstores, ate an early lunch though she was not hungry, drove to the Westminster Mall, window-shopped, ate a cone of frozen yogurt, drove to the Orange Mall, looked in a few shops, bought a square of fudge and ate half of it. "Shane," she told herself, "go home, or you'll be a double for Orson Welles by dinnertime."

As she parked in the carport at the apartment complex, she saw that Danny's car was gone. When she let herself into the apartment, she called his name but got no answer.

The script of *Shadrach* was piled on the dinette table.

She looked for a note. There was none.

"Oh, God," she said.

The book was bad. It stank. It reeked. It was mule puke. Poor Danny had gone out somewhere to have a beer and find the courage to tell her that she should study plumbing while she was still young enough to get launched on a new career.

She was going to throw up. She hurried to the bathroom, but the nausea passed. She washed her face with cold water.

The book was mule puke.

Okay, she would just have to live with that. She'd thought *Shadrach* was pretty good, better than *Jericho Nights* by a mile, but evidently she had been wrong. So she would write another book.

She went to the kitchen and opened a Coors. She had taken only two swallows when Danny came home with a gift-wrapped box about the right size to hold a basketball. He put it on the dinette table beside the manuscript, looked at her solemnly. "It's for you."

Ignoring the box, she said, "Tell me."

"Open your gift first."

"Oh, God, is it *that* bad? Is it so bad you have to soften the blow with a gift? Tell me. I can take it. Wait! Let me sit down." She pulled out a chair from the table and dropped into it. "Hit me with your best, big guy. I'm a survivor."

"You've got too strong a sense of drama, Laura."

"What're you saying? The book's melodramatic?"

"Not the book. You. Right now, anyway. Will you for God's sake stop being the shattered young artiste and open your gift?"

"All right, all right, if I've got to open the gift before you'll talk, then I'll open the bloody gift."

She put the box in her lap—it was heavy—and tore at the ribbon while Danny pulled up a chair and sat in front of her, watching.

The box was from an expensive shop, but she was not prepared for the contents: a large, gorgeous Lalique bowl; it was clear except for two handles that were partly clear green and partly frosted crystal; each handle was formed by two leaping toads, four toads altogether.

She looked up, wide-eyed. "Danny, I've never seen anything like this. It's the most beautiful piece ever."

"Like it, then?"

"Good God, how much was it?"

"Three thousand."

"Danny, we can't afford this!"

"Oh, yes, we can."

"No, we can't, really we can't. Just because I wrote a lousy book and you want to make me feel better—"

"You didn't write a lousy book. You wrote a toad-worthy book. A *four*-toad book on a scale of one to four, four being the best. We can afford that bowl precisely because you wrote *Shadrach*. This book is beautiful, Laura, infinitely better than the last one, and it's beautiful because it's you. This book is what you *are*, and it shines."

In her excitement and in her eagerness to hug him, she nearly dropped the three-thousand-dollar bowl.

## SIX

A skin of new snow covered the highway now. The Jeep wagon had four-wheel drive and was equipped with tire chains, so Stefan was able to make reasonably good time in spite of the road conditions.

But not good enough.

He estimated that the tavern, where he had stolen the Jeep, was about eleven miles from the Packard house, which was just off state route 330 a few miles south of Big Bear. The mountain roads were narrow, twisty, full of dramatic rises and falls, and blowing snow ensured poor visibility, so his average speed was about forty miles an hour. He could not risk driving faster or more recklessly, for he would be of no use at all to Laura, Danny, and Chris if he lost control of the Jeep and plunged over an embankment to his death. At his current speed, however, he would arrive at their place at least ten minutes after they had left.

His intention had been to delay them at their house until the danger had passed. That plan was no longer viable.

The January sky seemed to have sunk so low under the weight of the storm that it was no higher than the tops of the serried ranks of massive evergreens that flanked both sides of the roadway. Wind shook the trees and hammered the Jeep. Snow stuck to the windshield wipers and became ice, so he turned up the defroster and hunched over the wheel, squinting through the inadequately cleaned glass.

When he next glanced at his watch, he saw that he had less than fifteen minutes. Laura, Danny, and Chris would be getting into their Chevy Blazer. They might even be pulling out of their driveway already.

He would have to intercept them on the highway, scant seconds ahead of Death.

He tried to squeeze slightly more speed out of the Jeep without shooting wide of a turn and into an abyss.

# SEVEN

Five weeks after the day that Danny bought her the Lalique bowl, on August 15, 1979, a few minutes after noon, Laura was in the kitchen, heating a can of chicken soup for lunch, when she got a call from Spencer Keene, her literary agent in New York. Viking loved *Shadrach* and were offering a hundred thousand.

"*Dollars*?" she asked.

"Of course, dollars," Spencer said. "What do you think, Russian rubles? What would that buy you—a hat maybe?"

"Oh, God." She had to lean against the kitchen counter because suddenly her legs were weak.

Spencer said, "Laura, honey, only you can know what's best for you, but unless they're willing to let the hundred grand stand for a floor bid in an auction, I want you to consider turning this down."

"Turn down a hundred thousand dollars?" she asked in disbelief.

"I want to send this out to maybe six or eight houses, set an auction date, see what happens. I think I *know* what will happen, Laura, I think they'll all love this book as much as I do. On the other hand . . . maybe not. It's a hard decision, and you've got to go away and think about it before you answer me."

The moment Spencer said goodbye and hung up, Laura dialed Danny at work and told him about the offer.

He said, "If they won't make it a floor bid, turn it down."

"But, Danny, can we afford to? I mean, my car is eleven years old and falling apart. Yours is almost four years old—"

"Listen, what did I tell you about this book? Didn't I tell you that it was *you*, a reflection of what you are?"

"You're sweet, but—"

"Turn it down. Listen, Laura. You're thinking that scorning a hundred K is like spitting in the faces of all the gods of good fortune; it's like inviting that lightning you've spoken about. But you *earned* this payoff, and fate isn't going to cheat you out of it."

She called Spencer Keene and told him her decision.

Excited, nervous, already missing the hundred thousand dollars, she returned to the den and sat at her typewriter and stared at the unfinished short story for a while until she became aware of the odor of chicken soup and remembered she had left it on the stove. She hurried into the kitchen and found that all but half an inch of soup had boiled away; burnt noodles were stuck to the bottom of the pot.

At two-ten, which was five-ten New York time, Spencer called again to say that Viking had agreed to let the hundred thousand stand as a floor bid. "Now, that's the very least you make from *Shadrach*—a hundred grand. I think I'll set September twenty-sixth as the auction date. It's going to be a big one, Laura. I feel it."

She spent the remainder of the afternoon trying to be elated but unable to shake off her anxiety. *Shadrach* was already a big success, no matter what happened in the auction. She had no reason for her anxiety, but it held her in a tight grip.

Danny came home from work that day with a bottle of champagne, a bouquet of roses, and a box of Godiva chocolates. They sat on the sofa, nibbling chocolates, sipping champagne, and talking about the future, which seemed entirely bright; yet her anxiety lingered.

Finally she said, "I don't want chocolates or champagne or roses or a hundred thousand dollars. I want you. Take me to bed."

They made love for a long time. The late summer sun ebbed from the windows and the tide of night rolled in before they parted with a sweet, aching reluctance. Lying at her side in the darkness, Danny tenderly kissed her breasts, her throat, her eyes, and finally her lips. She realized that her anxiety had at last faded. It was not sexual release that expelled her fear. Intimacy, total surrender of self, and the sense of shared hopes and dreams and destinies had been the true medicines; the great, good feeling of *family* that she had with him was a talisman that effectively warded off cold fate.

On Wednesday, September 26, Danny took the day off from work to be at Laura's side as the news came in from New York.

At seven-thirty in the morning, ten-thirty New York time, Spencer Keene called to report that Random House had made the first offer above the auction floor. "One hundred and twenty-five thousand, and we're on our way."

Two hours later Spencer called again. "Everyone's off to lunch, so there'll be a lull. Right now, we're up to three hundred and fifty thousand and six houses are still in the bidding."

"Three hundred and fifty thousand?" Laura repeated.

At the kitchen sink where he was rinsing the breakfast dishes, Danny dropped a plate.

When she hung up and looked at Danny, he grinned and said, "Am I mistaken, or is this the book you were afraid might be mule puke?"

Four and a half hours later, as they were sitting at the dinette table pretending to be concentrating on a game of five-hundred rummy, their inattention betrayed by their mutual inability to keep score with any degree of mathematical accuracy whatsoever, Spencer Keene called again. Danny followed her into the kitchen to listen to her side of the conversation.

Spencer said, "You sitting down, honey?"

"I'm ready, Spencer. I don't need a chair. Tell me."

"It's over. Simon & Schuster. One million, two hundred and twenty-five thousand dollars."

Weak with shock, shaky, she spoke with Spencer for another ten minutes, and when she hung up, she wasn't sure of a thing that had been said after he had told her the price. Danny was staring at her expectantly, and she realized that he didn't know what had happened. She told him the name of the buyer and the figure.

For a moment they stared at each other in silence.

Then she said, "I think maybe now we can afford to have a baby."

# EIGHT

Stefan topped a hill and peered ahead at the half-mile stretch of snow-swept road on which it would happen. On his left, beyond the south-bound lane, the tree-covered mountainside sloped steeply down to the highway. On his right the northbound lane was edged by a soft shoulder only about four feet wide, beyond which the mountainside fell away again into a deep gorge. No guardrails protected travelers from that deadly drop-off.

At the bottom of the slope, the road turned left, out of sight. Between that turn below and the crest of the hill, which he had just topped, the two-lane blacktop was deserted.

According to his watch, Laura would be dead in a minute. Two minutes at most.

He suddenly realized that he should never have tried to drive toward the Packards, not after he had arrived so late. Instead he should have given up the idea of stopping the Packards and should have tried instead to identify and stop the Robertsons' vehicle farther back on the road to Arrowhead. That would have worked just as well.

Too late now.

Stefan had no time to go back, nor could he risk driving farther north toward the Packards. He did not know the exact moment of their deaths, not to the second, but that catastrophe was now approaching swiftly. If he tried to go even another half mile and stop them before they arrived at this fateful incline, he might reach the bottom of the slope and, in taking the turn, pass them going the other way, at which point he would not be able to swing around and catch up with them and stop them before the Robertsons' truck hit them head-on.

He braked gently and angled across the ascending southbound lane, stopping the Jeep on a wide portion of that shoulder of the road about halfway down the slope, so close to the embankment that he could not get out of the driver's door. His heart was thudding almost painfully as he shifted the Jeep into park, put on the emergency brake, cut the engine, slid across the seat, and got out the passenger-side door.

The blowing snow and icy air stung his face, and all along the mountainside the wind shrieked and howled like many voices, perhaps the voices of the three sisters of Greek myth, the Fates, mocking him for his desperate attempt to prevent what they had ordained.

# NINE

After receiving editorial suggestions, Laura undertook an easy revision of *Shadrach*, delivering the final version of the script in mid-December 1979, and Simon & Schuster scheduled the book for publication in September 1980.

It was such a busy year for Laura and Danny that she was only peripherally aware of the Iranian hostage crisis and presidential campaign, and even more vaguely cognizant of the countless fires, plane crashes, toxic spills, mass murders, floods, earthquakes, and other tragedies that constituted the news. That was the year the rabbit died. That was the year she and Danny bought their first house—a four-bedroom, two-and-a-half-bath, Spanish model in Orange Park Acres—and moved out of the apartment in Tustin. She started her third novel, *The Golden Eagle*, and one day when Danny asked her how it was going, she said, "Mule puke," and he said, "That's great!" The first of September, upon receipt of a substantial check for the film rights to *Shadrach*, which had sold to MGM, Danny quit his job at the brokerage house and became her full-time financial manager. On Sunday, September 21, three weeks after it arrived in the stores, *Shadrach* appeared on the *New York Times* bestseller list at number twelve. On October 5, 1980, when Laura gave birth to Christopher Robert Packard, *Shadrach* was in a third printing, sitting comfortably at number eight on the *Times*, and received what Spencer Keene called a "thunderously good" review on page five of that same book section.

The boy entered the world at 2:23 P.M in a greater rush of blood than that which usually carried babies out of their prenatal darkness. Pain-wracked and hemorrhaging, Laura required three pints during the afternoon and evening. She spent a better night than expected, however, and by morning she was sore, weary, but well out of danger.

The following day during visiting hours, Thelma Ackerson came to see the baby and the new mother. Still dressed punkish and ahead of her time—hair long on the left side of her head, with a white streak like the bride of Frankenstein, and short on the right side, with no streak—she breezed into Laura's private room, went straight to Danny, threw her arms around him, hugged him hard, and said, "God, you're big. You're a mutant. Admit it, Packard, your mother might have been human, but your father was a grizzly bear." She came to the bed where Laura was propped up against three pillows, kissed her on the forehead and then on the cheek. "I went to the nursery before I came here, had a peek at Christopher Robert through the glass, and he's adorable. But I think you're going to need all the millions you can make from your books, kiddo, because that boy is going to take after his father, and your food bill's going to run thirty thousand a month. Until you get him housebroken, he'll be eating your furniture."

Laura said, "I'm glad you came, Thelma."

"Would I miss it? Maybe if I was playing a Mafia-owned club in Bayonne, New Jersey, and had to cancel out part of a date to fly back, maybe *then* I'd miss it because if you break a contract with those guys they cut off your thumbs and make you use them as suppositories. But I was west of the Mississippi when I got the news last night, and only nuclear war or a date with Paul McCartney could keep me away."

Almost two years ago Thelma had finally gotten time on the stage at the Improv, and she'd been a hit. She landed an agent and began to get paid bookings in sleazy, third-rate—and eventually second-rate—clubs across the country. Laura and Danny had driven into Los Angeles twice to see her perform, and she had been hilarious; she wrote her own material and delivered it with the comic timing she had possessed since childhood but had honed in the intervening years. Her act had one unusual aspect that would either make her a national phenomenon or ensure her obscurity: Woven through the jokes was a strong thread of melancholy, a sense of the tragedy of life that existed simultaneously with the wonder and humor of it. In fact it was similar to the tone of Laura's novels, but what appealed to book readers was less likely to appeal to audiences who had paid for belly laughs.

Now Thelma leaned across the bed railing, peered closely at Laura and said, "Hey, you look pale. And those rings around your eyes . . . "

"Thelma, dear, I hate to shatter your illusions, but a baby isn't really brought by the stork. The mother has to expel it from her own womb, and it's a tight fit."

Thelma stared hard at her, then directed an equally hard stare at

Danny, who had come around the other side of the bed to hold Laura's hand. "What's wrong here?"

Laura sighed and, wincing with discomfort, shifted her position slightly. To Danny, she said, "See? I told you she's a bloodhound."

"It wasn't an easy pregnancy, was it?" Thelma demanded.

"The pregnancy was easy enough," Laura said. "It was the delivery that was the problem."

"You didn't . . . almost die or anything, Shane?"

"No, no, no," Laura said, and Danny's hand tightened on hers. "Nothing that dramatic. We knew from the start there were going to be some difficulties along the way, but we found the best doctor, and he kept a close watch. It's just . . . I won't be able to have any more. Christopher will be our last."

Thelma looked at Danny, at Laura, and said quietly, "I'm sorry."

"It's all right," Laura said, forcing a smile. "We have little Chris, and he's beautiful."

They endured an awkward silence, and then Danny said, "I haven't had lunch yet, and I'm starved. I'm going to slip down to the coffee shop for a half hour or so."

When Danny left, Thelma said, "He's not really hungry, is he? He just knew we wanted a girl-to-girl talk."

Laura smiled. "He's a lovely man."

Thelma put down the railing on one side of the bed and said, "If I hop up here and sit beside you, I won't shake up your insides, will I? You won't suddenly bleed all over me, will you, Shane?"

"I'll try not to."

Thelma eased up onto the high hospital bed. She took one of Laura's hands in both of hers. "Listen, I read *Shadrach*, and it's damned good. It's what all writers try to do and seldom achieve."

"You're sweet."

"I'm a tough, cynical, hard-nosed broad. Listen, I'm serious about the book. It's brilliant. And I saw Bovine Bowmaine in there, and Tammy. And Boone, the child-welfare psychologist. Different names but I saw them. You've captured them perfectly, Shane. God, there were times you brought it all back, times when chills ran up and down my back so bad I had to put down the book and go for a walk in the sun. And there were times when I laughed like a loon."

Laura ached in every muscle, in every joint. She did not have the strength to lean away from the pillows and put her arms around her friend. She just said, "I love you, Thelma."

"The Eel wasn't there, of course."

"I'm saving him for another book."

"And me, damn it. I'm not in the book, though I'm the most colorful character you've ever known!"

"I'm saving you for a book all your own," Laura said.

"You mean it, don't you?"

"Yes. Not the one I'm working on now but the one after it."

"Listen, Shane, you better make me *gorgeous*, or I'll sue your ass off. You hear me?"

"I hear you."

Thelma chewed her lip, then said, "Will you—"

"Yes. I'm going to put Ruthie in it too."

They were silent a while, just holding hands.

Unshed tears clouded Laura's vision, but she saw that Thelma was blinking back tears too. "Don't. It'll streak all that elaborate punk eye makeup."

Thelma raised one of her feet. "Are these boots freaky or what? Black leather, pointy toes, stud-ringed heels. Makes me look like a damned dominatrix, doesn't it?"

"When you walked in, the first thing I wondered was how many men you've whipped lately."

Thelma sighed and sniffed hard to clear her nose. "Shane, listen and listen good. This talent of yours is maybe more precious than you think. You're able to capture people's lives on the page, and when the people are gone, the page is still there, the life is still *there*. You can put feelings on the page, and anyone, anywhere, can pick up that book and *feel* those same feelings, you can touch the heart, you can remind us what it means to be human in a world that's increasingly bent on forgetting. That's a talent and a reason to live that's more than most people ever have. So . . . well, I know how much you want to have a family . . . three or four kids, you've said . . . so I know how bad you must be hurting right now. But you've got Danny and Christopher and this amazing talent, and that's so very much to have."

Laura's voice was unsteady. "Sometimes . . . I'm just so afraid."

"Afraid of what, baby?"

"I wanted a big family because . . . then it's less likely they'll all be taken away from me."

"Nobody's going to be taken away from you."

"With just Danny and little Chris . . . just two of them . . . something might happen."

"Nothing will happen."

"Then I'd be alone."

"Nothing will happen," Thelma repeated.

"Something always seems to happen. That's life."

Thelma slid farther onto the bed, stretched out beside Laura, and put her head against Laura's shoulder. "When you said it was a hard birth . . . and the way you look, so pale . . . I was scared. I have friends in LA, sure, but all of them are show-biz types. You're the only *real* person I'm close to, even though we don't see each other that much, and the idea that you might have nearly . . . ''

"But I didn't.''

"Might've, though.'' Thelma laughed sourly. "Hell, Shane, once an orphan, always an orphan, huh?''

Laura held her and stroked her hair.

Shortly after Chris's first birthday, Laura delivered *The Golden Edge*. It was published ten months later, and by the boy's second birthday, the book was number one on the *Times* bestseller list, which was a first for her.

Danny managed Laura's book income with such diligence, caution, and brilliance that within a few years, in spite of the savage bite of income taxes, they would be not just rich—they were already rich by most standards—but seriously rich. She didn't know what she thought about that. She had never expected to be rich. When she considered her enviable circumstances, she thought perhaps she should be thrilled or, given the want of much of the world, appalled, but she felt nothing much one way or the other about the money. The security that money provided was welcome; it inspired confidence. But they had no plans to move out of their quite pleasant four-bedroom house, though they could have afforded an estate. The money was *there*, and that was the end of it; she gave it little thought. Life was not money; life was Danny and Chris and, to a lesser extent, her books.

With a toddler in the house, she no longer had the ability or desire to work sixty hours a week at her word processor. Chris was talking, walking, and he exhibited none of the moodiness or mindless rebellion that the child-rearing books described as normal behavior for the year between two and three. Mostly he was a pleasure to be with, a bright and inquisitive boy. She spent as much time with him as she could without risk of spoiling him.

*The Amazing Appleby Twins*, her fourth novel, was not published until October 1984, two years after *The Golden Edge*, but there was none of the drop-off in audience that is sometimes the case when a writer does not publish a book each year. The advance sales were her biggest yet.

On October first, she was sitting with Danny and Chris on the sofa in the family room, watching old Road Runner cartoons on the VCR— "Vooom, vooom!'' Christopher said each time Road Runner took off in a flash of speed—eating popcorn, when Thelma called from Chicago, in tears. Laura took the call on the kitchen phone, but on the TV in the adjoining room the beleaguered coyote was trying to blow up his nemesis and was blowing himself up instead, so Laura said, "Danny, I better take this in the den.''

In the four years since Chris was born, Thelma's career had gone straight up. She had been booked in a couple of Vegas casino lounges. ("Hey, Shane, I must be pretty good because the cocktail waitresses are nearly naked, all boobs and butts, and sometimes the guys in the audience actually look at me instead of them. On the other hand maybe I only appeal to fags.") In the past year she had moved into the main showroom at the MGM Grand as an opening act for Dean Martin, and she had made four appearances on the *Tonight* show with Johnny Carson. There was talk of a movie or even a television series to be built around her, and she seemed poised for stardom as a comedienne. Now she was in Chicago, opening soon as the headliner at a major club.

Perhaps the long chain of positive developments in their lives was what panicked Laura when she heard Thelma crying. For some time she had been waiting for the sky to fall with a horrid suddenness that would have caught Chicken Little unaware. She dropped into the chair behind the desk in the den, snatched up the phone. "Thelma? What is it, what's wrong?"

"I just read . . . the new book."

Laura could not figure what in *The Amazing Appleby Twins* could have affected Thelma so profoundly, and then she suddenly wondered if something in the characterization of Carrie and Sandra Appleby had offended. Though none of the major events in the story mirrored those in the lives of Ruthie and Thelma, the Applebys were, of course, based on the Ackersons. But both characters had been drawn with great love and good humor; surely there was nothing about them that would offend Thelma, and in panic Laura tried to say as much.

"No, no, Shane, you hopeless fool," Thelma said between bouts of tears. "I'm not offended. The reason I can't stop crying is because you did the most wonderful thing. Carrie Appleby is Ruthie as sure as I ever knew her, but in your book you let Ruthie live a long time. You let Ruthie live, Shane, and that's a whole hell of a lot better job than God did in real life."

They talked for an hour, mostly about Ruthie, reminiscing, not with a lot of tears, now, but mostly with affection. Danny and Chris appeared in the open doorway of the den a couple of times, looking abandoned, and Laura blew them kisses, but she stayed on the telephone with Thelma because it was one of those rare times when remembering the dead was more important than tending to the needs of the living.

Two weeks before Christmas, 1985, when Chris was five and then some, the southern California rainy season started with a downpour that made palm fronds rattle like bones, battered the last remaining blossoms off the impatiens, and flooded streets. Chris could not play outside. His father was off inspecting a potential real estate investment, and the boy was in no mood to entertain himself. He kept finding excuses to bother Laura in her office, and by eleven o'clock she gave up trying to work on the current book. She sent him to the kitchen to get the baking sheets out of the cupboard, promising to let him help her make chocolate-chip cookies.

Before joining him, she got Sir Tommy Toad's webbed-foot boots, tiny umbrella, and miniature scarf from the dresser drawer in the bedroom, where she had been keeping them for just such a day as this. On her way to the kitchen she arranged those items near the front door.

Later, as she was slipping a tray of cookies into the oven, she sent him to the front door to see if the United Parcel deliveryman had left a package that she professed to be expecting, and Chris came back flushed with excitement. "Mommy, come look, come see."

In the foyer he showed her the three miniature items, and she said, "I suppose they belong to Sir Tommy. Oh, did I forget to tell you about the lodger we've taken in? A fine, upstanding toad from England here on the queen's business."

She had been eight when her father had invented Sir Tommy, and she had accepted the fabulous toad as a fun fantasy, but Chris was only five and took it more seriously. "Where's he going to sleep—the spare bedroom? Then what do we do when Grandpa comes to visit?"

"We've rented Sir Tommy a room in the attic," Laura said, "and we must not disturb him or tell anyone about him except Daddy because Sir Tommy is here on *secret* business for Her Majesty."

He looked at her wide-eyed, and she wanted to laugh but dared not. He had brown hair and eyes, like she and Danny, but his features were delicate, more his mother's than his father's. In spite of his smallness there was something about him that made her think he would eventually shoot up to be tall and solidly constructed like Danny. He leaned close and whispered: "Is Sir Tommy a *spy?*"

Throughout the afternoon, as they baked cookies, cleaned up, and played a few games of Old Maid, Chris was full of questions about Sir Tommy. Laura discovered that tale-telling for children was in some ways more demanding than writing novels for adults.

When Danny came home at four-thirty, he shouted a greeting on his way along the hall from the connecting door to the garage.

Chris jumped up from the breakfast-nook table, where he and Laura were playing cards, and urgently shushed his father. "Ssshhh, Daddy, Sir Tommy might be sleeping now, he had a long trip, he's the Queen of England, and he's spying in our attic!"

Danny frowned. "I go away from home for just a few hours, and while I'm gone we're invaded by scaly, transvestite, British spies?"

That night in bed, after Laura made love with a special passion that surprised even her, Danny said, "What's gotten into you today? All evening you were so . . . buoyant, so up."

Snuggling against him under the covers, enjoying the feel of his nude body against hers, she said, "Oh, I don't know, it's just that I'm *alive*, and Chris is alive, you're alive, we're all together. And it's this Tommy Toad thing."

"It tickles you?"

"Tickles me, yes. But it's more than that. It's . . . well, somehow it makes me feel that life goes on, that it always goes on, the cycle is renewed—does this sound crazy?—and that life is going to go on for us, too, for all of us, for a long time."

"Well, yeah, I think you're right," he said. "Unless you're that energetic *every* time you make love from now on, in which case you'll kill me in about three months."

In October, 1986, when Chris turned six, Laura's fifth novel, *Endless River,* was published to critical acclaim and bigger sales than any of her previous titles. Her editor had predicted the greater success: "It's got all the humor, all the tension, all the tragedy, that whole weird mix of a Laura Shane novel, but it's somehow not as *dark* as the others, and that makes it especially appealing."

For two years, Laura and Danny had been taking Chris up to the San Bernardino Mountains at least one weekend a month, to Lake Arrowhead and Big Bear, both during the summer and winter, to make sure he learned that the whole world was not like the pleasant but thoroughly urbanized and suburbanized realms of Orange County. With the continued flowering of her career and the success of Danny's investment strategies, and considering her recent willingness not only to entertain optimism but to *live* it, they decided it was time to indulge themselves, so they bought a second home in the mountains.

It was an eleven-room stone and redwood place on thirty acres just off state route 330, a few miles south of Big Bear. It was, in fact, a more expensive house than the one they lived in during the week in Orange Park Acres. The property was mostly covered with western juniper, Ponderosa pine, and sugar pine, and their nearest neighbor was far beyond sight. During their first weekend at the retreat, as they were making a snowman, three deer appeared at the edge of the looming forest, twenty yards away, and watched curiously.

Chris was thrilled at the sight of the deer, and by the time he had been tucked in bed that night, he was sure that they were Santa Claus's deer. *This* was where the jolly fat man went after Christmas, he insisted, and not, as legend had it, to the North Pole.

*Wind and Stars* appeared in October of '87, and it was a still bigger hit than any of her previous books. The movie of *Endless River* was released that Thanksgiving, enjoying the biggest opening-week box office of any film that year.

On Friday, January 8, 1988, buoyed by the knowledge that *Wind and Stars* would hold the number one spot on the *Times* list that Sunday for the fifth week in a row, they drove up to Big Bear in the afternoon, as soon as Chris came home from school. The following Tuesday was Laura's thirty-third birthday, and they intended to have an early cel-ebration, just the three of them, high in the mountains, with the snow like icing on a cake and the wind to sing for her.

Accustomed to them, the deer ventured within twenty feet of their house on Saturday morning. But Chris was seven now, and in school he heard the rumor that Santa Claus was not real, and he was no longer so sure that these were more than ordinary deer.

The weekend was perfect, perhaps the best they had spent in the mountains, but they had to cut it short. They had intended to leave at six o'clock Monday morning, returning to Orange County in time to deliver Chris to school. However a major storm moved into the area ahead of schedule late Sunday afternoon, and though they were little more than ninety minutes from the balmy temperatures nearer the coast, the weather report called for two feet of new snow by morning. Not wanting to risk being snowbound and causing Chris to miss a day of school—a possibility even with their four-wheel-drive Blazer—they closed up the big stone and redwood house and headed south on state route 330 at a few minutes past four o'clock.

Southern California was one of the few places in the world where you could drive from a winterscape to subtropical heat in less than two hours, and Laura always enjoyed—and marveled at—the jour-ney. The three of them were dressed for snow—wool socks, boots, thermal underwear, heavy slacks, warm sweaters, ski jackets—but in an hour and a quarter they would be in milder climes where no one was bundled up, and in two hours they would be in shirtsleeve weather.

Laura drove while Danny, sitting in front, and Chris, sitting behind him, played a word-association game that they had devised on previous trips to amuse themselves. Rapidly falling snow found even those sections of the highway that were largely protected by trees on both sides, and in unsheltered areas the hard-driven flakes sheeted and whirled by the millions in the capricious currents of the high-mountain winds, sometimes half obscuring the way ahead. She drove with caution, not caring if the two-hour drive home required three hours or four; since they had left early, they had plenty of time to spare, all the time in the world.

When she came out of the big curve a few miles south of their house and entered the half-mile incline, she saw a red Jeep station wagon parked on the right shoulder and a man in a navy peacoat in the middle of the road. He was coming down the hill, waving both arms to halt them.

Leaning forward and squinting between the thumping windshield wipers, Danny said, "Looks like he broke down, needs help."

"Packard's Patrol to the rescue!" Chris said from the back seat.

As Laura slowed, the guy on the road began frantically gesturing for them to pull to the right shoulder.

Danny said uneasily, "Something odd about him. . . . "

Yes, odd indeed. He was her special guardian. The sight of him after all these years shocked and frightened Laura.

# TEN

He had just gotten out of the stolen Jeep when the Blazer turned the bend at the bottom of the hill. As he rushed toward it, he saw Laura slow the Blazer to a crawl a third of the way up the slope, but she was still in the middle of the roadway, so he signaled her more frantically to get off onto the shoulder, as close to the embankment as possible. At first she continued to creep forward, as if unsure whether he was only a motorist in trouble or dangerous, but when they drew close enough to each other for her to see his face and perhaps recognize him, she immediately obeyed.

As she accelerated past him and whipped the Blazer onto the wider portion of the shoulder, only twenty feet downhill from Stefan's Jeep, he reversed direction and ran to her, yanked open her door. "I don't know if being off the road's good enough. Get out, up the embankment, quickly, *now!*"

Danny said, "Hey, wait just—"

"Do what he says!" Laura shouted. "Chris, come on, get out!"

Stefan gripped Laura's hand and helped her out of the driver's seat. As Danny and Chris also scrambled from the Blazer, Stefan heard a laboring engine above the skirling wind. He looked up the long hill and saw that a big pickup truck had topped the crest and was starting down toward them. Pulling Laura after him, he ran around the front of the Blazer.

\* \* \*

Her guardian said, "Up the embankment, come on," and began to climb the hard-packed, ice-crusted snow that had been shoved there by plows and that sloped steeply toward the nearby trees.

Laura looked up the highway and saw the truck, a quarter-mile from them and only a hundred feet below the crest, beginning a long, sickening slide on the treacherous pavement until it was coming sideways down the road. If they had not stopped, if her guardian had not delayed them, they would have been just below the crest when the truck went out of control; already they would have been hit.

Beside her, with Chris riding him piggyback and holding on tight, Danny obviously had seen the danger. The truck might come all the way down the hill without the driver in control, might slam into the Jeep and Blazer. Lugging Chris, he scrambled up the snow-packed embankment, yelling for Laura to *move*.

She climbed, grabbing for handholds, kicking footholds as she went. The snow was not only ice-mantled but ice-marbled and rotten in places, breaking away in chunks, and a couple of times she nearly fell backward to the shoulder of the highway below. By the time she joined her guardian, Danny, and Chris fifteen feet above the highway, on a narrow but snow-free shelf of rock near the trees, it seemed as if she had been climbing for minutes. But in fact her sense of time must have been distorted by fear, for when she looked up the highway, she saw that the truck was still sliding toward them, that it was two hundred feet away, had made one complete revolution, and was turning sideways again.

On it came through the streaming snow, as if in slow motion, fate in the form of a few tons of steel. A snowmobile stood in the big pickup's cargo bed, and it was apparently not secured by chains or in any way restrained; the driver foolishly had relied on inertia to keep it in place. But now the snowmobile was slamming from side to side against the walls of the cargo hold and forward into the back wall of the cab, and through the quarter-mile slide its violent shifts contributed to the destabilization of the vehicle under it, until it seemed as if the truck, leaning radically, would roll instead of spin through another complete turn.

Laura saw the driver fighting the wheel, and she saw a woman beside him, screaming, and she thought: Oh, my god, those poor people!

As if sensing her thoughts, her guardian shouted above the wind, "They're drunk, both of them, and no snow chains."

If you know that much about them, she thought, you must know who they are, so why didn't you stop them, why didn't you save them too?

With a terrible crash the front end of the truck rammed into the side of the Jeep, and unrestrained by a seat belt, the woman was thrown halfway through the windshield, where she hung partly in and partly out of the cab—

Laura yelled, "Chris!" But she saw that Danny had already taken the boy off his back and was holding him close, turning his head away from the ongoing accident.

—the collision didn't stop the truck; it had too much momentum, and the pavement was too slippery for chainless tread to grip. But the brutal impact did reverse the direction of the truck's slide: it abruptly whipped around to its driver's right, heading backward down the hill, and the snowmobile exploded through the tailgate, *flew* free, crashing onto the hood of the parked Blazer, smashing the windshield. An instant later the rear of the pickup slammed into the front of the Blazer with enough force to shove that vehicle ten feet backward in spite of its firmly engaged emergency brakes—

Though viewing the destruction from the safety of the embankment, Laura gripped Danny's arm, horrified by the thought that they surely would have been injured and perhaps killed if they had taken refuge either in front of or behind the Blazer.

—now the pickup bounced off the Blazer; the bloodied woman fell back into the cab; and, sliding more slowly but still out of control, the battered truck turned three hundred and sixty degrees in an eerily graceful ballet of death, angling down the slope and across the snowy pavement and over the far shoulder, over the unguarded brink, out into emptiness, down, out of sight, gone.

Though no horror remained to be seen, Laura covered her face with her hands, perhaps trying to block out the mental image of the pickup carrying its occupants down the rocky, nearly treeless wall of that gorge, tumbling hundreds upon hundreds of feet. The driver and his companion would be dead before they hit bottom. Even above the raging wind, she heard the truck strike an outcropping of rock, then another. But in seconds the noise of its violent descent faded, and the only sound was the mad shrieking of the storm.

Stunned, they slid and groped their way down the embankment to the shoulder of the road between the Jeep and the Blazer, where bits of glass and metal littered the snowy surface. Steam rose from under the Blazer as hot radiator fluid drizzled onto the frozen ground, and the ruined vehicle creaked under the weight of the snowmobile embedded in its hood.

Chris was crying. Laura reached for him. He came into her arms, and she lifted him, held him, while he sobbed against her neck.

Dazed, Danny turned to their savior. "Who . . . who in the name of God are you?"

Laura stared at her guardian, finding it difficult to cope with the fact that he really was there. She had not seen him in over twenty years, since she was twelve, that day in the cemetery when she had spotted him watching her father's interment from the grove of Indian laurels. She had not seen him close up for almost twenty-*five* years, since the day he had killed the junkie in her father's grocery. When he failed to save her from the Eel, when he left her to handle *that* one on her own, a loss of faith set in, and doubt was encouraged when he did nothing to save Nina Dockweiler, either—or Ruthie. With the passage of so much time, he had become a dream figure, more myth than reality, and in the last couple of years she had not thought about him at all, had abandoned belief in him just as Chris was currently abandoning belief in Santa Claus. She still had the note that he'd left on her desk, after her father's funeral. But she had long ago convinced herself that it had not in fact been written by a magical guardian but perhaps by Cora or Tom Lance, her father's friends. Now he had saved her again, miraculously, and Danny wanted to know who in the name of God he was, and that was what Laura wanted to know as well.

The strangest part of it was that he looked the same as when he had shot the junkie. *Exactly the same.* She had recognized him at once, even after the passage of so much time, because he had not aged. He still appeared to be in his middle to late thirties. Impossibly, the years had left no mark on him, no hint of gray in his blond hair, no wrinkles in his face. Though he had been her father's age that bloody day in the grocery store, he now was of her own generation or nearly so.

Before the man could answer Danny's question or find a way to avoid an answer, a car topped the hill and started down toward them. It was a late-model Pontiac equipped with tire chains that sang on the pavement. The driver apparently saw the damage to the Jeep and the Blazer and noted the pickup's still fresh skid marks that had not yet been obliterated by wind and snow; he slowed—with reduced speed the song of the chains quickly changed to a clatter—and pulled across the pavement into the southbound lane. Instead of going all the way to the shoulder and out of traffic, however, the car continued north in the wrong lane, stopping only fifteen feet from them, near the back of the Jeep. When he threw open the door and got out of the Pontiac, the driver—a tall man in dark clothing—was holding an object that, too late, Laura identified as a submachine gun.

Her guardian said, "Kokoschka!"

Even as his name was spoken, Kokoschka opened fire.

Though he was more than fifteen years from Vietnam, Danny reacted with the instincts of a soldier. As bullets ricocheted off the red Jeep in front of them and off the Blazer behind them, Danny grabbed Laura, pushing her and Chris to the ground between the two vehicles.

As Laura dropped below the line of fire, she saw Danny struck in the back. He was hit at least once, maybe twice, and she jerked as if the slugs had hit her. He fell against the front of the Blazer, dropped to his knees.

Laura cried out and, holding Chris with one arm, reached for her husband.

He was still alive, and in fact he swung toward her on his knees. His face was as white as the snow falling around them, and she had the bizarre and terrible feeling that she was looking into the countenance of a ghost rather than that of a living man. "Get under the Jeep," Danny said, pushing her hand away. His voice was thick and wet, as if something had broken in his throat. "Quick!"

One of the bullets had passed completely through him. Bright blood oozed down the front of his blue, quilted ski jacket.

When she hesitated, he moved to her on hands and knees, pushed her toward the Jeep just a few feet away.

Another loud burst of submachine-gun fire crackled through the wintry air.

The gunman would no doubt move cautiously forward toward the front of the Jeep and slaughter them as they cowered there. Yet they had nowhere to run: If they went up the embankment toward the trees, he would cut them down long before they reached the safety of the forest; if they crossed the road, he would blow them away before they reached the other side, and at the other side there was nothing but the steep-walled gorge, anyway; running uphill, they would be heading toward him; running downhill, they would be putting their backs to him, making even easier targets of themselves.

The submachine gun rattled. Windows burst. Bullets punctured sheet metal with a hard *pock-twang*.

Crawling to the front of the Jeep, dragging Chris with her, Laura saw her guardian slipping into the narrow space between that vehicle and the snow-packed embankment. He was crouched below the fender, out of sight of the man he had called Kokoschka. In his fear he no longer seemed magical, no guardian angel but merely a man; and in fact he was no longer a savior, either, but an agent of Death, for his presence here had attracted the killer.

At Danny's urging she frantically squirmed under the Jeep. Chris squirmed, too, not crying now, being brave for his father; but then he had not seen his father shot, for his face had been pressed to Laura's breast, buried in her ski jacket. It seemed useless to get under the Jeep because Kokoschka would find them anyway. He could not be so dim-witted as to fail to look under the Jeep when they could be found nowhere else, so at most they were just buying a little time, an extra minute of life at most.

When she was completely under the Jeep, pulling Chris against her to give him what little additional protection her body could provide, she heard Danny speak to her from the front of the vehicle. "I love you." Anguish pierced her as she realized that those three short words also meant goodbye.

Stefan slipped between the Jeep and the dirty, mounded snow along the embankment. There was little space, not enough for him to have gotten out of the driver's door on that side when he had parked there, but barely enough to squeeze along toward the rear bumper where Kokoschka might not expect him to show up, where he might get off one good shot before Kokoschka swung around and sprayed him with the submachine gun.

*Kokoschka.* He had never been so surprised in his life as when Kokoschka had gotten out of that Pontiac. It meant they were aware of his traitorous activities at the institute. And they were also aware that he had interposed himself between Laura and her true destiny. Kokoschka had taken the Lightning Road with the intention of eliminating the traitor and evidently Laura as well.

Now, keeping his head down, Stefan urgently forced his way between the Jeep and the embankment. The submachine gun chattered and windows blew out above him. At his back the snowbank was ice-crusted in many places, jabbing painfully into him; when he endured the pain and pressed hard with his body, the ice cracked, and the snow beneath it compacted just enough to give him passage. Wind streamed through the narrow space he occupied, shrieking between sheet metal and snow, so it seemed that he was not alone there but was in the company of some invisible creature that hooted and gibbered in his face.

He had seen Laura and Chris wriggling under the Jeep, but he knew that cover would provide only an additional minute of safety, perhaps even less. When Kokoschka got to the front of the Jeep and didn't find them there, he would look under the vehicle, get down at road level, and open fire, chopping them to pieces in their confinement.

And what of Danny? He was such a big man, barrel-chested, surely too big to slide swiftly under the Jeep. And already he'd been shot; he must be stiff with pain. Besides, Danny wasn't the kind of man who hid from trouble, not even trouble like this.

At last Stefan reached the rear bumper. Cautiously he looked out and saw the Pontiac parked eight feet away in the southbound lane with its driver's door standing open, engine running. No Kokoschka. So with his Walther PPK/S .380 in hand he eased away from the snowbank, moved behind the Jeep. He crouched against the tailgate and peered around the other rear bumper.

Kokoschka was in the middle of the roadway, moving toward the front of the Jeep where he believed everyone had taken cover. His weapon was an Uzi with an extended magazine, chosen for the mission because it would not be anachronistic. As Kokoschka reached the gap between the Jeep and the Blazer, he opened fire again, sweeping the submachine gun from left to right. Bullets screamed off metal, blew out tires, and thudded into the embankment.

Stefan fired at Kokoschka, missed.

Suddenly, with berserk courage, Danny Packard launched himself at Kokoschka, coming out from his hiding place tight up against the Jeep's grill, so low that he must have been lying flat, low enough to have been under the spray of bullets the submachine gun had just laid down. He was wounded from the initial burst of fire but still quick and powerful, and for a moment it seemed that he might even reach the gunman and disable him. Kokoschka was sweeping the Uzi from left to right, already moving away from his target when he saw Danny coming at him, so he had to reverse himself, bring the muzzle around. If he had been a few feet closer to the Jeep instead of in the middle of the highway, he would not have nailed Danny in time.

"Danny, no!" Stefan shouted, squeezing off three shots at Kokoschka even as Packard was going for him.

But Kokoschka had kept a cautious distance, and he brought the spitting muzzle around, straight at Danny, when they were still three or four feet apart. Danny was kicked backward by the impact of several slugs.

Stefan took no consolation from the fact that even as Danny was hit, Kokoschka was hit, too, taking two rounds from the Walther, one in his left thigh and one in his left shoulder. He was knocked down. He dropped the submachine gun as he fell; it spun along the pavement.

Under the Jeep, Laura was screaming.

Stefan rose from the cover of the rear bumper and ran toward Kokoschka, who was on the ground only thirty feet downslope, near the Blazer now. He slipped on the snowy pavement, struggled to keep his balance.

Badly wounded, no doubt in shock, Kokoschka nevertheless saw him coming. He rolled toward the Uzi carbine, which had come to rest by the rear tire of the Blazer.

Stefan fired three times as he ran, but he did not have the steadiness required for a good aim, and Kokoschka was rolling away from him, so he missed the son of a bitch. Then Stefan slipped again and fell to one knee in the middle of the road, landing so hard that pain shot up his thigh and into his hip.

Rolling, Kokoschka reached the submachine gun.

Realizing he'd never get to the man in time, Stefan dropped onto both knees and raised the Walther, holding it with both hands. He was twenty feet from Kokoschka, not far. But even a good marksman could miss at twenty feet if the circumstances were bad enough, and these were bad: a state of panic, a weird firing angle, gale-force wind to deflect the shot.

Downslope, lying on the ground, Kokoschka opened fire the instant he got his hands on the Uzi, even before he brought the weapon around, loosing the first twenty rounds under the Blazer, blowing out the front tires.

As Kokoschka swung the gun toward him, Stefan squeezed off his last three rounds with deliberation. In spite of the wind and the angle, he had to make them count, for if he missed he would have no time to reload.

The first round from the Walther missed.

Kokoschka continued to bring the submachine gun around, and the arc of fire reached the front of the Jeep. Laura was under the Jeep with Chris, and Kokoschka was shooting from ground level, so surely a couple of rounds had passed under the vehicle.

Stefan fired again. The slug hit Kokoschka in the upper body, and the submachine gun stopped firing. Stefan's next and last shot took Kokoschka in the head. It was over.

From beneath the Jeep, Laura saw Danny's incredibly brave charge, saw him go down again, flat on his back, unmoving, and she knew that he was dead, no possibility of a reprieve this time. A flash of grief like the terrible light from an explosion swept through her, and she glimpsed a future without Danny, a vision so starkly illuminated and of such dreadful power that she almost blacked out.

Then she thought of Chris, still alive and sheltering against her. She blocked out the grief, knowing she would return to it later—if she survived. The important thing right now was keeping Chris alive and, if possible, protecting him from the sight of his father's bullet-riddled corpse.

Danny's body blocked part of her view, but she saw Kokoschka hit by gunfire. She saw her guardian approaching the downed gunman, and for a moment it seemed the worst was over. Then her guardian slipped and fell to one knee, and Kokoschka rolled toward the submachine gun that he had dropped. More gunfire. A lot of it in a few seconds. She heard a couple of rounds passing under the Jeep, frighteningly close, lead cutting through the air with a deadly whisper that was louder than any other sound in the world.

The silence after the gunfire was at first perfect. Initially she could not hear the wind or her son's low sobbing. Gradually those sounds impinged upon her.

She saw her guardian was alive, and part of her was relieved, but part of her was irrationally angry that he had survived because he had drawn this Kokoschka with him, and Kokoschka had killed Danny. On the other hand Danny—and she and Chris—would surely have been killed in the collision with the truck, anyway, if her guardian had not come along. Who the hell was he? Where did he come from? Why was he so interested in her? She was frightened, angry, shocked, sick in her soul, and badly confused.

Clearly in pain, her guardian rose from his knees and hobbled to Kokoschka. Laura twisted farther around to look directly down the hill, just past Danny's unmoving head. She could not quite see what her guardian was doing, though he appeared to be tearing open Kokoschka's clothes.

After a while he hobbled back up the hill, carrying something he had taken off the corpse.

When he reached the Jeep, he crouched and looked under at her. "Come out. It's over." His face was pale, and in the past few minutes he seemed to have aged at least a couple of his twenty-five lost years. He cleared his throat. In a voice filled with what seemed like genuine, deeply felt remorse, he said, "I'm sorry, Laura. I'm so very sorry."

She squirmed on her belly toward the rear of the Jeep, bumping her head on the undercarriage. She pulled Chris and encouraged him to come with her, for if they wriggled out nearer the front, the boy might see his father. Her guardian pulled them into the open. Laura sat back against the rear bumper and clutched Chris to her.

Tremulously, the boy said, "I want Daddy."

I want him too, Laura thought. Oh, baby, I want him, too, I want him so bad, all I want in the world is your daddy.

The storm was a full-fledged blizzard now, pumping snow out of the sky under tremendous pressure. The afternoon was dying; light was fading, and all around the grim, gray day was succumbing to the queer, phosphorescent darkness of a snowy night.

In this weather few people would be traveling, but he was sure that someone would come along soon. No more than ten minutes had passed since he had stopped Laura in the Blazer, but even on this rural road in a storm, the gap in traffic would not last much longer. He needed to have a talk with her and leave before he got entangled in the aftermath of this bloody encounter.

Hunkering down in front of her and the weeping boy, behind the Jeep, Stefan said, "Laura, I've got to get out of here, but I'll be back soon, in just a couple of days—"

"Who are you?" she demanded angrily.

"There's no time for that now."

"I want to know, damn you. I have a right to know."

"Yes, you do, and I'll tell you in a few days. But right now we have to get your story straight, the way we did that day in the grocery store. Remember?"

"To hell with you."

Unfazed, he said, "It's for your own good, Laura. You can't tell the authorities the exact truth because it won't seem real, will it? They'll think you're making it all up. Especially when you see me leave . . . well, if you tell them how I went, they'll either be sure that you're somehow an accomplice to murder or a madwoman."

She glared at him and said nothing. He did not blame her for being angry. Perhaps she even wanted him dead, but he understood that too. The only emotions she stirred in him, however, were love and pity and a profound respect.

He said, "You'll tell them that when you and Danny turned the curve at the bottom of the hill and started up, there were *three* cars in the roadway: the Jeep parked here along the embankment, the Pontiac in the wrong lane just where it is now, and another car was stopped in the northbound lane. There were . . . four men, two of them with guns, and they seemed to have forced the Jeep off the road. You just came along at the wrong time, that's all. They pointed a submachine gun at you, made you pull off the road, made you and Danny and Chris get out of the car. At one point you heard talk about cocaine . . . somehow it involved drugs, you don't know how, but they were arguing over drugs, and they seemed to have chased down the man in the Jeep—"

"Drug dealers out here in the middle of nowhere?" she said scornfully.

"There could be processing labs out here—a cabin in the woods, processing PCP maybe. Listen, if the story makes at least *some* sense, they'll want to buy it. The *real* story makes no sense at all, so you can't rely on it. So you tell them the Robertsons came over the crest of the hill in their pickup—of course you don't know their name—and the road was blocked by all these cars, and when he braked the pickup it started to slide—"

"You've got an accent," she said angrily. "A slight one but I can hear it. Where are you from?"

"I'll tell you all of that in a few days," he said impatiently, looking up and down the snow-blasted road. "I really will, but now you've got to promise me you'll work with this false story, embellish it as best you can, and not tell them the truth."

"I don't have any choice, do I?"

"No," he said, relieved that she realized her position.

She clung to her son and said nothing.

Stefan had begun to feel the pain in his half-frozen feet again. The heat of action had dissipated, leaving him wracked by shivers. He handed her the belt that he had taken off Kokoschka. "Put this inside your ski jacket. Don't let anyone see it. When you get home, put it away somewhere."

"What is it?"

"Later. I'll try to return in a few hours. Only a few hours. Right now just promise me you'll hide it. Don't get curious, don't put it on, and for God's sake don't push the yellow button on it."

"Why not?"

"Because you don't want to go where it'll take you."

She blinked at him in confusion. "Take me?"

"I'll explain but not now."

"Why can't you take it with you, whatever it is?"

"Two belts, one body—it's an anomaly, it'll cause a disruption of some kind in the energy field, and God only knows where I might wind up or in what condition."

"I don't understand. What're you talking about?"

"Later. But, Laura, if for some reason I'm unable to come back, you better take precautions."

"What kind of precautions?"

"Arm yourself. Be prepared. There's no *reason* they should come after you if they get me, but they might. Just to teach me a lesson, to humble me. They thrive on vengeance. And if they come for you . . . there'll be a squad of them, well armed."

"Who the hell *are* they?"

Without answering, he got to his feet, wincing at the pain in his right knee. He backed away, taking one last, long look at her. Then he turned, leaving her on the ground, in the cold and snow, against the back of the battered and bullet-pocked Jeep, with her terrified child and her dead husband.

Slowly he walked out into the middle of the highway where more light seemed to come from the shifting snow on the pavement than from the sky overhead. She called to him, but he ignored her.

He holstered his empty gun beneath his coat. He reached inside his shirt, felt for and located the yellow button on his own travel belt, and hesitated.

They had sent Kokoschka to stop him. Now they would be waiting anxiously at the institute to learn the outcome. He would be arrested on arrival. He probably never again would have an opportunity to take the Lightning Road to return to her as he had promised.

The temptation to stay was great.

If he stayed, however, they would only send someone else to kill him, and he would spend the rest of his life running from one assassin after another—while watching the world around him change in ways that would be too horrible to endure. On the other hand, if he went back, there was a slim chance that he might still be able to destroy the institute. Dr. Penlovski and the others obviously knew everything about his meddling in the natural flow of events in this one woman's life, but perhaps they did not know that he had planted explosives in the attic and basement of the institute. In that case, if they gave him an opportunity to get into his office for just a moment, he could throw the hidden switch and blow the place—and all its files—to hell where it belonged. More likely than not, they had found the explosive charges and removed them. But as long as there was any possibility whatsoever that he could bring an end forever to the project and close the Lightning Road, he was morally obliged to return to the institute, even if it meant that he would never see Laura again.

As the day died, the storm seemed to come more fiercely alive. On the mountainside above the highway, the wind rumbled and keened through the enormous pines, and the boughs made an ominous rustling sound, as if some many-legged, giant creature were scuttling down the slope. The snowflakes had become fine and dry, almost like bits of ice, and they seemed to be abrading the world, smoothing it the way that sandpaper smoothed wood, until eventually there would be no peaks and valleys, nothing but a featureless, highly polished plain as far as anyone could see.

With his hand still inside his coat and shirt, Stefan pressed the yellow button three times in quick succession, triggering the beacon. With regret and fear he returned to his own time.

Holding Chris, whose sobbing had subsided, Laura sat on the ground at the back of the Jeep and watched her guardian walk into the slanting snow, past the rear of Kokoschka's Pontiac.

He stopped in the middle of the highway, stood for a long moment with his back to her, and then an incredible thing happened. First the air became heavy; she was aware of a strange pressure, something she had never felt before, as if the atmosphere of the earth were being condensed in some cosmic cataclysm, and abruptly she found it hard to draw breath. The air acquired a curious odor, too, exotic but familiar, and after a few seconds she realized it smelled like hot electrical wires and scorched insulation, much like what she had smelled in her own kitchen when a toaster plug had shorted out a few weeks ago; that stink was overlaid with the crisp but not unpleasant scent of ozone, which was the same odor that filled the air during any violent thunderstorm. The pressure grew greater, until she almost felt pinned to the ground, and the air shimmered and rippled as if it were water. With a sound like an enormous cork popping out of a bottle, her guardian vanished from the purple-gray, winter twilight, and simultaneously with that *pop* came a great *whoosh* of wind, as if massive quantities of air were rushing in to fill some void. Indeed for an instant she felt trapped in a vacuum, unable to breathe. Then the crushing pressure was gone, the air smelled only of snow and pine, and everything was normal again.

Except, of course, after what she had seen, nothing could ever be normal for her again.

The night grew very dark. Without Danny it was the blackest night of her life. Only one light remained to illuminate her struggle toward some distant hope of happiness: Chris. He was the last light in her darkness.

Later, at the top of the hill, a car appeared. Headlights bored through the gloom and the heavily falling snow.

She struggled to her feet and took Chris into the middle of the roadway. She waved for help.

As the descending car slowed, she suddenly wondered if when it stopped another man with another submachine gun would get out and open fire. She would never again feel safe.

# 4

◆ ◆ ◆

# The Inner Fire

## ONE

On Saturday, August 13, 1988, seven months after Danny was shot down, Thelma Ackerson came to the mountain house to stay for four days.

Laura was in the backyard, conducting target practice with her Smith & Wesson .38 Chief's Special. She had just reloaded, snapped the cylinder in place, and was about to put on her Hearing Guard headset when she heard a car approaching on the long gravel driveway from the state route. She picked up a pair of binoculars from the ground at her feet and took a closer look at the vehicle to be sure it was not an unwanted visitor. When she saw Thelma behind the wheel, she put the glasses down and continued firing at the target—an outline of a man's head and torso—that was lashed to a hay-bale backstop.

Sitting on the grass nearby, Chris plucked six more cartridges from the box and prepared to hand them to her when she had fired the last round currently in the cylinder.

The day was hot, clear, and dry. Wildflowers by the hundreds blazed along the edge of the yard where the mown area gave way to wild grass and weeds near the forest line. Squirrels had been at play on the grass a while ago, and birds had been singing, but the shooting had temporarily frightened them away.

Laura might have been expected to associate her husband's death with the high retreat and to sell it. Instead she had sold the house in Orange County four months ago and moved Chris to the San Bernardinos.

She believed that what had happened to them the previous January on route 330 could have happened anywhere. The place was not to blame; the fault lay in her destiny, in the mysterious forces at work in her strangely troubled life. Intuitively she knew that if her guardian had not stepped in to save her on that stretch of snowy highway, he would have entered her life elsewhere, at another moment of crisis. At *that* place Kokoschka would have shown up with a submachine gun, and the same set of violent, tragic events would have transpired.

Their other home had held more memories of Danny than did the stone and redwood place south of Big Bear. She was better able to deal with her grief in the mountains than in Orange Park Acres.

Besides, oddly enough, the mountains felt much safer to her. In the highly populated suburbs of Orange County, where the streets and freeways teemed with more than two million people, an enemy would not be perceived among the crowd until he chose to act. In the mountains, however, strangers were highly visible, especially since the house sat almost in the center of their thirty-acre property.

And she had not forgotten her guardian's warning: *Arm yourself. Be prepared. If they come for you . . . there'll be a squad of them.*

When Laura fired the last round in the .38 and pulled off the ear guards, Chris handed her six more cartridges. He removed his muffs, too, and ran to the target to check her accuracy.

The backstop consisted of hay bales piled seven feet high and four deep; it was fourteen feet wide. Behind it were acres of pine woods, her private land, so the need for an elaborate backstop was questionable, but she did not want to shoot anyone. At least not accidentally.

Chris lashed up a new target and returned to Laura with the old one. "Four hits out of six, Mom. Two deaders, two good wounds, but looks like you're pulling off to the left a little."

"Let's see if I can correct that."

"You're just getting tired, that's all," Chris said.

The grass around her was littered with over a hundred and fifty empty brass shell casings. Her wrists, arms, shoulders, and neck were beginning to ache from the cumulative recoil, but she wanted to get in another full cylinder before quitting for the day.

Back near the house, Thelma's car door slammed.

Chris put on his ear guards again and picked up the binoculars to watch the target while his mother fired.

Sorrow plucked at Laura as she paused to look at the boy, not merely because he was fatherless but because it seemed so unfair that a child two months short of his eighth birthday should already know how dangerous life was and should have to live in constant expectation of violence. She did her best to make sure there was as much fun in his life as possible: They still played with the Tommy Toad fantasy, though Chris no longer believed that Tommy was real; through a large personal library of children's classics, Laura also was showing him the pleasure and escape to be found in books; she even did her best to make target practice a game and thereby divert the focus from the deadly necessity of being able to protect themselves. Yet for the time being their lives were dominated by loss and danger, by a fear of the unknown. That reality could not be hidden from the boy, and it could not fail to have a profound and lasting effect on him.

Chris lowered the binoculars and looked at her to see why she was not shooting. She smiled at him. He smiled at her. He had such a sweet smile it almost broke her heart.

She turned to the target, raised the .38, gripped it with both hands, and squeezed off the first shot of the new series.

By the time Laura fired four rounds, Thelma stepped up beside her. She stood with her fingers in her ears, wincing.

Laura squeezed off the last two shots and removed her ear guards, and Chris retrieved the target. The roar of gunfire was still echoing through the mountains when she turned to Thelma and hugged her.

"What's all this gun stuff?" Thelma asked. "Are you going to write new movies for Clint Eastwood? No, hey, better yet, write the female equal of Clint's role—*Dirty Harriet*. And I'm just the broad to play it—tough, cold, with a sneer that would make Bogart cringe."

"I'll keep you in mind for the part," Laura said, "but what I'd really like to see is Clint play it in drag."

"Hey, you've still got a sense of humor, Shane."

"Did you think I wouldn't?"

Thelma frowned. "I didn't know what to think when I saw you blasting away, looking mean as a snake with fang decay."

"Self-defense," Laura said. "Every good girl should learn some."

"You were plinking away like a pro." Thelma noted the glitter of brass shell casings in the grass. "How often do you do this?"

"Three times a week, a couple of hours each time."

Chris returned with the target. "Hi, Aunt Thelma. Mom, you got four deaders out of six that time, one good wound, and a miss."

"Deaders?" Thelma said.

"Still pulling to the left, do you think?" Laura asked the boy.

He showed her the target. "Not so much as last time."

Thelma said, "Hey, Christopher Robin, is that all I get—just a lousy 'Hi, Aunt Thelma'?"

Chris put the target with the pile of others that he had taken down before it, went to Thelma, and gave her a big hug and a kiss. Noticing that she was no longer done up in punk style, he said, "Gee, what happened to you, Aunt Thelma? You look normal."

"I look normal? What is that—a compliment or an insult? Just you remember, kid, even if your old Aunt Thelma looks normal, she is no such a thing. She is a comic genius, a dazzling wit, a legend in her own scrapbook. Anyway, I decided punk was passé."

They enlisted Thelma to help them collect empty shell casings.

"Mom's a terrific shot," Chris said proudly.

"She better be terrific with all this practice. There's enough brass here to make balls for an entire army of Amazon warriors."

To his mother, Chris said, "What's that mean?"

"Ask me again in ten years," Laura said.

When they went into the house, Laura locked the kitchen door. Two deadbolts. She closed the Levelor blinds over the windows so no one could see them.

Thelma watched these rituals with interest but said nothing.

Chris put *Raiders of the Lost Ark* on the VCR in the family room and settled in front of the television with a bag of cheese popcorn and a Coke. In the adjacent kitchen Laura and Thelma sat at the table and drank coffee while Laura disassembled and cleaned the .38 Chief's Special.

The kitchen was big but cozy with lots of dark oak, used brick on two walls, a copper range hood, copper pots hung on hooks, and a dark blue, ceramic-tile floor. It was the kind of kitchen in which TV sitcom families worked out their nonsensical crises and attained transcendental enlightenment (with heart) in thirty minutes each week, minus commercials. Even to Laura it seemed like an odd place to be cleaning a weapon designed primarily to kill other human beings.

"Are you really afraid?" Thelma asked.

"Bet on it."

"But Danny was killed because you were unlucky enough to wander into the middle of a drug deal of some kind. Those people are long gone, right?"

"Maybe not."

"Well, if they were afraid that you might be able to identify them, they'd have come to get you long before this."

"I'm taking no chances."

"You got to ease up, kid. You can't live the rest of your life expecting someone to jump at you from the bushes. All right, you can keep a gun around the house. That's probably wise. But aren't you ever going to go out into the world again? You can't tote a gun with you everywhere you go."

"Yes, I can. I've got a permit."

"A permit to carry that cannon?"

"I take it in my purse wherever we go."

"Jesus, how'd you get a permit to carry?"

"My husband was killed under strange circumstances by persons unknown. Those killers tried to shoot my son and me—and they are still at large. On top of all that, I'm a rich and relatively famous woman. It'd be a little odd if I *couldn't* get a permit to carry."

Thelma was silent for a minute, sipping her coffee, watching Laura clean the revolver. Finally she said, "This is kind of spooky, Shane, seeing you so serious about this, so tense. I mean, it's seven months since . . . Danny died. But you're as skittish as if someone had shot at you yesterday. You can't maintain this level of tension or readiness or whatever you want to call it. That way lies madness. Paranoia. You've got to face the fact that you can't really be on guard the rest of your life, every minute."

"I can, though, if I have to."

"Oh, yeah? What about right now? Your gun's disassembled. What if some barbarian thug with tattoos on his tongue started kicking down the kitchen door?"

The kitchen chairs were on rubber casters, so when Laura suddenly shoved away from the table, she rolled swiftly to the counter beside the refrigerator. She pulled open a drawer and brought out another .38 Chief's Special.

Thelma said, "What—am I sitting in the middle of an arsenal?"

Laura put the second revolver back in the drawer. "Come on. I'll give you a tour."

Thelma followed her to the pantry. Hung on the back of the pantry door was an Uzi semiautomatic carbine.

"That's a machine gun. Is it legal to have one?"

"With federal approval, you can buy them at gunshops, though you can only get a semiautomatic; it's illegal to have them modified for full automatic fire."

Thelma studied her, then sighed. "Has this one been modified?"

"Yes. It's fully automatic. But I bought it that way from an illegal dealer, not a gunshop."

"This is too spooky, Shane. Really."

She led Thelma into the dining room and showed her the revolver that was clipped to the bottom of the sideboard. In the living room a fourth revolver was clipped under an end table next to one of the sofas. A second modified Uzi was hung on the back of the foyer door at the front of the house. Revolvers were also hidden in the desk drawer in the den, in her office upstairs, in the master bathroom, and in the nightstand in her bedroom. Finally, she kept a third Uzi in the master bedroom.

Staring at the Uzi that Laura pulled from under the bed, Thelma said, "Spookier and spookier. If I didn't know you better, Shane, I'd think you'd gone mad, a raving paranoid gun nut. But knowing you, if you're really *this* scared, you've got to have some reason. But what about Chris around all these guns?"

"He knows not to touch them, and I know he can be trusted. Most Swiss families have members in the militia—nearly every male citizen there is prepared to defend his country, did you know that?—with guns in almost every house, but they have the lowest rate of accidental shootings in the world. Because guns are a way of life. Children are taught to respect them from an early age. Chris'll be okay."

As Laura put the Uzi under the bed again, Thelma said, "How on earth do you find an illegal gun dealer?"

"I'm rich, remember?"

"And money can buy anything? Okay, maybe that's true. But, come on, how does a gal like you find an arms dealer? They don't advertise on Laundromat bulletin boards, I presume."

"I've researched the backgrounds to several complicated novels, Thelma. I've learned how to find anyone or anything I need."

Thelma was silent as they returned to the kitchen. From the family room came the heroic music that accompanied Indiana Jones on all of his exploits. While Laura sat at the table and continued cleaning the revolver, Thelma poured fresh coffee for both of them.

"Straight talk now, kiddo. If there's really some threat out there that justifies all this armament, then it's bigger than you can handle yourself. Why not bodyguards?"

"I don't trust anyone. Anyone but you and Chris, that is. And Danny's father, except he's in Florida."

"But you can't go on like this, alone, afraid . . . "

Working a spiral brush into the barrel of the revolver, Laura said, "I'm afraid, yeah, but I feel good about being prepared. All my life I've stood by while people I love have been taken from me. I've done nothing about it but endure. Well, to hell with that. From now on, I fight. If anyone wants to take Chris from me, they're going to have to go *through* me to get him, they'll have to fight a war."

"Laura, I know what you're going through. But listen, let me play psychoanalyst here and tell you that you're reacting less to any real threat than you are *over*reacting to a sense of helplessness in the face of fate. You can't thwart Providence, kid. You can't play poker with God and expect to win because you've got a .38 in your purse. I mean, you lost Danny to violence, yeah, and maybe you could say that Nina Dockweiler would have lived if someone had put a bullet in the Eel when he first deserved it, but those are the only cases where lives of people you loved might've been saved with guns. Your mother died in childbirth. Your father died of a heart attack. We lost Ruthie to fire. Learning to defend yourself with guns is fine, but you've got to keep perspective, you've got to have a sense of humor about our vulnerability as a species, or you'll wind up in an institution with people who talk to tree stumps and eat their belly-button lint. God forbid, but what if Chris got cancer? You're all prepared to blow away anyone who touches him, but you can't kill cancer with a revolver, and I'm afraid you're so crazy determined to protect him that you'll fall to pieces if something like that happens, something you can't deal with, that no one can deal with. I worry about you, kid."

Laura nodded and felt a rush of warmth for her friend. "I know you do, Thelma. And you can put your mind at ease. For thirty-three years I just endured; now I'm fighting back as best I can. If cancer were to strike me or Chris, I'd hire all the best specialists, seek the finest possible treatment. But if all failed, if for example Chris died of cancer, then I'd accept defeat. Fighting doesn't preclude enduring. I can fight, and if fighting fails, I can still endure."

For a long time Thelma stared at her across the table. At last she nodded. "That's what I hoped to hear. Okay. End of discussion. On to other things. When do you plan to buy a tank, Shane?"

"They're delivering it Monday."

"Howitzers, grenades, bazookas?"

"Tuesday. What about the Eddie Murphy movie?"

"We closed the deal two days ago," Thelma said.

"Really. My Thelma is going to star in a movie with Eddie Murphy?"

"Your Thelma is going to *appear* in a movie with Eddie Murphy. I don't think I qualify as a star yet."

"You had fourth lead in that picture with Steve Martin, third lead in the picture with Chevy Chase. And this is second lead, right? And how many times have you hosted the *Tonight* show? Eight times, isn't it? Face it, you're a star."

"Low magnitude, maybe. Isn't it weird, Shane? Two of us come from nothing, McIlroy Home, and we make it to the top. Strange?"

"Not so strange," Laura said. "Adversity breeds toughness, and the tough succeed. And survive."

# TWO

Stefan left the snow-filled night in the San Bernardino Mountains and an instant later was inside the gate at the other end of Lightning Road. The gate resembled a large barrel, not unlike one of those that were popular in carnival funhouses, except that its inner surface was of highly polished copper rather than wood, and it did not turn under his feet. The barrel was eight feet in diameter and twelve feet long, and in a few steps he walked out of it, into the main, ground-floor lab of the institute, where he was certain that he'd be met by armed men.

The lab was deserted.

Astonished, he stood for a moment in his snow-flecked peacoat and looked around in disbelief. Three walls of the thirty-by-forty-foot room were lined floor to ceiling with machinery that hummed and clicked unattended. Most of the overhead lamps were off, so the room was softly, eerily lit. The machinery supported the gate, and it featured scores of dials and gauges that glowed pale green or orange, for the gate—which was a breach in time, a tunnel to anywhen—was never shut down; once closed, it could be reopened only with great difficulty and a tremendous expenditure of energy, but once open it could be maintained with comparatively little effort. These days, because the primary research work was no longer focused on developing the gate itself, the main lab was attended by institute personnel only for routine maintenance of the machinery and, of course, when a jaunt was in progress. If different circumstances had pertained, Stefan would never have been able to make the scores of secret, unauthorized trips that he had taken to monitor—and sometimes correct—the events of Laura's life.

But though it was not unusual to find the lab deserted most times of the day, it was singularly strange now, for they had sent Kokoschka to stop him, and surely they would be waiting anxiously to learn how Kokoschka had fared in those wintry California mountains. They had to have entertained the possibility that Kokoschka would fail, that the wrong man would return from 1988, and that the gate would have to be guarded until the situation was resolved. Where were the secret police in their black trenchcoats with padded shoulders? Where were the guns with which he had expected to be greeted?

He looked at the large clock on the wall and saw that it was six minutes past eleven o'clock, local time. That was as it should have been. He'd begun the jaunt at five minutes till eleven that morning, and every jaunt ended exactly eleven minutes after it began. No one knew why, but no matter how long a time traveler spent at the other end of his journey, only eleven minutes passed at home base. He had been in the San Bernardinos for nearly an hour and a half, but only eleven minutes had transpired in his own life, in his own time. If he had stayed with Laura for months before pressing the yellow button on his belt, activating the beacon, he would still have returned to the institute only—and precisely—eleven minutes after he had left it.

But where were the authorities, the guns, his angry colleagues expressing their outrage? After discovering his meddling in the events of Laura's life, after sending Kokoschka to get him and Laura, why would they walk away from the gate when they had to wait only *eleven minutes* to learn the outcome of the confrontation?

Stefan took off his boots, peacoat, and shoulder holster, and tucked them out of sight in a corner behind some equipment. He had left his white lab coat in the same place when he had departed on the jaunt, and now he slipped into it again.

Baffled, still worried in spite of the lack of a hostile greeting committee, he stepped out of the lab into the ground-floor corridor and went looking for trouble.

# THREE

At two-thirty Sunday morning Laura was at her word processor in the office adjacent to the master bedroom, dressed in pajamas and a robe, sipping apple juice, and working on a new book. The only light in the room came from the electronic-green letters on the computer screen and from a small desk lamp tightly focused on a printout of yesterday's pages. A revolver lay on the desk beside the script.

The door to the dark hallway was open. She never closed any but the bathroom door these days because sooner or later a closed door might prevent her from hearing the stealthy progress of an intruder in another part of the house. The house had a sophisticated alarm system, but she kept interior doors open just in case.

She heard Thelma coming down the hallway, and she turned just as her friend looked through the door. "Sorry if I've made any noise that's kept you awake."

"Nah. We nightclub types work late. But I sleep till noon. What about you? You usually up at this hour?"

"I don't sleep well any more. Four or five hours a night is good for me. Instead of lying in bed, fidgeting, I get up and write."

Thelma pulled up a chair, sat, and propped her feet on Laura's desk. Her taste in sleepwear was even more flamboyant than it had been in her youth: baggy silk pajamas in a red, green, blue, and yellow abstract pattern of squares and circles.

"I'm glad to see you're still wearing bunny slippers," Laura said. "It shows a certain constancy of personality."

"That's me. Rock-solid. Can't buy bunny slippers in my size any more, so I have to buy a pair of furry adult slippers *and* a pair of kids' slippers, snip the eyes and ears off the little ones and sew them on the big ones. What're you writing?"

"A bile-black book."

"Sounds like just the thing for a fun weekend at the beach."

Laura sighed and relaxed in her spring-backed armchair. "It's a novel about death, about the injustice of death. It's a fool's project because I'm trying to explain the unexplainable. I'm trying to explain death to my ideal reader because then maybe I can finally understand it myself. It's a book about why we have to struggle and go on in spite of that knowledge of our mortality, why we have to fight and endure. It's a black, bleak, grim, moody, depressing, bitter, deeply disturbing book."

"Is there a big market for that?"

Laura laughed. "Probably no market at all. But once an idea for a novel seizes a writer . . . well, it's like an inner fire that at first warms you and makes you feel good but then begins to eat you alive, burn you up from within. You can't just walk away from the fire; it keeps burning. The only way to put it out is to write the damned book. Anyway, when I get stuck on this one, I turn to a nice little children's book I'm writing all about Sir Tommy Toad."

"You're nuts, Shane."

"Who's wearing the bunny slippers?"

They talked about this and that, with the easy camaraderie they had shared for twenty years. Perhaps it was Laura's loneliness, more acute than in the days immediately following Danny's murder, or maybe it was fear of the unknown, but for whatever reason she began to speak of her special guardian. In all the world only Thelma might believe the tale. In fact Thelma was spellbound, soon lowering her feet from the desk and sitting forward on her chair, never expressing disbelief, as the story unrolled from the day the junkie was shot until the guardian vanished on the mountain highway.

When Laura had quenched *that* inner fire, Thelma said, "Why didn't you tell me about this . . . this guardian years ago? Back in McIlroy?"

"I don't know. It seemed like something . . . magical. Something I should keep to myself because if I shared it I'd break the spell and never see him again. Then after he left me to deal with the Eel on my own, after he had done nothing to save Ruthie, I guess I just stopped believing in him. I never told Danny about him because by the time I met Danny my guardian was no more real to me than Santa Claus. Then suddenly . . . there he was again on the highway."

"That night on the mountain, he said he'd be back to explain everything in a few days . . . ?"

"But I haven't seen him since. I've been waiting seven months, and I figure that when someone suddenly materializes it might be my guardian or, just as likely, another Kokoschka with a submachine gun."

The story had electrified Thelma, and she fidgeted on her chair as if a current were crackling through her. Finally she got up and paced. "What about Kokoschka? The cops find out anything about him?"

"Nothing. He was carrying no identification whatsoever. The Pontiac he was driving was stolen, just like the red Jeep. They ran his fingerprints through every file they've got, came up empty-handed. And they can't interrogate a corpse. They don't know who he was or where he came from or why he wanted to kill us."

"You've had a long time to think about all this. So any ideas? Who is this guardian? Where did he come from?"

"I don't know." She had one idea in particular that she focused on, but it sounded mad, and she had no evidence to support the theory. She withheld it from Thelma not because it was crazy, however, but because it would sound so egomaniacal. "I just don't know."

"Where's this belt he left with you?"

"In the safe," Laura said, nodding toward the corner where a floor-set box was hidden under the carpet.

Together they pulled the wall-to-wall carpet off its tack strip in that corner, revealing the face of the safe, which was a cylinder twelve inches in diameter and sixteen inches deep. Only one item reposed within, and Laura withdrew it.

They moved back to the desk to look at the mysterious article in better light. Laura adjusted the flexible neck of the lamp.

The belt was four inches wide and was made of a stretchy, black fabric, perhaps nylon, through which were woven copper wires that formed intricate and peculiar patterns. Because of its width, the belt required two small buckles rather than one; those were also made of copper. In addition, sewn on the belt just to the left of the buckles, was a thin box the size of an old-fashioned cigarette case—about four inches by three inches, only three-quarters of an inch thick—and this, too, was made of copper. Even on close examination no way to open the rectangular copper box could be discerned; its only feature was a yellow button toward the lower left corner, less than an inch in diameter.

Thelma fingered the odd material. "Tell me again what he said would happen if you pushed the yellow button."

"He just told me for God's sake not to push it, and when I asked why not, he said, 'You won't want to go where it'll take you.' "

They stood side by side in the glow of the desk lamp, staring at the belt that Thelma held. It was after four in the morning, and the house was as silent as any dead, airless crater on the moon.

Finally Thelma said, "You ever been tempted to push the button?"

"No, never," Laura said without hesitation. "When he mentioned the place to which it would take me . . . there was a terrible look in his eyes. And I know he returned there himself only with reluctance. I don't know where he comes from, Thelma, but if I didn't misunderstand what I saw in his eyes, the place is just one step this side of hell."

Sunday afternoon they dressed in shorts and T-shirts, spread a couple of blankets on the rear lawn, and made a long, lazy picnic of potato salad, cold cuts, cheese, fresh fruit, potato chips, and plump cinnamon rolls with lots of crunchy pecan topping. They played games with Chris, and he enjoyed the day enormously, partly because Thelma was able to shift her comic engine into a lower gear, producing one-liners designed for eight-year-olds.

When Chris saw squirrels frolicking farther back in the yard, near the woods, he wanted to feed them. Laura gave him a pecan roll and said, "Tear it into little pieces and toss the pieces to them. They won't let you get too near. And you stay close to me, you hear?"

"Sure, Mom."

"Don't you go all the way to the woods. Only about halfway."

He ran thirty feet from the blanket, only a little more than halfway to the trees, then dropped to his knees. He tore pieces from the cinnamon roll and threw them to the squirrels, making those quick and cautious creatures edge a bit closer for each successive scrap.

"He's a good kid," Thelma said.

"The best." Laura moved the Uzi to her side.

"He's only ten or twelve yards away," Thelma said.

"But he's closer to the woods than to me." Laura studied the shadows under the serried pines.

Plucking a few potato chips from the bag, Thelma said, "Never been on a picnic with someone who brought a submachine gun. I sort of like it. Don't have to worry about bears."

"It's hell on ants, too."

Thelma stretched out on her side on the blanket, her head propped up on one bent arm, but Laura continued to sit with her legs crossed Indian-fashion. Orange butterflies, as bright as condensed sunshine, darted through the warm August air.

"The kid seems to be coping," Thelma said.

"More or less," Laura agreed. "There was a very bad time. He cried a lot, wasn't emotionally stable. But that passed. They're flexible at his age, quick to adapt, to accept. But as good as he seems . . . I'm afraid there's a darkness in him now that wasn't there before and that isn't going to go away."

"No," Thelma said, "it won't go away. It's like a shadow on the heart. But he'll live, and he'll find happiness, and there'll be times when he's not aware of the shadow at all."

While Thelma watched Chris luring the squirrels, Laura studied her friend's profile. "You still miss Ruth, don't you?"

"Every day for twenty years. Don't you still miss your dad?"

"Sure," Laura said. "But when I think of him, I don't believe what I feel is like what you feel. Because we *expect* our parents to die before us, and even when they die prematurely, we can accept it because we've always known it was going to happen sooner or later. But it's different when the one who dies is a wife, husband, child . . . or sister. We don't expect them to die on us, not early in life. So it's harder to cope. Especially, I suppose, if she's a twin sister."

"When I get a piece of good news—career news, I mean—the first thing I always think of is how happy Ruthie would have been for me. What about you, Shane? You coping?"

"I cry at night."

"That's healthy now. Not so healthy a year from now."

"I lie awake at night and listen to my heartbeat, and it's a lonely sound. Thank God for Chris. He gives me purpose. And you. I've got you and Chris, and we're sort of family, don't you think?"

"Not just sort of. We *are* family. You and me—sisters."

Laura smiled, reached out, and rumpled Thelma's tousled hair.

"But," Thelma said, "being sisters doesn't mean you get to borrow my clothes."

# FOUR

In the corridors and through the open doors of the institute's offices and labs, Stefan saw his colleagues at work, and none of them had any special interest in him. He took the elevator to the third floor where just outside his office he encountered Dr. Wladyslaw Januskaya, who was Dr. Vladimir Penlovski's longtime protégé and second in charge of the time-travel research which originally had been called Project Scythe but which for several months now had been known by the apt code name Lightning Road.

Januskaya was forty, ten years younger than his mentor, but he looked older than the vital, energetic Penlovski. Short, overweight, balding, with a blotchy complexion, with two bright gold teeth in the front of his mouth, wearing thick glasses that made his eyes look like painted eggs, Januskaya should have been a comic figure. But his unholy faith in the state and his zeal in working for the totalitarian cause were sufficient to counteract his comic potential; indeed he was one of the more disturbing men involved with Lightning Road.

"Stefan, dear Stefan," Januskaya said, "I've been meaning to tell you how grateful we are for your timely suggestion, last October, that the power supply to the gate should be provided by a secure generator. Your foresight has saved the project. If we were still drawing from the municipal power lines . . . why, the gate would have collapsed half a dozen times by now, and we'd be woefully behind schedule."

Having returned to the institute in expectation of arrest, Stefan was confused to find his treachery undiscovered and startled to hear himself being praised by this evil worm. He had suggested switching the gate to a secure generator not because he wanted to see their vile project achieve success but because he had not wanted his own jaunts into Laura's life to be interrupted by the failure of the public power supply.

"I would not have thought last October that by this time we would have come to such a situation as this, with ordinary public services no longer to be trusted," Januskaya said, shaking his head sadly, "the social order so thoroughly disturbed. What must the people endure to see the socialist state of their dreams triumph, eh?"

"These are dark times," Stefan said, meaning very different things than Januskaya meant.

"But we will triumph," Januskaya said forcefully. His magnified eyes filled with the madness that Stefan knew too well. "Through the Lightning Road, we will triumph."

He patted Stefan on the shoulder and continued down the hall.

After Stefan watched the scientist walk nearly to the elevators, he said, "Oh, Dr. Januskaya?"

The fat white worm turned and looked at him. "Yes?"

"Have you seen Kokoschka today?"

"Today? No, not yet today."

"He's here, isn't he?"

"Oh, I'd imagine so. He's here pretty much as long as there's anyone working, you know. He's a diligent man. If we had more like Kokoschka we'd have no doubt of ultimate triumph. Do you need to talk to him? If I see him, should I send him to you?"

"No, no," Stefan said. "It's nothing urgent. I wouldn't want to interrupt him in other work. I'm sure I'll see him sooner or later."

Januskaya continued to the elevators, and Stefan went into his office, closing the door behind him.

He crouched beside the filing cabinet that he had repositioned slightly to cover one-third of the grille in the corner ventilation chase. In the narrow space behind it, a bundle of copper wires was barely visible, coming out of the bottom slot in the grille. The wires were connected to a simple dial-type timer that was in turn plugged into a wall outlet farther behind the cabinet. Nothing had been disconnected. He could reach behind the cabinet, set the timer, and in one to five minutes, depending on how big a twist he gave the dial, the institute would be destroyed.

What the hell is going on? he wondered.

He sat for a while at his desk, staring at the square of sky that he could see from one of his two windows: scattered, dirty gray clouds moving sluggishly across an azure backdrop.

Finally he left his office, went to the north stairs, and climbed quickly past the fourth floor to the attic. The door opened with only a brief squeak. He flipped the light switch and entered the long, half-finished room, stepping as softly as possible on the board floor. He checked three of the charges of plastique that he had hidden in the rafters two nights ago. The explosives had not been disturbed.

He had no need to examine the charges in the basement. He left the attic and returned to his office.

Obviously no one knew about either his intention of destroying the institute or his attempts to turn Laura's life away from a series of ordained tragedies. No one except Kokoschka. Damn it, Kokoschka *had* to know because he had shown up on the mountain road with an Uzi.

So why hadn't Kokoschka told anyone else?

Kokoschka was an officer of the state's secret police, a true fanatic, obedient and eager servant of the government, and personally responsible for the security of Lightning Road. On discovering a traitor at the institute, Kokoschka would not have hesitated to call in squads of agents to encircle the building, guard the gate, and interrogate everyone.

Surely he would not have allowed Stefan to go to Laura's aid on that mountain highway, then follow with the intent of killing them all. For one thing, he would want to detain Stefan and interrogate him to determine if Stefan had conspirators in the institute.

Kokoschka had learned of Stefan's meddling in the ordained flow of events in one woman's life. And he had either discovered or had not discovered the explosives in the institute—probably not, or he would have at least unwired them. Then for reasons of his own he had not reacted as a policeman but as an individual. This morning he had followed Stefan through the gate, to that wintry afternoon in January of '88, with intentions that Stefan did not now understand at all.

It made no sense. Yet that was what had to have happened.

What had Kokoschka been up to?

He would probably never know.

Now Kokoschka was dead on a highway in 1988, and soon someone at the institute would realize that he was missing.

This afternoon at two o'clock, Stefan was scheduled to take an approved jaunt under the direction of Penlovski and Januskaya. He had intended to blow the institute—in two senses—at one o'clock, an hour before the scheduled event. Now, at 11:43, he decided that he would have to move faster than he originally intended, before Kokoschka's disappearance caused alarm.

He went to one of the tall files, opened the bottom drawer, which was empty, and disconnected it from its slides, lifting it all the way out of the cabinet. Wired to the back of the drawer was a pistol, a Colt Commander 9mm Parabellum with a nine-round magazine, acquired on one of his illicit jaunts and brought back secretly to the institute. From behind another drawer he removed two high-tech silencers and four additional, fully loaded magazines. At his desk, working quickly lest someone enter without knocking, he screwed one of the silencers onto the pistol, flicked off the safety, and distributed the other silencer and magazines in the pockets of his lab coat.

When he left the institute by way of the gate for the last time, he could not trust to the explosives to kill Penlovski, Januskaya, and certain other scientists. The blast would bring down the building and no doubt destroy all machinery and paper files, but what if just one of the key researchers survived? The necessary knowledge to rebuild the gate was in Penlovski's and Januskaya's minds, so Stefan planned to kill them and one other man, Volkaw, before he set the timer on the explosives and entered the gate to return to Laura.

With the silencer attached, the Commander was too long to fit all the way in the pocket of his lab coat, so he turned the pocket inside out and tore the bottom of it. With his finger on the trigger, he shoved the gun into his now bottomless pocket and held it there as he opened his office door and went into the hallway.

His heart pounded furiously. This was the most dangerous part of his plan, the killing, because there were so many opportunities for something to go wrong before he finished with the gun and returned to his office to set the timer on the explosives.

Laura was a long way off, and he might never see her again.

# FIVE

On Monday afternoon Laura and Chris dressed in gray sweat suits. After Thelma helped them unroll the thick gym mats on the patio at the back of the house, Laura and Chris sat side by side and did deep-breathing exercises.

"When does Bruce Lee arrive?" Thelma asked.

"At two," Laura said.

"He's not Bruce Lee, Aunt Thelma," Chris said exasperatedly. "You keep calling him Bruce Lee, but Bruce Lee is dead."

Mr. Takahami arrived promptly at two o'clock. He was wearing a dark blue sweat suit, on the back of which was the logo for his martial arts school: QUIET STRENGTH. When introduced to Thelma, he said, "You're a very funny lady. I love your record album."

Glowing from the praise, Thelma said, "And I can honestly tell you that I sincerely wish Japan had won the war."

Henry laughed. "I think we did."

Sitting on a sun lounger, sipping iced tea, Thelma watched while Henry instructed Laura and Chris in self-defense.

He was forty years old, with a well-developed upper body and wiry legs. He was a master of judo and karate, as well as an expert kick boxer, and he taught a form of self-defense based on various martial arts, a system which he had devised himself. Twice a week he drove out from Riverside and spent three hours with Laura and Chris.

The kicking, punching, poking, grunting, twisting, throwing, off-the-hip rolling combat was conducted gently enough not to cause injury but with enough force to teach. Chris's lessons were less strenuous and less elaborate than Laura's, and Henry gave the boy plenty of breaks to pause and recoup. But by the end of the session, Laura was, as always, dripping sweat and exhausted.

When Henry left, Laura sent Chris upstairs to shower while she and Thelma rolled up the mats.

"He's cute," Thelma said.

"Henry? I guess he is."

"Maybe I'll take up judo or karate."

"Have your audiences been *that* dissatisfied lately?"

"That one was below the belt, Shane."

"Anything's fair when the enemy's formidable and merciless."

The following afternoon, as Thelma was putting her suitcase in the trunk of her Camaro for the return trip to Beverly Hills, she said, "Hey, Shane, you remember that first foster family you were sent to from McIlroy?"

"The Teagels," Laura said. "Flora, Hazel, and Mike."

Thelma leaned against the sun-warmed side of the car next to Laura. "You remember what you told us about Mike's fascination with newspapers like the *National Enquirer*?"

"I remember the Teagels as if I lived with them yesterday."

"Well," Thelma said, "I've been thinking a lot about what's happened to you—this guardian, the way he never ages, the way he disappeared into thin air—and I thought of the Teagels, and it all seems sort of ironic to me. All those nights at McIlroy, we laughed at nutty old Mike Teagel . . . and now what you find yourself in the middle of is a prime bit of exotic news."

Laura laughed softly. "Maybe I'd better reconsider all those tales of aliens living secretly in Cleveland, huh?"

"I guess what I'm trying to say is . . . life is full of wonders and surprises. Some of them are nasty surprises, yeah, and some days are as dark as the inside of the average politician's head. But just the same, there are moments that make me realize we're all here for some reason, enigmatic as it might be. It's not meaningless. If it was meaningless, there'd be no mystery. It'd be as dull and clear and lacking in mystery as the mechanism of a Mr. Coffee machine."

Laura nodded.

"God, listen to me! I'm torturing the English language to come up with a half-baked philosophical statement that ultimately means nothing more than 'keep your chin up, kid.' "

"You're not half-baked."

"Mystery," Thelma said. "Wonder. You're in the middle of it, Shane, and that's what life's all about. If it's dark right now . . . well, this too shall pass."

They stood by the car, hugging, not needing to say more, until Chris ran out from the house with a crayon drawing he had done for Thelma and that he wanted her to take back to LA with her. It was a crude but charming scene of Tommy Toad standing outside a movie theater, gazing up at a marquee on which Thelma's name was huge.

He had tears in his eyes. "But do you really have to go, Aunt Thelma? Can't you stay one more day?"

Thelma hugged him, then carefully rolled up the drawing as if in possession of a priceless masterwork. "I'd love to stay, Christopher Robin, but I can't. My adoring fans are crying for me to make this movie. Besides, I've got a big mortgage."

"What's a mortgage?"

"The greatest motivator in the world," Thelma said, giving him a last kiss. She got into the car, started the engine, put down the side window, and winked at Laura. "Exotic news, Shane."

"Mystery."

"Wonder."

Laura gave her the split-finger greeting from *Star Trek*.

Thelma laughed. "You'll make it, Shane. In spite of the guns and all I've learned since I came here on Friday, I'm less worried about you now than I was then."

Chris stood at Laura's side, and they watched Thelma's car until it went down the long driveway and disappeared onto the state route.

# SIX

Dr. Vladimir Penlovski's large office suite was on the fourth floor of the institute. When Stefan entered the reception lounge, it was deserted, but he heard voices coming from the next room. He went to the inner door, which was ajar, pushed it all the way open, and saw Penlovski giving dictation to Anna Kaspar, his secretary.

Penlovski looked up, mildly surprised to see Stefan. He must have perceived the tension in Stefan's face, for he frowned and said, "Is something wrong?"

"Something's been wrong for a long time," Stefan said, "but it'll all be fine now, I think." Then, as Penlovski's frown deepened, Stefan pulled the silencer-equipped Colt Commander from the pocket of his lab coat and shot the scientist twice in the chest.

Anna Kaspar sprang up from her chair, dropping her pencil and dictation pad, a scream caught in her throat.

He did not like killing women—he did not like killing anyone—but there was no choice now, so he shot her three times, knocking her backward onto the desk, before the scream could tear free of her.

Dead, she slid off the desk and crumpled to the floor. The shots had been no louder than the hissing of an angry cat, and the sound of the body dropping had been insufficient to draw attention.

Penlovski was slumped in his chair, eyes and mouth open, staring sightlessly. One of the shots must have pierced his heart, for there was only a small spot of blood on his shirt; his circulation had been cut off in an instant.

Stefan backed out of the room, closed the door. He crossed the reception lounge and, stepping into the hall, shut the outer door too.

His heart was racing. With those two murders he had cut himself off forever from his own time, his own people. From here on, the only life for him was in Laura's time. Now there was no turning back.

With his hands—and the gun—jammed in his lab-coat pockets, he went down the hall toward Januskaya's office. As he neared the door, two of his other colleagues came out of it. They said hello as they passed him, and he stopped to see if they were heading for Penlovski's office. If they were, he'd have to kill them too.

He was relieved when they stopped at the elevators. The more corpses he left strewn around, the more likely someone would be to stumble across one of them and sound an alarm that would prevent him from setting the timer on the explosives and escaping by way of the Lightning Road.

He went into Januskaya's office, which also had a reception area. At the desk, the secretary—provided, as Anna Kaspar had been, by the secret police—looked up and smiled.

"Is Dr. Januskaya here?" Stefan asked.

"No. He's down in the documents room with Dr. Volkaw."

Volkaw was the third man whose overview of the project was great enough to require that he be eliminated. It seemed a good omen that he and Wladyslaw Januskaya were conveniently in the same place.

In the documents room, they stored and studied the many books, newspapers, magazines, and other materials that had been brought back by time travelers from scheduled jaunts. These days the men who had conceived of Lightning Road were engaged in an urgent analysis of the key points at which alterations in the natural flow of events could provide the changes in the course of history that they desired.

On the way down in the elevator, Stefan replaced the pistol's silencer with the unused spare. The first would muffle another dozen shots before its sound baffles were seriously damaged. But he did not want to overuse it. The second silencer was additional insurance. He also quickly exchanged the half-empty magazine for a full one.

The first-floor corridor was a busy place, with people coming and going from one lab and research room to another. He kept his hands in his pockets and went directly to the documents room.

When Stefan entered, Januskaya and Volkaw were standing at an oak table, bent over a copy of a magazine, arguing heatedly but in low voices. They glanced up, then immediately continued their discussion, assuming that he was there for research purposes of his own.

Stefan put two bullets in Volkaw's back.

Januskaya reacted with confusion and shock as Volkaw flew forward into the table, driven by the impact of the nearly silent gunfire.

Stefan shot Januskaya in the face, then turned and left the room, closing the door behind him. Not trusting himself to speak to one of his colleagues with any degree of self-control or coherence, he tried to appear to be lost in thought, hoping that would dissuade them from approaching him. He went to the elevators as quickly as possible without running, went to his third-floor office, reached behind the file cabinet, and twisted the dial on the timer as far as it would go, giving himself just five minutes to get to the gate and away before the institute was reduced to burning rubble.

# SEVEN

By the time the school year began, Laura had won approval for Chris to receive his education at home, from a state-accredited tutor. Her name was Ida Palomar, and she reminded Laura of Marjorie Main, the late actress in the Ma and Pa Kettle movies. Ida was a big woman, a bit gruff, but with a generous heart, and she was a good teacher.

By the Thanksgiving school break, instead of feeling as if they were imprisoned, both she and Chris had accommodated to the relative isolation in which they lived. In fact they had actually come to enjoy the special closeness that developed between them as a result of having so few other people in their lives.

On Thanksgiving Day Thelma called from Beverly Hills to wish them a happy holiday. Laura took the call in the kitchen, which was full of the aroma of roasting turkey. Chris was in the family room, reading Shel Silverstein.

"Besides wishing you a happy holiday," Thelma said, "I'm calling to invite you down here to spend Christmas week with me and Jason."

"Jason?" Laura said.

"Jason Gaines, the director," Thelma said. "He's the guy who's directing this film I'm making. I've moved in with him."

"Does he know it yet?"

"Listen, Shane, *I* make the wisecracks."

"Sorry."

"He says he loves me. Is that crazy or what? I mean, Jeez, here's this decent-looking guy, only five years older than me, with no visible mutations, who's a *hugely* successful film director, worth many millions, who could just about have any stacked little starlet he wanted, and the only one he wants is me. Now obviously he's brain-damaged, but you wouldn't know it to talk to him, he could pass for normal. He says what he loves about me is I've got a *brain*—"

"Does he know how diseased it is?"

"There you go again, Shane. He says he loves my brain and sense of humor, and he's even excited by my body—or if he isn't excited then he's the first guy in history who could *fake* an erection."

"You've got a perfectly lovely body."

"Well, I'm beginning to consider the possibility that it's not as bad as I always thought. That is, if you consider *boniness* to be the sine qua non of feminine beauty. But even if I am able to look at my bod in a mirror now, it's still got *this* face perched atop it."

"You've got a perfectly lovely face—especially now that it's not surrounded by green and purple hair."

"It's not *your* face, Shane. Which means I'm mad for inviting you here for Christmas week. Jason will see you, and the next thing I'll be sitting in a Glad trash bag at the curb. But what about it? Will you come? We're shooting the film in and around LA, and we'll finish principal photography December tenth. Then Jason's got a lot of work to do, what with the editing, the whole schmear, but Christmas week we're just *stopping*. We'd like you to be here. Say you will."

"I'd sure like to meet the man smart enough to fall for you, Thelma, but I don't know. I feel . . . safe here."

"What do you think—we're dangerous?"

"You know what I mean."

"You can bring an Uzi."

"What will Jason think of that?"

"I'll tell him you're a radical leftist, save-the-sperm-whale, get-toxic-preservatives-out-of-Spam, parakeet liberationist and that you keep an Uzi with you at all times in case the revolution comes without warning. He'll buy it. This is Hollywood, kid. Most of the actors he works with are politically crazier than that."

Through the family-room archway, Laura could see Chris curled up in the armchair with his book.

She sighed. "Maybe it is time we got out in the world once in a while. And it's going to be a difficult Christmas if it's just Chris and me, this being the first without Danny. But I feel uneasy . . . ."

"It's been over ten months, Laura," Thelma said gently.

"But I'm not going to let down my guard."

"You don't have to. I'm serious about the Uzi. Bring your whole arsenal if that'll make you feel better. Just come."

"Well . . . all right."

"Fantastic! I can't wait for you to meet Jason."

"Do I detect that the love this brain-damaged Hollywood maven feels for you is reciprocated?"

"I'm crazy about him," Thelma admitted.

"I'm happy for you, Thelma. In fact I'm standing here now with a grin that won't stop, and nothing's made me feel so good in months."

Everything she said was true. But after she hung up, she missed Danny more than ever.

# EIGHT

As soon as he set the timer behind the filing cabinet, Stefan left his third-floor office and went to the main lab on the ground floor. It was 12:14, and because the scheduled jaunt was not until two o'clock, the main lab was deserted. The windows were sealed, and most of the overhead lights were still off, as they had been little more than an hour ago, when he had returned from the San Bernardinos. The multitude of dials, gauges, and lighted graphs of the support machinery glowed green and orange. More in shadow than in the light, the gate awaited him.

Four minutes till detonation.

He went directly to the primary programming board and carefully adjusted the dials and switches and levers, setting the gate for the desired destination: southern California, near Big Bear, at eight o'clock on the night of January 10, 1988, just a few hours after Danny Packard had been killed. He had done the necessary calculations days ago and had them on a sheet of paper to which he referred, so he was able to program the machinery in only a minute.

If he could have traveled to the afternoon of the tenth, prior to the accident and the shoot-out with Kokoschka, he would have done so in the hope of saving Danny. However, they had learned that a time traveler could not revisit a place if he scheduled his second arrival shortly *before* his previous jaunt; there was a natural mechanism that prevented a traveler from being in a place where he might encounter himself on a previous jaunt. He could return to Big Bear *after* he had left Laura that January night, for having already departed from the highway, he was no longer at risk of encountering himself there. But if he set the gate for an arrival time that would make it possible for him to meet himself, he would simply bounce back to the institute without going anywhere. That was one of many mysterious aspects of time travel which they had learned, around which they worked, but which they did not understand.

When he finished programming the gate, he glanced at the latitude and longitude indicator to confirm that he would arrive in the general area of Big Bear. Then he looked at the clock that noted his arrival time, and he was startled to see that it showed 8:00 P.M., January 10,

1989, instead of 1988. The gate was now set to deliver him to Big Bear not hours after Danny's death but a full year later.

He was sure that his calculations were correct; he'd had plenty of time to make them and recheck them over the past couple of weeks. Evidently, nervous as he was, he had made a mistake when entering the numbers. He would have to reprogram the gate.

Less than three minutes until detonation.

He blinked sweat out of his eyes and studied the numbers on the paper, the end product of his extensive calculations. As he reached for a control knob to cancel out the current program and re-enter the first of the figures again, a shout of alarm went up in the ground-floor corridor. The cries sounded as if they were coming from the north end of the building, in the general area of the document room.

Someone had found the bodies of Januskaya and Volkaw.

He heard more shouting. People running.

Glancing nervously at the closed door to the hall, he decided he had no time to reprogram. He would have to settle for returning to Laura one year after he had last left her.

With the silencer-fitted Colt Commander in his right hand, he rose from the programming console and headed toward the gate—that eight-foot-high, twelve-foot-long, polished steel, open-ended barrel resting a foot off the floor on copper-plated blocks. He did not even want to risk taking time to recover his peacoat from the corner where he had left it an hour ago.

The commotion in the corridor was louder.

When he was only a couple of steps from the entrance to the gate, the lab door was thrown open behind him with such force that it hit the wall with a crash.

"Stop right there!"

Stefan recognized the voice, but he did not want to believe what he heard. He brought up the pistol as he swung around to confront his challenger: The man who had raced into the lab was Kokoschka.

Impossible. Kokoschka was dead. Kokoschka had followed him to Big Bear on the night of January 10, 1988, and he had killed Kokoschka on that snowswept highway.

Stunned, Stefan squeezed off two shots, both wide.

Kokoschka returned his fire. One slug took Stefan in the chest, high on the left side, knocking him backward against the edge of the gate. He stayed on his feet and got off three shots at Kokoschka, forcing the bastard to dive for cover and roll behind a lab bench.

There were less than two minutes from detonation.

Stefan felt no pain because he was in shock. But his left arm was useless; it hung limply at his side. And an insistent, oily blackness seeped in at the edges of his vision.

Only a few overhead lights had been left on, but suddenly even they flickered and went out, leaving the room vaguely illuminated by the wan glow of the many glass-covered dials and gauges. For an instant Stefan thought the dying light was a further surrender of his consciousness, a subjective development, but then he realized the public power supply had failed again, evidently due to the work of saboteurs, for there had been no sirens to warn of an air attack.

Kokoschka fired twice from darkness, the muzzle flash marking his position, and Stefan loosed the last three rounds in his pistol, though there was no hope of hitting Kokoschka through the marble lab bench.

Thankful that the gate was powered by a secure generator and still functional, Stefan threw away the pistol and with his good hand gripped the rim of the barrel-shaped portal. He pulled himself inside and crawled frantically toward the three-quarter point, where he would cross the energy field and depart this place for Big Bear, 1989.

As he hitched on two knees and one good arm through the gloomy interior of the barrel, he abruptly realized that the timer on the detonator in his office was connected to the public power supply. The countdown to destruction had been interrupted when the lights had gone out.

With dismay he understood why Kokoschka was not dead in Big Bear in 1988. *Kokoschka had not made that trip yet.* Kokoschka had only now learned of Stefan's perfidy, when he had discovered the bodies of Januskaya and Volkaw. Before the public power supply was restored, Kokoschka would search Stefan's office, find the detonator, and disarm the explosives. The institute would not be destroyed.

Stefan hesitated, wondering if he should go back.

Behind him he heard other voices in the lab, other security men arriving to reinforce Kokoschka.

He crawled forward.

And what of Kokoschka? The security chief evidently would travel to January 10, 1988, trying to kill Stefan on state route 330. But he would only manage to kill Danny before being killed himself. Stefan was pretty sure that Kokoschka's death was an immutable destiny, but he would need to think more about the paradoxes of time travel, to see if there was any way Kokoschka could escape being gunned down in 1988, a death that Stefan had already witnessed.

The complications of time travel were confusing even when one pondered them with a clear head. In his condition, wounded and struggling to remain conscious, he only grew dizzier thinking about such things. Later. He would worry about it later.

Behind him in the dark laboratory, someone began firing into the entrance of the gate, hoping to hit him before he reached the point of departure.

He crawled the last couple of feet. Toward Laura. Toward a new life in a distant time. But he had hoped to close forever the bridge between the era he was leaving and that to which he was now pledging himself. Instead the gate would remain open. And they could come across time to get him . . . and Laura.

# NINE

Laura and Chris spent Christmas with Thelma at Jason Gaines's house in Beverly Hills. It was a twenty-two-room, Tudor-style mansion on six, walled acres, a phenomenally large property in an area where the cost per acre had long ago escalated far beyond reason. During construction in the '40s—it had been built by a producer of screwball comedies and war movies—no compromises had been made in quality, and the rooms were marked by beautiful detail work that could not have been duplicated these days at ten times the original cost: There were intricately coffered ceilings, some made of oak, some of copper; crown moldings were elaborately carved; the leaded windows were of stained or beveled glass, and they were set so deep in the castle-thick walls that one could comfortably sit on the wide sills; interior lintels were decorated with hand-carved panels—vines and roses, cherubs and banners, leaping deer, birds with ribbons trailing from their bills; exterior lintels were of carved granite, and in two were set mortared clusters of colorful della Robbia-style ceramic fruits. The six-acre property around the house was a meticulously maintained private park where winding stone pathways led through a tropical landscape of palms, benjaminas, ficus nidida, azaleas laden with brilliant red blossoms, impatiens, ferns, birds of paradise, and seasonal flowers of so many species that Laura could identify only half of them.

When Laura and Chris arrived early on Saturday afternoon, the day before Christmas, Thelma took them on a long tour of the house and grounds, after which they drank hot cocoa and ate miniature pastries prepared by the cook and served by the maid in the airy sun porch that looked out upon the swimming pool.

"Is this a crazy life, Shane? Can you believe that the same girl who spent almost ten years in holes like McIlroy and Caswell could end up living *here* without first having to be reincarnated as a princess?"

The house was so imposing that it encouraged anyone who owned it to feel Important with a capital I, and anyone in possession of it would be hard-pressed to avoid smugness and pomposity. But when Jason Gaines came home at four o'clock, he proved to be as unpretentious as anyone Laura knew, amazingly so for a man who had spent seventeen years in the movie business. He was thirty-eight, five years older than Thelma, and he looked like a younger Robert Vaughn, which was a lot better than "decent-looking," as Thelma had referred to him. He was home less than half an hour before he and Chris huddled in one of his three hobby rooms, playing with an electric train set that covered a fifteen-by-twenty-foot platform, complete with detailed villages, rolling countryside, windmills, waterfalls, tunnels, and bridges.

That night, with Chris asleep in the room adjoining Laura's, Thelma visited her. In their pajamas they sat cross-legged on her bed, as if they were girls again, though they ate roasted pistachios and drank Christmas champagne instead of cookies and milk.

"The weirdest thing of all, Shane, is that in spite of where I came from, I feel as if I belong here. I don't feel out of place."

She did not look out of place, either. Though she was still recognizably Thelma Ackerson, she had changed in the past few months. Her hair was better cut and styled; she had a tan for the first time in her life; and she carried herself more like a woman and less like a comic trying to win laughter—meaning approval—with each funny gesture and posture. She was wearing less flamboyant—and sexier—pajamas than usual: clingy, unpatterned, peach-colored silk. She was, however, still sporting bunny slippers.

"Bunny slippers," she said, "remind me of who I am. You can't get a swelled head if you wear bunny slippers. You can't lose your sense of perspective and start acting like a star or a rich lady if you keep on wearing bunny slippers. Besides, bunny slippers give me confidence because they're so jaunty; they make a statement; they say, 'Nothing the world does to me can ever get me so far down that I can't be silly and frivolous.' If I died and found myself in hell, I could endure the place if I had bunny slippers."

Christmas Day was like a wonderful dream. Jason proved to be a sentimentalist with the undiminished wonder of a child. He insisted they gather at the Christmas tree in pajamas and robes, that they open their gifts with as much popping of ribbons and noisy tearing of paper and as much general drama as possible, that they sing carols, that while opening gifts they abandon the idea of a healthy breakfast and instead eat cookies, candy, nuts, fruitcake, and caramel popcorn. He proved that he had not just been trying to be a good host when he had spent the previous evening with Chris at the trains, for all Christmas Day he engaged the boy in one form of play or another, both inside and outside the house, and it was clear that he had a love of and natural rapport with kids. By dinnertime Laura realized Chris had laughed more in one day than in the entire past eleven months.

When she tucked the boy into bed that night, he said, "What a great day, huh, Mom?"

"One of the all-time greats," she agreed.

"All I wish," he said as he dropped toward sleep, "is that Daddy could've been here to play with us."

"I wish the same thing, honey."

"But in a way he was here,'cause I thought of him a lot. Will I always remember him, Mom, the way he was, even after dozens and dozens of years, will I remember him?"

"I'll help you remember, baby."

"Because sometimes already there are little things I don't quite remember about him. I have to think hard to remember them. But I don't want to forget 'cause he was my daddy."

When he was asleep, Laura went through the connecting door to her own bed. She was immensely relieved when a few minutes later Thelma came by for another girl-to-girl, because without Thelma, she would have had a few very bad hours there.

"If I had babies, Shane," Thelma said, climbing into Laura's bed, "do you think there's any chance at all that they'd be allowed to live in society, or would they be banished to some ugly-kid equivalent of a leper colony?"

"Don't be silly."

"Of course, I could afford *massive* plastic surgery for them. I mean, even if it turns out that their species is questionable, I could afford to have them made passably human."

"Sometimes your put-downs of yourself make me angry."

"Sorry. Chalk it up to not having a supportive mom and dad. I've got both the confidence and doubt of an orphan." She was quiet for a moment, then laughed and said, "Hey, you know what? Jason wants to marry me. I thought at first he was possessed by a demon and unable to control his tongue, but he assures me we've no need of an exorcist, though he's evidently suffered a minor stroke. So what do you think?"

"What do *I* think? What's that matter? But for what it's worth, he's a terrific guy. You are going to grab him, aren't you?"

"I worry that he's too good for me."

"No one's too good for you. Marry him."

"I worry that it won't work out, and then I'll be devastated."

"And if you don't give it a try," Laura said, "you'll be worse than devastated—you'll be alone."

# TEN

Stefan felt the familiar, unpleasant tingle that accompanied time travel, a peculiar vibration that passed inward from his skin, through his flesh, into the marrow of his bones, then swiftly back out again from bones to flesh to skin. With a *pop-whoooosh* he left the gate, and in the same instant he was stumbling down a steep, snow-covered slope in the California mountains on the night of January 10, 1989.

He tripped, fell on his wounded side, rolled to the bottom of the slope, where he came to rest against a rotted log. Pain flashed through him for the first time since he had been shot. He cried out and flopped onto his back, biting his tongue to keep from passing out, blinking up at the tumultuous night.

Another thunderbolt ripped the sky, and light seemed to pulse from the jagged wound. By the spectral glow of the snow-covered earth and by the fierce but fitful flashes of lightning, Stefan saw that he was in a clearing in a forest. Leafless, black trees thrust bare limbs toward the fulminous sky, as if they were fanatical cultists praising a violent god. Evergreens, boughs drooping under surplices of snow, stood like the solemn priests of a more decorous religion.

Arriving in a time other than his own, a traveler disrupted the forces of nature in some way that required the dissipation of tremendous energy. Regardless of the weather at the point of arrival, the imbalance was corrected by a sky-shattering display of lightning, which was why the ethereal highway on which time travelers journeyed was called the Lightning Road. For reasons no one had been able to ascertain, a return to the institute, to the traveler's own era, was marked by no celestial pyrotechnics.

The lightning subsided, as it always did, from bolts worthy of the Apocalypse to distant flickerings. In a minute the night was dark and calm again.

As the thunderbolts had faded, his pain had increased. It almost seemed as if the lightning that had cracked the vaults of heaven was now captured within his chest, left shoulder, and left arm, too great a power for mortal flesh to contain or endure.

He got onto his knees and rose shakily to his feet, worried that he had little chance of getting out of the woods alive. But for the phosphorescent glow of the snow-mantled clearing, the cloudy night was cellar-black, forbidding. Though undisturbed by wind, the winter air was icy, and he was wearing only a thin lab coat over shirt and pants.

Worse, he might be miles from a highway or any landmark by which he could reckon his position. If the gate was considered as a gun, its accuracy was remarkable for the temporal distance covered to the target, but it was far from perfect in its aim. A traveler usually arrived within ten or fifteen minutes of the *time* he intended, but not always with the desired geographic precision. Sometimes he touched down within a hundred yards of his physical destination, but on other occasions he was as far as ten or fifteen miles off, as on the day that he had traveled to January 10, 1988, to save Laura, Danny, and Chris from the Robertsons' sliding pickup truck.

On all previous trips, he had carried both a map of the target area and a compass, lest he find himself in just such a place of isolation as he had arrived at now. But this time, having left his peacoat in the corner of the lab, he had neither compass nor map, and the occluded sky deprived him of the hope of finding his way out of the forest with the help of the stars.

He stood in snow almost to his knees, wearing street shoes, no boots, and he felt as if he must start moving immediately or freeze to the ground. He looked around the clearing, hoping for inspiration, for a twinge of intuition, but at last he chose a direction at random and headed to his left, searching for a deer trail or other natural course that would provide him a passage through the forest.

His entire left side from neck to waist throbbed with pain. He hoped that the bullet, in passing through him, had torn no arteries and that the rate of blood loss was slow enough to allow him at least to reach Laura and see her face, the face he loved, one last time before he died.

The one-year anniversary of Danny's death fell on a Tuesday, and although Chris did not mention the significance of the date, he was aware of it. The boy was unusually quiet. He spent most of that somber day playing silently with his Masters of the Universe action figures in the family room, which was the kind of play ordinarily characterized by vocal imitations of laser weapons, clashing swords, and spaceship engines. Later he sprawled on his bed in his room, reading comic books. He resisted Laura's every effort to draw him out of his self-imposed isolation, which was probably for the best; any attempt she made to be cheerful would have been transparent, and he would have been further depressed by the perception that she was also struggling mightily to turn her thoughts away from their grievous loss.

Thelma, who had called only days before to report the good news that she had decided to marry Jason Gaines, called again at seven-fifteen that evening, just to chat, as if she were unaware of the importance of the date. Laura took the call in her office, where she was still struggling with the bile-black book that had occupied her for the past year.

"Hey, Shane, guess what? I met Paul McCartney! He was in LA to negotiate a recording contract, and we were at the same party Friday night. When I first saw him, he was stuffing an hors d'oeuvre in his mouth, he said hello, he had crumbs on his lip, and he was *gorgeous*.

He said he'd seen my movies, thought I was very good, and we talked—you believe this?—we must've chatted twenty minutes, and gradually the strangest thing happened.''

"You discovered that you'd undressed him while you were talking.''

"Well, he still looks very good, you know, still that cherub face we swooned over twenty years ago but marked now by experience, *très* sophisticated and with an extremely appealing touch of sadness about his eyes, and he was enormously amusing and charming. At first maybe I did want to tear his clothes off, yeah, and live out the fantasy at last. But then the longer we talked, the less he seemed like a god, the more he seemed like a person, and in *minutes*, Shane, the myth evaporated, and he was just this very nice, attractive, middle-aged man. Now what do you make of that?''

"What am I supposed to make of it?''

"I don't know,'' Thelma said. "I'm a little disturbed. Shouldn't a living legend continue to awe you longer than twenty minutes after you meet him? I mean, I've met lots of stars by now, and none of them have remained godlike, but this was *McCartney*.''

"Well, if you want my opinion, his swift loss of mythological stature says nothing negative about him, but it says plenty positive about you. You've achieved a new maturity, Ackerson.''

"Does this mean I've got to give up watching old Three Stooges movies every Saturday morning?''

"The Stooges are permitted, but food fights are definitely a thing of the past for you.''

By the time Thelma hung up at ten minutes till eight, Laura was feeling slightly better, so she switched from the bile-black book to the tale about Sir Tommy Toad. She had written only two sentences of the children's story when the night beyond the windows was lit by a bolt of lightning bright enough to spark dire thoughts of nuclear holocaust. The subsequent thunderclap shook the house from roof to foundation, as if a wrecker's ball had slammed into one of the walls. She came to her feet with a start, so surprised that she did not even hit the "save" key on the computer. A second bolt seared the night, making the windows as luminous as television screens, and the thunder that followed was louder than the first explosion.

"Mom!''

She turned and saw Chris standing in the doorway. "It's okay,'' she said. He ran to her. She sat in the spring-backed armchair and pulled him onto her lap. "It's all right. Don't be afraid, honey.''

"But it's not raining,'' he said. "Why's it booming like that if it's not raining?''

Outside, an incredible series of lightning bolts and overlapping thunderclaps continued for nearly a minute, then subsided. The power of the event had been so great, Laura was able to imagine that in the morning they would find the broken sky lying about in huge chunks like fragments of a giant eggshell.

Before he walked five minutes from the clearing in which he had arrived, Stefan was forced to pause and lean against the thick trunk of a pine whose branches began just above his head. The pain of his wound wrung streams of sweat from him, yet he was shivering in the bitter January cold, too dizzy to stand up, yet terrified of sitting down and falling into an endless sleep. With the drooping boughs of that mammoth pine overhead and all around, he felt as if he had taken refuge under Death's black robe, from which he might not emerge.

Before putting Chris to bed for the night, she made sundaes for them with coconut-almond ice cream and Hershey's syrup. They ate at the kitchen table, and the boy's depression seemed to have lifted. Perhaps by marking the end of that sad anniversary with such drama, the bizarre weather phenomenon had startled him out of thoughts of death and into the contemplation of wonders. He was filled with talk of the lightning that had crackled down a kite string and into Dr. Frankenstein's laboratory in the old James Whale film, which he'd seen for the first time a week ago, and of the lightning that had frightened Donald Duck in a Disney cartoon, and of the stormy night in *101 Dalmations* during which Cruella DeVille had posed such a dire threat to the title-role puppies.

By the time she tucked him in and kissed him goodnight, he was approaching sleep with a smile—a half smile, at least—rather than with the frown that had weighed upon his face all day. She sat in a chair by the side of his bed until he was fast asleep, though he was no longer afraid and did not require her presence. She stayed simply because she needed to look at him for a while.

She returned to her office at nine-fifteen, but before going to the word processor, she stopped at a window and stared out at the snow-swathed front lawn, at the black ribbon of the graveled driveway leading to the distant state route, and up at the starless, night sky. Something about the lightning deeply disturbed her: not that it had been so strange, not that it had been potentially destructive, but that the unprecedented and almost supernatural power of it had been some-how . . . familiar. She seemed to recall having witnessed a similar stormy display on another occasion, but she could not remember when. It was an uncanny feeling, akin to déjà vu, and it would not fade.

She went into the master bedroom and checked the security-control panel in her closet to be sure the perimeter alarm covering all the windows and doors was engaged. From beneath the bed, she withdrew the Uzi, which had an extended magazine holding four hundred exotic, lightweight, alloy-jacketed rounds. She took the gun back to her office and put it on the floor by her chair.

She was about to sit down when lightning split the night again, frightening her, and it was followed at once by a crack of thunder she felt in her bones. Another bolt and another and another blazed in the windows like a series of leering, ghostly faces formed of ectoplasmic light.

As the heavens quaked with scintillant shudders, Laura hurried to Chris's room to calm him. To her surprise, though the lightning and thunder were shockingly more violent than they had been previously, the boy was not awakened, perhaps because the din seemed a part of some dream he was having about Dalmation puppies on a stormy night of adventure.

Again, no rain fell.

The lightning and thunder quickly subsided, but her anxiety remained high.

He saw strange ebony shapes in the darkness, things that slipped between the trees and watched him with eyes blacker than their bodies, but though they startled and frightened him, he knew that they were not real, only phantoms spawned by his increasingly disoriented mind. He plodded onward in spite of outer cold, inner heat, prickling pine needles, sharp bramble thorns, icy ground that sometimes tilted out from beneath his feet and sometimes spun like a phonograph turntable. The pain in his chest and shoulder and arm was so intense that he was assailed by delirium images of rats gnawing at his flesh from within his body, though he could not figure how they had gotten *in* there.

After wandering for at least an hour—it seemed like many hours, even days, but could not have been days because the sun had not risen—he came to the perimeter of the forest and, at the far end of a sloping half acre of snow-mantled lawn, he saw the house. Lights were vaguely visible at the edges of the blind-covered windows.

He stood, disbelieving, at first convinced that the house was no more real than the Stygian figures that had accompanied him through the woods. Then he began moving toward the mirage—in case it wasn't a fever dream, after all.

When he had taken only a few steps, a lash of lightning whipped the night, scarred the sky. The whip cracked repeatedly, and each time a stronger arm seemed to power it.

Stefan's shadow leaped and writhed on the snow around him, though he was temporarily paralyzed by fear. Sometimes he had two shadows because lightning silhouetted him simultaneously from two directions. Already well-trained hunters had followed him on the Lightning Road, determined to stop him before he had a chance to warn Laura.

He looked back at the trees out of which he had come. Under the stroboscopic sky, the evergreens seemed to jump toward him, then back, then toward him again. He saw no hunters there.

As the lightning faded, he staggered toward the house again. He fell twice, struggled up, kept moving, though he was afraid that if he fell again he would not be able to get to his feet or shout loud enough to be heard.

Staring at the computer screen, trying to think about Sir Tommy Toad and thinking instead of the lightning, Laura suddenly recalled when she previously had seen such a preternaturally stormy sky: the very day on which her father had first told her about Sir Tommy, the day that the junkie had come into the grocery, the day that she had seen her guardian for the first time, that summer of her eighth year.

She sat up straight in her chair.

Her heart began to hammer hard, fast.

Lightning of that unnatural power meant trouble of a specific nature, trouble for *her*. She could recall no lightning on the day that Danny died or when her guardian appeared in the cemetery during her father's burial service. But with an absolute certainty that she could not explain, she knew that the phenomenon she had witnessed tonight held a terrible meaning for her; it was an omen and not a good one.

She grabbed the Uzi and made a circuit of the upstairs, checking all the windows, looking in on Chris, making sure everything was as it should be. Then she hurried downstairs to inspect those rooms.

As she stepped into the kitchen, something thumped against the back door. With a gasp of surprise and fear, she whirled in that direction, swung the Uzi around, and nearly opened fire.

But it was not the determined sound of someone breaking in. It was an unthreatening thump, barely louder than a knock, repeated twice. She thought she heard a voice, too, weakly calling her name.

Silence.

She edged to the door and listened for perhaps half a minute.

Nothing.

The door was a high-security model with a steel core sandwiched between two inch-thick slabs of oak, so she was not worried about being shot by a gunman on the other side. Yet she hesitated to move directly to it and peer through the fisheye lens because she feared seeing an eye pressed to the other side, trying to peer in at *her*. When at last she had the courage for it, the peephole gave her a wide-angled view of the patio, and she saw a man sprawled on the concrete, his arms flung out at his sides, as if he had fallen backward after knocking on the door.

Trap, she thought. Trap, trick.

She switched on the outdoor spotlights and crept to the Levelor-covered window above the built-in writing desk. Cautiously she lifted one of the slats. The man on the concrete patio was her guardian. His shoes and trousers were caked with snow. He wore what appeared to be a white lab coat, the front darkly stained with blood.

As far as she could see, no one was crouched on the patio or on the lawn beyond, but she had to consider the possibility that someone had dumped his body there as a lure to bring her out of the house. Opening the door at night, under these circumstances, was foolhardy.

Nevertheless she could not leave him out there. Not her guardian. Not if he was hurt and dying.

She pressed the alarm bypass button next to the door, disengaged the dead-bolt locks, and reluctantly stepped into the wintry night with the Uzi at the ready. No one shot at her. On the dimly snow-illumined lawn, all the way back to the forest, nothing moved.

She went to her guardian, knelt at his side, and felt for his pulse. He was alive. She peeled back one of his eyelids. He was unconscious. The wound high in the left side of his chest looked bad, though it did not appear to be bleeding at the moment.

Her training with Henry Takahami and her regular exercise program had dramatically increased her strength, but she was not strong enough to lift the wounded man with one arm. She propped the Uzi by the back door and found she could not lift him even with both arms. It seemed dangerous to move a man who was so badly hurt, but more dangerous to leave him in the frigid night, especially when someone was apparently in pursuit of him. She managed to half lift and half drag him into the kitchen, where she stretched him out on the floor. With relief she retrieved the Uzi, relocked the door, and engaged the alarm again.

He was frighteningly pale and cold to the touch, so the immediate necessity was to strip off his shoes and socks, which were crusted with snow. By the time she dealt with his left foot and was unlacing his right shoe, he was mumbling in a strange language, the words too slurred for her to identify the tongue, and in English he muttered about explosives and gates and "phantoms in the trees."

Though she knew that he was delirious and very likely could not understand her any more than she could understand him, she spoke to him reassuringly: "Easy now, just relax, you'll be all right; as soon as I get your foot out of this block of ice, I'll call a doctor."

The mention of a doctor brought him briefly out of his confusion.

He gripped her arm weakly, fixed her with an intense, fearful gaze. "No doctor. Get out . . . got to get out . . . "

"You're in no condition to go anywhere," she told him. "Except by ambulance to a hospital."

"Got to get out. Quick. They'll be coming . . . soon coming . . . "

She glanced at the Uzi. "Who will be coming?"

"Assassins," he said urgently. "Kill me for revenge. Kill you, kill Chris. Coming. Now."

At that moment there was no delirium in his eyes or voice. His pale, sweat-slick face was no longer slack but taut with terror.

All her training with guns and in the martial arts no longer seemed like hysterical precautions. "Okay," she said, "we'll get out as soon as I've had a look at that wound, see if it needs to be dressed."

"No! Now. Out now."

"But—"

"Now," he insisted. In his eyes was such a haunted look, she could almost believe that the assassins of whom he spoke were not ordinary men but creatures of some supernatural origin, demons with the ruthlessness and relentlessness of the soulless.

"Okay," she said. "We'll get out now."

His hand fell away from her arm. His eyes shifted out of focus, and he began to mumble thickly, senselessly.

As she hurried across the kitchen, intending to go upstairs and wake Chris, she heard her guardian speak dreamily yet anxiously of a "great, black, rolling machine of death," which meant nothing to her but frightened her nonetheless.

# PART TWO

# PURSUIT

*The long habit of living indisposeth us for dying.*

—SIR THOMAS BROWNE

# 5

◆ ◆ ◆

# An Army of Shadows

## ONE

Laura switched on a lamp and shook Chris awake. "Get dressed, honey. Quickly."

"What's happening?" he asked sleepily, rubbing his eyes with his small fists.

"Some bad men are coming, and we've got to get out of here before they arrive. Now hurry."

Chris had spent a year not only mourning his father but preparing for the moment when the deceptively placid events of daily life would be disrupted by another unexpected explosion of the chaos that lay at the heart of human existence, the chaos that from time to time erupted like an active volcano, as it had done the night his father had been murdered. Chris had watched his mother become a first-rate shot with a handgun, had seen her collect an arsenal, had taken self-defense classes with her, and through it all he had retained the point of view and attitudes of a child, had seemed pretty much like any other child, if understandably melancholy since the death of his father. But now in a moment of crisis he did not react like an eight-year-old; he did not whine, or ask unnecessary questions; he was not quarrelsome or stubborn or slow to obey. He threw back the covers, got out of bed at once, and hurried to the closet.

"Meet me in the kitchen," Laura said.

"Okay, Mom."

She was proud of his responsible reaction and relieved that he would not delay them, but she was also saddened that at eight years of age he understood enough about the brevity and harshness of life to respond to a crisis with the swiftness and equanimity of an adult.

She was wearing jeans and a blue-plaid, flannel shirt. When she went to her bedroom, she only had to slip into a wool sweater, pull off her Rockport walking shoes, and put on a pair of rubberized hiking boots with lace-up tops.

She had gotten rid of Danny's clothes, so she had no coat for the wounded man in the kitchen. She had plenty of blankets, however, and she grabbed two of those from the linen closet in the hall.

As an afterthought, she went to her office, opened the safe, and removed the strange black belt with copper fittings that her guardian had given her a year ago. She jammed it in her satchel-like purse.

Downstairs she stopped at the front foyer closet for a blue ski jacket and the Uzi carbine that hung on the back of the door. As she moved she was alert for unusual noises—voices in the night beyond the house or the sound of a car engine—but all remained silent.

In the kitchen she put the submachine gun on the table with the other one, then knelt beside her guardian, who was unconscious again. She unbuttoned his snow-wet lab coat, then his shirt, and looked at the gunshot wound in his chest. It was high in his left shoulder, well above the heart, which was good, but he had lost a lot of blood; his clothes were soaked with it.

"Mom?" Chris was in the doorway, dressed for a winter night.

"Take one of those Uzis from the table, get the third one from the back of the pantry door, and put them in the Jeep."

"It's him," Chris said, wide-eyed with surprise.

"Yes, it is. He showed up like this, hurt bad. Besides the Uzis, get two of the revolvers—the one in the drawer over there and the one in the dining room. And be careful not to accidentally—"

"Don't worry, Mom," he said, setting off on the errands.

As gently as possible she rolled her guardian onto his right side— he groaned but did not awaken—to see if there was an exit wound in his back. Yes. The bullet had gone through him, exiting under the scapula. His back was soaked with blood, too, but neither the entry nor exit point was bleeding heavily any longer; if there was serious bleeding, it was internal, and she could not detect or treat it.

Under his clothing he wore one of the belts. She unbuckled it. The belt wouldn't fit in the center compartment of her purse, so she had to stuff it into a zippered side compartment after dumping out the items she usually kept in there.

She rebuttoned his shirt and debated whether she should take off his damp lab coat. She decided it would be too difficult to wrestle the sleeves down his arms. Rolling him gently from side to side, she worked a gray wool blanket under and around him.

While Laura bundled up the wounded man, Chris made a couple of trips to the Jeep with the guns, using the inner door that connected the laundry room to the garage. Then he came in with a two-foot-wide, four-foot-long, flat dolly—essentially a wooden platform on casters—that had accidentally been left behind by some furniture deliverymen almost a year and a half ago. Riding it like a skateboard toward the pantry, he said, "We gotta take the ammo box, but it's too heavy for me to carry. I'll put it on this."

Pleased by his initiative and cleverness, she said, "We have twelve rounds in the two revolvers and twelve *hundred* rounds in the three Uzis, so I don't think we'll need more than that, no matter what happens. Bring the board here. Quick now. I've been trying to figure how we can get him to the Jeep without shaking him up too bad. That looks like the ticket."

They were moving fast, as if they had drilled for just this particular emergency, yet Laura felt that they were taking too much time. Her hands were shaking, and her belly fluttered continuously. She expected someone to hammer on the door at any moment.

Chris held the dolly still while Laura heaved the wounded man onto it. When she got the board under his head, shoulders, back, and buttocks, she was able to lift his legs and push him as if he were a wheelbarrow. Chris scooted along at a crouch by the front wheels, one hand on the unconscious man's right shoulder to keep him from sliding off and to prevent the board from rolling out from beneath him. They had a little trouble easing across the door sill at the end of the laundry room, but they got him into the three-car garage.

The Mercedes was on the left, the Jeep wagon on the right, with the middle slot empty. They wheeled her guardian to the Jeep.

Chris had opened the tailgate. He had also unrolled a small gym mat in there for a mattress.

"You're a great kid," she told him.

Together they managed to transfer the wounded man from the dolly into the cargo bed by way of the open tailgate.

"Bring the other blanket and his shoes from the kitchen," she told Chris.

By the time the boy returned with those items, Laura had gotten her guardian stretched out flat on his back on the gym mat. They covered his bare feet with the second blanket and put his soggy shoes beside him.

As Laura shut the tailgate, she said, "Chris, get in the front seat and buckle up."

She hurried back into the house. Her purse, which contained all of her credit cards, was on the table; she slipped the straps over her shoulder. She picked up the third Uzi and headed back toward the laundry room, but before she had taken three steps, something hit the rear door with tremendous force.

She whirled, bringing up the gun.

Something slammed into the door again, but the steel core and Schlage deadbolts could not be defeated easily.

Then the nightmare began in earnest.

A submachine gun chattered, and Laura threw herself against the side of the refrigerator, sheltering there. They were trying to blow open the back door, but the heavy steel core held against that assault too. The door shook, however, and bullets pierced the wall on both sides of the reinforced frame, tearing holes in the drywall.

Family-room and kitchen windows exploded as a second submachine gun opened fire. The metal Levelors danced on their mountings. Metal slats twanged as slugs passed between them, and some slats bent, but most of the shattered window glass was contained behind the blinds, where it rained on sills and from there to the floor. Cabinet doors splintered and cracked as bullets pierced them, and chips of brick flew off one wall, and bullets ricocheted off the copper range hood, leaving it dented, creased. Hanging from ceiling hooks, the copper pots and pans took a lot of hits, producing a variety of *clinks* and *ponks*. One overhead light blew out. The Levelor at the window above the writing desk was torn off its mountings at last, and half a dozen slugs plowed into the refrigerator door just inches from her.

Her heart was racing, and a flood of adrenaline had made her senses almost painfully sharp. She wanted to run for the Jeep in the garage and try to get out before they realized she was in the process of leaving, but a primal warrior instinct told her to stay put. She pressed flat against the side of the refrigerator, out of the direct line of fire, hoping that she would not be hit by a ricochet.

Who the hell *are* you people? she wondered angrily.

The firing stopped, and her instinct proved true: The barrage was followed by the gunmen themselves. They stormed the house. The first one clambered through the imploded window above the kitchen desk. She stepped away from the refrigerator and opened fire, blowing him back out onto the patio. A second man, dressed in black like the first, entered by the shattered sliding door in the family room—she saw him through the archway a second before he saw her—and she swung the Uzi in that direction, spraying bullets, destroying the Mr. Coffee machine, tearing the hell out of the kitchen wall beside the archway, then cutting him down as he brought his weapon around toward her. She had practiced with the Uzi but not recently, and she was surprised at how controllable it was. She was also surprised at how sickened she was by the need to kill them, though they were trying to slaughter her and her child; like a wave of oily sludge, nausea washed through her, but she choked down the gorge that rose in her throat. A third man started into the family room, and she was ready to kill him, too, and a hundred like him, no matter how sick the killing made her, but he threw himself backward, out of the line of fire, when he saw his companion blown away.

*Now* the Jeep.

She didn't know how many killers were outside, maybe only the three, two dead and one still living, maybe four or ten or a hundred, but regardless of how many there were, they would not have expected to be met with such a bold response and certainly not with so much firepower, no way, not from a woman and a small boy, and they had known that her guardian was wounded and unarmed. So right now they were stunned, and they'd be taking cover, assessing the situation, planning their next move. This might be her first and last chance to get away in the Jeep wagon. She sprinted through the laundry room into the garage.

She saw that Chris had started the Jeep's engine when he'd heard the gunfire; bluish exhaust fumes billowed from the tailpipes. As she ran to the Jeep, the garage door started up; Chris had evidently used the Genie remote-control unit the moment he saw her.

By the time she got behind the wheel, the garage door was a third open. She shifted into gear. "Get down!"

As Chris instantly obeyed, sliding down in his seat below window level, Laura let up on the brakes. She rammed the accelerator against the floorboards, peeled rubber on the concrete, and roared out into the night, clearing the still rising garage door by only an inch or two, ripping off the radio antenna.

The Jeep's big tires, though not swaddled in chains, had heavy winter tread. They dug into the frozen slush and gravel that formed the surface of the driveway, finding traction with no trouble, spewing shrapnel of stone and ice.

From off to her left came a dark figure, a man in black, running across the front lawn, kicking up snow, forty or fifty feet away, and he was such a featureless shape that he might have been just a shadow, except that over the screaming of the engine she heard the rattle of automatic gunfire. Slugs slammed into the side of the Jeep, and the window behind her blew in, but the window beside her remained intact, and then she was speeding away, heading out of range, a few seconds from safety now, with wind shrieking at the broken window. She prayed none of the tires would be hit, and she heard more rounds striking sheet metal, or maybe it was gravel and ice churned up by the Jeep.

When she reached the state route at the end of the driveway, she was certain that she was out of range. As she braked hard for the left turn, she glanced into the rearview mirror and saw, far back, a pair of headlights at the open garage. The killers had arrived at her house without a vehicle—God only knew how they had traveled, perhaps with the use of those strange belts—and they were using her Mercedes to pursue her.

She had intended to turn left on the state route, head down past Running Springs, past the turnoff to Lake Arrowhead, on to the superhighway and into the city of San Bernardino, where there were people and safety in numbers, where men dressed in black and toting automatic weapons would not stalk her so boldly, and where she could get medical treatment for her guardian. But when she saw the headlights behind her, she responded to an innate proclivity for survival, turning right instead, heading east-northeast toward Big Bear Lake.

If she had gone left they would have come to that fateful half mile of inclined highway on which Danny had been murdered a year ago; and Laura felt intuitively—almost superstitiously—that the most dangerous place in the world for them at the moment was that sloping length of two-lane blacktop. She and Chris had been meant to die twice on that hill: first, when the Robertsons' pickup slid out of control; second, when Kokoschka opened fire on them. Sometimes she perceived that there were both benign and ominous patterns in life and that, once thwarted, fate strove to reassert those predestined designs. Though she had no intellectually sound reason for believing that they would die if they headed down toward Running Springs, she knew in her heart that death in fact awaited them there.

As they pulled onto the state route and headed for Big Bear, tall evergreens rising darkly on both sides, Chris sat up and looked back.

"They're coming," Laura told him, "but we'll outrun them."

"Are they the ones that got Daddy?"

"Yes, I think so. But we didn't know about them then, and we weren't prepared."

The Mercedes was on the state route now, out of sight most of the time because the roadway rose and fell and twisted, putting hills and turns between the two vehicles. The car seemed to be about two hundred yards behind, but it was probably closing because it had a bigger engine and a lot more power than the Jeep.

"Who are they?" Chris asked.

"I'm not sure, honey. And I don't know why they want to hurt us, either. But I know *what* they are. They're thugs, they're scum, I learned all about their type a long time ago at Caswell Hall, and I know the only thing you can do with people like them is stand up to them, fight back, because they only respect toughness.''

"You were terrific back there, Mom."

"You were darned good yourself, kiddo. That was very smart of you to start the Jeep when you heard the gunfire, and to have the garage door on the way up by the time I got behind the wheel. That probably saved us.''

Behind them the Mercedes had closed the distance to about one hundred yards. It was a road-hugger, a 420 SEL, which handled as well as anything on the highway, much better than the Jeep.

"They're coming fast, Mom."

"I know.''

"Real fast.''

Approaching the eastern point of the lake, Laura pulled up behind a rattletrap Dodge pickup with one broken taillight and a rusted bumper that appeared to be held together by stickers with supposedly funny sayings—I BRAKE FOR BLONDES, MAFIA STAFF CAR. It chugged along at thirty miles an hour, below the speed limit. If Laura hesitated, the Mercedes would close the gap; when they were near enough the killers might use their guns again. They were in a no-passing zone, but she could see enough clear road ahead to risk the maneuver; she swung around the pickup, tramped the accelerator hard, got in front of the truck, and returned to the right lane. Immediately ahead was a Buick doing about forty, and she passed that, too, just before the road got too twisty to allow the Mercedes to get around the old truck.

"They're hung up back there!" Chris said.

Laura put the Jeep up to fifty-five, which was too fast for some of the turns, though she held it on the road and began to think they were going to escape. But the highway split at the lake, and neither the Buick nor the old Ford pickup followed her along the south shore toward Big Bear City; they both turned toward Fawnskin and the north shore, leaving the road empty between her and the Mercedes, which at once began to close the distance between them.

Houses were everywhere now, both on the high ground to the right and on the lower ground down toward the lake on her left. Some of them were dark, probably vacation homes used only on winter weekends and in the summers, but the lights of other places were visible among the trees.

She knew she could follow any of those lanes and driveways to a hundred different houses where she and Chris would have been taken in. People would open their doors without hesitation. This was not the city; in the small-town atmosphere of the mountains, people were not instantly suspicious of unannounced night visitors.

The Mercedes closed to within a hundred yards, and the driver flicked the headlights from low beam to high beam again and again, as if gleefully saying, *Hey, here we come, Laura, we're gonna get you, we're the boogeymen, the real thing, and nobody can run from us forever, here we come, here we come.*

If she tried to take refuge in one of the nearby houses, the killers probably would follow, murdering not only her and Chris but the people who sheltered them. The bastards might be reluctant to chase her to ground in the heart of San Bernardino or Riverside or even Redlands, where they were likely to encounter police response, but they would not be intimidated by a mere handful of bystanders because no matter how many people they slaughtered, they could no doubt elude capture by pushing the yellow buttons on their belts and vanishing as her guardian had vanished one year ago. She had no idea where they would be vanishing *to*, but she suspected that it was a place where the police could never touch them. She would not risk innocent lives, so she passed house after house without slowing.

The Mercedes was about fifty yards back, closing fast.

"Mom—"

"I see them, honey."

She was headed toward Big Bear City, but unfortunately the place was inaptly named. It was not only less than a city but not even much of a village, hardly a hamlet. There were not enough streets for her to hope to lose their pursuers, and the police presence was inadequate to deal with a couple of fanatics armed with submachine guns.

Light traffic passed them going the other way, and she got behind another car in their lane, a gray Volvo, around which she whipped on an almost blind stretch of road, but she had no choice because the Mercedes was within forty yards. The killers passed the Volvo with equal recklessness.

"How's our passenger?" she asked.

Without unfastening his safety harness, Chris turned to look into the back of the Jeep wagon. "He looks okay, I guess. He's getting bounced around a lot."

"I can't help that."

"Who is he, Mom?"

"I don't know much about him," she said. "But when we get out of this fix, I'm going to tell you what I do know. I haven't told you before because . . . I guess because I didn't know what was going on, and I was afraid it might be dangerous somehow for you to know anything about him at all. But it can't get more dangerous than this, huh? So I'll tell you later."

Assuming there was going to *be* a later.

When she was two-thirds of the way along the south shore of the lake, pushing the Jeep as fast as she dared, with the Mercedes just thirty-five yards behind, she saw the ridge-road turnoff ahead. It led up through the mountains past Clark's Summit, a ten-mile county road that cut off the thirty- or thirty-five-mile eastern loop of state route 38, rejoining that two-lane highway south near Barton Flats. As she recalled, the ridge road was paved for a couple of miles at each end but was only a graded dirt lane for six or seven miles in the middle. Unlike the Jeep, the Mercedes did not have four-wheel drive; it had winter tires, but they were not currently equipped with chains. The men driving the Mercedes were unlikely to know that the ridge road's pavement would give way to a rutted dirt surface patched with ice and in some places drifted over with snow.

"Hold on!" she told Chris.

She didn't use the brakes until the last moment, taking the right turn onto the ridge road so fast that the Jeep slid sideways with a tortured squeal of tires. It shuddered, too, as if it were an old horse that had been forced to make a frightening jump.

The Mercedes cornered better, though the driver had not known what she was going to do. As they headed into higher elevations and greater wilderness, the car closed the gap to about thirty yards.

Twenty-five. Twenty.

Thorny branches of lightning abruptly grew across the sky to the south. It was not as near to them as the lightning at the house but near enough to turn night to day around them. Even above the sound of the engine she could hear the roar of thunder.

Gaping at the stormy display, Chris said, "Mommy, what's going on? What's happening?"

"I don't know," she said, and she had to shout to be heard above the cacophony of the racing engine and clashing heavens.

She did not hear the gunfire itself but heard bullets smacking into the Jeep, and a slug punched a hole through the tailgate window and thudded into the back of the seat in which she and Chris were riding; she felt as well as heard its solid impact. She began to turn the wheel back and forth, weaving from one side of the road to the other, making as difficult a target as possible, which made her dizzy in the flickering light. Either the gunman stopped firing or missed them with every shot, because she did not hear any more incoming rounds. However, the weaving slowed her, and the Mercedes closed even faster.

She had to use the side mirrors instead of the rearview. Though most of the tailgate window was intact, the safety glass was webbed with thousands of tiny cracks that left it translucent and useless.

Fifteen yards, ten.

In the southern sky the lightning and thunder passed, as before.

She topped a rise, and the pavement ended halfway down the hill ahead of them. She stopped weaving, accelerated. When the Jeep left the blacktop, it shimmied for a moment, as if surprised by the change in road surface, but then streaked forward on the snow-spotted, ice-crusted, frozen dirt. They jolted across a series of ruts, through a short hollow where trees arched over them, and up the next hill.

In the side mirrors she saw the Mercedes cross the hollow on the dirt lane and start up the slope behind her. But as she reached the crest, the car began to founder in her wake. It slid sideways, its headlights swinging away from her. The driver overcorrected instead of turning the wheel into the slide, as he should have done. The car's tires began to spin uselessly. It slid not only off to the side but backward twenty yards, until the right rear wheel jolted into the drainage ditch that flanked the road; the headlight beams were canted up and angled across the dirt track.

"They're stuck!" Chris said.

"They'll need half an hour to get out of that mess." Laura continued over the crest, down the next slope of the dark ridge road.

Although she should have been exultant over their escape, or at least relieved, her fear was undiminished. She had a hunch that they were not yet safe, and she had learned to trust her hunches more than twenty years ago, when she had suspected the White Eel was going to come for her the night that she would have been alone in the end room by the stairs at McIlroy, the night when in fact he had left a Tootsie Roll under her pillow. After all, hunches were just messages from the subconscious, which was thinking furiously all the time and processing information she had not consciously noted.

Something was wrong. But what?

They made less than twenty miles an hour on that narrow, winding, potholed, rutted, frozen dirt track. For a while the road followed the rocky spine of a ridge where there were no trees, then traced the course of a declivity in the ridge wall, all the way to the floor of the parallel ravine, where trees were so thick on both sides that the headlights bouncing back from their trunks seemed to reveal phalanxes of pines as solid as board walls.

In the back of the wagon, her guardian murmured wordlessly in his fevered sleep. She was worried about him, and she wished that she could go faster, but she dared not.

For the first two miles after they lost their pursuers, Chris was silent. Finally he said, "At the house . . . did you kill any of them?"

She hesitated. "Yes. Two."

"Good."

Disturbed by the grim pleasure in the single word that he spoke, Laura said, "No, Chris, it isn't good to kill. It made me sick."

"But they deserved to be killed," he said.

"Yes, they did. But that doesn't mean it's pleasant to kill them. It's not. There's no satisfaction in it. Just . . . disgust at the necessity of it. And sadness."

"I wish I could've killed one of them," he said with tight, cold anger that was disturbing in a boy his age.

She glanced at him. With his face carved by shadows and the pale yellow light from the dashboard, he looked older than he was, and she had a glimpse of the man he would become.

When the ravine floor became too rocky to provide passage, the road rose again, following a shelf on the ridge wall.

She kept her eyes on the rude track. "Honey, we'll have to talk about this later at more length. Right now I just want you to listen carefully and try to understand something. There are a lot of bad philosophies in the world. You know what a philosophy is?"

"Sorta. No . . . not really."

"Then let's just say people believe in a lot of things that are bad for them to believe. But there are two things that different kinds of people believe that are the worst, most dangerous, *wrongest* of all. Some people believe the best way to solve a problem is with violence; they beat up or kill anyone who disagrees with them."

"Like these guys who're after us."

"Yes. Evidently that's the kind of people they are. That's a real bad way of thinking because violence leads to more violence. Besides, if you settle differences with a gun, there's no justice, no moment of peace, no hope. You follow me?"

"I guess so. But what's the other worst kind of bad thinking?"

"Pacifism," she said. "That's just the opposite of the first kind of bad thinking. Pacifists believe you should never lift a hand against another human being, no matter what he has done or what you know he's going to do. If a pacifist was standing beside his brother, and if he saw a man coming to kill his brother, he'd urge his brother to run, but he wouldn't pick up a gun and stop the killer."

"He'd let the guy go after his brother?" Chris asked, astonished.

"Yes. If worse came to worst, he'd let his brother be murdered rather than violate his own principles and become a killer himself."

"That's whacko."

They rounded the point of the ridge, and the road descended into another valley. The branches of overhanging pines were so low they scraped the roof; clumps of snow fell onto the hood and windshield.

Laura turned on the wipers and hunched over the steering wheel, using the change in terrain as an excuse not to talk until she had time to think how to make her point most clearly. They had endured a lot of violence in the past hour; much more violence no doubt lay ahead of them, and she was concerned that Chris develop a proper attitude toward it. She did not want him to get the idea that guns and muscle were acceptable substitutes for reason. On the other hand she did not want him to be traumatized by violence and learn to fear it at the cost of personal dignity and ultimate survival.

At last she said, "Some pacifists are cowards in disguise, but some really believe it's right to permit the murder of an innocent person rather than kill to stop it. They're wrong because by not fighting evil, they've become part of it. They're as bad as the guy who pulls the trigger. Maybe this is above your head right now, and maybe you'll have to do a lot of thinking before you understand, but it's important you realize there's a way to live that's in the middle, between killers and pacifists. You try to avoid violence. You never start it. But if someone else starts it, you defend yourself, friends, family, anyone who's in trouble. When I had to shoot those men at the house, it made me sick. I'm no hero. I'm not proud of having shot them, but I'm not ashamed of it, either. I don't want you to be proud of me for it, or think that killing them was satisfying, that revenge in any way makes me feel better about your dad's murder. It doesn't."

He was silent.

She said, "Did I dump too much on you?"

"No. I just gotta think about it a while," he said. "Right now, I'm thinking bad, I guess. 'Cause I want them all dead, all of them who had anything to do with . . . what happened to Dad. But I'll work on it, Mom. I'll try to be a better person."

She smiled. "I know you will, Chris."

During her conversation with Chris and for the few minutes of mutual silence that followed it, Laura continued to be plagued by the feeling that they were not yet out of imminent danger. They had gone about seven miles on the ridge road, with perhaps another mile of dirt track and two miles of pavement ahead before they connected with state route 38. The farther she drove, the more certain she became that she was overlooking something and that more trouble was drawing near.

She suddenly stopped on the spine of another ridge, just before the road dipped down again—and for the last time—toward lower land. She switched off the engine and the lights.

"What's wrong?" Chris asked.

"Nothing. I just need to think, have a look at our passenger."

She got out and went around to the back of the Jeep. She opened the tailgate, where a bullet had punched through the window. Chunks of safety glass broke out and fell on the ground at her feet. She climbed into the cargo bed and, lying next to her guardian, checked the wounded man's pulse. It was still weak, perhaps even slightly weaker than before, but it was regular. She put a hand to his head and found he was no longer cold; he seemed to be afire within. At her request Chris gave her the flashlight from the glove compartment. She pulled back the blankets to see if the man was bleeding worse than when they had loaded him into the Jeep. His wound looked bad, but there was not much fresh blood in spite of the bouncing that he had endured. She replaced the blankets, returned the flashlight to Chris, got out of the Jeep, and closed the tailgate.

She broke all of the remaining glass out of the tailgate window and out of the smaller rear window on the driver's side. With the glass missing completely, the damage was less conspicuous and less likely to draw the attention of a cop or anyone else.

For a while she stood in the cold air beside the wagon, staring out at the lightless wilderness, trying to force a connection between instinct and reason. Why was she so sure that she was heading for trouble and that the night's violence was not yet at an end?

The clouds were shredding in a high-altitude wind that harried them eastward, a wind that had not yet reached the ground, where the air was almost peculiarly still. Moonlight found its way through those ragged holes and eerily illuminated the snow-cloaked landscape of rising and falling hills, evergreens leached of their color by the night, and clustered rock formations.

Laura looked south where in a few miles the ridge road led to state route 38, and everything in that direction seemed serene. She looked east, west, then back to the north from which they had come, and on all sides the San Bernardino Mountains were without a sign of human habitation, without a single light, and seemed to exist in primeval purity and peace.

She asked herself the same questions and gave the same answers that had been part of an interior dialogue for the past year. Where did the men with the belts come from? Another planet, another galaxy? No. They were as human as she was. So maybe they came from Russia. Maybe the belts acted like matter transmitters, devices akin to the teleportation chamber in that old movie, *The Fly*. That might explain her guardian's accent—if he'd teleported from Russia—but it didn't explain why he had not aged in a quarter of a century; besides, she did not seriously believe that the Soviet Union or anyone else had been perfecting matter transmitters since she was eight years old. Which left time travel.

She had been considering that possibility for some months, though she'd not even felt confident enough about her analysis to mention it to Thelma. But if her guardian had been entering her life at crucial points by time travel, he could have made all of his journeys in the space of a single month or week in his own era while many years had passed for her, so he would have appeared not to have aged. Until she could question him and learn the truth, the time-travel theory was the only one on which she could operate: Her guardian had traveled to her from some future world; and evidently it was an unpleasant future, because when speaking of the belt had said, "You don't want to go where it'll take you," and there had been a bleak, haunted look in his eyes. She had no idea why a time traveler would come back from the future to protect her, of all people, from armed junkies and runaway pickup trucks, and she had no time to ponder the possibilities.

The night was quiet, dark, and cold.

They were heading straight into trouble.

She *knew* it, but she didn't know what it was or where it would come from.

When she got back into the Jeep, Chris said, "What's wrong now?"

"You're crazy about *Star Trek, Star Wars, Batteries Not Included*, all that stuff, so maybe what I've got here is the kind of background expert I seek out when I'm writing a novel. You're my resident expert in the weird."

The engine was switched off, and the interior of the Jeep was brightened only by the cloud-cloaked moonlight. But she was able to see Chris's face reasonably well because, during the few minutes she had been outside, her eyes had adapted to the night. He blinked at her and looked puzzled. "What're you talking about?"

"Chris, like I said earlier, I'm going to tell you all about the man lying back there, about the other strange appearances he's made in my life, but we don't have time for that now. So don't snow me under with lots of questions, okay? But just suppose my guardian—that's how I think of him, because he's protected me from terrible things when he could—suppose he was a time traveler from the future. Suppose he doesn't come in a big clumsy time machine. Suppose the whole machine is in a belt that he wears around his waist, under his clothes, and he just materializes out of thin air when he arrives here from the future. Are you with me so far?"

Chris was staring wide-eyed. "Is that what he is?"

"He might be, yes."

The boy freed himself from his safety harness, scrambled onto his knees on the seat, and looked back at the man lying in the compartment behind them. "Holy shit."

"Given the unusual circumstances," she said, "I'll overlook the foul language."

He glanced at her sheepishly. "Sorry. But a *time* traveler!"

If she had been angry with him, the anger would not have held, for she now saw in him a sudden rush of that boyish excitement and a capacity for wonder that he had not exhibited in a year, not even at Christmas when he had enjoyed himself immensely with Jason Gaines. The prospect of an encounter with a time traveler instantly filled him with a sense of adventure and joy. That was the splendid thing about life: Though it was cruel, it was also mysterious, filled with wonder and surprise; sometimes the surprises were so amazing that they qualified as miraculous, and by witnessing those miracles, a despondent person could discover a reason to live, a cynic could obtain unexpected relief from ennui, and a profoundly wounded boy could find the will to heal himself and medicine for melancholy.

She said, "Okay, suppose that when he wants to leave our time and return to his own, he presses a button on the special belt he wears."

"Can I see the belt?"

"Later. Remember, you promised not to ask a lot of questions just now."

"Okay." He looked again at the guardian, then turned and sat down, focusing his attention on his mother. "When he presses the button— what happens?"

"He just vanishes."

"Wow! And when he arrives from the future, does he just appear out of thin air?"

"I don't know. I've never seen him arrive. Though I think for some reason there's lightning and thunder—"

"The lightning tonight!"

"Yes, but there's not always lightning. All right. Suppose that he came back in time to help us, to protect us from certain dangers—"

"Like the runaway pickup."

"We don't know why he wants to protect us, can't know why until he tells us. Anyway, suppose other people from the future *don't* want us to be protected. We can't understand their motivations, either. But one of them was Kokoschka, the man who shot your father—"

"And the guys who showed up tonight at the house," Chris said, "they're from the future, too."

"I think so. They were planning to kill my guardian, you, and me. But we killed some of them instead and left two of them stranded in the Mercedes. So . . . what are they going to do next, kiddo? You're the resident expert on the weird. Do you have any ideas?"

"Let me think."

Moonlight gleamed dully on the dirty hood of the Jeep.

The interior of the station wagon was growing cold; their breath issued in frosty plumes, and the windows were beginning to fog over. Laura switched on the engine, heater, defroster, but not the lights.

Chris said, "Well, see, their mission failed, so they won't hang around. They'll go back to the future where they came from."

"Those two guys in our car?"

"Yeah. They probably already pushed the buttons on the belts of the guys you killed, sent the bodies back to the future, so there're no dead men at the house, no proof time travelers were ever there. Except maybe some blood. So when the last two or three guys got stuck in the ditch, they probably gave up and went home."

"So they aren't back there any more? They wouldn't walk back to Big Bear maybe, steal a car, and try to find us?"

"Nope. That would be too hard. I mean, they have an easier way to find us than to just drive around looking for us like regular bad guys would have to do."

"What way?"

The boy screwed up his face and squinted through the windshield at the snow and moon glow and darkness ahead. "See, Mom, as soon as they lost us, they'd push the buttons on their belts, go home to the future, and then make a *new* trip back to our time to set another trap for us. They knew we took this road. So what they probably did was make another trip back to our time, but earlier tonight, and, they set a trap at the other end of this road, and now they're waiting there for us. Yeah, that's where they are! I'll just bet that's where they are."

"But why couldn't they come back even earlier tonight, earlier than they came the first time, back to the house, and attack us before my guardian ever showed up to warn us?"

"Paradox," the boy said. "You know what that means?"

The word seemed too complex for a boy his age, but she said, "Yes, I know what a paradox is. Anything that's self-contradictory but possibly true."

"See, Mom, the neat thing is that time travel is full of all kinds of possible paradoxes. Things that couldn't be true, shouldn't be true— but then might be." Now he was talking in that excited voice with which he described scenes in his favorite fantastic films and comic books, but with more intensity than she had ever heard before, probably because this was not a story but reality even more amazing than fiction. "Like suppose you went back in time and married your own grandfather. See, then you'd be your own grandmother. If time travel was possible, maybe you could do that—but then how could you have ever been born if your *real* grandmother had never married your grandfather in the first place? Paradox! Or what if you went back in time and met up with your mom when she was a kid and accidentally killed her? Would you just cease to exist—*pop!*—like you'd never been born? But if you ceased to exist—then how could you have gone back in time in the first place? Paradox! Paradox!''

Staring at him in the moon-painted darkness of the Jeep, Laura felt as though she was looking at a different boy from the one she had always known. Of course, she had been aware of his great fascination with space-age tales, which seemed to preoccupy most kids these days, regardless of age. But until now she hadn't gotten a deep look inside the mind shaped by those influences. Evidently the American children of the late twentieth century not only lived interior fantasy lives richer than those of children at any other time in history, but they seemed to have gotten from their fantasies something not provided by the elves and fairies and ghosts with which earlier generations of kids had entertained themselves: the ability to think about abstract concepts like space and time in a manner far beyond their intellectual and emotional age. She had the peculiar feeling that she was speaking to a little boy and a rocket scientist coexisting in one body.

Disconcerted, she said, ''So . . . when these men failed to kill us on their first trip tonight, why wouldn't they make a second trip *earlier* than the first, to kill us before my guardian warned us that they were coming?''

''See, your guardian already showed up in the time stream to warn us. So if they came back *before* he warned us—then how could he have warned us in the first place, and how could we be here where we are now, alive? Paradox!''

He laughed and clapped his hands like a gnome chortling over some particularly amusing side-effect of a magical spell.

In contrast to his good humor, Laura was getting a headache from trying to sort out the complexities of this thing.

Chris said, ''Some people believe time travel isn't even possible 'cause of all the paradoxes. But some believe it's possible so long as the trip you make into the past doesn't create a paradox. Now if *that's* true, see, then the killers couldn't come back on a second, earlier trip 'cause two of them had already been killed on the *first* trip. They couldn't do it because they were already dead, and it was a paradox. But the guys you didn't kill and maybe some *new* time travelers could make another trip to cut us off at the end of this road.'' He leaned forward to peer through the streaked windshield again. ''That's what all that lightning was off to the south when we were weaving to keep them from shooting us—more guys from the future were arriving. Yeah, I'll bet they're waiting for us down there somewhere, down there in the dark.''

Rubbing her temples with her fingertips, Laura said, ''But if we turn around and go back, if we don't drive into the trap ahead, then they'll realize we've outthought them. And so they'll make a *third* trip back in time and return to the Mercedes and shoot us when we try to drive back that way. They'll get us no matter which way we go.''

He shook his head vigorously. ''No. Because by the time they realize we're on to them, maybe half an hour from now, we'll already have turned around and driven back past the Mercedes.'' The boy was bouncing up and down in his seat with excitement now. ''So if they try to make a *third* trip in time to go back to the beginning of this road and trap us there, they can't do it, because we'll already have driven back that way and out, we'll already be safe. Paradox! See, they got to play by the rules, Mom. They're not magical. They got to play by the rules, and they can be beat!''

In thirty-three years she had never had a headache that had gone from a mild throb to a pounding skull-splitter as quickly as this one. The more she tried to puzzle out the difficulties of avoiding a pack of time-traveling hitmen, the deeper rooted the pain became.

Finally she said, ''I give up. I guess I should've been watching *Star Trek* and reading Robert Heinlein all these years instead of being a serious adult, because I'm just not able to cope with this. So I'll tell you what: I'm going to rely on *you* to outsmart them. You'll have to try to keep one step ahead of them. They want us dead. So how can they try to kill us without creating one of these paradoxes? Where will they show up next . . . and next? Right now, we're going to go back the way we came, past the Mercedes, and if you're right, no one will be waiting there for us. So where will they show up after that? Will we see them again tonight? Think about those things, and when you have any ideas, let me know what they are.''

''I will, Mom.'' He slumped down in his seat, grinning broadly for a moment, then chewing on his lip as he settled deeper into the game.

Except it was not a game, of course. Their lives were really at stake. They had to elude killers with nearly superhuman abilities, and they were pinning their hopes of survival on nothing more than the richness of an eight-year-old boy's imagination.

Laura started the Jeep, put it in reverse, and backed up a couple of hundred yards until she found a place in the road wide enough to turn around. Then they headed back the way they had come, toward the Mercedes in the ditch, toward Big Bear.

She was beyond terror. Their situation contained such a large element of the unknown—and unknowable—that terror could not be sustained. Terror was not like happiness or depression; it was an *acute* condition that by its very nature had to be of a short term. Terror wilted fast. Or it escalated until you passed out or until you died of it, frightened to death; you screamed until a blood vessel burst in your brain. She wasn't screaming, and in spite of her headache she didn't think any vessels were going to burst. She settled into a low-key, chronic fear, hardly more than anxiety.

What a day this had been. What a year. What a life.

Exotic news.

## TWO

They passed the stranded Mercedes and drove all the way to the north end of the ridge road without encountering men with submachine guns. At the intersection with the lakeside highway, Laura stopped and looked at Chris. "Well?"

"As long as we're driving around," he said, "and as long as we go to a place where we've never been and don't usually go, we're pretty safe. They can't find us if they don't have any idea where we might be. Just like your regular-type scumbags."

Scumbags? she thought. What is this—H. G. Wells meets *Hill Street Blues*?

He said, "See, now that we've given them the slip, these guys are going to go back to the future and look over the records they've got about you, Mom, your history, and they're going to see where you show up next—like when you want to go live in the house again. Or if you hid out for a year and wrote another book and then went on a tour for it, they'd show up at a store where you're signing books because, see, there'd be a *record* of that in the future; they'd know you could be found in that store at a certain time on a certain day."

She frowned. "You mean the only way to avoid them for the rest of my life is to change my name, go on the run forever, and leave no trace of myself on any public records, just vanish from recorded history from here on out?"

"Yeah, I think maybe that's what you'll have to do," he said excitedly.

He was smart enough to have figured out how to defeat a pack of time-traveling hitmen but not adult enough to perceive how hard it would be for them to forsake everything they owned and start with only the cash in their pockets. In a way he was like an idiot savant, tremendously insightful and gifted in one narrow area, but naive and severely limited in all other ways. In matters of time-travel theory, he was a thousand years old, but otherwise he was going on nine.

She said, "I can never write another book because I'd have to have contact with editors, agents, even if by phone. So there'd be phone records that could be traced. And I can't collect royalties because no matter how many blinds I use, no matter how many different bank accounts I shift the money through, sooner or later I have to collect the funds personally, which would leave a public record. So then they'd have that record in the future, and they'd travel back to the bank to wipe me out when I showed up. How am I supposed to get my hands on the money we *already* have? How can I cash a check anywhere without leaving a record that they would have in the future?'' She blinked at him. ''Good God, Chris, we're in a box!''

Now it was the boy's turn to be baffled. He looked at her with little understanding of where money came from, how it was put aside for future use, or how difficult it was to obtain. ''Well, for a couple of days, we can just drive around, sleep in motels—''

''We can only sleep in motels if I pay cash. A credit card record might be all they need to find us. Then they'd come back in time to the night I used the credit card, and they'd kill us at the motel.''

''Yeah, so we use cash. Hey, we can eat at McDonald's all the time! That doesn't take much money, and it's *good*.''

They drove down from the mountains, out of the snow, into San Bernardino, a city of about 300,000, without encountering assassins. She needed to get their guardian to a doctor, not only because she owed him a debt of life, but also because without him she might never learn the truth of what was happening and might never find a way out of the box they were in.

She could not take him to a hospital because hospitals kept records, which might give her enemies from the future a way of finding her. She would have to obtain medical care secretly, from someone who would not have to be told her name or anything about the patient.

Shortly before midnight she stopped at a telephone booth near a Shell service station. The phone was at the corner of the property, away from the station itself, which was ideal because she could not risk an attendant noticing the Jeep's broken windows or the unconscious man.

In spite of the hour-long nap the boy had gotten earlier and in spite of the excitement, Chris had dozed off. In the compartment behind the front seat, their guardian was sleeping, too, but his sleep was neither restful nor natural. He was not mumbling much any more, but for minutes at a stretch he drew breath with a dismaying wheeze and rattle.

She left the Jeep in park, the engine running, and went into the telephone booth to look through the directory. She tore out the Yellow Pages' listings for physicians.

After obtaining a street map of San Bernardino from the attendant in the service station, she began searching for a doctor who did not operate out of a clinic or medical office building but from an office attached to his home, which was how most doctors in small towns and cities had worked in years gone by, though these days few continued to keep home and office together. She was acutely aware that the longer she took to find help, the smaller the chance that their guardian would survive.

At a quarter past one, in a quiet residential neighborhood of older homes, she pulled in front of a two-story, white, Victorian house built in another era, in a lost California, before everything had been constructed of stucco. It stood on a corner lot, with a two-car garage, shaded by alders that were leafless in the middle of winter, a touch that made it seem like a place transported entirely, landscaping and all, from the East. According to the pages she had torn from the telephone directory, this was the address for Dr. Carter Brenkshaw, and beside the driveway a small sign suspended between two wrought-iron posts confirmed the directory's accuracy.

She drove to the end of the block and parked at the curb. She got out of the Jeep, scooped a handful of damp earth from a flowerbed in front of a nearby house, and smeared the dirt over the front and back license plates as best she could.

By the time she wiped her hand in the grass and got back in the Jeep, Chris had awakened but was groggy and confused after being asleep for more than two hours. She patted his face and pushed his hair back from his forehead and rapidly talked him awake. The cold night air, flowing through the broken windows, helped too.

"Okay," she said when she was sure he was awake, "listen closely, partner. I've found a doctor. Can you act sick?"

"Sure." He made a face as if he was going to puke, then gagged and moaned.

"Don't overplay it." She explained what they were going to do.

"Good plan, Mom."

"No, it's nuts. But it's the only plan I've got."

She swung the car around and drove back to Brenkshaw's, where she parked in the driveway in front of the closed garage, which was set back from the house. Chris slid out by the driver's door, and she picked him up and held him against her left side, his head against her shoulder. He held on to her, so she only needed her left arm to keep him in place, though he was quite heavy; her baby was not a baby any more. In her free hand she gripped the revolver.

As she carried Chris along the walk, past the stark alders, with no light except a purplish glow from one of the widely spaced mercury-vapor streetlamps out at the curb, she hoped no one was at a window in any of the nearby houses. On the other hand it probably wasn't unusual for someone to visit a doctor's house in the middle of the night, needing treatment.

She went up the front steps, across the porch, and rang the bell three times, quick, as a frantic mother might do. She waited only a few seconds before ringing it three more times.

In a couple of minutes, after she had rung the bell again and was beginning to think that no one was home, the porch lights came on. She saw a man studying her through the three-pane, fan-shaped window in the top third of the door.

"Please," she said urgently, holding the revolver at her side where it could not be seen, "my boy, poison, he's swallowed poison!"

The man opened the door inward, and there was an outward-opening glass storm door, as well, so Laura stepped out of its way.

He was about sixty-five, white-haired, with a face that was Irish except for a strong Roman nose and dark brown eyes. He was dressed in a brown robe, white pajamas, and slippers. Peering at her over the rims of tortoiseshell glasses, he said, "What's wrong?"

"I live two blocks down, you're so close, and my boy—poison." At the height of her hysteria, she let go of Chris, and he got out of her way as she shoved the muzzle of the .38 against the man's belly. "I'll blow your guts out if you call for help."

She had no intention of shooting him, but she apparently sounded convincing, for he nodded and said nothing.

"Are you Dr. Brenkshaw?" He nodded again, and she said, "Who else is in the house, Doctor?"

"No one. I'm alone here."

"Your wife?"

"I'm a widower."

"Children?"

"All grown and gone."

"Don't lie to me."

"I've made a lifetime habit of not lying," he said. "It's gotten me in trouble a few times, but telling the truth generally makes life simpler. Look, it's chilly, and this robe's thin. You can intimidate me as well if you come inside."

She stepped across the threshold, keeping the gun in his belly and pushing him backward with it. Chris followed her. "Honey," she whispered, "go check out the house. Quietly. Start upstairs, and don't miss a room. If there's anyone here, tell them the doctor has an emergency patient and needs their help."

Chris headed for the stairs, and Laura kept Carter Brenkshaw in the foyer at gunpoint. Nearby a grandfather clock was ticking softly.

"You know," he said, "I've been a lifelong reader of thrillers."

She frowned. "What do you mean?"

"Well, I've often read a scene in which a gorgeous villainness held the hero against his will. As often as not, when he finally turned the tables on her, she surrendered to the inevitability of masculine triumph, and they made wild, passionate love. So when it happens to me, why do I have to be too old to enjoy the prospect of the second half of this little showdown?"

Laura held back a smile because she could not continue to pretend to be dangerous once she allowed herself to smile. "Shut up."

"Surely you can do better than that."

"Just shut up, all right? Shut up."

He did not go pale or begin to tremble. He smiled.

Chris returned from upstairs. "Nobody, Mom."

Brenkshaw said, "I wonder how many dangerous thugs have pint-size accomplices who call them Mom?"

"Don't misjudge me, Doctor. I'm desperate."

Chris disappeared into the downstairs rooms, turning on lights as he went.

To Brenkshaw, Laura said, "I've got a wounded man in the car—"

"Of course, a gunshot."

"—I want you to treat him and keep your mouth shut about it, 'cause if you don't, we'll come back some night and blow you away."

"This," he said almost merrily, "is perfectly delicious."

As Chris returned, he switched off the lights he had switched on moments ago. "Nobody, Mom."

"You have a stretcher?" Laura asked the physician.

Brenkshaw stared at her. "You really do have a wounded man?"

"What the hell else would I be doing here?"

"How peculiar. Well, all right, how badly is he bleeding?"

"A lot earlier, not so much now. But he's unconscious."

"If he's not bleeding badly now, we can roll him in. I've got a collapsible wheelchair in my office. Can I get an overcoat," he said, pointing to the foyer closet, "or do tough molls like you get a thrill out of making old men shiver in their peejays?"

"Get your coat, Doctor, but damn it, don't underestimate me."

"Yeah," Chris said. "She shot two guys already tonight." He imitated the sound of an Uzi. "She just cut 'em down, and they never had a chance to lay a hand on her."

The boy sounded so sincere that Brenkshaw looked at Laura with new concern. "There's nothing but coats in the closet. Umbrellas. A pair of galoshes. I don't keep a gun in there."

"Just be careful, Doctor. No fast moves."

"No fast moves—yes, I knew you'd say that." Though he still

seemed to find the situation to some degree amusing, he was not quite as lighthearted about it as he had been.

When he had pulled on his overcoat, they went with him through a door to the left of the foyer. Without snapping on a light, relying on the glow from the foyer and on his familiarity with the place, Dr. Brenkshaw led them through a patients' waiting room that contained straight-backed chairs and a couple of end tables. Another door led into his office—a desk, three chairs, medical books—where he did turn on a light, and a door from the office led farther back in the house to his examination room.

Laura had expected to see an examination table and equipment that had been in use and well maintained for thirty-odd years, a homely den of medicine straight out of a Norman Rockwell painting, but everything looked new. There was even an EKG machine, and at the far end of the room was a door with a sign that warned X-RAY: KEEP CLOSED IN USE.

"You have X-ray equipment here?" she asked.

"Sure. It's not as expensive as it once was. Every clinic has X-ray equipment these days."

"Every clinic, yes, but this is just a one-man—"

"I may look like Barry Fitzgerald playing at being a doctor in an old movie, and I may prefer the old-fashioned convenience of an office in my home, but I don't give patients outdated care just to be quaint. I dare say, I'm a more serious physician than you are a desperado."

"Don't bet on that," she said harshly, though she was getting tired of pretending to be cold-blooded.

"Don't worry," he said. "I'll play along. Seems like it'll be more fun if I do." To Chris, he said, "When we came through my office, did you notice a big, red-ceramic jar on the desk? It's full of orange-slice candies and Tootsie Pops if you want some."

"Wow, thanks!" Chris said. "Uh . . . can I have a piece, Mom?"

"A piece or two," she said, "but don't make yourself sick."

Brenkshaw said, "When it comes to giving sweet treats to young patients, I'm old-fashioned, I guess. No sugar-free gum here. What the hell fun is that stuff? Tastes like plastic. If their teeth rot out after they visit me, that's their dentists' problem."

While he talked, he got a folding wheelchair from the corner, unfolded it, and rolled it to the middle of the room.

Laura said, "Honey, you stay here while we go out to the Jeep."

"Okay," Chris said from the next room, where he was peering into the red-ceramic jar, selecting his treat.

"Your Jeep in the driveway?" Brenkshaw asked. "Then let's go out the back. Less conspicuous, I think."

Pointing the revolver at the physician but feeling foolish, Laura followed him out of a side door in the examination room, which opened onto a ramp, so there was no need to descend stairs.

"Handicapped entrance," Brenkshaw said quietly over his shoulder as he pushed the wheelchair along a walk toward the back of the house. His bedroom slippers made a crisp sound on the concrete.

The physician had a large property, so the neighboring house did not loom over them. Instead of being planted with alders as was the front lawn, the side yard was graced with ficus and pines, which were green all year. In spite of the screening branches and the darkness, however, Laura could see the blank windows of the neighboring place, so she supposed that she could be seen, as well, if anyone looked.

The world had the hushed quality that it possessed only between midnight and dawn. Even if she had not known it was going on two in the morning, she would have been able to guess the time within half an hour. Though faint city noises echoed in the distance, there was a cemeterial stillness that would have made her feel like a woman on a secret mission even if she had only been taking out the garbage.

The walk led around the house, crossing another walk that extended to the back of the property. They went past the rear porch, through an areaway between house and garage, into the driveway.

Brenkshaw halted at the back of the Jeep and chuckled. "Mud on the license plates," he whispered. "Convincing touch."

After she put the tailgate down, he got into the back of the Jeep to have a look at the wounded man.

She looked out toward the street. All was silent. Still.

But if a San Bernardino Police cruiser happened to drive by now on a routine patrol, the officer would surely stop to see what was up at kindly old Doc Brenkshaw's place. . . .

Brenkshaw was already crawling out of the Jeep. "By God, you *do* have a wounded man in there."

"Why the hell do you keep being surprised? Would I pull this kind of stunt for laughs?"

"Let's get him inside. Quickly," Brenkshaw said.

He could not handle her guardian by himself. In order to help him, Laura had to stick the .38 in the waistband of her jeans.

Brenkshaw made no attempt to run or to knock her down and get the weapon away from her. Instead, as soon as he had the wounded man in the wheelchair, he rolled him out of the drive, through the areaway, and around the house to the handicapped entrance at the far side.

She grabbed one of the Uzis from the front seat and followed Brenkshaw. She didn't think she'd have any use for the automatic carbine, but she felt better with it in her hands.

* * *

Fifteen minutes later, Brenkshaw turned from the developed X-rays that hung on a lightboard in a corner of his examination room. "The bullet didn't fragment, made a clean exit. Didn't nick any bones, so we don't have chips to worry about."

"Terrific," Chris said from a corner chair, happily sucking on a Tootsie Pop. In spite of the warm air in the house, Chris was still wearing his jacket, as was Laura, because she wanted them to be ready to get out on short notice.

"Is he in a coma or what?" Laura asked the doctor.

"Yes, he's comatose. Not from any fever associated with a bad infection of the wound. Too early for that. And now that he's gotten treatment, there probably won't be an infection. It's traumatic coma from being shot, the loss of blood, the shock and all. He shouldn't have been moved, you know."

"I had no choice. Will he come out of it?"

"Probably. In this case a coma is the body's way of shutting down to conserve energy, facilitate healing. He's not lost as much blood as it appears; he's got a good pulse, so this probably won't last long. When you see his shirt and lab coat soaked like that, you think he's bled quarts, but he hasn't. Not that it was a spoonful, either. He's had a bad time of it. But no major blood vessels were torn, or he'd be in worse shape. Still, he should be in a hospital."

"We've already been through that," Laura said impatiently. "We can't go to a hospital."

"What bank did you rob?" the physician asked teasingly, but with noticeably less twinkle in his eyes than there had been when he had made his other little jokes.

While he waited for the pictures to develop, he had cleaned the wound, flooded it with iodine, dusted it with antibiotic powder, and prepared a bandage. Now he got a needle, another implement she could not identify, and heavy thread from a cabinet and put them on a stainless-steel tray that he had hung on the side of the examination table. The wounded man lay there, unconscious, propped on his right side with the help of several foam pillows.

"What're you doing?" Laura asked.

"Those holes are fairly large, especially the exit wound. If you insist on endangering his life by keeping him out of a hospital, then the least I can do is throw a few stitches in him."

"Well, all right, but be quick about it."

"You expect G-men to break down the door any minute?"

"Worse than that," she said. "Far worse than that."

Since they had arrived at Brenkshaw's, she had been expecting a sudden, night-shattering display of lightning, thunder like the giant hooves of apocalyptic horsemen, and the arrival of more well-armed time travelers. Fifteen minutes ago, as the doctor had been X-raying her guardian's chest, she'd thought she heard thunder so distant that it was barely audible. She hurried to the nearest window to search the sky for far-off lightning, but she saw none through the breaks in the trees, perhaps because the sky over San Bernardino already had a ruddy glow from city lights or perhaps because she had not heard thunder in the first place. She had finally decided that she might have heard a jet passing overhead and, in her panic, had misinterpreted it as a more distant sound.

Brenkshaw stitched up his patient, snipped the thread—"sutures will dissolve"—and bound the bandages in place with wide adhesive tape that he repeatedly wound around the guardian's chest and back.

The air had a pungent, medicinal smell that made Laura slightly ill, but it did not bother Chris. He sat in the corner, happily working on another Tootsie Pop.

While waiting for the X-rays, Brenkshaw also had administered an injection of penicillin. Now he went to the tall, white, metal cabinets along the far wall and poured capsules from a large jar into a pill bottle, then from another large jar into a second small bottle. "I keep some basic drugs here, sell them to poorer patients at cost so they don't have to go broke at the pharmacy."

"What're these?" Laura asked when he returned to the examination table, where she stood, and gave her the two small plastic bottles.

"More penicillin in this one. Three a day, with meals—if he can take meals. I *think* he'll come around soon. If he doesn't he'll begin to dehydrate, and he'll need intravenous fluid. Can't give him liquid by mouth when he's in a coma—he'd choke. This other is a painkiller. Only when needed, and no more than two a day."

"Give me more of these. In fact give me your whole supply." She pointed to two quart jars that contained hundreds of both capsules.

"He won't need that much of either one. He—"

"No, I'm sure he won't," she said, "but I don't know what the hell other problems we're going to have. We may need both penicillin and painkillers for me—or my boy."

Brenkshaw stared at her for a long moment. "What in the name of God have you gotten into? It's like something in one of your books."

"Just give me—" Laura stopped, stunned by what he had said. "Like something in one of my books? *In one of my books!* Oh, my God, you know who I am."

"Of course. I've known almost from the moment I saw you on the porch. I read thrillers, as I said, and although your books aren't strictly in that genre, they're very suspenseful, so I read them, too, and your photograph's on the back of the jacket. Believe me, Ms. Shane, no man would forget your face once he'd seen it, even if he'd seen it only in pictures and even if he was an old crock like me.''

"But why didn't you say—''

"At first I thought it was a joke. After all, the melodramatic way you appeared on my doorstep in the dead of night, the gun, the corny, hard-boiled dialogue . . . it all seemed like a gag. Believe me, I have certain friends who might think of such an elaborate hoax and, if they knew you, might be able to persuade you to join in the fun.''

Pointing to her guardian, she said, "But when you saw him—''

"Then I knew it was no joke,'' the physician said.

Hurrying to his mother's side, Chris pulled the Tootsie Pop from his mouth. "Mom, if he tells on us . . . ''

Laura had drawn the .38 from her waistband. She began to raise it, then lowered her hand as she realized the gun no longer had any power to intimidate Brenkshaw; in fact it had never frightened him. For one thing she now realized he was not the kind of man who could be intimidated, and for another thing she could not convincingly portray a lawless, dangerous woman when he knew who she really was.

On the examination table her guardian groaned and tried to shift in his unnatural sleep, but Brenkshaw put a hand upon his chest and stilled him.

"Listen, Doctor, if you tell anyone what happened here tonight, if you can't keep my visit a secret for the rest of your life, it'll be the death of me and my boy.''

"Of course the law requires a physician to report any gunshot wounds he treats.''

"But this is a special case,'' Laura said urgently. "I'm not on the run from the law, Doctor.''

"Who are you running from?''

"In a sense . . . from the same men who killed my husband, Chris's father.''

He looked surprised and pained. "Your husband was killed?''

"You must've read about it in the papers,'' she said bitterly. "It made a sensational story there for a while, the kind of thing the press loves.''

"I'm afraid I don't read newspapers or watch television news,'' Brenkshaw said. "It's all fires, accidents, and crazed terrorists. They don't report real news, just blood and tragedy and politics. I'm sorry about your husband. And if these people who killed him, whoever they are, want to kill you now, you should go straight to the police.''

Laura liked this man and thought they shared more views and sympathies than not. He seemed reasonable, kind. Yet she had little hope of persuading Brenkshaw to keep his mouth shut. "The police can't protect me, Doctor. No one can protect me except *me*—and maybe that man whose wounds you just sewed up. These people who're after us . . . they're relentless, implacable, and they're beyond the law."

He shook his head. "No one is beyond the law."

"*They* are, Doctor. It'd take me an hour to explain to you why they are, and then you probably wouldn't believe me. But I beg of you, unless you want our deaths on your conscience, keep your mouth shut about our being here. Not just for a few days but forever."

"Well . . . "

Studying him, she knew it was no use. She remembered what he had told her in the foyer earlier, when she had warned him not to lie about the presence of other people in the house: He did not lie, he said, because always telling the truth made life simpler; telling the truth was a lifelong habit. Hardly forty-five minutes later, she knew him well enough to believe that he was indeed an unusually truthful man. Even now, as she begged him to keep their visit secret, he was not able to tell the lie that would placate her and get her out of his office. He stared at her guiltily and could not tease the falsehood from his tongue. He would do his duty when she left; he would file a police report. The cops would look for her at her house near Big Bear, where they would discover the blood if not the bodies of the time travelers, and where they would find hundreds of expended bullets, shattered windows, slug-pocked walls. By tomorrow or the next day the story would be splashed across the newspapers. . . .

The airliner that had flown overhead more than half an hour ago might not have been a passing jet, after all. It might well have been what she had first thought it was—very distant thunder, fifteen or twenty miles away.

More thunder on a night without rain.

"Doctor, help me get him dressed," she said, indicating her guardian on the table beside them. "Do at least that much for me, since you're going to betray me later."

He winced visibly at the word *betray*.

Earlier she'd sent Chris upstairs to get one each of Brenkshaw's shirts, sweaters, jackets, slacks, a pair of his socks, and shoes. The physician was not as muscular and trim as her guardian, but they were approximately the same size.

At the moment the wounded man was wearing only his blood-stained pants, but Laura knew there would not be time to put all the clothes on him. "Just help me get him into the jacket, Doctor. I'll take the rest and dress him later. The jacket will be enough to protect him from the cold."

Reluctantly lifting the unconscious man into a sitting position on the examination table, the doctor said, "He shouldn't be moved."

Ignoring Brenkshaw, struggling to pull the wounded man's right arm through the sleeve of the warmly lined corduroy jacket, Laura said, "Chris, go to the waiting room at the front of the house. It's dark in there. Don't turn on the lights. Go to the windows and give the street a good looking over, and for God's sake don't let yourself be seen."

"You think they're here?" the boy asked fearfully.

"If not now, they will be soon," she said, working her guardian's left arm through the other jacket sleeve.

"What're you talking about?" Brenkshaw asked, as Chris dashed into the adjoining office and on into the dark waiting room.

Laura didn't answer. "Come on, let's get him in the wheelchair."

Together, they lifted the wounded man off the examination table, into the chair, and buckled a restraining strap around his waist.

As Laura was gathering up the other clothes and the two quart-sized jars of drugs, making a bundle, padding the clothes around the jars and tying it all together in the shirt, Chris raced back from the waiting room. "Mom, they're just pulling up outside, it must be them, two cars full of men across the street, six or eight of 'em anyway. What're we going to do?"

"Damn," she said, "we can't get to the Jeep now. And we can't go out the side door because they might see us from the front."

Brenkshaw headed toward his office. "I'll call the police—"

"No!" She put the bundle of clothes and drugs on the wheelchair between her guardian's legs, put her purse there, too, and snatched up the Uzi and .38 Chief's Special. "There's no time, damn you. They'll be in here in a couple of minutes, and they'll kill us. You've got to help me get the wheelchair out the back, down the rear porch steps."

Apparently her terror was at last conveyed to the physician, for he did not hesitate or continue to work at cross purposes to her. He grabbed the chair and wheeled it swiftly through a door that connected the examination room to the downstairs hall. Laura and Chris followed him along the gloomy corridor, then across a kitchen lit only by the illuminated digital clocks on the oven and microwave oven. The chair thumped over the sill between the kitchen and the back porch, badly jarring the wounded man, but he had been through worse.

Slinging the Uzi over her shoulder and jamming the revolver into her waistband, Laura hurried around Brenkshaw to the bottom of the porch steps. She took hold of the wheelchair from the front, helping him trundle it to the concrete walk below.

She glanced at the areaway between the house and garage, half expecting to see an armed man coming through there already, and she whispered to Brenkshaw, "You'll have to go with us. They'll kill you if you stay here, I'm sure they will."

Again he offered no argument but followed Chris, as the boy led the way down the walk that struck across the rear lawn to the gate in the redwood fence at the back of the long property. Having unslung the Uzi from her shoulder, Laura came last, ready to turn and open fire if she heard a noise from the house behind them.

As Chris reached the gate, it opened in front of him, and a man dressed in black stepped through from the alley, darker than the night around them except for his moon-pale face and white hands, every bit as surprised by them as they were by him. He'd come along the street beside the house and into the alley to cover the place from the back. In his left hand, gleaming darkly, was a submachine gun, not at the ready, but he started to bring it up—Laura could not blow him away, not without cutting her son down as well—but Chris reacted as Henry Takahami had spent months teaching him to react. The boy spun and kicked the assassin's right arm, knocking the gun out of his grasp— it hit the lawn with a thump and soft clatter—then kicked again at his adversary's crotch, and with a grunt of pain, the man in black fell backward against the gatepost.

By then Laura had stepped around the wheelchair and interposed herself between Chris and the killer. She reversed the Uzi, raised it overhead, and brought the stock of it down on the assassin's skull, struck him again with all her might, and he dropped to the lawn, away from the walk, without having had a chance to cry out.

Events were moving fast now, too fast, they were on a downhill ride, and already Chris was going through the gate, so Laura followed, and they surprised a second man in black, eyes like holes in his white face, a vampiric figure, but this one was beyond the reach of a karate kick, so she had to open fire before he could use his own weapon. She shot over Chris's head, a tightly placed burst that pounded into the assassin's chest, throat, and neck, virtually decapitating him as it catapulted him backward onto the alley pavement.

Brenkshaw had come through the gate behind them, pushing the wheelchair into the alley, and Laura felt bad about having gotten him into this, but there was no going back now. The back street was narrow, flanked by the fenced yards of houses on both sides, with a few garages and clusters of garbage cans behind each property, poorly revealed by the lamps on the intersecting streets at each end of the block, with no lights of its own.

To Brenkshaw, Laura said, "Wheel him across the alley and down a couple of doors. Find a gate that's open and get him into somebody else's yard, out of sight. Chris, you go with them.''

"What about you?"

"I'll follow you in a second."

"Mom—"

"Go, Chris!" she said, for the physician had already rolled the wheelchair fifty feet, angling across the alleyway.

As the boy reluctantly followed the doctor, Laura returned to the open redwood gate at the rear of Brenkshaw's property. She was just in time to see two dark figures scuttle out of the areaway between the house and garage, thirty yards from her, barely visible, noticeable only because they were moving. They ran crouched, one of them heading toward the porch and the other toward the lawn because they didn't yet know exactly where the trouble was, where the gunfire had come from.

She stepped through the gate, onto the walk, and opened up on them before they saw her, spraying the back of the house with bullets. Though she was not on top of her targets, she was in range—ninety feet was not far—and they dove for cover. She could not tell if she hit them, and she didn't continue to fire because even with a magazine of four hundred rounds expended in short bursts, the Uzi could empty quickly; and now it was the only automatic weapon she still possessed. She backed out of the gate and ran after Brenkshaw and Chris.

They were just going through a wrought-iron gate at the back of a property on the other side of the alley, two doors down. When she got there and stepped into the yard, she found that old eugenias were planted along the iron fence to the left and right of the gate; they had grown into a dense hedge, so no one would spot her easily from the alley unless they were directly in front of the gate itself.

The physician had pushed the wheelchair all the way to the back of the house. It was Tudor, not Victorian like Brenkshaw's, but also built at least forty or fifty years ago. The doctor was starting around the side of the place, into the driveway, heading toward the next major street.

Lights winked on in houses all over the neighborhood. She was sure that faces were pressed to windows, including those where lights had not appeared, but she didn't think anyone would see much.

She caught up with Brenkshaw and Chris at the front of the house and halted them in shadows near some overgrown shrubbery. "Doc, I'd like you to wait here with your patient," she whispered.

He was shaking, and she hoped to God he didn't have a heart attack, but he was still game. "I'll be here."

She took Chris out to the next street, where at least a score of cars were parked at the near and far curbs along that block. In the rain of bluish light from the streetlamps, the boy looked bad but not as awful as she had feared, not as frightened as the physician; he was growing accustomed to terror. She said, "Okay, let's start trying car doors. You take this side, I'll take the far side. If the door is open, check the ignition, under the driver's seat, and behind the sun visor for keys."

"Gotcha."

Having once done research for a book in which a character had been a car thief, she had learned among other things that on average one out of seventeen drivers left his keys in his car overnight. She hoped the figure might be even more in their favor in a place like San Bernardino; after all, in New York and Chicago and LA and other big cities, nobody but masochists left their keys in their cars, so for the average to work out to one in seventeen, there had to be more trusting people among other Americans.

She attempted to keep an eye on Chris as she tried the doors of the cars along the far side of the street, but she soon lost track of him. Out of the first eight vehicles, four were unlocked, but no keys were in any of them.

In the distance rose the wail of sirens.

That would probably drive off the men in black. Anyway, they were most likely still searching along the alleyway behind Brenkshaw's house, moving cautiously, expecting to be fired upon again.

Laura moved boldly, with no caution whatsoever, not concerned about being seen by residents in the flanking houses. The street was lined with mature but squat, stunted date palms that provided a lot of cover. Anyway, if anyone had been aroused at this dead hour of the night, they were probably at second-floor windows, not trying to look down at their own street through the palms but over toward the next street, toward Brenkshaw's place, where all the shooting had been.

The ninth vehicle was an Oldsmobile Cutlass, and there were keys under the seat. Just as she started the engine and pulled her door shut, Chris opened the door on the passenger's side and showed her a set of keys that he had found.

"Brand new Toyota," he said.

"This'll do," she said.

The sirens were closer.

Chris pitched the Toyota's keys away, hopped into the car, and rode with her to the driveway of the house on the other side of the street, farther up toward the corner, where the doctor was waiting in the shadows along the driveway of a house in which no lights had yet come on. Maybe they were in luck; maybe no one was home at that place. They lifted her guardian out of the wheelchair and laid him on the rear seat of the Cutlass.

The sirens were very close now, and in fact a police cruiser shot past at the far end of that block, on the side street, red beacons flashing, heading toward Brenkshaw's block.

"You'll be okay, Doctor?" she asked, turning to him as she closed the back door of the Cutlass.

He had dropped into the wheelchair. "No apoplexy, if that's what you're afraid of. What the *hell* is going on with you, girl?"

"No time, Doc. I have to split."

"Listen," he said, "maybe I won't tell them anything."

"Yes, you will," she said. "You may think you won't, but you'll tell them everything. If you weren't going to tell them, then there wouldn't have been a police report or a newspaper story, and without that record in the future, those gunmen couldn't have found me."

"What're you jibbering about?"

She leaned down and kissed his cheek. "No time to explain, Doc. Thanks for your help. And, sorry, but I'd better take that wheelchair too."

He folded it and put it in the trunk for her.

The night was full of sirens now.

She got behind the wheel, slammed her door. "Buckle up, Chris."

"Buckled," he said.

She turned left at the end of the driveway and drove to the far corner of the block, away from Brenkshaw's end of the neighborhood, to the intersecting street on which a cruiser had flashed by only a moment ago. She figured that if police were converging in answer to reports of automatic-weapons fire, they would be coming from different areas of the city, from different patrols, so maybe no other car would approach by that same route. The avenue was nearly deserted, and the only other vehicles she saw were not fitted with rooftop emergency beacons. She turned right, heading steadily farther away from the Brenkshaw place, across San Bernardino, wondering where she would find sanctuary.

## THREE

Laura reached Riverside at 3:15 in the morning, stole a Buick from a quiet residential street, shifted her guardian to it with the wheelchair, and abandoned the Cutlass. Chris slept through the entire operation and had to be carried from one car to the other.

Half an hour later, in another neighborhood, exhausted and in need of sleep, she used a screwdriver from a tool pouch in the Buick's trunk to steal a set of license plates from a Nissan. She put the Nissan's plates on the Buick and put the Buick's plates in the trunk because they would eventually turn up on a police hot sheet.

A couple of days might pass before the Nissan's owner noticed his plates were missing, and even when he reported them stolen, the police would not treat that news with the same attention they gave to stolen cars. Plates were usually taken by kids playing a stupid prank or vandals, and their recovery was not a high priority for overworked police laboring under heavy caseloads of major crimes. That was one more useful fact she had learned while researching the book in which a car thief had played a secondary role.

She also paused long enough to dress her guardian in wool socks, shoes, and a pullover sweater to keep him from catching a chill. At one point he opened his eyes, blinked at her, and said her name, and she thought he was coming around, but then he slipped away again, muttering in a language that she could not identify because she could not hear any of the words clearly.

She drove from Riverside to Yorba Linda in Orange County, where she parked in a corner of a Ralph's Supermarket lot, behind a Goodwill collection station, at 4:50 in the morning. She killed the engine and lights, unbuckled her safety harness. Chris was still buckled up, leaning against the door, sound asleep. Lying on the back seat, her guardian was still unconscious, though his breathing was not quite as wheezy as it had been before they had visited Carter Brenkshaw. Laura did not think she would be able to doze off; she hoped just to collect her wits and rest her eyes, but in a minute or two she was asleep.

After killing at least three men, after being shot at repeatedly, after stealing two cars, after surviving a chase that had harried her through three counties, she might have expected to dream of death, of blasted bodies and blood, with the cold chatter of automatic-weapons fire as background music to the nightmare. She might have expected to dream of losing Chris, for he was one of the two remaining lights in her personal darkness, he and Thelma, and she dreaded the thought of going on without him. But instead she dreamed of Danny, and they were lovely dreams, not nightmares. Danny was alive again, and they were reliving the sale of *Shadrach* for more than one million dollars, but Chris was there, too, and he was eight years old, though in fact Chris had not been born at that time, and they were celebrating their good fortune by spending the day at Disneyland, where the three of them had their picture taken with Mickey Mouse, and in the Carnation Pavilion Danny told her he'd love her forever, while Chris pretended that he could speak in an all-snort pig language that he had learned from Carl Dockweiler, who was sitting at the next table with Nina and with Laura's father, and at another table the amazing Ackerson twins were eating strawberry sundaes. . . .

She woke more than three hours later at 8:26, feeling rested as much because of that familial communion, provided by her subconscious, as because of the sleep itself. Sunlight from a cloudless sky sparkled on the car's chrome and fell in a bright, brassy shaft through the rear window. Chris was still dozing. In the back seat the wounded man had not regained consciousness.

She risked a quick walk to a telephone booth beside the market, which was within sight of the car. With change she had in her purse, she called Ida Palomar, Chris's tutor in Lake Arrowhead, to tell her they would be away from home the rest of the week. She did not want poor Ida to walk unsuspecting into the bullet-riddled, blood-spattered house near Big Bear, where police forensic teams were no doubt hard at work. She did not tell Ida where she was calling from; nevertheless, she did not intend to remain in Yorba Linda much longer.

After she returned to the car, she sat yawning, stretching, and massaging the back of her neck, as she watched early shoppers entering and leaving the supermarket a couple of hundred feet away. She was hungry. With sleep-matted eyes and sour breath, Chris woke less than ten minutes later, and she gave him money to go into the market and buy a package of sweet rolls and two pints of orange juice, not the most nutritional breakfast but energy-giving.

"What about him?" Chris asked, indicating her guardian.

She remembered Dr. Brenkshaw's warning about the patient's risk of dehydration. But she also knew that she could not force-feed him liquids when he was comatose; he would choke to death. "Well . . . bring a third orange juice. Maybe I can coax him awake." As Chris got out of the car, she said, "Might as well get us something for lunch, something that won't spoil—say a loaf of bread and a jar of peanut butter. And get a can of spray deodorant and a bottle of shampoo."

He grinned. "Why won't you let me eat this way at home?"

"Because if you don't get good nutrition, you're going to wind up with a brain even more twisted than the one you've got now, kiddo."

"Even on the lam from hired killers, I'm surprised you didn't pack a microwave, fresh vegetables, and a bottle of vitamins."

"Are you saying I'm a good mother but a fussbudget? Compliment noted and point taken. Now go."

He started to close his door.

She said, "And, Chris . . . "

"I know," the boy said. "Be careful."

While Chris was gone, she started the engine and switched on the radio to listen to the nine o'clock news. She heard a story about herself: the scene at her house near Big Bear, the shoot-out in San Bernardino. Like most news stories it was inaccurate, disjointed, and made little sense. But it confirmed that the police were looking for her throughout southern California. According to the reporter, the authorities expected to locate her soon, largely because her face was already widely known.

She had been shocked last night when Carter Brenkshaw recognized her as Laura Shane, famous writer. She did not think of herself as a celebrity; she was only a storyteller, a weaver of tales, who worked with a loom of language, making a special fabric from words. She had done only one book tour for an early novel, had loathed that dreary trek, and had not repeated the experience. She was not a regular guest on television talkshows. She had never endorsed a product in a TV commercial, had never gone public in support of a politician, and had in general attempted to avoid being part of the media circus. She observed the tradition of having a dust jacket photograph on her books because it seemed harmless, and by the age of thirty-three she could admit without severe embarrassment that she was an unusually striking woman, but she never imagined, as the police put it, that her face was widely known.

Now she was dismayed not only because her loss of anonymity made her easier quarry for the police but because she knew that becoming a celebrity in modern America was tantamount to a loss of one's self-critical faculties and a severe decline of artistic power. A few managed to be both public figures and worthwhile writers, but most seemed to be corrupted by the media attention. Laura dreaded that trap almost as much as she dreaded being picked up by the police.

Suddenly, with some surprise, she realized that if she could worry about becoming a celebrity and losing her artistic center, she must still believe in a safe future in which she would write more books. At times during the night, she had vowed to fight to the death, to struggle to a bloody end to protect her son, but throughout she had felt that their situation was virtually hopeless, their enemy too powerful and un-reachable to be destroyed. Now something had changed her, had brought her around to a dim, guarded optimism.

Maybe it had been the dream.

Chris returned with a large package of pecan-cinnamon rolls, three one-pint containers of orange juice, and the other items. They ate the rolls and drank the juice, and nothing had ever tasted better.

When she finished her own breakfast, Laura got in the back seat and tried to wake her guardian. He could not be roused.

She gave the third carton of orange juice to Chris and said, "Keep it for him. He'll probably wake up soon."

"If he can't drink, he can't take his penicillin," Chris said.

"He doesn't need to take any for a few hours yet. Dr. Brenkshaw gave him a pretty potent shot last night; it's still working."

But Laura was worried. If he did not regain consciousness, they might never learn the true nature of the dangerous maze in which they were now lost—and might never find a way out of it.

"What next?" Chris asked.

"We'll find a service station, use the rest rooms, then stop at a gunshop and buy ammunition for the Uzi and the revolver. After that . . . we start looking for a motel, just the right kind of motel, a place where we can hide out."

When they settled in somewhere, they would be at least fifty miles from Dr. Brenkshaw's place, where their enemies had last found them. But did distance matter to men who measured their journeys strictly in days and years rather than miles?

Parts of Santa Ana, neighborhoods on the south side of Anaheim, and adjoining areas offered the greatest number of motels of the type she was seeking. She did not want a modern, gleaming Red Lion Inn or Howard Johnson's Motor Lodge with color television sets, deep-pile carpet, and a heated swimming pool, because reputable establishments required valid ID and a major credit card, and she dared not risk leaving a paper trail that would bring either the police or the assassins down on her. Instead she was seeking a motel that was no longer clean enough or in good enough repair to attract tourists, a seedy place where they were happy to get the business, eager to take cash, and reluctant to ask questions that would drive away guests.

She knew she would have a hard time finding a room, and she was not surprised to discover that the first twelve places she tried were unable or unwilling to accommodate her. The only people who could be seen going from or coming to those dead-end motels were young Mexican women with babies in their arms or young children in tow, and young or middle-aged Mexican men in sneakers, chinos, flannel shirts, and lightweight denim or corduroy jackets, some wearing straw cowboy hats and some baseball caps, and all of them with an air of watchfulness and suspicion. Most decrepit motels had become boarding houses for illegal immigrants, hundreds of thousands of whom had taken up not-so-secret residence in Orange County alone. Whole families lived in a single room, five or six or seven of them crowded into that cramped space, sharing one ancient bed and two chairs and a bathroom with minimally functional plumbing, for which they paid a hundred and fifty dollars or more every week, with no linen or maid service or amenities of any kind, but with cockroaches by the thousands. Yet they were willing to endure those conditions and let themselves be outrageously exploited as underpaid workers rather than return to their homeland and live under the rule of the "revolutionary people's government" that for decades had given them no brotherhood but that of despair.

At the thirteenth motel, The Bluebird of Happiness, the owner-manager still hoped to serve the lower end of the tourist trade, and he had not yet succumbed to the temptation to squeeze a rich living from the blood of poor immigrants. A few of the twenty-four units were obviously rented to illegals, but the management still provided fresh linen daily, maid service, television sets, and two spare pillows in every closet. However, the fact that the desk clerk took cash, did not press her for ID, and avoided meeting her eyes was sad proof that in another year The Bluebird of Happiness would be one more monument to political stupidity and human avarice in a world as crowded with such monuments as any old, city cemetery was crowded with tombstones.

The motel had three wings in a U-shape, with parking in the middle, and their unit was in the right rear corner of the back wing. A big fan palm flourished near the door to their room, not visibly touched by smog or limited by its small patch of ground midst so much concrete and blacktop, bristling with new growth even in winter, as if nature had chosen it as a subtle omen of her intention to seize every corner of the earth again when humankind passed on.

Laura and Chris unfolded the wheelchair and got the wounded man into it, making no effort to conceal what they were doing, as if they were simply caring for a disabled person. Fully dressed, with his wounds concealed, her guardian could pass for a paraplegic—except for the way his head lolled against his shoulder.

Their room was small though passably clean. The carpet was worn but recently shampooed, and a pair of dustballs in one corner were far from the size of tumbleweeds. The maroon-plaid spread on the queen-size bed was tattered at the edges, and its pattern was not quite busy enough to conceal two patches, but the sheets were crisp and smelled faintly of detergent. They moved her guardian from the wheelchair to the bed and put two pillows under his head.

The seventeen-inch television set was firmly bolted to a table with a scarred, laminated top, and the back legs of the table were in turn bolted to the floor. Chris sat in one of the two mismatched chairs, switched on the set, and turned the cracked dial in search of either a cartoon show or reruns of an old sitcom. He settled for *Get Smart* but complained that it was "too stupid to be funny," and Laura wondered how many boys his age would have thought so.

She sat in the other chair. "Why don't you get a shower?"

"Then just get back in these same clothes?" he asked doubtfully.

"I know it sounds like purest folly, but try it. I guarantee you'll feel cleaner even without fresh clothes."

"But all that trouble to shower, then get into *wrinkled* clothes?"

"When did you become such a fashion plate that you're offended by a few wrinkles?"

He grinned, got up from his chair, and pranced to the bathroom as he thought a hopeless fop might prance. "The king and queen would be shocked to see me such a mess."

"We'll make them put on blindfolds when they visit," she said.

He returned from the bathroom in a minute. "There's a dead bug in the toilet bowl. I think it's a cockroach, but I'm not really sure."

"Does the species matter? Will we be notifying next of kin?"

Chris laughed. God, she loved to hear him laugh. He said, "What should I do—flush him?"

"Unless you want to fish him out, put him in a matchbox, and bury him in the flowerbed outside."

He laughed again. "Nope. Burial at sea." In the bathroom, he hummed "Taps," then flushed the john.

While the boy was showering, *Get Smart* ended and a movie came on, *The Harlem Globetrotters on Gilligan's Island*. Laura was not actually watching the set; she left it on for background, but there were limits to what even a woman on the lam could endure, so she quickly switched to channel eleven and *Hour Magazine*.

She stared at her guardian for a while, but his unnatural slumber depressed her. From her chair she reached to the drapes a few times, parting them far enough to scan the motel's parking lot, but no one on earth could know where she was; she was in no imminent danger. So she stared at the TV screen, uninterested in what it offered, until she was half hypnotized by it. The *Hour Magazine* host was interviewing a young actor who droned on about himself, not always making much sense, and after a while she was vaguely aware that he kept saying something about water, but now she was beginning to doze off, and his insistent talk of water was both mesmeric and annoying.

*"Mom?"*

She blinked, sat up, and saw Chris in the bathroom doorway. He'd just gotten out of the shower. His hair was damp, and he was dressed only in his briefs. The sight of his thin, boyish body—all ribs and elbows and knees—pulled at her heart, for he looked so innocent and vulnerable. He was so small and fragile that she wondered how she could ever protect him, and renewed fear rose in her.

"Mom, he's talking," Chris said, pointing to the man on the bed. "Didn't you hear him? He's talking."

"Water," her guardian said thickly. "Water."

She went quickly to the bed and bent over him. He was no longer comatose. He was trying to sit up, but he had no strength. His blue eyes were open, and although they were bloodshot, they focused on her, alert and observant.

"Thirsty," he said.

She said, "Chris—"

He was already there with a glass of water from the bathroom.

She sat on the bed beside her guardian, lifted his head, took the water from Chris, and helped the wounded man drink. She allowed him only small sips; she didn't want him to choke. His lips were fever-chapped, and his tongue was coated with a white film, as if he had eaten ashes. He drank more than a third of a glass of water, then indicated that he'd had enough.

After she lowered his head to the pillow, she put a hand to his forehead. "Not so hot as he was."

He rolled his head from side to side, trying to look at the room. In spite of the water, his voice was dry, burnt out. "Where are we?"

"Safe," she said.

"Nowhere . . . is safe."

"We may have figured out more of this crazy situation than you realize," she told him.

"Yeah," Chris said, sitting on the bed beside his mother. "We know you're a time traveler!"

The man looked at the boy, managed a weak smile, winced in pain.

"I've got drugs," Laura said. "A painkiller."

"No," he said. "Not now. Later maybe. More water?"

Laura lifted him once more, and this time he drank most of what remained in the glass. She remembered the penicillin and put a capsule between his teeth. He washed it down with the last two swallows.

"When do you come from?" Chris asked, intensely interested, oblivious of the droplets of bathwater that tracked out of his damp hair and down his face. "When?"

"Honey," Laura said, "he's very weak, and I don't think we should bother him with too many questions just yet."

"He can tell us that much, anyway, Mom." To the wounded man, Chris said, "When do you come from?"

He stared at Chris, then at Laura, and the haunted look was in his eyes again.

"When do you come from? Huh? The year 2100? 3000?"

In his paper-dry voice, her guardian said, "Nineteen forty-four."

The little bit of activity had clearly tired him already, for his eyelids looked heavy, and his voice was fainter than it had been, so Laura was certain that he had lapsed into delirium again.

"When?" Chris repeated, baffled by the answer he had been given.

"Nineteen forty-four."

"That's impossible," Chris said.

"Berlin," her guardian said.

"He's delirious," Laura told Chris.

His voice was slurred now as weariness dragged him down, but what he said was unmistakable: "Berlin."

"Berlin?" Chris said. "You mean—Berlin, Germany?"

Sleep claimed the wounded man, not the unnatural sleep of a coma but restful sleep that was immediately marked by soft snoring, though in the moment before he slipped away, he said, "*Nazi* Germany."

# FOUR

*One Life to Live* was on the television, but neither she nor Chris was paying any attention to the soap opera. They had drawn the two chairs closer to the bed, where they could watch the sleeping man. Chris was dressed, and his hair was mostly dry, though it remained damp at the nape of his neck. Laura felt grimy and longed for a shower, but she was not going to leave her guardian in case he woke again and was able to talk. She and the boy spoke in whispers:

"Chris, it just occurred to me, if these people were from the future, why wouldn't they have been carrying laser guns or something futuristic when they came for us?"

"They wouldn't want everyone to *know* they were from the future," Chris said. "They'd bring weapons and wear clothes that wouldn't be out of place here. But, Mom, he said he was from—"

"I know what he said. But it doesn't make sense, does it? If they had time travel in 1944, we'd know about it by now, wouldn't we?"

At one-thirty her guardian woke and seemed briefly confused as to his whereabouts. He asked for more water, and Laura helped him drink. He said he was feeling a little better, though very weak and still surprisingly sleepy. He asked to be propped up higher. Chris got the two spare pillows from the closet and helped his mother raise the wounded man.

"What is your name?" Laura asked.

"Stefan. Stefan Krieger."

She repeated the name softly, and it was all right, not melodic but solid, a masculine-sounding name. It was just not the name of a guardian angel, and she was mildly amused to realize that after so many years, including two decades during which she had professed to have no belief in him, she still expected his name to be musical and unearthly.

"And you really come from—"

"Nineteen forty-four," he repeated. Just the effort required to move to a sitting position had wrung fine beads of perspiration from his brow—or perhaps the sweat resulted in part from thoughts of the time and place where his long journey had begun. "Berlin, Germany. There was a brilliant Polish scientist, Vladimir Penlovski, considered a madman by some, and very likely mad in fact—very mad, I think—but also a genius. He was in Warsaw, working on certain theories about the nature of time for more than twenty-five years before Germany and Russia collaborated to invade Poland in 1939 . . . ''

Penlovski, according to Stefan Krieger, was a Nazi sympathizer and welcomed Hitler's forces. Perhaps he knew that from Hitler he would receive the kind of financial backing for his researches that he could not get from sources more rational. Under the personal patronage of Hitler himself, Penlovski and his closest assistant, Wladyslaw Januskaya, went to Berlin to establish an institute for temporal research, which was so secret that it was given no name. It was simply called the institute. There, in association with German scientists no less committed and no less farsighted than he, financed by a seemingly inexhaustible river of funds from the Third Reich, Penlovski had found a way to pierce the artery of time and move at will through that bloodstream of days and months and years.

*"Blitzstrasse,"* Stefan said.

*"Blitz*—that part of it means lightning," Chris said. "Like *Blitzkrieg*—lightning war—in all those old movies."

"Lightning Road in this case," Stefan said. "The road through time. The road to the future."

It literally could have been called *Zukunftstrasse*, or Future Road, Stefan explained, for Vladimir Penlovski had been unable to discover a way to send men backward in time from the gate he had invented. They could travel only forward, into their future, and return automatically to their own era.

"There seems to be some cosmic mechanism that prohibits time travelers from meddling with their own pasts in order to change their present-day circumstances. You see, if they *could* travel back in time to their own past, there would develop certain—''

"Paradoxes!" Chris said excitedly.

Stefan looked surprised to hear the boy speak that word.

Smiling, Laura said, "As I told you, we've had rather a long discussion about your possible origins, and time travel turned out to be the most logical. And in Chris here, you're looking at my resident expert on the weird."

"Paradox," Stefan agreed. "It's the same word in English and German. If a time traveler could go back in time to his own past and affect some event in history, that change would have tremendous ramifications. It would alter the future from which he had come. Therefore he wouldn't be able to return to the same world he'd left—''

"Paradox!" Chris said gleefully.

"Paradox," Stefan agreed. "Apparently nature abhors a paradox and generally will not permit a time traveler to create one. And thank God for that. Because . . . suppose, for example, Hitler sent an assassin back in time to kill Franklin Roosevelt and Winston Churchill long before they rose to high office, which would have resulted in the election of different men in the U.S. and England, men who might have been less brilliant and more easily dealt with, leading to Hitler's triumph by '44 or sooner."

He was speaking now with a passion that his physical condition would not allow him to sustain, and Laura could see it taking a toll on him word by word. The perspiration had almost dried on his brow; but now, although he was not even gesturing, a new thin film of sweat silvered his pale forehead again. The circles of fatigue around his eyes appeared to grow darker. But she could not stop him and order him to rest, because she wanted and needed to hear everything he had to say—and because he would not have allowed her to stop him.

"Suppose *der Führer* could send back assassins to kill Dwight Eisenhower, George Patton, Field Marshal Montgomery, kill them in their *cradles*, when they were babies, eliminating them and others, all the best military minds the Allies possessed. Then most of the world would have been his by '44, in which case time travelers would have been going back in time to kill those men *who had already long been dead and posed no threat*. Paradox, you see. And thank God that nature permits no such paradox, no such tampering with the time traveler's own past, for otherwise Adolf Hitler would have turned the entire world into a concentration camp, a crematorium."

They were silent a while, as the possibility of such hell on earth struck each of them. Even Chris responded to the picture of an altered world that Stefan painted, for he was a child of the eighties, in which the villains of film and television melodramas were usually either voracious aliens from a distant star or Nazis. The Swastika, the silver death's-head symbol and black uniforms of the SS, and that strange fanatic with the small mustache were to Chris especially terrifying because they were part of the media-created mythology on which he had been raised. Laura knew that real people and events, once subsumed by mythology, were somehow *more* real to a child than the very bread he ate.

Stefan said, "So from the institute we could go only forward in time, but that had its uses too. We could leap forward a few decades to discover if Germany had held on in the dark days of the war and had somehow turned the tide. But of course we found that Germany had not done any such thing, that the Third Reich had been defeated. Yet with all the knowledge of the future to draw from, could not that tide be turned, after all? Surely there were things Hitler could do to save the Reich even as late as '44. And there were things that might be brought back from the future with which the war might be won—''

''Such as,'' Chris said, ''atomic bombs!''

''Or the knowledge of how they were built,'' Stefan said. ''The Reich already had a nuclear research program, you know, and if they'd had a breakthrough early enough, had split the atom . . . ''

''They'd have won the war,'' Chris said.

Stefan asked for water and drank half a glass this time. He wanted to hold the glass in his good hand, but he was shaking too much; water slopped on the bedclothes, and Laura had to help him.

When he spoke again, Stefan's voice wavered at times. ''Because the time traveler exists *outside* of time during his journey, he is not only able to move in time but geographically, as well. Picture him hanging above the earth, unmoving, as the globe turns below him. That's not what he does, of course, but it's easier to see that image than to imagine him hovering in another dimension. Now, as he hangs above the world, it turns below him, and if his journey to the future is gauged properly, he can travel to a precise time at which he will find himself in Berlin, the same city he left years before. But if he chooses to travel a few hours more or less, the world will have turned that much more beneath him, and he will arrive at a different place on its surface. The calculations to achieve a precise arrival are monumentally difficult in my era, 1944—''

''But they'd be easy these days,'' Chris said, ''with computers.''

Shifting in discomfort against the pillows that propped him up, putting his trembling right hand against his wounded left shoulder as if to quell the pain by his own touch, he said, ''Teams of German physicists, accompanied by Gestapo, were sent secretly to various cities in Europe and the United States in the year 1985, to accumulate vital information on the making of nuclear weapons. The material they were after was not classified or difficult to find. With what they already knew from their own researches, they could obtain the rest from textbooks and scientific publications readily available at any major university library in '85. Four days before I departed the institute for the last time, those teams returned from '85 to March 1944, with material that would give the Third Reich a nuclear arsenal before the autumn of that year. They were to spend a few weeks studying the material at the institute before deciding how and where to introduce that knowledge into the German nuclear program without revealing how it had been obtained. I knew then that I had to destroy the institute and everything it contained, key personnel as well as files, to prevent a future shaped by Adolf Hitler.''

As Laura and Chris listened, rapt, Stefan Krieger told them how he

had planted explosives in the institute, how on the last of his days in
'44 he had shot Penlovski, Januskaya, and Volkaw, and had programmed the time gate to bring him to Laura in present-day America.

But something had gone wrong at the last minute, as Stefan was
leaving. The public power supply failed. The RAF had bombed Berlin
for the first time in January that year, and the U.S. bombers had made
the first daylight runs on March 6, so the power supply had been
interrupted often, not merely due to bomb damage but also because
of the work of saboteurs. It was to guard against such interruptions
that the gate itself was powered by a secure generator. Stefan heard
no bombers that day when, wounded by Kokoschka, he had crawled
into the gate, so apparently the power failed because of saboteurs.

"And the timer on the explosives stopped. The gate was not destroyed. It's still open back there, and they can come after us. And
. . . they can still win the war."

Laura was getting another headache. She put her fingertips to her
temples. "But wait. Hitler can't have succeeded in building atomic
weapons and winning World War Two, because we don't live in a
world where that happened. You don't have to worry. Somehow, in
spite of all the knowledge they took back through the gate, they obviously failed to develop a nuclear arsenal."

"No," he said. "They've failed so far, but we can't assume they
will continue to fail. To those men at the institute in Berlin in 1944,
their past is immutable, as I have said. They cannot travel backward
in time and change their own past. But they can change their future
and ours, because a time traveler's future is mutable; he can take steps
to alter it."

"But *his* future is *my* past," Laura said. "And if the past can't be
changed, how can he change mine?"

"Yeah," Chris said. "Paradox."

Laura said, "Listen, I haven't spent the last thirty-four years in a
world ruled by Adolf Hitler and his heirs; therefore, in spite of the
gate, Hitler failed."

Stefan's expression was dismal. "If time travel were invented now,
in 1989, that past of which you speak—World War Two and every
event since—would be unalterable. You could not change it, for nature's rule against backward time-travel and time-travel paradoxes
would apply to you. But time travel has not been discovered here—
or rediscovered. The time travelers at the institute in Berlin in '44 are
free to change *their* future, apparently, and though they will simultaneously be changing your past, nothing in the laws of nature will
stop them. And there you have the greatest paradox of all—the only
one that for some reason nature seems to allow."

"You're saying they could still build nuclear weapons back then with the information they got in '85," Laura said, "and win the war?"

"Yes. Unless the institute is destroyed first."

"And what then? Suddenly, all around us, we find things changed, find ourselves living under Nazism?"

"Yes. And you won't even know what's happened, because you will be a different person than you are now. Your entire past will never have occurred. You will have lived a *different* past altogether, and you will remember nothing else, none of what has happened to you in *this* life because this life will never have existed. You will think the world has always been as it is, that there was never a world in which Hitler lost."

What he was proposing terrified and appalled her because it made life seem even more fragile than she had always thought it was. The world under her feet suddenly seemed no more real than the world of a dream; it was apt to dissolve without warning and send her tumbling into a great, dark void.

With growing horror she said, "If they change the world in which I grew up, I might never have met Danny, never married."

"I might never have been born," Chris said.

She reached to Chris and put a hand on his arm, not only to reassure him but to reassure herself of his current solidity. "I might not have been born myself. Everything I've seen, the good and bad of the world that's been since 1944 . . . it'll all wash away like an elaborate sand-castle, and a new reality will exist in its place."

"A new and worse reality," Stefan said, clearly exhausted by the effort he had made to explain what was at stake.

"In that new world, I might never have written my novels."

"Or if you wrote novels," Stefan said, "they would be different from those you've done in this life, grotesque works produced by an artist laboring under the rule of an oppressive government, in the iron fist of Nazi censorship."

"If those guys build the atom bomb in 1944," Chris said, "then we'll all just crumble into dust and blow away."

"Not literally. But like dust, yes," Stefan Krieger agreed. "Gone, with no trace that we've ever been."

"We've gotta stop them," Chris said.

"If we can," Stefan agreed. "But first we've got to stay alive in *this* reality, and that might not be easy."

Stefan needed to relieve himself, and Laura helped him into the motel bathroom, handling him as if she were a nurse accustomed to matter-of-fact dealings with the plumbing of sick men. By the time she returned him to the bed, she was worried about him again; though he was muscular, he felt limp, clammy, and he was frighteningly weak.

She told him briefly about the shoot-out at Brenkshaw's, through which he had remained comatose. "If these assassins are coming from the past instead of the future, how do they know where to find us? How did they know in 1944 that we'd be at Dr. Brenkshaw's when we were, forty-five years later?"

"To find you," Stefan said, "they made two trips. First, they went farther into the future, a couple of days farther, to this coming weekend perhaps, to see if you had shown up anywhere by then. If you hadn't— and apparently you had not—then they started checking the public record. Back issues of newspapers, for one thing. They looked for the stories about the shooting at your house last night, and in those stories they read that you'd taken a wounded man to Brenkshaw's place in San Bernardino. So they simply returned to '44 and made a second trip—this time to Dr. Brenkshaw's in the early hours of this morning, January 11."

"They can hopscotch around us," Chris told Laura. "They can pop ahead in time to see where we show up, then they pick and choose the easiest place along the time stream to ambush us. It's sorta like . . . if we were cowboys and the Indians were all psychic."

"Who was Kokoschka?" Chris wanted to know. "Who was the man who killed my dad?"

"Head of institute security," Stefan said. "He claimed to be a distant relation of Oskar Kokoschka, the noted Austrian expressionist painter, but I doubt if it was true because in *our* Kokoschka there was no hint of an artist's sensitivity. *Standartenführer*—which means Colonel—Heinrich Kokoschka was an efficient killer for the Gestapo."

"Gestapo," Chris said, awestruck. "Secret police?"

"State police," Stefan said. "Widely known to exist but allowed to operate in secrecy. When he showed up on that mountain road in 1988, I was as surprised as you. There'd been no lightning. He must have arrived far away from us, fifteen or twenty miles, in some other valley of the San Bernardinos, and the lightning had been beyond our notice." The lightning associated with time travel was in fact a very localized phenomenon, Stefan explained. "After Kokoschka showed up there, on my trail, I thought I would return to the institute and find all of my colleagues outraged at my treason, but when I got there, no one took special notice of me. I was confused. Then after I killed Penlovski and the others, when I was in the main lab preparing for my final jaunt into the future, Heinrich Kokoschka burst in and shot me. He wasn't dead! Not dead on that highway in 1988. Then I realized that Kokoschka had obviously only just learned of my treason when he'd found the men I'd shot. He would travel to 1988 and try to kill me—and all of you—at a later time. Which meant that the gate would have to remain open to allow him to do so, and that I was destined to fail to destroy it. At least at that time.''

"God, this headache," Laura said.

Chris seemed to have no trouble whatsoever following the tangled threads of time travel. He said, "So after you traveled to our house last night, Kokoschka traveled to 1988 and killed my dad. Jeez! In a way, Mr. Krieger, you killed Kokoschka forty-three years *after* he shot you in that lab . . . yet you had shot him *before* he shot you. This is wild stuff, Mom, isn't this wild? Isn't this great?''

"It's something," she agreed. "And how did Kokoschka know to find you on that mountain road?''

"After he discovered I'd shot Penlovski, and after I escaped through the gate, Kokoschka must have found the explosives in the attic and basement. Then he must have dug into the automatic records the machinery keeps of all the times the gate is used. That was a bit of data tracking that was *my* responsibility, so no one previously had noticed all my jaunts into your life, Laura. Anyway, Kokoschka must have done some time traveling of his own, must have taken a lot of trips to see where I'd been going, secretly watching me watch you, watching me alter your destiny for the better. He must have been watching the day I came to the cemetery when your father was buried, and he must have been watching when I beat Sheener, but I never saw him. So from all the trips I made into your life, from all the times I just observed you and the times I acted to save you, he picked a place at which to kill us. He wanted to kill me because I was a traitor, and he wanted to kill you and your family because . . . well because he realized you were so important to me.''

Why? she thought. Why am I so important to you, Stefan Krieger? Why have you intruded in my destiny, trying to give me a better life?

She would have asked those questions then, but he had more to say about Kokoschka. His strength seemed to be fading fast, and he was having some difficulty holding on to the thread of his reasoning. She did not want to interrupt and confuse him.

He said, "From the clocks and graphs on the gate's programming board, Kokoschka could have discovered my final destination: last night, your house. But, you see, I actually had intended to return to the night that Danny died, as I promised you I would, and instead I returned one year later only because I made some mistake when entering my calculations in the machine. After I left through the gate, wounded, Heinrich Kokoschka would have found those calculations.

He would have realized my mistake, and would have known where to find me not only last night but on the night that Danny died. In a way, by coming to save you from that runaway truck last year, I brought Danny's killer with me. I feel responsible for that, even though Danny would have died in the accident, anyway. At least you and Chris are alive. For now.''

''Why wouldn't Kokoschka have followed you to 1989, to our house last night? He knew you were already wounded, easy prey.''

''But he also knew that I would expect him to follow me, and he was afraid I was armed and would be prepared for him. So he went to 1988, where I was not expecting him, where he had the advantage of surprise. Also, Kokoschka probably figured if he followed me to 1988 and killed me there, I would not therefore have ever returned to the institute from that mountain highway and would not have had a chance to kill Penlovski. He no doubt thought he could pull a trick with time and *undo* those murders, thereby saving the head of the project. But of course he could not do so, because then he would be altering his *own* past, an impossibility. Penlovski and the others were already dead by then and would stay dead. If Kokoschka had better understood the laws of time travel, he would have known that I would kill him in 1988 when he followed me there, because by the time he made that jaunt to avenge Penlovski, I had already returned to the institute from that night, safe!''

Chris said, ''Are you all right, Mom?''

''Do they make Excedrin in one-pound tablets?'' she asked.

''I know it's a lot to absorb,'' Stefan said. ''But that's who Heinrich Kokoschka is. Or who he was. He removed the explosives I'd planted. Because of him—and that inconvenient power failure that stopped the timer on the detonator—the institute still stands, the gate is still open, and Gestapo agents are trying to track us here in our own time—and kill us.''

''Why?'' Laura asked.

''For revenge,'' Chris said.

''They're crossing forty-five years of time to kill us just for revenge?'' Laura said. ''Surely there's more than that.''

''There is,'' Stefan said. ''They want to kill us because they believe we are the only people in existence who can find a way to close the gate before they win the war and alter their future. And in that assumption, they're correct.''

''How?'' she asked, astounded. ''How can we destroy the institute forty-five years ago?''

''I'm not sure yet,'' he said. ''But I'll think about it.''

She began to ask more questions, but Stefan shook his head. He pleaded exhaustion and soon drifted off to sleep again.

* * *

Chris made a late lunch of peanut butter sandwiches with the fixings he had bought at the supermarket. Laura had no appetite.

She could see that Stefan was going to sleep for a few hours, so she showered. She felt better afterward, even in wrinkled clothes.

Throughout the afternoon the television fare was relentlessly idiotic: soap operas, game shows, more soap operas, reruns of *Fantasy Island, The Bold and the Beautiful*, and Phil Donahue dashing back and forth through the studio audience, exhorting them to raise their consciousness about—and find compassion for—the singular plight of transvestite dentists.

She replenished the Uzi's magazine with the ammunition she had bought at a gunshop that morning.

Outside, as the day waned, clots of dark clouds formed and grew until no blue sky could be seen. The fan palm beside the stolen Buick seemed to pull its fronds closer together in expectation of a storm.

She sat in one of the chairs, propped her feet up on the edge of the bed, closed her eyes, and dozed for a while. She woke from a bad dream in which she had discovered she was made of sand and was swiftly dissolving in a rainstorm. Chris was sleeping in the other chair, and Stefan was still snoring softly on the bed.

Rain was falling, drumming hollowly on the motel roof, pattering in the puddles on the parking lot outside, a sound like bubbling-hot grease, though the day was cool. It was a typical southern California storm, tropically heavy and steady but lacking thunder and lightning. Occasionally such pyrotechnics accompanied rain in this part of the world, but less often than elsewhere. Now Laura had special reason to be thankful for that climatological fact, because if there had been thunder and lightning, she would not have known whether it was natural or signaled the arrival of Gestapo agents from another era.

Chris woke at five-fifteen, and Stefan Krieger came around five minutes later. Both said they were hungry, and in addition to his appetite, Stefan showed other signs of recovery. His eyes had been bloodshot and watery; now they were clear. He was able to raise himself up in bed with his good arm. His left hand, which had been numb and virtually useless, was full of feeling now, and he was able to flex it, wriggle his fingers, and make a weak fist.

Instead of dinner she wanted answers to her questions, but she'd led a life that had taught her patience—among other things. When they had checked into the motel shortly after eleven that morning, Laura had noticed a Chinese restaurant across the street. Now, though reluctant to leave Stefan and Chris, she went out into the rain to get some take-out food.

She carried the .38 under her jacket and left the Uzi on the bed with

Stefan. Though the carbine was too big and powerful for Chris to handle, Stefan might be able to brace himself against the headboard and trigger a burst even with just his right hand, though the shock of recoil would shatter through his wound.

When she returned, dripping rain, they put the waxed-cardboard containers of food on the bed—except for the two orders of egg-flower soup, which were for Stefan, and which she put on the nightstand near him. Upon walking into the aromatic restaurant, she had found her own appetite, and naturally she had ordered far too much food: lemon chicken, beef with orange flavor, brown-pepper shrimp, moo goo gai pan, moo shu pork, and two containers of rice.

As she and Chris sampled all of the dishes with plastic forks and washed the food down with Cokes that she had gotten from the motel's soda machine, Stefan drank his soup. He had thought he could not hold down more solid food, but with the soup disposed of, he cautiously began to try the moo goo gai pan and the lemon chicken.

At Laura's request he told them about himself while they ate. He had been born in 1909 in the German town of Gittelde in the Harz Mountains, which made him thirty-five years old. ("Well," Chris said, "on the other hand, if you count the forty-five years you skipped when you traveled in time from '44 to '89, you're actually eighty years old!" He laughed, pleased with himself. "Boy, you sure look *good* for an eighty-year-old geezer!") After moving the family to Munich following the First World War, Stefan's father, Franz Krieger, had been an early supporter of Hitler in 1919, a member of the German Workers' Party from the very week that Hitler began his political career in that organization. He even worked with Hitler and Anton Drexler to write the platform with which that group, essentially a debating society, was eventually transformed into a true political party, later to become the National Socialists.

"I was one of the first members of the Hitler Youth in 1926, when I was seventeen," he said. "Less than a year later I joined the *Sturmabteilung* or the SA, the brown shirts, the enforcement arm of the party, virtually a private army. By 1928, however, I was a member of the *Schutzstaffel*—"

"The SS!" Chris said, speaking in the same tone of horror mixed with strange attraction that he would have used if he had been talking of vampires or werewolves. "You were a member of the SS? You wore the black uniform and the silver death's-head, carried the dagger?"

"I'm not proud of it," Stefan Krieger said. "Oh, at the time I was proud, of course. I was a fool. My father's fool. In the early days the SS was a small group, the essence of elitism, and our purpose was to protect *der Führer* with our own lives if that was necessary. We were all eighteen to twenty-two, young and ignorant and hotheaded. In my own defense I'll say that I was not particularly hotheaded, not as committed as those around me. I was doing what my father wanted, but of ignorance I'll admit to having more than my fair share."

Windblown rain rattled against the window and gurgled noisily in a downspout beyond the outside wall against which the bed stood.

Since awakening from his nap, Stefan had looked healthier, and he had perked up even more with the hot soup. But now, as he recalled a youth spent in a cauldron of hatred and death, he paled again, and his eyes seemed to sink deeper into the darkness under his brow. "I never left the SS because it was such a desired position and there was no way to leave without arousing suspicion that I'd lost my faith in our revered leader. But year by year, month by month, then day by day I became sickened by what I saw, by the madness and murder and terror."

Neither the brown-pepper shrimp nor the lemon chicken tasted too good any longer, and Laura's mouth was so dry that the rice stuck to the roof of it. She pushed the food aside, sipped her Coke. "But if you never left the SS . . . when did you go to college, when did you get involved in scientific research?"

"Oh," he said, "I wasn't at the institute as a researcher. I've no university education. Except . . . for two years I received intensive instruction in English, trying to learn to speak with an acceptable American accent. I was part of a project that dropped hundreds of deep-cover agents into Britain and the United States. But I never could quite cast off the accent, so I was never sent overseas; besides, because my father was an early supporter of Hitler, they felt I was trustworthy, so they found other uses for me. I was on special assignment to *der Führer*'s staff, where I was given sensitive jobs, usually as a liaison between squabbling factions of the government. It was an excellent position from which to obtain information useful to the British, which I did from 1938 on."

"You were a spy?" Chris asked excitedly.

"Of a sort. I had to do what little I could to bring down the Reich, to make up for ever having been a willing part of it. I had to atone— though atoning seemed impossible. And then, in the autumn of 1943, when Penlovski began to have some success with his time gate, sending animals off to God-knew-where and bringing them back, I was assigned to the institute as an observer, as *der Führer*'s personal representative. Also as a guinea pig, as the first human to be sent forward in time. You see, when they were ready to send a man into the future, they did not want to risk Penlovski or Januskaya or Helmut Volkaw or

Mitter or Shenck or one of the other scientists whose loss would damage the project. No one knew if a man would come back as reliably as the animals did—or if he would come back sane and whole.''

Chris nodded solemnly. "It's possible time travel might've been painful or mentally unbalancing or something, yeah. Who could know?''

Who could know indeed? Laura thought.

Stefan said, "They also wanted whomever they sent to be reliable and capable of keeping his mission a secret. I was the ideal choice.''

"An SS officer, a spy, and the first chrononaut," Chris said. "Wow, what a fascinating life.''

"May God give you a life far less eventful," Stefan Krieger said. Then he looked at Laura more directly than previously. His eyes were a beautiful, pure blue, yet they revealed a tortured soul. "Laura . . . what do you think of your guardian now? Not an angel but an aide to Hitler, an SS thug.''

"No thug," she said. "Your father, your time, and your society may have tried to make a thug of you, but there was an inner core they couldn't bend. Not a thug, Stefan Krieger. Never. Not you.''

"No angel, though," he said. "Far from an angel, Laura. Upon my death, when the stains on my soul are read by He who sits in judgment, I'll be given my own small space in hell.''

The rain drumming on the roof seemed like time flowing away, many millions of precious minutes, hours and days and years pouring through gutters and downspouts, draining away, wasted.

After she had gathered up the unfinished food and thrown it in a dumpster behind the motel office, after she'd gotten three more Cokes from the machine, one for each of them, she at last asked her guardian the question she had wanted to ask him from the moment he had come out of his coma: "Why? Why did you focus on me, on my life, and why did you want to help me along, to save my butt now and then? For God's sake, how does my fate tie up with Nazis, time travelers, the fate of the world?''

On his third trip into the future, he explained, he had traveled to California in 1984. California because his previous two trips—two weeks in 1954, two weeks in 1964—had shown him that California was perhaps the coming cultural and current scientific center of the most advanced nation on earth. Nineteen eighty-four because it was a neat forty years from his own time. He was not the only man going through the gate by then; four others began making jaunts as soon as it was proved safe. On that third trip Stefan had still been scouting the future, learning in detail what had happened to the world during and after the war. He was also learning what scientific developments of the intervening forty years would most likely be taken back to Berlin in '44 to win the war for Hitler, not because he intended to help in that design but because he hoped to sabotage it. His researches involved reading newspapers, watching television, and just circulating in American society, getting a feel for the late twentieth century.

Leaning back on his pillows now, recalling that third journey in a voice utterly different from the gloom with which he had described his grim life up to 1944, he said, "You can't imagine what it was like for me to walk the streets of Los Angeles for the first time. If I had traveled one thousand years into the future instead of forty, it couldn't have seemed more wondrous. The cars! Cars everywhere—and so many of them German, which seemed to indicate a certain forgiveness for the war, acceptance of the new Germany, and I was moved by that."

"We have a Mercedes," Chris said. "It's neat, but I like the Jeep better."

"The cars," Stefan said, "the styles, the amazing advancements everywhere: digital watches, home computers, videotape recorders for watching movies in your own living room! Even after five days of my visit had passed, I was in a state of pleasant shock, and looked forward each morning to new wonders. On the sixth day, as I passed a bookstore in Westwood, I saw a line of people waiting to have copies of a novel signed by the author. I went inside to browse and to see what kind of book was so popular, to help me a bit in understanding American society. And there you were, Laura, at a table piled with copies of your third novel and your first major success, *Ledges*."

Laura leaned forward, as if puzzlement were a force drawing her to the edge of her chair. "*Ledges*? But I've never written a book with that title."

Again, Chris understood. "That was a book you wrote in the life you would've lived if Mr. Krieger hadn't meddled in it."

"You were twenty-nine years old when I saw you for the first time at that book-signing party in Westwood," Stefan said. "You were in a wheelchair because your legs were twisted, useless. Your left arm was partly paralyzed, as well."

"Crippled?" Chris said. "Mom was crippled?"

Laura was literally on the edge of her chair now, for though what her guardian said seemed too fantastic to be believed, she sensed that it was true. On a deep level even more primitive than instinct, she perceived a *rightness* to the image of herself in a wheelchair, her legs useless and wasted; perhaps what she apprehended was the faint echo of destiny thwarted.

"You'd been that way since birth," Stefan said.

"Why?"

"I only learned that much later, after conducting much research into your life. The doctor who had delivered you in Denver, Colorado, in 1955—Markwell was his name—had been an alcoholic. Yours was a difficult birth anyway—"

"My mother died delivering me."

"Yes, in *that* reality she died too. But in that reality Markwell botched the delivery, and you received a spinal injury that crippled you for life."

A shudder passed through her. As if to prove to herself that she had indeed escaped the life that fate had originally planned for her, she got up and walked to the window, using her legs, her undamaged and blessedly useful legs.

To Chris, Stefan said, "That day I saw her in the wheelchair, your mother was so beautiful. Oh, so very beautiful. Her face, of course, was the same as it is now. But it wasn't the face alone that made her beautiful. There was such an aura of *courage* about her, and she was in such good humor in spite of her handicaps. Each person who came to her with *Ledges* was sent away not only with a signature but with a laugh. In spite of being condemned to a life in a wheelchair, your mother was so amusing, lighthearted. I watched from a distance and was charmed and profoundly moved, as I'd never been before."

"She's great," Chris said. "Nothing scares my mom."

"Everything scares your mom," Laura said. "This whole crazy conversation is scaring your mom half to death."

"You never run from anything or hide," Chris said, turning to look at her. He blushed; a boy his age was supposed to be cool, at a stage where he was beginning to wonder if he was not infinitely wiser than his mother. In an ordinary relationship, such expressions of admiration for one's mother seldom were expressed so directly short of the child's fortieth birthday or the mother's death, whichever came first. "Maybe you're afraid, but you never *act* afraid."

She had learned young that those who showed fear were seen as easy targets.

"I bought a copy of *Ledges* that day," Stefan said, "and took it back to the hotel where I was staying. I read it overnight, and it was so beautiful that in places I wept . . . and so amusing that in other places I laughed out loud. The next day I got your other two books, *Silverlock* and *Fields of Night*, which were as fine, as moving, as the book that made you famous, *Ledges*."

It was strange to listen to favorable reviews of books that in this life she had never written. But she was less concerned about learning the storylines of those novels than hearing the answer to a chilling question that had just occurred to her: "In this life I was meant to live, in this other 1984 . . . was I married?"

"No."

"But I'd met Danny and—"

"No. You had never met Danny. You had never married."

"I'd never been born!" Chris said.

Stefan said, "All of those things happened because I went back to Denver, Colorado, in 1955, and prevented Dr. Markwell from delivering you. The doctor who took Markwell's place couldn't save your mother, but he brought you into the world whole and sound. And everything in your life changed from that point on. It was your past that I was changing, yes, but it was *my* future, therefore flexible. And thank God for that peculiarity of time travel, for otherwise I wouldn't have been able to save you from a life as a paraplegic."

The wind gusted, and another barrage of rain rattled against the window at which Laura stood.

She was plagued again by the feeling that the room in which she stood, the earth on which it was built, and the universe in which it turned were as insubstantial as smoke, subject to sudden change.

"I monitored your life thereafter," Stefan said. "Between mid-January of '44 and mid-March, I made over thirty secret jaunts to see how you were getting along. On the fourth of those trips, when I went to 1964, I discovered you had been dead for one year, you and your father, killed by that junkie who had held up the grocery store. So I journeyed to 1963 and killed him before he could kill you."

"Junkie?" Chris said, baffled.

"I'll tell you about it later, honey."

Stefan said, "And until that night that Kokoschka showed up on that mountain road, I was pretty successful, I think, at making your life easier and better. Yet my interference did not deprive you of your art or result in books that were any less beautiful than the ones that you'd written in that other life. Different books but not lesser ones, books in the same voice, in fact, that you write in now."

Feeling weak-kneed, Laura returned to her chair. "But *why*? Why did you go to such great lengths to improve my life?"

Stefan Krieger looked at Chris, then at her, then closed his eyes when he finally spoke. "After seeing you in that wheelchair, signing copies of *Ledges*, and after reading your books, I fell in love with you . . . deeply in love with you."

Chris squirmed in his chair, obviously embarrassed to hear such feelings expressed when the object of affection was his own mother.

"Your mind was even more beautiful than your face," Stefan said softly. His eyes were still closed. "I fell in love with your great courage, perhaps because real courage was something I'd seen none of in my own world of strutting, uniformed fanatics. They committed atrocities in the name of the people and called that courage. They were willing to die for a twisted totalitarian ideal, and they called *that* courage when it was really stupidity, insanity. And I fell in love with your dignity, for I had none of my own, no self-respect like that I saw shining in you. I fell in love with your compassion, which was so rich a part of your books, for in my world I had seen little compassion. I fell in love, Laura, and realized that I could do for you what all men would do for those they loved if they had the power of gods: I did my best to spare you the worst that fate had planned for you."

He opened his eyes at last.

They were a beautiful blue. And tortured.

She was immeasurably grateful to him. She did not love him in return, for she hardly knew him. But in stating the depth of his love, a passion that had caused him to transform her destiny and that had driven him to sail across vast tides of time to be with her, he had to some degree restored the magical aura in which she had once viewed him. Again he seemed larger than life, a demigod if not a god, elevated from mere mortal status by the degree of his selfless commitment to her.

That night Chris shared the creaky-springed bed with Stefan Krieger. Laura tried to sleep in one chair with her feet propped on the other.

Rain fell in ceaseless, lulling rhythms that soon put Chris to sleep. Laura could hear him snoring softly.

After she sat for perhaps an hour in darkness, she said quietly, "Are you asleep?"

"No," Stefan said at once.

"Danny," she said. "My Danny . . . "

"Yes?"

"Why didn't you . . . "

"Make a second trip to that night in 1988 and kill Kokoschka before he could kill Danny?"

"Yes. Why didn't you?"

"Because . . . you see, Kokoschka was from the world of 1944, so his killing of Danny and his own death were a part of *my* past, which I could not undo. If I'd attempted to travel again to that night in '88, to an earlier point in the evening, to stop Kokoschka *before* he killed Danny—I would have bounced immediately back through the gate, back to the institute, without going anywhere; nature's law against paradox would have prevented me from going in the first place."

Laura was silent.

Stefan said, "Do you understand?"

"Yes."

"Do you accept it?"

"I'll never accept his death."

"But . . . do you believe me?"

"I think I do, yes."

"Laura, I know how much you loved Danny Packard. If I could have saved him, even at the cost of my own life, I would have done so. I would not have hesitated."

"I believe you," she said. "Because without you . . . I'd never have had Danny at all."

"The Eel," she said.

"Destiny struggles to reassert the pattern that was meant to be," Stefan said in the darkness. "When you were eight years old, I shot that junkie, prevented him from raping and killing you, but inevitably fate brought you to another pedophile who had the potential to be a murderer. Willy Sheener. The Eel. But fate also determined that you would be a writer and a successful one, that you would bring the same message to the world in your books regardless of what I did to change your life. That's a *good* pattern. There's something frightening yet reassuring in the way some power tries to reestablish destiny's broken designs . . . almost as if there's meaning in the universe, something that in spite of its insistence on our suffering, we might even call God."

For a while they listened to the rain and wind sweep clean the world outside.

She said, "But why didn't you take care of the Eel for me?"

"I waited for him one night in his apartment—"

"You gave him a bad beating. Yes, I knew that was you."

"Beat him and warned him to stay away from you. I told him I'd kill him the next time."

"But the beating only made him more determined to have me. Why didn't you kill him right off?"

"I should have. But . . . I don't know. Perhaps I'd seen so much killing and participated in enough of it that . . . I just hoped for once that killing wouldn't be necessary."

She thought of his world of war, concentration camps, genocide, and she could understand why he might have hoped to avoid murder even though Sheener had hardly deserved to live.

"But when Sheener came after me at the Dockweilers' house, why weren't you there to stop him?"

"The next time I monitored your life was when you were thirteen, after you'd already killed Sheener yourself and survived, so I decided not to go back and deal with him for you."

"I survived," she said. "But Nina Dockweiler didn't. Maybe if she hadn't come home and seen the blood, the body . . . "

"Maybe," he said. "And maybe not. Destiny struggles to restore the ordained pattern as best it can. Maybe she'd have died anyway. Besides, I couldn't protect you from every trauma, Laura. I would have needed ten thousand trips through time to have done that. And perhaps that degree of tampering wouldn't have been good for you. Without any adversity in your life, perhaps you wouldn't have become the woman with whom I fell in love."

Silence settled between them.

She listened to the wind, the rain.

She listened to her heartbeat.

At last she said, "I don't love you."

"I understand."

"Seems like I should—a little."

"You don't even really know me yet."

"Maybe I can never love you."

"I know."

"In spite of all you've done for me."

"I know. But if we live through this . . . well, there's always time."

"Yes," she said, "I suppose there's always time."

# 6

◆◆◆

# Night's Companion

## ONE

On Saturday, March 18, 1944, in the main, ground-floor lab of the institute, SS *Obersturmführer* Erich Klietmann and his squad of three highly trained men were prepared to jump into the future and eliminate Krieger, the woman, and the boy. They were dressed to pass as young California executives in 1989: pinstripe suits by Yves St. Laurent, white shirts, dark ties, black Bally loafers, black socks, and Ray-Ban sunglasses if the weather required them; they had been told that in the future this was called the "power look," and though Klietmann didn't know what that meant exactly, he liked the sound of it. Their clothes had been purchased in the future by institute researchers on previous jaunts; nothing about them, down to their underwear, was anachronistic.

Each of the four was carrying a Mark Cross attaché case, as well, a smart-looking model made of calfskin with gold-plated fixtures. The cases had also been brought back from the future, as had the modified Uzi carbine and spare magazines that were packed in each attaché.

A team of institute researchers had been on a mission to the U.S. in the year and month when John Hinckley had attempted to assassinate Ronald Reagan. While watching the film of the attack on television, they had been immensely impressed by the compact automatic weapons that the Secret Service agents had been carrying in attaché cases. The agents had been able to withdraw those submachine guns and bring them into firing position in but a second or two. Now the Uzi was not only the automatic carbine of choice in many of the police agencies and armies of 1989, but was the preferred weapon of the time-traveling *Schutzstaffel* commandos.

Klietmann had practiced with the Uzi. He regarded the weapon with as much affection as he had ever lavished upon a human being. The only thing about it that bothered him was the fact that it was an Israeli-designed and manufactured gun, the product of a bunch of Jews. On the other hand, within a few days the new directors of the institute were likely to approve the integration of the Uzi into the world of 1944, and German soldiers equipped with it would be better able to drive back the subhuman hordes who would depose *der Führer*.

He looked at the clock on the gate's programming board and saw that seven minutes had passed since the research team had left for California on February 15, 1989. They were there to search public records—mostly back issues of newspapers—to discover if Krieger, the woman, and the boy had been found by police and detained for questioning in the month following the shoot-outs at Big Bear and San Bernardino. Then they would return to '44 and tell Klietmann the day, time, and place where Krieger and the woman could be found. Because every time traveler returned from a jaunt exactly eleven minutes after departing, regardless of how long he spent in the future, Klietmann and his squad had only four more minutes to wait.

# TWO

Thursday, January 12, 1989, was Laura's thirty-fourth birthday, and they spent it in the same room at The Bluebird of Happiness Motel. Stefan needed another day of rest to regain his strength and let the penicillin do its work. He also needed the time to think; he had to devise a plan for destroying the institute, and that problem was sufficiently knotty to require hours of intense concentration.

The rain had stopped, but the sky still looked bruised, swollen. The forecast was for another storm to follow the first by midnight.

They watched the local five o'clock television news and saw a story about her and Chris and the wounded mystery man they had taken to Dr. Brenkshaw. Police were still looking for her, and the best guess anyone could make about the situation was that the drug dealers who had killed her husband were after her and her son, either because they were afraid she would eventually identify them in a police lineup or because she was somehow involved in drug traffic herself.

"My mom a drug dealer?" Chris said, offended by that insinuation. "What a bunch of bozos!"

Although no bodies had been found at Big Bear or San Bernardino, there had been a sensational development that guaranteed the media's continued interest. Reporters had learned that considerable blood had been found at both scenes—and that a man's severed head had been discovered in the alleyway behind the Brenkshaw house, between two garbage cans.

Laura remembered stepping through the redwood gate behind Carter Brenkshaw's property, seeing the second surprised gunman, and opening fire on him with the Uzi. The burst had taken him in the throat and head, and at the time she had thought that the concentrated automatic fire might well have decapitated him.

"The surviving SS men pushed the call-home button on the dead man's belt," Stefan said, "and sent his body back."

"But why not his head?" Laura said, sickened by the subject but too curious not to ask the question.

"It must've rolled away from the body, between the garbage cans," Stefan said, "and they couldn't find it in the few seconds they had to look. If they'd located it, they could have laid it on the corpse and folded his arms around it. Anything a time traveler wears or carries is taken with him on a jaunt. But with the sirens approaching and the darkness in the alley . . . they didn't have time to find the head."

Chris, who might have been expected to revel in these bizarre complications, slumped in his chair, legs curled up under him, and was silent. Perhaps the hideous image of a severed head had made Death's presence more real for him than had all the gunfire directed at him.

Laura made a special point of hugging him and subtly reassuring him that they were going to come out of this together and unscathed. The hugs, however, were as much for her as for him, and the pep talks she gave him must have seemed at least somewhat false, for she had not yet convinced herself that in fact they would triumph.

For lunch and dinner she got take-out from the Chinese restaurant just across the street. The previous night none of the restaurant's employees recognized her as either the famous author or the fugitive, so she felt reasonably safe there. It seemed foolish to go elsewhere and risk being spotted.

At the end of dinner, while Laura was cleaning up the cardboard containers, Chris produced two chocolate cupcakes with a yellow candle on each. He had bought the packet of Hostess pastries and a box of birthday candles at the Ralph's supermarket yesterday morning and had hidden them until now. With great ceremony he carried the cupcakes from the bathroom, where he had secretly inserted and lit the candles, and golden reflections of the two flames shimmered brightly in his eyes. He grinned when he saw that he had surprised and delighted her. In fact she had to strive to hold back tears. She was moved that even in the thrall of fear, in the midst of danger, he'd still had the presence of mind to think of her birthday, and the desire to please her; it seemed, to her, to be the essence of what mothers and children were all about.

The three of them ate wedges of the cupcakes. In addition five fortune cookies had come with the take-out food.

From his pillowed perch upon the bed, Stefan opened his cookie. "If only this were true: 'You'll live in times of peace and plenty.' "

"It might turn out to be true," Laura said. She cracked her cookie and withdrew the slip of paper. "Oh, well, I think I've had enough of this, thank you: 'Adventure will be your companion.' "

When Chris opened his cookie, there was no slip of paper inside, no fortune.

A flicker of fear passed through Laura, as if the empty cookie actually meant that he had no future. Superstitious nonsense. But she could not suppress her sudden anxiety.

"Here," she said, quickly handing him both of the remaining cookies. "Getting none in that one just means you get *two* fortunes."

Chris opened the first, read it to himself, laughed, then read it to them: " 'You will achieve fame and fortune.' "

"When you're stinking rich, will you support me in my old age?" Laura asked.

"Sure, Mom. Well . . . as long as you'll still cook for me, and especially your vegetable soup."

"Going to make your old mom *earn* her way, huh?"

Smiling at the interplay between Laura and Chris, Stefan Krieger said, "He's a tough customer, isn't he?"

"He'll probably have me scrubbing his floors when I'm eighty," Laura said.

Chris opened the second cookie. " 'You'll have a good life of little pleasures—books, music, art.' "

Neither Chris nor Stefan seemed to notice that the two fortunes made opposed predictions, effectively canceling each other, which in a way confirmed the ominous meaning of the empty cookie.

Hey, you're losing your mind, Shane, you really are, she thought. They're just fortune cookies. They don't *really* predict anything.

Hours later, after the lights were out and Chris was asleep, Stefan spoke to Laura from the darkness. "I've devised a plan."

"A way to destroy the institute?"

"Yes. But it's very complicated, and there are many things we'll need. I don't know for sure . . . but I suspect some of these items can't be purchased by private citizens."

"I can get anything you need," she said confidently. "I have the contacts. Anything."

"We'll have to have quite a lot of money."

"That's thorny. I've only got forty bucks left, and I can't go to the bank and withdraw funds because that would leave a record—"

"Yes. That would draw them straight to us. Is there someone you can trust and who trusts you, someone who would give you a lot of their own money and tell no one they'd seen you?"

"You know all about me," Laura said, "so you know about Thelma Ackerson. But, God, I don't want to drag her into this. If anything happened to Thelma—"

"It can be arranged without risk to her," he insisted.

Outside, the promised rain arrived in a sudden downpour.

Laura said, "No."

"But she's our only hope."

"No."

"Where else can you raise the money?"

"We'll find another way that doesn't require a lot of financing."

"Whether we come up with another plan or not, we'll need money. Your forty dollars won't last another day. And I have nothing."

"I won't risk Thelma," she said adamantly.

"As I said, we can do it without risk, without—"

"No."

"Then we're defeated," he said dismally.

She listened to the rain, which in her mind became the heavy roar of World War II bombers—and then the sound of a chanting, maddened crowd.

At last she said, "But even if we could arrange it without any risk to Thelma, what if the SS has a tail on her? They must know she's my best friend—my only real friend. So why wouldn't they have sent one of their teams forward in time to just keep a watch on Thelma with the hope she'd lead them to me?"

"Because that's an unnecessarily tedious way to find us," he said. "They can just send research teams into the future, to February of this year and then March and April, month after month, to check the newspapers until they found out where we first showed up. Each of those jaunts only takes eleven minutes in *their* time, remember, so it's quick; and that method is almost certain to work sooner or later because it's doubtful we could stay in hiding the rest of our lives."

"Well . . ."

He waited a long time. Then he said, "You're like sisters, you two. And if you can't turn for help to a sister at a time like this, who can you turn to, Laura?"

"If we can get Thelma's help without putting her at risk . . . I guess we have to try."

"First thing in the morning," he said.

That was a night of rain, and rain also filled her dreams, and in those dreams were explosive thunderclaps and lightning, as well. She woke in terror, but the rainy night in Santa Ana was unmarred by those bright, noisy omens of death. It was a comparatively peaceful storm, without thunder, lightning, and wind, though she knew that it would not always be so.

# THREE

The machinery clicked and hummed.

Erich Klietmann looked at the clock. In just three minutes the research team would return to the institute.

Two scientists, heirs of Penlovski and Januskaya and Volkaw, stood at the programming board, studying the myriad dials and gauges.

All the light in the room was unnatural, for the windows were not merely blacked out to avoid providing beacons for night-flying enemy bombers, but were bricked in for security reasons. The air was stuffy.

Standing in one corner of the main lab, near the gate, Lieutenant

Klietmann anticipated his trip to 1989 with excitement, not because that future was filled with wonders but because the mission gave him an opportunity to serve *der Führer* in a way that few men ever could. If he succeeded in killing Krieger, the woman, and the boy, he would have earned a personal meeting with Hitler, a chance to see the great man face to face, to know the touch of his hand and through that touch to feel the power, the tremendous power of the German state and people and history and destiny. The lieutenant would have risked death ten times, a thousand times, for the chance to be brought to the personal attention of *der Führer*, to make Hitler aware of him, not aware of him as just another SS officer, but aware of him as an individual, as Erich Klietmann, the man who saved the Reich from the dire fate that it had almost been forced to endure.

Klietmann was not the Aryan ideal, and he was acutely aware of his physical shortcomings. His maternal grandfather had been Polish, a disgusting slavic mongrel, which made Klietmann only three-quarters German. Furthermore, though his other three grandparents and both of his parents had been blond, blue-eyed, with Nordic features, Erich had hazel eyes, dark hair, and the heavier, more sensuous features of his barbarian grandfather. He loathed the way he looked, and he tried to compensate for his physical shortcomings by being the most vigilant Nazi, most courageous soldier, and most ardent supporter of Hitler in the entire *Schutzstaffel*, which was tough because he had so much competition for that honor. Sometimes he had despaired of ever being singled out for glory. But he never gave up, and now here he was, on the brink of heroism that would earn him Valhalla.

He wanted to kill Stefan Krieger personally, not only because that would win *der Führer*'s favor but because Krieger *was* the Aryan ideal, blond and blue-eyed, every feature truly Nordic, and from fine breeding stock. With every advantage, the hateful Krieger had chosen to betray his *Führer*, and that enraged Klietmann, who had to labor toward greatness under the burden of mongrel genes.

Now, with little more than two minutes left before the research team would return through the gate from 1989, Klietmann looked at his three subordinates, all dressed as young executives of another age, and he felt both a fierce and a sentimental pride in them so strong it almost brought tears to his eyes.

They had all come from humble beginnings. *Unterscharführer* Felix Hubatsch, Klietmann's sergeant and second in command of the unit, was the son of an alcoholic lathe operator and a slattern mother, both of whom he despised. *Rottenführer* Rudolph von Manstein was the son of a poor farmer whose lifetime of failure shamed him, and *Rottenführer* Martin Bracher was an orphan. In spite of coming from four different corners of Germany, the two corporals, the sergeant, and lieutenant Klietmann shared one thing that made them as close as brothers: They understood that a man's truest, deepest, and dearest relationship was not to his family but to the state, to the fatherland, and to their leader in whom the fatherland was embodied; the state was the only family that mattered; this single bit of wisdom elevated them and made them worthy fathers of the superrace to come.

Klietmann discreetly dabbed at the corners of his eyes with his thumb, blotting the nascent tears that he was not able to suppress.

In one minute the research team would return.

The machinery clicked and hummed.

# FOUR

At three o'clock, Friday afternoon, January 13, a white pickup entered the rainswept motel lot, came straight to the rear wing, and parked next to the Buick that bore a Nissan's license plates. The truck was about five or six years old. The passenger-side door was dented, and that rocker panel was spotted with rust. The owner was evidently refinishing the pickup in a patchwork fashion, because some spots had been sanded and primed but not yet repainted.

Laura watched the truck from behind the barely parted drapes at the motel-room window. She held the Uzi in one hand at her side.

The truck's headlights blinked off, and its windshield wipers stopped, and a moment later a woman with frizzy blond hair got out and walked to the door of Laura's unit. She rapped three times.

Chris was standing behind the door, looking at his mother.

Laura nodded.

Chris opened the door and said, "Hi, Aunt Thelma. Jeez, that's an ugly wig."

Stepping inside, hugging Chris fiercely, Thelma said, "Well, thanks a lot. And what would you say if I told you that was a monumentally ugly nose you were born with, but you're stuck with it, while I'm not stuck with the wig? Huh? What would you say then?"

Chris giggled. "Nothing. 'Cause I know I've got a cute nose."

"Cute nose? God, kid, you've got an actor's ego." She let go of him, glanced at Stefan Krieger, who was sitting in one of the chairs near the TV set, then turned to Laura. "Shane, did you see the heap I pulled up in? Am I clever? As I was getting in my Mercedes, I said to myself, Thelma—I call myself Thelma—I said, Thelma, isn't it going to draw a hell of a lot of attention at that sleazy motel when you pull up in a sixty-five-thousand-dollar car? So I tried to borrow the butler's car, but you know what *he* drives? A Jaguar. Is Beverly Hills the Twilight Zone, or what? So I had to borrow the gardener's truck. But here I am, and what do you think of this disguise?''

She was wearing a kinky blond wig glittering with droplets of rain, horn-rimmed glasses, and a pair of false dentures that gave her an overbite.

''You look better this way,'' Laura said, grinning.

Thelma popped out the fake teeth. ''Listen, once I turned up a set of wheels that wouldn't draw attention, I realized that I'd draw some attention myself, being a major star and everything. And since the media's already dug up the fact that you and I are friends and have tried to ask me some pointed questions about you, the famous machine-gun-packing authoress, I decided to come incognito.'' She dropped her purse and the stage teeth on the bed. ''This getup was for a new character I created in my nightclub act, tried it about eight times at Bally's in Vegas. It was a primo flop, that character. The audience *spat* at me, Shane, they brought in the casino's security guard and tried to have me arrested, they questioned my right to share the same planet with them—oh, they were rude, Shane, they were—''

Suddenly she halted in the middle of her patter and burst into tears. She rushed to Laura, threw her arms around her. ''Oh, Jesus, Laura, I was scared, I was so scared. When I heard the news about San Bernardino, machine guns, and then the way they found your house at Big Bear, I thought you . . . or maybe Chris . . . I was so worried . . . ''

Holding Thelma as tightly as Thelma was holding her, Laura said, ''I'll tell you all about it, but the main thing is we're all right, and we think maybe we have a way to get out of the hole we're in.''

''Why didn't you call me, you silly bitch?''

''I did call you.''

''Only this morning! Two *days* after you're splashed all over the newspapers. I nearly went crazy.''

''I'm sorry. I should've called sooner. I just didn't want to get you involved if I could avoid it.''

Reluctantly Thelma let go of her. ''I'm inevitably, deeply, and hopelessly involved, you idiot, because *you're* involved.'' She pulled a Kleenex from a pocket of her suede jacket and blotted her eyes.

''You have another one of those?'' Laura asked.

Thelma gave her a Kleenex, and they both blew their noses.

''We were on the lam, Aunt Thelma,'' Chris said. ''It's hard to stay in touch with people when you're on the lam.''

Taking a deep, shuddery breath, Thelma said, ''So, Shane, where are you keeping your collection of severed heads? In the bathroom? I heard you left one behind in San Bernardino. Sloppy. Is this a new hobby of yours, or have you always had an appreciation for the beauty of the human head unencumbered by all the messy extremities?''

"I want you to meet someone," Laura said. "Thelma Ackerson, this is Stefan Krieger."

"Pleased to meet you," Thelma said.

"You'll excuse me if I don't get up," Stefan said. "I'm still recuperating."

"If you can excuse this wig, I can excuse anything." To Laura, Thelma said, "Is he who I think he is?"

"Yes."

"Your guardian?"

"Yes."

Thelma went to Stefan and kissed him wetly on both cheeks. "I've no idea where you come from or who the hell you are, Stefan Krieger, but I love you for all the times you've helped my Laura." She stepped back and sat on the foot of the bed beside Chris. "Shane, this man you have here is gorgeous. Look at him, he's a hunk. I'll bet *you* shot him just so he couldn't get away. He looks just like a guardian angel ought to look." Stefan was embarrassed, but Thelma would not be stopped. "You're a real dish, Krieger. I want to hear all about you. But first, here's the money you asked for, Shane." She opened her voluminous purse and withdrew a thick wad of hundred-dollar bills.

Examining the money, Laura said, "Thelma, I asked you for four thousand. There's at least twice that here."

"Ten or twelve thousand, I think." Thelma winked at Chris and said, "When my friends are on the lam, I *insist* they go first class."

Thelma listened to the story, never expressing disbelief. Stefan was surprised by her open-mindedness, but she said, "Hey, once you've lived at McIlroy Home and Caswell Hall, the universe holds no more surprises. Time travelers from 1944? Pah! At McIlroy I could've shown you a woman as big as a sofa, who wore clothes made of bad upholstery fabric, and who was paid a handsome civil-service wage to treat orphaned children like vermin. Now *there* is an amazement." She was clearly affected by Stefan's origins, chilled and amazed by the trap they were in, but even under these circumstances she was Thelma Ackerson, always looking for the laugh in everything.

At six o'clock she put in the stage teeth again and went up the street to get take-out from a Mexican restaurant. "When you're on the run from the law, you need beans in your belly, tough-guy food." She came back with rain-dampened bags of tacos, containers of enchiladas, two orders of nachos, burritos, and chimichangas. They spread the food out on the bottom half of the bed, and Thelma and

Chris sat on the top half. Laura and Stefan sat in chairs at the foot of the bed.

"Thelma," Laura said, "there's enough food here for ten."

"Well, I figured that would feed us and the cockroaches. If we didn't have food for the cockroaches, they might get mean, might go outside and overturn my gardener's pickup. You *do* have cockroaches here, don't you ? I mean, after all, a swell place like this without cockroaches would be like the Beverly Hills Hotel without tree rats."

As they ate, Stefan outlined the plan he had devised for closing the gate and destroying the institute. Thelma interrupted with wisecracks, but when he was finished, she was solemn. "This is damned dangerous, Stefan. Brave enough to be foolish, maybe."

"There's no other way."

"I can see that," she said. "So what can I do to help?"

Pausing with a wad of corn chips halfway to his mouth, Chris said, "We need you to buy the computer, Aunt Thelma."

Laura said, "An IBM PC, their best model, the same one I have at home, so I'll know how to use all the software. We don't have time to learn the operating procedures of a new machine. I've written it all down for you. I could go buy it myself, I guess, with money you gave me, but I'm afraid of showing my face too many places."

"And we'll need a place to stay," Stefan said.

"We can't stay here," Chris said, enjoying being a part of the discussion, "not if we're going to be doing stuff with a computer. The maid would see it no matter how hard we tried to hide it, and she'd talk about it because that would be weird, people holing up in a place like this with a computer."

Stefan said, "Laura tells me that you and your husband have a second house in Palm Springs."

"We have a house in Palm Springs, a condo in Monterey, another condo in Vegas, and it wouldn't surprise me if we owned—or at least had time shares in—our very own Hawaiian volcano. My husband is too rich. So take your pick. My houses are your houses. Just don't use the towels to polish the hubcaps on your car, and if you must chew tobacco and spit on the floors, try to keep it in the corners."

"I thought the house in Palm Springs would be ideal," Laura said. "You've told me it's fairly secluded."

"It's on a large property with lots of trees, and there're other show-biz people on that block, all of 'em busy, so they don't tend to drop over for a cup of coffee. No one'll disturb you there."

"All right," Laura said, "there's just a few other things. We need changes of clothes, comfortable shoes, some basic necessities. I've made a list, sizes and everything. And, of course, when this is all over, I'll pay you back the cash you gave me and whatever you spend on the computer and these other things.''

"Damn right you will, Shane. And forty percent interest. Per week. Compounded hourly. Plus your child. Your child will be mine.''

Chris laughed. "My Aunt Rumpelstiltskin.''

"You won't make smart remarks when you're *my* child, Christopher Robin. Or at least you'll call me Mother Rumpelstiltskin, Sir.''

"Mother Rumpelstiltskin, Sir!'' Chris said, and saluted her.

At eight-thirty Thelma prepared to leave with the shopping list that Laura had composed and the information about the computer. "I'll be back tomorrow afternoon, as soon as I can,'' she said, giving Laura and then Chris one last hug. "You'll really be safe here, Shane?''

"I think we will. If they'd discovered we were staying here, they would've shown up sooner.''

Stefan said, "Remember, Thelma, they're time travelers; once they discover where we've been hiding, they could just jaunt forward to the moment when we first arrived here. In fact they could've been waiting for us when we pulled into the motel on Wednesday. The fact that we've stayed here so long unmolested is almost proof there'll never be public knowledge that this was our hideout.''

"My head spins,'' Thelma said. "And I thought reading a major studio's contract was complicated!''

She went out into the night and rain, still wearing the wig and the horn-rimmed glasses but carrying her stage teeth in her pocket, and she drove away in her gardener's truck.

Laura, Chris, and Stefan watched her from the big window, and Stefan said, "She's a special person.''

"Very,'' Laura said. "I hope to God I haven't endangered her.''

"Don't worry, Mom,'' Chris said. "Aunt Thelma's a tough broad. She always says so.''

That night at nine o'clock, shortly after Thelma left, Laura drove to Fat Jack's place in Anaheim. The rain was not as heavy as it had been but fell in a steady drizzle. The macadamized pavement glistened silver-black, and gutters still overflowed with water that looked like oil in the queer light of the sodium-vapor streetlamps. Fog had crept in, too, not on little cat feet but slithering like a snake on its belly.

She had been loath to leave Stefan at the motel. But it was not wise for him to spend much time in the chilly, rainy January night in his debilitated condition. Besides, he could do nothing to help her.

Though Stefan remained behind, Chris accompanied Laura, for she would not be separated from him for the time it would take to cut a deal for the weapons. The boy had gone with her when she had first visited Fat Jack a year ago, when she'd bought the illegally modified Uzis, so the fat man would not be surprised to see him. Displeased, yes, since Fat Jack was no lover of children, but not surprised.

As she drove, Laura looked frequently in the rearview mirror, in the side mirrors, and took the measure of the other drivers around her with a diligence that gave new meaning to the term defensive driving. She could not afford to be broadsided by a dunderhead who was driving too fast for the road conditions. Police would put in an appearance at the scene of the crash, would routinely check out her license plates, and before they even arrested her, men carrying submachine guns would materialize and kill her and Chris.

She had left her own Uzi with Stefan, although he had protested. However, she was unable to abandon him with no means of self-defense. She still carried the .38 Chief's Special. And fifty spare rounds were distributed in the zippered pockets of her ski jacket.

Near Disneyland, when the neon-drenched phantasmagoria of Fat Jack's Pizza Party Palace appeared in the fog like the starship in *Close Encounters of the Third Kind* descending from clouds of its own making, Laura was relieved. She pulled into the crowded parking lot and switched off the engine. The windshield wipers stopped thumping, and rain washed down the glass in rippling sheets. Orange, red, blue, yellow, green, white, purple, and pink reflections of neon glimmered in that flowing film of water, so Laura felt curiously as if she were inside one of those old-fashioned, gaudy jukeboxes from the 1950s.

Chris said, "Fat Jack's put up more neon since we were here."

"I think you're right," Laura said.

They got out of the car and looked up at the blinking, flashing, rippling, winking, grotesquely flamboyant façade of Fat Jack's Pizza Party Palace. Neon was not reserved solely for the name of the place. It was also used to outline the building, the roofline, every window, and the front doors. In addition there were a pair of giant neon sunglasses on one end of the roof, and a huge neon rocketship poised for takeoff on the other end, with neon vapors perpetually curling and sparkling beneath its exhaust jets. The ten-foot-diameter neon pizza was an old feature, but the grinning neon clown's face was new.

The quantity of neon was so great that every falling raindrop was brightly tinted, as if it was part of a rainbow that had broken apart at nightfall. Every puddle shimmered with rainbow fragments.

The effect was disorienting, but it prepared the visitor for the inside of Fat Jack's, which seemed to be a glimpse of the chaos out of which the universe had formed trillions of years ago. The waiters and waitresses were dressed as clowns, ghosts, pirates, spacemen, witches, gypsies, and vampires, and a singing trio in bear costumes moved from table to table, delighting young children with pizza-smeared faces. In alcoves off the main room, older kids were at banks of videogames, so the *beep-zing-zap-bong* of that electronic play served as background music to singing bears and shouting children.

"Asylum," Chris said.

They were met inside the front door by the host, Dominick, who was Fat Jack's minority partner. Dominick was tall, cadaverous, with mournful eyes, and he seemed out of place midst the forced hilarity.

Raising her voice to be heard over the din, Laura asked for Fat Jack and said, "I called earlier. I'm an old friend of his mother's," which was what you were to say to indicate you wanted guns not pizza.

Dominick had learned to project his voice clearly through the cacophony without shouting. "You've been here before, I believe."

"Good memory," she said. "A year ago."

"Please follow me," Dominick said in a funereal voice.

They did not have to go through the cyclonic commotion of the dining room, which was good because that meant Laura was less likely to be seen and recognized by one of the customers. A door off the other side of the host's foyer opened onto a corridor that led past the kitchen and the storeroom to Fat Jack's private office. Dominick knocked on the door, ushered them inside, and said to Fat Jack, "Old friends of your mother," then left Laura and Chris with the big man.

Fat Jack took his nickname seriously and tried to live up to it. He was five feet ten and weighed about three hundred and fifty pounds. Wearing immense gray sweatpants and sweatshirt that fit him almost as tightly as Spandex, he looked like the fat man in that magnetized photograph that dieters could buy to put on refrigerators to scare them off food; in fact, he looked like the refrigerator.

He sat in a baronial swivel chair behind a desk sized for him, and he did not get up. "Listen to the little beasts." He spoke to Laura, ignored Chris. "I put my office at the back of the building, had it specially soundproofed, and I can still hear them out there, shrieking, squealing; it's as if I'm just down the hall from hell."

"They're only children having fun," Laura said, standing with Chris in front of the desk.

"And Mrs. O'Leary was just an old lady with a clumsy cow, but she burned down Chicago," Fat Jack said sourly. He was eating a Mars bar. In the distance children's voices, insulated by soundproofing, rose in a dull roar, and as if talking to that unseen multitude, the fat man said, "Ah, choke on it, you little trolls."

"It's a nuthouse out there," Chris said.

"Who asked you?"

"Nobody, sir."

Jack had a grainy complexion with gray eyes nearly buried in a puff-adder face. He focused on Laura and said, "You see my new neon?"

"The clown is new, isn't it?"

"Yeah. Isn't it a beauty? I designed it, had it made, and then had it erected in the dead of night, so the next morning it was too late for anybody to get a restraining order to stop me. The damn city council just about croaked, all of them at once."

Fat Jack had been embroiled in a decade-long legal battle with the Anaheim Zoning Commission and the city council. The authorities disapproved of his garish neon displays, especially now that the area around Disneyland was slated for urban renewal. Fat Jack had spent tens if not hundreds of thousands of dollars fighting them in the courts, paying fines, being sued, countersuing, and he had even spent time in jail for contempt of court. He was a former libertarian who now claimed to be an anarchist, and he would not tolerate infringement on his rights—real and imagined—as a free-thinking individual.

He dealt in illegal weapons for the same reason he erected neon signs that violated city codes: as a statement against authority, to champion individual rights. He could talk for hours about the evils of government, any kind of government, in any degree whatsoever, and on Laura's last visit with Chris, in order to get the modified Uzis she wanted, she had listened to a lengthy explanation of why the government did not even have the right to pass laws forbidding murder.

Laura had no great love of big government, whether of the left or right, but she had little sympathy with Fat Jack, either. He did not acknowledge the legitimacy of any authority whatsoever, not that of proven institutions, not even that of family.

Now, after she gave Fat Jack her new shopping list, after he quoted a price and counted her money, he led her and Chris through the hidden door in the back of his office closet, down a narrow stairwell—he seemed in danger of becoming wedged tight—to the basement where he kept his illegal stock. Though his restaurant was a madhouse, his arsenal was stored with fetishistic neatness: cartons upon cartons of handguns and automatic weapons were stacked on metal shelves, arranged according to caliber and also according to price; he kept at least a thousand guns in the basement of the Pizza Party Palace.

He was able to provide her with two modified Uzis—"An immensely popular gun since the attempt to kill Reagan," he said—and another .38 Chief's Special. Stefan had hoped to obtain a Colt Commander 9mm Parabellum with a nine-round magazine and the barrel machined for a silencer. "Don't have it," Fat Jack said, "but

I can let you have a Colt Commander Mark IV in .38 Super, which has a nine-round magazine, and I've got two of those machined for silencers. Got the silencers, too, plenty of 'em.'' She already knew that he wasn't able to provide her with ammunition, but as he finished his Mars bar, he explained anyway: "Don't stock ammunition or explosives. Look, I don't believe in authority, but I'm not totally irresponsible. I got a restaurant full of shrieking, snot-faced kids upstairs, and I can't risk blowing them to bits, even if that'd bring more peace to the world. Besides, I'd destroy all my pretty neon too.''

"All right," Laura said, putting one arm around Chris to keep him at her side, "what about the gas on my list?"

"You sure you don't mean tear gas?"

"No. Vexxon. That's the stuff I want." Stefan had given her the name of the gas. He said it was one of the chemical weapons that was on the list of items the institute hoped to bring back to 1944 and introduce into the German military arsenal. Now perhaps it could be used *against* the Nazis. "We need something that will kill fast."

Fat Jack leaned his backside against the metal worktable in the middle of the room, where he had laid out the Uzis, revolvers, pistol, and silencers. The table creaked ominously. "Well, what we're talking about here is army ordnance, tightly controlled stuff."

"You can't get it?"

"Oh, sure, I can get you some Vexxon," Fat Jack said. He moved away from the table, which creaked in relief as his weight was lifted from it, and went to a set of metal shelves where he withdrew a couple of Hershey bars from between boxes of guns, a secret stash. He did not offer one to Chris, but put the second bar in the side pocket of his sweatpants and began to eat the other. "I don't have that sort of crap here; just as dangerous as explosives. But I can have it for you late tomorrow, if that's not inconvenient."

"That'll be fine."

"It'll cost you."

"I know."

Fat Jack grinned. Bits of chocolate were stuck between his teeth. "Don't get much call for this kind of thing, not from someone like yourself, a small buyer. Tickles me to try to figure what you'd be up to with it. Not that I expect you to tell me. But usually it's big buyers from South America or the Middle East who want these neuroactive and respiractive gases. Iraq and Iran used plenty the last few years."

"Neuroactive, respiractive? What's the difference?"

"Respiractive—they have to breathe it in; it kills them seconds after it hits the lungs and spreads through the bloodstream. When you release it, you've got to be wearing a gas mask. Your neuroactive, on the other hand, kills even quicker, just on touching the skin, and with certain types of it—like Vexxon—you won't need a gas mask or protective clothing,'cause you can take a couple of pills before you use it, and they're like an advance antidote.''

"Yes, I was supposed to ask for the pills, too,'' Laura said.

"Vexxon. Easiest-to-use gas on the market. You're a real smart shopper,'' Fat Jack said.

Already he had finished the candy bar, and he appeared to have grown noticeably since Laura and Chris had entered his office half an hour ago. She realized that Fat Jack's commitment to political anarchy was reflected not only in the atmosphere of his pizza parlor but in the condition of his body, for his flesh swelled unrestrained by social or medical considerations. He seemed to revel in his size, as well, frequently patting his gut or grabbing the rolls of fat on his sides and kneading them almost affectionately, and he walked with belligerent arrogance, pushing the world away from him with his belly. She had a vision of Fat Jack growing ever more huge, soaring past four hundred pounds, past five hundred, even as the wildly pyramiding neon structures on the roof grew ever more elaborate, until one day the roof collapsed and Fat Jack exploded simultaneously.

"I'll have the gas by five o'clock tomorrow,'' he said as he put the Uzis, .38 Chief's Special, Colt Commander, and silencers in a box labeled BIRTHDAY PARTY FAVORS, which had probably contained paper hats or noisemakers for the restaurant. He slipped the lid on the box and indicated that Laura was to carry it upstairs; among other things, Fat Jack did not believe in chivalry.

Back in Fat Jack's office, when Chris opened the door to the hall for his mother, Laura was pleased by the squealing of the children in the pizza parlor. That sound was the first normal, sane thing she had heard in more than half an hour.

"Listen to the little cretins,'' Fat Jack said. "They're not children; they're shaved baboons trying to pass for children.'' He slammed his soundproofed office door behind Chris and Laura.

In the car on the way back to the motel, Chris said, "When this is all over . . . what're you going to do about Fat Jack?''

"Turn his butt into the cops,'' Laura said. "Anonymously.''

"Good. He's a nut.''

"He's worse than a nut, honey. He's a fanatic.''

"What's a fanatic exactly?''

She thought for a moment, then said, "A fanatic is a nut who has something to believe in.''

# FIVE

Lieutenant Erich Klietmann, SS, watched the second hand on the programming-board clock, and when it neared the twelve, he turned and looked at the gate. Inside that twelve-foot-long, gloom-filled tube, something shimmered, a fuzzy gray-black patch that resolved into the silhouette of a man—then three more men, one behind the other. The research team came out of the gate, into the room, and were met by the three scientists who had been monitoring the programming board.

They had returned from February 1989, and were smiling, which made Klietmann's heart pound because they would not be smiling if they had not located Stefan Krieger, the woman, and the boy. The first two assassination squads that had been sent into the future—the one that had attacked the house near Big Bear and the one in San Bernardino—had been composed of Gestapo officers. Their failures had led *der Führer* to insist the third team be *Schutzstaffel*, and now Erich judged the researchers' smiles to mean that his squad was going to have a chance to prove the SS was filled with better men than the Gestapo.

The failures of the two previous squads were not the only black marks on the Gestapo's record in this affair. Heinrich Kokoschka, the head of the institute's security, had been a Gestapo officer, as well, and he had apparently turned traitor. Available evidence seemed to support the theory that two days ago, on March 16, he had defected to the future with five other members of the institute's staff.

On the evening of March 16, Kokoschka had jaunted alone to the San Bernardino Mountains with the claimed intention of killing Stefan Krieger there in the future before Krieger returned to 1944 and killed Penlovski, thereby undoing the deaths of the project's best men. But Kokoschka never came back. Some argued that Kokoschka had been killed up there in 1988, that Krieger had won the confrontation—but that did not explain what had happened to the five other men in the institute that evening: the two Gestapo agents waiting for Kokoschka's return and the three scientists monitoring the gate's programming board. All vanished, and five homing belts were missing; so the evidence pointed to a group of traitors within the institute who had become convinced that Hitler would lose the war even with the advantage of exotic weapons brought back from the future, and who had defected to another age rather than stay in a doomed Berlin.

But Berlin was not doomed. Klietmann would not entertain that possibility. Berlin was the new Rome; the Third Reich would last a thousand years. Now that the SS was being given the chance to find and kill Krieger, *der Führer*'s dream would be protected and fulfilled. Once they had eliminated Krieger, who was the main threat to the gate and whose execution was the most urgent task before them, they would then focus on finding Kokoschka and the other traitors. Wherever those swine had gone, in whatever distant year and place they had taken refuge, Klietmann and his SS brethren would exterminate them with extreme prejudice and great pleasure.

Now Dr. Theodore Juttner—director of the institute since the murders of Penlovski, Januskaya, and Volkaw, and the disappearances on March 16—turned to Erich and said, "We've perhaps found Krieger, *Obersturmführer* Klietmann. Get your men ready to go."

"We're ready, Doctor," Erich said. Ready for the future, he thought, ready for Krieger, ready for glory.

# SIX

At three-forty on Saturday afternoon, January 14, little more than one day after her first visit, Thelma returned to The Bluebird of Happiness Motel in her gardener's battered white pickup. She had two changes of clothes for each of them, suitcases in which to pack all the stuff, and a couple of thousand rounds of ammunition for the revolvers and the Uzis. She also had the IBM PC in the truck, plus a printer, a variety of software, a box of diskettes, and everything else they would need to make the system work for them.

With the wound in his shoulder only four days old, Stefan was recuperating surprisingly fast, although he was not ready to do any lifting, heavy or otherwise. He stayed in the motel room with Chris and packed the suitcases while Laura and Thelma moved the computer boxes to the trunk and back seat of the Buick.

The storm had passed during the night. Shredded gray clouds hung beardlike from the sky. The day had warmed to sixty-five degrees, and the air smelled clean.

Closing the Buick's trunk on the last of the boxes, Laura said, "You went shopping in that wig and those glasses, those *teeth?*"

"Nah," Thelma said, removing the stage teeth and putting them in a jacket pocket because they made her lisp when she talked. "Up close a salesclerk might've recognized me, and being disguised would arouse more attention than if I shopped as myself. But after I'd bought everything, I drove the truck to the deserted end of another shopping center's parking lot and made myself look like a cross between Harpo Marx and Bucky Beaver before heading here, just in case someone in another car looked over at me in traffic. You know, Shane, I sorta like this kind of intrigue. Maybe I'm the reincarnation of Mata Hari,'cause when I think about seducing men to learn their secrets and then selling the secrets to a foreign government, I get delicious chills.''

''It's the part about seducing men that gives you chills,'' Laura said, ''not the secret-selling part. You're no spy, just a lech.''

Thelma gave her the keys to the house in Palm Springs. ''There's no full-time staff there. We just call a housekeeping service to spruce the place up a couple of days before we go. I didn't call them this time, of course, so you're liable to find some dust, but no real filth, and none of the severed heads *you* tend to leave behind.''

''You're a love.''

''There's a gardener. Not full-time like the one at our house in Beverly Hills. This guy just comes around once a week, Tuesday, to mow the lawn, trim the hedges, and trample some flowers so he can charge us to replace them. I'd advise staying away from windows and keeping a low profile on Tuesday, until he comes and goes.''

''We'll hide under the beds.''

''You'll notice a lot of whips and chains under the bed, but don't get the idea Jason and I are kinky. The whips and chains belonged to his mother, and we keep them strictly for sentimental reasons.''

They brought the packed suitcases out of the motel room and put those in the back seat with the other packages that would not fit in the Buick's trunk. After a round of hugs, Thelma said, ''Shane, I'm between night-club appearances for the next three weeks, so if you need me for anything more, you can get hold of me at the house in Beverly Hills, night or day. I'll stay by the phone.'' Reluctantly she left.

Laura was relieved when the truck disappeared in traffic; Thelma was safe, out of it. She dropped the room keys at the motel office, then drove away in the Buick with Chris in the other front seat and Stefan in the back seat with the luggage. She regretted leaving The Bluebird of Happiness because they had been safe there for four days, and there was no guarantee they'd be safe anywhere else in the world.

They stopped at a gunshop first. Because it was best to keep Laura out of sight as much as possible, Stefan went in to buy a box of ammunition for the pistol. They had not put that item on the shopping list they had given Thelma, for at that time they had not known whether they would get the 9mm Parabellum that Stefan wanted. And in fact they had gotten the .38 Colt Commander Mark IV instead.

After the gunshop they drove to Fat Jack's Pizza Party Palace to pick up two canisters of deadly nerve gas. Stefan and Chris waited in the car, under neon signs that were already burning at twilight, though they would not be in their full glory until nightfall.

The canisters were on Jack's desk. They were the size of small household fire extinguishers with a stainless-steel finish instead of fire-red, with a skull-and-crossbones label that said VEXXON/AEROSOL/ WARNING—DEADLY NERVE TOXIN/UNAUTHORIZED POSSESSION IS A FEL-ONY UNDER U.S. LAW, followed by a lot of fine print.

With a finger as plump as an overstuffed sausage, Jack pointed to a half-dollar-size dial on the top of each cylinder. "These here are timers, calibrated in minutes, one to sixty. If you set the timer and push the button in the center of it, you can release the gas remote, sort of like setting off a time bomb. But if you want to release it manually, then you hold the bottom of the canister in one hand, take this pistol-grip handle in your other hand, and just squeeze this loop the way you would a trigger. This crap, released under pressure, will disperse through a five-thousand-square-foot building in a minute and a half, faster if the heating or air conditioning is running. Exposed to light and air, it breaks down fast into nontoxic components, but it remains deadly for forty to sixty minutes. Just three milligrams on the skin kills in thirty seconds."

"The antidote?" Laura asked.

Fat Jack smiled and tapped the sealed, four-inch-square, blue-plastic bags that were fixed to the handles of the cylinders. "Ten capsules in each bag. Two will protect one person. Instructions are in the bag, but I was told you have to take the pills at least one hour before dispersing the gas. Then they'll protect you for three to five hours."

He took her money and put the Vexxon cylinders in a cardboard box labeled MOZZARELLA CHEESE—KEEP REFRIGERATED. As he put the lid on the box, he laughed and shook his head.

"What's wrong?" Laura asked.

"It just tickles me," Fat Jack said. "A looker like you, clearly well educated, with a little boy . . . if someone like *you* is involved in shit like this, society must be really coming apart at the seams a lot faster than I ever hoped. Maybe I will live to see the day when the establishment falls, when anarchy rules, when the only laws are those that individuals make between themselves and seal with a handshake."

As an afterthought, he lifted the lid on the box, plucked a few green slips of paper from a desk drawer, and dropped them on top of the cylinders of Vexxon.

"What're those?" Laura asked.

"You're a good customer," Fat Jack said, "so I'm throwing in a few coupons for free pizza."

Thelma and Jason's house in Palm Springs was indeed secluded. It was a curious but attractive cross between Spanish and Southwest adobe-style architecture on a one-acre property surrounded by a nine-foot-tall, peach-colored stucco wall that was interrupted only by the entrance and exit from the circular driveway. The grounds were heavily planted with olive trees, palms, and ficus, so neighbors were screened out on three sides, with only the front of the house revealed.

Though they arrived at eight o'clock that Saturday night, after driving into the desert from Fat Jack's place in Anaheim, the house and grounds were visible in detail because they were illuminated by cunningly designed, photocell-controlled landscape lighting that provided both security and aesthetic value. Palm and fern shadows made dramatic patterns on stucco walls.

Thelma had given them the remote garage door opener, so they drove the Buick into the three-car garage and entered the house through the connecting door to the laundry room—after deactivating the alarm system with the code Thelma had also given them.

It was far smaller than the Gaines's mansion in Beverly Hills, but still sizable, with ten rooms and four baths. The unique stamp of Steve Chase, the interior designer of choice in Palm Springs, was on every room: dramatic spaces dramatically lit; simple colors—warm apricot, dusty salmon—accented with turquoise here and there; suede walls, cedar ceilings; here, copper tables with a rich patina; there, granite tables contrasting interestingly with comfortably upholstered furniture in a variety of textured fabrics; elegant yet livable.

In the kitchen Laura found most of the pantry bare except for one shelf of canned goods. As they were all too tired to go grocery shopping, they made a dinner of what was at hand. Even if Laura had broken into the house without a key and had not known who owned the place, she would have realized it belonged to Thelma and Jason as soon as she looked in the pantry, for she could not imagine that any other pair of millionaires would still be so childlike at heart as to stock their larder with Chef Boyardee canned ravioli and spaghetti. Chris was delighted. For dessert they finished off two boxes of chocolate-covered Klondike ice-cream nuggets that they found in the otherwise empty freezer.

Laura and Chris shared the king-size bed in the master bedroom, and Stefan bunked across the hall in a guest room. Though she had reengaged the perimeter alarm system that monitored every door and window, though a loaded Uzi was on the floor beside her, though a loaded .38 was on the nightstand, and though no one in the world but Thelma could know where they were, Laura slept only fitfully. Each time she woke, she sat straight up in bed, listening for noises in the night—stealthy footsteps, whispering voices.

Toward morning, when she could not get back to sleep, she stared at the shadowy ceiling for a long time, thinking about something that Stefan had said a couple of days ago when explaining some of the fine points of time travel and the changes that travelers could effect in their futures: *Destiny struggles to reassert the pattern that was meant to be.* When Stefan had saved her from the junkie in the grocery store in 1963, fate eventually had brought her to another pedophile, Willy Sheener, in 1967. She had been destined to be an orphan, so when she found a new home with the Dockweilers, fate had conspired to shock Nina Dockweiler with a fatal heart attack, sending Laura back to the orphanage again.

*Destiny struggles to reassert the pattern that was meant to be.*

What next?

In the pattern that was meant to be, Chris had never been born. Therefore would fate arrange his death soon, to bring events back as close as possible to those which had been ordained and with which Stefan Krieger had meddled? She had been destined to spend her life in a wheelchair before Stefan held Dr. Paul Markwell at gunpoint and prevented him from delivering her. So perhaps now fate would put her in the way of Gestapo gunfire that would sever her spine and render her paraplegic in accordance with the original plan.

How long did the forces of destiny strive to reassert the pattern after a change had been made in it? Chris had been alive for more than eight years. Was that long enough for destiny to decide that his existence was acceptable? She had lived thirty-four years out of a wheelchair. Was destiny still troubling itself with that unnatural squiggle in the ordained design?

*Destiny struggles to reassert the pattern that was meant to be.*

As dawn's light glowed softly at the edges of the drapes, Laura tossed and turned, growing angry but not sure at whom or what her anger could be directed. What *was* destiny? What was the power that shaped the patterns and attempted to enforce them? God? Should she be raging at God—or begging Him to let her son live and to spare her from the life of a cripple? Or was the power behind destiny merely a natural mechanism, a force no different in origin from gravity or magnetism?

Because there was no logical target at which her emotions could be vented, Laura felt her anger slowly metamorphosing to fear. They seemed to be safe at the Gaines's Palm Springs house. After passing one uneventful night in the place, they almost could be assured that their presence would never be public knowledge, for otherwise killers from the past no doubt already would have appeared. Yet Laura was afraid.

Something bad was going to happen. Something very bad.

Trouble was coming, but she did not know from what direction.

Lightning. Soon.

Too bad the old saw wasn't true: In fact lightning did strike twice in the same place, three times, a hundred, and she was the reliable rod that drew it.

# SEVEN

Dr. Juttner entered the last of the numbers in the programming board that controlled the gate. To Erich Klietmann, he said, "You and your men will be traveling to the vicinity of Palm Springs, California, in January 1989."

"Palm Springs?" Klietmann was surprised.

"Yes. Of course, we had expected you'd have to go somewhere in the Los Angeles or Orange County area, where you would have found your young-executive dress more appropriate than in a resort town, but you'll still pass without notice. For one thing, it's winter there, and even in the desert dark suits will be appropriate for the season." Juttner handed Klietmann a sheet of paper on which he had written directions. "Here's where you'll find the woman and the boy."

Folding the paper and putting it in an inside coat pocket, the lieutenant said, "What about Krieger?"

"The researchers didn't find mention of him," Juttner said, "but he must be with the woman and the boy. If you don't see him, then do your best to take the woman and boy captive. If you have to torture them to learn Krieger's whereabouts, so be it. And if worse comes to worst and they won't give you Krieger—kill them. That might draw him into the open somewhere down the time line."

"We'll find him, Doctor."

Klietmann, Hubatsch, von Manstein, and Bracher were all wearing their homing belts beneath their Yves St. Laurent suits. Carrying their Mark Cross attaché cases, they walked to the gate, stepped up into that giant barrel, and moved toward the two-thirds point where they would pass in a wink from 1944 to 1989.

The lieutenant was afraid but also exhilarated. He was the iron fist of Hitler, from which Krieger could not hide even forty-five years in the future.

# EIGHT

On their first full day in the Palm Springs house, Sunday the fifteenth of January, they set up the computer, and Laura instructed Stefan in its use. IBM's operating program and the software for the tasks they needed to perform were extremely user-friendly, and though by nightfall Stefan was far from expert at operating the computer, he was able to understand how it functioned, how it thought. He would not be doing most of the work with the machine, anyway; that would be left to Laura, who was already experienced with the system. His job would be to explain to her the calculations that would have to be done, so she would be able to apply the computer to the solution of the many problems ahead of them.

Stefan's intention was to go back to 1944, using the gate-homing belt he had taken off Kokoschka. The belts were not time machines. The gate itself was the machine, the vehicle of transport, and it remained always in 1944. The belts were in tune with the temporal vibrations of the gate, and they simply brought the traveler home when he pushed the button to activate that link.

"How?" Laura asked when he explained the use of the belt. "How does it take you back?"

"I don't know. Would you know *how* a microchip functions inside a computer? No. But that doesn't prevent you from using the computer any more than my ignorance prevents me from using the gate."

Having returned to the institute in 1944, having seized control of the main lab, Stefan would make two crucial jaunts, each only days into the future from March of '44, to arrange the destruction of the institute. Those two trips had to be meticulously planned, so he would arrive at each destination in *exactly* the geographical location and *precisely* at the time that he desired. Such refined calculations were impossible to make in 1944, not only because computer assistance was unavailable but because in those days marginally—but vitally—less was known then about the angle and rate of rotation of the earth and about other planetary factors that affected a jaunt, which was why time travelers from the institute frequently arrived off schedule by minutes and out of place by miles. With the ultimate numbers provided by the IBM, he could program the gate to deliver him within one yard and within a split second of his desired point of arrival.

They used all of the books that Thelma had bought. These were not merely science and mathematics texts, but histories of the Second World War, in which they could pinpoint the whereabouts of certain major figures on certain dates.

In addition to performing complex calculations for the jaunts, they had to allow time for Stefan to heal. When he returned to 1944, he would be reentering the wolf's lair, and even equipped with nerve gas and a first-rate firearm, he would have to be quick and agile to avoid being killed. "Two weeks," he said. "I think I'll have enough flexibility in the shoulder and arm to go back in two more weeks."

It did not matter if he took two weeks or ten, for when he used Kokoschka's homing belt, he would return to the institute only eleven minutes after Kokoschka had left it. His date of departure from current time would not affect his date of return in 1944.

The only worry was that the Gestapo would find them first and send a hit squad to 1989 to eliminate them before Stefan could return to his era to implement his plan. Though it was their only worry—it was worry enough.

With considerable caution, more than half expecting a sudden flash of lightning and a roll of thunder, they took a break and went grocery shopping Sunday afternoon. Laura, still the object of media attention, remained in the car while Chris and Stefan went into the market. No lightning struck, and they returned to the house with a trunkful of groceries.

Unpacking the market bags in the kitchen, Laura discovered that a third of the sacks contained nothing but snack food: three different kinds of ice-cream bars, plus one quart each of chocolate, rocky road, butter almond, and almond fudge; family-size bags of M&Ms, Kit Kats, Reese's Cups, and Almond Joys; potato chips, pretzels, tortilla chips, cheese popcorn, peanuts; four kinds of cookies; one chocolate cake, one cherry pie, one box of doughnuts, four packages of Ding Dongs.

Stefan was helping her put things away, and she said, "You must have the world's biggest sweet tooth."

"See, this is another thing I find so amazing and wonderful about this future of yours," he said. "Just imagine—there's no longer any nutritional difference between a chocolate cake and a steak. Just as many vitamins and minerals in these potato chips as in a green salad. You can eat nothing but desserts and remain as healthy as a man who eats balanced meals. Incredible! How was this advance achieved?"

Laura turned in time to see Chris slinking out of the kitchen. "Whoa, you little con artist."

Looking sheepish, he said, "Doesn't Mr. Krieger get some funny ideas about our culture?"

"I know where he got this one," she said. "What a sneaky thing to have done."

Chris sighed and tried to sound mournful. "Yeah. But I figure . . . if we're being hunted down by Gestapo agents, we ought to be able to eat as many Ding Dongs as we want, at least, 'cause every meal could be our last." He looked at her sideways to see if she was buying his condemned-man routine.

In fact what the boy said contained enough truth to make his trickery understandable if not excusable, and she could not find the will to punish him.

That night after dinner, Laura changed the dressing on Stefan's wound. The impact of the slug had left an enormous bruise on his chest with the bullet hole at its approximate center, a smaller bruise around the exit point. The suture threads and the inside of the old bandage were crusted with fluid that had seeped from him and dried. After she carefully bathed the wounds, cleaning that material away as much as possible without disturbing the scab, she gently palpated the flesh, producing a trace of clear seepage, but there was no sign of pus formation that would indicate a serious infection. Of course, he might have an abscess within the wound, draining internally, but that was not likely because he had no fever.

"Keep taking the penicillin," she said, "and I think you'll be fine. Doc Brenkshaw did a good job."

While Laura and Stefan spent long hours at the computer Monday and Tuesday, Chris watched television, looked through the bookshelves for something to read, puzzled over a hardcover collection of old Barbarella cartoons—

"Mom, what does orgasm mean?"

"What're you reading? Give me that."

—and generally entertained himself without a fuss. He came to the den once in a while and stood for a minute or two at a time, watching them use the computer. After about a dozen visits he said, "In *Back to the Future* they just had this time-traveling car, and they pushed a few buttons on the dashboard, and they were *off—Pow!*—like that. How come nothing in real life's ever as easy as it is in the movies?"

On Tuesday, January 19, they kept a low profile while the gardener mowed the lawn and trimmed some shrubbery. In four days he was the only person they had seen; no door-to-door salesmen had called, not even a Jehovah's Witness pushing *Watchtower* magazine.

"We're safe here," Stefan said. "Obviously, our presence in the house never becomes public knowledge. If it did, the Gestapo would have visited us already."

Nevertheless Laura kept the perimeter alarm system switched on nearly twenty-four hours a day. And at night she dreamed of destiny reasserting itself, of Chris erased from existence, of waking up to find herself in a wheelchair.

# NINE

They were supposed to arrive at eight o'clock to give them plenty of time to reach the location at which the researchers had pinpointed the woman and the boy, if not Krieger. But when Lieutenant Klietmann blinked and found himself forty-five years beyond his own era, he knew at once that they were a couple of hours late. The sun was too high above the horizon. The temperature was about seventy-five, too warm for an early, winter morning in the desert.

Like a white crack in a blue-glazed bowl, lightning splintered down the sky. Other cracks opened, and sparks flashed above as if struck from the hooves of a bull loose in some celestial china shop.

As the thunder faded, Klietmann turned to see if von Manstein, Hubatsch, and Bracher had made the journey safely. They were with him, all carrying attaché cases, with sunglasses stuck in the breast pockets of their expensive suits.

The problem was that thirty feet beyond the sergeant and the two corporals, a pair of elderly, white-haired women in pastel stretch pants and pastel blouses were standing at a white car near the rear door to a church, staring in astonishment at Klietmann and his squad. They were holding what appeared to be casseroles.

Klietmann glanced around and saw that he and his men had arrived in the parking lot behind the church. There were two other cars in addition to the one that seemed to belong to the women, but there were no other onlookers. The lot was encircled by a wall, so the only way out was past the women and along the side of the church.

Deciding that boldness was the best course, Klietmann walked straight toward the women, as if there was nothing whatsoever unusual about his having materialized out of thin air, and his men followed him. Mesmerized, the women watched them approach.

"Good morning, ladies." Like Krieger, Klietmann had learned to speak English with an American accent in hopes of serving as a deep-cover agent, but he'd been unable to lose his accent entirely, no matter how hard he studied and practiced. Though his own watch was set to local time, he knew he could no longer trust it, so he said, "Could you please be so kind as to tell me what time it is?"

They stared at him.

"The time?" he repeated.

The woman in yellow pastel twisted her wrist without letting go of the casserole, looked at her watch, and said, "Uh, it's ten-forty."

They were two hours and forty minutes late. They couldn't waste time searching for a car to hot-wire, especially not when a perfectly good one was available, with keys, right in front of them. Klietmann was prepared to kill both women for the car. He could not leave their bodies in the parking lot; an alarm would go up when they were found, and shortly thereafter the police would be looking for their car—a nasty complication. He'd have to stuff the bodies in the trunk and take them with him.

The woman in blue pastels said, "Why've you come to us, are you angels?"

Klietmann wondered if she was senile. Angels in pinstripe suits? Then he realized that they were in the vicinity of a church and had appeared miraculously, so it might be logical for a religious woman to assume they were angels, regardless of their clothing. Maybe it would not be necessary to waste time killing them, after all. He said, "Yes, ma'am, we are angels, and God needs your car."

The woman in yellow said, "My Toyota here?"

"Yes, ma'am." The driver's door was standing open, and Klietmann put his attaché on the front seat. "We're on an urgent mission for God, you saw us step through the pearly gate from Heaven right before your eyes, and we must have transportation."

Von Manstein and Bracher had gone around to the other side of the Toyota, opened those doors, and gotten inside.

The woman in blue said, "Shirley, you've been *chosen* to give your car."

"God will return it to you," Klietmann said, "when our work here is done." Remembering the gasoline shortages of his own war-torn era and not sure how plentiful fuel was in 1989, he added: "Of course, no matter how much gas is in the tank now, it'll be full when we return it and perpetually full thereafter. The loaves and fishes thing."

"But there's potato salad in there for the church brunch," the woman in yellow said.

Felix Hubatsch had already opened the rear door on the driver's side and had found the potato salad. Now he took it out of the car and put it on the macadam at the woman's feet.

Klietmann got in, closed the door, heard Hubatsch slam the door behind him, found the keys in the ignition, started the car, and drove out of the church lot. When he looked in the rearview mirror just before turning into the street, the old women were still back there, holding their casseroles, staring after him.

# TEN

Day by day they refined their calculations, and Stefan exercised his left arm and shoulder as much as he dared, trying to prevent it from growing stiff as it healed, hoping to maintain as much muscle tone as possible. On Saturday afternoon, January 21, as their first week in Palm Springs drew to a close, they completed the calculations and arrived at the precise time and space coordinates that Stefan would require for the jaunts he would make once he returned to 1944.

"Now I just need a bit more time to heal," he said, as he stood up from the computer and testingly moved his left arm in circles.

She said, "It's been eleven days since you were shot. Do you still have pain?"

"Some. A deeper, duller pain. And not all the time. But the strength isn't back. I think I'd better wait a few days yet. If it feels all right by next Wednesday, the twenty-fifth, I'll return to the institute then. Sooner, if I improve faster, but certainly no later than next Wednesday.''

That night, Laura woke from a nightmare in which she was confined yet again to a wheelchair and in which destiny, in the form of a faceless man in a black robe, was busily erasing Chris from reality, as if the boy was only a crayon drawing on a pane of glass. She was soaked in sweat, and for a while she sat up in bed, listening for noises in the house but hearing nothing other than her son's steady, low breathing on the bed beside her.

Later, unable to get back to sleep, she lay thinking about Stefan Krieger. He was an interesting man, extremely self-contained and at times hard to figure.

Since Wednesday of the previous week, when he explained that he had become her guardian because he had fallen in love with her and wanted to improve the life she had been meant to live, he'd said nothing more of love. He had not restated his feelings for her, had not subjected her to meaningful looks, had not played the part of a pining suitor. He made his case and was willing to give her time to think about him and get to know him before she decided what she thought of him. She suspected he would wait years, if necessary, and without complaint. He had the patience born of extreme adversity, which was something she understood.

He was quiet, pensive a lot of the time, occasionally downright melancholy, which she supposed was a result of the horrors he had seen in his long-ago Germany. Perhaps that core of sadness had its roots in things he had done himself and had come to regret, things for which he felt he could never atone. After all, he had said that a place in hell was reserved for him. He had revealed no more about his past than what he had told her and Chris in the motel room more than ten days ago. She sensed, however, that he was willing to tell her all the details, those that were a discredit to him as well as those that reflected well on him; he would not conceal anything from her; he was merely waiting for her to decide what she thought of him and whether, in any case, she wanted to know more.

In spite of the sorrow in him, deep as marrow and dark as blood, he had a quiet sense of humor. He was good with Chris and could make the boy laugh, which Laura counted in his favor. His smile was warm and gentle.

She still did not love him, and she did not think that she ever would. She wondered how she could be so sure of that. In fact she lay in the dark bedroom for a couple of hours, wondering, until at last she began to suspect that the reason she could not love him was because he was not Danny. Her Danny had been a unique man, and with him she had known a love as close to perfection as the world allowed. Now, in seeking her affections, Stefan Krieger would be forever in competition with a ghost.

She recognized the pathos in their situation, and she was glumly aware of the loneliness that her attitude assured. In her heart she wanted to be loved and to love in return, but in her relationship with Stefan, she saw only his passion unrequited, her hope unfulfilled.

Beside her, Chris murmured in his sleep, then sighed.

I love you, honey, she thought. I love you so much.

Her son, the only child she could ever have, was the center of her existence now and for the foreseeable future, her primary reason for going on. If anything happened to Chris, Laura knew she would no longer be able to find relief in the dark humor of life; this world in which tragedy and comedy were married in all things would become, for her, exclusively a place of tragedy, too black and bleak to be endured.

# ELEVEN

Three blocks from the church Erich Klietmann pulled the white Toyota to the curb and parked on a side street off Palm Canyon Drive in Palm Springs's main shopping district. Scores of people strolled along the sidewalks, window-shopping. Some of the younger women were wearing shorts and brief tops that Klietmann found not only scandalous but embarrassing, casually displaying their bodies in a way unknown in his own age. Under the iron rule of *der Führer's* National Socialist Workers' Party, such shameless behavior wouldn't be permitted; Hitler's triumph would result in a different world, where morality would be strictly enforced, where these bare-limbed, brassiereless women would parade themselves only at the risk of imprisonment and reeducation, where decadent creatures wouldn't be tolerated. As he watched their buttocks clench and flex beneath their tight shorts, as he watched unrestrained breasts swaying under the thin fabric of T-shirts, what most disturbed Klietmann was that he desperately wanted to lay with every one of these women even if they were representatives of the deviant strains of humanity that Hitler would abolish.

Beside Klietmann, Corporal Rudy von Manstein had unfolded the map of Palm Springs provided by the team of researchers that had located the woman and the boy. He said, "Where do we make the hit?"

From an inside pocket of his suit jacket, Klietmann withdrew the folded paper that Dr. Juttner had given him in the lab. He opened it and read aloud: "On state route 111, approximately six miles north of the Palm Springs city limits, the woman will be arrested by an officer of the California Highway Patrol at eleven-twenty, Wednesday morning, January 25. She will be driving a black Buick Riviera. The boy will be with her and will be taken into protective custody. Apparently Krieger is there, but we're not sure; apparently he escapes from the police officer, but we don't know how."

Von Manstein had already traced a route on the map that would take them out of Palm Springs and onto highway 111.

"We've got thirty-one minutes," Klietmann said, glancing at the dashboard clock.

"We'll make it easily," von Manstein said. "Fifteen minutes at the most."

"If we get there early," Klietmann said, "we can kill Krieger before he slips away from the highway-patrol officer. In any event we have to get there before the woman and boy are taken into custody because it'll be far more difficult to get at them once they're in jail." He turned around to look at Bracher and Hubatsch in the back seat. "Understood?"

They both nodded, but then Sergeant Hubatsch patted the breast pocket of his suit and said, "Sir, what about these sunglasses?"

"What about them?" Klietmann asked impatiently.

"Should we put them on now? Will that help us blend with the local citizenry? I've been studying the people on the street, and though a lot of them are wearing dark glasses, many of them aren't."

Klietmann looked at the pedestrians, trying not to be distracted by scantily clad women, and he saw that Hubatsch was correct. More to the point, he realized that not even one of the men in sight was dressed in the power look preferred by young executives. Maybe all young executives were in their offices at this hour. Whatever the reason for the lack of dark suits and black Bally loafers, Klietmann felt conspicuous even though he and his men were in a car. Because many pedestrians were wearing sunglasses, he decided that wearing his own would give him one thing in common with some of the locals.

When the lieutenant put on his Ray-Bans, so did von Manstein, Bracher, and Hubatsch.

"All right, let's go," Klietmann said.

But before he could pop the emergency brake and put the car in gear, someone knocked on the driver's window beside him. It was a Palm Springs police officer.

# TWELVE

Laura sensed that, one way or the other, their ordeal was soon coming to an end. They would succeed in destroying the institute or die trying, and she had almost reached the point at which an end to fear was desirable regardless of how it was achieved.

Wednesday morning, January 25, Stefan still suffered deep-muscle soreness in his shoulder but no sharp pain. No numbness remained in his hand or arm, which meant the bullet had not damaged any nerves. Because he cautiously had exercised every day, he had more than half of his usual strength in his left arm and shoulder, just enough to make him confident that he would be able to implement his plan. But Laura could see that he was afraid of the trip ahead of him.

He put on Kokoschka's gate-homing belt, which Laura had taken from her safe the night that Stefan had arrived wounded on her doorstep. His fear remained apparent, but the moment that he put on the belt, his anxiety was overlaid with a steely determination.

In the kitchen at ten o'clock, each of them, including Chris, took two of the capsules that would render them impervious to the effects of the nerve gas, Vexxon. They washed down the preventive with glasses of Hi-C orange drink.

The three Uzis, one of the .38 revolvers, the silencer-equipped Colt Commander Mark IV, and a small nylon backpack full of books had been loaded into the car.

The two pressurized, stainless-steel bottles of Vexxon were still in the Buick's trunk. After studying the informational pamphlets in the blue plastic bags attached to the containers, Stefan had decided he would need only one cylinder for the job. Vexxon was a designer gas tailored primarily for use indoors—to kill the enemy in barracks, shelters, and bunkers deep underground—rather than against troops in the field. In the open air the stuff dispersed too fast—and broke down too quickly in sunlight—to be effective beyond a radius of two hundred yards from point of release. However, when opened full-cock, a single cylinder could contaminate a fifty-thousand-square-foot structure in a few minutes, which was good enough for his purposes.

At 10:35 they got in the car and left the Gaines's house, heading for the desert off route 111, north of Palm Springs. Laura made sure

Chris's safety harness was buckled, and the boy said, "See, if you had a car that was a time machine, we'd drive back to 1944 in comfort."

Days ago they had taken a night drive to the open desert to find a spot suitable for Stefan's departure. They needed to know the exact geographical location in advance in order to do the calculations that would make it possible for him to return conveniently to them after his work in 1944 was done.

Stefan intended to open the valve on the Vexxon cylinder *before* he pushed the button on the gate-homing belt, so the nerve gas would be dispersing even as he returned through the gate to the institute, killing everyone who was in the lab at the 1944 end of the Lightning Road. Therefore he would be releasing a quantity of the toxin at his point of departure, too, and it seemed prudent to do so only in an isolated place. The street in front of the Gaines's house was less than two hundred yards away, within Vexxon's effective range, and they did not want to kill innocent bystanders.

Besides, though the gas was supposed to remain poisonous only for forty to sixty minutes, Laura was concerned that the deactivated residue, although not lethal, might have unknown, long-range toxic effects. She did not intend to leave any such substance in Thelma and Jason's house.

The day was clear, blue, serene.

When they had driven only a couple of blocks and were descending into a hollow where the road was flanked by huge date palms, Laura thought she saw a strange pulse of light in the fragment of sky that was captured by her rearview mirror. What would lightning be like in a bright, cloudless sky? Not as dramatic as on a storm-clouded day, for it would be competing with the brightness of the sun. What it might look like in fact was the very thing she thought she had seen—a strange, brief *pulse* of brightness.

Though she braked, the Buick was into the bottom of the hollow, and she could no longer see the sky in the rearview mirror, just the hill behind them. She thought she heard a rumble, too, like distant thunder, but she could not be sure because of the roar of the car's air conditioner. She pulled quickly to the side of the road, fumbling with the ventilation controls.

"What's wrong?" Chris asked as she put the car in park, threw open her door, and got out.

Stefan opened the rear door and got out too. "Laura?"

She was looking at the limited expanse of sky that she could see from the bottom of the hollow, using her flattened hand as a visor over her eyes. "You hear that, Stefan?"

In the warm, desert-dry day, a faraway rumble slowly died.

He said, "Could be jet noise."

"No. The last time I thought it might be a jet, it was *them*."

The sky pulsed again, one last time. She did not actually see the lightning itself, not the jagged bolt scored on the heavens, but just the reflection of it in the upper atmosphere, a faint wave of light flushing across the blue vault above.

"They're here," she said.

"Yes," he agreed.

"Somewhere on our way out to route 111, someone's going to stop us, maybe a traffic cop, or maybe we'll be in an accident, so there'll be a public record, and then *they'll* show up. Stefan, we've got to turn around, go back to the house."

"It's no use," he said.

Chris had gotten out of the other side of the car. "He's right, Mom. It doesn't matter what we do. Those time travelers came here 'cause they've already peeked into the future and know where they're gonna find us maybe half an hour from now, maybe ten minutes from now. It doesn't matter if we go back to the house or go on ahead; they've already seen us someplace—maybe even back at the house. See, no matter how much we change our plans, we'll cross their path."

Destiny.

"Shit!" she said and kicked the side of the car, which didn't do any good, didn't even make her feel better. "I *hate* this. How can you hope to win against goddamn time travelers? It's like playing blackjack when the dealer is God."

No more lightning flared.

She said, "Come to think of it, all of life is a blackjack game with God as the dealer, isn't it? So this is no worse. Get in the car, Chris. Let's get on with it."

As she drove through the western neighborhoods of the resort city, Laura's nerves were as taut as garroting wire. She was alert for trouble on all sides, though she knew it would come when and where she least expected it.

Without incident they connected with the northern end of Palm Canyon Drive, then state route 111. Ahead lay twelve miles of mostly barren desert before 111 intersected Interstate 10.

# THIRTEEN

Hoping to avoid catastrophe, Lieutenant Klietmann lowered the driver's window and smiled up at the Palm Springs policeman who had rapped on the glass to get his attention and who was now bending down, squinting in at him. "What is it, officer?"

"Didn't you see the red curb when you parked here?"

"Red curb?" Klietmann said, smiling, wondering what the hell the cop was talking about.

"Now, sir," the officer said in a curiously playful tone, "are you telling me you didn't see the red curb?"

"Yes, sir, of course I saw it."

"I didn't think *you'd* fib," the cop said as if he knew Klietmann and trusted his reputation for honesty, which baffled the lieutenant. "So if you saw the red curb, sir, why'd you park here?"

"Oh, I see," Klietmann said, "parking is restricted to curbs that aren't red. Yes, of course."

The patrolman blinked at the lieutenant. He shifted his attention to von Manstein in the passenger's seat, then to Bracher and Hubatsch in the rear, smiled and nodded at them.

Klietmann did not have to look at his men to know they were on edge. The air in the car was heavy with tension.

When he shifted his gaze to Klietmann, the police officer smiled tentatively and said, "Am I right—you fellas are four preachers?"

"Preachers?" Klietmann said, disconcerted by the question.

"I've got a bit of a deductive mind," the cop said, his tentative smile still holding. "I'm no Sherlock Holmes. But the bumper stickers on your car say 'I Love Jesus' and 'Christ Has Risen.' And there's a Baptist convention in town, and you're all dressed in dark suits."

That was why he had thought he could trust Klietmann not to fib: He believed they were Baptist ministers.

"That's right," Klietmann said at once. "We're with the Baptist convention, officer. Sorry about the illegal parking. We don't have red curbs where I come from. Now if—"

"Where *do* you hail from?" the cop asked, not with suspicion but in an attempt to be friendly.

Klietmann knew a lot about the United States but not enough to carry on a conversation of this sort when he did not control its direction to any degree whatsoever. He believed that Baptists were from the southern part of the country; he wasn't sure if there were any of them in the north or west or east, so he tried to think of a southern state. He said, "I'm from Georgia," before he realized how unlikely that claim seemed when spoken in his German accent.

The smile on the cop's face faltered. Looking past Klietmann to von Manstein, he said, "And where you from, sir?"

Following his lieutenant's lead, but speaking with an even stronger accent, von Manstein said, "Georgia."

From the back seat, before they could be asked, Hubatsch and Bracher said, "Georgia, we're from Georgia," as if that word was magic and would cast a spell over the patrolman.

The cop's smile had vanished altogether. He frowned at Erich Klietmann and said, "Sir, would you mind stepping out of the car for a moment?"

"Certainly, officer," Klietmann said, as he opened his door, noticing how the cop backed up a couple of steps and rested his right hand on the butt of his holstered revolver. "But we're late for a prayer meeting—"

In the back seat Hubatsch snapped open his attaché case and snatched the Uzi from it as quickly as a presidential bodyguard might have done. He did not roll down the window but put the nuzzle against the glass and opened fire on the cop, giving him no time to draw his revolver. The car window blew out as bullets pounded through it. Struck by at least twenty rounds at close range, the cop pitched backward into traffic. Brakes squealed as a car made a hard stop to avoid the body, and across the street display windows shattered as bullets hit a men's clothing shop.

With the cool detachment and quick thinking that made Klietmann proud to be in the *Schutzstaffel,* Martin Bracher got out of the Toyota on his side and loosed a wide arc of fire from the Uzi to add to the chaos and give them a better chance of escaping. Windows imploded in the exclusive shops not only on the side street at the end of which they were parked but all the way across the intersection on the east flank of Palm Canyon Drive as well. People screamed, dropped to the pavement, scuttled for the cover of doorways. Klietmann saw passing cars hit by bullets out on Palm Canyon, and maybe a few drivers were hit or maybe they only panicked, but the vehicles swung wildly from lane to lane; a tan Mercedes sideswiped a delivery truck, and a sleek, red sportscar jumped the curb, crossed the sidewalk, grazed the bole of a palm tree, and plowed into the front of a gift shop.

Klietmann got behind the wheel again and released the emergency brake. He heard Bracher and Hubatsch leap into the car, so he threw the white Toyota in gear and shot forward onto Palm Canyon, hanging a hard left, heading north. He discovered at once that he was on a one-way street, going in the wrong direction. Cursing, he dodged oncoming cars. The Toyota rocked wildly on bad springs, and the glove compartment popped open, emptying its contents in von Manstein's lap. Klietmann turned right at the next intersection. A block later he ran a red light, narrowly avoiding pedestrians in the crosswalk, and turned left onto another avenue that allowed northbound traffic.

"We only have twenty-one minutes," von Manstein said, pointing at the dashboard clock.

"Tell me where to go," Klietmann said. "I'm lost."

"No, you're not," von Manstein said, brushing the contents of the glove compartment—spare keys, paper napkins, a pair of white gloves, individual packets of catsup and mustard, documents of various kinds—off the map that he was still holding open in his lap. "You're not lost. This will connect with Palm Canyon where it becomes a two-way street. From there we head straight north onto route 111."

# FOURTEEN

Approximately six miles north of Palm Springs, where the barren land looked particularly empty, Laura pulled to the shoulder of the highway. She slowly proceeded a few hundred yards until she found the place where the embankment declined almost to the level of the surrounding desert and sloped sufficiently to allow her to drive out onto the flat plain. Aside from a little bunchgrass that bristled in dry clumps and a few gnarly mesquite bushes, the only vegetation was tumbleweed—some green and rooted, some dry and rolling free. The fixed weeds scraped softly against the Buick, and the loose ones flew away on the wind that the car created.

The hard ground had a shale base over which an alkaline sand was drifted and whorled in places. As she had done when they found the place a few nights ago, Laura stayed away from the sand, kept to the bare gray-pink shale. She did not stop until she was three hundred yards from the highway, putting that well-traveled road beyond the radius of Vexxon's open-air effectiveness. She parked not far from an arroyo, a twenty-foot-wide and thirty-foot-deep natural drainage channel formed by flash floods during hundreds of the desert's brief rainy seasons; previously, at night, proceeding with caution but guided only by headlights, they'd been fortunate not to drive into that enormous ditch.

Though the lightning had not been followed by any sign of armed men, urgency informed the moment; Laura, Chris, and Stefan moved as if they could hear a clock ticking toward an impending detonation. While Laura removed one of the thirty-pound Vexxon cylinders from the trunk of the Buick, Stefan put his arms through the straps on the small, green nylon backpack that was full of books, pulled the chest strap in place, and pressed the Velcro fasteners together. Chris carried one of the Uzis twenty feet from the car to the center of a circle of utterly barren shale where not even a tuft of bunchgrass grew, which looked like a good staging area for Stefan's debarkation from 1989. Laura joined the boy there, and Stefan followed, holding the silencer-fitted Colt Commander in his right hand.

*   *   *

North of Palm Springs on state route 111, Klietmann was pushing the Toyota as hard as it would go, which was not hard enough. The car had forty thousand miles on the odometer, and no doubt the old woman who owned it never drove faster than fifty, so it wasn't responding well to the demands Klietmann made on it. When he tried to go faster than sixty, the Toyota began to shimmy and sputter, forcing him to ease up.

Nevertheless, just two miles north of the Palm Springs city limits, they fell in behind a California Highway Patrol cruiser, and Klietmann knew they must have caught up with the officer who was going to encounter and arrest Laura Shane and her son. The cop was doing just under fifty-five in a fifty-five-mile-per-hour zone.

"Kill him," Klietmann said over his shoulder to Corporal Martin Bracher, who was in the right rear seat.

Klietmann glanced in the rearview mirror, saw no traffic behind; there was oncoming traffic, but it was in the southbound lanes. He swung into the northbound passing lane and began to move around the patrol car at sixty.

In the back Bracher rolled down his window. The other rear window was already open because Hubatsch had shot it out when he had killed the Palm Springs cop, so wind roared noisily through the back of the Toyota and reached into the front seat to flutter the map that was still in von Manstein's lap.

The CHP officer glanced over in surprise, for motorists probably seldom dared pass a policeman who was already driving within a couple of miles of the speed limit. When Klietmann pressed the Toyota past sixty, it shimmied and coughed, still accelerating but grudgingly. The policeman took note of this indication of Klietmann's determined breaking of the law, and he tapped his siren lightly, making it whoop and die, which apparently meant that Klietmann was to fall back and pull to the shoulder of the road.

Instead the lieutenant nursed the protesting Toyota up to sixty-four miles an hour, where it seemed in danger of shaking itself apart, and that was just fast enough to pull slightly ahead of the startled CHP officer, bringing Bracher's rear window in line with the patrol car's front window. The corporal opened fire with his Uzi.

The police cruiser's windows imploded, and the officer was dead in an instant. He had to be dead, for he had not seen the attack coming and surely had taken several rounds in the head and upper body. The patrol car swung toward the Toyota and brushed it before Klietmann could get out of the way, then veered toward the shoulder of the road.

Klietmann braked, falling back from the out-of-control cruiser.

The four-lane highway was elevated about ten feet above the desert floor, and the patrol car shot past the unguarded brink of the shoulder. It was airborne for a few seconds, then came down so hard that some of its tires no doubt blew out on impact. Two doors popped open, including that on the driver's side.

As Klietmann moved into the right lane and drove slowly by the wreckage, von Manstein said, "I can see him in there, slumped over the wheel. He's no more trouble to us."

Oncoming drivers had witnessed the patrol car's spectacular flight. They pulled to the verge on their side of route 111. When Klietmann glanced in his rearview mirror, he saw people getting out of those vehicles, good Samaritans hurrying across the highway to the CHP officer's rescue. If some of them realized why the cruiser had crashed, they had decided not to pursue Klietmann and bring him to justice. Which was wise.

He accelerated again, glanced at the odometer, and said, "Three miles from here, that cop would've arrested the woman and boy. So be on the lookout for a black Buick. Three miles."

Standing in the bright desert sun on the patch of barren shale near the Buick, Laura watched Stefan slip the strap of the Uzi over his right shoulder. The carbine hung freely and did not interfere with the back-pack full of books.

"But now I wonder if I should take it," he said. "If the nerve gas works as well as it ought to, I probably won't even need the pistol, let alone a submachine gun."

"Take it," Laura said grimly.

He nodded. "You're right. Who knows."

"Too bad you don't have a couple of grenades too," Chris said. "Grenades would be good."

"Let's hope it doesn't get *that* nasty back there," Stefan said.

He switched off the pistol's safeties and held it ready in his right hand. Gripping the canister of Vexxon by its heavy-duty, fire-extinguisher-type handle, he picked it up with his left hand and tested its weight to see how his injured shoulder would react.

"Hurts a little," he said. "Pulls at the wound. But it's not bad, and I'll be able to control it."

They had cut the wire on the canister's trigger, which allowed the manual venting of the Vexxon. He curled his finger through that release loop.

When he finished his work in 1944, he would make a final jaunt to their time again, 1989, and the plan was for him to arrive only five minutes after he departed. Now he said, "I'll see you very soon. You'll hardly know I'm gone."

Suddenly Laura was afraid that he would never return. She put a hand to his face and kissed him on the cheek. "Good luck, Stefan."

It was not a kiss that a lover might have given, nor was there even a promise of passion; it was just the affectionate kiss of a friend, the kiss of a woman who owed eternal gratitude but who did not owe her heart. She saw an awareness of that in his eyes. At the core, in spite of flashes of humor, he was a melancholy man, and she wished that she could make him happy. She regretted that she could not at least pretend to feel more for him; yet she knew he would see through any such pretense.

"I want you to come back," she said. "I really do. Very much."

"That's enough." He looked at Chris and said, "Take care of your mother while I'm gone."

"I'll try," Chris said. "But she's pretty good at taking care of herself."

Laura pulled her son to her side.

Stefan lifted the thirty-pound Vexxon cylinder higher, squeezed the release loop.

As the gas vented under high pressure with a sound like a dozen snakes hissing at once, Laura was seized by a brief panic, certain that the capsules they had taken would not protect them from the nerve toxin, that they would drop to the ground, twitching in the grip of muscle spasms and convulsions, where they would die in thirty seconds. Vexxon was colorless but not odorless or tasteless; even in the open air, where it dispersed quickly, she detected a sweet odor of apricots and a tart, nauseating taste that seemed half lemon juice and half spoiled milk. But in spite of what she could smell and taste, she felt no adverse effects.

Holding the pistol across his body, Stefan reached beneath his shirt with a free finger of his gun hand and pressed the button on the homing belt three times.

Von Manstein was the first to spot the black car standing in that expanse of white sand and pale rock, a few hundred yards east of the highway. He called it to their attention.

Of course, Lieutenant Klietmann could not see the make of the car from so far away, but he was sure it was the one for which they were searching. Three people stood together near the car; they were hardly more than stick figures at that distance, and they appeared to shimmer like mirages in the desert sun, but Klietmann could see that two of them were adults, the other a child.

Abruptly one of the adults vanished. It was not a trick of the desert air and light. The figure did not shimmer into view again a moment later. It was gone, and Klietmann knew that it had been Stefan Krieger.

"He went back!" Bracher said, astonished.

"Why would he go back," von Manstein said, "when everyone at the institute wants his ass?"

"Worse," Hubatsch said from behind the lieutenant. "He came to 1989 days before we did. So that belt of his will have taken him back to the same point, to the day that Kokoschka shot him—to just eleven minutes after Kokoschka shot him. Yet we know for a fact he never returned that day. What the hell's going on here?"

Klietmann was worried, too, but he didn't have time to figure out what was going on. His job was to kill the woman and her son if not Krieger. He said, "Get ready," and he slowed the Toyota to look for a way down the embankment.

Hubatsch and Bracher had already withdrawn the Uzis from their attaché cases in Palm Springs. Now von Manstein armed himself with his weapon.

The land rose to meet the highway. Klietmann swung the Toyota off the pavement, down the sloped embankment, and onto the desert floor, heading toward the woman and the boy.

When Stefan activated the homing belt, the air became heavy, and Laura felt a great, invisible weight pressing on her. She grimaced at the stench of hot electrical wiring and burnt insulation, overlaid by the scent of ozone, underlaid by the apricot smell of the Vexxon. The air pressure grew, the blend of odors intensified, and Stefan left her world with a sudden, loud *pop*. For an instant there seemed to be no air to breathe, but the brief vacuum was followed by a blustery inrush of hot wind tainted by the faintly alkaline smell of the desert.

Standing close at her side and holding fast to her, Chris said, "Wow! Wasn't that something, Mom, wasn't that great?"

She did not answer because she noticed a white car driving off state route 111, onto the desert floor. It turned toward them and leaped forward as its driver accelerated.

"Chris, get in front of the Buick. Stay down!"

He saw the oncoming vehicle and obeyed her without question.

She ran to the open door of the Buick and snatched one of the submachine guns off the seat. She stepped to the rear, standing by the open trunk, and faced the oncoming car.

It was less than two hundred yards away, closing fast. Sunlight starred and flashed off the chrome, coruscated across the windshield.

She considered the possibility that the occupants were not German agents from 1944 but innocent people. However that was so unlikely, she could not allow the possibility to inhibit her.

*Destiny struggles to reassert the pattern that was meant to be.*

No. Damn it, no.

When the white car was within one hundred yards, she squeezed off two solid bursts from the Uzi and saw bullets punch at least two holes in the windshield. The rest of the tempered glass instantly crazed.

The car—she could see now that it was a Toyota—spun out, turning a full three hundred and sixty degrees, then ninety degrees more, throwing up clouds of dust, tearing through a couple of still green tumbleweeds. It came to rest about sixty yards away, the front end pointed north, the passenger's side toward her.

Doors flew open on the far side, and Laura knew the occupants were scrambling out of the car where she could not see them, staying low. She opened fire again, not with the hope of hitting them through the Toyota but with the intention of puncturing the fuel tank; then perhaps a lucky spark, struck by a bullet passing through sheet metal, might ignite the gasoline and catch some or all of those men in the sudden flames as they huddled against the far flank of the vehicle. But she emptied the Uzi's extended magazine without igniting a fire, even though she had almost certainly riddled the fuel tank.

She threw down the gun, pulled open the back door of the Buick, and snatched up the other, fully loaded Uzi. She got the .38 Chief's Special from the front seat, too, never taking her eyes off the white Toyota for more than a second or two. She wished that Stefan had left the third submachine gun, after all.

From the other car, sixty yards away, one of the gunmen opened fire with an automatic weapon, and now there was no doubt who they were. As Laura crouched against the side of the Buick, bullets thudded into the open trunk lid, blew out the rear window, tore into the rear fenders, ricocheted off the bumper, bounced off surrounding shale with sharp *cracks,* and kicked up puffs of powdery, white sand.

She heard a couple of rounds cutting the air close to her head—deadly, high-pitched, whispery whines—and she began to edge backward toward the front of the Buick, staying close to it, trying to make as small a target of herself as possible. In a moment she joined Chris where he huddled against the Buick's grille.

The gunman at the Toyota ceased firing.

"Mom?" Chris said fearfully.

"It's all right," she said, trying hard to believe what she told him. "Stefan will be back in less than five minutes, honey. He's got another Uzi, and that'll even the odds a lot. We'll be okay. We only have to hold them off for a few minutes. Just a few minutes."

# FIFTEEN

Kokoschka's belt returned Stefan to the institute in a blink, and he entered the gate with the nozzle on the Vexxon cylinder wide open. He was squeezing the handle and trigger so hard that his hand ached, and the pain already was beginning to travel up his arm into his wounded shoulder.

From within the gloom of the barrel, he could see only a small portion of the lab. He glimpsed two men in dark suits, who were peering in the far end of the gate. They very much resembled Gestapo agents—all of the bastards looked as if they'd been cloned from the same small group of degenerates and fanatics—and he was relieved to know that they could not see him as clearly as he could see them; for a moment at least they would think he was Kokoschka.

He moved forward, the noisily hissing canister of Vexxon held before him in his left hand, the pistol in his right hand, and before the men in the lab realized something was wrong, the nerve gas hit them. They dropped to the floor, below the elevated gate, and by the time Stefan stepped down into the laboratory, they were writhing in agony. They had vomited explosively. Blood was running from their nostrils. One of them was on his side, kicking his legs and clawing at his throat; the other was curled fetally on his side and, with fingers hooked like claws, was ripping horribly at his eyes. Near the gate-programming board three men in lab coats—Stefan knew them: Hoepner, Eicke, Schmauser—had collapsed. They tore at themselves as if mad or rabid. All five dying men were trying to scream, but their throats had swollen shut in an instant; they were able to make only faint, pathetic, chilling sounds like the newling of small, tortured animals. Stefan stood among them, physically unaffected but appalled, horrified, and in thirty to forty seconds they were dead.

A cruel justice was served in the use of Vexxon against these men, for it had been Nazi-sponsored researchers who had synthesized the first nerve gas in 1936, an organophosphorous ester called Tabun. Virtually all subsequent nerve gases—which killed by interfering with the transmission of electrical nerve impulses—had been related to that original chemical compound. Including Vexxon. These men in 1944 had been killed by a futuristic weapon, yet it was a substance that had its origins in their own twisted, death-centered society.

Nevertheless Stefan took no satisfaction from these five deaths. He had seen so much killing in his life that even the extermination of the guilty to protect the innocent, even murder in the service of justice, repulsed him. But he could do what he had to do.

He put the pistol on a lab bench. He shrugged the Uzi off his shoulder and put that aside as well.

From a pocket of his jeans, he withdrew a few inches of wire, which he used to lock open the trigger on the Vexxon. He stepped into the ground-floor corridor and put the canister in the center of that hallway. In a few minutes the gas would spread through the building by way of stairwells, elevator shafts, and ventilation ducts.

He was surprised to see that only the night lights illuminated the hallway and that the other labs on the ground floor appeared to be deserted. Leaving the gas to disperse, he returned to the gate-programming board in the main lab to learn the date and time to which Heinrich Kokoschka's homing device had brought him. It was eleven minutes past nine o'clock on the night of March 16.

This was a piece of singularly good luck. Stefan had expected to return to the institute at an hour when most of its staff—some of whom began work as early as six in the morning and some of whom stayed as late as eight o'clock—would be in residence. That would have meant as many as a hundred bodies scattered throughout the four-floor building; and when they were discovered, it would be known that only Stefan Krieger, using Kokoschka's belt and penetrating the institute from the future by way of the gate, could have been responsible. They would realize that he had not come back merely to kill as many of the staff as were on the premises, that he had been up to something else, and they would launch a major investigation to discover the nature of his scheme and undo what damage he had done. But now . . . if the building was mostly empty, he might be able to dispose of the few bodies in a fashion that would cover his presence and direct all suspicion to these dead men.

After five minutes the Vexxon cylinder was empty. The gas had spread throughout the structure, with the exception of the two guard foyers at the front and back entrances, which did not share even ventilation ducts with the rest of the building. Stefan went from floor to floor, room to room, looking for more victims. The only bodies he found were those of the animals in the basement, the first time-travelers, and the sight of their pathetic corpses disturbed him as much or more than the five gassed men.

Stefan returned to the main lab, took five of the special belts from a white cabinet, and buckled the devices on the dead men, over their clothes. He quickly reprogrammed the gate to send the bodies roughly six billion years into the future. He had read somewhere that the sun would have gone nova or would have died in six billion years, and he wanted to dispose of the five men in a place where no one would exist to notice them or to use their belts to home in on the gate.

Dealing with the dead in that silent, deserted building was an eerie business. Repeatedly he froze, certain that he'd heard stealthy movement. A couple of times he even paused in his labors to go in search of the imagined sound but found nothing. Once he looked at one of the dead men behind him, half convinced that the lifeless thing had started to rise, that the soft scrape he'd heard had been its cool hand clawing for a grip on the machinery, as it tried to drag itself erect. That was when he realized how deeply disturbed he had been by bearing witness to so many deaths over so many years.

One by one he dragged the reeking corpses into the gate, shoved them along to the point of transmission, and heaved them across that energy field. Tumbling through the invisible doorway in time, they vanished. At an unimaginably distant point they would reappear— either on an earth long cold and dead, where not even one plant or insect lived, or in the airless and empty space where the planet had existed before being consumed by the exploding sun.

He was exceedingly careful not to venture across the transmission point. If he was suddenly transported to the vacuum of deep space, six billion years hence, he would be dead before he had a chance to press the button on his homing belt and return to the lab.

By the time he disposed of the five cadavers and cleaned up all traces of their messy deaths, he was weary. Fortunately the nerve gas left no apparent residue; there was no need to wipe down every surface in the institute. His wounded shoulder throbbed as badly as in the days immediately after he had been shot.

But at least he had cleverly covered his trail. In the morning it might appear as if Kokoschka, Hoepner, Eicke, Schmauser, and the two Gestapo agents had decided that the Third Reich was doomed and had defected to a future in which peace and plenty could be found.

He remembered the animals in the basement. If he left them in their cages, tests would be run to discover what had killed them, and perhaps the results would cast doubt on the theory that Kokoschka and the others had defected through the gate. Then once again the primary suspect would be Stefan Krieger. Better the animals should disappear. That would be a mystery, but it would not point directly toward the truth, as would the condition of their carcasses.

The hot, pounding pain in his shoulder became hotter, as he used clean lab coats for burial shrouds, bundling groups of animals together, tying them up with cord. Without belts he sent them six billion years into the future. He retrieved the empty nerve-gas canister from the hall and sent that to the far end of time as well.

At last he was ready to make the two crucial jaunts that he hoped would lead to the utter destruction of the institute and the certain defeat of Nazi Germany. Moving to the gate-programming board again, he took a folded sheet of paper from the hip pocket of his jeans; it contained the results of days of calculations that he and Laura had done on the IBM PC in the house in Palm Springs.

If he had been able to return from 1989 with enough explosives to reduce the institute to smoldering rubble, he would have done the job himself, right here, right now. However, in addition to the heavy canister of Vexxon, the rucksack filled with six books, the pistol, and the Uzi, he would have been unable to carry more than forty or fifty pounds of plastique, which was insufficient to the task. The explosives he had planted in the attic and basement had been removed by Ko- koschka a couple of days ago, of course, in local time. He might have come back from 1989 with a couple of cans of gasoline, might have attempted to burn the place to the ground; but many research documents were locked in fireproof file cabinets to which even he did not have access, and only a devastating explosion would split them open and expose their contents to flames.

He could no longer destroy the institute alone.

But he knew who could help him.

Referring to the numbers arrived at with the aid of the IBM PC, he re- programmed the gate to take him three and a half days into the future from that night of March 16. Geographically, he would be arriving on British soil in the heart of the extensive underground shelters beneath the government offices overlooking St. James's Park by Storey's Gate, where bombproof offices and quarters for the prime minister and other officials had been constructed during the Blitz, and where the War Room was still located. Specifically Stefan hoped to arrive in a particu- lar conference room at 7:30 A.M., a jaunt of such precision that only the knowledge and computers available in 1989 could allow the complex calculations to determine the necessary time and space coordinates.

Carrying no weapons, taking with him only the rucksack full of books, he entered the gate, crossed the point of transmission, and materialized in the corner of a low-ceilinged conference room in the center of which stood a large table encircled by twelve chairs. Ten of the chairs were empty. Only two men were present. The first was a male secretary in a British army uniform, a pen in one hand and a pad of paper in the other. The second man, engaged in the dictation of an urgent message, was Winston Churchill.

# SIXTEEN

As he crouched against the Toyota, Klietmann decided they could not have been more inappropriately dressed for their mission if they had been made up as circus clowns. The surrounding desert was mostly white and beige, pale pink and peach, with little vegetation and only a few rock formations significant enough to provide cover.

In their black suits, as they tried to circle and get behind the woman, they would be as visible as bugs on a wedding cake.

Hubatsch, who had been standing near the front of the Toyota, directing short barrages of automatic fire at the Buick, dropped down. "She's gone to the front of the car with the boy, out of sight."

"Local authorities will show up soon," Bracher said, looking west toward state route 111, then southwest in the general direction of the patrol car they had blown off the road four miles back.

"Remove your coats," Klietmann said, stripping out of his own. "White shirts will blend with the landscape better. Bracher, you stay here, prevent the bitch from doubling back this way. Von Manstein and Hubatsch, try to circle around on the right side. Stay well apart and don't move from one point of cover until you've picked out the next. I'll go north and east, around on the left."

"Do we kill her without trying to find out what Krieger is up to?" Bracher asked.

"Yes," Klietmann said at once. "She's too heavily armed to be taken alive. Anyway, I'd bet my honor that Krieger will be coming back to them, returning here through the gate in a few minutes, and we'll be better able to deal with him when he arrives if we've already taken out the woman. Now go. *Go.*"

Hubatsch, followed a few seconds later by von Manstein, left the cover of the Toyota, staying low, moving fast, and heading south-southeast.

Lieutenant Klietmann went north from the Toyota, holding his submachine gun in one hand, running in a crouch, making for the meager cover of a sprawling mesquite bush upon which a few tumbleweeds had gotten hung up.

Laura rose slightly and peered around the front fender of the Buick just in time to see two men in white shirts and black trousers sprint away from the Toyota, heading east toward her but also angling to the south, obviously intending to circle behind her. She stood and squeezed off a short burst at the first man, who made for the cover of a toothlike formation of rock, behind which he safely vanished.

At the sound of gunfire, the second man sprawled flat in a shallow depression that did not entirely conceal him, but the angle of fire and the distance made him a hard target. She did not intend to waste any more rounds.

Besides, even as she saw where the second man had gone to ground, a third gunman opened fire on her from behind the Toyota. Bullets cracked off the Buick, missing her by inches, and she was forced to drop down again.

Stefan would be back in just three or four minutes. Not long. Not long at all. But an eternity.

Chris was sitting with his back against the front bumper of the Buick, his knees drawn up against his chest, hugging himself, and shaking visibly.

"Hang on, kiddo," she said.

He looked at her but said nothing. Through all the terrors they had endured in the past couple of weeks, she had not seen him look so dispirited. His face was pale and slack. He realized that this game of hide and seek had never been a game at all for anyone but him, that nothing *was* in fact as easy as in the movies, and this frightening perception brought to his gaze a bleak detachment that scared Laura.

"Hang on," she repeated, then scrambled past him to the other front fender, on the driver's side, where she crouched to study the desert to the north of them.

She was worried that other men were circling her on that flank. She could not let them do that because then the Buick would be of no use as a barricade, and there would be no place to run except into the open desert, where they would kill her and Chris within fifty yards. The Buick was the only good cover around. She had to keep the Buick between her and them.

She could see no one out there on her north flank. The land was more uneven in that direction, with a few low spines of rock, a few drifts of white sand, and no doubt many man-size depressions in the desert floor that were not visible from her position, places where a stalker might even now be taking cover. But the only things that moved were three dry tumbleweeds; they rolled slowly, erratically, in the mild, inconstant breeze.

She slipped past Chris and returned to the other fender in time to see that the two men to the south were already on the move again. They were thirty yards south of her but only twenty yards in front of the Buick, closing with frightening speed. Though the leader was staying low and weaving as he ran, the follower was bolder; perhaps he thought Laura's attention would be focused on the front man.

She fooled him, stood up, leaned out from the Buick as far as she had to, using it for cover as best she could, and squeezed off a two-second burst. The gunman at the Toyota opened fire on her, giving his buddies cover, but she hit the second running man hard enough to lift him off his feet and pitch him through a bristling manzanita.

Though not dead, he was clearly out of action, for his screams were so shrill and agonized, there could be no doubt he was mortally wounded.

As she dropped down below the line of fire again, she found that she was grinning fiercely. She was intensely pleased by the pain and horror that the wounded man's screams conveyed. Her savage reaction, the primitive power of her thirst for blood and revenge, startled her, but she held fast to it because she sensed that she would be a better and more clever fighter while in the spell of that primal rage.

One down. Perhaps only two more to go.

And soon Stefan would be here. No matter how long his work required in 1944, Stefan would program the gate to bring him back here shortly after he had left. He would rejoin her—and enter the fight—in only two or three minutes.

# SEVENTEEN

The prime minister happened to be looking directly at Stefan when he materialized, but the man in uniform—a sergeant—became aware of him because of the discharge of electrical energy that accompanied his arrival. Thousands of bright snakes of blue-white light wriggled away from Stefan, as if his very flesh had generated them. Perhaps deep crashes of thunder and bolts of lightning shattered the sky in the world above these underground rooms, but some of the displaced energy of time travel was expended here, as well, in a sizzling display that brought the uniformed man straight to his feet in surprise and fear. The hissing serpents of electricity streaked across the floor, up the walls, coalesced briefly on the ceiling, then dissipated, leaving everyone unharmed; the only damage was to a large wall map of Europe, which had been seared in several places but not set aflame.

"Guards!" the sergeant shouted. He was unarmed but evidently quite sure that his cry would be heard and answered swiftly, for he repeated it only once and made no move toward the door. "Guards!"

"Mr. Churchill, please," Stefan said, ignoring the sergeant, "I'm not here to do you any harm."

The door flew open and two British soldiers entered the room, one holding a revolver, the other an automatic carbine.

Speaking hastily, afraid he was about to be shot, Stefan said, "The future of the world depends on your hearing me out, sir, please."

Throughout the excitement, the prime minister had remained seated in the armchair at the end of the table. Stefan believed that he had seen a brief flash of surprise and perhaps even a glimmer of fear on the great man's face, but he would not have bet on it. Now the prime minister looked as bemused and implacable as in every photograph that Stefan had ever seen of him. He raised one hand to the guards: "Hold a moment." When the sergeant began to protest, the prime minister said, "If he had meant to kill me, certainly he would have done so already, on arrival." To Stefan he said, "And that was *some* entrance, sir. As dramatic as any that young Olivier has ever made."

Stefan could not help but smile. He stepped out of the corner, but when he moved toward the table, he saw the guards stiffen, so he stopped and spoke from a distance. "Sir, by the very manner that I've arrived here, you know I'm no ordinary messenger and that what I have to tell you must be . . . unusual. It's also highly sensitive, and you may not wish to have my information conveyed to any ears but yours."

"If you expect us to leave you alone with the PM," the sergeant said, "you're . . . you're mad!"

"He may be mad," the prime minister said, "but he's got flair. You must admit that much, Sergeant. If the guards search him and find no weapons, I'll give the gentleman a bit of my time, as he asks."

"But, sir, you don't know who he is. You don't know *what* he is. The way he exploded into—"

Churchill cut him off. "I know how he arrived, Sergeant. And please remember that only you and I *do* know. I will expect you to remain as tight-lipped about what you've seen here as you would about any other bit of war information that might be considered classified."

Chastened, the sergeant stood to one side and glowered at Stefan while the guards conducted a body search.

They found no weapons, only the books in the rucksack and a few papers in Stefan's pockets. They returned the papers and stacked the books in the middle of the long table, and Stefan was amused to see that they had not noticed the nature of the volumes they'd handled.

Reluctantly, carrying his pencil and dictation pad, the sergeant accompanied the guards out of the room, as the prime minister had instructed. When the door closed, Churchill motioned Stefan to the chair that the sergeant had vacated. They sat in silence a moment, regarding each other with interest. Then the prime minister pointed to a steaming pot that stood on a serving tray. "Tea?"

Twenty minutes later, when Stefan had told only half of the condensed version of his story, the prime minister called for the sergeant in the corridor. "We'll be here a while yet, Sergeant. I will have to delay the War Cabinet meeting by an hour, I'm afraid. Please see that everyone is informed—and with my apologies."

Twenty-five minutes after *that,* Stefan finished.

The prime minister asked a few more questions—surprisingly few but well-thought and to the heart of the matter. Finally he sighed and said, "It's terribly early for a cigar, I suppose, but I'm in the mood to have one. Will you join me?"

"No, thank you, sir."

As he prepared the cigar for smoking, Churchill said, "Aside from your spectacular entrance—which really proves nothing but the existence of a revolutionary means of travel, which might or might not be *time* travel—what evidence do you have to convince a reasonable man that the particulars of your story are true?"

Stefan had expected such a test and was prepared for it. "Sir, because I have been to the future and read portions of your account of the war, I knew you would be in this room at this hour on this day. Furthermore I knew what you would be doing here in the hour before your meeting with the War Cabinet."

Drawing on his cigar, the prime minister raised his eyebrows.

"You were dictating a message to General Alexander in Italy, expressing your concerns about the conduct of the battle for the town of Cassino, which has been dragging on at a terrible cost of life."

Churchill remained inscrutable. He must have been surprised by Stefan's knowledge, but he would not provide encouragement even with a nod or a narrowing of his eyes.

Stefan needed no encouragement because he knew that what he said was correct. "From the account of the war that you will eventually write, I memorized the opening of that message to General Alexander—which you had not even finished dictating to the sergeant when I arrived a short while ago: 'I wish you would explain to me why this passage by Cassino Monastery Hill, et cetera, all on a front of two or three miles, is the only place which you must keep butting at.' "

The prime minister drew on his cigar again, blew out smoke, and studied Stefan intensely. Their chairs were only a few feet apart, and being the object of Churchill's thoughtful scrutiny was more unnerving than Stefan would have expected.

At last the prime minister said, "And you got that information from something I will write in the future?"

Stefan rose from his chair, retrieved the six thick books that the guards had taken from his rucksack—Houghton Mifflin Company's trade-paperback reprints published at $9.95 each—and spread them out on the end of the table in front of Winston Churchill. "This, sir, is your six-volume history of the Second World War, which will stand as the definitive account of that conflict and be hailed as both a great work of history and literature." He was going to add that those books were largely responsible for Churchill's being awarded the Nobel Prize for literature in 1953, but decided not to make that revelation. Life would be less interesting if robbed of such grand surprises.

The prime minister examined the covers of all six books, front and back, and permitted himself a smile when he read the three-line excerpt from the review that had appeared in the *Times Literary Supplement*. He opened one volume and swiftly riffled the pages, not pausing to read anything.

"They aren't elaborate forgeries," Stefan assured him. "If you will read any page at random, you'll recognize your own unique and unmistakable voice. You will—"

"I've no need to read them. I believe you, Stefan Krieger." He pushed the books away and leaned back in his chair. "And I believe I understand why you've come to me. You want me to arrange an aerial bombardment of Berlin, targeted tightly to the district in which this institute of yours is located."

"Yes, Prime Minister, that's exactly right. It must be done before the scientists working at the institute have finished studying the material on nuclear weapons that's been brought back from the future, before they agree upon a means of introducing that information into the German scientific community at large—which they may do any day now. You must act before they come back from the future with something else that might turn the tide against the Allies. I'll give you the precise location of the institute. American and RAF bombers have been making both daylight and night runs on Berlin since the first of the year, after all—"

"There has been considerable uproar in Parliament about bombing cities, even enemy cities," Churchill noted.

"Yes, but it's not as if Berlin can't be hit. Because of the narrowly defined target, of course, this mission will have to take place in daylight. But if you strike that district, if you utterly pulverize that block—"

"Several blocks on all sides of it would have to be reduced to rubble," the prime minister said. "We can't strike with sufficient accuracy to surgically remove the buildings on one block alone."

"Yes, I understand. But you *must* order it, sir. More tons of explosives must be dropped on that district—and within the next few days—than will be dropped on any other scrap of land in the entire European theater at any time in the entire war. Nothing must be left of the institute but *dust*."

The prime minister was silent for a minute or so, watching the thin, bluish plume of his cigar smoke, thinking. Finally: "I'll need to consult with my advisers, of course, but I believe the earliest we could prepare and launch the bombardment would be two days hence, on the twenty-second, but perhaps as late as the twenty-third."

"I think that'll be soon enough," Stefan said with great relief. "But no later. For God's sake, sir, no later."

# EIGHTEEN

As the woman crouched by the driver's-side fender of the Buick and surveyed the desert to the north of her position, Klietmann was watching her from behind a tangle of mesquite and tumbleweed. She did not see him. When she moved to the other fender and turned her back to Klietmann, he got up at once and ran in a crouch toward the next bit of cover, a wind-scalloped knob of rock narrower than he was.

The lieutenant silently cursed the Bally loafers he was wearing, because the soles were too slippery for this kind of action. It now seemed foolish to have come on a mission of assassination dressed like young executives—or Baptist ministers. At least the Ray-Bans were useful. The bright sun glared off every stone and slope of drifted sand; without the sunglasses, he would not have been able to see the ground ahead of him as clearly as he could now, and he certainly would have put a foot wrong and fallen more than once.

He was about to dive for cover again when he heard the woman open fire in the other direction. With this proof that she was distracted, he kept going. Then he heard screaming so shrill and ululant that it hardly sounded like the screaming of a man; it was more like the cry of a wild animal gutted by another creature's claws but still alive.

Shaken, he took cover in a long, narrow basin of rock that was below the woman's line of sight. He crawled on his belly to the end of that trough and lay there, breathing hard. When he raised his head to bring his eyes up to the level of the surrounding ground, he saw that he was fifteen yards directly north of the Buick's rear door. If he could move just a few more yards east, he would be behind the woman, in the perfect position to cut her down.

The screaming faded.

Figuring that the other man to the south of her would lie low for a while because he would be spooked by the death of his partner, Laura shifted again to the other front fender. As she passed Chris, she said, "Two minutes, baby. Two minutes at most."

Crouching against the corner of the car, she surveyed their north flank. The desert out there still seemed untenanted. The breeze had died, and not even the tumbleweed moved.

If there were only three of them, they surely would not leave one man at the Toyota while the other two tried to circle her from the *same* direction. If there were only three, then the two on her south side would have split, one of them going north. Which meant there had to be a fourth man, perhaps even a fifth, out there in the shale and sand and desert scrub to the northwest of the Buick.

But where?

# NINETEEN

As Stefan expressed his gratitude to the prime minister and got up to leave, Churchill pointed to the books on the table and said, ''I wouldn't want you to forget those. If you left them behind—what a temptation to plagiarize myself!''

''It's a mark of your character,'' Stefan said, ''that you haven't importuned me to leave them with you for that very purpose.''

''Nonsense.'' Churchill put his cigar in an ashtray and rose from his chair. ''If I possessed those books now, all written, I'd not be content to have them published just as they are. Undoubtedly I would find things needing improvement, and I'd spend the years immediately after the war tinkering endlessly with them—only to find, upon completion and publication, that I had destroyed the very elements of them that in your future have made them classics.''

Stefan laughed.

''I'm quite serious,'' Churchill said. ''You've told me that my history will be the definitive one. That's enough foreknowledge to suit me. I'll write them as I wrote them, so to speak, and not risk second-guessing myself.''

''Perhaps that's wise,'' Stefan agreed.

As Stefan packed the six books in the rucksack, Churchill stood with his hands behind his back, rocking slightly on his feet. ''There are so many things I'd like to ask you about the future that I'm helping to shape. Things that are of more interest to me than whether I will write successful books or not.''

''I really must be going, sir, but—''

''I know, yes,'' the prime minister said. ''I won't detain you. But tell me at least one thing. Curiosity's killing me. Let's see . . . well, for instance, what of the Soviets after the war?''

Stefan hesitated, closed the rucksack, and said, ''Prime Minister, I'm sorry to tell you that the Soviets will become far more powerful than Britain, rivaled only by the United States.''

Churchill looked surprised for the first time. ''That abominable system of theirs will actually produce economic success, abundance?''

''No, no. Their system will produce economic ruin—but tremendous military power. The Soviets will relentlessly militarize their entire society and eliminate all dissidents. Some say their concentration camps rival those of the Reich.''

The expression on the prime minister's face remained inscrutable, but he could not conceal the troubled look in his eyes. ''Yet they are allies of ours now.''

''Yes, sir. And without them perhaps the war against the Reich wouldn't have been won.''

''Oh, it would be won,'' Churchill said confidently, ''just not as quickly.'' He sighed. ''They say politics makes strange bedfellows, but the alliances necessitated by war make stranger ones yet.''

Stefan was ready to depart.

They shook hands.

''Your institute shall be reduced to pebbles, splinters, dust, and ashes,'' the prime minister said. ''You've my word on that.''

''That's all the assurance I need,'' Stefan said.

He reached beneath his shirt and pushed three times on the button that activated the homing belt's link with the gate.

In what seemed like the same instant, he was in the institute in Berlin. He stepped out of the barrel-like gate and returned to the programming board. Exactly eleven minutes had elapsed on the clock since he had departed for those bombproof rooms below London.

His shoulder still ached, but the pain had not increased. The relentless throbbing, however, was gradually taking a toll on him, and he sat in the programmer's chair for a while, resting.

Then, using more numbers provided by the IBM computer in 1989, he programmed the gate for his next-to-last jaunt. This time he would go five days into the future, arriving at eleven o'clock at night, March 21, in other bombproof, underground quarters—not in London but in his own city of Berlin.

When the gate was ready, he entered it, taking no weapons. This time he did not take the six volumes of Churchill's history, either.

When he crossed the point of transmission inside the gate, the familiar unpleasant tingle passed inward from his skin, through his flesh, into his marrow, then instantly back out again from marrow to flesh to skin.

The windowless, subterranean room in which Stefan arrived was lit by a single lamp on the corner desk and briefly by the crackling light he brought with him. In that weird glow Hitler was clearly revealed.

# TWENTY

One minute.

Laura huddled with Chris against the Buick. Without shifting her position she looked first toward the south where she knew one man was hiding, then to the north where she suspected that other enemies lay concealed.

A preternatural calm had befallen the desert. Windless, the day had no more breath than a corpse. The sun had shed so much of itself upon the arid plain that the land seemed as full of light as the sky; at the far edges of the world, the bright heavens blended into the bright earth with so little demarcation that the horizon effectively disappeared. Though the temperature was only in the high seventies, everything—every bush and rock and weed and sweep of sand—appeared to have been welded by the heat to the object beside it.

One minute.

Surely only a minute or less remained until Stefan would return from 1944, and somehow he would be of great help to them, not only because he had an Uzi but because he was her guardian. Her *guardian*. Although she understood his origins now and was aware that he was not supernatural, in some ways he remained for her a figure larger than life, capable of working wonders.

No movement to the south.

No movement to the north.

"They're coming," Chris said.

"We'll be okay, honey," she said softly. However, her heart not only raced with fear but ached with a sense of loss, as if she knew on some primitive level that her son—the only child she could ever have, the child who had never been meant to live—was already dead, not because of her failure to protect him so much as because destiny would not be thwarted. No. Damn it, no. She would beat fate this time. She would hold on to her boy. She would not lose him as she had lost so many people she had loved over the years. He was hers. He did not belong to destiny. He did not belong to fate. He was hers. He was *hers*. "We'll be okay, honey."

Only half a minute now.

Suddenly she saw movement to the south.


# TWENTY-ONE


In the private study of Hitler's Berlin bunker, the displaced energy of time travel hissed and squirmed away from Stefan in snakes of blazing light, tracing hundreds of serpentine paths across the floor and up the concrete walls, as it had done in the subterranean conference room in London. That bright and noisy phenomenon did not draw guards from other chambers, however, for at that moment Berlin was enduring another bombing by Allied planes; the bunker shook with the impact of blockbusters in the city far above, and even at that depth the thunder of the attack masked the particular sounds of Stefan's arrival.

Hitler turned in his swivel chair to face Stefan. He showed no more surprise than Churchill, though of course he knew about the work of the institute, as Churchill had not, and he understood at once how Stefan had materialized within these private quarters. Furthermore he knew Stefan both as the son of a loyal and early supporter and as an SS officer who had worked long for the cause.

Though Stefan had not expected to see surprise on Hitler's face, he had hoped to see those vulturine features twist with fear. After all, if *der Führer* had read Gestapo reports on recent events at the institute— which he had certainly done—he knew that Stefan stood accused of having killed Penlovski, Januskaya, and Volkaw six days ago, on March 15, fleeing thereafter into the future. He probably thought that Stefan had made this trip illicitly just six days ago, shortly before killing those scientists, and was going to kill him as well. Yet if he was frightened, he controlled his fear; remaining seated, he calmly opened a desk drawer and withdrew a Luger.

Even as the last of the electricity discharged, Stefan threw his arm forth in the Nazi salute, and said with all the false passion he could muster, "Heil Hitler!" To prove quickly that his intentions were not hostile, he dropped to one knee, as if genuflecting before the altar of a church, and bowed his head, making of himself an easy and un-resisting target. *"Mein Führer*, I come to you to clear my name and to alert you to the existence of traitors in the institute and in the Gestapo contingent responsible for the institute's security."

For a long moment the dictator did not speak.

From far above, the shockwaves of the night bombardment passed through the earth, through twenty-foot-thick steel and concrete walls, and filled the bunker with a continuous, low, ominous sound. Each time that a blockbuster hit nearby, the three paintings—removed from the Louvre following the conquest of France—rattled against the walls, and on *der Führer*'s desk a hollow, vibrant sound rose from a tall copper pot filled with pencils.

"Get up, Stefan," Hitler said. "Sit there." He indicated a maroon leather armchair, one of only five pieces of furniture in the cramped, windowless study. He put the Luger on his desk—but within easy reach. "Not just for your honor but for your father's honor and that of the SS, as well, I hope you're as innocent as you claim."

Stefan spoke forcefully because he knew Hitler greatly admired forcefulness. But at all times he also spoke with feigned reverence, as if he truly believed he was in the presence of the man in whom the very spirit of the German people, past and present and future, was embodied. Even more than forcefulness, Hitler was pleased by the awe in which certain of his subordinates held him. It was a thin line to tread, but this was not Stefan's first encounter with the man; he'd had some practice ingratiating himself with this megalomaniac, this viper cloaked in a human disguise.

"*Mein Führer*, it was not I who killed Vladimir Penlovski, Januskaya, and Volkaw. It was Kokoschka. He was a traitor to the Reich, and I caught him in the documents room at the institute just after he had shot Januskaya and Volkaw. He shot me there, as well." Stefan put his right hand against the upper left side of his chest. "I can show you the wound if you wish. Shot, I fled from him to the main lab. I was stunned, not sure how many in the institute were involved in his subversion. I didn't know to whom I could safely turn, so there was only one way to save myself—I fled through the gate to the future before Kokoschka could catch me and finish me off."

"Colonel Kokoschka's report tells a quite different story. He said that he shot you *as* you fled through the gate, after *you* had killed Penlovski and the others."

"If that were so, *Mein Führer*, would I have returned here to attempt to clear my name? If I were a traitor with more faith in the future than I have in you, would I not have stayed in that future, where I was safe, rather than return to you?"

"But were you safe there, Stefan?" Hitler said, and smiled slyly. "As I understand, two Gestapo squads and later an SS squad were sent after you in that distant time."

Stefan was jolted by the mention of an SS squad because he knew it must have been the group that arrived in Palm Springs less than an hour before he left, the group that had occasioned the lightning in the clear desert sky. He was suddenly more worried for Laura and Chris than he had been, because his respect for the dedication and murderous abilities of the SS was far greater than that with which he regarded the Gestapo.

He also realized Hitler had not been told that the Gestapo squads had been outgunned by a woman; he thought Stefan had gone up against them himself, not realizing that Stefan had been comatose throughout those encounters. That played into the lies that Stefan intended to tell, so he said, "My *Führer*, I dealt with those men when they came after me, yes, and did so in good conscience because I knew they were all traitors to you, intent on killing me so that I would not be able to return to you and warn you of the nest of subversives who were—and still are—at work within the institute. Kokoschka has since vanished—am I correct? And so have five other men at the institute, as I understand. They had no faith in the future of the Reich, and fearing that their roles in the murders of March fifteenth would soon be revealed, they fled to the future, to hide in another era."

Stefan paused to let what he had said sink in.

As the explosions far overhead subsided and a lull developed in bombardment, Hitler studied him intently. This man's scrutiny was every bit as direct as that of Winston Churchill, but there was none of the clean, straightforward, man-to-man assessment in it that had marked the prime minister's attitude. Instead Hitler appraised Stefan from the perspective of a self-appointed god viewing one of his own creations for indications of a dangerous mutation. And this was a malign god who had no love for his creatures; he loved only the fact of their obedience.

At last *der Führer* said, "If there are traitors at the institute, what is their goal?"

"To mislead you," Stefan said. "They are presenting you with information about the future in hopes of encouraging you to make serious military blunders. They've told you that in the last year and a half of the war, virtually all of your military decisions will prove to be mistakes, but that's not true. As the future stands now, you will lose the war by only the thinnest of margins. With but a few changes in your strategies, you can *win*."

Hitler's face hardened, and his eyes narrowed, not because he was suspicious of Stefan but because suddenly he was suspicious of those at the institute who had told him he would make fatal military misjudgments in the days ahead. Stefan was encouraging him to believe again in his infallibility, and the madman was only too eager to trust once more in his genius.

"With a few *small* changes in my strategies?" Hitler asked. "And what might those changes be?"

Stefan quickly summarized six alterations in military strategy that he claimed would be decisive in certain key battles to come; in fact those changes would make no difference to the outcome, and the battles of which he spoke were not to be the major engagements of the remainder of the war.

But *der Führer* wanted to believe that he had been very nearly a winner rather than a certain loser, and now he seized upon Stefan's advice as the truth, for it suggested bold strategies only slightly different from those the dictator would have endorsed himself. He rose from his chair and paced the small room in excitement. "From the first reports presented to me by the institute, I've felt there was a *wrongness* in the future they portrayed. I sensed that I could not have managed this war as brilliantly as I have—then suddenly be plagued by such a long string of misjudgments. Oh, yes, we are in a dark period now, but this will not last. When the Allies launch their long-awaited invasion of Europe, they will fail; we will drive them back into the sea.'' He spoke almost in a whisper, though with the mesmerizing passion so familiar from his many public speeches. ''In that failed assault they will have expended most of their reserves; they will have to retreat on a broad front, and they will not be able to regain their strength and mount a new offensive for many months. During that time we will strengthen our hold on Europe, defeat the Russian barbarians, and be stronger than we have ever been!'' He stopped pacing, blinked as if rising from a self-induced trance, and said, ''Yes, what of the invasion of Europe? D-Day as I'm told it came to be called. Reports from the institute tell me that the Allies will land at Normandy.''

''Lies,'' Stefan said. Now they had come to the issue that was the entire purpose behind Stefan's trip to this bunker on this night in March. Hitler had learned from the institute that the beaches of Normandy would be the site of the invasion. In the future that fate had ordained for him, *der Führer* would misjudge the Allies and would prepare for a landing elsewhere, leaving Normandy inadequately defended. He must be encouraged to stick with the strategy that he would have followed had the institute never existed. He must lose the war as fate intended, and it was up to Stefan to undermine the influence of the institute and thereby assure the success of the Normandy invasion.

## TWENTY-TWO

Klietmann had managed to ease a few more yards east, past the Buick, outflanking the woman. He lay prone behind a low spine of white rock veined with pale blue quartz, waiting for Hubatsch to make a move on the south of her. When the woman was thus distracted, Klietmann would spring from concealment and close on her, firing the Uzi as he ran. He would cut her to pieces before she even had a chance to turn and see the face of her executioner.

Come on, Sergeant, don't huddle out there like a cowardly Jew, Klietmann thought savagely. Show yourself. Draw her fire.

An instant later Hubatsch broke from cover, and the woman saw him running. As she focused on Hubatsch, Klietmann leaped up from behind the quartz-veined rock.

# TWENTY-THREE

Leaning forward in the leather armchair in the bunker, Stefan said, "Lies, all lies, my *Führer*. This attempt to misdirect you toward Normandy is the key part of the plot by the subversives at the institute. They want to force you to make the sort of major mistake that you're not really destined to make. They want you to focus on Normandy, when the real invasion will come at—"

"Calais!" Hitler said.

"Yes."

"I have believed it will be in the area of Calais, farther north than Normandy. They will cross the Channel where it's narrowest."

"You're correct, my *Führer*," Stefan said. "Troops *will* be put ashore at Normandy on June seventh—"

Actually it would be June 6, but the weather would be so bad on the sixth that the German High Command would not believe the Allies capable of conducting the operation in such rough seas.

"—but that will be a minor force, a diversion, to pull your elite Panzer divisions to the Normandy coast while the real front subsequently opens near Calais."

This information played to all of the dictator's prejudices and to his belief in his own infallibility. He returned to his chair and thumped his desk with one fist. "*This* has the feel of reality, Stefan. But . . . I have seen documents, selected pages from histories of the war that were brought back from the future—"

"Forgeries," Stefan said, counting on the man's paranoia to make the lie seem plausible. "Rather than show you the real documents from the future, they created forgeries to mislead you."

With luck, Churchill's promised bombardment of the institute would take place tomorrow, eradicating the gate, everyone who knew how to re-create the gate, and every scrap of material that had been brought back from the future. Then *der Führer* would never have the opportunity to conduct a thorough investigation to test Stefan's truthfulness.

Hitler sat in silence for perhaps a minute, staring at the Luger on his desk, thinking intently.

Overhead the bombing began to escalate once more, rattling the paintings on the walls and the pencils in the copper pot.

Stefan waited anxiously to discover if he would be believed.

"How have you come to me?" Hitler asked. "How could you use the gate now? I mean, it has been so closely guarded since the defection of Kokoschka and the other five."

"I didn't come to you by way of the gate," Stefan said. "I came to you straight from the future, using only the time-travel belt."

This was the boldest lie of all, for the belt was not a time machine, only a homing device that could do nothing but bring the wearer back to the institute. He was counting on the ignorance of politicians to save him: They knew a little bit about everything that was done under their rule, but there were no matters that they understood in depth. Hitler knew of the gate and of the nature of time travel, of course, but perhaps only in a general sense; he might lack knowledge of most of the details, such as how the belts actually functioned.

If Hitler realized that Stefan had come from the institute after returning there with Kokoschka's device, he would know that Kokoschka and the other five had been dispatched by Stefan and had not been defectors, after all, at which point the entire elaborate tale of conspiracy would collapse. And Stefan would be a dead man.

Frowning, the dictator said, "You used the belt without the gate? Is that possible?"

Dry-mouthed with fear but speaking with conviction, Stefan said, "Oh, yes, my *Führer,* it is quite simple to . . . adjust the belt and use it not merely to home in on the beacon of the gate but to skip through time as one wishes. And we are fortunate that such is the case, for otherwise, if I'd had to return to the gate to get here, I would have been stopped by the Jews who control it."

"Jews?" Hitler said, startled.

"Yes, sir. The conspiracy within the institute is organized, I believe, by staff members who have Jewish blood but have concealed their heritage."

The madman's face hardened further in a look of sudden anger. "Jews. Always the same problem. Everywhere, the same problem. Now in the institute as well."

Upon hearing that statement, Stefan knew that he had pushed the course of history back toward the proper path.

Destiny struggles to reassert the pattern that was meant to be.

# TWENTY-FOUR

Laura said, "Chris, I think you better hide under the car."

Even as she spoke, the gunman to the southwest of her rose from concealment and sprinted along the edge of the arroyo, angling toward her and toward the meager cover offered by another low dune.

She leaped to her feet, confident that the Buick would shelter her from the man at the Toyota, and opened fire. The first dozen rounds kicked up sand and chips of shale at the running man's heels, but then the bullets caught up with him, tearing into his legs. He went down, screaming, and was hit on the ground as well. He rolled twice and fell over the edge of the arroyo to the floor thirty feet below.

Even as the gunman slipped over that brink, Laura heard automatic fire, not from the Toyota but behind her. Before she could turn to meet the threat, she took several bullets in the back and was thrown forward, facedown on the hard shale.

# TWENTY-FIVE

"Jews," Hitler said again, angrily. Then: "What of this nuclear weapon that they say may win the war for us?"

"Another lie, my *Führer*. Though many attempts to develop such a weapon were made in the future, there were never any successes. This is a fantasy the conspirators have created to further misdirect the resources and energies of the Reich."

A rumbling came through the walls, as if they were not underground but suspended high in the heavens, in a thunderstorm.

The heavy frames of the paintings thumped against the concrete.

The pencils jiggled in the copper pot.

Hitler met Stefan's eyes and studied him for a long time. Then: "I suppose that if you were not loyal to me, you'd simply have come armed and would have killed me the instant you arrived."

He had considered doing just that, for only in killing Adolf Hitler might he expunge some of the stain on his own soul. But that would have been a selfish act, for by killing Hitler he would have radically changed the course of history and would have put the future as he knew it at extreme risk. He could not forget that his future was also Laura's past; if he meddled sufficiently to change the series of events that fate ordained, perhaps he would change the world for the worse in general and for Laura in particular. What if he killed Hitler here and, upon returning to 1989, found a world so drastically altered that for some reason Laura had never even been born?

He wanted to kill this snake in human skin, but he could not take the responsibility for the world that might follow. Common sense said that only a better world could result, but he knew that common sense and fate were mutually exclusive concepts.

"Yes," he said, "had I been a traitor, my *Führer*, I could've done just that. And I worry that the *real* traitors at the institute may sooner or later think of just such a method of assassination."

Hitler paled. "Tomorrow, I shut the institute down. The gate will be closed until I know the staff is purged of traitors."

Churchill's bombers may beat you to the punch, Stefan thought.

"We will win, Stefan, and we'll do so by retaining faith in our destiny, not by playing fortune teller. We will win because it is our fate to win."

"It's our destiny," Stefan agreed. "We're on the side of truth."

Finally the madman smiled. Overcome by a sentimentality that was strange because of the extremely sudden change of mood, Hitler spoke of Stefan's father, Franz, and the early days in Munich: the secret meetings in Anton Drexler's apartment, the public meetings at the beer halls—the *Hofbräuhaus* and *Eberlbräu*.

Stefan listened for a while, pretending to be enthralled, but when Hitler expressed his continued and unshakable faith in the son of Franz Krieger, Stefan seized the opportunity to leave. "And I, my *Führer*, have undying faith in you and will be, forever, your loyal disciple." He stood, saluted the dictator, put one hand under his shirt to the button on the belt, and said, "Now I must return to the future, for I've more work to do in your behalf."

"Go?" Hitler said, rising from the desk chair. "But I thought you'd stay now in your own time? Why go there now that you've cleared your name with me?"

"I think I may know where the traitor Kokoschka has gone, in what corner of the future he's taken refuge. I've got to find him, bring him back, for perhaps only Kokoschka knows the names of the traitors at the institute and can be made to reveal them."

He saluted quickly, pushed the button on the belt, and left the bunker before Hitler could respond.

He returned to the institute on the night of March 16, the night Kokoschka had set out for the San Bernardinos in pursuit of him, never to return. To the best of his ability, he had arranged for the destruction of the institute and had almost ensured Hitler's distrust of any information that came from it. He would have been exhilarated if he had not been so worried about the SS squad that apparently was stalking Laura in 1989.

At the programming board, he entered the computer-derived numbers for the last jaunt that he would ever make: to the desert outside of Palm Springs, where Laura and Chris waited for him on the morning of January 25, 1989.

# TWENTY-SIX

Even as she fell to the ground, Laura knew that her spinal column had been severed or shattered by one of the bullets, for she felt no pain whatsoever—nor any sensation of any kind in any part of her body below the neck.

*Destiny struggles to reassert the pattern that was meant to be.*
The gunfire ceased.

She could move only her head, and only enough to turn and see Chris on his feet in front of the Buick, as paralyzed by terror as she was by the bullet that had cracked her spine. Beyond the boy, hurrying toward them from the north, only fifteen yards away, was a man in sunglasses, a white shirt, and black slacks, carrying a sub-machine gun.

"Chris," she said thickly, "run! *Run!*"

His face twisted with an expression of purest grief, as if he knew he was leaving her to die. Then he ran as fast as his small legs would carry him, east into the desert, and he was smart enough to weave back and forth as he ran, making as difficult a target of himself as possible.

Laura saw the killer raise the submachine gun.

In the main lab, Stefan opened the hinged panel that covered the automatic jaunt-recorder.

A spool of two-inch-wide paper indicated that tonight's uses of the gate had included a jaunt to January 10, 1988, which was the trip Heinrich Kokoschka had made to the San Bernardinos, when he had killed Danny Packard. The tape additionally recorded eight trips to the year A.D. 6,000,000,000—the five men and three bundles of lab animals. Also noted were Stefan's own jaunts: to March 20, 1944, with the latitudes and longitudes of the bomb-proof underground facility near St. James's Park in London; to March 21, 1944, with the precise latitudes and longitudes of Hitler's bunker; and the destination of the jaunt that he had just programmed but not yet made—Palm Springs, January 25, 1989. He tore the tape, pocketed the evidence, and re-spooled the blank paper. He'd already set the programming-board clocks to clear themselves and reset to zero when he passed through the gate. They would know someone had tampered with the records, but they would think it had been Kokoschka and the other defectors covering their trail.

He closed the panel and strapped on the backpack that was filled with Churchill's books. He slipped the strap of the Uzi over his shoulder and picked up the silencer-fitted pistol from the lab bench.

He quickly scanned the room to see if he had left anything behind that might betray his presence here tonight. The IBM printouts were folded away in the pockets of his jeans again. The Vexxon cylinder had long ago been sent into a future where the sun was dead or dying. As far as he could see, he had overlooked nothing.

He stepped into the gate and approached the point of transmission with more hope than he had dared entertain in many years. He had been able to assure the destruction of the institute and the defeat of Nazi Germany through a series of Machiavellian manipulations of time and people, so surely he and Laura would be able to deal with that single squad of SS gunmen who were somewhere in Palm Springs in 1989.

Lying paralyzed upon the desert shale, Laura screamed, "No!" The word came out as a whisper, for she didn't have the strength or power to make more of it.

The submachine gun opened fire on Chris, and for a moment she was sure that the boy was going to weave his way out of range, which was a last desperate fantasy, of course, because he was only a small boy, such a very small boy, with short legs, and he was well within range when the bullets found him, stitching a pattern across the center of his frail back, pitching him into the sand where he lay motionless in spreading blood.

All the unfelt pain of her ruined body would have been as a pinprick compared to the anguish that wrenched her at the sight of her little boy's lifeless body. Through all the tragedies of her life, she had known no pain to equal this. It was as if all the losses she had experienced—the mother she had never known, her sweet father, Nina Dockweiler, gentle Ruthie, and Danny, for whom she would gladly have sacrificed herself—were manifested again in this new brutality that fate insisted she endure, so she felt not only the shattering grief at Chris's death but felt anew the terrible agony of all the deaths that had come before it. She lay paralyzed and unfeeling but in torment, spiritually lacerated, at last emotionally broken on the hateful wheel of fate, no longer able to be brave, no longer able to hope or care. Her boy was dead. She had failed to save him, and with him all prospects of joy had died. She felt horribly alone in a cold and hostile universe, and all she hoped for now was death, emptiness, infinite nothingness, and at last an end to all loss and grief.

She saw the gunman approaching her.

She said, "Kill me, please kill me, finish me," but her voice was so faint that he probably did not hear her.

What had been the point of living? What had been the point of enduring all the tragedies that she had endured? Why had she suffered and gone on with life if it was all to end like this? What cruel consciousness lay behind the workings of the universe that it could even conceive of forcing her to struggle through a troubled life that turned out, in the end, to have no apparent meaning or purpose?

Christopher Robin was dead.

She felt hot tears spilling down her face, but that was all she could feel physically—that and the hardness of the shale against the right side of her face.

In a few steps the gunman reached her, stood over her, and kicked her in the side. She knew he kicked her, for she was looking back along her own immobile body and saw his foot land in her ribs, but she felt nothing whatsoever.

"Kill me," she murmured.

She was suddenly terrified that destiny would try too faithfully to reassert the pattern that was meant to be, in which case she might be permitted to live but only in the wheelchair that Stefan had saved her from when he had meddled with the ordained circumstances of her birth. Chris was the child who had never been a part of destiny's plans, and now he had been scrubbed from existence. But she might not be erased, for it had been *her* destiny to live as a cripple. Now she had a vision of her future: alive, paraplegic or quadriplegic, confined to a wheelchair, but trapped in something else far worse—trapped in a life of tragedy, of bitter memories, of endless sorrow, of unendurable longing for her son, her husband, her father, and all the others she had lost.

"Oh, God, please, please kill me."

Standing over her, the gunman smiled and said, "Well, I must be God's messenger." He laughed unpleasantly. "Anyway, I'm answering your prayer."

Lightning flashed and thunder crashed across the desert.

Thanks to the calculations performed on the computer, Stefan returned to the precise spot in the desert from which he had departed for 1944, exactly five minutes after he had left. The first thing he saw in the too-bright desert light was Laura's bloody body and the SS gunman standing over it. Then beyond them, he saw Chris.

The gunman reacted to the thunder and lightning. He began to turn in search of Stefan.

Stefan pushed the button on his homing belt three times. The air pressure instantly increased; the odor of hot electric wires and ozone filled the day.

The SS thug saw him, brought up the submachine gun, and opened fire, wide of him at first, then bringing the muzzle around to bear straight on him.

Before the bullets hit, Stefan popped out of 1989 and back to the institute on the night of March 16, 1944.

"Shit!" Klietmann said when Krieger slipped into the time stream and away, unhurt.

Bracher was running over from the Toyota, shouting, "That was him! That was him!"

"I know it was him," Klietmann said when Bracher arrived. "Who else would it be—Christ on His second coming?"

"What's he up to?" Bracher said. "What's he doing back there, where's he been, what's this all about?"

"I don't know," Klietmann said irritably. He looked down at the badly wounded woman and said to her, "All I know is that he saw you and your boy's dead body, and he didn't even make an attempt to kill me for what I'd done to you. He cut and ran to save his own skin. What do you think of your hero now?"

She only continued to beg for death.

Stepping back from the woman, Klietmann said, "Bracher, get out of the way."

Bracher moved, and Klietmann squeezed off a burst of perhaps ten or twenty rounds, all of which pierced the woman, killing her instantly.

"We could have questioned her," Corporal Bracher said. "About Krieger, about what he was doing here—"

"She was paralyzed," Klietmann said impatiently. "She could feel nothing. I kicked her in the side, must've broken half her ribs, and she didn't even cry out. You can't torture information from a woman who can feel no pain."

March 16, 1944. The institute.

His heart hammering like a blacksmith's sledge, Stefan jumped down from the gate and ran to the programming board. He pulled the list of computer-derived numbers from his pocket and spread it out on the small programmer's desk that filled a niche in the machinery.

He sat in the chair, picked up a pencil, pulled a tablet from the drawer. His hands shook so badly that he dropped the pencil twice.

He already had the numbers that would put him in that desert five minutes after he had first left it. He could work backward from those figures and find a new set that would put him in the same place four minutes and fifty-five seconds earlier, only five seconds after he had originally left Laura and Chris.

If he was gone only five seconds, the SS assassins would not yet have killed her and the boy by the time Stefan returned. He would be able to add his firepower to the fight, and perhaps that would be enough to change the outcome.

He had learned the necessary mathematics when first assigned to the institute in the autumn of 1943. He could do the calculations. The work was not impossible because he didn't have to begin from scratch;

he had only to refine the computer's numbers, work backward a few minutes.

But he stared at the paper and could not *think* because Laura was dead and Chris was dead.

Without them he had nothing.

You can get them back, he told himself. Damn it, shape up. You can stop it before it happens.

He bent himself to the task, working for nearly an hour. He knew that no one was likely to come to the institute so late at night and discover him, but he repeatedly imagined that he heard footsteps in the ground-floor hall, the *click-click-click* of SS boots. Twice he looked toward the gate, half convinced he had heard the five dead men returning from A.D. 6,000,000,000, somehow revitalized and in search of him.

When he had the numbers and doubled-checked them, he entered them in the board. Carrying the submachine gun in one hand and the pistol in the other, he climbed into the gate and passed through the point of transmission—

—and returned to the institute.

He stood for a moment in the gate, surprised, confused. Then he stepped through the energy field again—

—and returned to the institute.

The explanation hit him with such force that he bent forward as if he actually had been punched in the stomach. He could *not* go back earlier now, for he had already showed up at that place five minutes after leaving it; if he went back now he would be creating a situation in which he would surely be there to see himself arrive the first time. Paradox! The mechanism of the cosmos would not permit a time traveler to encounter himself anywhere along the time stream; when such a jaunt was attempted, it invariably failed. Nature despised a paradox.

In memory he could hear Chris in the sleazy motel room where they had first discussed time travel: "Paradox! Isn't this wild stuff, Mom? Isn't this wild? Isn't this great?" And the charming, excited, boyish laughter.

But there had to be a way.

He returned to the programming board, dropped the guns on the work desk, and sat down.

Sweat was pouring off his brow. He blotted his face on his shirtsleeves.

*Think.*

He stared at the Uzi and wondered if he could send *that* back to her at least. Probably not. He had been carrying the machine gun and the pistol when he had returned to her the first time, so if he sent either of the guns back four minutes and fifty seconds earlier, they would exist twice in the same place when he showed up just four minutes and fifty seconds later. Paradox.

But maybe he could send her something else, something that came from this room, something he had not been carrying with him and that would not, therefore, create a paradox.

He pushed the guns aside, picked up a pencil, and wrote a brief message on a sheet of tablet paper: THE SS WILL KILL YOU AND CHRIS IF YOU STAY AT THE CAR. GET AWAY. HIDE. He paused, thinking. Where could they hide on that flat desert plain? He wrote: MAYBE IN THE ARROYO. He tore the sheet of paper from the tablet. Then as an afterthought he hastily added: THE SECOND CANISTER OF VEXXON. IT'S A WEAPON TOO.

He searched the drawers of the lab bench for a glass beaker with a narrow top, but there were no such vessels in that lab, where all of the research had been related to electromagnetism rather than to chemistry. He went down the hall, searching through other labs, until he found what he needed.

Back in the main lab, carrying the beaker with the note inside it, he entered the gate and approached the point of transmission. He threw the object through the energy field as if he were a man stranded on an island, throwing a bottled message into the sea.

It did not bounce back to him.


—but the brief vacuum was followed by a blustery inrush of hot wind tainted by the faintly alkaline smell of the desert.

Standing close at her side, holding fast to her, delighted by Stefan's magical departure, Chris said, "Wow! Wasn't that something, Mom, wasn't that great?"

She did not answer because she noticed a white car driving off state route 111, onto the desert floor.

Lightning flared, thunder shook the day, startling her, and a glass bottle appeared in midair, fell at her feet, shattering on the shale, and she saw that there had been a paper inside.

Chris snatched the paper from among the shards of glass. With his usual aplomb in these matters, he said, "It must be from Stefan!"

She took it from him, read the words, aware that the white car had turned toward them. She did not understand how and why this message had been sent, but she believed it implicitly. Even as she finished reading, with the lightning and thunder still flickering and rumbling through the sky, she heard the engine of the white car roar.

She looked up and saw the vehicle leap toward them as its driver accelerated. They were almost three hundred yards away, but were closing as fast as the rough desert terrain permitted.

"Chris, get both Uzis from the car and meet me at the edge of the arroyo. Hurry!"

As the boy sprinted to the open door of the nearby Buick, Laura raced to the open trunk. She grabbed the canister of Vexxon, lifted it out, and caught up with Chris before he had reached the brink of the deep, naturally carved water channel, which was a raging river during a flash flood but dry now.

The white car was less than a hundred and fifty yards away.

"Come on," she said, leading him eastward along the brink, we've got to find a way down into the arroyo."

The walls of the channel sloped slightly to the bottom thirty feet below, but only slightly. They were carved by erosion, filled with miniature vertical channels leading down to the main channel, some as narrow as a few inches, some as wide as three and four feet; during a rainstorm, water poured off the surface of the desert, down those gulleys to the floor of the arroyo, where it was carried away in great, surging torrents. In some of the downsloping drains the soil had washed away to reveal rocks here and there that would impede a swift descent, while others were partially blocked by hardy mesquite bushes that had taken root in the very wall of the arroyo.

Little more than a hundred yards away, the car strayed off the shale into sand that pulled at the tires and slowed it down.

When Laura had gone only twenty yards along the edge of the arroyo, she discovered a wide channel leading straight down to the floor of that dry river, unobstructed by rocks or mesquite. What lay before her was essentially a four-foot-wide, thirty-foot-long, water-smoothed, dirt slide.

She dropped the canister of Vexxon into that natural run, and it slipped down halfway before halting.

She took one of the Uzis from Chris, turned to the approaching car, which was now about seventy-five yards away, and opened fire. She saw bullets punch at least two holes in the windshield. The rest of the tempered glass instantly crazed.

The car—she could see now that it was a Toyota—spun out, turning a full three hundred and sixty degrees, then ninety degrees more, throwing up clouds of dust, tearing through a couple of still green tumbleweeds. It came to rest about forty yards from the Buick, sixty yards from her and Chris, the front end pointed north. Doors flew open on the far side. Laura knew the occupants were scrambling out of the car where she would not see them, staying low.

She took the other Uzi from Chris and said, "Into the slide, kiddo.

When you reach the canister of gas, push it ahead of you all the way to the bottom.''

He went down the wall of the arroyo, pulled most of the way by the force of gravity but having to scoot along a couple of times when friction stopped him. It was exactly the kind of daredevil stunt that would have raised a mother's ire under other circumstances, but now she cheered him on.

She pumped at least a hundred rounds into the Toyota, hoping to pierce the fuel tank and set off the gasoline with a bullet-made spark, roasting the bastards as they huddled against the far side. But she emptied the magazine without the desired result.

When she stopped shooting, they took a crack at her. She did not stay long enough to give them a target. With the second Uzi held before her in both hands, she sat on the edge of the arroyo and shoved off into the slide that Chris had already used. In seconds she was at the bottom.

Dry tumbleweeds had blown down to the floor of the gulch from the desert above. Gnarled driftwood, some time-grayed lumber washed from the distant ruins of an old desert shack, and a few stones littered the powder-soft soil that formed the bed of the arroyo. None of those things offered a place to hide or protection from the gunfire that would soon be directed down at them.

"Mom?" Chris said, meaning: What now?

The arroyo would have scores of tributaries spread out across the desert, and many of those tributaries would have tributaries of their own. The drainage network was like a maze. They could not hide in it forever, but perhaps by putting a few branches of the system between themselves and their pursuers, they would gain time to plan an ambush.

She said, "Run, baby. Follow the main arroyo, take the first right-hand branch you come to, and wait there for me."

"What're you going to do?"

"I'll wait for them to look over the edge up there," she said, pointing to the top of the palisades, "then pick them off if I can. Now go, *go*."

He ran.

Leaving the canister of Vexxon in plain sight, Laura returned to the wall of the arroyo down which they'd slid. She went to a different vertical channel, however, one that was carved deeper into the wall, had less of a slope, and was half-blocked at its midpoint by a mesquite bush. She stood in the bottom of that deep hollow, confident that the bush overhead blocked their view of her from the desert above.

To the east, Chris vanished around a turn into a tributary of the main channel.

A moment later she heard voices. She waited, waited, giving them time to feel confident that both she and Chris were gone. Then she stepped out from the erosion channel in the arroyo wall, turned, and swept the top of the cliff with bullets.

Four men were there, peering down, and she killed the first two, the third and fourth leaped backward, out of sight before the arc of fire reached them. One of the bodies lay at the top of the arroyo wall, one arm and leg over the brink. The other fell all the way to the floor of the channel, losing his sunglasses on the way.

March 16, 1944. The institute.

When the bottle with the message did not bounce back to him, Stefan was reasonably confident that it had reached Laura before she had been killed, only seconds after he had first departed for 1944.

Now he returned to the programmer's desk and set to work on the calculations that would return him to the desert a few minutes *after* his previous arrival there. He could make that trip because he would be arriving subsequent to his previous hasty departure, and there would be no possibility of encountering himself, no paradox.

Again the calculations were not terribly difficult because he needed only to work forward from the numbers that the IBM PC had provided him. Though he knew that the time he spent here was not passing in equal measure in the desert of 1989, he was eager to rejoin Laura nevertheless. Even if she had taken the advice of the message in the bottle, even if the future he had seen had been changed and she was still alive, she would have to deal with those SS gunmen, and she would need help.

In forty minutes he had the numbers that he required, and he re-programmed the gate.

Again he opened the panel on the jaunt recorder and tore the evidence off that spool of paper.

Carrying the Uzi and the pistol, gritting his teeth as the dull throbbing in his half-healed shoulder grew worse, he entered the gate.

Lugging both the Vexxon canister and the Uzi, Laura joined Chris in the narrower tributary off the main channel, about sixty feet from the point at which they had descended into the system. Crouching at the corner formed by the two earth walls, she looked back into the primary arroyo from which she had come.

On the desert above, one of the surviving assassins shoved the dangling corpse off the brink, into the deep gulch, apparently to see if she was still immediately below them and if she would be tricked into opening fire. When there was no fire, the two survivors became bolder. One lay at the brink with a submachine gun, covering the other man while he slid down. Then the first gunman covered the second's descent.

When the second man joined the first, Laura stepped boldly around the corner and squeezed off a two-second burst. Both of her pursuers were so startled by her aggressiveness that they did not return fire but threw themselves toward the deep, vertical erosion channels in the arroyo wall, seeking shelter there as she had sheltered while waiting for the opportunity to shoot them off the top of the cliff. Only one of them made it to cover. She blew the other one away.

She stepped back around the corner, picked up the cylinder of nerve gas, and said to Chris, "Come on. Let's hustle."

As they ran along the tributary, seeking yet another branch in the maze, lightning and thunder split the blue sky above.

"Mr. Krieger!" Chris said.

He returned to the desert seven minutes after he had originally departed for his meetings with Churchill and Hitler in 1944, just *two* minutes after his initial return when he had seen Laura and Chris dead at the hands of SS gunmen. There were no bodies this time, just the Buick—and the bullet-riddled Toyota in a different position.

Daring to hope that his scheme had worked, Stefan hurried to the arroyo and ran along the brink, searching for someone, anyone, friend or foe. Before long he saw the three dead men on the floor of the channel, thirty feet below.

There would be a fourth. No SS squad would have been composed of only three men. Somewhere in the network of zigzagging arroyos that crossed the desert like a chain of jagged lightning bolts, Laura was still on the run from the last man.

In the arroyo wall Stefan found a vertical channel that appeared to have been used already; he stripped off his book-filled rucksack, slid to the bottom. On the way down, his back scraped against the earth, and hot pain flared in the partly healed exit wound. At the end of the slope, when he stood up, a wave of dizziness washed through him, and bile rose in his throat.

Somewhere in the maze to the east, automatic weapons chattered.

She halted just inside the mouth of a new tributary and signaled Chris to be quiet.

Breathing through her open mouth, she waited for the last killer to turn the corner into the channel that she had just left. Even in the soft soil, his running footsteps were audible.

She leaned out to gun him down. But he was extremely cautious now; he entered low and at a dead run. When her gunfire alerted him to her position, he crossed the channel and hid against the same wall off which her new tributary opened, so she could get a clear shot at him only if she stepped out into the arroyo where he waited.

In fact she tried that, risking his fire, but when she squeezed off a two-second burst, it ended in less than a second. The Uzi spat out its last ten or twelve rounds, then failed her.

Klietmann heard her Uzi go empty. He looked out from the crevice in the arroyo wall where he was sheltering and saw her throw the gun down. She disappeared into the mouth of the tributary where she had been laying for him.

He considered what he had seen in the Buick, up on the desert: a .38 revolver lying on the driver's seat. He assumed that she had not had time to grab it or, in her haste to get that curious canister from the trunk, had forgotten about the handgun.

She'd had two Uzis, both discarded now. Could she have had two handguns—and left only one in the car?

He thought not. Two automatic carbines made sense because they were useful at a distance and in a variety of circumstances. But unless she was an expert marksman, a handgun would be of little use except at close range, where six shots was about all she would need before she either dealt with her assailant or died at his hands. A second revolver would be superfluous.

Which meant that for self-defense she had—what? That canister? It had looked like nothing more than a chemical fire extinguisher.

He went after her.

The new tributary was narrower than the one before it, just as that one had been narrower than the main channel. It was twenty-five feet deep and only ten feet wide at the mouth, growing shallower and half that narrow as it cut a crooked path through the desert floor. In a hundred yards, it funneled to an end.

At the terminus, she looked for a way out. On two sides the cliffs were too steep, soft, and crumbly to be easily climbed, but the wall behind her sloped at a scalable angle and was studded with mesquite that offered handholds. She knew, however, that they would be only halfway up the slope when their pursuer found them; suspended on that high ground, they would make easy targets.

This was where she would have to make her last stand.

Cornered at the bottom of this big, natural ditch, she looked up at the rectangular patch of blue sky and thought they might have been at the bottom of an enormous grave in a cemetery where only giants were buried.

*Destiny struggles to reassert the pattern that was meant to be.*

She pushed Chris behind her, into the point of the dead-end arroyo. Ahead of her, she could see forty feet back the way they had come, along the five-foot-wide channel, to the point where it angled to the left. He would appear at that turn within a minute or two.

She dropped to her knees with the canister of Vexxon, intending to strip the safety wire off the manual trigger. But the wire was not merely looped and braided through the trigger; it was repeatedly wound and then sealed with solder. It could not be unwound; it had to be cut, and she had nothing with which to cut it.

Maybe a stone. A sharp-edged stone might wear through the wire if scraped across it often enough.

"Get me a stone," she said urgently to the boy behind her. "One with a rough, sharp edge."

As he searched the soft, flood-carried soil that had washed down from the desert floor, looking for a suitable scrap of slate, she examined the automatic timer on the canister, which provided a second means of releasing the gas. It was a simple device: a rotating dial was calibrated in minutes; if you wanted to set the timer for twenty minutes, you twisted the dial until the 20 was lined up with the red mark on the dial frame; when you pushed the button in the center, the countdown began.

The problem was that the dial could be set for no fewer than five minutes. The gunman would reach them sooner than that.

Nevertheless she twisted the dial to 5 and pushed the button that started it ticking.

"Here, Mom," Chris said, presenting her with a blade of slate that just might do the job.

Though the timer was ticking, she set to work, frantically sawing at the strong, twined wire that prevented manual release. Every few seconds she looked up to see if the assassin had found them, but the narrow arroyo ahead of them remained deserted.

Stefan followed the footprints in the soft soil that formed the bed of the arroyo. He had no idea how far behind them he might be. They had only a few minutes' head start, but they were probably moving faster than he was because the pain in his shoulder, exhaustion, and dizziness slowed him.

He had unscrewed the silencer from the pistol, thrown it away, and tucked the handgun under his belt. He carried the Uzi in both hands, at the ready.

Klietmann had thrown away his Ray-Bans because the floor of the arroyo network was shadow-swaddled in many places, especially as they moved into narrower tributaries, where the walls closed in and left less of an opening above for sunlight to enter.

His Bally loafers filled with sand and provided no surer footing here than on the slate of the desert above. Finally he paused, kicked off the shoes, stripped off the socks, and proceeded barefoot, which was a great improvement.

He was not tracking the woman and the boy as swiftly as he would have liked, partly because of the shoes that he had discarded, but mainly because he kept a watch on his backside every step of the way. He had heard and seen the recent display of thunder and lightning; he knew Krieger must have returned. Most likely, as Klietmann stalked the woman and boy, Krieger was stalking him. He did not intend to be meat for *that* tiger.

On the timer two minutes had ticked off.

Laura had sawed almost as long at the wire, initially with the blade of slate that Chris had found, then with a second that he turned up when the first piece crumbled in her fingers. The government could not make a postage stamp that could be trusted to stay on an envelope, could not build a battle tank that was capable of crossing a river on every attempt, could not protect the environment or eliminate poverty, but it sure as hell knew how to procure indestructible wire; this stuff must be some wonder material which they had developed for the space shuttle and for which they'd eventually found more mundane uses; it was the wire God would use to guy the tilting pillars that held up the world.

Her fingers were raw, the second chip of slate was slick with her blood, and only half the strands of wire were cut when the barefoot man in black slacks and a white shirt rounded the bend in the narrow arroyo, forty feet away.

Klietmann edged forward warily, wondering why the hell she was struggling so frantically with the fire extinguisher. Did she really think a blast of chemical fog would disorient him and protect her from submachine-gun fire?

Or was the extinguisher not what it appeared to be? Since arriving in Palm Springs less than two hours ago, he had encountered several things that were not what they appeared to be. A red curb, for instance, did not mean EMERGENCY PARKING, as he had thought, but NO PARKING AT ANY TIME. Who could know? And who could know for sure about this canister with which she was struggling?

She looked up at him, then went right back to work on the handle of the extinguisher.

Klietmann edged along the narrow arroyo, which was now not even wide enough for two men to walk abreast. He would not have gone any closer to her except that he could not see the boy. If she had tucked the boy in some crevice along the way, he would have to force her to reveal the child's whereabouts, for his orders were to kill them all—Krieger and the woman and the boy. He did not think the boy could be a danger to the Reich, but he was not one to question orders.

Stefan found a discarded pair of shoes and a tangled pair of black socks caked with sand. Earlier he had found a pair of sunglasses.

He had never before pursued a man who had undressed during a chase, and at first there seemed to be something funny about it. But then he thought of the world portrayed in the novels of Laura Shane, a world in which comedy and terror were intermingled, a world in which tragedy frequently struck in the middle of a laugh, and suddenly the discarded shoes and socks scared him *because* they were funny; he had the crazy idea that if he laughed, that would be the catalyst of Laura and Chris's deaths.

And if they died this time, he would not be able to save them by going back in time and sending them another message sooner than the one he had sent in the bottle, for the remaining window for such a feat was only five seconds. Even with an IBM PC, he could not split a hair that fine.

In the silt, the prints of the barefoot man led away to the mouth of a tributary. Although the pain in Stefan's half-healed shoulder had wrung sweat from him and left him dizzy, he followed that trail as Robinson Crusoe had followed Friday but with more dread.

With growing despair Laura watched the Nazi assassin approach through the shadows along the earthen corridor. His Uzi was trained on her, but for some reason he did not immediately blow her away. She used that inexplicable period of grace to saw relentlessly at the safety wires on the trigger of the Vexxon canister.

Even in those circumstances she held on to hope, largely because of a line from one of her own novels that had come back to her just a moment ago: *In tragedy and despair, when an endless night seems to have fallen, hope can be found in the realization that the companion of night is not another night, that the companion of night is day, that darkness always gives way to light, and that death rules only half of creation, life the other half.*

Only twenty feet away now, the killer said, "Where is the boy? The boy. Where is the boy?"

She felt Chris against her back, curled in the shadows between her and the wall of the cul-de-sac. She wondered if her body would protect him from the bullets and that if, after killing her, this man would leave without realizing that Chris lived in the dark niche at her back.

The timer on the cylinder clicked. Nerve gas erupted from the nozzle with the rich odor of apricots and the disgusting taste of lemon juice mixed with sour milk.

Klietmann could see nothing escaping the canister, but he could hear it: like a hissing score of serpents.

An instant later he felt as if someone had shoved a hand through his midsection, had seized his stomach in a viselike grip, and had torn that organ loose of him. He doubled over, vomiting explosively on the ground and on his bare feet. With a painful flash that seared the *backs* of his eyes, something seemed to burst in his sinuses, and blood gushed from his nose. As he fell to the floor of the arroyo, he reflexively triggered the Uzi; aware that he was dying and losing all control of himself in the process, he tried as a last effort of will to fall on his side, facing the woman, so the final burst from the submachine gun would take her with him.

Soon after Stefan entered the narrowest of all the tributaries, where the walls seemed to tilt in above him instead of sloping away toward the sky, as they had in the other channels, he heard a long rattle of submachine-gun fire, very near, and he hurried forward. He stumbled a lot and bounced off the earthen walls, but he followed the crooked corridor into the cul-de-sac, where he saw the SS officer dead of Vexxon poisoning.

Beyond the corpse, Laura sat splay-legged, with the canister of nerve gas between her thighs, her bloodied hands hooked around it. Her head hung down, her chin on her breast; she looked as limp and lifeless as a doll made of rags.

"Laura, no," he said in a voice that he hardly recognized as his own. "No, no."

She raised her head and blinked at him, shuddered, and finally smiled weakly. Alive.

"Chris," he said, stepping over the dead man. "Where's Chris?"

She pushed the still hissing canister of nerve gas away from her and moved to one side.

Chris looked out from the dark niche behind her and said, "Mr. Krieger, are you all right? You look like shit. Sorry, Mom, but he really does."

For the first time in more than twenty years—or for the first time in more than *sixty-five* years if you wanted to count those over which he had jumped when he had come to live with Laura in her time—

Stefan Krieger wept. He was surprised by his own tears, for he thought that his life under the Third Reich had left him incapable of weeping for anyone or anything ever again. More surprising still—these first tears in decades were tears of joy.

# 7

◆ ◆ ◆

# Ever After

## ONE

More than an hour later, when the police moved north from the site of the machine-gun attack on the CHP patrolman along route 111, when they found the bullet-riddled Toyota and saw blood on the sand and shale near the brink of the arroyo, when they saw the discarded Uzi, and when they saw Laura and Chris struggling out of the channel near the Buick with the Nissan plates, they expected to find the immediate area littered with bodies, and they were not disappointed. The first three were at the bottom of the nearby gulch, and the fourth was in a distant tributary to which the exhausted woman directed them.

In the days that followed she appeared to cooperate fully with local, state, and federal authorities—yet none of them was satisfied that she was telling the whole truth. The drug dealers who had killed her husband a year ago had finally sent hired killers after her, she said, for they had evidently been afraid that she would identify them. They had attacked with such force at her house near Big Bear and had been so relentless that she'd had to run, and she'd not gone to the police because she did not believe that the authorities could protect her and her son adequately. She had been on the move for fifteen days, ever since that submachine-gun assault on the night of January 10, the first anniversary of her husband's murder; in spite of every precaution she had taken, hitmen found her in Palm Springs, pursued her on route 111, forced her off the highway into the desert, and chased her on foot into the arroyos where she finally got the best of them.

That story—one woman wiping out four experienced hitmen, plus at least the one additional whose head had been found in the alley behind Brenkshaw's house—would have been unbelievable if she had not proved to be a superb marksman, the beneficiary of considerable martial-arts training, and the owner of an illegal arsenal the envy of some third-world countries. During interrogation to determine how she had obtained illegally modified Uzis and a nerve gas kept under lock and key by the army, she had said, "I write novels. It's part of my job to do a lot of research. I've learned how to find out anything I want to know, how to obtain anything I need." Then she gave them Fat Jack, and the raid on his Pizza Party Palace turned up everything she had said it would.

"I don't hold it against her," Fat Jack told the press at his arraignment. "She owes me nothing. None of us owes anybody nothing that we don't *want* to owe them. I'm an anarchist, I love broads like her. Besides, I won't go to prison. I'm too fat, I'd die, it'd be cruel and unusual punishment."

She would not tell them the name of the man she had brought to Carter Brenkshaw's house in the early morning hours of January 11, the man whose bullet wounds the physician had treated. She would only say that he was a good friend who had been staying with her at the house near Big Bear when the hitmen had struck. He was, she insisted, an innocent bystander whose life would be wrecked if she involved him in this sordid affair, and she implied that he was a married man with whom she had been having an affair. He was recovering from the bullet wound quite well, and he had suffered enough.

The authorities pressed her hard on the issue of this nameless lover, but she would not budge, and they were limited in the pressures that they could apply to her, especially since she could afford the finest legal counsel in the country. They never believed the claim that the mystery man was her lover. Little investigation was required to learn that her husband, only one year deceased, had been unusually close to her and that she had not recovered from the loss of him sufficiently to convince anyone that she was able to conduct an affair in the shadow of Danny Packard's memory.

No, she could not explain why none of the dead hitmen carried identification or why they were all dressed identically, or why they had been without their own car and had been forced to steal one from two women at a church, or why they had panicked in downtown Palm Springs and killed a policeman there. The abdominal flesh on two of the bodies had borne the marks of what appeared to be tightly fitted trusses of some kind, yet neither had been wearing such a device, and she knew nothing of that, either. Who knew, she asked, what reasons men like that had for their antisocial actions? That was a mystery that the finest criminologists and sociologists could not adequately explain.

And if all those experts could not begin to shed light on the deepest and truest reasons for such sociopathic behavior, how could she be expected to provide an answer to the more mundane but also more bizarre mystery of the disappearing trusses? Confronted by the woman whose Toyota had been stolen and who claimed that the hitmen had been angels, Laura Shane listened with evident interest, even fascination, but subsequently inquired of the police if they were going to subject her to the cuckoo fantasies of every nut who took an interest in her case.

She was granite.

She was iron.

She was steel.

She could not be broken. The authorities hammered at her as relentlessly and with as much force as the god Thor had wielded his hammer Mjollnir but with no effect. After several days they were angry with her. After several weeks they were furious. After three months they loathed her and wanted to punish her for not shivering in awe of their power. In six months they were weary. In ten months they were bored. In a year they forced themselves to forget her.

In the meantime, of course, they had seen her son, Chris, as the weak link. They had not pounded at him as they had at her, choosing instead to use false affection, guile, trickery, and deceit to lure the boy into making the revelations that his mother refused to make. But when they questioned him about the missing, wounded man, he told them all about Indiana Jones and Luke Skywalker and Han Solo instead. When they tried to pry from him a few details about the events in the arroyos, he told them all about Sir Tommy Toad, servant of the queen, who rented quarters in his house. When they sought to elicit at least a hint of where his mother and he had hidden out—and what they had done—in the sixteen days between January 10 and 25, the boy said, "I slept through it all, I was in a coma, I think I had malaria or maybe even Mars fever, see, and now I got amnesia like Wile E. Coyote got that one time when the Road Runner tricked him into dropping a boulder on his own head." Eventually, frustrated with their inability to get the point, he said, "This is *family* stuff, see. Don't you know about family stuff? I can only talk with my mom about this stuff, and it's nobody else's business. If you start talking family stuff with strangers, pretty soon where do you go when you want to go home?"

To complicate matters for the authorities, Laura Shane publicly apologized to everyone whose property she had appropriated or damaged during the course of her attempts to escape from the hired killers who had been sent after her. To the family whose Buick she had stolen, she gave a new Cadillac. To the man whose Nissan plates she had taken, she gave a new *Nissan*. In every case she made restitution to excess and won friends at every hand.

Her old books went back to press repeatedly, and some of them reappeared on paperback bestseller lists now, years after their original successes. Major film studios bid competitively for the few movie rights to her books that had remained unsold. Rumors, perhaps encouraged by her own agent but very likely true, circulated to the effect that publishers were standing six deep for a chance to pay her a record advance for her next novel.

# TWO

During that year Stefan Krieger missed Laura and Chris terribly, but life at the Gaines's mansion in Beverly Hills was not a hardship. The accommodations were superb; the food was delicious; Jason enjoyed teaching him how film could be manipulated in his home editing studio; and Thelma was unfailingly amusing.

"Listen, Krieger," she said one summer day by the pool. "Maybe you would rather be with them, maybe you're getting tired of hiding here, but consider the alternative. You could be stuck back there in your own age, when there weren't plastic garbage bags, Pop Tarts, Day-Glo underwear, Thelma Ackerson movies, or reruns of *Gilligan's Island*. Count your blessings, that you should find yourself in this enlightened era."

"It's just that . . . ." He stared for a while at the spangles of sunlight on the chlorine-scented water. "Well, I'm afraid that during this year of separation, I'm losing any slim chance I might have had to win her."

"You can't win her, anyway, *Herr* Krieger. She's not a set of cereal containers raffled off at a Tupperware party. A woman like Laura can't be won. She decides when she wants to *give* herself, and that's that."

"You're not very encouraging."

"Being encouraging is not my job—"

"I know—"

"—my job—"

"—yes, yes—"

"—is comedy. Although with my devastating looks, I'd probably be just as successful as a traveling slut—at least in really remote logging camps."

At Christmas Laura and Chris came to stay at the Gaines's house, and her gift to Stefan was a new identity. Although rather closely monitored by various authorities for the better part of the year, she had managed through surrogates to obtain a driver's license, social security card, credit cards, and a passport in the name of Steven Krieger.

She presented them to him on Christmas morning, wrapped in a box from Neiman-Marcus. "All the documents are valid. In *Endless River*, two of my characters are on the run, in need of new identities—"

"Yes," Stefan said, "I read it. Three times."

"The same book three times?" Jason said. They were all sitting around the Christmas tree, eating junk food and drinking cocoa, and Jason was in his cheeriest mood of the year. "Laura, beware this man. He sounds like an obsessive-compulsive to me."

"Well, of course," Thelma said, "to you Hollywood types, anyone who reads *any* book, even once, is viewed either as an intellectual giant or a psychopath. Now, Laura, how *did* you come up with all these convincing-looking, phony papers?"

"They're not phony," Chris said. "They're *real*."

"That's right," Laura said. "The driver's license and everything else is supported by government files. In researching *Endless River,* I had to find out how you go about obtaining a new identity of high quality, and I found this interesting man in San Francisco who runs a veritable document industry from the basement beneath a topless night-club—"

"It doesn't have a roof?" Chris asked.

Laura ruffled the boy's hair and said, "Anyway, Stefan, if you look deeper into that box, you'll find a couple of bank books as well. I've opened accounts for you under your new identity at Security Pacific Bank and Great Western Savings."

He was startled. "I can't take money from you. I can't—"

"You save me from a wheelchair, repeatedly save my life, and I can't give you money if I feel like it? Thelma, what's wrong with him?"

"He's a man," Thelma said.

"I guess that explains it."

"Hairy, Neanderthalic," Thelma said, "perpetually half-crazed from excessive levels of testosterone, plagued by racial memories of the lost glory of mammoth-hunting expeditions—they're all alike."

"Men," Laura said.

"Men," Thelma said.

To his surprise and almost against his will, Stefan Krieger felt some of the darkness fading from within him, and light began to find a pane through which to shine into his heart.

In late February of the next year, thirteen months after the events in the desert outside Palm Springs, Laura suggested that he come to stay with her and Chris at the house near Big Bear. He went the next day, driving there in the sleek new Russian sports car that he had bought with some of the money she had given him.

For the next seven months he slept in the guest room. Every night. He needed nothing more. Just being with them, day after day, being accepted by them, being included, was all the love he could handle for a while.

In mid-September, twenty months after he had appeared on her doorstep with a bullet hole in his chest, she asked him into her bed. Three nights later he found the courage to go.

## THREE

The year that Chris was twelve, Jason and Thelma bought a getaway house in Monterey, overlooking the most beautiful coastline in the world, and they insisted that Laura, Stefan, and Chris visit them for the month of August, when they were both between film projects. The mornings on the Monterey peninsula were cool and foggy, the days warm and clear, the nights downright chilly in spite of the season, and that daily pattern of weather was invigorating.

On the second Friday of the month, Stefan and Chris went for a beach walk with Jason. On the rocks not far from shore, sea lions were sunning themselves and barking noisily. Tourists were parked bumper to bumper along the road that served the beach; they ventured onto the sand to take photographs of the sun-worshiping "seals," as they called them.

"Year by year," Jason said, "there's more foreign tourists. It's a regular invasion. And you notice—they're mostly either Japanese, Germans, or Russians. Less than half a century ago, we fought the greatest war in history against all three of them, and now they're all more prosperous than we are. Japanese electronics and cars, Russian cars and computers, German cars and quality machinery of all kinds ...Honest to God, Stefan, I think Americans frequently treat old enemies better than they do old friends."

Stefan paused to watch the sea lions that had drawn the interest of the tourists, and he thought of the mistake that he had made in his meeting with Winston Churchill.

*But tell me at least one thing. Curiosity's killing me. Let's see ... well, for instance, what of the Soviets after the war?*

The old fox had spoken so casually, as if the question was one that had occurred to him by chance, as if he might as likely have asked whether the cut of men's suits would change in the future, when in fact his query had been calculated and the answer of intense interest to him. Operating on what Stefan had told him, Churchill had rallied the Western Allies to continue fighting in Europe after the Germans were defeated. Using the Soviets' land grab of Eastern Europe as an excuse to turn against them, the other Allies had fought the Russians, driving them back into their motherland and ultimately defeating them entirely; in fact, throughout the war with Germany, the Soviets had been propped up with weapons and supplies from the United States, and when that support was withdrawn they collapsed in a matter of months. After all, they had been exhausted after the war with their old ally, Hitler. Now the modern world was far different from what destiny had intended, and all because Stefan had answered Churchill's one question.

Unlike Jason or Thelma or Laura or Chris, Stefan was a man out of time, a man for whom this era was not his destined home; the years since the Great Wars were his future, while those same years were in these people's past; therefore he recalled both the future that had once been and the future that had now come to pass in place of the old. They, however, could remember no different world but this one in which no great world powers were hostile toward one another, in which no huge nuclear arsenals awaited launch, in which democracy flourished even in Russia, in which there were plenty and peace.

Destiny struggles to reassert the pattern that was meant to be. But sometimes, happily, it fails.

Laura and Thelma remained in rocking chairs on the porch, watching their menfolk walk down to the sea and then north along the beach, out of sight.

"Are you happy with him, Shane?"

"He's a melancholy man."

"But lovely."

"He'll never be Danny."

"But Danny is gone."

Laura nodded. They rocked.

"He says I redeemed him," Laura said.

"Like grocery coupons, you mean?"

Finally Laura said, "I love him."

"I know," Thelma said.

"I never thought I would . . . again. I mean, love a man that way."

"What way is that, Shane? Are you talking about some kinky new position? You're heading toward middle age, Shane; you'll be forty before too many moons, so isn't it time you reformed your libidinous ways?"

"You're incorrigible."

"I try to be."

"How about you, Thelma? Are you happy?"

Thelma patted her large belly. She was seven months pregnant.

"Very happy, Shane. Did I tell you—maybe twins?"

"You told me."

"Twins," Thelma said, as if the prospect awed her. "Think how pleased Ruthie would be for me."

Twins.

Destiny struggles to reassert the pattern that was meant to be, Laura thought. And sometimes, happily, it succeeds.

They sat for a while in companionable silence, breathing the healthful sea air, listening to the wind sough softly in the Monterey pines and cypress.

After a while Thelma said, "Remember that day I came to your house in the mountains, and you were taking target practice in the backyard?"

"I remember."

"Blasting away at those human silhouettes. Snarling, daring the world to tackle you, guns hidden everywhere. That day you told me you'd spent your life enduring what fate threw at you, but you were not just going to endure any more—you were going to fight to protect your own. You were very angry that day, Shane, and very bitter."

"Yes."

"Now, I know you're still an endurer. And I know you're still a fighter. The world is still full of death and tragedy. In spite of all that, somehow you just aren't bitter any more."

"No."

"Share the secret?"

"I've learned the third great lesson, that's all. As a kid I learned to endure. After Danny was killed, I learned to fight. Now I'm still an endurer and a fighter—but I've also learned to accept. Fate *is*."

"Sounds very Eastern-mystic-transcendental-bullshit, Shane. Jeez. 'Fate *is*.' Next you'll be telling me to chant a mantra and contemplate my navel."

"Stuffed with twins, as you are," Laura said, "you can't even see your navel."

"Oh, yes, I can—with just the right arrangement of mirrors."

Laura laughed. "I love you, Thelma."

"I love you, Sis."

They rocked and rocked.

Down on the shore, the tide was coming in.

# THE FACE OF FEAR

◆ ◆ ◆

*For Barbara Norville*

# PART ONE

# FRIDAY
# 12:01 A.M.
# 8:00 P.M.

◆

# 1
## ❖ ❖ ❖

Wary, not actually expecting trouble but prepared for it, he parked his car across the street from the four-story brownstone apartment house. When he switched off the engine, he heard a siren wail in the street behind him.

They're coming for me, he thought. Somehow they've found out I'm the one.

He smiled. He wouldn't let them put the handcuffs on him. He wouldn't go easily. That wasn't his style.

Frank Bollinger was not easily frightened. In fact, he couldn't remember *ever* having been frightened. He knew how to take care of himself. He had reached six feet when he was thirteen years old, and he hadn't quit growing until he was six-four. He had a thick neck, broad shoulders and the biceps of a young weightlifter. At thirty-seven he was in virtually the same good condition, at least outwardly, as he had been when he was twenty-seven—or even seventeen. Curiously enough, he never exercised. He had neither the time nor the temperament for endless series of push-ups and sit-ups and running in place. His size and his hard-packed muscles were nature's gifts, simply a matter of genetics. Although he had a voracious appetite and never dieted, he was not girdled with rings of extra weight in the hips and stomach, as were most men his age. His doctor had explained to him that, because he suffered constantly from extreme nervous tension and because he refused to take the drugs that would bring his condition under control, he would most likely die young of hypertension. Strain, anxiety, nervous tension—these were what kept the weight off him, said the doctor. Wound tight, roaring inside like a perpetually accelerating engine, he burned away the fat, regardless of how much he ate.

But Bollinger found that he could agree with only half of that diagnosis. Nervous: no. Tension: yes. He was never nervous; that word had no meaning for him. However, he was always tense. He *strove* for tension, worked at building it, for he thought of it as a survival factor. He was always watchful. Always aware. Always tense. Always ready. Ready for anything. That was why there was nothing that he feared: nothing on earth could surprise him.

As the siren grew louder, he glanced at the rear-view mirror. A bit more than a block away, a revolving red light pulsed in the night.

He took the .38 revolver out of his shoulder holster. He put one hand on the door and waited for the right moment to throw it open.

The squad car bore down on him—then swept past. It turned the corner two blocks away.

They weren't on his trail after all.

He felt slightly disappointed.

He put the gun away and studied the street. Six mercury vapor street lamps—two at each end of the block and two in the middle—drenched the pavement and the automobiles and the buildings in an eerie purple-white light. The street was lined with three- and four-story townhouses, some of them brownstones and some brick, most of them in good repair. There didn't seem to be anyone at any of the lighted windows. That was good; he did not want to be seen. A few trees struggled for life at the edges of the sidewalks, the scrawny plane trees and maples and birches that were all that New York City could boast beyond the boundaries of its public parks, all of them stunted trees, skeletal, their branches like charred bones reaching for the midnight sky. A gentle but chilly January wind pushed scraps of paper along the gutters; and when the wind gusted, the branches of the trees rattled like children's sticks on a rail fence. The other parked cars looked like animals huddling against the cold air; they were empty. Both sidewalks were deserted for the length of the block.

He got out of the car, quickly crossed the street and went up the front steps of the apartment house.

The foyer was clean and brightly lighted. The complex mosaic floor—a garland of faded roses on a beige background—was highly polished, and there were no pieces of tile missing from it. The inner foyer door was locked and could only be opened by key or with a lock-release button in one of the apartments.

There were three apartments on the top floor, three on the second floor and two on the ground level. Apartment 1A belonged to Mr. and Mrs. Harold Nagly, the owners of the building, who were on their annual pilgrimage to Miami Beach. The small apartment at the rear of the first floor was occupied by Edna Mowry, and he supposed that right now Edna would be having a midnight snack or a well-deserved martini to help her relax after a long night's work.

He had come to see Edna. He knew she would be home. He had followed her for six nights now, and he knew that she lived by strict routine, much too strict for such a young and attractive woman. She always arrived home from work at twelve, seldom more than five minutes later.

Pretty little Edna, he thought. You've got such long and lovely legs.

He smiled.

He pressed the call button for Mr. and Mrs. Yardley on the third floor.

A man's voice echoed tinnily from the speaker at the top of the mailbox. "Who is it?"

"Is this the Hutchinson apartment?" Bollinger asked, knowing full well that it was not.

"You pressed the wrong button, mister. The Hutchinsons are on the second floor. Their mailbox is next to ours."

"Sorry," Bollinger said as Yardley broke the connection.

He rang the Hutchinson apartment.

The Hutchinsons, apparently expecting visitors and less cautious than the Yardleys, buzzed him through the inner door without asking who he was.

The downstairs hall was pleasantly warm. The brown tile floor and tan walls were spotless. Halfway along the corridor, a marble bench stood on the left, and a large beveled mirror hung above it. Both apartment doors, dark wood with brassy fixtures, were on the right.

He stopped in front of the second door and flexed his gloved fingers. He pulled his wallet from an inside coat pocket and took a knife from an overcoat pocket. When he touched the button on the burnished handle, the spring-hinged blade popped into sight; it was seven inches long, thin and nearly as sharp as a razor.

The gleaming blade transfixed Bollinger and caused bright images to flicker behind his eyes.

He was an admirer of William Blake's poetry; indeed, he fancied himself an intimate spiritual student of Blake's. It was not surprising, then, that a passage from Blake's work should come to him at that moment, flowing through his mind like blood running down the troughs in an autopsy table.

*Then the inhabitants of those cities*
*Felt their nerves change into marrow,*
*And the hardening bones began*
*In swift diseases and torments,*
*In shootings and throbbings and grindings*
*Through all the coasts; till, weakened,*
*The senses inward rushed, shrinking*
*Beneath the dark net of infection.*

I'll change their bones to marrow, sure as hell, Bollinger thought. I'll have the inhabitants of *this* city hiding behind their doors at night. Except that I'm not the infection; I'm the cure. I'm the cure for all that's wrong with this world.

He rang the bell. After a moment he heard her on the other side of the door, and he rang the bell again.

"Who is it?" she asked. She had a pleasant, almost musical voice, marked now with a thin note of apprehension.

"Miss Mowry?" he asked.

"Yes?"

"Police."

She didn't reply.

"Miss Mowry? Are you there?"

"What's it about?"

"Some trouble where you work."

"I never cause trouble."

"I didn't say that. The trouble doesn't involve you. At least not directly. But you might have seen something important. You might have been a witness."

"To what?"

"That will take a while to explain."

"I couldn't have been a witness. Not me. I wear blinders in that place."

"Miss Mowry," he said sternly, "if I must get a warrant in order to question you, I will."

"How do I know you're really the police?"

"New York," Bollinger said with mock exasperation. "Isn't it just wonderful? Everyone suspects everyone else."

"They have to."

He sighed. "Perhaps. Look, Miss Mowry, do you have a security chain on the door?"

"Of course."

"Of course. Well, leave the chain on and open up. I'll show you my identification."

Hesitantly, she slid back a bolt lock. The chain lock allowed the door to open an inch and no farther.

He held up his wallet. "Detective Bollinger," he said. The knife was in his left hand, pointed at the floor, pressed flat against his overcoat.

She squinted through the narrow crack. She peered for a moment at the badge that was pinned to the inside of his wallet, then carefully studied the photo-identification card in the plastic window below the badge.

When she stopped squinting at the ID and looked up at him, he saw that her eyes were not blue, as he had thought—having seen her no closer than when she was on stage and he was in the shadowed audience—but a deep shade of green. They were truly the most attractive eyes he had ever seen. "Satisfied?" he asked.

Her thick dark hair had fallen across one eye. She pushed it away from her face. Her fingers were long and perfectly formed, the nails painted blood red. When she was on stage, bathed in that intense spotlight, her nails appeared to be black. She said, "What's this trouble you mentioned?"

"I have quite a number of questions to ask you, Miss Mowry. Must we discuss this through a crack in the door for the next twenty minutes?"

Frowning, she said, "I suppose not. Wait there just a minute while I put on a robe."

"I can wait. Patience is the key to content."

She looked at him curiously.

"Mohammed," he said.

"A cop who quotes Mohammed?"

"Why not?"

"Are you—of that religion?"

"No." He was amused at the way she phrased the question. "It's just that I've acquired a considerable amount of knowledge for the sole purpose of shocking those people who think all policemen are hopelessly ignorant."

She winced. "Sorry." Then she smiled. He had not seen her smile before, not once in the entire week since he had first seen her. She had stood in that spotlight, moving with the music, shedding her clothes, bumping, grinding, caressing her own bare breasts, observing her audience with the cold eyes and almost lipless expression of a snake. Her smile was dazzling.

"Get your robe, Miss Mowry."

She closed the door.

Bollinger watched the foyer door at the end of the hall, hoping no one would come in or go out while he was standing there, exposed.

He put away his wallet.

He kept the knife in his left hand.

In less than a minute she returned. She removed the security chain, opened the door and said, "Come in."

He stepped past her, inside.

She closed the door and put the bolt lock in place and turned to him and said, "Whatever trouble—"

Moving quickly for such a large man he slammed her against the door, brought up the knife, shifted it from his left hand to his right hand, and lightly pricked her throat with the point of the blade.

Her green eyes were very wide. She'd had the breath knocked out of her and could not scream.

"No noise," Bollinger said fiercely. "If you try to call for help, I'll push this pig sticker straight into your lovely throat. I'll ram it right out the back of your neck. Do you understand?"

She stared at him.

*"Do you understand?"*

"Yes," she said thinly.

"Are you going to cooperate?"

She said nothing. Her gaze traveled down from his eyes, over his proud nose and full lips and strong jawline, down to his fist and to the handle of the knife.

"If you aren't going to cooperate," he said quietly, "I can skewer you right here. I'll pin you to the damn door." He was breathing hard.

A tremor passed through her.

He grinned.

Still trembling, she said, "What do you want?"

"Not much. Not very much at all. Just a little loving."

She closed her eyes. "Are you—him?"

A slender, all but invisible thread of blood trickled from beneath the needlelike point of the knife, slid along her throat to the neck of her bright red robe. Watching the minuscule flow of blood as if he were a scientist observing an extremely rare bacterium through a microscope, pleased by it, nearly mesmerized by it, he said, "Him? Who is 'him'? I don't know what you're talking about."

"You know," she said weakly.

"I'm afraid not."

"Are you *him*?" she bit her lip. "The one who—who's cut up all those other women?"

Looking up from her throat, he said, "I see. I see how it is. Of course. You mean the one they call the Butcher. You think I'm the Butcher."

"Are you?"

"I've been reading a great deal about him in the *Daily News*. He slits their throats, doesn't he? From one ear to the other. Isn't that right?" He was teasing her and enjoying himself immensely. "Sometimes he even disembowels them. Doesn't he? Correct me if I'm wrong. But that's what he does sometimes, isn't it?"

She said nothing.

"I believe I read in the *News* that he sliced the ears off one of them. When the police found her, her ears were on the nightstand beside her bed."

She shuddered more violently than ever.

"Poor little Edna. You think I'm the Butcher. No wonder you're so frightened." He patted her shoulder, smoothed her dark hair as if he were quieting an animal. "I'd be scared too if I were in your shoes right now. But I'm not. I'm not in your shoes and I'm not this guy they call the Butcher. You can relax."

She opened her eyes and searched his, trying to tell whether he spoke the truth.

"What kind of man do you think I am, Edna?" he asked, pretending to have been hurt by her suspicion. "I don't want to harm you. I will if I must. I will cause you a great deal of harm if you don't cooperate with me. But if you're docile, if you're good to me, I'll be good to you. I'll make you very happy, and I'll leave you just like I found you. Flawless. You are flawless, you know. Perfectly beautiful. And your breath smells like strawberries. Isn't that nice? That's such a wonderful way for us to begin, such a nice touch, that scent of strawberries on your breath. Were you eating when I knocked?"

"You're crazy," she said softly.

"Now, Edna, let's have cooperation. Were you eating strawberries?"

Tears began to form in the corners of her eyes.

He pressed a bit harder with the knife.

She whimpered.

"Well?" he said.

"Wine."

"What?"

"It was wine."

"Strawberry wine?"

"Yes."

"Is there any left?"

"Yes."

"I'd like to have some."

"I'll get it for you."

"I'll get it myself," he said. "But first I've got to take you into the bedroom and tie you up. Now, now. Don't be scared. If I didn't tie you up, sooner or later you'd try to escape. If you tried to escape, I'd have to kill you. So, you see, I'm going to tie you up for your own good, so that you won't make it necessary for me to hurt you.''

Still holding the knife at her throat, he kissed her. Her lips were cold and stiff.

"Please don't," she said.

"Relax and enjoy yourself, Edna." He untied the sash at her waist. The robe fell open. Under it, she was naked. He gently squeezed her breasts. "If you cooperate you'll come out of this just fine. And you'll have a lot of fun. I'm not going to kill you unless you force me to it. I'm no butcher, Edna. Me . . . I'm nothing but your ordinary, everyday rapist.''

# 2
◆◆◆

Graham Harris sensed that there was trouble coming. He shifted in his chair but could not get comfortable. He glanced at the three television cameras and suddenly felt as if he were surrounded by intelligent and hostile robots. He almost laughed at that bizarre image; the tension made him slightly giddy.

"Nervous?" Anthony Prine asked.

"A little."

"No need to be."

"Maybe not while the commercials are running, but—"

"Not when we're back on the air again, either," Prine said. "You've handled yourself well so far." Although he was as American as Harris, Prine managed to look like the stereotypical British gentleman: sophisticated, rather jaded yet just a bit stuffy, completely relaxed, a model of self-confidence. He was sitting in a high-backed leather armchair, an exact copy of the chair in which Graham had suddenly found himself so uncomfortable. "You're a most interesting guest, Mr. Harris."

"Thank you. You're interesting yourself. I don't see how you can keep your wits about you. I mean, doing this much *live* television, five nights a week—''

"But the fact that it's live is what makes it so exciting," Prine said. "Being on the air *live*, risking all, taking a chance of making a fool of yourself—that keeps the juices flowing. That's why I hesitate to accept one of these offers to syndicate the show or to go network with it. They'd want it on tape, all neatly edited down from two hours to ninety minutes. And that wouldn't be the same.''

The program director, a heavyset man in a white turtle-neck sweater and houndstooth-check slacks, said, "Twenty seconds, Tony."

"Relax," Prine told Harris. "You'll be off in fifteen more minutes."

Harris nodded. Prine seemed friendly—yet he could not shake the feeling that the night was going to go sour for him, and soon.

Anthony Prine was the host of *Manhattan at Midnight*, an informal two-hour-long interview program that originated from a local New York City station. *Manhattan at Midnight* provided the same sort of entertainment to be found on all other talk shows—actors and actresses plugging their latest movies, authors plugging their latest books, musicians plugging their latest records, politicians plugging their latest campaigns (as yet unannounced campaigns and thus unfettered by the equal-time provisions of the election laws)—except that it presented a greater number of mind readers and psychics and UFO "experts" than did most talk shows. Prine was a *Believer*. He was also damned good at his job, so good there were rumors ABC wanted to pick him up for a nationwide audience. He was not so witty as Johnny Carson or so homey as Mike Douglas, but no one asked better or more probing questions than he did. Most of the time he was serene, in lazy command of his show; and when things were going well, he looked somewhat like a slimmed-down Santa Claus: completely white hair, a round face and merry blue eyes. He appeared to be incapable of rudeness. However, there were occasions—no more often than once a night, sometimes only once a week—when he would lash out at a guest, prove him a liar or in some other way thoroughly embarrass and humiliate him with a series of wickedly pointed questions. The attack never lasted more than three or four minutes, but it was as brutal and as relentless as it was surprising.

*Manhattan at Midnight* commanded a large and faithful audience primarily because of this element of surprise that magnified the ferocity of Prine's interrogations. If he had subjected every guest to this abuse, he would have been a bore; but his calculated style made him as fascinating as a cobra. Those millions of people who spend most of their leisure hours in front of a television set apparently enjoyed secondhand violence more than they did any other form of entertainment.

They watched the police shows to see people beaten, robbed and murdered; they watched Prine for those unexpected moments when he bludgeoned a guest with words that were nearly as devastating as clubs.

He had started twenty-five years earlier as a nightclub comic and impressionist, doing old jokes and mimicking famous voices in cheap lounges. He had come a long way.

The director signaled Prine. A red light shone on one camera.

Addressing his unseen audience, Prine said, "I'm talking with Mr. Graham Harris, a resident of Manhattan who calls himself a 'clairvoyant,' a seer of visions. Is that the proper definition of the term, Mr. Harris?"

"It'll do," Graham said. "Although when you put it that way, it sounds a bit religious. Which it isn't. I don't attribute my extrasensory perception to God—nor to any other supernatural force."

"As you said earlier, you're convinced that the clairvoyance is a result of a head injury you received in a rather serious accident. Subsequent to that, you began to have these visions. If that's God's work, His methods are even more roundabout than we might have thought."

Graham smiled. "Precisely."

"Now, anyone who reads the newspapers knows that you've been asked to assist the police in uncovering a clue to the identity of this man they call the Butcher. But what about your last case, the murder of the Havelock sisters in Boston? That was very interesting too. Tell us about that."

Graham shifted uneasily in his chair. He still sensed trouble coming, but he couldn't imagine what it might be or how he might avoid it. "The Havelock sisters . . ."

Nineteen-year-old Paula and twenty-two-year-old Paige Havelock had lived together in a cozy Boston apartment near the university where Paula was an undergraduate student and where Paige was working for her master's degree in sociology. On the morning of last November second, Michael Shute had stopped by the apartment to take Paige to lunch. The date had been made by telephone the previous evening. Shute and the elder Havelock sister were lovers, and he had a key to the apartment. When no one responded to the bell, he decided to let himself in and wait for them. Inside, however, he discovered that they *were* at home. Paula and Paige had been awakened in the night by one or more intruders who had stripped them naked; pajamas and robes were strewn on the floor. The women had been tied with a heavy cord, sexually molested and finally shot to death in their own living room.

Because the proper authorities were unable to come up with a single major lead in the case, the parents of the dead girls got in touch with Graham on the tenth of November and asked for his assistance. He arrived in Boston two days later. Although the police were skeptical of his talents—a number of them were downright hostile toward him—they were anxious to placate the Havelocks, who had some political influence in the city. He was taken to the sealed apartment and permitted to examine the scene of the crime. But he got absolutely nothing from that: no emanations, no psychic visions—just a chill that slithered down his spine and coiled in his stomach. Later, under the suspicious gaze of a police property officer, he was allowed to handle the pillow that the killer had used to muffle the gunshots—and then the pajamas and the robes that had been found next to the bodies. As he caressed the blood-stiffened fabric, his paranormal talent abruptly blossomed; his mind was inundated with clairvoyant images like a series of choppy, frothing waves breaking on a beach.

Anthony Prine interrupted Graham. "Wait a minute. I think we need some elaboration on this point. We need to make it much clearer. Do you mean that the simple act of touching the bloodstained pajamas caused your clairvoyant visions?"

"No. It didn't cause them. It *freed* them. The pajamas were like a key that unlocked the clairvoyant part of my mind. That's a quality common to nearly all murder weapons and to the last garments worn by the victims."

"Why do you think that is?"

"I don't know," Graham said.

"You've never thought about it?"

"I've thought about it endlessly," Graham said. "But I've never reached any conclusions."

Although Prine's voice held not even the slightest note of hostility, Graham was almost certain that the man was searching for an opening to launch one of his famous attacks.

For a moment he thought *that* might be the oncoming trouble which he had known about, in a somewhat psychic fashion, for the past quarter of an hour. Then he suddenly understood, through the powers of his sixth sense, that the trouble would happen to someone else, beyond the walls of this studio.

"When you touched the pajamas," Prine said, "did you see the murders as if they were actually taking place in front of you at that very moment?"

"Not exactly. I saw it all take place—well, *behind* my eyes."

"What do you mean by that? Are your visions sort of like daydreams?"

"In a way. But much more vivid than daydreams. Full of color and sound and texture."

"Did you see the Havelocks' killer in this vision?"

"Yes. Quite clearly."

"Did you also intuit his name?"

"No," Graham said. "But I was able to give the police a thorough description of him. He was in his early thirties, not shorter than five-ten or taller than six feet. Slightly heavy. Receding hairline. Blue eyes. A thin nose, generally sharp features. A small strawberry birthmark on his chin. . . . As it turned out, that was a perfect description of the building superintendent."

"And you'd never seen him?"

"My first glimpse of him was in that vision."

"You'd never seen a photograph of him?"

"No."

"Had he been a suspect before you gave the police this description?" Prine asked.

"Yes. But the murders took place in the early morning hours of his day off. He swore that he had gone to his sister's house to spend the night, hours before the Havelock girls were killed; and his sister supported his story. Since she lived over eighty miles away, he seemed out of the running."

"Was his sister lying?"

"Yes."

"How did you prove it?"

While handling the dead girls' clothing, Graham sensed that the killer had gone to his sister's house a full two hours after the murder had taken place—not early the previous evening as she insisted. He also sensed that the weapon—a Smith & Wesson Terrier .32— was hidden in the sister's house, in the bottom drawer of a china closet.

He accompanied a Boston city detective and two state troopers to the sister's place. Arriving unannounced and uninvited, they told her they wanted to question her on some new evidence in the case. Ten seconds after he stepped into her house, while the woman was still surprised at the sight of them, Graham asked her why she had said that her brother had come to stay on the evening of November first when in fact he actually had not arrived until well after dawn on November second. Before she could answer that, before she could get her wits about her, he asked her why she was hiding the murder weapon in the bottom drawer of her china closet. Shocked by his knowledge, she withstood only half a dozen questions from the detective before she finally admitted the truth.

"Amazing," Prine said. "And you had never seen the inside of her house before you had that vision?"

"I'd never even seen the outside of it," Graham said.

"Why would she protect her brother when she knew he was guilty of such a horrible crime?"

"I don't know. I can see things that have happened—and very occasionally, things that soon will happen—in places where I've never been. But I can't read minds. I can't explain human motivations."

The program director signaled Prine: five minutes until they broke for the commercials.

Leaning toward Harris, Prine said, "Who asked you to help catch this man they're calling the Butcher? Parents of one of the murdered women?"

"No. One of the detectives assigned to the case isn't as skeptical as most policemen. He believes that I can do what I say I can do. He wants to give me a chance."

"Have you gone to the scenes of the nine murders?"

"I've seen five of them."

"And handled the clothes of the victims?"

"Some of them."

Prine slid forward on his chair, leaning conspiratorially toward Harris. "What can you tell us about the Butcher?"

"Not much," Graham Harris said, and he frowned, because that bothered him. He was having more trouble than usual on this case. "He's a big man. Good-looking. Young. Very sure of himself and sure of the—"

"How much are you being paid?" Prine asked.

Confused by the question, Graham said, "For what?"

"For helping the police," Prine said.

"I'm not being paid anything."

"You're just doing it for the good of society, then?"

"I'm doing it because I *have* to. I'm compelled—"

"How much did the Havelocks pay you?"

He realized that Prine had been leaning toward him not conspiratorially but hungrily, like a beast preparing to pounce on its prey. His hunch had been correct: that son of a bitch had chosen him for the nightly trouncing. But *why?*

"Mr. Harris?"

Graham had temporarily forgotten the cameras (and the audience beyond), but now he was uncomfortably aware of them again. "The Havelocks didn't pay me anything."

"You're certain of that?"

"Of course I'm certain."

"You *are* sometimes paid for your services, aren't you?"

"No. I earn my living by—"

"Sixteen months ago a young boy was brutally murdered in the

Midwest. We'll skip the name of the town to spare the family publicity. His mother asked for your assistance in uncovering the killer. I spoke with her yesterday. She says that she paid you slightly more than one thousand dollars—and then you failed to find the killer.''

What the hell is he trying to prove? Graham wondered. He knows I'm far from poor. He knows I don't need to run halfway across the country to hustle a few hundred dollars. "First of all, I *did* tell them who killed the child and where they could look for the evidence that would make their case. But both the police and this woman refused to follow up on the lead that I gave them.''

"Why would they refuse?''

"Because the man I fingered for the murder is the son of a wealthy family in that town. He's also a respected clergyman in his own right, and the stepfather of the dead boy.''

Prine's expression was proof enough that the woman had not told him this part of it. Nevertheless, he pressed the attack. That was uncharacteristic of him. Ordinarily, he was vicious with a guest only when he *knew* that he had evidence enough to ruin him. He was not entirely an admirable man; however, he usually didn't make mistakes. "But she did pay you the thousand dollars?''

"That was for my expenses. Airline fares, car rentals, meals and lodging while I was working on the case.''

Smiling as if he had made his point, Prine said, "Do they usually pay your expenses?''

"Naturally. I can't be expected to travel all about, spending thousands of my own money for—''

"Did the Havelocks pay you?''

"My expenses.''

"But didn't you just tell us a minute ago that the Havelocks didn't pay you anything?''

Exasperated, Graham said, "They didn't *pay* me. They just reimbursed me for—''

"Mr. Harris, forgive me if I seem to be accusing you of something you haven't done. But it occurs to me that a man with your reputation for performing psychic miracles could easily take many thousands of dollars a year from the gullible. If he was unscrupulous, that is.''

"Look here—''

"When you're on one of these investigations, do you ever pad your expenses?'' Prine asked.

Graham was stunned. He slid forward on his chair, leaned toward Prine. "That's outrageous!'' He realized that Prine had settled back and crossed his legs the instant that he got a strong reaction. That was a clever maneuver that made Graham's response seem exaggerated.

He suddenly felt as if *he* were the predator. He supposed that his justifiable indignation looked like the desperate and weak self-defense of a guilty man. "You know I don't need the money. I'm not a millionaire, but I'm well fixed. My father was a successful publisher. I received a substantial trust fund. Furthermore, I've got a moderately successful business of my own."

"I know you publish two expensive magazines about mountain climbing," Prine said. "But they *do* have small circulations. As for the trust fund. . . . I hadn't heard about that."

He's lying, Graham thought. He prepares meticulously for these shows. When I walked into this studio, he knew almost as much about me as I know about myself. So why is he lying? What will he gain by slandering me? What in hell is happening here?

*The woman has green eyes, clear and beautiful green eyes, but there is terror in them now, and she stares up at the blade, the shining blade, and she sucks in her breath to scream, and the blade starts its downward arc. . . .*

The images passed as suddenly as they had come, leaving him badly shaken. He knew that some clairvoyants—including the two most famous, Peter Hurkos and his fellow Dutchman Gerard Croiset—could receive, interpret and catalogue their psychic perceptions while holding an uninterrupted conversation. Only rarely could Graham manage that. Usually he was distracted by the visions. Occasionally, when they had to do with a particularly violent murder, he was so overwhelmed by them that he blanked out reality altogether. The visions were more than an intellectual experience; they affected him emotionally and spiritually as well. For a moment, seeing the green-eyed woman behind his eyes, he had not been *fully* aware of the world around him: the television audience, the studio, the cameras, Prine. He was trembling.

"Mr. Harris?" Prine said.

He looked up from his hands.

"I asked you a question," Prine said.

"I'm sorry. I didn't hear it."

*As the blood explodes from her throat and her scream dies unborn, he pulls the blade free and raises it high and brings it down, down again, with all of his strength, down between her bare breasts, and he neither scowls nor grins, and he does not laugh maniacally, but goes about the killing in a workmanlike manner, as if this is his profession, as if this is just a job, as if this is no different from a man selling cars for a living or washing windows, merely a task to be finished, stab and rip and tear and bring the blood welling up in pools . . . and then stand up and go home and sleep contentedly, satisfied with a job well done. . . .*

Graham was shaking uncontrollably. His face was greasy with perspiration, yet he felt as if he were sitting in a cool draft. His own power scared him. Ever since the accident in which he had nearly died, he had been frightened of many things; but these inexplicable visions were the ultimate fear.

"Mr. Harris?" Prine said. "Are you feeling all right?"

The second wave of impressions had lasted only three or four seconds, although it had seemed much longer than that. During that time he was totally unaware of the studio and the cameras.

"He's doing it again," Graham said softly. "Right now, this minute."

Frowning, Prine said, "Who? Doing what?"

"Killing."

"You're talking about—the Butcher?"

Graham nodded and licked his lips. His throat was so dry that it hurt him a bit to speak. There was an unpleasant metallic taste in his mouth.

Prine was excited. He faced one of the cameras and said, "Remember, New York, you heard it and saw it here first." He turned back to Graham and said, "Who is he killing?" He was suddenly charged with ghoulish anticipation.

"A woman. Green eyes. Pretty."

"What's her name?"

Perspiration trickled into the corners of Graham's eyes and stung them. He wiped his forehead with the back of his hand—and wondered how foolish he looked to the hundreds of thousands who were watching.

"Can you tell me her name?" Prine asked.

*Edna . . . pretty little Edna . . . poor little Edna. . . .*

"Edna," Graham said.

"Last name?"

"I don't . . . can't see it."

"Try. You must try."

"Maybe . . . dancer."

"Edna Dancer?"

"I don't . . . maybe not . . . maybe the dancer part isn't right . . . maybe just . . . just the Edna . . . "

"Reach for it," Prine said. "Try harder. Can't you force it out?"

"No use."

"*His* name?"

"Daryl . . . no . . . Dwight."

"Like Dwight Eisenhower?"

"I'm not certain that's actually his first name . . . or even first or last . . . but people have called him that . . . Dwight . . . yes . . . and he's answered to it.''

''Incredible,'' Prine said, apparently having forgotten that he had been in the process of destroying his guest's reputation. ''Do you see his other name, first or last?''

''No. But I sense . . . the police already know him . . . somehow . . . and they . . . they know him well.''

''You mean that he's already a suspect?'' Prine asked.

The cameras seemed to move in closer.

Graham wished they would go away. He wished Prine would go away. He should never have come here tonight. Most of all, he wished his clairvoyant powers would go away, vanish back into that lockbox, deep within his mind, from which they had been sprung by the accident.

''I don't know,'' Graham said. ''I suppose . . . he must be a suspect. But whatever the situation . . . they know him. They—'' He shuddered.

''What is it?'' Prine asked.

''Edna . . . ''

''Yes?''

''She's dead now.''

Graham felt as if he were going to be sick.

''*Where* did it happen?'' Prine asked.

Graham sank back in his armchair, struggling to keep control of himself. He felt almost as if he were Edna, as if the knife had been plunged into him.

''Where was she murdered?'' Prine asked again.

''In her apartment.''

''What's the address?''

''I don't know.''

''But if the police could get there in time—''

''I've lost it,'' Graham said. ''It's gone. I'm sorry. It's all gone for now.''

He felt cold and hollow inside.

# 3

### ◆ ◆ ◆

Shortly before two o'clock in the morning, after a conference on the set with the director, Anthony Prine left the studio and went down the hall to his suite, which served him as office, dressing room and home away from home. Inside, he walked straight to the bar, put two ice cubes in a glass and reached for the bottle of bourbon.

His manager and business partner, Paul Stevenson, was sitting on the couch. He wore expensive, well-tailored clothes. Prine was a smart dresser, and he appreciated that quality in other men. The problem was that Stevenson always destroyed the effect of his outfit with one bizarre accessory. Tonight he was wearing a Saville Row suit—a hard-finished gray worsted with a midnight-blue Thai silk lining—a hand-sewn light blue shirt, maroon tie, black alligator shoes. And bright pink socks—with green clocks on the sides. Like cockroaches on a wedding cake.

For two reasons, Stevenson was a perfect business partner: he had money, and he did what he was told to do. Prine had great respect for the dollar. And he did not believe that anyone lived who had the experience, the intelligence or the right to tell *him* what to do.

"Were there any calls for me on the private line?" Prine asked.

"No calls."

"You're certain?"

"Of course."

"You were here all the time?"

"Watching the show on that set," Stevenson said.

"I was expecting a call."

"I'm sorry. There wasn't one."

Prine scowled.

"Terrific show," Stevenson said.

"Just the first thirty minutes. Following Harris, the other guests looked duller than they were. Did we get viewer calls?"

"Over a hundred, all favorable. Do you believe he really saw the killing take place?"

"You heard the details he gave. The color of her eyes. Her name. He convinced me."

"Until the next victim's found, you don't know that his details were accurate."

"They were accurate," Prine said. He finished his bourbon and refilled his glass. He could drink a great deal of whiskey without becoming drunk. Likewise, when he ate he gorged himself, yet he had never been overweight. He was constantly on the prowl for pretty young women, and when he paid for sex he usually went to bed with two call girls. He was not simply a middle-aged man desperately trying to prove his youth. He *needed* those fuels—whiskey, food and women—in large doses. For most of his life he had been fighting ennui, a deep and abiding boredom with the way the world was. Pacing energetically, sipping his bourbon, he said, "A green-eyed woman named Edna. . . . He's right about that. We'll be reading it in the papers tomorrow."

"You can't *know*—"

"If you'd been sitting there beside him, Paul, you'd have no doubts about it."

"But wasn't it odd that he had his 'vision' just when you about had him nailed?"

"Nailed for what?" Prine asked.

"Well . . . for taking money. For—"

"If he's ever been paid more than his expenses for that kind of work, I've no proof of it," Prine said.

Perplexed, Stevenson said, "Then why did you go after him?"

"I wanted to break him. Reduce him to a babbling, defenseless fool." Prine smiled.

"But if he wasn't guilty—"

"He's guilty of other things."

"Like what?"

"You'll know eventually."

Stevenson sighed. "You enjoy humiliating them right there on television."

"Of course."

"Why?"

"Why not?"

"Is it the sense of power?"

"Not at all," Prine said. "I enjoy exposing them as fools because they *are* fools. Most men are fools. Politicians, clergymen, poets, philosophers, businessmen, generals and admirals. Gradually, I'm exposing the leaders in every profession. I'm going to show the ignorant masses that their leaders are as dull-witted as they are." He swallowed some bourbon. When he spoke again, his voice was hard. "Maybe someday all those fools will go at one another's throats and leave the world to the few of us who can appreciate it.''

''What are you saying?''

''I spoke English, didn't I?''

''You sound so—bitter.''

''I've got a right to.''

''You? After your success?''

''Aren't you drinking, Paul?''

''No. Tony, I don't understand—''

''I think you should have a drink.''

Stevenson knew when he was expected to change the subject. ''I really don't want a drink.''

''Have you ever gotten blind drunk?''

''No. I'm not much of a drinker.''

''Ever gone to bed with two girls at once?''

''What's that got to do with anything?''

''You don't reach out for life like you should,'' Prine said. ''You don't *experience*. You don't get loose enough often enough. That's the only thing wrong with you, Paul—other than your socks.''

Stevenson looked at his feet. ''What's wrong with my socks?''

Prine went to the windows. He didn't look at the bright city beyond but stared instead at his reflection in the glass. He grinned at himself. He felt marvelous. Better than he had felt in weeks, and all thanks to Harris. The clairvoyant had brought some excitement and danger into his life, new purpose and interest. Although Graham Harris didn't know it as yet, he was the most important target of Prine's career. We'll destroy him, Prine thought happily; wipe him out, finish him off for good. He turned to Stevenson. ''Are you certain about the phone? I *must* have gotten a call.''

''No. Nothing.''

''Maybe you stepped out of here for a minute.''

''Tony, *I'm* not a fool. Give me some credit. I was here all the time, and the private line never rang.''

Prine finished his second bourbon. It burned his throat. A welcome and pleasant heat rose in him. ''Why don't you have a drink with me?''

Stevenson stood and stretched. ''No. I've really got to go.''

Prine went to the bar.

''You're drinking those awfully fast, Tony.''

''Celebrating,'' Prine said as he added ice and bourbon to his glass.

''Celebrating what?''

''The downfall of another fool.''

# 4

### ◆ ◆ ◆

Connie Davis was waiting for Graham when he came home to the townhouse they shared in Greenwich Village. She took his coat and hung it in the closet.

She was pretty. Thirty-four years old. Slender. Brunette. Gray eyes. Proud nose. Wide mouth. Sexy.

She owned a prosperous hole-in-the-wall antique shop on Tenth Street. In business she was every bit as tough as she was pretty.

For the past eighteen months she and Graham had lived together. Their relationship was the closest thing to genuine romance that either of them had ever known.

However, it was more than a romance. She was his doctor and nurse as well as his lover. Since the accident five years ago, he had been losing faith in himself. His self-respect faded year by year. She was here to help him, to heal him. She was not certain that he understood this; but she saw it as the most important task of her life.

"Where have you been?" she asked. "It's two-thirty."

"I had to think. I went walking. You saw the program?"

"We'll talk about it. But first you need to get warm."

"Do I ever. It must be twenty below out there."

"Go into the study and sit down. Relax," she said. "I've got a fire going. I'll bring you a drink."

"Brandy?"

"What else on a night like this?"

"You're nearly perfect."

*"Nearly?"*

"Mustn't give you a swelled head."

"I'm too perfect to be immodest."

He laughed.

She turned from him and went to the bar at the far end of the living room.

With a sixth sense of her own, she knew that he stared after her for a moment before he left the room. Good. Just as planned. He was *meant* to watch. She was wearing a clinging white sweater and tight blue jeans that accentuated her waistline and her bottom. If he hadn't stared after her, she would have been disappointed. After what he had been through tonight, he needed more than a seat in front of the fireplace and a snifter of brandy. He needed her. Touching. Kissing. Making love. And she was willing—more than willing, delighted—to provide it.

She was not merely plunging into her Earth Mother role again. Unquestionably, she *did* have a tendency to overwhelm her men, to be so excessively affectionate and understanding and dependable that she smothered their self-reliance. However, this affair was different from all the others. She wanted to depend on Graham as much as he depended on her. This time she wanted to receive as much as she gave. He was the first man to whom she had ever responded in quite that fashion. She wanted to make love to him in order to soothe him, but she wanted to soothe herself as well. She had always had strong, healthy sexual drives, but Graham had put a new and sharper edge on her desire.

She carried the glasses of Remy Martin into the den. She sat beside him on the sofa.

After a moment of silence, still staring at the fire, he said, "Why the interrogation? What was he after?"

"Prine?"

"Who else?"

"You've seen his show often enough. You know what he's like."

"But he usually has a reason for his attacks. And he's always got proof of what he says."

"Well, at least you shut him up with your visions of the tenth murder."

"They were real," he said.

"I know they were."

"It was so vivid . . . as if I were right there."

"Was it bad? Bloody?"

"One of the worst. I saw him . . . ram the knife into her throat and then twist it." He quickly sipped his brandy.

She leaned against him, kissed him on the cheek.

"I can't figure this Butcher," he said worriedly. "I've never had so much trouble getting an image of a killer."

"You sensed his name."

"Maybe. Dwight. . . . I'm not entirely sure."

"You've given the police a fairly good description of him."

"But I can't pick up much more about him," he said. "When the visions come and I try to force an image of this man, this Butcher, to the center of them, all I get are waves of . . . evil. Not illness, not an impression of a sick mind. Just overwhelming evil. I don't know how to explain this—but the Butcher isn't a lunatic. At least not in the classical sense. He doesn't kill in a maniacal frenzy.''

"He's chopped up nine innocent women,'' Connie said. *"Ten* if you count the one they haven't found yet. He cuts off their ears and fingers sometimes. Sometimes he disembowels them. And you say he isn't *crazy?''*

"He's not a lunatic, not by any definition we have of the word. I'd stake my life on it.''

"Maybe you don't sense mental illness because he doesn't know he's sick. Amnesia—''

"No. No amnesia. No schizophrenia. He's very aware of his murders. He's no Dr. Jekyll and Mr. Hyde. I'll bet he'd pass any psychiatric examination you'd care to give him, and with flying colors. This isn't easy to explain. But I have the feeling that if he *is* a lunatic, he's a whole new breed. No one's ever encountered anything like him before. I think—dammit, I *know*—he's not even angry or particularly excited when he kills these women. He's just—methodical.''

"You're giving me the shivers.''

"You? I feel as if I've been inside his head. I've got a *chronic* case of shivers.''

A coal popped in the fireplace.

She took hold of his free hand. "Let's not talk about Prine or the killings.''

"After tonight, how can I not talk about them?''

"You looked wonderful on television,'' she said, working him away from the subject.

"Oh, yeah. Wonderful. Sweating, pale, shaking—''

"Not during the visions. Before them. You're a natural for television. Even for movies. Leading-man type.''

Graham Harris was handsome. Thick reddish-blond hair. Blue eyes, heavily crinkled at the corners. Leathery skin with sharply carved lines from all the years he had spent in an outdoor life. Five-ten; not tall, but lean and hard. He was thirty-eight, yet he still had a trace of boyish vulnerability about him.

"Leading-man type?'' he said. He smiled at her. "Maybe you're right. I'll give up the publishing business and all this messy psychic stuff. I'll go into the movies.''

"The next Robert Redford.''

"Robert Redford? I was thinking maybe the next Boris Karloff.''

"Redford,'' Connie insisted.

"Come to think of it, Karloff was a rather elegant-looking man out of makeup. Perhaps I'll try for being the next Wallace Beery."

"If you're Wallace Beery, then I'm Marie Dressler."

"Hi, Marie."

"Do you really have an inferiority complex, or do you cultivate it as part of your charm?"

He grinned, then sipped the brandy. "Remember that Tugboat Annie movie with Beery and Dressler? Do you think Annie ever went to bed with her husband?"

"Sure!"

"They were always fighting. He lied to her every chance he got—and most of the time he was drunk."

"But in their own way they *loved* each other," Connie said. "They couldn't have been married to anyone else."

"I wonder what it was like for them. He was such a weak man, and she was such a strong woman."

"Remember, though, he was always strong when the chips were down: right near the end of the picture, for example."

"Some good in all of us, huh?"

"He could have been strong from the start. He just didn't respect himself enough."

Graham stared at the fire. He turned the brandy snifter around and around in his hand.

"What about William Powell and Myrna Loy?" she asked.

"The Thin Man movies."

"Both of them were strong," she said. "That's who we could be. Nick and Nora Charles."

"I always liked their dog. Asta. Now *that* was a good part."

"How do you think Nick and Nora made love?" she asked.

"Passionately."

"But with a lot of fun."

"Little jokes."

"That's it." She took the brandy glass out of his hand and put it on the hearth with her own snifter. She kissed him lightly, teasing his lips with her tongue. "I bet we could play Nick and Nora."

"I don't know. It's such a strain making love and being witty at the same time."

She sat in his lap. She put her arms around his neck and kissed him more fully this time and drew back and smiled when he slid a hand beneath her sweater.

"Nora?" he said.

"Yes, Nicky?"

"Where's Asta?"

"I put him to bed."

"We wouldn't want him interrupting."

"He's asleep."

"Might traumatize the little fella if he saw—"

"I made sure he'd be asleep."

"Oh?"

"I drugged his Alpo."

"Such a smart girl."

"And now *we* belong in bed."

"Such a *very* smart girl."

"With a lovely body," she said.

"Yes, you're ravishing."

"Am I?"

"Oh, yes."

"Ravish me, then."

"With pleasure."

"I would hope so."

# 5
◆◆◆

An hour later he was asleep, but Connie was not. She lay on her side, studying his face in the soft glow of the bedside lamp.

His experience and attitudes were stamped on his features. His toughness shone through clearly, yet there was the boyish quality too. Kindness. Intelligence. Humor. Sensitivity. He was a deep-down *good* man. But the fear shone through as well, the fear of falling, and all of the ugly things that had grown from it.

During his twenties and early thirties, Graham had been one of the best mountain climbers in the world. He lived for the vertical trek, for the risk and the triumph. Nothing else in his life mattered half so much as that. He had been an active climber from the age of thirteen, year by year setting higher and more difficult goals for himself. At twenty-six he was organizing parties to scale the most taxing peaks in Europe, Asia, and South America. When he was thirty he led an expedition up the South Col route of Everest, climbed the West Ridge to traverse the mountain, and returned down the South Col. At thirty-one he tackled the Eiger Direct with an Alpine-style single push up the hideously sheer face without using fixed ropes. Accomplishments such as these, his good looks, his wit, and his reputation as a Casanova (exaggerated by both his friends and the press) made him the most colorful and popular figure in mountaineering at that time.

Five years ago, with only a few challenging climbs remaining, he put together a team to assault the most dangerous wall of rock known to man, the Southwest Face of Everest, a route that had never been taken to the top. Two-thirds of the way through the climb, he fell, breaking sixteen bones and suffering internal injuries. He was given first aid in Nepal, then flown to Europe with a doctor and two friends at his side in what everyone assumed would conclude as a death watch. Instead of adding one more outstanding achievement to his record, he spent seven months in a private Swiss clinic. However, the ordeal was not at an end when he left the hospital. This Goliath had not been beaten, and had left this David with a warning: Graham limped.

The doctors told him he could still scale easy cliffs and ridges as a weekend sport if he wished. With sufficient practice he might even learn to compensate for his partially game right leg and move on to more ambitious climbs. Not Eiger. Not Everest, by any route. But there were hundreds of lesser palisades that should interest him.

At first he was convinced that he would be back on Everest within a year. Three times he tried to climb, and three times he was reduced to panic in the first hundred feet of the ascent. Forced to retreat from even the simplest climbs, he quickly saw that Everest or anything remotely like it would most likely scare him to death.

Over the years, that fear had undergone a metamorphosis, had grown and spread like a fungus. His fear of climbing had become a generalized fear that affected every aspect of his life. He was convinced that his inheritance would be lost in bad investments, and he began following the stock market with a nervous interest that made him the bane of his broker. He started his three low-circulation, high-priced mountain-climbing magazines as a hedge against a collapse of the market; and although they were quite profitable, he periodically predicted their demise. He began to see the dread specter of cancer in every cold, case of flu, headache and bout with acid indigestion. His clairvoyance frightened him, and he attempted to deal with it only because he could not run from it. At times the fear intruded between him and Connie in the most intimate moments, leaving him impotent.

Recently he had sunk into a depression far deeper than any that had come before it, and for several days he had seemed unable and unwilling to claw his way out of it. Two weeks ago he had witnessed a mugging, heard the victim's cries for help—and walked away. Five years ago he would have waded into the fight without hesitation. He came home and told Connie about the mugging, belittled himself, called himself names, and argued with her when she tried to defend him. She was afraid that he had come to loathe himself, and she knew that for a man like Graham such an attitude would lead inevitably to some form of madness.

She knew that she was not particularly qualified to put him back together again. Because of her strong will, because of her competitive and fiercely self-sufficient nature, she felt that she had done more harm than good to her previous lovers. She had never thought of herself as a women's liberationist and certainly not as a ball breaker; she simply had been, from the age of consent, sharper and tougher and more self-reliant than most men of her acquaintance. In the past her lovers had been emotionally and intellectually weaker than she. Few men seemed able to accept a woman as anything but an inferior. She had nearly destroyed the man she lived with before Graham, merely by assuming her equality and—in his mind, at least—invalidating the male role he needed to sustain himself.

With Graham's ego in a fragile state, she had to modify her basic personality to an extent she would have thought impossible. It was worth the strain, because she saw the man he had been prior to the accident. She wanted to break his shell of fear and let out the old Graham Harris. What he had once been was what she had hoped for so long to find: a man who was her equal and who would not feel threatened by a woman who was his match. However, while trying to bring that Graham back to life, she had to be cautious and patient, for *this* Graham could be shattered so very easily.

A gust of wind rattled the window.

Although she was warm under the covers, she shivered.

The telephone rang.

Startled, she rolled away from Graham.

The phone was strident. Like the cry of a halidon, it echoed eerily in the room.

She snatched up the receiver to stop the ringing before it woke him. "Hello?" she said softly.

"Mr. Harris, please."

"Who's calling?"

"Ira Preduski."

"I'm sorry, but I—"

"Detective Preduski."

"It's four in the morning," she said.

"I apologize. Really. I'm sorry. Sincerely. If I've wakened you . . . terrible of me. But, you see, he wanted me to call him immediately if we had any—major developments in the Butcher case."

"Just a minute." She looked at Graham.

He was awake, watching her.

She said, "Preduski."

He took the receiver. "Harris speaking."

A minute later, when he was finished, she hung up for him. "They found number ten?"

"Yeah."

"What's her name?" Connie asked.

"Edna. Edna Mowry."

# 6
◆ ◆ ◆

The bedclothes were sodden with blood. The carpet at the right of the bed was marred by a dark stain like a Rorschach blot. Dried blood spotted the wall behind the brass headboard.

Three police lab technicians were working in the room under the direction of the coroner. Two of them were on their hands and knees beside the bed. One man was dusting the nightstand for fingerprints, although he must have known that he would not find any. This was the work of the Butcher, and the Butcher always wore gloves. The coroner was plotting the trajectory of the blood on the wall in order to establish whether the killer was left-handed or right-handed.

"Where's the body?" Graham asked.

"I'm sorry, but they took it to the morgue ten minutes ago," Detective Preduski said, as if he felt responsible for some inexcusable breach of manners. Graham wondered if Preduski's entire life was an apologia. The detective was quick to take the blame for everything— and to find fault with himself even when he behaved impeccably. He was a nondescript man with a pale complexion and watery brown eyes. In spite of his appearance and his apparent inferiority complex, he was a highly respected member of the Manhattan homicide detail. More than one of the detective's associates had made it clear to Graham that he was working with the best, that Ira Preduski was the top man in the department. "I held the ambulance as long as I could. You took so much time to get here. Of course I woke you in the dead of night. I shouldn't have done that. And then you probably had to call a cab and wait around for it. I'm so sorry. Now I've probably ruined everything for you. I should have tried to keep the body here just a bit longer. I *knew* you'd want to see it where it was found."

"That doesn't matter," Graham said. "In a sense, I've already had a firsthand look at her."

"Of course you have," Preduski said. "I saw you on the Prine show earlier."

"Her eyes were green, weren't they?"

"Just as you said."

"She was found nude?"

"Yes."

"Stabbed many times?"

"Yes."

"With a particularly brutal wound in the throat?"

"That's right."

"He mutilated her, didn't he?"

"Yes."

"How?"

"Awful thing," Preduski said. "I wish I didn't have to tell you. Nobody should have to hear it." Preduski seemed about to wring his hands. "He cut a plug of flesh out of her stomach. It's almost like a cork, with her navel in the center of it. Terrible."

Graham closed his eyes and shuddered. "This . . . cork . . . " He was beginning to perspire. He felt ill. He wasn't receiving a vision, just a strong sense of what had happened, a hunch that was difficult to ignore. "He put this cork . . . in her right hand and closed her fingers around it. That's where you found it."

"Yes."

The coroner turned away from the blood-spattered wall and stared curiously at Graham.

Don't look at me that way, Graham thought. I don't *want* to know these things.

He would have been delighted if his clairvoyance had allowed him to predict sharp rises in the stock market rather than isolated pockets of maniacal violence. He would have preferred to see the names of winning horses in races not yet run rather than the names of victims in murders he'd never seen committed.

If he could have wished away his powers, he would have done that long ago. But because that was impossible, he felt as if he had a responsibility to develop and interpret his psychic talent. He believed, perhaps irrationally, that by doing so he was compensating, at least in part, for the cowardice that had overwhelmed him these past five years.

"What do you make of the message he left us?" Preduski asked.

On the wall beside the vanity bench there were lines of poetry printed in blood.

> *Rintah roars and shakes his fires*
> *in the burden'd air;*
> *Hungry clouds swag on the deep*

"Have any idea what it means?" Preduski asked.

"I'm afraid not."

"Recognize the poet?"

"No."

"Neither do I." Preduski shook his head sorrowfully. "I'm not very well educated. I only had one year of college. Couldn't afford it. I read a lot, but there's so *much* to read. If I were educated, maybe I'd know whose poetry that is. I should know. If the Butcher takes the time to write it down, it's something important to him. It's a lead. What kind of detective am I if I can't follow up a lead as plain as that?" He shook his head again, clearly disgusted with himself. "Not a good one. Not a very good one."

"Maybe it's his own poetry," Graham said.

"The Butcher's?"

"Maybe."

"A murderous poet? T. S. Eliot with a homicidal urge?"

Graham shrugged.

"No," Preduski said. "A man usually commits this sort of crime because it's the only way he can express the rage inside him. Slaughter releases pressures that have built in him. But a poet can express his feelings with words. No. If it were doggerel, perhaps it could be the Butcher's own verse. But this is too smooth, too sensitive, too good. Anyway, it rings a bell. Way back in this thick head of mine, it rings a bell." Preduski studied the bloody message for a moment, then turned and went to the bedroom door. It was standing open; he closed it. "Then there's this one."

On the back of the door, five words were printed in the dead woman's blood.

> *a rope over an abyss*

"Has he ever left anything like this before?" Graham asked.

"No. I would have told you if he had. But it's not unusual in this sort of crime. Certain types of psychopaths like to communicate with whoever finds the corpse. Jack the Ripper wrote notes to the police. The Manson family used blood to scrawl one-word messages on the walls. 'A rope over an abyss.' What is he trying to tell us?"

"Is it from the same poem as the other?"

"I haven't the faintest idea." Preduski sighed, thrust his hands into his pockets. He looked dejected. "I'm beginning to wonder if I'm *ever* going to catch him."

The living room of Edna Mowry's apartment was small but not mean. Indirect lighting bathed everything in a relaxing amber glow. Gold velvet drapes. Textured light tan burlap-pattern wallpaper. Plush brown carpet. A beige velour sofa and two matching armchairs. A heavy glass coffee table with brass legs. Chrome and glass shelves full of books and statuary. Limited editions of prints by some fine contemporary artists. It was tasteful, cozy and expensive.

At Preduski's request, Graham settled down in one of the armchairs.

Sarah Piper was sitting on one end of the sofa. She looked as expensive as the room. She was wearing a knitted pantsuit—dark blue with Kelly green piping—gold earrings and an elegant watch as thin as a half dollar. She was no older than twenty-five, a strikingly lovely, well-built blonde, marked by experience.

Earlier she had been crying. Her eyes were puffy and red. She was in control of herself now.

"We've been through this before," she said.

Preduski was beside her on the couch. "I know," he said. "And I'm sorry. Truly sorry. It's terribly late, too late for this. But there *is* something to be gained by asking the same questions two and even three times. You think you've told me all the pertinent facts. But it's possible you overlooked something. God knows, *I'm* forever over-looking things. This questioning may seem redundant to you, but it's the way I work. I have to go over things again and again to make sure I've done them right. I'm not proud of it. That's just the way I am. Some other detective might get everything he needs the first time he speaks to you. Not me, I'm afraid. It was your misfortune that the call came in while I was on duty. Bear with me. I'll be able to let you go home before much longer. I promise."

The woman glanced at Graham and cocked her head as if to say, *Is this guy for real?*

Graham smiled.

"How long had you known—the deceased?" Preduski asked.

She said, "About a year."

"How well did you know her?"

"She was my best friend."

"Do you think that in her eyes you were *her* best friend?"

"Sure. I was her only friend."

Preduski raised his eyebrows. "People didn't like her?"

"Of course they liked her," Sarah Piper said. "What wasn't to like? She just didn't make friends easily. She was a quiet girl. She kept mostly to herself."

"Where did you meet her?"

"At work."

"Where is work?"

"You know that. The Rhinestone Palace."

"And what did she do there?"

"You know that too."

Nodding, patting her knee in a strictly fatherly manner, the detective said, "That's correct. I know it. But, you see, Mr. Harris doesn't know it. I neglected to fill him in. My fault. I'm sorry. Would you tell him?"

She turned to Graham. "Edna was a stripper. Just like me."

"I know the Rhinestone Palace," Graham said.

"You've been there?" Preduski asked.

"No. But I know it's fairly high class, not like most strip-tease clubs."

For a moment Preduski's watery brown eyes seemed less out of focus than usual. He stared intently at Graham. "Edna Mowry was a stripper. How about that?"

He knew precisely what the detective was thinking. On the Prine show he had said that the victim's name might be Edna Dancer. He had not been right—but he had not been altogether wrong either; for although her name was Mowry, *she earned her living as a dancer*.

According to Sarah Piper, Edna had reported for work at five o'clock the previous evening. She performed a ten-minute act twice every hour for the next seven hours, peeling out of a variety of costumes until she was entirely nude. Between acts, dressed in a black cocktail dress, sans bra, she mixed with the customers—mostly men, alone and in groups—hustling drinks in a cautious, demure and stylish way that skipped successfully along the edge of the state's B-girl laws. She had finished her last performance at twenty minutes of twelve and left the Rhinestone Palace no more than five minutes after that.

"You think she came straight home?" Preduski asked.

"She always did," Sarah said. "She never wanted to go out and have fun. The Rhinestone Palace was all the night life she could stomach. Who could blame her?"

Her voice wavered, as if she might begin to cry again.

Preduski took her hand and squeezed it reassuringly. She let him hold it, and that appeared to give him an innocent pleasure. "Did you dance last evening?"

"Yeah. Till midnight."

"When did you come here?"

"A quarter of three."

"Why would you be visiting at that hour?"

"Edna liked to sit and read all night. She never went to bed until eight or nine in the morning. I told her I'd stop around for breakfast and gossip. I often did."

"You've probably already told me..." Preduski made a face: embarrassment, apology, frustration. "I'm sorry. This mind of mine—like a sieve. Did you tell me why you didn't come here at midnight, when you got off work?"

"I had a date," she said.

Graham could tell from her expression and from the tone of her voice that the "date" had been a paying customer. That saddened him a bit. He liked her already. He couldn't help but like her. He was receiving low-key waves, threshold psychic vibrations from her; they were very positive, mellow and warm vibrations. She was a damned nice person. He *knew*. And he wanted only pleasant things to happen to her.

"Did Edna have a date tonight?" Preduski asked.

"No. I told you. She came right home."

"Maybe her boyfriend was waiting for her."

"She was between boyfriends."

"Maybe an old boyfriend stopped in to talk."

"No. When Edna dropped a guy, he *stayed* dropped."

Preduski sighed, pinched the bridge of his nose, shook his head sadly. "I hate to have to ask this.... You were her best friend. But what I'm going to say—please understand I don't mean to put her down. Life is tough. We all have to do things we'd rather not do. I'm not proud of every day of my life. God knows. Don't judge. That's my motto. There's only one crime I can't rationalize away. Murder. I really hate to ask this.... Well, was she... do you think she ever..."

"Was she a prostitute?" Sarah asked for him.

"Oh, I wouldn't put it that way! That's such an awful... I really meant..."

"Don't worry," she said. She smiled sweetly. "I'm not offended."

Graham was amused to see her squeeze the detective's hand. Now *she* was comforting *Preduski*.

"I do some light hooking myself," Sarah said. "Not much. Once a week, maybe. I've got to like the guy, and he's got to have two hundred bucks to spare. It's all the same as stripping to me, really. But it wouldn't have been something Edna could do. She was surprisingly straight.''

"I shouldn't have asked. It was none of my business," said Preduski. "But it occurred to me that in her line of work there would be a lot of temptation for a girl who needed money.''

"She made eight hundred a week stripping and hustling drinks," Sarah said. "She only spent money on her books and apartment. She was socking it in the bank. She didn't need more.''

Preduski was somber. "But you see why I had to ask? If she opened the door to the killer, he must have been someone she knew, however briefly. That's what puzzles me most about this whole case. How does the Butcher get them to open the door?''

Graham had never thought about that. The dead women were all young, but they were from varied backgrounds. One was a housewife. One was a lawyer. Two were schoolteachers. Three secretaries, one model, one sales clerk. . . . How *did* the Butcher get so many different women to open their doors to him late at night?

The kitchen table was littered with the remains of a hastily prepared and hastily eaten meal. Bits of bread. The dried edge of a slice of bologna. Smears of mustard and mayonnaise. Two apple cores. A can of cling peaches empty of everything except an inch of packing syrup. A drumstick gnawed to the bone. Half a doughnut. Three crushed beer cans. The Butcher had been ravenous and sloppy.

"Ten murders," Preduski said, "and he always goes to the kitchen for a snack afterward.''

Stifled by the psychic atmosphere of the kitchen, by the incredibly strong, lingering presence of the killer which was nearly as heavy here as it had been in the dead woman's bedroom, Graham could only nod. The mess on the table, in contrast with the otherwise tidy kitchen, disturbed him deeply. The peach can and the beer can were covered with reddish-brown stains; the killer had eaten while wearing his bloody gloves.

Preduski shuffled forlornly to the window by the sink. He stared at the neighboring apartment house. "I've talked to a few psychiatrists about these feasts he has when he's done the dirty work. As I understand it, there are two basic ways a psychopath will act when he's finished with his victim. Number one, there's Mr. Meek. The killing is everything for him, his whole reason for living, the only color and desire in his life. When he's done killing, there's nothing, he's nothing. He goes home and watches television. Sleeps a lot. He sinks into a deep pit of boredom until the pressures build up and he kills again. Number two, there's the man who gets psyched up by the murder. His real excitement comes not during the killing but after it. He'll go straight from the scene of the crime to a bar and drink everyone under the table. His adrenaline is up. His heartbeat is up. He eats like a lumberjack and sometimes picks up whores by the six-pack. Apparently, our man is number two. Except . . .''

''Except what?'' Graham asked.

Turning away from the window, Preduski said, ''Seven times he's eaten a big meal in the dead women's own homes. But the other three times, he's taken the food out of the refrigerator and faked a big meal.''

''Faked it? What do you mean?''

''The fifth murder, the Liedstrom woman,'' Preduski said. He closed his eyes and grimaced as if he could still see her body and blood. ''We were aware of his style by then. We checked the kitchen right away. There was an empty pear can on the table, an empty cottage cheese container, the remains of an apple and several other items. But there wasn't a mess. The first four times, he'd been sloppy—like he was tonight. But in the Liedstrom kitchen, he hadn't left a lot of crumbs. No smears of butter or mustard or mayonnaise or ketchup. No bloodstains on the beer cans.''

He opened his eyes and walked to the table. ''We'd found well-gnawed apple cores in two of the first four kitchens.'' He pointed at an apple core on the table in front of him. ''Like that one. The lab had even studied the teeth marks on them. But in the Liedstrom kitchen he peeled the apple and removed the center with a corer. The skins and the core were piled neatly on one corner of his dinner plate. That was a change from what we'd seen previously, and it got me thinking. Why had he eaten like a Neanderthal the first four times—and like a gentleman the fifth? I had the forensic boys open the plumbing under the sink and take out the garbage disposal unit. They ran tests on it and found that each of the eight kinds of food on the table had been put through the disposal within the past few hours. In short, the Butcher hadn't taken a bite of anything in the Liedstrom kitchen. He got the food from the refrigerator and tossed it down the drain. Then he set the table so it would look as if he'd had a big meal. He did the same thing at the scene of murders seven and eight.''

That sort of behavior struck Graham as particularly eerie. The air in the room seemed suddenly more moist and oppressive than before. ''You said his eating after a murder was part of a psychotic compulsion.''

''Yes.''

''If for some reason he didn't feel that compulsion at the Liedstrom house, why would he bother to fake it?''

''I don't know,'' Preduski said. He wiped one slender hand across his face as if he were trying to pull off his weariness. "It's too much for me. It really is. Much too much. If he's crazy, why isn't he crazy in the same way all of the time?"

Graham hesitated. Then: "I don't think any court-appointed psychiatrist would find him insane."

"Say again?"

"In fact, I think even the best psychiatrist, if not informed of the murders, would find this man saner and more reasonable than he would most of us."

Preduski blinked his watery eyes in surprise. "Well, hell. He carves up ten women and leaves them for garbage, and you don't think he's crazy?"

"That's the same reaction I got from a lady friend when I told her."

"I don't wonder."

"But I'll stick by it. Maybe he *is* crazy. But not in any traditional, recognizable way. He's something altogether new."

"You sense this?"

"Yes."

"Psychically?"

"Yes."

"Can you be more specific?"

"Sorry."

"Sense anything else?"

"Just what you heard on the Prine show."

"Nothing new since you came here?"

"Nothing."

"If he's not insane *at all*, then there's a reason behind the killings," Preduski said thoughtfully. "Somehow they're connected. Is that what you're saying?"

"I'm not sure *what* I mean."

"I don't see how they could be connected."

"Neither do I."

"I've been looking for a connection, really looking. I was hoping you could pick up something here. From the bloody bedclothes. Or from this mess on the table."

"I'm blank," Harris said. "That's why I'm positive that either he is sane, or he is insane in some whole new fashion. Usually, when I study or touch an item intimately connected with the murder, I can pick up on the emotion, the mania, the passion behind the crime. It's like leaping into a river of violent thoughts, sensations, images. . . . This time all I get is a feeling of cool, implacable, evil *logic*. I've never had so much trouble drawing a bead on this kind of killer."

"Me either," Preduski said. "I never claimed to be Sherlock

Holmes. I'm no genius. I work slow. Always have. And I've been lucky. God knows. It's luck more than skill that's kept my arrest record high. But this time I'm having no luck at all. None at all. Maybe it's time for me to be put out to pasture.''

On his way out of the apartment, having left Ira Preduski in the kitchen to ponder the remnants of the Butcher's macabre meal, Graham passed through the living room and saw Sarah Piper. The detective had not yet dismissed her. She was sitting on the sofa, her feet propped on the coffee table. She was smoking a cigarette and staring at the ceiling, smoke spiraling like dreams from her head; her back was to Graham.

The instant he saw her, a brilliant image flashed behind his eyes, intense, breathtaking: *Sarah Piper with blood all over her*.

He stopped. Shaking. Waiting for more.

Nothing.

He strained. Tried to pluck more pictures from the ether.

Nothing. Just her face. And the blood. Gone now as quickly as it had come to him.

She became aware of him. She turned around and said, ''Hi.''

He licked his lips, forced a smile.

''You predicted this?'' she asked, waving one hand toward the dead woman's bedroom.

''I'm afraid so.''

''That's spooky.''

''I want to say . . . ''

''Yes?''

''It was nice meeting you.''

She smiled too.

''I wish it could have been under other circumstances,'' he said, stalling, wondering how to tell her about the brief vision, wondering whether he should tell her at all.

''Maybe we will,'' she said.

''What?''

''Meet under other circumstances.''

''Miss Piper . . . be careful.''

''I'm always careful.''

''For the next few days . . . be especially careful.''

''After what I've seen tonight,'' she said, no longer smiling, ''you can bet on it.''

# 7
◆ ◆ ◆

Frank Bollinger's apartment near the Metropolitan Museum of Art was small and Spartan. The bedroom walls were cocoa brown, the wooden floor polished and bare. The only furniture in the room was a queen-size bed, one nightstand, and a portable television set. He had built shelves into the closets to hold his clothes. The living room had white walls and the same shining wood floor. The only furniture was a black leather couch, a wicker chair with black cushions, a mirrored coffee table, and shelves full of books. The kitchen held the usual appliances and a small table with two straight-backed chairs. The windows were covered with venetian blinds, no drapes. The apartment was more like a monk's cell than a home, and that was how he liked it.

At nine o'clock Friday morning he got out of bed, showered, plugged in the telephone, and brewed a pot of coffee.

He had come directly to his apartment from Edna Mowry's place and had spent the early morning hours drinking Scotch and reading Blake's poetry. Halfway through the bottle, still not drunk but so happy, very happy, he went to bed and fell asleep reciting lines from *The Four Zoas*. When he awoke five hours later, he felt new and fresh and pure, as if he had been reborn.

He was pouring his first cup of coffee when the telephone rang.

"Hello?"

"Dwight?"

"Yeah."

"This is Billy."

"Of course."

Dwight was his middle name—Franklin Dwight Bollinger—and had been the name of his maternal grandfather, who had died when Frank was less than a year old. Until he met and came to know Billy, until he trusted Billy, his grandmother had been the only one who ever used his middle name. Shortly after his fourth birthday, his father abandoned the family, and his mother discovered that a four-year-old interfered with the hectic social life of a divorcee. Except for a few scattered and agonizing months with his mother—who managed to provide occasional bursts of affection only when her conscience began to bother her—he had spent his childhood with his grandmother. She not only wanted him, she cherished him. She treated him as if he were the focus not just of her own life but of the very rotation of the earth.

"Franklin is such an ordinary name," his grandmother used to say. "But *Dwight* . . . well, now, that's *special*. It was your grandfather's name, and he was a wonderful man, not at all like other people, one of a kind. You're going to grow up to be just like him, set apart, set above, more important than others. Let everyone call you Frank. To me you'll always be Dwight." His grandmother had died ten years ago. For nine and a half years no one had called him Dwight; then, six months ago, he'd met Billy. Billy understood what it was like to be one of the new breed, to have been born superior to most men. Billy was superior too, and had a right to call him Dwight. He liked hearing the name again after all this time. It was a key to his psyche, a pleasure button that lifted his spirits each time it was pushed, a reminder that he was destined for a dizzyingly high station in life.

"I tried calling you several times last night," Billy said.

"I unplugged the phone so I could drink some Scotch and sleep in peace."

"Have you seen the papers this morning?"

"I just got up."

"You haven't heard anything about Harris?"

"Who?"

"Graham Harris. The psychic."

"Oh. No. Nothing. What's to hear?"

"Get the papers, Dwight. And then we'd better have lunch. You are off work today, aren't you?"

"I'm always off Thursdays and Fridays. But what's wrong?"

"The *Daily News* will tell you what's wrong. Be sure to get a copy. We'll have lunch at The Leopard at eleven-thirty."

Frowning, Bollinger said, "Look—"

"Eleven-thirty, Dwight."

Billy hung up.

The day was dreary and cold. Thick dark clouds scudded southward; they were so low they seemed to skim the tops of the highest buildings.

Three blocks from the restaurant, Bollinger left his taxi and bought the *Daily News* at a kiosk. In his bulky coat and sweaters and gloves and scarves and wool toboggan cap, the vendor looked like a mummy.

The lower half of the front page held a publicity photograph of Edna Mowry provided by the Rhinestone Palace. She was smiling, quite lovely. The upper half of the page featured bold black headlines:

*BUTCHER KILLS NUMBER 10*
*PSYCHIC PREDICTS MURDER*

At the corner he turned to the second page and tried to read the story while waiting for the traffic light to change. The wind stung his eyes and made them water. It rattled the paper in his hands and made it impossible for him to read.

He crossed the street and stepped into the sheltered entranceway of an office building. His teeth still chattering from the cold, but free of the wind, he read about Graham Harris and *Manhattan at Midnight*.

His name is Dwight, Harris had said.

The police already know him, Harris had said.

*Christ!* How could the son of a bitch possibly know so much? Psychic powers? That was a lot of bullshit. There weren't such things. Were there?

Worried now, Bollinger walked to the corner, threw the newspaper into a litter basket, hunched his shoulders against the wind, and hurried toward the restaurant.

The Leopard, on Fiftieth Street near Second Avenue, was a charming restaurant with only a handful of tables and excellent food. The dining area was no larger than an average living room. A hideous display of artificial flowers filled the center of the room, but that was the only really outrageous element in a generally bland decor.

Billy was sitting at a choice table by the window. In an hour The Leopard would be full of diners and noisy conversation. This early, fifteen minutes or more before the executive lunch crowd could slip away from conference rooms and desks, Billy was the only customer. Bollinger sat opposite him. They shook hands and ordered drinks.

"Nasty weather," Billy said. His Southern accent was heavy.

"Yes."

They stared at each other over the bud vase and single rose that stood in the center of the table.

"Nasty news," Billy said at last.

"Yes."

"What do you think?"

"This Harris is incredible," Bollinger said.

"Dwight. . . . Nobody but me knows you by that name. He hasn't given them much of a clue."

"My middle name's on all my records—on my employee file at the department."

Unfolding a linen napkin, Billy said, "They've got no reason to believe the killer's a policeman."

"Harris told them they already knew the Butcher."

"They'll just suppose that he's someone they've already questioned."

Frowning, Bollinger said, "If he gives them one more bit of detail, one more clue, I'm blown."

"I thought you didn't believe in psychics."

"I was wrong. You were right."

"Apology accepted," Billy said, smiling thinly.

"This Harris—can we reason with him?"

"No."

"He wouldn't understand?"

"He's not one of us."

The waiter came with their drinks.

When they were alone again, Bollinger said, "I've never seen this Harris. What does he look like?"

"I'll describe him to you later. Right now . . . do you mind telling me what you're going to do?"

Bollinger didn't have to think about that. Without hesitation he said, "Kill him."

"Ah," Billy said softly.

"Objections?"

"Absolutely none."

"Good." Bollinger swallowed half of his drink. "Because I'd do it even if you had objections."

The captain came to the table and asked if they would like to hear the menu.

"Give us five minutes," Billy said. When the captain had gone, he said, "When you've killed Harris, will you leave him like the Butcher would?"

"Why not?"

"Well, the others have been women."

"This will confuse and upset them even more," Bollinger said.

"When will you do it?"

"Tonight."

Billy said, "I don't think he lives alone."

"With his mother?" Bollinger asked sourly.

"No. I believe he lives with a woman."

"Young?"

"I would imagine so."

"Pretty?"

"He *does* seem to be a man of good taste."

"Well, that's just fine," Bollinger said.

"I thought you'd see it that way."

"A double-header," Bollinger said. "That just adds to the fun." He grinned.

# 8
◆ ◆ ◆

"Detective Preduski is on the line, Mr. Harris."

"I'll talk to him. Put him through. Hello?"

"Sorry to bother you, Graham. Can we be less formal than we've been? May I call you Graham?"

"Sure."

"Please call me Ira."

"I'd be honored."

"You're very kind. I hope I didn't interrupt something."

"No."

"I know you're a busy man. Would you rather I called you back later? Or would you like to call me back at your convenience?"

"You didn't interrupt. What is it you want?"

"You know that writing we found on the walls of the Mowry apartment?"

"Too clearly."

"Well, I've been trying to track down the source for the past few hours, and—"

"You're still on duty at two in the afternoon?"

"No, no. I'm at home."

"Don't you ever sleep?"

"I wish I could. I haven't been able to sleep more than four or five hours a day for the past twenty years. I'm probably ruining my health. I *know* I am. But I've got this twisted brain. My head's full of garbage, thousands of useless facts, and I can't stop thinking about them. I keep picking at the damndest things. Like the writing on the walls at the Mowry apartment. I couldn't sleep for thinking about it."

"And you've come up with something?"

"Well, I told you last night the poetry rang a bell. 'Rintah roars and shakes his fires in the burden'd air; Hungry clouds swag on the deep.' As soon as I saw it I said to myself, 'Ira, that's from something

William Blake wrote.' You see, when I was in college for that one year, my major was literature. I had to write a paper on Blake. Twenty-five years ago. You see what I mean about garbage in my head? I remember the most useless things. Anyway this morning I bought the Erdman edition of Blake's poetry and prose. Sure enough, I found those lines in 'The Argument,' part of *The Marriage of Heaven and Hell*. Do you know Blake?''

"I'm afraid not.''

"He was a mystic and a psychic.''

"Clairvoyant?''

"No. But with a psychic bent. He thought men had the power to be gods. For an important part of his career he was a poet of chaos and cataclysm—and yet he was fundamentally a table-pounding optimist. Now, do you remember the line the Butcher printed on the bedroom door?''

"Yes. 'A rope over an abyss.' ''

"Do you have any idea what that's from?''

"None.''

"Neither did I. My head is full of garbage. There's no room for anything important. And I'm not a well-educated man. Not well educated at all. So I called a friend of mine, a professor in the Department of English at Columbia. He didn't recognize the line either, but he passed it around to a few of his colleagues. One of them thought he knew it. He got a concordance of the major philosophers and located the full quotation. 'Man is rope stretched between the animal and the Superman—a rope over an abyss.' ''

"Who said it?''

"Hitler's favorite philosopher.''

"Nietzsche.''

"You know his work?''

"In passing.''

"He believed men could be gods—or at least that certain men could be gods if their society allowed them to grow and exercise their powers. He believed mankind was evolving toward godhood. You see, there's a superficial resemblance between Blake and Nietzsche. That's why the Butcher might quote both of them. But there's a problem, Graham.''

"What's that?''

"Blake was an optimist all the way. Nietzsche was a raving pessimist. Blake thought mankind had a bright future. Nietzsche thought mankind *should* have a bright future, but he believed that it would destroy itself before the Supermen ever evolved from it. Blake apparently liked women. Nietzsche despised them. In fact, he thought women constituted one of the greatest obstacles standing between man and his climb to godhood. You see what I'm getting at?''

"You're saying that if the Butcher subscribes to both Blake and Nietzsche's philosophies, then he's a schizophrenic.''

"Yet you say he's not even crazy.''

"Wait a minute.''

"Last night—''

"All I said was that if he's a maniac, he's a *new kind* of maniac. I said he wasn't crazy in any traditional sense.''

"Which rules out schizophrenia?''

"I guess it does, Ira.''

"But I think it's a good bet . . . maybe I'm wrong . . . God knows . . . but maybe he looks at himself as one of Nietzsche's Supermen. A psychiatrist would call that delusions of grandeur. And delusions of grandeur characterize schizophrenia and paranoia. Do you *still* think the Butcher could pass any psychiatric test we could give him?''

"Yes.''

"You sense this psychically?''

"That's right.''

"Have you ever sensed something and been wrong?''

"Not seriously wrong. No worse than thinking Edna Mowry's name was Edna Dancer.''

"Of course. I know your reputation. I know you're good. I didn't mean to imply anything. You understand? But still—now where do I stand?''

"I don't know.''

"Graham . . . if you were to sit down with a book of Blake's poems, if you were to spend an hour or so reading them, would that maybe put you in tune with the Butcher? Would it spark something—if not a vision, at least a hunch?''

"It might.''

"Would you do me a favor then?''

"Name it.''

"If I send a messenger right over with an edition of Blake's work, will you sit down with it for an hour and see what happens?''

"You can send it over today if you want, but I won't get to it until tomorrow.''

"Maybe just *half* an hour.''

"Not even that. I've got to finish working on one of my magazines and get it off to the printer tomorrow morning. I'm already three days late with the issue. I'll be working most of tonight. But tomorrow afternoon or evening, I'll make time for Blake.''

"Thank you. I appreciate it. I really do. I'm counting on you. You're my only hope. This Butcher is too much for me, too sharp for me. I'm getting nowhere. Absolutely nowhere. If we don't get a solid lead soon, I don't know what's going to happen.''

# 9
◆ ◆ ◆

Paul Stevenson was wearing a hand-sewn blue shirt, a blue-and-black-striped silk tie, an expensive black suit, black socks, and light brown shoes with white stitching. When he came into Anthony Prine's office at two o'clock Friday afternoon, unaware that Prine winced when he saw the shoes, he was upset. Because he was incapable of shouting and screaming at Prine, he pouted. "Tony, why are you keeping secrets from me?''

Prine was stretched out on the couch, his head propped on a bolster pillow. He was reading *The New York Times*. "Secrets?''

"I just found out that at your direction the company has hired a private detective agency to snoop on Graham Harris.''

"They're not snooping. All I've asked them to do is establish Harris's whereabouts at certain hours on certain days.''

"You asked the detectives not to approach Harris or his girlfriend directly. That's snooping. And you asked them for a forty-eight-hour rush job, which triples the cost. If you want to know where he was, why don't you ask him yourself?''

"I think he'd lie to me.''

"Why should he lie? What certain hours? What certain dates?''

Prine put down the paper, sat up, stood up, stretched. "I want to know where he was when each of those ten women was killed.''

Perplexed, blinking somewhat stupidly, Stevenson said, "Why?''

"If on all ten occasions he was alone—working alone, seeing a movie alone, walking alone—then maybe he could have killed them.''

"*Harris?* You think Harris is the Butcher?''

"Maybe.''

"You hire detectives on a maybe?''

"I told you, I've distrusted that man from the start. And if I'm right about this, what a scoop we'll have!"

"But Harris isn't a killer. He *catches* killers."

Prine went to the bar. "If a doctor treats fifty patients for influenza one week and fifty more the next, would it surprise you if he got influenza himself during the third week?"

"I'm not sure I get your point."

Prine filled his glass with bourbon. "For years Harris has been tuning in to murder with the deepest levels of his mind, exposing himself to trauma as few of us ever do. He has been literally delving into the minds of wife killers, child killers, mass murderers. . . . He's probably seen more blood and violence than most career cops. Isn't it conceivable that a man, unstable to begin with, could crack from all the violent input? Isn't it conceivable that he could become the kind of maniac he's worked so hard to catch?"

"Unstable?" Stevenson frowned. "Graham Harris is as stable as you or me."

"How well do you know him?"

"I saw him on the show."

"There's a bit more you should know." Prine caught sight of himself in the mirror behind the bar cabinet; he smoothed his lustrous white hair with one hand.

"For example?"

"I'll indulge myself in amateur psychoanalysis—amateur but probably accurate. First of all, Graham Harris was born into borderline poverty and—"

"Hold on. His old man was Evan Harris, the publisher."

"His stepfather. His real father died when Graham was a year old. His mother was a cocktail waitress. She had trouble keeping a roof over their heads because she had to pay off her husband's medical bills. For years they lived day to day, on the edge of disaster. That would leave marks on a child."

"How did she meet Evan Harris?" Stevenson asked.

"I don't know. But after they were married, Graham took his step-father's name. He spent the latter part of his childhood in a mansion. After he got his university degree, he had enough time and money to become one of the world's leading climbers. Old man Harris encouraged him. In some circles, Graham was famous, a star. Do you realize how many beautiful women are drawn to the sport of climbing?"

Stevenson shrugged.

"Not as participants," Prine said. "As companions to the partici-pants, as bedmates. More women than you'd think. I guess it's the nearness of death that attracts them. For more than a decade, Graham was adored, made over. Then he took a bad fall. When he recovered, he was terrified of climbing." Prine was listening to his own voice, fascinated by the theory he had developed. "Do you understand, Paul? He was born a nobody, lived the first six years of his life as a nobody— then overnight he became a somebody when his mother married Evan Harris. Now is it any wonder that he's afraid of being a nobody again?"

Stevenson went to the bar and poured himself some bourbon. "It's not likely he'll be a nobody again. He *did* inherit his stepfather's money."

"Money isn't the same as fame. Once he'd been a celebrity, even within the tight circle of climbing enthusiasts, maybe he developed a habit for it. Maybe he became a fame junkie. It can happen to the best. I've seen it."

"So have I."

"If that's what he is . . . well, maybe he's decided that being infamous is as good as being famous. As the Butcher, he's grabbing headlines; he's infamous, even if only under a *nom de guerre*."

"But he was with you in the studio last night when the Mowry girl was murdered."

"Maybe not."

"What? He predicted her death."

"Did he? Or did he simply tell us who he had selected for his next victim?"

Stevenson stared at him as if he were mad.

Laughing, Prine said, "Of course Harris was in the studio with me—but perhaps not when the murder took place. I used a source in the police department and got a copy of the coroner's report. According to the pathologist, Edna Mowry was murdered sometime between eleven-thirty Thursday night and one-thirty Friday morning. Now, Graham Harris left the studio at twelve-thirty Friday morning. He had an hour to get to Edna Mowry."

Stevenson swallowed some bourbon. "Jesus, Tony, if you're right, if you break a story like this, ABC will give you a late-night talk show and let you do it your way, *live*!"

"They might."

Stevenson finished his bourbon. "But you don't have any proof. It's just a theory. And a pretty far-out theory at that. You can't convict a man because he was born to poor parents. Hell, your childhood was worse than his, and you're not a killer."

"At the moment I've got no proof," Prine said. But if it can't be found, it can be manufactured, he thought.

# 10
### ◆ ◆ ◆

Sarah Piper spent the early part of Friday afternoon packing for a five-day trip to Las Vegas. Ernie Nolan, a men's clothing manufacturer who had been on her special list of customers for three years, went to Vegas every six months and took her with him. He paid her fifteen hundred dollars for her time in bed and gave her five hundred as a gambling stake. Even if Ernie had been a beast, which he was not, it would have been a good vacation for her.

Beginning today, she was on a week's leave from the Rhinestone Palace, and she was glad that she hadn't tried to squeeze in one more night's work before catching the flight to Vegas tomorrow morning. She'd had only two hours' sleep after returning from Edna's place, and those two hours had been plagued by nightmares. She would need to rest well tonight if she was going to be at the top of her form for Ernie.

As she packed, she wondered if there was something missing from her. Heart? Normal emotions? She had cried last night, had been deeply affected by Edna's death. But already her spirits were high again. She was excited, pleased to be getting away from New York. Introspection didn't give rise to any guilt. She had seen too much of the world—too much violence, desperation, selfishness, and grubbiness—to chastise herself for being unable to sustain her grief. That was the way people were built: forgetfulness was the hub of the wheel, the core of the mind, the thing that kept you sane. Maybe that was not pleasant to contemplate, but it was true.

At three o'clock, as she was locking the third suitcase, a man called. He wanted to set up a date for that evening. She didn't know him, but he claimed to have gotten her name from one of her regular clients. Although he sounded quite nice—a genuine Southern gentleman with a mellow accent—she had to turn him down.

"If you've got something else going," he said, "I can make it worth your while to drop him for tonight."

"There's no one else. But I'm going to Vegas in the morning, and I need my rest."

"What's your usual rate?" he asked.

"Two hundred. But—"

"I'll give you three hundred."

She hesitated.

"Four hundred."

"I'll give you the names of a couple of girls—"

"I want to spend the evening with *you*. I hear you're the loveliest woman in Manhattan."

She laughed. "You'd be in for a big disappointment."

"I've made up my mind. When I've made up my mind, nothing on God's earth can change it. Five hundred dollars."

"That's too much. If you—"

"Young lady, five hundred is peanuts. I've made millions in the oil business. Five hundred—and I won't tie you up all evening. I'll be there around six o'clock. We'll relax together—then go out to dinner. You'll be home by ten, plenty of time to rest up for Vegas."

"You don't give up easily, do you?"

"That's my trademark. I'm blessed with perseverance. Down home they call it pure mule-headed stubbornness."

Smiling, she said, "All right. You win. Five hundred. But you promise we'll be back by ten?"

"Word of honor," he said.

"You haven't told me your name."

"Plover," he said. "Billy James Plover."

"Do I call you Billy James?"

"Just Billy."

"Who recommended me?"

"I'd rather not use his name on the phone."

"Okay. Six o'clock it is."

"Don't you forget."

"I'm looking forward to it," she said.

"So am I," Billy said.

# 11
◆ ◆ ◆

Although Connie Davis had slept late and hadn't opened the antique shop until after lunch, and although she'd had only one customer, it was a good day for business. She had sold six perfectly matched seventeenth-century Spanish chairs. Each piece was of dark oak with bowed legs and claw feet. The arms ended in snarling demon heads, elaborately carved gargoyles the size of oranges. The woman who purchased the chairs had a fourteen-room apartment overlooking Fifth Avenue and Central Park; she wanted them for the room in which she sometimes held séances.

Later, when she was alone in the shop, Connie went to her alcove office at the rear of the main room. She opened a can of fresh coffee, prepared the percolator.

At the front of the room the big windows rattled noisily. Connie looked up from the percolator to see who had come in. No one was there. The windows were trembling from the sudden violence of the winter weather; the wind had picked up and was gusting fiercely.

She sat down at a neatly kept Sheraton desk from the late 1780s and dialed the number of Graham's private office phone, bypassing his secretary. When he answered she said, "Hello, Nick."

"Hi, Nora."

"If you've made any headway with your work, let me take you to dinner tonight. I just sold the Spanish chairs, and I feel a need to celebrate."

"Can't do, I'm afraid. I'm going to have to work most of the night to finish here."

"Can't the staff work a bit of overtime?" she asked.

"They've done their job. But you know how I am. I have to double-check and triple-check everything."

"I'll come help."

"There's nothing you can help with."

"Then I'll sit in the corner and read."

"Really, Connie, you'd be bored. You go home and relax. I'll show up sometime around one or two in the morning."

"Nothing doing. I won't get in your way, and I'll be perfectly comfortable reading in an office chair. Nora needs her Nick tonight. I'll bring supper."

"Well . . . okay. Who am I kidding? I knew you'd come."

"A large pizza and a bottle of wine. How's that?"

"Sounds good."

"When?" she asked.

"I've been dozing over my typewriter. If I'm to get this work done tonight, I'd better take a nap. As soon as the staff clears out for the day, I'll lie down. Why don't you bring the pizza at seven-thirty?"

"Count on it."

"We'll have company at eight-thirty."

"Who?"

"A police detective. He wants to discuss some new evidence in the Butcher case."

"Preduski?" she asked.

"No. One of Preduski's lieutenants. A guy named Bollinger. He called a few minutes ago and wanted to come to the house this evening. I told him that you and I would be working here until late."

"Well, at least he's coming after we eat," she said. "Talking about the Butcher *before* dinner would spoil my appetite."

"See you at seven-thirty."

"Sleep tight, Nicky."

When the percolator shut off, she poured steaming coffee into a mug, added cream, went to the front of the store and sat in a chair near one of the mullioned show windows. She could look over and between the antiques for a many-paned view of a windswept section of Tenth Street.

A few people hurried past, dressed in heavy coats, their hands in their pockets, heads tucked down.

Scattered snowflakes followed the air currents down between the buildings and ricocheted along the pavement.

She sipped her coffee and almost purred as the warmth spread through her.

She thought about Graham and felt warmer still. Nothing could chill her when Graham was on her mind. Not wind. Not snow. Not the Butcher. She felt safe with Graham—even with just the thought of him. Safe and protected. She knew that, in spite of the fear that had grown in him since his fall, he would lay down his life for her if that was ever required of him. Just as she would give her life to save his.

It wasn't likely that either of them would be presented with such a dramatic choice; but she was convinced that Graham would find his courage gradually in the weeks and months ahead, would find it without the help of a crisis.

Suddenly the wind exploded against the window, howled and moaned and pasted snow, like specks of froth and spittle, to the cold glass.

# 12
### ◆◆◆

The room was long and narrow with a brown tile floor, beige walls, a high ceiling and fluorescent lights. Two metal desks stood just inside the door; they held typewriters, letter trays, vases full of artificial flowers, and the detritus of a day's work. The two well-dressed matronly women behind the desks were cheerful in spite of the drab institutional atmosphere. There were five cafeteria tables lined up, short end to short end, so that whoever sat at them would always be sideways to the desks. The ten metal chairs were all on the same side of the table row. Except for the relationship of the tables to the desks, it might have been a schoolroom, a study hall monitored by two teachers.

Frank Bollinger identified himself as Ben Frank and said he was an employee of a major New York City firm of architects. He asked for the complete file on the Bowerton Building, took off his coat and sat at the first table.

The two women, as efficient as they appeared to be, quickly brought him the Bowerton material from an adjacent storage room: original blueprints, amendments to the blueprints, cost estimates, applications for dozens of different building permits, final cost sheets, remodeling plans, photographs, letters . . . Every form—and everything else required by law—that was related to the Bowerton highrise and that had passed officially through a city bureau or department was in that file. It was a formidable mound of paper, even though each piece was carefully labeled and both categorically and sequentially arranged.

The forty-two-story Bowerton Building, facing a busy block of Lexington Avenue, had been completed in 1929 and stood essentially unchanged. It was one of Manhattan's art deco masterpieces, even more effectively designed than the justly acclaimed art deco Chanin Building which was only a few blocks away. More than a year ago a group of concerned citizens had launched a campaign to have the building declared a landmark in order to keep its most spectacular art deco features from being wiped away during sporadic flurries of "modernization." But the most important fact, so far as Bollinger was concerned, was that Graham Harris had his offices on the fortieth floor of the Bowerton Building.

For an hour and ten minutes, Bollinger studied the paper image of the structure. Main entrances. Service entrances. One-way emergency exits. The placement and operation of the bank of sixteen elevators. The placement of the two stairwells. A minimal electronic security system, primarily a closed-circuit television guard station, had been installed in 1969; and he went over and over the paper on that until he was certain that he had overlooked no detail of it.

At four forty-five he stood up, yawned and stretched. Smiling, humming softly, he put on his overcoat.

Two blocks from City Hall he stepped into a telephone booth and called Billy. "I've checked it out."

"Bowerton?"

"Yeah."

"What do you think?" Billy asked anxiously.

"It can be done."

"My God. You're sure?"

"As sure as I can be until I start it."

"Maybe I should be more help. I could—"

"No," Bollinger said. "If anything goes wrong, I can flash my badge and say I showed up to investigate a complaint. Then I can slip quietly away. But if we were both there, how could we explain our way out of it?"

"I suppose you're right."

"We'll stick to the original plan."

"All right."

"You be in that alleyway at ten o'clock."

Billy said, "What if you get there and discover it won't work? I don't want to be waiting—"

"If I have to give it up," Bollinger said, "I'll call you well before ten. But if you don't get the call, *be in that alley.*"

"Of course. What else? But I won't wait past ten-thirty. I *can't* wait longer than that."

"That'll be long enough."

Billy sighed happily. "Are we going to stand this city on its ear?"

"Nobody will sleep tomorrow night."

"Have you decided what lines you'll write on the wall?"

Bollinger waited until a city bus rumbled past the booth. His choice of quotations was clever; and he wanted Billy to appreciate them. "Yeah. I've got a long one from Nietzsche. 'I want to teach men the sense of their existence, which is Superman, the lightning out of the dark cloud man.'"

"Oh, that's excellent," Billy said. "I couldn't have chosen better myself."

"Thank you."

"And Blake?"

"Just a fragment from the alternate seventh night of *The Four Zoas*. 'Hearts laid open to the light . . .' "

Billy laughed.

"I knew you'd like it."

"I suppose you *do* intend to lay their hearts open?"

"Naturally," Bollinger said. "Their hearts and everything else, from throat to crotch."

# 13
◆ ◆ ◆

Promptly at six o'clock, the doorbell rang.

Sarah Piper answered it. Her professional smile slipped when she saw who was standing in the hall. "What are *you* doing here?" she asked, surprised.

"May I come in?"

"Well . . ."

"You look beautiful tonight. Absolutely stunning."

She was wearing a tight burnt-orange pantsuit, flimsy, with a low neckline that revealed too much of her creamy breasts. Self-consciously she put one hand over her cleavage. "I'm sorry, but I can't ask you in. I'm expecting someone."

"You're expecting me," he said. "Billy James Plover."

"What? That's not your name."

"It surely is. It's the name I was born with. I changed it years ago, of course."

"Why didn't you give me your real name on the phone?"

"I've got to protect my reputation."

Still confused, she stepped back to let him pass. She closed the door and locked it. Aware that she was being rude but unable to control herself, she stared openly at him. She couldn't think what to say.

"You seem shocked, Sarah."

"Yeah," she said. "I guess I am. It's just that you don't seem like the sort of man who would come to a woman—to someone like me."

He had been smiling from the moment she'd opened the door. Now his face broke into a broad grin. "What's wrong with someone like you? You're gorgeous."

This is crazy, she thought.

She said, "Your voice."

"The Southern accent?"

"Yeah."

"That's also part of my youth, just like the name. Would you prefer I dropped it?"

"Yeah. Your talking like that—it's not right. It's creepy." She hugged herself.

"Creepy? I thought you'd be amused. And when I'm Billy . . . I don't know . . . I kind of have fun with it . . . kind of feel like someone altogether new." He stared hard at her and said, "Something's wrong. We're off on the wrong foot. Or maybe worse than that. Is it worse than that? If you don't want to go to bed with me, say so. I'll understand. Maybe something about me repels you. I haven't always been successful with women. I've lost out many times. God knows. So just tell me. I'll leave. No hard feelings."

She put on her professional smile again and shook her head. Her thick blond hair bounced prettily. "I'm sorry. There's no need for you to go. I was just surprised, that's all."

"You're sure?"

"Positive."

He looked at the living room beyond the foyer arch, reached down to finger the antique umbrella stand beside the door. "You have a nice place."

"Thank you." She opened the foyer closet, plucked a hanger from the clothes rod. "Let me take your coat."

He took it off, handed it to her.

As she put the coat in the closet, she said, "Your gloves too. I'll put them in a coat pocket."

"I'll keep my gloves," he said.

When she turned back to him, he was standing between her and the front door, and he was holding a wicked switchblade knife in his right hand.

She said, "Put that away."

"What did you say?"

*"Put that away!"*

He laughed.

"I mean it," she said.

"You're the coolest bitch I've ever met."

"Put that knife in your pocket. Put it away and then get out of here."

Waving the knife at her, he said, "When they realize I'm going to slit them open, they say some silly things. But I don't believe any of them ever *seriously* thought she could talk me out of it. Until you. So very cool."

She twisted away from him. She ran out of the foyer, into the living room. Her heart was pounding; she was shaking badly; but she was determined not to be incapacitated by fear. She kept a gun in the top drawer of her nightstand. If she could get into the bedroom, close and lock the door between them, she could hold him off long enough to put her hands on the pistol.

Within a few steps he caught her by the shoulder.

She tried to jerk free.

He was stronger than he looked. His fingers were like talons. He swung her around and shoved her backward.

Off balance, she collided with the coffee table, fell over it. She struck her hip on one of the heavy wooden legs; pain like an incandescent bulb flashed along her thigh.

He stood over her, still holding the knife, still grinning.

"Bastard," she said.

"There are two ways you can die, Sarah. You can try to run and resist, forcing me to kill you now—painfully and slowly. Or you can cooperate, come into the bedroom, let me give you some fun. Then I promise you'll die quickly and painlessly."

Don't panic, she told herself. You're Sarah Piper, and you came out of nothing, and you made something of yourself, and you have been knocked down dozens of times before, knocked down figuratively and literally, and you've always gotten up, and you'll get up this time, and you'll survive, you will, dammit, you will.

"Okay," she said. She stood up.

"Good girl." He held the knife out at his side. He unbuttoned the bodice of her pantsuit and slipped his free hand under the thin material. "Nice," he said.

She closed her eyes as he moved nearer.

"I'll make it fun for you," he said.

She drove her knee into his crotch.

Although the blow didn't land squarely, he staggered backward.

She grabbed a table lamp and threw it. Without waiting to see if it hit him, she ran into the bedroom and shut the door. Before she could lock it, he slammed against the far side and pushed the door open two or three inches.

She tried to force it shut again so that she could throw the lock, but he was stronger than she. She knew she couldn't hold out against him for more than a minute or two. Therefore, when he was pressing the hardest and would expect it the least, she let go of the door altogether and ran to the nightstand.

Surprised, he stumbled into the room and nearly fell.

She pulled open the nightstand drawer and picked up the gun. He knocked it out of her hand. It clattered against the wall and dropped to the floor, out of reach.

Why didn't you scream? she asked herself. Why didn't you yell for help while you could hold the door shut? It's unlikely anyone would hear you in soundly built apartments like these, but at least it was worth a try when you had a chance.

But she knew why she didn't cry out. She was Sarah Piper. She had never called for help in her life. She had always solved her own problems, had always fought her own battles. She was tough and proud of it. She did not scream.

She was terrified, trembling, sick with fear, but she knew that she had to die the same way she had lived. If she broke now, whimpered and mewled when there wasn't any chance of salvation, she would be making a lie of her life. If her life was to have meant anything, anything at all, she would have to die as she had lived: resolute, proud, tough.

She spat in his face.

# 14
◆ ◆ ◆

"Homicide."

"I want to speak to a detective."

"What's his name?"

"Any detective. I don't care."

"Is this an emergency?"

"Yes."

"Where are you calling from?"

"Never mind. I want a detective."

"I'm required to take your address, telephone number, name—"

"Stuff it! Let me talk to a detective or I'll hang up."

"Detective Martin speaking."

"I just killed a woman."

"Where are you calling from?"

"Her apartment."

"What's the address?"

"She was very beautiful."

"What's the address?"

"A lovely girl."

"What was her name?"

"Sarah."

"Do you know her last name?"

"Piper."

"Will you spell that?"

"P-i-p-e-r."

"Sarah Piper."

"That's right."

"What's your name?"

"The Butcher."

"What's your real name?"

"I'm not going to tell you."

"Yes, you are. That's why you called."

"No. I called to tell you I'm going to kill some more people before the night's out."

"Who?"

"One of them is the woman I love."

"What's her name?"

"I wish I didn't have to kill her."

"Then don't. You—"

"But I think she suspects."

"Why don't we—"

"Nietzsche was right."

"Who?"

"Nietzsche."

"Who's he?"

"A philosopher."

"Oh."

"He was right about women."

"What did he say about women?"

"They just get in our way. They hold us back from perfection. All those energies we put into courting them and screwing them—wasted! All that wasted sex energy could be put to other use, to thought and study. If we didn't waste our energies on women, we could evolve into what we were meant to be."

"And what were we meant to be?"

"Are you trying to trace this call?"

"No, no."

"Yes. Of course you are."

"No, really we aren't."

"I'll be gone from here in a minute. I just wanted to tell you that tomorrow you'll know who I am, who the Butcher is. But you won't catch me. I'm the lightning out of the dark cloud man."

"Let's try to—"

"Good-bye, Detective Martin."

# 15
◆ ◆ ◆

At seven o'clock Friday evening, a fine dry snow began to fall in Manhattan, not merely flurries but a full-scale storm. The snow sifted out of the black sky and made pale, shifting patterns on the dark streets.

In his living room, Frank Bollinger watched the millions of tiny flakes streaming past the window. The snow pleased him no end. With the weekend ahead, and now especially with the change of weather, it was doubtful that anyone other than Harris and his woman would be working late in the Bowerton Building. He felt that his chances of getting to them and pulling off the plan without a hitch had improved considerably. The snow was an accomplice.

At seven-twenty, he took his overcoat from the hall closet, slipped into it and buttoned up.

The pistol was already in the right coat pocket. He wasn't using his police revolver, because bullets from that could be traced too easily. This was a Walther PPK, a compact .38 that had been banned from importation into the United States since 1969. (A slightly larger pistol, the Walther PPK/S, was now manufactured for marketing in the United States; it was less easily concealed than the original model.) There was a silencer on the piece, not homemade junk but a precision-machined silencer made by Walther for use by various elite European police agencies. Even with the silencer screwed in place, the gun fit easily out of sight in the deep overcoat pocket. Bollinger had taken the weapon off a dead man, a suspect in a narcotics and prostitution investigation. The moment he saw it he knew that he must have it; and he failed to report finding it as he should have done. That was nearly a year ago; he'd had no occasion to use it until tonight.

In his left coat pocket, Bollinger was carrying a box of fifty bullets. He didn't think he'd need more than were already in the pistol's magazine, but he intended to be prepared for any eventuality.

He left the apartment and took the stairs two at a time, eager for the hunt to begin.

Outside, the grainy, wind-driven snow was like bits of ground glass.

The night howled spectrally between the buildings and rattled the branches of the trees.

Graham Harris's office, the largest of the five rooms in the Harris Publications suite on the fortieth floor of the Bowerton Building, didn't look like a place where business was transacted. It was paneled in dark wood—real and solid wood, not veneer—and had a textured beige acoustical ceiling. The forest-green ceiling-to-floor drapes matched the plush carpet. The desk had once been a Steinway piano; the guts had been ripped out, the lid lowered and cut to fit the frame. Behind the desk rose bookshelves filled with volumes about skiing and climbing. The light came from four floorlamps with old-fashioned ceramic sconces and glass chimneys that hid the electric bulbs. There were also two brass reading lamps on the desk. A small conference table and four armchairs occupied the space in front of the windows. A richly carved seventeenth-century British coatrack stood by the door to the corridor, and an antique bar of cut glass, beveled mirrors and inlaid woods stood by the door to the reception lounge. On the walls were photographs of climbing teams in action, and there was one oil painting, a mountain snowscape. The room might have been a study in the home of a retired professor, where books were read and pipes were smoked and where a spaniel lay curled at the feet of its master.

Connie opened the foil-lined box on the conference table. Steam rose from the pizza; a spicy aroma filled the office.

The wine was chilled. In the pizzeria, she had made them keep the bottle in their refrigerator until the pie was ready to go.

Famished, they ate and drank in silence for a few minutes.

Finally she said, "Did you take a nap?"

"Did I ever."

"How long?"

"Two hours."

"Sleep well?"

"Like the dead."

"You don't look it."

"Dead?"

"You don't look like you'd slept."

"Maybe I dreamed it."

"You've got dark rings under your eyes."

"My Rudolph Valentino look."

"You should go home to bed."

"And have the printer down my throat tomorrow?"

"They're *quarterly* magazines. A few days one way or the other won't matter."

"You're talking to a perfectionist."

"Don't I know it."

"A perfectionist who loves you."

She blew him a kiss.


Frank Bollinger parked his car on a side street and walked the last three blocks to the Bowerton Building.

A skin of snow, no more than a quarter inch but growing deeper, sheathed the sidewalks and street. Except for a few taxicabs that spun past too fast for road conditions, there was not much traffic on Lexington Avenue.

The main entrance to the Bowerton Building was set back twenty feet from the sidewalk. There were four revolving glass doors, three of them locked at this hour. Beyond the doors the large lobby rich with marble and brasswork and copper trim was overflowing with warm amber light.

Bollinger patted the pistol in his pocket and went inside.

Overhead, a closed-circuit television camera was suspended from a brace. It was focused on the only unlocked door.

Bollinger stamped his feet to knock the snow from his shoes and to give the camera time to study him. The man in the control room wouldn't find him suspicious if he faced the camera without concern.

A uniformed security guard was sitting on a stool behind a lectern near the first bank of elevators.

Bollinger walked over to him, stepped out of the camera's range.

"Evening," the guard said.

As he walked, he took his wallet from an inside pocket and flashed the gold badge. "Police." His voice echoed eerily off the marble walls and the high ceiling.

"Something wrong?" the guard asked.

"Anybody working late tonight?"

"Just four."

"All in the same office?"

"No. What's up?"

Bollinger pointed to the open registry on the lectern. "I'd like all four names."

"Let's see here . . . Harris, Davis, Ott and MacDonald."

"Where would I find Ott?"

"Sixteenth floor."

"What's the name of the office?"

"Cragmont Imports."

The guard's face was round and white. He had a weak mouth and a tiny Oliver Hardy mustache. When he tried for an expression of curiosity, the mustache nearly disappeared up his nostrils.

"What floor for MacDonald?" Bollinger asked.

"Same. Sixteenth."

"He's working with Ott?"

"That's right."

"Just those four?"

"Just those four."

"Maybe someone else is working late, and you don't know it."

"Impossible. After five-thirty, anyone going upstairs has to sign in with me. At six o'clock we go through every floor to see who's working late, and then they check out with us when they leave. The building management has set down strict fire-prevention rules. This is part of them." He patted the registry. "If there's ever a fire, we'll know exactly who's in the building and where we can find them."

"What about maintenance crews?"

"What about them?"

"Janitors. Cleaning women. Any working now?"

"Not on Friday night."

"You're sure?"

"Sure I'm sure." He was visibly upset by the interrogation and beginning to wonder if he should cooperate. "They come in all day tomorrow."

"Building engineer?"

"Schiller. He's night engineer."

"Where is Schiller?"

"Downstairs."

"Where downstairs?"

"Checking one of the heat pumps, I think."

"Is he alone?"

"Yeah."

"How many other security guards?"

"Are you going to tell me what's up?"

"For God's sake, this is an emergency!" Bollinger said. "How many security guards besides you?"

"Just two. What emergency?"

"There's been a bomb threat."

The guard's lips trembled. The mustache seemed about to fall off. "You're kidding."

"I wish I were."

The guard slid off his stool, stepped from behind the lectern.

At the same time Bollinger took the Walther from his pocket.

The guard blanched. "What's that?"

"A gun. Don't go for yours."

"Look, this bomb threat . . . *I* didn't call it in."

Bollinger laughed.

"It's true."

"I'm sure it is."

"Hey . . . that gun has a silencer on it."

"Yeah."

"But policemen don't—"

Bollinger shot him twice in the chest.

The impact of the bullets threw the guard into the sheet marble. For an instant he stood very straight, as if he were waiting for someone to measure his height and mark it on the wall. Then he collapsed.

# PART TWO

# FRIDAY
# 8:00 P.M.
# 8:30 P.M.

◆◆◆

# 16
◆◆◆

Bollinger turned immediately from the dead man and looked at the revolving doors. Nobody was there, no one on the sidewalk beyond, no one who might have seen the killing.

Moving quickly but calmly, he tucked the pistol into his pocket and grabbed the body by the arms. He dragged it into the waiting area between the first two banks of elevators. Now, anyone coming to the doors would see only an empty lobby.

The dead man stared at him. The mustache seemed to have been painted on his lip.

Bollinger turned out the guard's pockets. He found quarters, dimes, a crumpled five-dollar bill, and a key ring with seven keys.

He returned to the main part of the lobby.

He wanted to go straight to the door, but he knew that was not a good idea. That would put him in camera range. If the men monitoring the closed-circuit system saw him locking the door, they would be curious. They'd come to investigate, and he would lose the advantage of surprise.

Keeping in mind the details of the plans he had studied at City Hall that afternoon, he walked quietly to the rear of the lobby and stepped into a short corridor on the left. Four rooms led off the hall. The second on the right was the guards' room, and the door was open.

Wondering if the squeaking of his wet shoes sounded as loud to the guards as it did to him, he edged up to the open door.

Inside, two men were talking laconically about their jobs, complaining, but only halfheartedly.

Bollinger took the pistol from his coat pocket. He walked through the doorway.

The men were sitting at a small table in front of three television screens. They weren't watching the monitors. They were playing two-handed pinochle.

The older of the two was in his fifties. Heavy. Gray-haired. He had a prizefighter's lumpy face. The name "Neely" was stitched on his left shirt pocket. He was slow. He looked up at Bollinger, failed to react as he should have to the gun, and said without fear, "What's this?"

The other guard was in his thirties. Trim. Ascetic face. Pale hands. As he turned to see what had caught Neely's attention, Bollinger saw "Faulkner" stitched on his shirt.

He shot Faulkner first.

Reaching with both hands for his ruined throat, too late to stop the life from gushing out of him, Faulkner toppled backward in his chair.

"Hey!" Fat Neely was finally on his feet. His holster was snapped shut. He grappled with it.

Bollinger shot him twice.

Neely did an ungraceful pirouette, fell on the table, collapsed it, and went to the floor in a flutter of pinochle cards.

Bollinger checked their pulses.

They were dead.

When he left the room, he closed the door.

At the front of the big lobby, he locked the last revolving door and put the keys into his pocket.

He went to the lectern, sat on the stool. He took the box of bullets from his left coat pocket and replenished the pistol's magazine.

He looked at his watch. 8:10. He was right on schedule.

# 17
### ◆ ◆ ◆

"That was good pizza," Graham said.

"Good wine, too. Have another glass."

"I've had enough."

"Just a little one."

"No. I've got to work."

"Dammit."

"You knew that when you came."

"I was trying to get you drunk."

"On one bottle of wine?"

"And then seduce you."

"Tomorrow night," he said.

"I'll be blind with desire by then."

"Doesn't matter. Love is a Braille experience."

She winced.

He got up, came around the table, kissed her cheek. "Did you bring a book to read?"

"A Nero Wolfe mystery."

"Then read."

"Can I look at you from time to time?"

"What's to look at?"

"Why do *men* buy *Playboy* magazine?" she asked.

"I won't be working in the nude."

"You don't have to be."

"Pretty dull."

"You're even sexy with your clothes on."

"Okay," he said, smiling. "Look but don't talk."

"Can I drool?"

"Drool if you must."

He was pleased with the flattery, and she was delighted by his reaction. She felt that she was gradually chipping away at his inferiority complex, peeling it layer by layer.

# 18
◆ ◆ ◆

The building engineer for the night shift was a stocky, fair-skinned blond in his late forties. He was wearing gray slacks and a gray-white-blue checkered shirt. He was smoking a pipe.

When Bollinger came down the steps from the lobby corridor, the gun in his right hand, the engineer said, "Who the hell are you?" He spoke with a slight German accent.

*"Sie sind Herr Schiller, nicht wahr?"* Bollinger asked. His grandfather and grandmother had been German-Americans; he had learned the language when he was young and had never forgotten it.

Surprised to hear German spoken, worried about the gun but confused by Bollinger's smile, Schiller said, *"Ja, ich bin's."*

*"Es freut mich sehr Sie kennenzulernen."*

Schiller took the pipe from his mouth. He licked his lips nervously. *"Die Pistole?"*

*"Fur den Mord,"* Bollinger said. He squeezed off two shots.

Upstairs, on the lobby floor, Bollinger opened the door directly across the hall from the guards' room. He switched on the lights.

The narrow room was lined with telephone and power company equipment. The ceiling and walls were unfinished concrete. Two bright red fire extinguishers were hung where they could be reached quickly.

He went to the far side of the room, to a pair of yard-square metal cabinets that were fixed to the wall. The lid of each cabinet bore the insignia of the telephone company. Although the destruction of the contents would render useless all other routing boxes, switchboards and backup systems, neither of the cabinets was locked. Each housed twenty-six small levers, circuit breakers in a fuse box. They were all inclined toward the "on" mark. Bollinger switched them off, one by one.

He moved to a box labeled "Fire Emergency," forced it open, and tinkered with the wires inside.

That done, he went to the guards' room across the hall. He stepped around the bodies and picked up one of the two telephones that stood in front of the closed-circuit television screens.

No dial tone.

He jiggled the cut-off spikes.

Still no dial tone.

He hung up, picked up the other phone: another dead line.

Whistling softly, Bollinger entered the first elevator.

There were two keyholes in the control panel. The top one opened the panel for repairs. The one at the bottom shut down the lift mechanism.

He tried the keys that he had taken from the dead guard. The third one fit the bottom lock.

He pushed the button for the fifth floor. The number didn't light; the doors didn't close; the elevator didn't move.

Whistling louder than before, he proceeded to shut down fourteen of the remaining fifteen elevators. He would use the last one to go to the sixteenth floor, where Ott and MacDonald were working, and later to the fortieth floor, where Harris and his woman were waiting.

# 19
◆ ◆ ◆

Although Graham hadn't spoken, Connie knew that something was wrong. He was breathing heavily. She looked up from her book and saw that he had stopped working and was staring at empty air, his mouth slightly open, his eyes sort of glazed. "What's the matter?"

"Nothing."

"You're pale."

"Just a headache."

"You're shaking."

He said nothing.

She got up, put down her book, went to him. She sat on the corner of his desk. "Graham?"

"It's okay. I'm fine now."

"No, you aren't."

"I'm fine."

"There for a minute you weren't."

"For a minute I wasn't," he agreed.

She took his hand; it was icy. "A vision?"

"Yeah," Graham said.

"Of what?"

"Me. Getting shot."

"That's not the least bit funny."

"I'm not joking."

"You've never had a *personal* vision before. You've always said the clairvoyance works only when other people are involved."

"Not this time."

"Maybe you're wrong."

"I doubt it. I felt as if I had been hit between the shoulders with a sledgehammer. The wind was knocked out of me. I saw myself falling." His blue eyes grew wide. "There was blood. A great deal of blood."

She felt sick in her soul, in her heart. He had never been wrong, and now he was predicting he would be shot.

He squeezed her hand tightly, as if he were trying to press strength from her into him.

"Do you mean shot—and killed?"

"I don't know," he said. "Maybe killed or maybe just wounded. Shot in the back. That much is clear."

"Who did it—will do it?"

"The Butcher, I think."

"You saw him?"

"No. Just a strong impression."

"Where did it happen?"

"Someplace I know well."

"Here?"

"Maybe . . ."

"At home?"

"Maybe."

A fierce gust of wind boomed along the side of the highrise. The office windows vibrated behind the drapes.

"When will it happen?" she asked.

"Soon."

"Tonight?"

"I can't be sure."

"Tomorrow?"

"Possibly."

"Sunday?"

"Not as late as that."

"What are we going to do?"

# 20

◆ ◆ ◆

The lift stopped at the sixteenth floor.

Bollinger used the key to shut off the elevator before he stepped out of it. The cab would remain where it was, doors open, until he needed it again.

For the most part, the sixteenth floor was shrouded in darkness. An overhead fluorescent tube brightened the elevator alcove, but the only light in the corridor came from two dim red emergency exit bulbs, one at each end of the building.

Bollinger had anticipated the darkness. He took a pencil flashlight from an inside coat pocket, flicked it on.

Ten small businesses maintained offices on the sixteenth floor, six to the right and four to the left of the elevators. He went to the right. Two suites down the hall he found a door that bore the words CRAG-MONT IMPORTS.

He turned off the flashlight and put it away.

He took out the Walther PPK.

Christ, he thought, it's going so smoothly. So easily. As soon as he finished at Cragmont Imports, he could go after the primary targets. Harris first. Then the woman. If she was good-looking . . . well, he was so far ahead of schedule now that he had an hour to spare. An hour for the woman if she rated it. He was ready for a woman, full of energy and appetite and excitement. A woman, a table filled with good food, and a lot of fine whiskey. But mostly a woman. In an hour he could use her up, really use her up.

He tried the door to Cragmont Imports. It wasn't locked.

He walked into the reception lounge. The room was gloomy. The only light came from an adjacent office where the door was standing halfway open.

He went to the shaft of light, stood in it, listened to the men talking in the inner office. At last he pushed open the door and went inside.

They were sitting at a conference table that was piled high with papers and bound folders. They weren't wearing their suit jackets or their ties, and their shirt sleeves were rolled up; one was wearing a blue shirt, the other a white shirt. They saw the pistol at once, but they needed several seconds to adjust before they could raise their eyes to look at his face.

"This place smells like perfume," Bollinger said.

They stared at him.

"Is one of you wearing perfume?"

"No," said blue shirt. "Perfume's one of the things we import."

"Is one of you MacDonald?"

They looked at the gun, at each other, then at the gun again.

"MacDonald?" Bollinger asked.

The one in the blue shirt said, "He's MacDonald."

The one in the white shirt said, "*He's* MacDonald."

"That's a lie," said the one in the blue shirt.

"No, *he's* lying," said the other.

"I don't know what you want with MacDonald," said the one in the blue shirt. "Just leave me out of it. Do what you have to do to him and go away."

"Christ almighty!" said the one in the white shirt. "I'm *not* MacDonald! You want *him*, that son of a bitch there, not me!"

Bollinger laughed. "It doesn't matter. I'm also here to get Mr. Ott."

"*Me?*" said the one in the blue shirt. "Who in the hell would want *me* killed?"

# 21
### ◆ ◆ ◆

Connie said, "You'll have to call Preduski."

"Why?"

"To get police protection."

"It's no use."

"He believes in your visions."

"I know he does."

"He'll give you protection."

"Of course," Graham said. "But that's not what I meant."

"Explain."

"Connie, I've seen myself shot in the back. It's going to happen. Things I see *always* happen. Nobody can do anything to stop this."

"There's no such thing as predestination. The future can be changed."

"Can it?"

"You know it can."

A haunted look filled his bright blue eyes. "I doubt that very much."

"You can't be sure."

"But I am sure."

This attitude of his, this willingness to ascribe all of his failings to predestination, worried and upset her more than anything else about him. It was an especially pernicious form of cowardice. He was rejecting all responsibility for his own life.

"Call Preduski," she said.

He lowered his eyes and stared at her hand but didn't seem to see how tightly he was gripping it.

She said, "If this man comes to the *house* to kill you, I'll probably be there too. Do you think he's going to shoot you, then just walk away and let *me* live?"

Shocked, as she had known he would be, by the thought of her under the Butcher's knife, he said, "My God."

"Call Preduski."

"All right." He let go of her hand. He picked up the receiver, listened for a moment, played with the dial, jiggled the buttons.

"What's wrong?"

Frowning, he said, "No dial tone." He hung up, waited a few seconds, picked up the receiver again. "Still nothing."

She slid off the desk. "Let's try your secretary's phone."

They went out to the reception room.

That phone was dead too.

"Funny," he said.

Her heartbeat quickening, she said, "Is he going to come after you tonight?"

"I told you, I don't know for sure."

"Is he in the building right now?"

"You think he cut the telephone line."

She nodded.

"That's pretty farfetched," he said. "It's just a breakdown in service."

She went to the door, opened it, stepped into the hall. He came behind her, favoring his injured leg.

Darkness lay on most of the corridor. Dim red emergency lights shone at each end of the hall, above the doors to the staircases. Fifty feet away a pool of wan blue light marked the elevator alcove.

Except for the sound of their breathing, the fortieth floor was silent.

"I'm not a clairvoyant," she said, "but I don't like the way it feels. I sense it, Graham. Something's wrong."

"In a building like this, the telephone lines are in the walls. Outside of the building they're underground. All the lines are underground in this city. How would he get to them?"

"I don't know. But maybe *he* knows."

"He'd be taking such a risk," Graham said.

"He's taken risks before. Ten times before."

"But not like this. We're not alone. The security guards are in the building."

"They're forty stories below."

"A long way," he agreed. "Let's get out of here."

"We're probably being silly."

"Probably."

"We're probably safe where we are."

"Probably."

"I'll grab our coats."

"Forget the coats." He took hold of her hand. "Come on. Let's get to those elevators."

* * *

Bollinger needed eight shots to finish off MacDonald and Ott. They kept ducking behind the furniture.

By the time he had killed them, the Walther PPK was no longer firing silently. No silencer could function at peak efficiency for more than a dozen shots; the baffles and wadding were compacted by the bullets, and sound escaped. The last three shots were like the sharp barks of a medium-sized guard dog. But that didn't matter. The noise wouldn't carry to the street or up to the fortieth floor.

In the outer office of Cragmont Imports, he switched on a light. He sat on a couch, reloaded the Walther's magazine, unscrewed the silencer and put it into his pocket. He didn't want to risk fouling the barrel with loose steel fibers from the silencer; besides, there was no one left in the building to hear shots when he killed Harris and the woman. And a shot fired on the fortieth floor would not penetrate walls and windows and travel all the way down to Lexington Avenue.

He looked at his watch. 8:25.

He turned off the light, left Cragmont Imports, and went down the hall to the elevator.

Eight elevators served the fortieth floor, but none of them was working.

Connie pushed the call button on the last lift. When nothing happened, she said, "The telephone, and now this."

In the spare yet harsh fluorescent light, Graham's laugh lines looked deeper and sharper than usual; his face resembled that of a kabuki actor painted to represent extreme anxiety. "We're trapped."

"It could be just an ordinary breakdown of some sort," she said. "Mechanical failure. They might be making repairs right now."

"The telephones?"

"Coincidence. Maybe there's nothing sinister about it."

Suddenly the numerals above the elevator doors in front of them began to light up, one after the other: 16 . . . 17 . . . 18 . . . 19 . . . 20 . . .

"Someone's coming," Graham said.

A chill passed down her spine.

. . . 25 . . . 26 . . . 27 . . .

"Maybe it's the security guards," she said.

He said nothing.

She wanted to turn and run, but she could not move. The numbers mesmerized her.

. . . 30 . . . 31 . . . 32. . . .

She thought of women lying in bloody bedclothes, women with their throats cut and their fingers chopped off and their ears cut off.

...33....

"The stairs!" Graham said, startling her.

"Stairs?"

"The emergency stairs."

...34....

"What about them?"

"We've got to go down."

"Hide out a few floors below?"

...35....

"No. All the way down to the lobby."

"That's too far!"

"That's where there's help."

...36....

"Maybe we don't need help."

"We need it," he said.

...37....

"But your leg—"

"I'm not a *complete* cripple," he said sharply.

...38....

He grabbed her by the shoulder. His fingers hurt her, but she knew he wasn't aware of how fiercely he was gripping her. "Come on, Connie!"

...39....

Frustrated with her hesitation, he gave her a shove, propelled her out of the alcove. She stumbled, and for an instant she thought she would fall. He kept her upright.

As they hurried down the dark corridor, she heard the elevator doors open behind them.

When Bollinger came out of the elevator alcove, he saw two people running away from him. They were nothing but ghostly shapes, vaguely silhouetted against the eerie glow of the red emergency light at the end of the corridor.

Harris and the woman? he wondered. Have they been alerted? Do they know who I am? How can they know?

"Mr. Harris?" Bollinger called.

They stopped two-thirds of the way down the hall, in front of the open door to the Harris Publications suite. They turned toward him, but he could not see their faces even with the red light spilling over their shoulders.

"Mr. Harris, is that you?"

"Who are you?"

"Police," Bollinger said. He took a step toward them, then another.

As he moved he took the wallet with his badge from his inside coat pocket. With the elevator light behind him, he knew they could see more than he could.

"Don't come any closer," Harris said.

Bollinger stopped. "What's the matter?"

"I don't want you to come closer."

"Why?"

"We don't know who you are."

"I'm a detective. Frank Bollinger. We have an appointment for eight-thirty. Remember?" Another step. Then another.

"How did you get up here?" Harris's voice was shrill.

He's scared to death, Bollinger thought. He smiled and said, "Hey, what's going on with you? Why are you so uptight? You were expecting me." Bollinger took slow steps, easy steps, so as not to frighten the animals.

"How did you get up here?" Harris asked again. "The elevators aren't working."

"You're mistaken. I came up on an elevator." He held the badge in front of him in his left hand, arm extended, hoping the light from behind would gleam on the gold finish. He had covered perhaps a fifth of the distance between them.

"The telephones are out," Harris said.

"They are?" Step. Step.

He put his right hand in his coat pocket and gripped the butt of the pistol.

Connie couldn't take her eyes off the shadowy form moving steadily toward them. To Graham she said softly, "You remember what you said on the Prine show?"

"What?" His voice cracked.

Don't let the fear take you, she thought. Don't break down and leave me to handle this alone.

She said, "In your vision you saw that the police know the killer well."

"What about it?"

"Maybe the Butcher is a cop."

"Christ, that's it!"

He spoke so softly that she could barely hear him.

Bollinger kept coming, a big man, bearish. His face was in shadow. He had closed the distance between them by at least half.

"Stop right there," Graham said. But there was no force in his voice, no authority.

Bollinger stopped anyway. "Mr. Harris, you're acting very strange.

I'm a *policeman*. You know . . . you're acting as if you've just done something that you want to hide from me.'' He took a step, another, a third.

''The stairs?'' Connie asked.

''No,'' Graham said. ''We don't have enough of a lead. With my game leg, he'd catch us in a minute.''

''Mr. Harris?'' Bollinger said. ''What are you two saying? Please don't whisper.''

''Where then?'' Connie whispered.

''The office.''

He nudged her, and they ducked quickly into the Harris Publications suite, slammed and locked the reception room door.

A second later, Bollinger hit the outside of the door with his shoulder. It trembled in its frame. He rattled the knob violently.

''He's probably got a gun,'' Connie said. ''He'll get in sooner or later.''

Graham nodded. ''I know.''

# PART THREE

# FRIDAY
# 8:30 P.M.
# 10:30 P.M.

◆

# 22
◆ ◆ ◆

Ira Preduski parked at the end of a string of three squad cars and two unmarked police sedans that blocked one half of the two-lane street. Although there was no one in any of the five vehicles, all the engines were running, headlights blazing; the trio of black-and-whites were crowned with revolving red beacons. Preduski got out of his car and locked it.

A half inch of snow made the street look clean and pretty. As he walked toward the apartment house, Preduski scuffed his shoes against the sidewalk, sending up puffs of white flakes in front of him. The wind whipped the falling snow into his back, and cold flakes found their way past his collar. He was reminded of that February, in his fourth year, when his family moved to Albany, New York, where he saw his first winter storm.

A uniformed patrolman in his late twenties was standing at the bottom of the outside steps to the apartment house.

"Tough job you've got tonight," Preduski said.

"I don't mind it. I like snow."

"Yeah? So do I."

"Besides," the patrolman said, "it's better standing out here in the cold than up there in all that blood."

The room smelled of blood, excrement and dusting powder.

Fingers bent like claws, the dead woman lay on the floor beside the bed. Her eyes were open.

Two lab technicians were working around the body, studying it carefully before chalking its position and moving it.

Ralph Martin was the detective handling the on-scene investigation. He was chubby, completely bald, with bushy eyebrows and dark-rimmed glasses. He avoided looking at the corpse.

"The call from the Butcher came in at ten of seven," Martin said. "We tried your home number immediately, but we weren't able to get through until almost eight o'clock."

"My phone was off the hook. I just got out of bed at a quarter past eight. I'm working graveyard." He sighed and turned away from the corpse. "What did he say—this Butcher?"

Martin took two folded sheets of paper from his pocket, unfolded them. "I dictated the conversation, as well as I could recall it, and one of the girls made copies."

Preduski read the two pages. "He gave you no clue to who else he's going to kill tonight?"

"Just what's there."

"This phone call is out of character."

"And it's out of character for him to strike two nights in a row," Martin said.

"It's also not like him to kill two women who knew each other and worked together."

Martin raised his eyebrows. "You think Sarah Piper knew something?"

"You mean, did she know who killed her friend?"

"Yeah. You think he killed Sarah to keep her from talking?"

"No. He probably just saw both of them at the Rhinestone Palace and couldn't make up his mind which he wanted the most. She didn't know who murdered Edna Mowry. I'd bet my life on that. Of course I'm not the best judge of character you'll ever meet. I'm pretty dense when it comes to people. God knows. Dense as stone. But this time I think I'm right. If she had known, she would have told me. She wasn't the kind of girl who could hide a thing like that. She was open. Forthright. Honest in her way. She was damned nice."

Glancing at the dead woman's face, which was surprisingly unmarked and clear of blood in the midst of so much gore, Martin said, "She was lovely."

"I didn't mean just nice-looking," Preduski said. "She was a nice *person*."

Martin nodded.

"She had a soft Georgia accent that reminded me of home."

"Home?" Martin was confused. "*You're* from Georgia?"

"Why not?"

"Ira Preduski from Georgia?"

"They *do* have Jews and Slavs down there."

"Where's your accent?"

"My parents weren't born in the South, so they didn't have an accent to pass on to me. And we moved North when I was four, before I had time to pick it up."

For a moment they stared at the late Sarah Piper and at the pair of technicians who bent over her like Egyptian attendants of death.

Preduski turned away from the corpse, took a handkerchief from his pocket and blew his nose.

"The coroner's in the kitchen," Martin said. His face was pale and greasy with sweat. "He said he wanted to see you when you checked in."

"Give me a few minutes," Preduski said. "I want to look around here a bit and talk with these fellows."

"Mind if I wait in the living room?"

"No. Go ahead."

Martin shuddered. "This is a rotten job."

"Rotten," Preduski agreed.

# 23
◆ ◆ ◆

The gunshot boomed and echoed in the dark corridor.

The lock shattered, and the wood splintered under the impact of the bullet.

Wrinkling his nose at the odor of burnt powder and scorched metal, Bollinger pushed open the ruined door.

The reception lounge was dark. When he found the light switch and flipped it up, he discovered that the room was also deserted.

Harris Publications occupied the smallest of three business suites on the fortieth floor. In addition to the hall door by which he had entered, two other doors opened from the reception area, one to the left and one to the right. Five rooms. Including the lounge. That didn't leave Harris and the woman with many places to hide.

First he tried the door to the left. It led to a private corridor that served three large offices: one for an editor and his secretary, one for an advertising space salesman, and one for the two-man art department.

Neither Harris nor the woman was in any of those rooms.

Bollinger was cool, calm, but at the same time enormously excited. No sport could be half so dramatic and rewarding as hunting down people. He actually enjoyed the chase more than he did the kill. Indeed, he got an even greater kick out of the first few days immediately *after* a kill than he did from either the hunt or the murder itself. Once the act was done, once blood had been spilled, he had to wonder if he'd made a mistake, if he'd left behind a clue that would lead the police straight to him. The tension kept him sharp, made the juices bubble. Finally, when sufficient time had passed for him to be certain that he had gotten away with murder, a sense of well-being—of great importance, towering superiority, godhood—filled him like a magic elixir flowing into a long-empty pitcher.

The other door connected the reception room and Graham Harris's private office. It was locked.

He stepped back and fired two shots into the lock. The soft metal twisted and tore; chunks of wood spun into the air.

He still could not open it. They had pushed a heavy piece of furniture against the far side.

When he leaned on the door, pushed with all of his strength, he could not budge it; however, he *could* make the unseen piece of furniture rock back and forth on its base. He figured it was something high, at least as wide as the doorway, but not too deep. Perhaps a bookshelf. Something with a high center of gravity. He began to force the door rhythmically: push hard, relax, push hard, relax, push hard. . . . The barricade tipped faster and farther each time he wobbled it— and suddenly it fell away from the door with a loud crash and the sound of breaking glass.

Abruptly the air was laden with whiskey fumes.

He squeezed through the door which remained partly blocked. He stepped over the antique bar they had used as a barrier and put his foot in a puddle of expensive Scotch.

The lights were on, but no one was there.

At the far end of the room there was another door. He went to it, opened it. Beyond lay the gloomy fortieth-floor corridor.

While he had wasted time searching the offices, they had slipped back into the hall by this circuitous route, gaining a few minutes lead on him.

Clever.

But not clever enough.

After all, they were nothing but ignorant game, while he was a master hunter.

He laughed softly.

Bathed in red light, Bollinger went to the nearest end of the hall and opened the fire door without making a sound. He stepped onto the landing in the emergency stairwell, closing the door quietly behind him. A dim white bulb burned above the exit on this side.

He heard their footsteps reverberating from below, amplified by the cold concrete walls.

He went to the steel railing and peered into the alternate layers of light and shadow: landings hung with bulbs, and stairs left dark. Ten or twelve flights down, five or six floors below, the woman's hand appeared on the railing, moving along less quickly than it should have. (If he had been in their place, he would have taken the steps two at a time, perhaps even faster.) Because the open core was so narrow—as long as a flight of stairs, but only one yard wide—Bollinger wasn't able to see at an angle into the tiers of steps beneath him. All he could see was the serpentine railing winding to infinity, and nothing of his prey except her white hand. A second later Harris's hand emerged from the velvety shadows, into the light that spilled out from a landing; he gripped the railing, followed the woman through the hazy light and into the darkness once again, descending.

For an instant Bollinger considered going down the steps behind them, shooting them in the back, but he rejected that thought almost as soon as it occurred to him. They would hear him coming. They would most likely scuttle out of the stairwell, seeking a place to hide or another escape route. He wouldn't know for certain at which floor they had left the stairs, and he couldn't run after them and watch their hands on the railing at the same time.

He didn't want to lose track of them. Although he wouldn't mind an interesting and complicated hunt, he didn't want it to drag on all night. For one thing, Billy would be waiting in the car, outside in the alley, at ten o'clock. For another, he wanted time with the woman, at least half an hour if she was at all good-looking.

Her pale hand slipped into sight on a light-swathed patch of railing. Then Harris's hand.

They were still not moving as fast as they should have.

He tried to count flights of stairs. Twelve to fourteen. . . . They were six, maybe seven floors below.

Where did that put them?

Thirty-third floor?

Bollinger turned away from the railing, opened the door and left the stairwell. He ran down the fortieth-floor corridor to the elevator cab he was using. He switched it on with his key, hesitated, then put his thumb on the button for the twenty-sixth floor.

# 24
◆◆◆

To Connie the stairwell seemed endless. As she passed through alternating levels of purple darkness and wan light, she felt as if she were following a long pathway to hell, the Butcher fulfilling the role of the grinning hellhound that harried her ever downward.

The stale air was cool. Nevertheless, she was perspiring.

She knew they should be going faster, but they were hampered in their flight by Graham's lame left leg. At one point she was almost overcome with anger, furious at him for being a hindrance to their escape. However, her fury vanished in the same instant, leaving her surprised by it and flushed with guilt. She had thought that no pressure, however great, could cause her to react to him so negatively. But filled with—nearly consumed by—the survival instinct, she clearly was capable of responses and attitudes that she would have criticized in others. Extreme circumstances could alter anyone's personality. That insight forced her to understand and appreciate Graham's fear to an extent she had never done before. After all, he had not *wanted* to fall on Everest; he hadn't *asked* for the injury. And indeed, considering the dull pain he suffered when he tried to climb or descend more than two flights of stairs, he was responding to this challenge damned well.

From behind her, Graham said, "You go on ahead." He had said it several times before. "You move faster."

"I'm staying," she said breathlessly.

The echoes of their low-pitched voices were eerie, soft and sibilant.

She reached the landing at the thirty-first floor, waited for him to catch up, then went ahead. "I won't leave you alone. Two of us . . . have a better chance against him . . . better than one of us would."

"He's got a gun. We've *no* chance."

She said nothing. She just kept taking the steps one at a time.

"Go on," he said, sucking breath between phrases. "You bring back . . . security guard . . . in time to keep . . . him from . . . killing me."

"I think the guards are dead."

"What?"

She hadn't wanted to say it, as if saying would make it so. "How else . . . would he get past them?"

"Sign the registry."

"And leave his name . . . for the cops to find?"

A dozen steps later he said, "Christ!"

"What?"

"You're right."

"No help . . . to be had," she said. "We've just got . . . to get out of . . . the building."

Somehow he found new strength in his left leg. When she reached the thirtieth-floor landing, Connie didn't have to wait for him to catch up.

A minute later, a cannonlike sound boomed up from below, halting them within the fuzzy circle of light at the twenty-ninth floor.

"What was that?"

Graham said, "A fire door. Someone slammed it . . . down there."

"Him?"

"*Ssshh.*"

They stood perfectly still, trying to hear movement above the noise of their own labored breathing.

Connie felt as if the circle of light were shrinking around her, rapidly pulling back to a tiny point of brilliance. She was afraid of being blind and helpless, an easy target in pitch blackness. In her mind the Butcher had the quality of a mythical being; he could see in darkness.

As they got control of their breathing, the stairwell became silent.

Too silent.

Unnaturally silent.

Finally Graham said, "Who's there?"

She jumped, startled by his voice.

The man below said, "Police, Mr. Harris."

Under her breath Connie said, "Bollinger."

She was at the outer edge of the steps; she looked down the open core. A man's hand was on the railing, four flights below, in the meager illumination just two or three steps up from the landing. She could also see the sleeve of his overcoat.

"Mr. Harris," Bollinger said. His voice was cold, hollow, distorted by the shaft.

"What do you want?" Graham asked.

"Is she pretty?"

"What?"

"Is she *pretty?*"

"Who?"

"Your woman."

With that, Bollinger started up. Not hurrying. Leisurely. One step at a time.

She was more frightened by his slow, casual approach than if he had rushed them. By *not* hurrying, he was telling them that they were trapped, that he had the whole night to get them if he wished to stretch it out that long.

If only we had a gun, she thought.

Graham took hold of her hand, and they climbed the steps as fast as he was able. It wasn't easy for either of them. Her back and legs ached. With each step, Graham either gritted his teeth or moaned loudly.

When they had gone two floors, four flights, they were forced to stop and rest. He bent over, massaging his bum leg. She went to the railing, peered down.

Bollinger was four flights under them. Evidently he had run when he heard them running, but now he had stopped again. He was leaning over the railing, framed in a pool of light, the gun extended in his right hand.

He smiled at her and said, "Hey now, you *are* pretty."

She screamed, jerked back.

He fired.

The shot passed up the core, ricocheted off the top of the rail, smashed into the wall over their heads and ricocheted once more into the steps above them.

She grabbed Graham; he held her.

"I could have killed you," Bollinger called to her. "I had you dead on, sweetheart. But you and I are going to have a lot of fun later."

Then he started up again. As before. Slowly. Shoes scraping ominously on the concrete: *shuss . . . shuss . . . shuss . . . shuss. . . .* He began to whistle softly.

"He's not just chasing us," Graham said angrily. "The son of a bitch is playing with us."

"What are we going to do?"

*Shuss . . . shuss. . . .*

"We can't outrun him."

"But we've got to."

*Shuss. . . . shuss. . . .*

Harris pulled open the landing door. The thirty-first floor lay beyond. "Come on."

Not convinced that they gained anything by leaving the stairs, but having nothing better to suggest, she went out of the white light into the red.

*Shuss . . . shuss. . . .*

Graham shut the door and stooped beside it. A collapsible doorstop was fixed to the bottom right-hand corner of the door. He pushed it all the way down, until the rubber-tipped shank was hard against the floor and the braces were locked in place. His hands were trembling, so that for a moment it looked as if he wouldn't be able to handle even a simple task like this.

"What are you doing?" she asked.

He stood up. "It might not work if the stop didn't have locking hinges. But it does. See the doorsill? It's an inch higher than the floor on either side. When he tries to open the door, the stop will catch on the sill. It'll be almost as good as a bolt latch."

"But he's got a gun."

"Doesn't matter. He can't shoot through a heavy metal fire door."

Although she was terrified, at the same time Connie was relieved that Graham had taken charge—for however brief a time—and was functioning in spite of his fear.

The door rattled as Bollinger depressed the bar handle on the far side. The stop caught on the sill; its hinges didn't fold up; the door refused to open.

"He'll have to go up or down a floor," Harris said, "and come at us by the stairs at the other end of the building. Or by the elevator. Which gives us a few minutes."

Cursing, Bollinger shook the door, putting all his strength into it. It wouldn't budge.

"What good will a few minutes do us?" Connie asked.

"I don't know."

"Graham, are we ever going to get out of here?"

"Probably not."

# 25

### ◆ ◆ ◆

Dr. Andrew Enderby, the medical examiner on the scene, was suave, even dashing, extremely fit for a man in his fifties. He had thick hair going white at the temples. Clear brown eyes. A long aristocratic nose, generally handsome features. His salt-and-pepper mustache was large but well kept. He was wearing a tailored gray suit with tastefully matched accessories that made Preduski's sloppiness all the more apparent.

"Hello, Andy," Preduski said.

"Number eleven," Enderby said. "Unusual. Like numbers five, seven and eight." When Enderby was excited, which wasn't often, he was impatient to express himself. He sometimes spoke in staccato bursts. He pointed at the kitchen table and said, "See it? No butter smears. No jelly stains. No crumbs. Too damned neat. Another fake."

A lab technician was disconnecting the garbage-disposal unit from the pipes under the sink.

"Why?" Preduski said. "Why does he fake it when he isn't hungry?"

"I know why. Sure of it."

"So tell me," Preduski said.

"First of all, did you know I'm a psychiatrist?"

"You're a coroner, a pathologist."

"Psychiatrist too."

"I didn't know that."

"Went to medical school. Did my internship. Specialized in oto-laryngology. Couldn't stand it. Hideous way to make a living. My family had money. Didn't have to work. Went back to medical school. Became a psychiatrist."

"That must be interesting work."

"Fascinating. But I couldn't stand it. Couldn't stand associating with the patients."

"Oh?"

"All day with a bunch of neurotics. Began to feel that half of them should be locked up. Got out of the field fast. Better for me *and* the patients.''

''I should say so.''

''Kicked around a bit. Twenty years ago, I became a police pathologist.''

''The dead aren't neurotic.''

''Not even a little bit.''

''And they don't have ear, nose, and throat infections.''

''Which they don't pass on to me,'' Enderby said. ''No money in this job, of course. But I've got all the money I need. And the work is right for me. I'm perfect for the work, too. My psychiatric training gives me a different perspective. Insights. I have insights that other pathologists might not have. Like the one I had tonight.''

''About why the Butcher sometimes eats a hearty meal and sometimes *fakes* a hearty meal?''

''Yes,'' Enderby said. He took a breath. Then: ''It's because there are two of him.''

Preduski scratched his head. ''Schizophrenia?''

''No, no. I mean . . . there isn't just one man running around killing women. There are *two*.'' He smiled triumphantly.

Preduski stared at him.

Slamming his fist into his open hand, Enderby said, ''I'm right! I know I am. Butcher number one killed the first four victims. Killing them gave him an appetite. Butcher number two killed the fifth woman. Cut her up as Butcher number one had done. But he was ever so slightly more tender-hearted than the first Butcher. Killing *spoiled* his appetite. So he faked the meal.''

''Why bother to fake it?''

''Simple. He wanted to leave no doubt about who killed her. Wanted us to think it was the Butcher.''

Preduski was suddenly aware of how precisely Enderby's necktie had been knotted. He touched his own tie self-consciously. ''Pardon me. Excuse me. I don't quite understand. My fault. God knows. But, you see, we've never told the newspapers about the scene in the kitchens. We've held that back to check false confessions against real ones. If this guy, Butcher number two, wanted to imitate the real Butcher, how would he know about the kitchen?''

''You're missing my point.''

''I'm sure I am.''

''Butcher number one and Butcher number two know each other. They're in this together.''

Amazed, Preduski said, ''They're friends? You mean they go out and murder—like other men go out bowling?''

''I wouldn't put it like that.''

"They're killing women, trying to make it look like the work of one man?"

"Yes."

"Why?"

"Don't know. Maybe they're creating a composite character in the Butcher. Giving us an image of a killer that isn't really like either of them. Throw us off the track. Protect themselves."

Preduski started to pace in front of the littered table. "Two psychopaths meet in a bar—"

"Not necessarily a bar."

"They get chummy and sign a pact to kill all the women in Manhattan."

"Not all," Enderby said. "But enough."

"I'm sorry. Maybe I'm not very bright. I'm not well educated. Not a doctor like you. But I can't swallow it. I can't see psychopaths working together so smoothly and effectively."

"Why not? Remember the Tate murders in California? There were several psychopaths in the Manson family, yet they all worked smoothly and efficiently together, committing a large number of murders."

"They were caught," Preduski said.

"Not for quite some time."

# 26
◆ ◆ ◆

Six business offices occupied the thirty-first floor of the Bowerton Building. Graham and Connie tried a few doors, all of which proved to be locked. They knew the others would be shut tight as well.

However, in the main hall near the elevator alcove, Connie discovered an unmarked, unlocked door. She opened it. Graham felt for the light switch, found it. They went inside.

The room was approximately ten feet deep and six or seven feet wide. On the left was a metal door that had been painted bright red; and to one side of the door, mops and brooms and brushes were racked on the wall. On the right, the wall was lined with metal storage shelves full of bathroom and cleaning supplies.

"It's a maintenance center," Graham said.

Connie went to the red door. She took one step out of the room, holding the door behind her. She was surprised and excited by what she saw. "Graham! Hey, look at this."

He didn't respond.

She stepped back into the room, turned and said, "Graham, look what—"

He was only a foot away, holding a large pair of scissors up to his face. He gripped the instrument in his fist, in the manner of a man holding a dagger. The blades gleamed; and like polished gems, the sharp points caught the light.

"Graham?" she said.

Lowering the scissors, he said, "I found these on the shelf over there. I can use them as a weapon."

"Against a gun?"

"Maybe we can set up a trap."

"What kind of trap?"

"Lure him into a situation where I can surprise him, where he won't have time enough to use the damned gun."

"For instance?"

His hand was shaking. Light danced on the blades. "I don't know," he said miserably.

"It wouldn't work," she said. "Besides, I've found a way out of the building."

He looked up. "You have?"

"Come look. You won't need the scissors. Put them down."

"I'll look," he said. "But I'll keep the scissors just in case."

She was afraid that when he saw the escape route she'd found he would prefer to face the Butcher armed only with the scissors.

He followed her through the red door, onto a railed platform that was only eighteen inches wide and four feet long. A light glowed overhead; and other lights lay some distance away in a peculiar, at first unidentifiable void.

They were suspended on the side of one of the two elevator shafts that went from the ground floor to the roof. It served four cabs, all of which were parked at the bottom. Fat cables dangled in front of Connie and Graham. On this side and on the opposite wall of the cavernous well, from roof to basement at the odd-numbered floors, other doors opened onto other tiny platforms. There was one directly across from Graham and Connie, and the sight of it made them realize the precarious nature of their perch. On both sides of the shaft, metal rungs were bolted to the walls: ladders connecting the doors in each tier to other exits in the same tier.

The system could be used for emergency maintenance work or for moving people off stalled elevators in case of fire, power failure, or other calamity. A small white light burned above each door; otherwise, the shaft would have been in absolute darkness. When Connie looked up, and especially when she looked down from the thirty-first floor, the sets of farther lights appeared to be closer together than the sets of nearer lights. It was a long way to the bottom.

His voice wavered when he said, "*This* is a way out?"

She hesitated, then said, "We can climb down."

"No."

"We can't use the stairs. He'll be watching those."

"Not this."

"It won't be like mountain climbing."

His eyes shifted quickly from left to right and back again. "No."

"We'll have the ladder."

"And we'll climb down thirty-one floors?" he asked.

"Please, Graham. If we start now, we might make it. Even if he finds that the maintenance room is unlocked, and even if he sees this red door—well, he might not think we'd have enough nerve to climb down the shaft. And if he *did* see us, we could get off the ladder, leave the shaft at another floor. We'd gain more time."

"I can't." He was gripping the railing with both hands, and with such force that she would not have been surprised if the metal had bent like paper in his hands.

Exasperated, she said, "Graham, what *else* can we do?"

He stared into the concrete depths.

When Bollinger found that Harris and the woman had locked the fire door, he ran down two flights to the thirtieth floor. He intended to use that corridor to reach the far end of the building where he could take the second stairwell back up to the thirty-first level and try the *other* fire door. However, at the next landing the words "Hollowfield Land Management" were stenciled in black letters on the gray door: the entire floor belonged to a single occupant. That level had no public corridor; the fire door could be opened only from the inside. The same was true of the twenty-ninth and twenty-eighth floors, which were the domain of Sweet Sixteen Cosmetics. He tried both entrances without success.

Worried that he would lose track of his prey, he rushed back to the twenty-sixth floor. That was where he had originally entered the stairwell, where he had left the elevator cab.

As he pulled open the fire door and stepped into the hall, he looked at his watch. 9:15. The time was passing too fast, unnaturally fast, as if the universe had become unbalanced.

Hurrying to the elevator alcove, he fished in his pocket for the dead guard's keys. They snagged on the lining. When he jerked them loose, they spun out of his hand and fell on the carpet with a sleighbell jingle.

He knelt and felt for them in the darkness. Then he remembered the pencil flashlight, but even with that he needed more than a minute to locate the keys.

As he got up, angry with himself, he wondered if Harris and the woman were waiting here for him. He put away the flashlight and snatched the pistol from his pocket. He stood quite still. He studied the darkness. If they were hiding there, they would have been silhouetted by the bright spot farther along at the alcove.

When he thought about it, he realized that they couldn't have known on which floor he'd left the elevator. Furthermore, they couldn't have gotten down here in time to surprise him.

The thirty-first floor was a different story. They might have time to set a trap for him up there. When the elevator doors slid open, they might be waiting for him; he would be most vulnerable at that moment.

Then again, *he* was the one with the pistol. So what if they were waiting with makeshift weapons? They didn't stand a chance of overpowering him.

At the elevator he put the key in the control board and activated the circuit.

He looked at his watch. 9:19.

If there were no more delays, he could kill Harris and still have twenty minutes or half an hour with the woman.

Whistling again, he pushed one of the buttons: 31.

# 27
◆◆◆

The lab technician disconnected the garbage disposal, wrapped it in a heavy white plastic sheet, and carried it out of the apartment.

Preduski and Enderby were left alone in the kitchen.

In the foyer, a grandfather clock struck the quarter hour: two soft chimes, running five minutes late. In accompaniment, the wind fluted musically through the eaves just above the kitchen windows.

"If you find it hard to accept the idea of two psychopaths working so smoothly together," Enderby said, "then consider the possibility that they aren't psychopaths of any sort we've seen before."

"Now you sound like Graham Harris."

"I know."

"The Butcher is mentally ill, Harris says. But you wouldn't know it to look at him, Harris says. Either the symptoms of his mania don't show, or he knows how to conceal them. He'd pass any psychiatric exam, Harris says."

"I'm beginning to agree with him."

"Except you say there are two Butchers."

Enderby nodded.

Preduski sighed. He went to the nearest window and drew the outline of a knife in the thin gray-white film of moisture that coated the glass. "If you're right, I can't hold onto my theory. That he's just your ordinary paranoid schizophrenic. Maybe a lone killer could be operating in a psychotic fugue. But not two of them simultaneously."

"They're not suffering any psychotic fugue," Enderby agreed. "Both of these men know precisely what they're doing. Neither of them suffers from amnesia."

Turning from the window, from the drawing of the knife which had begun to streak as droplets of water slid down the pane, Preduski said, "Whether this is a new type of psychotic or not, the crime is familiar. Sex murders are—"

"These aren't sex murders," Enderby said.

Preduski cocked his head. "Come again?"

"These aren't *sex* murders."

"They only kill women."

"Yes, but—"

"And they rape them first."

"Yes. It's murder with sex *associated*. But these aren't *sex* murders."

"I'm sorry. I'm lost. My fault. Not yours."

"Sex isn't the motivating force. Sex isn't the whole or even the primary reason they have for attacking these women. The opportunity for rape is there. So they take it. Going to kill the women anyway. They aren't adding to their legal risks by raping them first. Sex is secondary. They aren't killing out of some psychosexual impulse."

Shaking his head, Preduski said, "I don't see how you can say that. You've never met them. What evidence do you have that their motives aren't basically sexual?"

"Circumstantial," Enderby said. "For instance, the way they mutilate the corpses."

"What about it?"

"Have you studied the mutilations carefully?"

"I had no choice."

"All right. Found any sign of anal mutilation?"

"No."

"Mutilation of the genitalia?"

"No."

"Mutilation of the breasts?"

"In some cases he's cut open the abdomen and chest cavity."

"Mutilation of the breasts alone?"

"When he opens the chest—"

"I mean has he ever cut off a woman's nipples, or perhaps her entire breasts, as Jack the Ripper did?"

A look of loathing came over his face. "No."

"Has he ever mutlilated the mouth of a victim?"

"The mouth?"

"Has he ever cut off the lips?"

"No. Never."

"Has he ever cut out a tongue?"

"God, no! Andy, do we have to go on like this? It's morbid. And I don't see where it's leading."

"If they were maniacal *sex* killers with a desire to cut their victims," Enderby said, "they'd have disfigured one of those areas."

"Anus, breasts, genitalia, or mouth?"

"Unquestionably. At least one of them. Probably all of them. But they didn't. So the mutilation is an afterthought. Not a sexual compulsion. Window dressing."

Preduski closed his eyes, pressed his fingertips to them, as if he were trying to suppress unpleasant images. "Window dressing? I'm afraid I don't understand."

"To impress us."

"The police?"

"Yes. And the newspapers."

Preduski went to the window where he had drawn the knife. He wiped away the film of moisture and stared at the snow sheeting through the glow around the street lamp. "Why would he want to impress us?"

"I don't know. Whatever the reason, whatever the need behind his desire to impress—*that* is the true motivation."

"If we knew what it was, we might be able to see a pattern in the killings. We might be able to anticipate him."

Suddenly excited, Enderby said, "Wait a minute. Another case. Two killers. Working together. Chicago. Nineteen twenty-four. Two young men were the murderers. Both sons of millionaires. In their late teens."

"Leopold and Loeb."

"You know the case?"

"Slightly."

"They killed a boy, Bobby Franks. Fourteen years old. Son of another rich man. They had nothing against him. None of the usual reasons. No classic motive. Newspapers said it was for kicks. For thrills. Very bloody murder. But they killed Franks for other reasons. For more than kicks. For a philosophical ideal."

Turning away from the window, Preduski said, "I'm sorry. I must have missed something. I'm not making sense of this. *What* philosophical ideal?"

"They thought they were special. Supermen. The first of a new race. Leopold idolized Nietzsche."

Frowning, Preduski said, "One of the quotes in there on the bedroom wall is probably from Nietzsche's work, the other from Blake. There was a quote from Nietzsche written in blood on Edna Mowry's wall last night."

"Leopold and Loeb. Incredible pair. They thought that committing the perfect crime was proof that they were supermen. Getting away with murder. They thought that was *proof* of superior intelligence, superior cunning."

"Weren't they homosexuals?"

"Yes. But that doesn't make Bobby Franks the victim of a sex killing. They didn't molest him. Never had any intention of molesting him. They weren't motivated by lust. Not at all. It was, as Loeb called it, 'an intellectual exercise.' "

In spite of his excitement, Enderby noticed that his shirt cuffs were not showing beyond the sleeves of his suit jacket. He pulled them out, one at a time, until the proper half inch was revealed. Although he had worked for some time in the blood-splashed bedroom and then in the messy kitchen, he didn't have a stain on him.

His back to the window, leaning against the sill, conscious of his own scuffed shoes and wrinkled trousers, Preduski said, "I'm having trouble understanding. You'll have to be patient with me. You know how I am. Dense sometimes. But if these two boys, Leopold and Loeb, thought that murder was an intellectual exercise, then they were crazy. Weren't they? Were they mad?"

"In a way. Mad with their own power. Both real and imagined power."

"Would they have appeared to be mad?"

"Not at all."

"How is that possible?"

"Remember, Leopold graduated from college when he was just seventeen. He had an IQ of two hundred or nearly so. He was a genius. So was Loeb. They were bright enough to keep their Nietzschean fantasies to themselves, to hide their grandiose self-images."

"What if they'd taken psychiatric tests?"

"Psychiatric tests weren't very well developed in nineteen twenty-four."

"But if there had been tests back then as sophisticated as those we have today, would Leopold and Loeb have passed them?"

"Probably with flying colors."

"Have there been others like Leopold and Loeb since nineteen twenty-four?" Preduski asked.

"Not that I know of. Not in a pure sense, anyway. The Manson family killed for murky political and religious reasons. They thought Manson was Christ. Thought killing the rich would help the down-trodden. Unmitigated crazies, in my book. Think of some other killers, especially mass murderers. Charles Starkweather. Richard Speck. Albert DeSalvo. All of them were psychotic. All of them were driven by psychoses that had grown and festered in them, that had slowly corrupted them since childhood. In Leopold and Loeb, there were apparently no serious childhood traumas that could have led to psychotic behavior. No black seed to bear fruit later."

"So if the Butcher is two men," Preduski said forlornly, "we've got a new Leopold and Loeb. Killing to prove their superiority."

Enderby began to pace. "Maybe. But then again, maybe it's more than that. Something more complex than that."

"Like what?"

"I don't know. But I feel it's not *exactly* a Leopold and Loeb sort of thing." He went to the table and stared at the remains of the meal that had never been eaten. "Have you called Harris?"

Preduski said, "No."

"You should. He's been trying to get an image of the killer. Hasn't had any luck. Maybe that's because he's focusing on a single image, trying to envision just one face. Tell him there are *two* killers. Maybe that'll break it open for him. Maybe he'll finally get a handle on the case."

"We don't *know* there are two. That's just a theory."

"Tell him anyway," Enderby said. "What harm can it do?"

"I should tell him tonight. I really should. But I just can't," Preduski said. "He's gotten behind in his work because of this case. That's my fault. I'm always calling him, talking to him, pressuring him about it. He's working late, trying to get caught up. I don't want to disturb him.''

In the foyer by the front door, the grandfather clock chimed the half hour, five minutes late again.

Preduski glanced at his wristwatch and said, ''It'll soon be ten o'clock. I've got to be going.''

''Going? There's work to do here.''

''I'm not on duty yet.''

''Graveyard?''

''Yeah.''

''I never knew you to hesitate about a bit of overtime.''

''Well, I just got out of bed. I was cooking spaghetti when Head-quarters called me about this. Never got a chance to eat any of it. I'm starving.''

Enderby shook his head. ''As long as I've known you, I don't believe I've ever seen you eat a square meal. You're always grabbing sand-wiches so you don't have to stop working to eat. And at home you're cooking spaghetti. You need a wife, Ira.''

''A wife?''

''Other men have them.''

''But me? Are you kidding?''

''Be good for you.''

''Andy, look at me.''

''I'm looking.''

''Look closer.''

''So?''

''You must be blind.''

''What should I see?''

''What woman in her right mind would marry me?''

''Don't give me your usual crap, Ira,'' Enderby said with a smile. ''I know that under all of that self-deprecating chatter, you've got a healthy and proper respect for yourself.''

''You're the psychiatrist.''

''That's right. I'm not a suspect or a witness; you can't charm me with that blather.''

Preduski grinned.

''I'll bet there have been more than a few women who've fallen for that calculated little-boy look of yours.''

''A few,'' Preduski admitted uncomfortably. ''But never the *right* woman.''

''Who said anything about the *right* one? Most men are happy to settle for half-right.''

"Not me." Preduski looked at his watch again. "I really have to be going. I'll come back around midnight. Martin probably won't even have finished questioning the other tenants by then. It's a big building."

Dr. Enderby sighed as if the troubles of the world were on his shoulders alone. "We'll be here too. Dusting the furniture for prints, vacuuming the carpets for hairs and threads, finding nothing, but working hard. The same old circus."

# 28
◆◆◆

Graham's foot slipped off the rung.

Although he was still holding tightly with both hands, he panicked. He struck out at the ladder with his feet, scrabbling wildly, as if the ladder were alive, as if he had to kick it into submission before he could regain his foothold on it.

"Graham, what's wrong?" Connie asked from her position on the ladder above him. "Graham?"

Her voice sobered him. He stopped kicking. He hung by his hands until he was breathing almost normally, until the vivid memories of Everest had faded.

"Graham?"

With his feet he probed for a rung, found one after several seconds that seemed like hours. "I'm all right. My foot slipped. I'm okay now."

"Don't look down."

"I didn't. I won't."

He sought the next rung, stepped to it, continued the descent.

He felt feverish. The hair was damp at the back of his neck. Perspiration beaded his forehead, jeweled his eyebrows, stung the corners of his eyes, filmed his cheeks, brought a salty taste to his lips. In spite of the perspiration, he was cold. He shivered as he moved down the long ladder.

He was as much aware of the void at his back as he would have been of a knife pressed between his shoulder blades.

* * *

On the thirty-first floor, Frank Bollinger entered the maintenance supply room.

He saw the red door. Someone had put down the doorstop that was fixed to it, so that it was open an inch or two. He knew immediately that Harris and the woman had gone through there.

But why was the door ajar?

It was like a signpost. Beckoning him.

Alert for a trap, he advanced cautiously. He held the Walther PPK in his right hand. He kept his left hand out in front of him, arm extended all the way, to stop the door in case they tried to throw it open in his face. He held his breath for those few steps, listening for the slightest sound other than the soft squeak of his own shoes.

Nothing. Silence.

He used the toe of his shoe to push up the doorstop; then he pulled open the door and walked onto the small platform. He had just enough time to realize where he was, when the door closed behind him and all the lights in the shaft went out.

At first he thought Harris had come into the maintenance room after him. But when he tried the door, it was not locked. And when he opened it, all the lights came on. The emergency lighting didn't burn twenty-four hours a day; it came on only when one of the service entrances was open, and that was why Harris had left the door ajar.

Bollinger was impressed by the system of lights and platforms and ladders. Not every building erected in the 1920s would have been designed with an eye toward emergencies. In fact, damned few skyscrapers built since the war could boast *any* safety provisions. These days, they expected you to wait in a stalled elevator until it was repaired, no matter if that took ten hours or ten days; and, if the lift couldn't be repaired, you could risk a manually cranked descent, or you could rot in it.

The more time he spent in the building, the deeper he penetrated it, the more fascinating he found it to be. It was not on the scale of those truly gargantuan stadiums and museums and highrises that Hitler had designed for the ''super race'' just prior to and during the first days of World War Two. But then Hitler's magnificent edifices had never been realized in stone and mortar, whereas this place *had* risen. He began to feel that the men who had designed and constructed it were Olympians. He found his appreciation strange, for he knew that had he been restricted to the halls and offices during the day, when the building was full of people and buzzing with commerce, he would not have noticed the great size and high style of the structure. One took for granted that which was commonplace; and to New Yorkers, there was nothing unusual about a forty-two-story office building.

Now, however, abandoned for the night, the tower seemed incredibly huge and complex; in solitude and silence one had time to contemplate it and see how magnificent and extraordinary it was. He was like a microbe wandering through the veins and bowels of a living creature, a behemoth almost beyond measurement.

He felt in league with the minds that could conceive of a monument like this. He was one of them, a mover and shaker, a superior man. The Olympian nature of the building—and of the architects responsible for it—struck a responsive chord in him, made him reverberate with the knowledge of his own special godlike stature. Brimming with a sense of glory, he was more determined than ever to kill Harris and the woman. They were animals. Lice. Parasites. Because of Harris's freakish psychic gift, they posed a threat to Bollinger. They were trying to deny him his rightful place in this new and forceful current of history: the at first gradual but ever-quickening rise of the new men.

He pushed the doorstop against the floor to keep the door open and the lights burning. Then he went to the edge of the platform and peered down the ladder.

They were three floors under him. The woman on top, nearest by a few rungs. Harris below her, going first. Neither of them looked up. They certainly were aware of the momentary loss of light and understood the significance of it. They were hurrying toward the next platform, where they could get out of the shaft.

Bollinger knelt, tested the railing. It was strong. He leaned against it, using it like a safety harness to keep him from tumbling to his death.

He didn't want to kill them here. The place and method of murder were extremely important tonight. Here, they would drop to the bottom of the well, and that would ruin the scheme that he and Billy had come up with this afternoon. He wasn't here just to kill them any way he could; he had to dispose of them in a certain manner. If he brought it off just right, the police would be confused, misled; and the people of New York would begin to experience a spiraling reign of terror unlike anything in their worst nightmares. He and Billy had worked out a damned clever gambit, and he wouldn't abandon it so long as there was a chance of bringing it off as planned.

It was a quarter of ten. In fifteen minutes Billy would be in the alleyway outside, and he would wait only until ten-thirty. Bollinger saw that he probably wouldn't have time for the woman, but he was pretty sure he'd be able to carry out the plan in forty-five minutes.

Besides, he didn't know what Harris looked like, and he felt there was something cowardly about killing a man whose face he'd never seen. It was akin to shooting someone in the back. That sort of killing— even of an animal, even of a louse like Harris—didn't fit Bollinger's image of a superman. He liked to meet his prey head-on, to get close, so that there was at least a hint of danger.

The trick was to force them out of the shaft without killing them; to herd them to other ground where the plan could be carried out. He pointed the pistol down, aimed wide of the woman's head and squeezed the trigger.

The shot exploded; ear-splitting noise assaulted Connie from every side. Over the diminishing echoes, she could hear the bullet ricocheting from one wall to the other, farther down the shaft.

The situation was so unreal that she had to wonder if it was transpiring in her mind. She supposed it was possible that she was in a hospital and that all of this was the product of a fevered imagination, the delusions of madness.

Descending the ladder, she repeatedly caught herself murmuring softly: sometimes it was jumbled phrases that made little sense, sometimes strings of utterly meaningless sounds. Her stomach rolled over like a fish on a wet boat dock. Her bowels quivered. She felt as if a bullet had already ripped into her, already had torn apart her vital organs.

Bollinger fired again.

The shot seemed less sharp than the one before it. Her ears were desensitized, still ringing from the first explosion.

For a woman who had experienced little emotional—and *no* physical—terror in her life, she was handling herself surprisingly well.

When she looked down, she saw Graham let go of the ladder with one hand. He grabbed the railing that ringed the platform. He took one foot off the ladder; hesitated, leaning at a precarious angle; started to bring his foot back; suddenly found the courage to put it on the edge of the platform. For a moment, fighting his own terror, he stayed that way, crucified between the two points of safety. She was about to call to him, urge him on, when he finally freed himself of the ladder altogether, wobbled on the brink of the platform as if he would fall, then got his balance and climbed over the railing.

She descended the last dozen rungs much too fast and reached the platform as Bollinger fired a third shot. She hurried through the red door that Graham held open for her, into the maintenance supply room on the twenty-seventh level.

The first thing she saw was the blood on his trousers. A bright spot of it. As big as a silver dollar. Glistening on the gray fabric. "What happened?"

"Had these in my pocket," he said, holding up the scissors. "A couple of floors back, when I almost fell, the blades tore through the lining and gouged my thigh."

"Is it bad?"

"No."

"Hurt?"

"Not much."

"Better get rid of them."

"Not just yet."

Bollinger watched until they left the shaft. They had gotten out two platforms down. Because there was only a service entrance at every second floor, that put them on the twenty-seventh level.

He got up, hurried toward the elevator.

"Come on," Graham said. "Let's make a run for the stairs."

"No. We've got to go back up the shaft."

Incredulity showed on his face, anguish in his eyes. "That's crazy!"

"He won't be looking for us in the shaft. At least not for a couple of minutes. We can go up two floors, then use the stairs when he comes back to check the shaft." She opened the red door through which they'd come only seconds ago.

"I don't know if I can do it again," he said.

"Of course you can."

"You said *up* the shaft?"

"That's right."

"We have to go down to escape."

She shook her head; her hair formed a brief dark halo. "You remember what I said about the night guards?"

"They might be dead."

"If Bollinger killed them so he could have a free hand with us, wouldn't he also have sealed off the building? What if we get to the lobby, with Bollinger hot on our heels, and we find the doors are locked? Before we could break the glass and get out, he'd have killed us."

"But the guards might not be dead. He might have gotten past them somehow."

"Can we take that chance?"

He frowned. "I guess not."

"I don't want to get to the lobby until we're certain of having a long lead on Bollinger."

"So we go up. How's that better?"

"We can't play cat and mouse with him for twenty-seven floors. The next time he catches us in the shaft or on the stairs, he won't make any mistakes. But if he doesn't realize we're going *up*, we might be able to alternate between the shaft and the stairs for thirteen floors, long enough to get to your office."

"Why there?"

"Because he won't expect us to backtrack."

Graham's blue eyes were not as wide with fear as they had been; they had narrowed with calculation. In spite of himself, the will to survive was flowering in him; the first signs of the old Graham Harris were becoming visible, pushing through his shell of fear.

He said, "Eventually, he'll realize what we've done. It'll buy us only fifteen minutes or so."

"Time to think of another way out," she said. "Come on, Graham. We're wasting too much time. He'll be on this floor any second now."

Less reluctantly than the first time, but still without enthusiasm, he followed her into the elevator shaft.

On the platform he said, "You go first. I'll bring up the rear, so I won't knock you off the ladder if I fall."

For the same reason, he had insisted on going first when they descended.

She put her arms around him, kissed him, then turned and started to climb.

As soon as he got off the elevator on the twenty-seventh floor, Bollinger investigated the stairs at the north end of the building. They were deserted.

He ran the length of the corridor and opened the door to the south stairs. He stood on the landing for almost a minute, listening intently for movement. He heard none.

In the corridor again, he searched for an unlocked office door until he realized they might have gone back into the elevator shaft. He located the maintenance supply room; the red door was ajar.

He approached it cautiously, as before. He was opening the door all the way when the shaft beyond was filled with the sound of another door closing on it.

On the platform, he bent over the railing. He stared down into the vertiginous depths, wondering which one of the doors they had used.

How many floors had they gained on him?

*Dammit!*

Cursing aloud, overcoat flapping around his legs, Bollinger went back to the south stairs to listen for them.

By the time they had climbed two flights on the north stairs, Graham was wincing with each step. From sole to hip, pain coruscated through his bad leg. In anticipation of each jolt, he tensed his stomach. Now his entire abdomen ached. If he had continued to work out and climb after his fall on Mount Everest, as the doctors had urged him to do, he would have been in shape for this. He had given his leg more punishment tonight than it ordinarily received in a year. Now he was paying in pain for five years of inactivity.

"Don't slow down," Connie said.

"Trying not to."

"Use the rail as much as you can. Pull yourself along."

"How far are we going?"

"One more floor."

"Eternity."

"After that we'll switch back to the elevator shaft."

He liked the ladder in the shaft better than he did the stairs. On the ladder he could use his good leg and pull with both hands to keep nearly all of his weight off the other leg. But on the stairs, if he didn't use the lame leg at all, he would have to hop from one step to the other; and that was too slow.

"One more flight," she said encouragingly.

Trying to surprise himself, trying to cover a lot of ground before the pain transmitted itself from leg to brain, he put on a burst of speed, staggered up ten steps as fast as he could. That transformed the pain into agony. He had to slow down, but he kept moving.

Bollinger stood on the landing, listening for sound in the south stairwell.

Nothing.

He looked over the railing. Squinting, he tried to see through the layers of darkness that filled the spaces between the landing.

Nothing.

He went back into the hall and ran toward the north stairs.

# 29

◆◆◆

Billy drove into the alley. His car made the first tracks in the new snow.

A forty-foot-long, twenty-foot-deep service courtyard lay at the back of the Bowerton Building. Four doors opened onto it. One of these was a big green garage door, where delivery could be taken on office furniture and other items too large to fit through the public entrance. A sodium vapor lamp glowed above the green door, casting a harsh light on the stone walls, on the rows of trash bins awaiting pickup in the morning, and on the snow; the shadows were sharply drawn.

There was no sign of Bollinger.

Prepared to leave at the first indication of trouble, Billy backed the car into the courtyard. He switched off the headlights but not the engine. He rolled down his window, just an inch, to keep the glass from steaming.

When Bollinger didn't come out to meet him, Billy looked at his watch. 10:02.

Clouds of dry snow swirled down the alley in front of him. In the courtyard, out of the worst of the wind, the snow was relatively undisturbed.

Most nights, squad cars conducted random patrols of poorly lighted back streets like this one, always on the lookout for business-district burglars with half-filled vans, muggers with half-robbed victims, and rapists with half-subdued women. But not tonight. Not in this weather. The city's uniformed patrolmen would be occupied elsewhere. The majority of them would be busy cleaning up after the usual foul-weather automobile accidents, but as much as a third of the evening shift would be squirreled away in favorite hideouts, on a side street or in a park; they would be drinking coffee—in a few cases, something stronger— and talking about sports and women, ready to go to work only if the radio dispatcher insisted upon it.

Billy looked at his watch again. 10:04.

He would wait exactly twenty-six minutes. Not one minute less, and certainly not one more. That was what he had promised Dwight.

Once again, Bollinger reached the elevator shaft just as it was filled with the sound of another door closing on it.

He bent over the railing, looked down. Nothing but other railings, other platforms, other emergency light bulbs, and a lot of darkness. Harris and the woman had gone.

He was tired of playing hide-and-seek with them, of dashing from stairwell to stairwell to shaft. He was sweating profusely. Under his overcoat, his shirt clung to him wetly. He left the platform, went to the elevator, activated it with a key, pushed the button marked "Lobby."

On the ground level, he took off his heavy overcoat and dropped it beside the elevator doors. Sweat trickled down his neck, down the center of his chest. He didn't remove his gloves. With the back of his left hand and then with his shirt sleeve he wiped his dripping forehead.

Out of sight of anyone who might come to the street doors, he leaned against the marble wall at the end of the offset that contained the four banks of elevators. From that position, he could see two white doors with black stenciled letters on them, one at the north end and one at the south end of the lobby. These were the exits from the stairwells. When Harris and the woman came through one of them, he would blow their goddamned brains out. Oh, yes. With pleasure.

Hobbling along the fortieth-floor corridor toward the light that came from the open reception-room door of the Harris Publications suite, Harris saw the fire-alarm box. It was approximately nine inches on a side, set flush with the wall. The metal rim was painted red, and the face of it was glass.

He couldn't imagine why he hadn't thought of this before.

Ahead of him, Connie realized that he had stopped. "What's the matter?"

"Look here."

She came back.

"If we set it off," Graham said, "it'll bring the security guards up from downstairs."

"If they aren't dead."

"Even if they are dead, it'll bring the fire department on the double. Bollinger will have the crimps put to him."

"Maybe he won't run when he hears the bells. After all, we know his name. He might hang on, kill us, sneak out past the firemen."

"He might," Graham agreed, unsettled by the thought of being stalked through dark halls full of clanging, banging bells.

They stared through the glass at the steel alarm lever that glinted in the red light.

He felt hope, like a muscle relaxant, relieve a fraction of the tension in his shoulders, neck, and face. For the first time all night, he began to think they might escape.

Then he remembered the vision. The bullet. The blood. He was going to be shot in the back.

She said, "The alarms will probably be so loud that we won't hear him if he comes after us."

"But it works both ways," he said eagerly. "*He* won't be able to hear *us*."

She pressed her fingertips to the cool plate of glass, hesitated, then took her hand away. "Okay. But there's no little hammer to break the glass." She held up the chain that was supposed to secure a hammer to the side of the alarm. "What do we use instead?"

Smiling, he took the scissors from his pocket and held them up as if they were a talisman.

"Applause, applause," she said, beginning to feel just enough hope to allow herself a little joke.

"Thank you."

"Be careful," she said.

"Stand back."

She did.

Graham held the scissors by the closed blades. Using the heavy handles as a hammer, he smashed the thin glass. A few pieces held stubbornly to the frame. So as not to cut himself, he broke out the jagged splinters before he put one hand into the shallow alarm box and jerked the steel lever from green to red.

No noise.

No bells.

Silence.

*Christ!*

"Oh, no," she said.

Frantically, the flame of hope flickering in him, he pushed the lever up, back to the green safety mark, then slammed it down again.

Still nothing.

Bollinger had been as thorough with the fire alarm as he had been with the telephones.

The wipers swept back and forth, clearing the snow from the windshield. The rhythmic *thump-thump-thump* was getting on his nerves.

Billy glanced over his shoulder, through the rear window, at the green garage door, then at the other three doors.

The time was 10:15.

Where in the hell was Dwight?

Graham and Connie went to the magazine's art department in search of a knife and other sharp draftsmen's tools that would make better weapons than the scissors. He found a pair of razor-edged scalpel-like instruments in the center drawer of the art director's big metal desk.

When he looked up from the drawer, he saw that Connie was lost in thought. She was standing just inside the door, staring at the floor in front of a light blue photographic backdrop. Climbing equipment— coils of rope, pitons, étriers, carabiners, klettershoes, nylon jackets lined with down, and perhaps thirty other items—lay in a disordered heap before the screen.

"See what I found?" he said. He held up the blades.

She wasn't interested. "What about this stuff?" she asked, pointing to the climbing equipment.

Coming from behind the desk, he said, "This issue we're running a buyer's guide. Each of those pieces was photographed for the article. Why'd you ask?" Then his face brightened. "Never mind. I see why." He hunkered in front of the equipment, picked up an ice ax. "This makes a better weapon than any draftsman's tool."

"Graham?"

He looked up.

Her expression was peculiar: a combination of puzzlement, fear and amazement. Although she clearly had thought of something interesting and important, her gray eyes gave no indication of what was going through her mind. She said, "Let's not rush out to fight him. Can we consider all of our options?"

"That's why we're here."

She stepped into the short, private hallway, cocked her head and listened for Bollinger.

Graham stood up, prepared to use the ice ax.

When she was satisfied that there was nothing to listen for but more silence, she came back into the room.

He lowered the ax. "I thought you heard something."

"Just being cautious." She glanced at the climbing equipment before she sat down on the edge of the desk. "As I see it, there are five different things we can do. Number one, we can make a stand, try to fight Bollinger."

"With this," he said, hefting the ice ax.

"And with anything else we can find."

"We can set a trap, surprise him."

"I see two problems with that approach."

"The gun."

"That's sure one."

"If we're clever enough, he won't have time to shoot."

"More important," she said, "neither of us is a killer."

"We could just knock him unconscious."

"If you hit him on the head with an ax like that, you're bound to kill him."

"If it's kill or be killed, I suppose I could do it."

"Maybe. But if you hesitate at the last instant, we're dead."

He didn't resent the limits of her faith in him; he knew that he didn't deserve her complete trust. "You said there were five things we could do."

"Number two, we can try to hide."

"Where?"

"I don't know. Maybe look for an office that someone forgot to lock, go inside and lock it after us."

"No one forgot."

"Maybe we *can* continue to play cat and mouse with him."

"For how long?"

"Until a new shift of guards finds the dead ones."

"If he didn't kill the guards, then the new guards won't know what's going on up here."

"That's right."

"Besides, I think maybe they work twelve-hour shifts, four days a week. I know one of the night men. I've heard him curse the long shifts and at the same time praise the eight hours of overtime he gets each week. So if they come on duty at six, they won't be off until six in the morning."

"Seven and a half hours."

"Too long to play cat and mouse in the elevator shaft and on the stairs. Especially with this bum leg of mine."

"Number three," she said. "We could open one of your office windows and shout for help."

"From the fortieth floor? Even in good weather, they probably couldn't hear you on the sidewalk. With this wind, they wouldn't hear you even two floors away."

"I know that. And on a night like this, there's not going to be anyone out walking anyway."

"Then why'd you suggest it?"

"Number five is going to surprise you," she said. "When I get to it, I want you to understand that I've thought of every other possible out."

"What's number five?"

"Number four first. We open the office window and throw furniture into the street, try to catch the attention of anyone who's driving past on Lexington."

"If anyone *is* driving in this weather."

"Someone will be. A taxi or two."

"But if we toss out a chair, we won't be able to calculate the effect of the wind on it. We won't be able to gauge where it'll land. What if it goes through the windshield of a car and kills someone?"

"I've thought of that."

"We can't do it."

"I know."

"What's number five?"

She slid off the desk and went to the pile of climbing equipment. "We've got to get rigged out in this stuff."

"Rigged out?"

"Boots, jackets, gloves, ropes—the works."

He was perplexed. "Why?"

Her eyes were wide, like the eyes of a startled doe. "For the climb down."

"Down what?"

"Down the outside of the building. All the way to the street."

# PART FOUR

# FRIDAY
# 10:30 P.M.

# SATURDAY
# 4:00 A.M.

◆ ◆ ◆

# 30
### ◆ ◆ ◆

Promptly at ten-thirty, Billy drove out of the service courtyard behind the highrise.

The snowfall had grown heavier during the past half hour, and the wind had become downright dangerous. Roiling in the headlight beams, the sheets of powder-dry flakes were almost as dense as a fog.

At the mouth of the alley, as he was pulling onto the side street, the tires spun on the icy pavement. The car slewed toward the far curb. He turned the wheel in the direction of the slide and managed to stop just short of colliding with a panel truck parked at the curb.

He had been driving too fast, and he hadn't even been aware of it until he'd almost crashed. That wasn't like him. He was a careful man. He was never reckless. Never. He was angry with himself for losing control.

He drove toward the avenue. The traffic light was with him, and the nearest car was three or four blocks away, a lone pair of headlights dimmed and diffused by the falling snow. He turned the corner onto Lexington.

In three hundred feet, he came to the front of the Bowerton Building. Ferns and flowers, molded in a twenty-foot-long rectangular bronze plaque, crowned the stonework above the four revolving doors. Part of the enormous lobby was visible beyond the entrance, and it appeared to be deserted. He drove near the curb, in the parking lane, barely moving, studying the building and the sidewalks and the calcimined street, looking for some sign of trouble and finding none.

Nevertheless, the plan had failed. Something had gone wrong in there. Terribly, terribly wrong.

Will Bollinger talk if he's caught? Billy wondered uneasily. Will he implicate me?

He would have to go to work without knowing how badly Dwight had failed, without knowing whether or not Bollinger would be—had been?—apprehended by the police. He was going to find it difficult to concentrate on his job tonight; but if he was going to construct an alibi to counter a possible confession from Dwight, it would help his case if he was calm tonight, as much like himself as he could be, as thorough and diligent as those who knew him expected him to be.

Franklin Dwight Bollinger was getting restless. He was bathed in a thin, oily sweat. His fingers ached from the tight grip he had kept on the Walther PPK. He'd been watching the stairwell exits for more than twenty minutes, but there was no sign of Harris or the woman.

Billy was gone by now, the schedule destroyed. Bollinger hoped he might salvage the plan. But at the same time he knew that wasn't possible. The situation had degenerated to this: slaughter them and get the hell out.

Where *is* Harris? he wondered. Has he sensed that I'm waiting here for him? Has he used his carnival act, his goddamned clairvoyance to anticipate me?

He decided to wait five minutes more. Then he would be forced to go after them.

Staring out of the office window at an eerie panorama of gigantic, snow-swept buildings and fuzzy lights, Graham said, "It's impossible."

Beside him, Connie put one hand on his arm. "*Why* is it impossible?"

"It just is."

"That's not good enough."

"I can't climb it."

"It's not a climb."

"What?"

"It's a descent."

"Doesn't matter."

"Can it be done?"

"Not by me."

"You climbed the ladder in the shaft."

"That's different."

"How?"

"Besides, you've never climbed."

"You can teach me."

"No."

"Sure you can."

"You can't learn on the sheer face of a forty-story building in the middle of a blizzard."

"I'd have a damned good teacher," she said.

"Oh, yeah. One who hasn't climbed in five years."

"You still know how. You haven't forgotten."

"I'm out of shape."

"You're a strong man."

"You forget my leg."

She turned away from the window and went back to the door so that she could listen for Bollinger while she talked. "Remember when Abercrombie and Fitch had a man scale their building to advertise a new line of climbing equipment?"

He didn't look away from the window. He was transfixed by the night. "What about it?"

"At that time, you said what that man did wasn't really so difficult."

"Did I?"

"You said a building, with all its ledges and setbacks, is an easy climb compared to almost any mountain."

He said nothing. He remembered telling her that, and he knew he had been right. But when he'd said it he never thought he'd be called upon to *do* it. Images of Mount Everest and of hospital rooms filled his mind.

"This equipment you chose for the buyer's guide—"

"What about it?"

"It's the best, isn't it?"

"The best, or close to it."

"We'd be perfectly outfitted."

"If we try it, we'll die."

"We'll die if we stay here."

"Maybe not."

"I think so. Absolutely."

"There has to be an alternative."

"I've outlined them already."

"Maybe we *can* hide from him."

"Where?"

"I don't know. But—"

"And we can't hide for seven hours."

"This is crazy, dammit!"

"Can you think of anything better?"

"Give me time."

"Bollinger will be here any minute."

"The wind speed must be forty miles an hour at street level. At least when it's gusting. Fifty miles an hour up this high."

"Will it blow us off?"

"We'd have to fight it every inch."

"Won't we anchor the ropes?"

He turned away from the window. "Yes, but—"

"And won't we be wearing those?" She pointed to a pair of safety harnesses that lay atop the pile of equipment.

"It'll be damned cold out there, Connie."

"We've got the down-lined jackets."

"But we don't have quilted, insulated pants. You're wearing ordinary jeans. So am I. For all the good they'll do us, we might as well be naked below the waist."

"I can stand the cold."

"Not for very long. Not cold as bitter as that."

"How long will it take us to get to the street?"

"I don't know."

"You must have *some* idea."

"An hour. Maybe two hours."

"That long?"

"You're a novice."

"Couldn't we rappel?"

"Rappel?" He was appalled.

"It looks so easy. Swinging out and back, dropping a few feet with every swing, bouncing off the stone, dancing along the side of the building . . ."

"It looks easy, but it isn't."

"But it's fast."

"Jesus! You've never climbed before, and you want to rappel down."

"I've got guts."

"But no common sense."

"Okay," she said. "We don't rappel."

"We definitely don't rappel."

"We go slow and easy."

"We don't go at all."

Ignoring him, she said, "I can take two hours of the cold. I know I can. And if we keep moving, maybe it won't bother us so much."

"We'll freeze to death." He refused to be shaken from that opinion.

"Graham, we have a simple choice. Go or stay. If we make the climb, *maybe* we'll fall or freeze to death. If we stay here, we'll sure as hell be killed."

"I'm not convinced it *is* that simple."

"Yes, you are."

He closed his eyes. He was furious with himself, sick of his inability to accept unpleasant realities, to risk pain, and to come face to face with his own fear. The climb would be dangerous. Supremely dangerous. It might even prove to be sheer folly; they could die in the first few minutes of the descent. But she was correct when she said they had no choice but to try it.

"Graham? We're wasting time."

"You know the real reason why the climb isn't possible."

"No," she said. "Tell me."

He felt color and warmth come into his face. "Connie, you aren't leaving me with any dignity."

"I never took that from you. You've taken it from yourself." Her lovely face was lined with sorrow. He could see that it hurt her to have to speak to him so bluntly. She came across the room, put one hand to his face. "You've surrendered your dignity and your self-respect. Piece by piece." Her voice was low, almost a whisper; it wavered. "I'm afraid for you, afraid that if you don't stop throwing it away, you'll have nothing left. Nothing."

"Connie . . ." He wanted to cry. But he had no tears for Graham Harris. He knew precisely what he had done to himself. He had no pity; he *despised* the man he'd become. He felt that, deep inside, he had always been a coward, and that his fall on Mount Everest had given him an excuse to retreat into fear. Why else had he resisted going to a psychiatrist? Every one of his doctors had suggested psychoanalysis. He suspected that he was comfortable in his fear; and that possibility sickened him. "I'm afraid of my own shadow. I'd be no good to you out there."

"You're not so frightened today as you were yesterday," she said tenderly. "Tonight, you've coped damned well. What about the elevator shaft? This morning, the thought of going down that ladder would have overwhelmed you."

He was trembling.

"This is your chance," she said. "You can overcome the fear. I know you can."

He licked his lips nervously. He went to the pile of gear in front of the photographic backdrop. "I wish I could be half as sure of me as you are."

Following him, she said, "I understand what I'm asking of you. I know it'll be the hardest thing you've ever done."

He remembered the fall vividly. He could close his eyes any time—even in a crowded room—and experience it again: his foot slipping, pain in the chest as the safety harness tightened around him, pain abruptly relieved as the rope snapped, breath caught like an unchewed lump of meat in his throat, then floating and floating and floating. The fall was only three hundred feet, and it had ended in a thick cushion of snow; it had seemed a mile.

She said, "If you stay here, you'll die; but it'll be an easier death. The instant Bollinger sees you, he'll shoot to kill. He won't hesitate. It'll be over within a second for you." She took hold of his hand. "But it won't be like that for me."

He looked up from the equipment. Her gray eyes radiated a fear as primal and paralyzing as his own.

"Bollinger will use me," she said.

He was unable to speak.

"He'll cut me," she said.

Unbidden, an image of Edna Mowry came to him. She had been holding her own bloody navel in her hand.

"He'll disfigure me."

"Maybe—"

"He's the Butcher. Don't forget. Don't forget who he is. What he is."

"God help me," he said.

"I don't want to die. But if I *have* to die, I don't want it to be like that." She shuddered. "If we're not going to make the climb, if we're just going to wait for him here, then I want you to kill me. Hit me across the back of the head with something. Hit me very hard."

Amazed, he said, "What are you talking about?"

"Kill me before Bollinger can get to me. Graham, you owe me that much. You've got to do it."

"I love you," he said weakly. "You're everything. There's nothing else for me."

She was somber, a mourner at her own execution. "If you love me, then you understand why you've got to kill me."

"I couldn't do it."

"We don't have much time," she said. "Either we get ready for the climb right now—or you kill me. Bollinger will be here any minute."

Glancing at the main entrance to see if anyone was trying to get in, Bollinger crossed the marble floor and opened the white door. He stood at the bottom of the north stairs and listened for footsteps. There were none. No footsteps, no voices, no noise at all. He peered up the narrow, open core of the shaft, but he didn't see anyone moving alongside the switchback railing.

He went to the south stairs.

Those too were deserted.

He looked at his watch. 10:38.

Running some of Blake's verses through his mind to calm himself, he went to the elevator.

# 31
◆ ◆ ◆

Well-made boots are essential to a serious climber. They should be five to seven inches high, crafted from the best grade of leather, lined with leather, preferably hand-sewn, with foam-padded tongues. Most important of all, the soles should be hard and stiff, with tough lugs made of Vibram.

Graham was wearing just such a pair of boots. They were a perfect fit, more like gloves than footwear. Although putting them on and lacing them up brought him closer to the act that he regarded with terror, he found the boots strangely comforting, reassuring. His familiarity with them, with climbing gear in general, seemed like a touchstone against which he could test for the old Graham Harris, test for a trace of the courage he'd once shown.

Both pairs of boots in the pile of equipment were four sizes too large for Connie. She couldn't wear either of them. If she stuffed paper into the toes and along the sides, she would feel as if she were wearing blocks of concrete; and she would surely misstep at some crucial point in the climb.

Fortunately, they found a pair of klettershoes that fitted well enough. The klettershoe—an anglicization of *Kletterschuh*, German for "climbing shoe"—was lighter, tighter, more flexible, and not so high as standard climbing boots. The sole was of rubber, and the welt did not protrude, making it possible for the wearer to gain toeholds on even the narrowest ledges.

Although they would have to serve for want of something better, the klettershoes weren't suited for the climb that lay ahead. Because they were made of suede and were not waterproof, they should be used only in the fairest weather, never in a snowstorm.

To protect her feet from becoming wet and from the inevitable frostbite, Connie wore both socks and plastic binding. The socks were thick, gray, woolen; they came to mid-calf. The plastic was ordinarily used to seal up the dry food that a climber carried in his rucksack. Graham had wrapped her feet in two sheets of plastic, securing the waterproof material at her ankles with rubber bands.

They were both wearing heavy, bright red nylon parkas with hoods that tied under the chin. Between the outer nylon surface and the inner nylon lining, his jacket was fitted with man-made insulation, sufficient for autumn climbing but not for the cold that awaited them tonight. Her parka was much better—although he hadn't explained that to her for fear she would insist that *he* wear it—because it was insulated with one hundred percent goose down. That made it the warmest garment, for its size and weight, that she could have worn.

Over the parka, each of them was wearing a klettergurtel, a climbing harness, for protection in the event of a fall. This piece of equipment was a great improvement over the waistband that climbers had once used, for in a fall the band sometimes jerked so tight that it damaged the heart and lungs. The simple leather harness distributed the pressure over the entire body trunk, reducing the risk of a severe injury and virtually guaranteeing the climber that he would not turn upside down.

Connie was impressed by the *Klettergürtel*. As he strapped her into it, she said, "It's perfect insurance, isn't it? Even if you fall, it brings you up short."

Of course, if she didn't just slip or misplace her foot, if instead the rope broke, and if she was on a single line, the harness would not stop her fall. However, Connie didn't have to worry about that, for he was taking extraordinary safety measures with her: she would be going down on two independent lines. In addition to the main rope, he intended to fix her to a second which he would belay all the way to the street.

He would not be so well looked after as she was. There was no one to belay him. He would be descending last—on a single line.

He didn't explain that to her. When she got outside, the less she had to worry about, the better her chances were of coming out of this alive. Tension was good for a climber; but too much tension could cause him to make mistakes.

Both harnesses had accessory loops at the waist. Graham was carrying pitons, carabiners, expansion bolts, a hammer, and a compact battery-powered drill the size of two packs of cigarettes. In her harness loops, Connie had a variety of extra pitons and carabiners.

Besides the equipment hung on their harnesses, they were both burdened with rope. Connie had hundred-foot lengths of it at each hip;

it was heavy, but so tightly coiled that it did not restrict her movements. Graham had another hundred-foot coil at his right hip. They were left with two shorter lengths: and these they would use for the first leg of the descent.

Last of all, they put on their gloves.

At every floor, Bollinger got off the elevator. If the entire level was occupied by one business firm, he tried the locked doors at opposite ends of the alcove. If it was an ''open'' floor, he stepped out of the alcove to make certain there was no one in the corridor.

At every fifth floor, he looked not only into the corridor but into the stairs and the elevator shafts as well. On the first twenty floors, four elevator shafts served the building; from the twentieth to the thirty-fifth floors, two shafts; and from the thirty-fifth to the forty-second, only one shaft. In the first half of his vertical search, he wasted far more time than he could afford, opening the emergency doors to all of those shafts.

At ten-fifty he was on the fifteenth floor.

He had not found a sign of them. He was beginning to wonder if he was conducting the search properly. However, at the moment he was unable to see any other way to go about it.

He went to the sixteenth floor.

Connie pulled on the heavy cord and drew back the office draperies.

Graham unlatched the center window. The two rectangular panes wouldn't budge at first, then abruptly gave with a squeal, opened inward like casement windows.

Wind exploded into the room. It had the voice of a living creature; its screams were piercing, demonic. Snowflakes swirled around him, danced across the top of the conference table and melted on its polished surface, beaded like dew on the grass-green carpet.

Leaning over the sill, he looked down the side of the Bowerton Building. The top five floors—and the four-story decorative pinnacle above them—were set back two yards from the bottom thirty-seven levels. Just three floors below, there was a six-foot-wide ledge that ringed the structure. The lower four-fifths of the building's face lay beyond the ledge, out of his line of sight.

The snow was falling so thickly that he could barely see the street lamps on the far side of Lexington Avenue. Under the lights, not even a small patch of pavement was visible.

In the few seconds he needed to survey the situation, the wind battered his head, chilled and numbed his exposed face.

''That's damned cold!'' As he spoke, breath pluming out of him, he turned from the window. "We're bound to suffer at least *some* frostbite."

"We've got to go anyway," she said.

"I know. I'm not trying to back out."

"Should we wrap our faces?"

"With what?"

"Scarves—"

"The wind would cut through any material we've got handy, then paste it to our faces so we'd have trouble breathing. Unfortunately, the magazine didn't recommend any face masks in that buyer's guide. Otherwise, we'd have exactly what we need."

"Then what can we do?"

He had a sudden thought and went to his desk. He stripped off his bulky gloves. The center drawer contained evidence of the hypochondria that had been an ever-growing component of his fear: Anacin, aspirin, half a dozen cold remedies, tetracycline capsules, throat lozenges, a thermometer in its case . . . He picked up a small tube and showed it to her.

"Chap Stick?" she asked.

"Come here."

She went to him. "That stuff's for chapped lips. If we're going to be frostbitten, why worry about a little thing like chapped lips?"

He pulled the cap off the tube, twisted the base to bring up the waxy stick, and coated her entire face—forehead, temples, cheeks, nose, lips and chin. "With even a thin shield of this, the wind will need more time to leach the warmth out of you. And it'll keep your skin supple. Loss of heat is two-thirds of the danger. But loss of moisture along with loss of heat is what causes severe frostbite. The moisture in bitterly cold air doesn't get to your skin; in fact, subzero wind can dry out your face almost as thoroughly as desert air."

"I was right," she said.

"Right about what?"

"There's some Nick Charles in you."

At eleven o'clock, Bollinger entered the elevator, switched it on, and pressed the button for the twenty-second floor.

# 32
◆ ◆ ◆

The window frame was extremely sturdy, not cold-pressed and not of aluminum as were most of the window frames in buildings erected during the past thirty years. The grooved, steel center post was almost an inch thick and appeared to be capable of supporting hundreds of pounds without bending or breaking loose from the sash.

Harris hooked a carabiner to the post.

This piece of hardware was one of the most important that a climber carried. Carabiners were made of steel or alloy and came in several shapes—oval D, offset D, and pear or keyhole—but the oval was used more often than any of the others. It was approximately three and a half inches by one and three-quarter inches, and it resembled nothing so much as an oversized key ring or perhaps an elongated chain link. A spring-loaded gate opened on one side of the oval, making it possible for the climber to connect the carabiner to the eye of a piton; he could also slip a loop of rope onto the metal ring. A carabiner, which was sometimes referred to as a "snap link," could be employed to join two ropes at any point along them, which was essential when the ends of those lines were secured above and below. A vital—but not the only—function of the highly polished snap links was to prevent ropes from chaffing each other, to guard against their fraying through on the rough, unpolished eye of a piton or on the sharp edge of a rock; carabiners saved lives.

At Graham's direction, Connie had stripped the manufacturer's plastic bands from an eighty-foot coil of red and blue hawser-laid nylon rope.

"It doesn't look strong," she said.

"It's got a breaking strength of four thousand pounds."

"So thin."

"Seven-sixteenths of an inch."

"I guess you know what you're doing."

Smiling reassuringly, he said, "Relax."

He tied a knot in one end of the rope. That done, he grasped the double loop that sprouted above the knot and slipped it through the gate of the carabiner that was attached to the window post.

He was surprised at how quickly he was working, and by the ease with which he had fashioned the complex knot. He seemed to be operating on instinct more than on knowledge. In five years he had not forgotten anything.

"This will be your safety line," he told her.

The carabiner was one of those that came with a metal sleeve that fitted over the gate to guard against an accidental opening. He screwed the sleeve in place.

He picked up the rope and pulled it through his hands, quickly measuring eleven yards of it. He took a folding knife from a pocket of his parka and cut the rope, dropped one piece to the floor. He tied the cut end of the shorter section to her harness, so that she was attached to the window post by a thirty-foot umbilical. He took one end of the other piece of rope and tied it around her waist, using a bowline knot.

Patting the windowsill, he said, "Sit up here."

She sat facing him, her back to the wind and snow.

He pushed the thirty-foot rope out of the window; and the loop of slack, from the post to Connie's harness, swung in the wind. He arranged the forty-five-foot length on the office floor, carefully coiled it to be certain that it would pay out without tangling, and finally tied the free end around his waist.

He intended to perform a standing hip belay. On a mountain, it was always possible that a belayer might be jerked from his standing position if he was not anchored by another rope and a well-placed piton; he could lose his balance and fall, along with the person whom he was belaying. Therefore, a standing belay was considered less desirable than one accomplished from a sitting position. However, because Connie weighed sixty pounds less than he, and because the window was waist high, he didn't think she would be able to drag him out of the room.

Standing with his legs spread to improve his balance, he picked up the forty-five-foot line at a point midway between the neatly piled coil and Connie. He had knotted the rope at his navel; now, he passed it behind him and across the hips at the belt line. The rope that came from Connie went around his left hip and then around his right; therefore, his left hand was the guide hand, while the right was the braking hand.

From his anchor point six feet in front of her he said, "Ready?"

She bit her lip.

"The ledge is only thirty feet below."

"Not so far," she said weakly.

"You'll be there before you know it."

She forced a smile.

She looked down at her harness and tugged on it, as if she thought it might have come undone.

"Remember what to do?" he asked.

"Hold the line with both hands above my head. Don't try to help. Look for the ledge, get my feet on it right away, don't let myself be lowered past it."

"And when you get there?"

"First, I untie myself."

"But only from this line."

"Yes."

"Not from the other."

She nodded.

"Then, when you've untied yourself—"

"I jerk on this line twice."

"That's right. I'll put you down as gently as I can."

In spite of the stinging cold wind that whistled through the open window on both sides of her, her face was pale. "I love you," she said.

"And I love you."

"You can do this."

"I hope so."

"I *know.*"

His heart was pounding.

"I trust you," she said.

He realized that if he allowed her to die during the climb, he would have no right or reason to save himself. Life without her would be an unbearable passage through guilt and loneliness, a gray emptiness worse than death. If she fell, he might as well pitch himself after her.

He was scared.

All he could do was repeat what he had already said, "I love you."

Taking a deep breath, leaning backward, she said, "Well . . . woman overboard!"

The corridor was dark and deserted.

Bollinger returned to the elevator and pressed the button for the twenty-seventh floor.

# 33
◆ ◆ ◆

The instant that Connie slipped backward off the windowsill, she sensed the hundreds of feet of open space beneath her. She didn't need to look down to be profoundly affected by that great, dark gulf. She was even more terrified than she had expected to be. The fear had a physical as well as a mental impact on her. Her throat constricted; she found it hard to breathe. Her chest felt tight, and her pulse rate soared. Suddenly acidic, her stomach contracted sickeningly.

She resisted the urge to clutch the windowsill before it was out of her grasp. Instead, she reached overhead and gripped the rope with both hands.

The wind rocked her from side to side. It pinched her face and stung the thin rim of ungreased skin around her eyes.

In order to see at all, she was forced to squint, to peer out through the narrowest of lash-shielded slits. Otherwise, the wind would have blinded her with her own tears. Unfortunately, the pile of climbing equipment in the art director's office had not contained snow goggles.

She glanced down at the ledge toward which she was slowly moving. It was six feet wide, but to her it looked like a tightrope.

His feet slipped on the carpet.

He dug in his heels.

Judging by the amount of rope still coiled beside him, she was not even halfway to the ledge. Yet he felt as if he had lowered her at least a hundred feet.

Initially, the strain on Graham's arms and shoulders had been tolerable. But as he payed out the line, he became increasingly aware of the toll taken by five years of inactivity. With each foot of rope, new aches sprang up like sparks in his muscles, spread toward each other, fanned into crackling fires.

Nevertheless, the pain was the least of his worries. More important, he was facing away from the office doors. And he could not forget the vision: a bullet in the back, blood, and then darkness.

Where was Bollinger?

The farther Connie descended, the less slack there was in the line that connected her to the window post. She hoped that Graham had estimated its length correctly. If not, she might be in serious trouble. A too-long safety line posed no threat; but if it was too short, she would be hung up a foot or two from the ledge. She would have to climb back to the window so that Graham could rectify the situation—or she would have to give up the safety line altogether, proceed to the setback on just the belayer's rope. Anxiously, she watched the safety line as it gradually grew taut.

Overhead, the main rope was twisting and untwisting with lateral tension. As the thousands of nylon strands repeatedly tightened, relaxed, tightened, she found herself turning slowly in a semicircle from left to right and back again. This movement was in addition to the pendulumlike swing caused by the wind; and of course it made her increasingly ill.

She wondered if the rope would break. Surely, all of that twisting and untwisting began where the rope dropped away from the window. Was the thin line even now fraying at its contact point with the sill?

Graham had said there would be some dangerous friction at the sill. But he had assured her that she would be on the ledge before the nylon fibers had even been slightly bruised. Nylon was tough material. Strong. Reliable. It would not wear through from a few minutes—or even a quarter-hour—of heavy friction.

Still, she wondered.

At eight minutes after eleven, Frank Bollinger started to search the thirtieth floor.

He was beginning to feel that he was trapped in a surreal landscape of doors; hundreds upon hundreds of doors. All night long he had been opening them, anticipating sudden violence, overflowing with that tension that made him feel *alive*. But all of the doors opened on the same thing: darkness, emptiness, silence. Each door promised to deliver what he had been hunting for, but not one of them kept the promise.

It seemed to him that the wilderness of doors was a condition not merely of this one night but of his entire life. Doors. Doors that opened on darkness. On emptiness. On blind passages and dead ends of every sort. Each day of his life, he had expected to find a door that, when flung wide, would present him with all that he deserved. Yet that golden door eluded him. He had not been treated fairly. After all, he was one of the new men, superior to everyone he saw around him. Yet what had he become in thirty-seven years? Anything? Not a president. Not even a senator. Not famous. Not rich. He was nothing but a lousy vice detective, a cop whose working life was spent in the grimy subculture of whores, pimps, gamblers, addicts, and petty racketeers.

That was why Harris (and tens of millions like him) had to die. They were subhumans, vastly inferior to the new breed of men. Yet for every new man, there were a million old ones. Because there was strength in numbers, these pitiful creatures—risking thermonuclear destruction to satisfy their greed and their fondness for childish posturing—held on to the world's power, money, and resources. Only through the greatest slaughter in history, only in the midst of Armageddon, could the new men seize what was rightfully theirs.

The thirtieth level was deserted, as were the stairs and the elevator shafts.

He went up one floor.

Connie's feet touched the ledge. Thanks to the scouring wind, the stone was pretty much free of snow; therefore, there had been no chance for the snow to be pressed into ice. She wasn't in any danger of sliding off her perch.

She put her back to the face of the building, staying as far from the brink as she could.

Surprisingly, with stone under her feet, she was more impressed by the gulf in front of her than when she was dangling in empty space. Swinging at the end of the rope, she had not been able to see the void in the proper perspective. Now, with the benefit of secure footing, she found the thirty-eight-story drop doubly terrifying; it seemed a bottomless pit.

She untied the knot at her harness, freed herself of the main line. She jerked on the rope twice, hard.

Immediately Graham reeled it up.

In a minute he would be on his way to her.

Would he panic when he got out here?

I trust him, she told herself. I really do. I *have* to.

Nonetheless, she was afraid he would get only part of the way out of the window before he turned and fled, leaving her stranded.

# 34
◆ ◆ ◆

Graham took off his gloves, leaned out of the window, and felt the stone below the sash. It was planed granite, a rock meant to withstand the ages. However, before the icy wind could numb his fingertips, he discovered a tiny horizontal fissure that suited his purpose.

Keeping one hand on the crack in order not to lose it, he took the hammer and a piton from the tool straps at his waist. Balanced on the sill, leaning out as far as he dared, he put the sharp tip of the steel peg into the crack and pounded it home.

The light he had to work by was barely adequate. It came from the aircraft warning lights that ringed the decorative pinnacle of the building just thirty feet above him; it alternated between red and white.

From his upside-down position, the work went more slowly than he would have liked. When he finished at last, he looked over his shoulder to see if Bollinger was behind him. He was still alone.

The piton felt as if it were well placed. He got a good grip on it, tried to wiggle it. It was firm.

He snapped a carabiner through the eye of the piton.

He snapped another carabiner to the center post of the window, above the one that secured Connie's safety line.

Next, he pulled the knots out of the belaying rope. He took it from around his waist and dropped it on the floor by the window.

He closed one of the tall, rectangular panes as best he could; the carabiners fixed to the center post would not permit it to close all the way. He would attempt to shut the other half of the window from the outside.

He hurried to the draw cords and pulled the green velvet drapes into place.

Eventually, Bollinger would come back to this office and would realize that they had gone out of the window. But Graham wanted to conceal the evidence of their escape as long as possible.

Stepping behind the drapes, he sidled along to the window. Wind roared through the open pane and billowed the velvet around him.

He picked up an eleven-yard line that he had cut from another hundred-foot coil. He tied it to his harness and to the free carabiner on the window post. There was no one here to belay him as he had done Connie, but he had worked out a way to avoid a single-line descent; he would have a safety tether exactly like Connie's.

He quickly tied a figure-eight knot in one end of the forty-five-foot line. Leaning out of the window once more, he hooked the double loops of rope through the carabiner that was linked to the piton. Then he screwed the sleeve over the gate, locking the snap link. He tossed the rope into the night and watched to be sure that it hung straight and unobstructed from the piton. This would be his rappelling line.

He was not adhering strictly to orthodox mountain climbing procedure. But then this "mountain" certainly was not orthodox either. The situation called for flexibility, for a few original methods.

After he had put on his gloves again, he took hold of the thirty-foot safety line. He wrapped it once around his right wrist and then seized it tightly with the same hand. Approximately four feet of rope lay between his hand and the anchor point on the window post. In the first few seconds after he went through the window, he would be hanging by his right arm, four feet under the sill.

He got on his knees on the window ledge, facing the lining of the office drapes. Slowly, cautiously, reluctantly, he went out of the room backward, feet first. Just before he overbalanced and slid all the way out, he closed the open half of the window as far as the carabiners would allow. Then he dropped four feet.

Memories of Mount Everest burst upon him, clamored for his attention. He shoved them down, desperately forced them deep into his mind.

He tasted vomit at the back of his mouth. But he swallowed hard, swallowed repeatedly until his throat was clear. He *willed* himself not to be sick, and it worked. At least for the moment.

With his left hand he plucked the rappelling line from the face of the building. Holding that loosely, he reached above his head and grabbed the safety rope that he already had in his right hand. Both hands on the shorter line, he raised his knees in a fetal position and planted his boots against the granite. Pulling hand over hand on the safety tether, he took three small steps up the sheer wall until he was balanced against the building at a forty-five-degree angle. The toes of his boots were jammed into a narrow mortar seam with all the force he could apply.

Satisfied with his precarious position, he let go of the safety tether with his left hand.

Although he remained securely anchored, the very act of letting go of anything at that height made the vomit rise in his throat once more. He gagged, held it down, quickly recovered.

He was balanced on four points: his right hand on the shorter rope, now only two feet from the window post; his left hand on the line with which he would rappel down; his right foot; his left foot. He clung like a fly to the side of the highrise.

Keeping his eyes on the piton that thrust up between his spread feet, he jerked on the rappelling line several times. Hard. The piton didn't move. He shifted his weight to the longer line but kept his right-hand grip on the safety tether. Even with a hundred and fifty pounds of downward drag, the piton did not shift in the crack.

Convinced that the peg was well placed, he released the safety tether.

Now he was balanced on three points: left hand on the long line, both feet on the wall, still at a forty-five-degree angle to the building.

Although he would not be touching it again before he reached the ledge, the safety rope would nevertheless bring him up short of death if the longer line broke while he was rappelling down to Connie.

He told himself to remember that. Remember and stave off panic. Panic was the real enemy. It could kill him faster than Bollinger could. The tether was there. Linking his harness to the window post. He must remember . . .

With his free hand, he groped under his thigh, felt behind himself for the long rope that he already held in his other hand. After a maddening few seconds, he found it. Now, the line on which he would rappel came from the piton to his left hand in front of him, passed between his legs at crotch level to his right hand behind him. With that hand he brought the rope forward, over his right hip, across his chest, over his head, and finally over his left shoulder. It hung down his back, passed through his right hand, and ran on into empty space.

He was perfectly positioned.

The left hand was his guiding hand.

The right hand was his braking hand.

He was ready to rappel.

For the first time since he had come through the window, he took a good look around him. Dark monoliths, gigantic skyscrapers rose eerily out of the winter storm. Hundreds of thousands of points of light, made hazy and even more distant by the falling snow, marked the night on every side of him. Manhattan to his left. Manhattan to his right. Manhattan behind him. Most important—Manhattan *below* him. Six hundred feet of empty night waiting to swallow him. Strangely, for an instant he felt as if this were a miniature replica of the city, a tiny reproduction that was forever frozen in plastic; he felt as if he were also tiny, as if he were suspended in a paperweight, one of those clear hemispheres that filled with artificial snow when it was shaken. As unexpectedly as it came, the illusion passed; the city became huge again; the concrete canyon below appeared to be bottomless; however, while all else returned to normal, he remained tiny, insignificant.

When he first came out of the window, he had focused his attention on pitons, ropes and technical maneuvers. Thus occupied, he had been able to ignore his surroundings, to blunt his awareness of them.

That was no longer possible. Suddenly, he was *too* aware of the city and of how far it was to the street.

Inevitably, such awareness brought unwanted memories: *his foot slipping, harness jerking tight, rope snapping, floating, floating, floating, floating, striking, darkness, splinters of pain in his legs, darkness again, a hot iron in his guts, pain breaking like glass in his back, blood, darkness, hospital rooms*. . . .

Although the bitterly cold wind pummeled his face, sweat popped out on his brow and along his temples.

He was trembling.

He knew he couldn't make the climb.

*Floating, floating* . . .

He couldn't move at all.

Not an inch.


In the elevator, Bollinger hesitated. He was about to press the button for the twenty-third floor, when he realized that, after he lost track of them, Harris and the woman apparently had not continued down toward the lobby. They had vanished on the twenty-seventh level. He had searched that floor and all those below it; and he was as certain as he could be, short of shooting open every locked door, that they were not in the lower three-fourths of the building. They'd gone up. Back to Harris's office? As soon as that occurred to him, he knew it was true, and he knew why they had done it. They'd gone up because that was the last thing he would expect them to do. If they had continued down the stairs or elevator shaft, he would have nailed them in minutes. Sure as hell. But, in going up, they had confused him and gained time.

Forty-five minutes of time, he thought angrily. That bastard has made a fool out of me. Forty-five minutes. But not one goddamned minute more.

He pushed the button for the fortieth floor.


Six hundred feet.

Twice as far as he had fallen on Everest.

And this time there would be no miracle to save him, no deep snowdrift to cushion the impact. He would be a bloody mess when the police found him. Broken. Ruined. Lifeless.

Although he could see nothing of it, he stared intently at the street. The darkness and snow obscured the pavement. Yet he could not look away. He was mesmerized not by what he saw, but by what he didn't *need* to see, transfixed by what he *knew* lay below the night and below the shifting white curtains of the storm.

He closed his eyes. Thought about courage. Thought about how far he had come. Toes pressed into the shallow mortar-filled groove between two blocks of granite. Left hand in front. Right hand behind. Ready, get set . . . but he couldn't go.

When he opened his eyes, he saw Connie on the ledge.

She motioned for him to hurry.

If he didn't move, she would die. He would fail her utterly. She didn't deserve that after the eighteen months she'd given him, eighteen months of tender care and saint-like understanding. She hadn't once criticized him for whining, for his paranoia or his self-pity or his selfishness. She had put herself in emotional jeopardy that was no less terrifying than the physical risk demanded of him. He knew that mental anguish was every bit as painful as a broken leg. In return for those eighteen months, he had to make this climb for her. He owed her that much; hell, he owed her *everything*.

The perspiration had dissolved some of the coating of Chap Stick on his forehead and cheeks. As the wind dried the sweat, it chilled his face. He realized again how little time they could spend out here before the winter night sapped their strength.

He looked up at the piton that anchored him.

*Connie will die if you don't do this.*

He was squeezing the line too tightly with his left hand, which ought to be used only to guide him. He should hold the line *loosely,* using his right hand to pass rope and to brake.

*Connie will die. . . .*

He relaxed his left-hand grip.

He told himself not to look down. Took a deep breath. Let it out. Started to count to ten. Told himself he was stalling. Pushed off the wall.

*Don't panic!*

As he swung backward into the night, he slid down the rope. When he glided back to the wall, both feet in front of him and firmly planted against the granite, pain zigzagged through his game leg. He winced, but he knew he could bear it. When he looked down, he saw that he had descended no more than two feet, but the fact that he had gotten anywhere at all made the pain seem unimportant.

He had intended to thrust away from the stone with all his strength and to cover two yards on each long arc. But he could not do it. Not yet. He was too scared to rappel as enthusiastically as he had done in the past; furthermore, a more vigorous descent would make the pain in his leg unbearable.

Instead, he pushed from the wall again, swung backward, dropped two feet along the line, swooped back to the wall. And again: just a foot or eighteen inches this time. Little mincing steps. A cautious dance of fear along the face of the building. Out, down, in; out, down, in; out, down, in . . .

The terror had not evaporated. It was in him yet, bubbling, thick as stew. A cancer that had fed upon him and grown for years was not likely to vanish through natural remission in a few minutes. However, he was no longer overwhelmed by fear, incapacitated by it. He could see ahead to a day when he might be cured of it, and that was a fine vision.

When he finally dared to look down, he saw that he was so near the ledge that he no longer needed to rappel. He let go of the rope and dropped the last few feet.

Connie pressed close to him. She had to shout to be heard above the wind. "You did it!"

"I did it!"

"You've beaten it."

"So far."

"Maybe this is far enough."

"What?"

She pointed to the window beside them. "What if we break in here?"

"Why should we?"

"It's somebody's office. We could hide in it."

"What about Bollinger?"

She raised her voice a notch to compensate for a new gust of wind. "Sooner or later, he'll go to your office."

"So?"

"He'll see the window. Carabiners and ropes."

"I know."

"He'll think we went all the way to the street."

"Maybe he will. I doubt it."

"Even if he doesn't think that, he won't know where we stopped. He can't blast open every door in the building, looking for us."

The wind *whooshed* between them, rebounded from the building, rocked them as if they were toy figures. It wailed: a banshee.

Snowflakes sliced into Graham's eyes. They were so fine and cold that they affected him almost as grains of salt would have done. He squeezed his eyes shut, trying to force out the sudden pain. He had some success; but the pain was replaced by a copious flow of tears that temporarily blinded him.

They pressed their foreheads together, trying to get closer so they wouldn't have to yell at each other.

"We can hide until people come to work," she said.

"Tomorrow's Saturday."

"*Some* people will work. The custodial crews, at least."

"The city will be paralyzed by morning," he said. "This is a blizzard! No one will go to work."

"Then we hide until Monday."

"What about water? Food?"

"A big office will have water coolers. Coffee and soda-vending machines. Maybe even a candy and cracker vendor."

"Until Monday?"

"If we have to."

"That's a long time."

She jerked one hand to the void at her left side. "And that's a long *climb!*"

"Agreed."

"Come on," she said impatiently. "Let's smash in the window."

Bollinger stepped over the fallen liquor cabinet and looked around Harris's office.

Nothing out of the ordinary. No sign of the prey.

Where in the name of God *were* they?

He was turning to leave when the green velvet drapes billowed out from the wall.

He brought up the Walther PPK, almost opened fire.

Before he could squeeze off the first shot, the drapes fell back against the wall. Nobody could be hiding behind them; there wasn't enough room for that.

He went to one end of the drapes and found the draw cords. The green velvet folded back on itself with a soft hiss.

As soon as the middle window was revealed, he saw that something was wrong with it. He went to it and opened the tall, rectangular panes.

The wind rushed in at him, fluttered his unbuttoned collar, mussed his hair, moaned to him. Hard-driven flakes of snow peppered his face.

He saw the carabiners on the center post, and the ropes leading from them.

He leaned out of the window, looked down the side of the building.

"I'll be damned!" he said.

*   *   *

Graham was trying to unhook the hammer from the accessory strap on his safety harness, but he was hampered by his heavy gloves. Without the gloves, it would have been an easy chore, but he didn't want to take them off out here for fear they would slip away from him and disappear over the edge. If something went wrong and they were forced to continue the climb, he would need gloves desperately.

Above him, the wind made a strange sound. *Whump!* A loud, blunt noise. Like a muffled crack of thunder.

He finally got the hammer off the strap.

*Whump!*

Connie grabbed his arm. "Bollinger!"

At first he didn't know what she meant. He looked up only because she did.

Thirty feet above them, Bollinger was leaning out of the window.

To Connie, Graham said, "Stand against the wall!"

She didn't move. She seemed stunned. This was the first time she had ever *looked* frightened.

"Don't make a target of yourself!" he shouted.

She pressed her back to the building.

"Untie yourself from the safety line," he said.

Overhead, a tongue of flame licked out of the pistol's muzzle: *whump!*

Graham swung the hammer, struck the window.

Glass exploded inward.

Frantically, unable to forget the vision of himself being shot in the back, he smashed the stubborn, jagged shards that clung to the frame.

*Whump!*

The sharp sound of a ricochet made Graham jump. The bullet skipped off the stone inches from his face.

He was sweating again.

Bollinger shouted something.

The wind tore his words apart, transformed them into meaningless sounds.

Graham didn't look up. He kept working at the spiked edges of the window.

*Whump!*

"Go!" he shouted as he shattered the last dangerous piece of glass.

Connie scrambled over the windowsill, disappeared into the dark office.

He slipped the safety line knot at his harness.

*Whump!*

The shot was so close that he cried out involuntarily. The slug plucked at the sleeve of his parka. He was unbalanced by the surprise, and for an instant he thought he would fall off the ledge.

*Whump!*
*Whump!*

He plunged forward, through the broken window, expecting to be stopped at the last second by a bullet in the spine.

# 35
◆◆◆

In the unlighted office on the thirty-eighth floor, the glass crunched under their feet.

Connie said, "How could he miss us?"

As he patted the sweat from his face with the palm of his glove, Graham said, "Wind's near gale force. Could have deflected the bullets slightly."

"In just thirty feet?"

"Maybe. Besides, he was firing from a bad angle. Leaning out the window, shooting down and in. Light was bad. Wind was in his face. He'd have been damned lucky if he'd hit us."

"We can't stay here as we planned," she said.

"Of course not. He knows which floor we're on. He's probably running for the elevator right now."

"We go back out?"

"I sure don't want to."

"He'll keep popping up along the way, trying to shoot us off the side of the building."

"Do we have a choice?"

"None," she said. "Ready to climb?"

"As I'll ever be."

"You've done well."

"I'm not all the way down yet."

"You'll make it."

"Are you the clairvoyant now?"

"You'll make it. Because you aren't afraid anymore."

"Who? Me?"

"You."

"I'm scared to death."

"Not like you once were. Not that bad. Anyway, there's good reason to be afraid right now. It's a healthy fear you've got this time."

"Oh, yeah. I'm brimming with healthy fear."

"I was right."

"About what?"

"You're the man I've always wanted."

"Then you haven't wanted much."

In spite of what he said, she detected pleasure in his voice. He didn't sound as if he were seriously denigrating himself; at worst, he was poking fun at the sort of inferiority complex he'd displayed before tonight. Already, he had regained some of his self-respect.

He pulled open the second half of the window and said, "You wait here. I'll set another piton, tie up a new line." He took off his gloves. "Hold these for me."

"Your hands will freeze."

"Not in just a minute or two. I can work faster with bare hands."

Cautiously he put his head out of the window, looked up.

"Is he still there?" she asked.

"No."

He crawled onto the six-foot-wide ledge, stretched out on his stomach. His feet were toward her, his head and shoulders over the brink.

She took a few steps away from the window. Stood very still. Listened for Bollinger.

In the Harris Publications suite, Bollinger paused to reload the Walther PPK before going to the elevator.

Graham hammered the piton into the tight horizontal mortar line between two granite blocks. He tested it, found it to be secure, and snapped a carabiner to it.

Sitting up, he took the hundred-foot length of rope from his right hip and quickly arranged it in a coil that would unravel without a hitch. The wind had sufficient force to disturb the coil; he would have to watch it all the while he was belaying Connie. If it got fouled on itself, they would both be in trouble. He tied a knot in one end of the line, a knot with two small loops rising above it.

Lying down again, he reached over the brink and hooked the loops of rope through the carabiner. He shut the gate on the snap link and screwed the sleeve in place.

He sat up, his back to the wind. He felt as if strong hands were trying to shove him off the ledge.

Already, his fingers were numb with cold.

The two safety lines they had used during their descent from the fortieth floor were dangling beside him. He took hold of one.

Overhead, the line had been fixed to the carabiner in such a fashion that it could be tugged loose and retrieved from below. As long as there was heavy tension on the line, the knot remained tight and safe; in fact, the more tension there was—and the greater the climber's weight, the greater the tension—the firmer the knot. However, when the climber left the rope, releasing the tension, and when the rope was tugged in the proper manner, the knot would slip open. He jerked on the line, then again, and a third time. Finally it freed itself from the snap link and tumbled down into his lap.

He took a folding knife from a pocket of his parka, opened it. He cut two five-foot pieces from the eleven-yard safety line, then put the knife away.

He stood up, tottering slightly as pain shimmered through his bad leg.

One of the five-foot lines was for him. He tied an end of it to his harness. He tied the other end to a carabiner and snapped the carabiner to the window post.

Leaning in the window, he said, "Connie?"

She stepped out of the shadows, into the wan fan of light. "I was listening."

"Hear anything?"

"Not yet."

"Come out here."

He wished Billy could be here for the kill. He felt that Billy was half of him, fifty percent of his flesh and blood and mind. Without Billy, he wasn't fully alive at moments like this. Without Billy, he could experience only a part of the thrill, half of the excitement.

On his way to the elevator, Bollinger thought about Billy, mostly about the first few nights they had known each other.

They had met on a Friday and spent nine hours in a private all-night club on Forty-fourth Street. They had left well after dawn, and they were amazed at how the time had flown. The bar was a favorite hangout for city detectives and was always busy; however, it seemed to Bollinger that he and Billy had been the only people in the place, all alone in their corner booth.

From the start they weren't awkward with each other. He felt as if they were twin brothers, as if they shared that mythical oneness of twins in addition to years of daily contact. They talked rapidly, eagerly. No chitchat or gossip. Conversation. Honest-to-God conversation. It was an exchange of ideas and sentiments that Bollinger had never enjoyed with anyone else. Nothing was taboo. Politics. Religion. Poetry. Sex. Self-appraisal. They found a phenomenal number of things about which they held the same unorthodox opinions. After nine hours, they knew each other better than either of them had ever known another human being.

The following night they met at the bar, talked, drank, picked up a good-looking whore and took her to Billy's apartment. The three of them had gone to bed together, but not in a bisexual sense. In fact, it would be more accurate to say that the two of them had gone to bed with her, for although they performed, sometimes separately and sometimes simultaneously, a wide variety of sex acts with and upon her, Billy did not touch Bollinger, nor did Bollinger touch Billy.

That night, sex was more dynamic, exhilarating, frenzied, manic, and ultimately more exhausting than Bollinger had ever imagined it could be. Billy certainly didn't look like a stud. Far from it. But he was precisely that, insatiable. He delighted in withholding his orgasm for hours, for he knew that the longer he denied himself, the more shattering the climax when it finally came. A sensualist, he preferred to refuse immediate satisfaction in favor of a far greater series of sensations later on. Bollinger realized from the moment he climbed into bed that he was being tested. Rated. Billy was watching. He found it difficult to match the pace set by the older man, but he did. Even the girl complained of being worn out, used up.

He vividly recalled the position in which he'd been when he'd climaxed, because afterward he suspected that Billy had maneuvered him into it. The girl was on hands and knees in the center of the bed. Billy knelt in front of her. Bollinger knelt behind, stroking her dog-fashion. He faced Billy across her back; later, he knew that Billy had wanted to finish while confronting him.

He watched himself moving in and out of the girl, then looked up and saw Billy staring at him. Staring intently. Eyes wide, electric. Eyes that weren't entirely sane. Although he was frightened by it, he returned the stare—and was plunged into an hallucinogenic experience. He imagined he was rising out of his body, felt as if he were floating toward Billy. And as he floated, he shrank until he was so small he could tumble into those eyes. Knowing that it was an illusion in no way detracted from the impact of it; he could have sworn that he actually *was* sinking into Billy's eyes, sinking down, down. . . .

His climax was considerably more than a biological function; it joined him to the whore on a physical level, but it also tied him to Billy on a much higher plane. He spurted deep into her vagina, and precisely at that moment Billy spilled seed into her mouth. In the throes of an intense orgasm, Bollinger had the odd notion that he and Billy had grown incredibly inside of the girl, had swelled and lengthened until they were touching at the center of her. Then he went one step further, lost all awareness of the woman; so far as he was concerned, he and Billy were the only people in the room. In his mind he saw them standing with the tips of their organs pressed together, ejaculating into each other's penis. The image was powerful but strangely asexual. There was certainly nothing *homosexual* about it. Absolutely nothing. He wasn't queer. He had no doubt about that. None at all. The imaginary act that preoccupied him was similar to the ritual by which members of certain American Indian tribes had once become blood brothers. The Indians cut their hands and pressed the cuts together; because they believed that the blood flowed from the body of one into that of the other, they felt that they would be part of each other forever. Bollinger's bizarre vision was like the Indians' blood-brother ceremony. It was an oath, a most sacred bond. And he knew that a metamorphosis had taken place; henceforth, they were not two men but one.

Now, feeling incomplete without Billy beside him, he reached the elevator cab and switched it on.

Connie clambered through the window, onto the thirty-eighth-floor setback.

Graham quickly tied the free end of the hundred-foot main line to her harness.

"Ready?" she asked.

"Not quite."

His hands were getting numb. His fingertips stung, and his knuckles ached as if they were arthritic.

He tied carabiners to both ends of one of the five-foot pieces of rope he had cut. He snapped both carabiners to a metal ring on her harness. The rope between them looped all the way to her knees.

He clipped the hammer to the accessory strap on the waist belt of her harness.

"What's all this for?" she asked.

"The next setback is five stories down. Looks about half as wide as this one. I'll lower you the same way I got you here. I'll be anchored to the window post." He tugged on his own five-foot tether. "But we don't have time to rig a seventy-five-foot safety line for you. You'll have to go on just a single rope."

She chewed her lower lip, nodded.

"As soon as you reach that ledge," Graham said, "look for a narrow, horizontal masonry seam between blocks of granite. The narrower the better. But don't waste too much time comparing cracks. Use the hammer to pound in a piton."

"This short rope you just hooked onto me: is that to be my safety line when I get down there?"

"Yes. Unclip one end of it from your harness and snap the carabiner to the piton. Make sure the sleeve is screwed over the gate."

"Sleeve?"

He showed her what he meant. "As soon as you've got the sleeve in place, untie yourself from the main line so that I can reel it up and use it."

She gave him his gloves.

He put them on. "One more thing. I'll be letting the rope out much faster than I did the first time. Don't panic. Just hold on, relax, and keep your eyes open for the ledge coming up under you."

"All right."

"Any questions?"

"No."

She sat on the edge of the setback, dangled her legs over the gulf.

He picked up the rope, flexed his cold hands several times to be certain he had a firm grip. A meager trace of warmth had begun to seep into his fingers. He spread his feet, took a deep breath, and said, "Go!"

She slid off the ledge, into empty space.

Pain pulsated through his arms and shoulders as her full weight suddenly dragged on him. Gritting his teeth, he payed out the rope as fast as he dared.

In the thirty-eighth-floor corridor, Frank Bollinger had some difficulty deciding which business lay directly under Harris's office. Finally, he settled on two possibilities: Boswell Patent Brokerage and Dentonwick Mail Order Sales.

Both doors were locked.

He pumped three bullets into the lock on the Dentonwick office. Pushed open the door. Fired twice into the darkness. Leaped inside, crouched, fumbled for the wall switch, turned on the overhead lights.

The first of the three rooms was deserted. He proceeded cautiously to search the other two.

The tension went out of the line.

Connie had reached the ledge five stories below.

Nevertheless, he kept his hands on the rope and was prepared to belay her again if she slipped and fell before she had anchored her safety tether.

He heard two muffled shots.

The fact that he could hear them at all above the howling wind meant that they were frighteningly close.

But what was Bollinger shooting at?

The office behind Graham remained dark; but suddenly, lights came on beyond the windows of the office next door.

Bollinger was too damned close.

Is this where it happens? he wondered. Is this where I get the bullet in the back?

Sooner than he had expected, the signal came on the line: two sharp tugs.

He reeled in the rope, wondering if he had as much as a minute left before Bollinger found the correct office, the broken window—and him.

If he was going to reach that ledge five stories below before Bollinger had a chance to kill him, he would have to rappel much faster than he had done the first time.

Once more, the rope passed over regularly spaced windows. He would have to be careful not to put his feet through one of them. Because he'd have to take big steps rather than little ones, and because he'd have to descend farther on each arc and take less time to calculate his movements, avoiding the glass would be far more difficult than it had been from the fortieth to the thirty-eighth floor.

His prospects rekindled his terror. Perhaps it was fortunate that he needed to hurry. If he'd had time to delay, the fear might have grown strong enough to immobilize him again.

Harris and the woman were not in the offices of Dentonwick Mail Order Sales.

Bollinger returned to the corridor. He fired two shots into the door of the Boswell Patent Brokerage suite.

# 36
◆ ◆ ◆

Boswell Patent Brokerage occupied three small rooms, all of them shabbily furnished—and all of them deserted.

At the broken window, Bollinger leaned out, looked both ways along the snow-swept six-foot-wide setback. They weren't there either.

Reluctantly, he brushed the shards of glass out of his way and crawled through the window.

The storm wind raced over him, pummeled him, stood his hair on end, dashed snowflakes in his face and shoved them down his shirt, under his collar, where they melted on his back. Shivering, he regretted having taken off his overcoat.

Wishing he had handholds of some sort, he stretched out on his belly. The stone was so cold that he felt as if he had lain down bare-chested on a block of ice.

He peered over the edge. Graham Harris was only ten feet below, swinging away from the building on a thin rope, slipping down the line as he followed his arc, swinging back to the building: rappelling.

He reached down, gripped the piton. It was so cold that his fingers almost froze to it. He tried to twist it loose but discovered it was well planted.

Even in the pale, almost nonexistent light, he could see that there was a gate in the snap link that was fixed to the piton. He fingered it, tried to open it, but couldn't figure out how it worked.

Although he was right on top of Harris, Bollinger knew he could not get off an accurate shot. The cold and the wind had brought tears to his eyes, blurring his vision. The light was poor. And the man was moving too fast to make a good target.

Instead, he put down the Walther PPK, rolled onto his side, and quickly extracted a knife from his trousers pocket. He flicked it open. It was the same razor-sharp knife with which he had murdered so many women. And now, if he could cut the rappelling line before Harris got down to the ledge, he would have claimed his first male victim with it. Reaching to the piton, he began to saw through the loop of the knot that was suspended from the jiggling carabiner.

The wind struck the side of the building, rose along the stone, buffeted his face.

He was breathing through his mouth. The air was so cold that it made his throat ache.

Completely unaware of Bollinger, Harris pushed away from the building once more. Swung out, swung back, descended six or eight feet in the process. Pushed out again.

The carabiner was moving on the piton, making it difficult for Bollinger to keep the blade at precisely the same cutting point on the rope.

Harris was rappelling fast, rapidly approaching the ledge where Connie waited for him. In a few seconds he would be safely off the rope.

Finally, after Harris had taken several more steps along the face of the highrise, Bollinger's knife severed the nylon rope; and the line snapped free of the carabiner.

As Graham swooped toward the building, his feet in front of him, intending to take brief possession of a narrow window ledge, he felt the rope go slack.

He knew what had happened.

His thoughts accelerated. Long before the rope had fallen around his shoulders, before his forward momentum was depleted, even as his feet touched the stone, he had considered his situation and decided on a course of action.

The ledge was two inches deep. Just the tips of his boots fit on it. It wasn't large enough to support him.

Taking advantage of his momentum, he flung himself toward the window and pushed in that direction with his toes—up and in, with all of his strength—the instant he made contact with the window ledge. His shoulder hit one of the tall panes. Glass shattered.

He had hoped to thrust an arm through the glass, then throw it around the center post. If he could do that, he might hold on long enough to open the window and drag himself inside.

However, even as the glass broke, he lost his toehold on the icy two-inch-wide sill. His boots skidded backward, sank through empty air.

He slid down the stonework. He pawed desperately at the window as he went.

His knees struck the sill. The granite tore his trousers, gouging his skin. His knees slipped off the impossibly shallow indention just as his feet had done.

He grabbed the sill with both hands as gravity drew him over it. He held on as best he could. By his fingers. Dangling over the street. Kicking at the wall with his feet. Trying to find a toehold where there was none. Gasping.

The setback where Connie waited was only fifteen feet from the sill to which he clung, just seven or eight feet from the bottoms of his boots. Eight feet. It looked like a mile to him.

As he contemplated the long fall to Lexington Avenue, he hoped to God that his vision of a bullet in the back had been correct.

His gloves were too thick to serve him well in a precarious position like this. He lost his grip on the ice-sheathed stone.

He dropped onto the yard-wide setback. Landed on his feet. Cried out in pain. Tottered backward.

Connie shouted.

With one foot he stepped into space. Felt death pulling at him. Screamed. Windmilled his arms.

Connie was tethered to the wall and willing to test the piton that she had hammered between the granite blocks. She jumped at Graham, clutched the front of his parka, jerked at him, tried to stagger to safety with him.

For what must have been only a second or two but seemed like an hour, they swayed on the brink.

The wind shoved them toward the street.

But at last she proved sufficiently strong to arrest his backward fall. He brought his foot in from the gulf. They stabilized on the last few inches of stone. Then he threw his arms around her, and they moved back to the face of the building, to safety, away from the concrete canyon.

# 37

"He may have cut the rope," Connie said, "but he isn't up there now."

"He's coming for us."

"Then he'll cut the rope again."

"I guess he will. So we'll just have to be too damned fast for him."

Graham stretched out on the yard-wide ledge, parallel to the side of the building.

His bad leg was filled with a steady, almost crippling pain from ankle to hip. Considering all the rappelling he would have to do to reach the street, he was certain the leg would give out at some crucial point in the climb, probably just when his life most depended on surefootedness.

He took a piton from one of the accessory straps at his waist. He held out one hand to Connie. "Hammer."

She gave it to him.

He twisted around a bit, lay at an angle to the building, his head and one arm over the edge of the setback.

Far below, an ambulance moved cautiously on Lexington Avenue, its lights flashing. Even from the thirty-third floor, the street was not entirely visible. He could barely make out the lines of the ambulance in the wash of its own emergency beacons. It drew even with the Bowerton Building, then drove on into the snowy night.

He found a mortar seam even without removing his bulky gloves, and he started to pound in a piton.

Suddenly, to one side, two floors below, movement caught his eye. A window opened inward. One of two tall panes. No one appeared at it. However, he sensed the man in the darkness of the office beyond.

A chill passed along his spine; it had nothing to do with the cold or the wind.

Pretending that he had seen nothing, he finished hammering the piton in place. Then he slid away from the edge, stood up. "We can't go down here," he told Connie.

She looked puzzled. "Why not?"

"Bollinger is below us."

"What?"

"At a window. Waiting to shoot us—or at least you—as we go past him."

Her gray eyes were wide. "But why didn't he come here to get us?"

"Maybe he thought we'd already started down. Or maybe he thought we'd run out of his reach along this setback the moment he came into an office on this floor."

"What now?"

"I'm thinking."

"I'm scared."

"Don't be."

"Can't help it."

Her eyebrows were crusted with snow, as was the fringe of fur lining that escaped her hood. He held her. The wind moaned incessantly.

He said, "This is a corner building."

"Does that matter?"

"It faces on another street besides Lexington."

"So?"

"So we follow the setback," he said excitedly. "Turn the corner on the setback."

"And climb down the other face, the one that overlooks the side street?"

"You've got it. That's no harder to climb than this wall."

"And Bollinger can only see Lexington Avenue from his window," she said.

"That's right."

"Brilliant."

"Let's do it."

"Sooner or later, he'll figure out what we've done."

"Later."

"It had better be."

"Sure. He'll wait right where he is for a few minutes, expecting to pick us off. Then he'll waste time checking this entire floor."

"And the stairwells."

"And the elevator shafts. We might get most of the way down before he finds us."

"Okay," she said. She unhooked her safety tether from the window post.

# 38
◆◆◆

At the open window on the thirty-first floor, Frank Bollinger waited. Apparently they were preparing the rope which they would hook to the piton that Harris had just pounded into place.

He looked forward to shooting the woman as she came past him on the line. The image excited him. He would enjoy blowing her away into the night.

When that happened, Harris would be stunned, emotionally destroyed, unable to think fast, unable to protect himself. Then Bollinger could go after him at will. If he could kill Harris where he chose, kill him cleanly, he could salvage the plan that he and Billy had devised this afternoon.

As he waited for his prey, he thought again of that second night of his relationship with Billy. . . .

After the whore left Billy's apartment, they ate dinner in the kitchen. Between them they consumed two salads, four steaks, four rashers of bacon, six eggs, eight pieces of toast, and a large quantity of Scotch. They approached the food as they had the woman: with intensity, with single-mindedness, with appetites that were not those of men but those of supermen.

At midnight, over brandy, Bollinger had talked about the years when he had lived with his grandmother.

Even now he could remember any part of that conversation he wished. He was blessed with virtually total recall, a talent honed by years of memorizing complex poetry.

"So she called you Dwight. I like that name."

"Why are you talking that way?"

"The Southern accent? I was born in the South. I had an accent until I was twenty. I made a concerted effort to lose it. Took voice lessons. But I can recall it when I want. Sometimes the drawl amuses me."

"Why did you take voice lessons in the first place? The accent is nice."

"Nobody up North takes you seriously when you've got a heavy drawl. They think you're a redneck. Say, what if I call you Dwight?"

"If you want."

"I'm closer to you than anyone's been since your grandmother. Isn't that true?"

"Yeah."

"I should call you Dwight. In fact, I'm closer to you than your grandmother was."

"I guess so."

"And you know me better than anyone else does."

"Do I? I suppose I do."

"Then we need special names for each other."

"So call me Dwight. I like it."

"And you call me—Billy."

"Billy?"

"Billy James Plover."

"Where'd you get that?"

"I was born with it."

"You changed your name?"

"Just like I did the accent."

"When?"

"A long time ago."

"Why?"

"I went to college up North. Didn't do as well as I should have done. Didn't get the grades I deserved. Finally dropped out. But by then I knew why I didn't make it. In those days, Ivy League professors didn't give you a chance if you spoke with a drawl and had a redneck name like Billy James Plover."

"You're exaggerating."

"How would you know? How in the hell would you know? You've always had a nice white Anglo-Saxon Protestant Northern name. Franklin Dwight Bollinger. What would you know about it?"

"I guess you're right."

"At that time, all the Ivy League intellectuals were involved in a *conspiracy of sorts against the South, against Southerners. They still are, except that the conspiracy isn't so broad or so vicious as it once was. Back then, the only way you could succeed in a Northern university or community was to have an Anglo-Saxon name like yours—or else one that was out-and-out Jewish. Frank Bollinger or Sol Cohen. You could be accepted with either name. But not with Billy James Plover.''*

*''So you stopped being Billy.''*

*''As soon as I could.''*

*''And did your luck improve?''*

*''The same day I changed my name.''*

*''But you want me to call you Billy.''*

*''It wasn't the* name *that was wrong. It was the people who reacted negatively to the name.''*

*''Billy . . .''*

*''Shouldn't we have special names for each other?''*

*''Doesn't matter. If you want.''*

*''Aren't we special ourselves, Frank?''*

*''I think so.''*

*''Aren't we different from other people?''*

*''Quite different.''*

*''So we shouldn't use between us the names they call us by.''*

*''If you say so.''*

*''We're supermen, Frank.''*

*''What?''*

*''Not like Clark Kent.''*

*''I sure don't have X-ray vision.''*

*''Supermen as Nietzsche meant.''*

*''Nietzsche?''*

*''You aren't familiar with his work?''*

*''Not particularly.''*

*''I'll lend you a book by him.''*

*''Okay.''*

*''In fact, since Nietzsche should be read over and over again, I'll give* you *a book by him.''*

*''Thank you . . . Billy.''*

*''You're welcome, Dwight.''*

At the half-open window, Bollinger glanced at his watch. The time was 12:30.

Neither Harris nor the woman had started down from the thirty-third-floor setback.

He couldn't wait any longer. He had squandered too much time already. He would have to go looking for them.

# 39

◆ ◆ ◆

Connie hammered a piton into a horizontal mortar seam. She hooked the safety tether to the piton with a carabiner, then untied herself from the main line.

The moment it was free, Graham reeled up the rope.

Climbing this face of the building was proving easier than scaling the front on Lexington Avenue. Not that there was a greater number of setbacks, ledges or footholds here than there; the distribution of those was the same. However, the wind was much less fierce on the side street than it had been on Lexington. Here, the snowflakes that struck her face *felt* like snowflakes and not like tiny bullets. The cold air hugged her legs, but it did not press *through* her jeans; it didn't pinch her thighs and stab painfully into her calves as it had done earlier.

She had descended ten floors—and Graham five—since they had seen Bollinger waiting for them at the window. Graham had lowered her to the yard-wide twenty-eighth-floor setback and had rappelled down after her. Below that point there was only one other setback, this one at the sixth floor, three hundred and thirty feet down. At the twenty-third level, there was an eighteen-inch-wide decorative ledge— quintessential art deco; the stone was carved into a band of connected, abstract bunches of grapes—and they made that their next goal. Graham belayed her, and she found that the carved ledge was large and strong enough to support her. In less than a minute, powered by his newfound confidence, he would be beside her.

She had no idea what they would do after that. The sixth-floor setback was still a long way off; figuring five yards to a floor, that haven lay two hundred and fifty-five feet below. Their ropes were only one hundred feet long. Between this ledge of stone grapes and the sixth story, there was nothing but a sheer wall and impossibly narrow window ledges.

Graham had assured her that they were not at a dead end. Nevertheless, she was worried.

Overhead, he began to rappel through the falling snow. She was fascinated by the sight. He seemed to be creating the line as he went, weaving it out of his own substance; he resembled a spider that was swinging gracefully, smoothly on its own silk from one point to another on a web that it was constructing.

In seconds he was standing beside her.

She gave him the hammer.

He placed two pitons in the wall between the windows, in different horizontal mortar seams.

He was breathing hard; mist plumed from his open mouth.

"You all right?" she asked.

"So far."

Without benefit of a safety line, he sidled along the ledge, away from her, his back to the street, his hands pressed against the stone. On this side of the building, the gentler wind had formed miniature drifts on the ledges and on the windowsills. He was putting his feet down in two or three inches of snow and, here and there, on patches of brittle ice.

Connie wanted to ask him where he was going, what he was doing; but she was afraid that if she talked she would distract him and he would fall.

Past the window, he stopped and pounded in another piton, then hung the hammer on the accessory strap at his waist.

He returned, inch by inch, to where he had placed the first two pegs. He snapped his safety harness to one of those pitons.

"What was all that for?" she asked.

"We're going to rappel down a few floors," he said. "Both of us. At the same time. On two separate ropes."

Swallowing hard, she said, "Not me."

"Yes, you."

Her heart was thumping so furiously that she thought it might burst. "I can't do it."

"You can. You will."

She shook her head: no.

"You won't rappel the way I've done."

"That's for damned sure."

"I've been doing a body rappel. You'll go down in a seat rappel. It's safer and easier."

Although none of her doubts had been allayed, Connie said, "What's the difference between a body rappel and a seat rappel?"

"I'll show you in a minute."

"Take your time."

He grabbed the hundred-foot line on which he had descended from the twenty-eighth-floor setback. He tugged on it three times, jerked it to the right. Five stories above them, the knot came loose; the rope snaked down.

He caught the line, piled it beside him.

He examined the end of it to see if it was worn, and was satisfied that it wasn't. He tied a knot in it, looped the rope through the gate of the carabiner. He snapped the carabiner to the free piton that was one mortar seam above the peg that anchored his safety tether.

"We can't rappel all the way to the street," Connie said.

"Sure we can."

"The ropes aren't long enough."

"You'll rappel just five floors at a time. Brace yourself on a window ledge. Then let go of the rappelling line with your right hand—"

"Brace myself on a two-inch sill?"

"It can be done. Don't forget, you'll still be holding onto the line with your left hand."

"Meanwhile, what will my right hand be doing?"

"Smashing in both panes of the window."

"And then?"

"First, attach your safety tether to the window. Second, snap another carabiner to the center post. As soon as that's done, you take your weight off the main line and then—"

"Tug on it," Connie said, "pull apart the overhead knot like you did just a minute ago."

"I'll show you how."

"I catch the line as it falls?"

"Yes."

"And tie it to the carabiner that I've linked to the window post."

"That's right."

Her legs were cold. She stamped her feet on the ledge. "I guess then I unhook my safety line and rappel down five more floors."

"And brace yourself in another window and repeat the entire routine. We'll go all the way to the street, but only five stories at a time."

"You make it sound simple."

"You'll manage better than you think. I'll show you how to use a seat rappel."

"There's another problem."

"What?"

"I don't know how to tie one of those knots that can be jerked loose from below."

"It isn't difficult. I'll show you."

He untied the main line from the carabiner in front of him.

She leaned close to him and bent over the rope that he held in both hands. The world-famous glow of Manhattan's millions of bright lights was screened by the storm. Below, the rimed pavement of the street reflected the light from the many street lamps; but that illumination scarcely affected the purple shadows twenty-three floors above. Nevertheless, if she squinted, she could see what Graham was doing.

In a few minutes, she learned how to attach the rope to the anchor point so that it could be retrieved. She tied it several times to make sure she would not forget how it was done.

Next, Graham looped a sling around her hips and through her crotch. He joined the three end-points of the rope with yet another carabiner.

"Now, about this rappelling," she said as she gripped the main line. She manufactured a smile that he probably did not see, and she tried not to sound terrified.

Taking another snap link from the accessory strap at his waist, Graham said, "First, I've got to link the main line to the sling. Then I'll show you how you should stand to begin the rappel. I'll explain—"

He was interrupted by the muffled report of a gun: *whump!*

Connie looked up.

Bollinger wasn't above them.

She wondered if she actually had heard a gun or whether the noise might have been produced by the wind.

Then she heard it again: *whump!* There was no doubt. A shot. Two shots. Very close. Inside the building. Somewhere on the twenty-third floor.

Frank Bollinger pushed open the broken door, went into the office, switched on the lights. He stepped around the receptionist's desk, around a typewriter stand and a Xerox copier. He hurried toward the windows that overlooked the side street.

When the lights came on behind the windows on both sides of them, Graham unhooked his safety tether from the piton and told Connie to unhook her own five-foot line.

There was a noise at the window on their right as Bollinger pushed up the rusty latch.

"Follow me," Graham said.

He was perspiring again. His face was slick with sweat. Under the hood, his moist scalp itched.

He turned away from Connie, from the window that Bollinger was about to open, turned to his left, toward Lexington Avenue. Without benefit of a safety line, he walked the narrow ledge instead of sidling along it. He kept his right hand on the granite for what little sense of security it gave him. He had to place each foot directly in front of the other, as if he were on a tightrope, for the ledge was not wide enough to allow him to walk naturally.

He was fifty feet from the Lexington Avenue face of the highrise. When he and Connie turned the corner on the ledge, they would be out of the line of fire.

Of course, Bollinger would find an office with windows that had a view of Lexington. At most they would gain only a minute or two. But right now, an extra minute of life was worth any effort.

He wanted to look back to see if Connie was having any difficulty, but he didn't dare. He had to keep his eyes on the ledge ahead of him and carefully judge the placement of each boot.

Before he had gone more than ten feet, he heard Bollinger shouting.

He hunched his shoulders, remembering the psychic vision, anticipating the bullet.

With a shock he realized that Connie was shielding him. He should have sent her ahead, should have placed himself between her and the pistol. If she stopped a bullet that was meant for him, he didn't want to live. However, it was much too late for him to relinquish the lead. If they stopped they would make even better targets than they already were.

A shot cracked in the darkness.

Then another.

He began to walk faster than was prudent, aware that a misstep would plummet him to the street. His feet slipped on the snow-sheathed stone.

The corner was thirty feet away.

Twenty-five. . . .

Bollinger fired again.

Twenty feet. . . .

He felt the fourth shot before he heard it. The bullet ripped open the left sleeve of his parka, seared through the upper part of his arm.

The impact of the slug made him stumble a bit. He lumbered forward a few quick, unplanned steps. The street appeared to spin wildly below him. With his right hand he pawed helplessly at the side of the building. He put one foot down on the edge of the stone, his heel in empty air. He heard himself shouting but hardly knew what he was saying. His boots gripped in the drifted snow, but they skidded on a patch of ice. When he regained his balance within half a dozen steps, he was amazed that he hadn't fallen.

At first there was no pain in his arm. He was numb from the shoulder down. It was as if his arm had been blown off. For an instant he wondered if he had been mortally wounded; but he realized that a direct hit would have had more force, would have knocked him off his feet and pitched him off the ledge. In a minute or two the wound would begin to hurt like hell, but it wouldn't kill him.

Fifteen feet. . . .

He was dizzy.

His legs felt weak.

Probably shock, he thought.

Ten feet. . . .

Another shot. Not so loud as the ones that had come before it. Not as frighteningly close. Fifteen yards away.

At the corner, as he started to inch around onto the Lexington Avenue face of the highrise where a violent wind wrenched at him, he was able to glance back the way he had come. Behind him, the ledge was empty.

Connie was gone.

# 40

◆ ◆ ◆

Connie was four or five yards below the thirty-third-floor ledge of stone grapes, swinging slightly, suspended over the street. She couldn't bear to look down.

Arms extended above her, she held the nylon rope with both hands. She had considerable difficulty maintaining her grip. Strain had numbed her fingers, and she could no longer be certain that she was clutching the line tightly enough to save herself. A moment ago, relaxing her hands without realizing what she was doing, she had slipped down the rope as if it were well greased, covering two yards in a split second before she was able to halt herself.

She had tried to find toeholds. There were none.

She fixed her gaze on the ledge overhead. She expected to see Bollinger.

Minutes ago, when he opened the window on her right and leaned out with the pistol in one hand, she had known at once that he was too close to miss her. She couldn't follow Graham toward the Lexington Avenue corner. If she tried that, she would be shot in the back.

Instead, she gripped the main line and tried to anticipate the shot. If she had even the slimmest chance of escaping—and she was not convinced that she had—then she would have to act only a fraction of a second *before* the explosion came. If she didn't move until or after he fired, she might be dead, and she would certainly be too late to fool him. Fortunately, her timing was perfect; she jumped backward into the void just as he fired, so he must have thought he hit her.

She prayed he would think she was dead. If he had any doubt, he would crawl part of the way through the window, lean over the ledge, see her—and cut the rope.

Although her own plight was serious enough to require all of her attention, she was worried about Graham. She knew that he hadn't been shot off the ledge, for she would have seen him as he fell past her. He was still up there, but he might be badly wounded.

Whether or not he was hurt, her life depended on his coming back to look for her.

She was not a climber. She didn't know how to rappel. She didn't know how to secure her position on the rope. She didn't know how to do anything but hang there; and she wouldn't be able to do even that much longer.

She didn't want to die, *refused* to die. Even if Graham had been killed already, she didn't want to follow him into death. She loved him more than she had ever loved anyone else. At times she became frustrated because she could not find the words to express the breadth and depth of her feeling for him. The language of love was inadequate. She ached for him. But she cherished life as well. Getting up in the morning and making French toast for breakfast. Working in the antique shop. Reading a good book. Going out to an exciting movie. So many small delights. Perhaps it was true that the little joys of daily life were insignificant when compared to the intense pleasures of love, but if she was to be denied the ultimate, she would settle willingly for second best. She knew that her attitude in no way cheapened her love for Graham or made suspect the bonds between them. Her love of life was what had drawn him to her and made her so right for him. To Connie, there was but one obscenity, and that was the grave.

Fifteen feet above, someone moved in the light that radiated through the open window.

Bollinger?

*Oh, Jesus, no!*

But before she could give in to despair, Graham's face came out of the shadows. He saw her and was stunned. Obviously, he had expected her to be twenty-three stories below, a crumpled corpse on the snow-covered pavement.

"Help me," she said.

Grinning, he began to reel her up.

In the twenty-third-floor corridor, Frank Bollinger stopped to reload his pistol. He was nearly out of ammunition.

*"So you read Nietzsche last night. What did you think?"*

*"I agree with him."*

*"About what?"*

*"Everything."*

*"Supermen?"*

*"Especially that."*

*"Why especially?"*

*"He has to be right. Mankind as we know it has to be an intermediate stage in evolution. Otherwise, everything is so pointless."*

*"Aren't we the kind of men he was talking about?"*

*"It sure as hell seems to me that we are. But one thing bothers me. I've always thought of myself as a liberal. In politics."*

*"So?"*

*"How do I reconcile liberal, left-of-center politics with a belief in a superior race?"*

*"No problem, Dwight. Pure, hard-core liberals believe in a superior race. They think they're it. They believe they're more intelligent than the general run of mankind, better suited than the little people are to manage the little people's lives. They think they have the one true vision, the ability to solve all the moral dilemmas of the century. They prefer big government because that is the first step to totalitarianism, toward unquestioned rule by the elite. And of course they see themselves as the elite. Reconcile Nietzsche with liberal politics? That's no more difficult than reconciling it with extreme right-wing philosophy."*

Bollinger stopped in front of the door to Opway Electronics, because that office had windows that overlooked Lexington Avenue. He fired the Walther PPK twice; the lock disintegrated under the bullets' impact.

Suggesting ways that she could help herself, favoring his injured left arm, Graham pulled Connie onto the ledge.

Weeping, he hugged her with both arms, squeezed her so tightly that he would have cut off her breath if they hadn't been wearing the goose-down parkas. They swayed on the narrow ledge; and for the moment they were unaware of the long drop beside them, temporarily unimpressed by the danger. He didn't want to let go of her, not ever. He felt as if he had taken a drug, an upper, something to boost his spirits. Considering their circumstances, his mood was unrealistic.

Although they were a long way, both in time and in distance, from safety, he was elated; she was alive.

"Where's Bollinger?" she asked.

Behind Graham, the office was full of light, the window opened. But there was no sign of the killer.

"He probably went to look for me on the Lexington side," Graham said.

"Then he *does* think I'm dead."

"He must. *I* thought you were."

"What's happened to your arm?"

"He shot me."

"Oh, no!"

"It hurts. And it feels stiff, but that's all."

"There's a lot of blood."

"Not much. The bullet probably cauterized the wound; that's how shallow it is." He held out his left hand, opened and closed it to show her that he wasn't seriously affected. "I can climb."

"You shouldn't."

"I'll be fine. Besides, I don't have a choice."

"We could go inside, use the stairs again."

"As soon as Bollinger checks the Lexington side and doesn't find me, he'll come back. If I'm not here, he'll look on the stairs. He'd nail us if we tried to go that way."

"Now what?"

"Same as before. We'll walk this ledge to the corner. By the time we get to Lexington, he'll have looked over that face of the building and be gone. Then we'll rappel."

"With your arm like this?"

"With my arm like this."

"The vision you had about being shot in the back—"

"What about it?"

She touched his left arm. "Was this it?"

"No."

Bollinger turned away from the window that opened onto Lexington Avenue. He hurried out of the Opway Electronics suite and down the hall toward the office from which he had shot at Harris a few minutes ago.

*"Chaos, Dwight."*

*"Chaos?"*

*"There are too damned many of these subhumans for the supermen to take control of things in ordinary times. Only in the midst of Armageddon will men like us ascend."*

*"You mean . . . after a nuclear war?"*

*"That's one way it could happen. Only men like us would have the courage and imagination to lead civilization out of the ruins. But wouldn't it be ridiculous to wait until they've destroyed everything we should inherit?"*

*"Ridiculous."*

*"So it's occurred to me that we could generate the chaos we need, bring about Armageddon in a less destructive form."*

*"How?"*

*"Well . . . does the name Albert DeSalvo mean anything to you?"*

*"No."*

*"He was the Boston Strangler."*

*"Oh, yeah. He murdered a lot of women."*

*"We should study DeSalvo's case. He wasn't one of us, of course. He was an inferior and a psychotic to boot. But I think we should use him as a model. Single-handedly, he created so much fear that he almost threw the city of Boston into a state of panic. Fear would be our basic tool. Fear can be stoked into panic. A handful of panic-stricken people can transmit their hysteria to the entire population of a city or country."*

*"But DeSalvo didn't come close to creating the kind of—or the degree of—chaos that would lead to the collapse of society."*

*"Because that wasn't his goal."*

*"Even if it had been—"*

*"Dwight, suppose an Albert DeSalvo . . . better yet, suppose a Jack the Ripper were loose in Manhattan. Suppose he murdered not just ten women, not twenty, but a hundred. Two hundred. In a particularly brutal fashion. With clear evidence of aberrant sex in every case. So there was no doubt that they all died by the same hand. And what if he did all of this in a few months?"*

*"There would be fear. But—"*

*"It would be the biggest news story in the city, in the state, and probably in the country. Then suppose that after we murdered the first hundred women, we began to spend half of our time killing men. Each time, we'd cut off the man's sex organ and leave behind a message attributing the murder to a fictitious militant feminist group."*

*"What?"*

*"We'd make the public think the men were being murdered in re-taliation for the murders of the hundred women."*

*"Except women don't typically commit crimes like that."*

*"Doesn't matter. We're not trying to create a typical situation."*

*"I'm not sure I understand what sort of situation we are trying to create."*

*"Don't you see? There are damned ugly tensions between men and*

*women in this country. Hideous tensions. Year by year, as the women's liberation movement has grown, those tensions have become almost unbearable, because they're repressed, hidden. We'll make them boil to the surface.''*

*''It's not bad. You're exaggerating.''*

*''I'm not. Believe me. I know. And don't you see what else? There are hundreds of potential psychotic killers out there. All they need is to be given some direction, a little push. They'll hear about and read about the killings so much that they'll get ideas of their own. Once we've cut up a hundred women and twenty or so men,* pretending *to be psychotic ourselves, we'll have a dozen imitators doing our work for us.''*

*''Maybe.''*

*''Definitely. All mass murderers have had their imitators. But none of them has ever committed crimes grand enough to inspire legions of mimics. We will. And then when we've turned out a squad of sex killers, we'll shift the direction of our own activities.''*

*''Shift to what?''*

*''We'll murder white people at random and use a fictitious black revolutionary group to claim credit. After a dozen killings of that sort—''*

*''We could knock off some blacks and leave everyone under the impression they were killed in retaliation.''*

*''You've got it. Fan the flames.''*

*''I'm beginning to see your point. In a city this size, there are countless factions. Blacks, whites, Puerto Ricans, Orientals, men, women, liberals, conservatives, radicals and reactionaries, Catholics and Jews, rich and poor, young and old . . . We could try to turn each against its opposite and all of them against one another. Once factional violence begins, whether it's religious or political or economic, it usually escalates endlessly.''*

*''Exactly. If we planned carefully enough, we could do it. In six months, you'd have at least two thousand dead. Maybe five times that number.''*

*''And you'd have martial law. That would put an end to it before there was chaos on the scale you've talked about.''*

*''We might have martial law. But we'd still have chaos. In Northern Ireland they've had soldiers on street corners for years, but the killing goes on. Oh, there'd be chaos, Dwight. And it would spread to other cities as—''*

*''No. I can't swallow that.''*

*''All over the country, people would be reading and hearing about New York. They'd—''*

*''It wouldn't spread that easily, Billy.''*

*"All right. All right. But there would be chaos here, at least. The voters would be ready to elect a tough-talking mayor with new ideas."*

*"Certainly."*

*"We could elect one of us, one of the new race. The mayoralty of New York is a good political base for a smart man who wants the presidency."*

*"The voters might elect a political strongman. But not every political strongman is going to be one of our people."*

*"If we planned the chaos, we could also plan to run one of our men in the wake of it. He would know what was coming; he'd have an inside track."*

*"One of our men? Hell, we don't know any but you and me."*

*"I'd make an excellent mayor."*

*"You?"*

*"I have a good base for a campaign."*

*"Christ, come to think of it, you do."*

*"I could win."*

*"You'd have a fair chance, anyway."*

*"It would be a step up the ladder of power for our kind, our race."*

*"Jesus, the killing we'd have to do!"*

*"Haven't you ever killed?"*

*"A pimp. Two drug pushers who pulled guns on me. A whore that nobody knows about."*

*"Did killing disturb you?"*

*"No. They were scum."*

*"We'd be killing scum. Our inferiors. Animals."*

*"Could we get away with it?"*

*"We both know cops. What would cops look for? Known mental patients. Known criminals. Known radicals. People with some sort of motive. We have a motive, but they'd never figure it in a million years."*

*"If we worked out every detail, planned carefully—hell, we might do it."*

*"Do you know what Leopold wrote to Loeb before they murdered Bobby Franks? 'The superman is not liable for anything he may do, except for the one crime that it is possible for him to commit—to make a mistake.' "*

*"If we did something like this—"*

*"If?"*

*"You're committed to it?"*

*"Aren't you, Dwight?"*

*"We'd start with women?"*

*"Yes."*

*"Kill them."*

*"Yes."*

*"Billy . . . ?"*

*"Yes?"*

*"Rape them first?"*

*"Oh, yes."*

*"It could even be fun."*

Bollinger leaned out of the window, looked both ways along the ledge. Harris was not on the face of the building that overlooked the side street.

Although the pitons were wedged in the stone beside the window, as they had been when he'd fired at Harris, the rope that had been attached to one of them was gone.

Bollinger crawled onto the windowsill, leaned out much too far, peered over the ledge. The woman's body should have been on the street below. But there was no corpse. Nothing but the smooth sheen of fresh snow.

Dammit, she hadn't fallen! He hadn't shot the bitch after all!

Why wouldn't these people *die?*

Furious, he stumbled back into the room, out of the wind-whipped snow. He left the office and followed the corridor to the nearest stairwell.

Connie wished that she could rappel with her eyes closed. Balanced on the side of the highrise, twenty-three stories above Lexington Avenue, without a safety tether, she was unnerved by the scene.

Right hand behind.

Left hand in front.

Right hand to brake.

Left hand to guide.

Feet spread and planted firmly on the wall.

Repeating to herself all that Graham had taught her, she pushed away from the building. And gasped. She felt as if she had taken a suicidal leap.

As she swung out, she realized that she was clenching the rope too tightly with her left hand. Left to guide. *Right* to brake. She relaxed her grip on the rope in front of her and slid down a few feet before braking.

She approached the building improperly. Her legs were not straight out in front of her, and they weren't rigid enough. They buckled. She twisted to the right, out of control, and struck the granite with her shoulder. The impact was not great enough to break a bone, but it was much too hard.

It dazed her, but she didn't let go of the rope. Got her feet against the stone once more. Got into position. Shook her head to clear it. Glanced to her left. Saw Graham three yards away on that side. Nodded so he would know that she was all right. Then pushed outward. Pushed hard. Slid down. Swung back. She didn't make any mistakes this time.

Grinning, Graham watched as Connie took a few more steps down the stone. Her endurance and determination delighted him. There really was some Nora Charles in her. And a hell of a lot of Nick too.

When he saw that she had pretty much gotten the knack of rappelling—her style was crude but adequate—he kicked away from the wall. He descended farther than she did on each arc and reached the eighteenth floor ahead of her.

He braced himself on the almost nonexistent window ledge. He smashed in the two tall panes of glass and fixed a snap link to the metal center post. When he had attached his safety tether to that carabiner, he released the main line, pulled it free of the overhead anchor. He caught the rope, tied it to the carabiner in front of him, and took up a rappelling position.

Beside him, nine feet away, Connie was also ready to rappel.

He flung himself into space.

He was amazed not only at how well he remembered the skills and techniques of a climber, but at how quickly the worst of his fear had vanished. He was still afraid, but not unnaturally so. Necessity and Connie's love had produced a miracle that no psychiatrist could have matched.

He was beginning to think they might escape. His left arm ached where the bullet had grazed it, and the fingers of that hand were stiff. The pain in his bad leg had subsided to a continuous dull throb that made him grit his teeth occasionally but which didn't interfere too much with his rappelling.

In a couple of steps he reached the seventeenth floor. In two more jumps he came to rest against the sixteenth-story window ledge—where Frank Bollinger had decided to set up an ambush.

The window was closed. However, the drapes had been drawn back. One desk lamp glowed dimly in the office.

Bollinger was on the other side of the glass, a huge silhouette. He was just lifting the latch.

*No!* Graham thought.

In the same instant that his boots touched the window ledge, he kicked away from it.

Bollinger saw him and pulled off a shot without bothering to open the rectangular panes. Glass sliced into the night.

Although Bollinger reacted fast, Graham was already out of his line of fire. He swung back to the wall seven or eight feet below Bollinger, rappelled again, stopped at the fifteenth-story window.

He looked up and saw flame flicker briefly from the muzzle of the pistol as Bollinger shot at Connie.

The gunfire threw her off her pace. She hit the wall with her shoulder again. Frantic, she got her feet under her and rappelled.

Bollinger fired again.

Bollinger knew that he hadn't scored a hit on either of them.

He left the office, ran to the elevator. He switched on the control panel and pushed the button for the tenth floor.

As the lift descended, he thought about the plan that he and Billy had formulated yesterday.

*"You'll kill Harris first. Do what you want with the woman, but be sure to cut her up."*

*"I always cut them up. That was my idea in the first place."*

*"You should kill Harris where it'll cause the least mess, where you can clean up after."*

*"Clean up?"*

*"When you're done with the woman, you'll go back to Harris, wipe up every speck of blood around him, and wrap his body in a plastic tarp. So don't kill him on a carpet where he'll leave stains. Take him into a room with a tile floor. Maybe a bathroom."*

*"Wrap him in a tarp?"*

*"I'll be waiting behind the Bowerton Building at ten o'clock. You'll bring the body to me. We'll put it in the car. Later, we can take it out of the city, bury it upstate someplace."*

*"Bury it? Why?"*

*"We're going to try to make the police think that Harris has killed his own fiancée, that he's the Butcher. I'll disguise my voice and call Homicide. I'll claim to be Harris, and I'll tell them I'm the Butcher."*

*"To mislead them?"*

*"You've got it."*

*"Sooner or later they'll smell a trick."*

*"Yes, they will. Eventually. But for a few weeks, maybe even for a few months, they'll be after Harris. There wouldn't be any chance whatsoever that they'd follow a good lead, one that might bring them to us."*

*"A classic red herring."*

*"Precisely."*

*"It'll give us time."*

*"Yes."*

*"To do everything we want."*

*"Nearly everything."*

The plan was ruined.

The clairvoyant was too damned hard to kill.

The doors of the lift slid apart.

Bollinger tripped coming out of the elevator. He fell. The pistol flew out of his hand, clattered against the wall.

He got to his knees and wiped the sweat out of his eyes.

He said, "Billy?"

But he was alone.

Coughing, sniffling, he crawled to the pistol, clutched it in his right hand and stood up.

He went into the dark hall, to the door of an office that would have a view of Lexington.

Because he was worried about running out of ammunition, he used only one shot on the door. He aimed carefully. The *boom!* echoed and reechoed in the corridor. The lock was damaged, but it wouldn't release altogether. The door rattled in its frame. Rather than use another bullet, he put his shoulder to the panel, pressed until it gave inward.

By the time he reached the Lexington Avenue windows, Harris and the woman had passed him. They were two floors below.

He returned to the elevator. He was going to have to go outside and confront them when they reached the street. He pushed the button for the ground floor.

# 42
◆ ◆ ◆

Braced against the eighth-floor windows, they agreed to cover the final hundred and twenty feet in two equal rappels, using the fourth-floor window posts as their last anchor points.

At the fourth level, Graham smashed in both rectangular panes. He snapped a carabiner to the post, hooked his safety tether to the carabiner, and jerked involuntarily as a bullet slapped the stone a foot to the right of his head.

He knew at once what had happened. He turned slightly and looked down.

Bollinger, in shirt sleeves and looking harried, stood on the snow-shrouded sidewalk, sixty feet below.

Motioning to Connie, Graham shouted, "Go in! Get inside! Through the window!"

Bollinger fired again.

*A burst of light, pain, blood: a bullet in the back. . . .*

Is this where it happens? he wondered.

Desperately, Graham used his gloved fist to punch out the shards of glass that remained in the window frame. He grabbed the center post and was about to drag himself inside when the street behind him was suddenly filled with a curious rumbling.

A big yellow road grader turned the corner into Lexington Avenue. Its large black tires churned through the slush and spewed out an icy liquid behind. The plow on the front of the machine was six feet high and ten feet across. Emergency beacons flashed on the roof of the operator's cab. Two headlights the size of dinner plates popped up like the eyes of a frog, glared through the falling snow.

It was the only vehicle in sight on the storm-clogged street.

Graham glanced at Connie. She seemed to be having trouble disentangling herself from the lines and getting through the window. He turned away from her, waved urgently at the driver of the grader. The man could barely be seen behind the dirty windshield. "Help!" Graham shouted. He didn't think the man could hear him over the roar of the engine. Nevertheless, he kept shouting. "Help! Up here! Help us!"

Connie began to shout too.

Surprised, Bollinger did exactly what he should not have done. He whirled and shot at the grader.

The driver braked, almost came to a full stop.

"Help!" Graham shouted.

Bollinger fired at the machine again. The slug ricocheted off the steel that framed the windshield of the cab.

The driver shifted gears and gunned the engine.

Bollinger ran.

Lifted by hydraulic arms, the plow rose a foot off the pavement. It cleared the curb as the machine lumbered onto the sidewalk.

Pursued by the grader, Bollinger ran thirty or forty feet along the walk before he sprinted into the street. Kicking up small clouds of snow with each step, he crossed the avenue, with the plow close behind him.

Connie was rapt.

Bollinger let the grader close the distance between them. When only two yards separated him from the shining steel blade, he dashed to one side, out of its way. He ran past the machine, came back toward the Bowerton Building.

The grader didn't turn as easily as a sports car. By the time the driver had brought it around and was headed back, Bollinger was standing under Graham again.

Graham saw him raise the gun. It glinted in the light from the street lamp.

At ground level where the wind was a bit less fierce, the shot was very loud. The bullet cracked into the granite by Graham's right foot.

The grader bore down on Bollinger, horn blaring.

He put his back to the building and faced the mechanical behemoth.

Sensing what the madman would do, Graham fumbled with the compact, battery-powered rock drill that was clipped to his waist belt. He got it free of the strap.

The grader was fifteen to twenty feet from Bollinger, who aimed the pistol at the windshield of the operator's cab.

From his perch on the fourth floor, Graham threw the rock drill. It arced through sixty feet of falling snow and hit Bollinger—not a solid blow on the head, as Graham had hoped, but on the hip. It glanced off him with little force.

Nevertheless, the drill startled Bollinger. He jumped, put a foot on ice, pitched forward, stumbled off the curb, skidded with peculiar grace in the snow, and sprawled face-down in the gutter.

The driver of the grader had expected his quarry to run away; instead, Bollinger fell toward the machine, into it. The operator braked, but he could not bring the grader to a full stop within only eight feet.

The huge steel plow was raised twelve inches off the street; but that was not quite high enough to pass safely over Bollinger. The bottom of the blade caught him at the buttocks and gouged through his flesh, rammed his head, crushed his skull, jammed his body against the raised curb.

Blood sprayed across the snow in the circle of light beneath the nearest street lamp.

# 43
◆ ◆ ◆

MacDonald, Ott, the security guards and the building engineer had been tucked into heavy plastic body bags supplied by the city morgue. The bags were lined up on the marble floor.

Near the shuttered newsstand at the front of the lobby, half a dozen folding chairs had been arranged in a semicircle. Graham and Connie sat there with Ira Preduski and three other policemen.

Preduski was in his usual condition: slightly bedraggled. His brown suit hung on him only marginally better than a sheet would have done. Because he had been walking in the snow, his trouser cuffs were damp. His shoes and socks were wet. He wasn't wearing galoshes or boots; he owned a pair of the former and two pairs of the latter, but he never remembered to put them on in bad weather.

"Now, I don't mean to mother you," Preduski said to Graham. "I know I've asked before. And you've told me. But I'm worried. I can't help it. I worry unnecessarily about a lot of things. That's another fault of mine. But what about your arm? Where you were shot. Is it all right?"

Graham lightly patted the bandage under his shirt. A paramedic with bad breath but sure hands had attended to him an hour ago. "I'm just fine."

"What about your leg?"

Graham grimaced. "I'm no more crippled now than I was before all this happened."

Turning to Connie, Preduski said, "What about you? The doc with the ambulance says you've got some bad bruises."

"Just bruises," she said almost airily. She was holding Graham's hand. "Nothing worse."

"Well, you've both had a terrible night. Just awful. And it's my fault. I should have caught Bollinger weeks ago. If I'd had half a brain, I'd have wrapped up this case long before you two got involved." He looked at his watch. "Almost three in the morning." He stood up, tried unsuccessfully to straighten the rumpled collar of his overcoat. "We've kept you here much too long. Much too long. But I'm going to have to ask you to hang around fifteen or twenty minutes more to answer any questions that the other detectives or forensics men might have. Is that too much to ask? Would you mind? I know it's a terrible, terrible imposition. I apologize."

"It's all right," Graham said wearily.

Preduski spoke to another plainclothes detective sitting with the group. "Jerry, will you be sure they aren't kept more than fifteen or twenty minutes?"

"Whatever you say, Ira." Jerry was a tall, chunky man in his late thirties. He had a mole on his chin.

"Make sure they're given a ride home in a squad car."

Jerry nodded.

"And keep the reporters away from them."

"Okay, Ira. But it won't be easy."

To Graham and Connie, Preduski said, "When you get home, unplug your telephones first thing. You'll have to deal with the press tomorrow. But that's soon enough. They'll be pestering you for weeks. One more cross to bear. I'm sorry. I really am. But maybe we can keep them away from you tonight, give you a few hours of peace before the storm."

"Thank you," Connie said.

"Now, I've got to be going. Work to do. Things that ought to have been done long ago. I'm always behind in my work. Always. I'm not cut out for this job. That's the truth."

He shook hands with Graham and performed an awkward half bow in Connie's direction.

As he walked across the lobby, his wet shoes squished and squeaked.

Outside, he dodged some reporters and refused to answer the questions of others.

His unmarked car was at the end of a double line of police sedans, black-and-whites, ambulances, and press vans. He got behind the wheel, buckled his safety belt, started the engine.

His partner, Detective Daniel Mulligan, would be busy inside for a couple of hours yet. He wouldn't miss the car.

Humming a tune of his own creation, Preduski drove onto Lexington, which had recently been plowed. There were chains on his tires; they crunched in the snow and sang on the few bare patches of pavement. He turned the corner, went to Fifth Avenue, and headed downtown.

Less than fifteen minutes later, he parked on a tree-lined street in Greenwich Village.

He left the car. He walked a third of a block, keeping to the shadows beyond the pools of light around the street lamps. With a quick backward glance to be sure he wasn't observed, he stepped into a narrow passageway between two elegant townhouses.

The roofless walkway ended in a blank wall, but there were high gates on both sides. He stopped in front of the gate on his left.

Snowflakes eddied gently in the still night air. The wind did not reach down here, but its fierce voice called from the rooftops above.

He took a pair of lock picks from his pocket. He had found them a long time ago in the apartment of a burglar who had committed suicide. Over the years there had been rare but important occasions on which the picks had come in handy. He used one of them to tease up the pins in the cheap gate lock, used the other pick to hold the pins in place once they'd been teased. In two minutes he was inside.

A small courtyard lay behind Graham Harris's house. A patch of grass. Two trees. A brick patio. Of course, the two flower beds were barren during the winter; however, the presence of a wrought-iron table and four wrought-iron chairs made it seem that people had been playing cards in the sun just that afternoon.

He crossed the courtyard and climbed three steps to the rear entrance.

The storm door was not locked.

As delicately, swiftly and silently as he could manage, he picked the lock on the wooden door.

He was dismayed by the ease with which he had gained entry. Wouldn't people *ever* learn to buy good locks?

Harris's kitchen was warm and dark. It smelled of spice cake, and of bananas that had been put out to ripen and were now overripe.

He closed the door soundlessly.

For a few minutes he stood perfectly still, listening to the house and waiting for his eyes to adjust to the darkness. Finally, when he could identify every object in the kitchen, he went to the table, lifted a chair away from it, put the chair down again without making even the faintest noise.

He sat down and took his revolver from the shoulder holster under his left arm. He held the gun in his lap.

# 44
◆ ◆ ◆

The squad car waited at the curb until Graham opened the front door of the house. Then it drove away, leaving tracks in the five-inch snowfall that, in Greenwich Village, had not yet been pushed onto the sidewalks.

He switched on the foyer light. As Connie closed the door, he went into the unlighted living room and located the nearest table lamp. He turned it on—and froze, unable to find the strength or the will to remove his fingers from the switch.

A man sat in one of the easy chairs. He had a gun.

Connie put one hand on Graham's arm. To the man in the chair, she said, "What are *you* doing here?"

Anthony Prine, the host of *Manhattan at Midnight,* stood up. He waved the gun at them. "I've been waiting for you."

"Why are you talking like that?" Connie asked.

"The Southern accent? I was born with it. Got rid of it years ago. But I can recall it when I want. It was losing the accent that got me interested in mimicry. I started in show business as a comic who did imitations of famous people. Now I imitate Billy James Plover, the man I used to be."

"How did you get in here?" Graham demanded.

"I went around the side of the house and broke a window."

"Get out. I want you out of here."

"You killed Dwight," Prine said. "I drove by the Bowerton Building after the show. I saw all the cops. I know what you did." He was very pale. His face was lined with strain.

"Killed who?" Graham asked.

"Dwight. Franklin Dwight Bollinger."

Perplexed, Graham said, "He was trying to kill us."

"He was one of the best people. One of the very best there ever was. I did a program about vice cops, and he was one of the guests. Within minutes we knew we were two of a kind."

"He was the Butcher, the one who—"

Prine was extremely agitated. His hands were shaking. His left cheek was distorted by a nervous tic. He interrupted Connie and said, "Dwight was *half* the Butcher."

"Half the Butcher?" Connie said.

Graham lowered his hand from the switch and gripped the pillar of the brass table lamp.

"I was the other half," Prine said. "We were identical personalities, Dwight and I." He took one step toward them. Then another. "More than that. We were incomplete without each other. We were halves of the same organism." He pointed the pistol at Graham's head.

"Get out of here!" Graham shouted. "Run, Connie!" And as he spoke he threw the lamp at Prine.

The lamp knocked Prine back into the easy chair.

Graham turned to the foyer.

Connie was opening the front door.

As he followed her, Prine shot him in the back.

*A terrible blow on the right shoulder blade, a burst of light, blood spattering the carpet all around him . . .*

He fell and rolled onto his side in time to see Ira Preduski come out of the hallway that led to the kitchen.

He floated on a raft of pain in a sea that grew darker by the second. What was happening?

The detective shouted at Prine and then shot him in self-defense. Once. In the chest.

The talk-show host collapsed against a magazine rack.

Pain. Just the first twitches of pain.

Graham closed his eyes. Wondered if that was the wrong thing to do. If you go to sleep, you'll die. Or was that only with a head injury? He opened his eyes to be on the safe side.

Connie was wiping the sweat from his face.

Kneeling beside him, Preduski said, "I called an ambulance."

Some time must have passed. He seemed to fade out in the middle of one conversation and in on the middle of the next.

He closed his eyes.

Opened them.

"Medical examiner's theory," Preduski said. "Sounded crazy at first. But the more I thought about it . . ."

"I'm thirsty," Graham said. He was hoarse.

"Thirsty? I'll bet you are," Preduski said.

"Get me . . . drink."

"That might be the wrong thing to do for you," Connie said. "We'll wait for the ambulance."

The room spun. He smiled. He rode the room as if it were a carousel.

"I shouldn't have come here alone," Preduski said miserably. "But you see why I thought I had to? Bollinger was a cop. The other half of the Butcher might be a cop too. Who could I trust? Really. Who?"

Graham licked his lips and said, "Prine. Dead?"

"I'm afraid not," Preduski said.

"Me?"

"What about you?"

"Dead?"

"You'll live."

"Sure?"

"Bullet wasn't near the spine. Didn't puncture any vital organs, I'll bet."

"Sure?"

"*I'm* sure," Connie said.

Graham closed his eyes.

# EPILOGUE

# SUNDAY

◆ ◆ ◆

Ira Preduski stood with his back to the hospital window. The late afternoon sun framed him in soft gold light. "Prine says they wanted to start racial wars, religious wars, economic wars . . . ''

Graham was lying on his side in the bed, propped up with pillows. He spoke somewhat slowly because of the pain killers he had been given. "So they could gain power in the aftermath."

"That's what he says."

From her chair at Graham's bedside, Connie said, "But that's crazy. In fact, didn't Charles Manson's bunch of psychos kill all those people for the same reason?"

"I mentioned Manson to Prine," Preduski said. "But he tells me Manson was a two-bit con man, a cheap sleazy hood."

"While Prine is a superman."

Preduski shook his head sadly. "Poor Nietzsche. He was one of the most brilliant philosophers who ever lived—and also the most misunderstood." He bent over and sniffed at an arrangement of flowers that stood on the table by the window. When he looked up again, he said, "Excuse me for asking. It's none of my business. I know that. But I'm a curious man. One of my faults. But—when's the wedding?"

"Wedding?" Connie said.

"Don't kid me. You two are getting married."

Confused, Graham said, "How could you know that? We just talked about it this morning. Just the two of us."

"I'm a detective," Preduski said. "I've picked up clues."

"For instance?" Connie said.

"For instance, the way the two of you are looking at each other this afternoon."

Delighted at being able to share the news, Graham said, "We'll be married a few weeks after I'm released from the hospital, as soon as I have my strength back."

"Which he'll need," Connie said, smiling wickedly.

Preduski walked around the bed, looked at the bandages on Graham's left arm and on the upper right quarter of his back. "Every time I think of all that happened Friday night and Saturday morning, I wonder how you two came out of it alive."

"It wasn't much," Connie said.

"Not much?" Preduski said.

"No. Really. It wasn't so much, what we did, was it, Nick?"

Graham smiled and felt very good indeed. "No, it wasn't much, Nora."

# THE VISION

◆

*For Gerda*

# MONDAY, DECEMBER 21

◆◆◆

# 1

## ◆ ◆ ◆

"Gloves of blood."

The woman raised her hands and stared at them, stared *through* them.

Her voice was soft but tense. "Blood on his hands." Her own hands were clean and pale.

Her husband leaned forward from the back seat of the patrol car. "Mary?"

She didn't respond.

"Mary, can you hear me?"

"Yes."

"Whose blood do you see?"

"I'm not sure."

"The victim's blood?"

"No. In fact . . . it's his own."

"The killer's?"

"Yes."

"He has his own blood on his hands?"

"That's right," she said.

"He's hurt himself?"

"But not badly."

"How?"

"I don't know."

"Try to get inside of him."

"I am already."

"Get deeper."

"I'm not a mind reader."

"I know that, darling. But you're the next best thing."

The perspiration on Mary Bergen's face was like the ceramic glaze on the plaster countenance of an altar saint. Her smooth skin gleamed in the green light from the instrument panel. Her dark eyes also shone, but they were unfocused, blank.

Suddenly she leaned forward and shuddered.

In the driver's seat Chief of Police Harley Barnes shifted uneasily. He flexed his big hands on the steering wheel.

"He's sucking the wound," she said. "Sucking his own blood."

After thirty years of police work, Barnes didn't expect to be surprised or frightened. Now, in a single evening, he had been surprised more than once and had felt his heartbeat accelerate with fear.

The tree-shrouded streets were as familiar to him as the contours of his own face. However, tonight, cloaked in a rainstorm, they seemed menacing. The tires hissed on the slick pavement. The windshield wipers thumped, an eerie metronome.

The woman beside Barnes was distraught, but her appearance was less disturbing than the changes she had wrought inside the patrol car. The humid air became clearer when she entered her trance. He was certain he was not imagining that. The ordinary sounds of the storm and the car were overlaid with the soft humming of ghost frequencies. He sensed an indescribable power radiating from her. He was a practical man, not at all superstitious. But he could not deny what he felt so strongly.

She bent as far toward the dashboard as her seat belt would allow. She hugged herself and groaned as if she were having labor pains.

Max Bergen reached out from the rear seat, touched her.

She murmured and relaxed slightly.

His hand looked enormous on her slender shoulder. He was tall, angular, hard-muscled, hard-faced, forty years old, ten years older than his wife. His eyes were his most arresting feature; they were gray, cold, humorless.

Chief Barnes had never seen him smile. Clearly, Bergen harbored powerful and complex feelings for Mary, but he gave no indication that he felt anything but contempt for the rest of the world.

The woman said, "Turn at the next corner."

Barnes braked gently. "Left or right?"

"Right," she said.

Well-kept, thirty-year-old stucco houses and bungalows, most of them California-Spanish in style, lay on both sides of the street. Yellow lights glowed vaguely behind drapes that had been drawn against the chill of the damp December night. The road was much darker than the one they had left. Sodium vapor lamps stood only at the corners, and purple-black, rain-pooled shadows filled the long blocks between them.

After he made the turn, Barnes drove no faster than ten miles an hour. From the woman's attitude, he gathered that the chase would end nearby.

Mary sat up straight. Her voice was louder and clearer than it had been since she began to use her strange talent, her clairvoyance. "I get an impression . . . of a . . . a fence. Yes . . . I see it now . . . he's cut his hand . . . on a fence."

Max stroked her hair. "And it's not a serious wound?"

"No . . . just a cut . . . his thumb . . . deep . . . but not disabling." She raised one thin hand, forgot what she meant to do with it, let it flutter back into her lap.

"But if he's bleeding from a deep cut, won't he give up tonight?" Max asked.

"No," she said.

"You're sure?"

"He'll go on."

"The bastard's killed five women so far," Barnes said. "Some of them fought like hell, scratched him and cut him and even tore out his hair. He doesn't give up easily."

Ignoring the policeman, Max soothed his wife, caressed her face with one hand and prompted her with another question. "What kind of fence do you see?"

"Chain-link," she said. "Sharp and unfinished at the top."

"Is it high?"

"Five feet."

"What does it surround?"

"A yard."

"Storage yard?"

"No. Behind a house."

"Can you see the house?"

"Yes."

"What's it like?"

"It's a two-story."

"Stucco?"

"Yes."

"What about the roof?"

"Spanish tile."

"Any unique features?"

"I can't quite see . . . "

"A veranda?"

"No."

"A courtyard maybe?"

"No. But I see . . . a winding tile walkway."

"Front or back?"

"Out front of the house."

"Any trees?"

"Matched magnolias . . . on either side of the walk."

"Anything else?"

"A few small palms . . . farther back."

Harley Barnes squinted through the rain-dappled windshield. He was searching for a pair of magnolias.

Initially he had been skeptical. In fact, he'd been certain the Bergens were frauds. He played his role in the charade because the *mayor* was a believer. The mayor brought them to town and insisted the police cooperate with them.

Barnes had read about psychic detectives, of course, and most especially about that famous Dutch clairvoyant, Peter Hurkos. But using ESP to track down a psychopathic killer, to catch him in the act? He didn't put much faith in that.

Or do I? he wondered. This woman was so lovely, charming, earnest, so convincing that perhaps she'd made a believer of him. If she hasn't, he thought, why am I looking for magnolia trees?

She made a sound like an animal caught in a sawtoothed trap for a long time. Not a screech of agony, but a nearly inaudible mewl.

When an animal made that noise, it meant, "This still hurts, but I'm resigned to it now."

Many years ago, as a boy in Minnesota, Barnes had hunted and trapped. It was that same pitiful, stifled moan of the wounded prey that caused him to give up his sport.

Until tonight, he had never heard precisely the same sound issue from a human being. Apparently, as she used her talent to zero in on the killer, she suffered from contact with his deranged mind.

Barnes shivered.

"Mary," her husband said. "What's the matter?"

"I see him . . . at the back door of the house. His hand on the door . . . and blood . . . his blood on a white door frame. He's talking to himself."

"What's he saying?"

"I don't . . . ."

"Mary?"

"He's saying filthy things about the woman."

"The woman in the house—the one he's after tonight?"

"Yes."

"He knows her?"

"No. She's a stranger . . . random target. But he's been . . . watching her . . . watching her for several days . . . knows her habits and routines."

With those last few words she slumped against the door. She took several deep breaths. She was forced to relax periodically to regroup her energies if she were to maintain the psychic thread. For some clairvoyants, Barnes knew, the visions came without strain, virtually without effort; but apparently not for this one.

Phantom voices whispered and crackled, came and went in staccato bursts on the police radio.

The wind carried fine sheets of rain across the roadway.

The wettest rainy season in years, Barnes thought. Twenty years ago it would have seemed normal. But California had steadily become a drought state. This much rain was unnatural now. Like everything else that's happening tonight, he thought.

Waiting for Mary to speak, he slowed to less than five miles an hour.

*Matched magnolia trees flanking a winding tile walk . . .*

He found it taxing to see what lay in the headlights directly in front of him, and extremely difficult to discern the landscaping on either side. They might already have passed the magnolias.

Brief as it was, Mary Bergen's hesitation elicited Dan Goldman's first words in more than an hour. "We haven't much time left, Mrs. Bergen."

Goldman was a reliable young officer, the chief's most trusted subordinate. He was sitting beside Max Bergen, behind Barnes, his eyes fixed on the woman.

Goldman believed in psychic powers. He was impressionable. And as Barnes could see in the rearview mirror, the events of the evening had left a haunted look on his broad, plain face.

"We don't have much time," Goldman said again. "If this madman's already at the woman's back door—"

Abruptly, Mary turned to him. Her voice was freighted with concern. "Don't get out of this car tonight—not until the man is caught."

"What do you mean?" Goldman asked.

"If you try to help capture him, you'll be hurt."

"He'll kill me?"

She shuddered convulsively. New beads of sweat popped out at her hairline.

Barnes felt perspiration trickle down his face, too.

She said to Goldman, "He'll stab you . . . with the same knife he's used on all the women . . . hurt you badly . . . but not kill you." Closing her eyes, speaking between clenched teeth, she said, *"Stay in the car!"*

"Harley?" Goldman asked worriedly.

"It'll be all right," Barnes assured him.

"You'd better listen to her," Max told Goldman. "Don't leave the car."

"If I need you," Barnes told Goldman, "you'll come with me. No one will be hurt." He was concerned that the woman was undermining his authority. He glanced at her. "We need a number for the house you've described, a street address."

"Don't press," her husband said sharply. With everyone but Mary he had a voice like two rough steel bars scraped against each other. "It won't do any good whatsoever to press her. It'll only interfere."

"It's okay, Max," she said.

"But I've told them before," he said.

She faced front once more. "I see . . . the rear door of the house. It's open."

"Where's the man, the killer?" Max asked.

"He's standing in a dark room . . . small . . . the laundry room . . . that's what it is . . . the laundry room behind the kitchen."

"What's he doing?"

"He's opening another door . . . to the kitchen . . . no one in there . . . a dim light on over the gas range . . . a few dirty dishes on the table . . . he's standing . . . just standing there and listening . . . left hand in a fist to stop the thumb from bleeding . . . listening . . . Benny Goodman music on a stereo in the living room . . . " Touching Barnes' arm, a new and urgent tone in her voice, she said, "Just two blocks from here. On the right. The second house . . . no, the third from the corner."

"You're positive?"

"For God's sake, *hurry!*"

Am I about to make a fool of myself? Barnes wondered. If I take her seriously and she's wrong, I'll be the punch line of bad jokes for the rest of my career.

Nevertheless, he switched on the siren and tramped the accelerator to the floor. The tires spun on the pavement. With a squeal of rubber, the car surged forward.

Breathlessly she said, "I still see . . . he's crossing the kitchen . . . moving slowly . . . "

If she's faking all this, Barnes thought, she's a hell of a good actress.

The Ford raced along the poorly lit street. Rain snapped against the windshield. They swept through a four-way stop, then toward another.

"Listening . . . listening between steps . . . cautious . . . nervous . . . taking the knife out of his overcoat pocket . . . smiling at the sharp edge of the blade . . . such a big knife . . . "

In the block she had specified they fishtailed to a stop at the curb in front of the third house on the right: a pair of matched magnolias, a winding walk, a two-story stucco with lights on downstairs.

"Goddamn," Goldman said, more reverently than not. "It fits her description perfectly."

# 2

♦ ♦ ♦

Barnes got out of the car as the siren moaned into silence.

The revolving red emergency lights cast frenetic shadows on the wet pavement. Another black-and-white had pulled in behind the first, adding its beacons to the cascade of bloody color.

Several men had already climbed out of the second car. Two uniformed officers, Malone and Gonzales, hurried toward Barnes. Mayor Henderson, round and shiny in his black vinyl rain slicker, looked like a balloon bouncing along the street. Close behind him was whip-thin little Harry Oberlander, Henderson's most vocal critic on the city council.

The last man was Alan Tanner, Mary Tanner Bergen's brother. Ordinarily, he would have been in the first car with his sister; but he and Max had argued earlier and were keeping away from each other.

"Malone, Gonzales . . . split up," Barnes said. "Flank the house. Go around it and meet at the rear door. I'll take the front. Now move it!"

"What about me?" Goldman asked.

Barnes sighed. "You better stay here."

Goldman was relieved.

Taking the .357 Magnum from his holster, Barnes hurried up the tile walk. The name "Harrington" was printed on the mailbox. As he rang the doorbell, the rain suddenly lost most of its power. The downpour became a drizzle.

Alerted by the sirens, she had watched his approach from the window. She answered the door at once.

"Mrs. Harrington?"

"*Miss* Harrington. After the divorce, I took my maiden name."

She was a petite blonde in her early forties. She had a lush figure, but she wasn't carrying any excess weight.

Apparently, her primary occupation was taking good care of herself. Although she wore jeans and a T-shirt and didn't appear to be going out for the evening, her hair looked as if it had been styled minutes ago; her false eyelashes and makeup were perfectly applied; and her nails were freshly painted the color of orange sherbet.

"Are you alone?" Barnes asked.

Lasciviously, she said, "Why do you ask?"

"This is police business, Miss Harrington."

"What a shame." She had a drink in one hand. He knew it wasn't her first of the night.

"Are you alone?" he asked again.

"I live by myself."

"Is everything all right?"

"I don't like living by myself."

"That's not what I meant. Are you all right? Is there any trouble here?"

She looked at the revolver that he held at his side. "Should there be?"

Exasperated with her and with having to talk above the loud swing music that boomed behind her, he said, "Maybe. We think your life's in danger."

She laughed.

"I know it sounds melodramatic, but—"

"Who's after me?"

"The newspapers call him 'The Slasher.' "

She frowned, then instantly dropped the expression as if she had remembered that frowning caused wrinkles. "You're kidding."

"We have reason to believe you're his target tonight."

"What reason?"

"A clairvoyant."

"A what?"

Malone entered the living room behind her and switched off the stereo.

She turned, surprised.

Malone said, "We found something, Chief."

Barnes stepped into the house, uninvited. "Yeah?"

"The back door was open."

"Did you leave it open?" Barnes asked the woman.

"On a night like this?"

"Was it locked?"

"I don't know."

"There's blood on the door frame," Malone said. "More of it on the door between the laundry room and the kitchen."

"But he's gone?"

"Must have run when he heard the sirens."

Sweating, aware of his too-rapid heartbeat, wondering how to fit clairvoyance and the other psychic phenomena into his previously uncomplicated view of life, Barnes followed the younger officer through the kitchen and laundry room. The woman stayed close beside him, asking questions that he didn't bother answering.

Hector Gonzales was waiting at the back door.

"There's an alleyway behind that chain-link fence," Barnes told him. "Get back there and search for our man, two blocks in each direction."

The woman said, "I'm bewildered."

So am I, Barnes thought.

To Malone he said, "Beat the shrubs around both sides of the house. And check out that line of bushes near the fence."

"Right."

"And both of you, keep your guns drawn."

Waiting by the squad cars in front of the house, Harry Oberlander was baiting the mayor. He shook his head as if the very sight of Henderson amazed him. "What a mayor you are," he said with heavy sarcasm. "Hiring a witch to do police work."

Henderson responded like a weary giant spotting yet one more tiny challenger with delusions of grandeur. "She's not a witch."

"Don't you know there's no such thing as a witch?"

"Like I said, Councilman, she's not a witch."

"She's a fake."

"A clairvoyant."

"Clairvoyant, shmairvoyant."

"So clever with language."

"It's just a fancier name for a witch."

Dan Goldman watched Oberlander, as weary of the argument as the mayor was. There are no worse enemies, he thought, than two men who used to be best friends. He would have to separate them if Harry became dissatisfied with words and started to throw a few fast but largely ineffective punches at the mayor's well-padded belly. It had happened before.

"You know why I sold you my half of the furniture business?" Oberlander asked Henderson.

"You sold out because you didn't have any vision," Henderson said smugly.

"Vision, smision. I sold out because I knew a superstitious fool like you would run it into the ground sooner or later."

"The store's more profitable now than ever before," Henderson said.

"Luck! Blind luck!"

Fortunately, before the first punch could be thrown, Harley Barnes came to the front door of the house and shouted, "It's all right. Come on."

"Now we'll see who's the fool," Henderson said. "They must have caught him." He ran across the sidewalk and the slippery wet lawn with that unexpected grace peculiar to certain very fat men.

Oberlander scurried after him, an angry mouse snapping at the heels of a behemoth.

Suppressing a laugh, Goldman followed.

Alan Tanner sat behind the steering wheel in order to be in the front seat with his sister. When he saw Harley Barnes at the door of the house, he said, "Did they get the killer, Mary?"

"I don't know," she said. Her voice was hollow; she sounded drained.

"Wouldn't there have been a shot?"

"I don't know."

"There would have been *some* commotion."

"I guess so."

From the rear seat Max said urgently, "Mary, is it safe for Goldman?"

She sighed and shook her head and pressed her fingertips to her eyes. "I really can't say. I've lost the thread. I don't see anything else."

Max rolled down his window. The damp air carried his voice well. "Hey, Goldman!"

The officer was halfway across the lawn. He stopped and looked back.

"Maybe you'd better stay here," Max said.

"Harley wants me," Goldman said.

"Remember what my wife told you."

"It's all right," Goldman said. "Nothing's going to happen. They caught him."

"Are you sure of that?" Max asked.

But Goldman had already turned and was headed for the house again.

Alan said, "Mary?"

"Hmmmm?"

"Are you feeling well?"

"Well enough."

"You don't sound good."

"Just tired."

"He presses you much too hard," Alan told her solicitously. He didn't even glance back at Max. He spoke as if he and his sister were alone in the car. "He doesn't realize how fragile you are."

"I'm okay," she said.

Alan wouldn't quit. "He doesn't know how to prompt you, how to help you refine the visions. He doesn't have any finesse. He always presses too hard."

You creepy little bastard, Max thought, staring hard at his brother-in-law.

For Mary's sake, he said nothing. She was easily upset when the two men in her life argued. She preferred to pretend that they were charmed by each other. And while she never entirely took Alan's side, she always blamed Max when the argument became particularly bitter.

To get his mind off Alan, he studied the house. A shaft of light thrust through the open door, silhouetted some of the dense lumps of shrubbery. "Maybe we should lock the car doors," he said.

Mary turned sideways in her seat and stared at him. "Lock the doors?"

"For protection."

"I don't understand."

"For protection from what?" Alan asked.

"The cops are all up at the house, and none of us has a weapon."

"You think we'll need one?"

"It's a possibility."

"Are *you* getting psychic now?" Alan asked.

Max forced himself to smile. "Nothing psychic about it, I'm afraid. Just good sense." He locked his and Mary's doors, and when he saw that Alan wouldn't cooperate, he latched both doors on the driver's side.

"Feel safe now?" Alan asked.

Max watched the house.


Barnes, Henderson, and Oberlander crowded into the laundry room to examine the smears of blood that the killer had left behind.

Miss Harrington squeezed in beside the chief, determined not to miss any of the excitement. She appeared to be delighted to have been the madman's choice.

Dan Goldman preferred to remain in the kitchen. As Barnes explained how these few pieces of physical evidence matched the clairvoyant's visions, the mayor would begin to gloat. Harry Oberlander would be embarrassed, then outraged. The nasty bickering would quickly escalate into a loud and vicious exchange. Goldman had had enough of that.

Besides, the big kitchen deserved an appreciative inspection. It had been designed and furnished by someone who enjoyed cooking and who could afford the best.

Miss Harrington? Goldman wondered. She didn't seem to be a woman who would welcome the opportunity to pass several hours in front of a stove. No doubt, the cook had been her ex-husband.

Quite a lot of money had been spent to create a professional kitchen with a country home atmosphere. The floor was of Mexican tile with brown grouting. There were oak cabinets with porcelain hardware, white ceramic counter tops, two standard ovens and a microwave oven, two large refrigerator-freezers, two double sinks, an island cooking surface, a built-in appliance center, and a dozen other machines, tools, and gadgets.

Goldman liked to cook, but he had to make do with a battered gas range and the cheapest pots, pans, and utensils on the market.

His envious appraisal of the kitchen was interrupted when, from the corner of his eye, he saw a door opening beside and somewhat behind him, no more than a yard away. It had been ajar when he'd entered the room, but he hadn't thought anything of it. Now he turned and saw a man in a raincoat stepping out of a pantry that was lined with canned goods. The stranger's left hand was bloody, the thumb tucked into a tight fist.

She was right, Goldman thought. *Christ!*

In his raised right hand the killer held a butcher knife by its thick wooden handle.

Time ceased to have meaning for Goldman. Each second extended itself a hundredfold. Each moment expanded like a soap bubble, encapsulated him, separated him from the rest of the world where clocks maintained their proper pace.

In the distance Henderson and Oberlander were arguing again. It didn't seem possible that they were only one room away. They sounded extremely odd, as if they had been recorded at seventy-eight revolutions per minute and were being played back at forty-five.

The stranger stepped forward. Light slithered along the well-honed edge of the blade.

As if moving against incredible resistance, Goldman reached for the revolver at his hip.

The knife ripped into his chest. High and to the left. Too deep to contemplate.

Curiously he felt no pain, but the front of his shirt was suddenly soaked with blood.

Mary Bergen, he thought. How could you know? What are you?

He unsnapped his holster.

Too slow. Too damned slow!

Although he didn't realize that the blade had been wrenched loose from him, he watched with horror as the knife arched down again. The stranger jerked the weapon free, and Goldman collapsed against the wall, framed by a spray of his own blood.

There was still no pain, but his strength was draining out of him as if there was a tap in his ankle.

Can't fall down, he told himself. Don't dare fall down. Wouldn't have a chance.

But the killer was finished. He turned and ran toward the dining room.

Clutching his wounds with his weakening left hand, Goldman staggered after the man. By the time he reached the archway and leaned against it to catch his breath, the killer was nearly to the living room. Goldman had the gun out of his holster, but he found it too heavy to lift. To get Harley's attention, he fired into the floor. With that explosion time resumed its normal flow and pain finally smashed through his chest, and suddenly he found it difficult to breathe and his knees buckled and he went down.

Alan interrupted himself in the middle of a sentence. "What was that?"

"A shot," Max said.

Mary said, "Something's happened to Goldman. I know it as sure as I'm sitting here."

Someone rushed out of the house. His raincoat flapped and billowed like a cape.

"That's *him*," Mary said.

When he saw the squad cars, the man stopped. Confused, he looked left and right, didn't seem to trust either route, and turned back toward the house.

Harley Barnes appeared at the open door. Even from where he sat, even through the dirty window and the shadows and the thin rain, Max could see the oversized revolver in the cop's hand. Obscenely, fire licked from the muzzle.

The madman spun as if in an inept ballet, then fell, rolled along the walk. Surprisingly, he scrambled to his feet and headed for the street again. He hadn't been hit. If he'd taken a bullet from the .357 Magnum, he would have stayed down.

Max was certain of that. He knew a great deal about firearms. He owned an extensive collection of guns.

Barnes fired again.

"Dammit!" Max said furiously. "Small town cops. Overarmed and undertrained. If that ass misses his man, he'll kill one of us!"

The third shot took the killer in the back as he reached the sidewalk.

Max could tell two things about the bullet. Because it didn't exit from the killer's chest and pierce the car window, it had been insufficiently packed with powder. It was designed for use on crowded streets; it had just enough punch to stop a guilty man without passing through him and harming others. Secondly, considering how it had lifted the man off his feet, the bullet was surely hollow-nosed.

After an instant of graceless flight, the killer slammed hard into the police cruiser. For a moment he clung to Mary's door. He slid down until he was peering at her. "Mary Bergen . . . " His voice was hoarse. He clawed at the window. "Mary Bergen." Blood spouted from his mouth and painted the glass.

Mary screamed.

The corpse dropped to the sidewalk.

The ambulance carrying Dan Goldman turned the corner as fast as it could without flipping on its side.

Max hoped the siren was fading more rapidly than the young patrolman's life.

On the sidewalk the dead man lay on his back. He stared at the sky and waited patiently for the coroner.

"She's upset about the killer knowing her name," Alan said.

"He saw her picture in her newspaper column," Max said. "Somehow he heard she was coming to town to find him."

"But only the mayor and the city council knew. And the cops."

"Somehow this guy heard. He knew she was in town and he recognized her. There's nothing supernatural about it. Is that what she thinks?"

"I know there's a simple explanation, and you know it. Deep down she knows it, too. But considering what she's seen in her life, she can't help wondering. Now, I've talked to Barnes. He can spare a man and a car for us. We should get Mary back to the hotel so she can lie down."

"We will," Max said, "when everything's settled with the mayor."

"That could be hours."

"Half an hour at most," Max said. "Now, if that's all you wanted to talk to me about—"

"She's dead tired."

"Aren't we all? She'll be okay."

"The loving husband."

"Go to hell."

They were standing behind the first squad car. Mary still sat inside with her eyes closed and her hands folded in her lap.

The rain had stopped. The air was moist and fragrant.

Glancing nervously at the people who had come out of their homes to gather around the pathetic scene, Alan said, "There'll be reporters here any minute. I don't think she should have to put up with a lot of reporters tonight."

Max knew what his brother-in-law wanted. Tomorrow Alan began a two-week vacation. Before leaving he hoped to have a final conversation with his sister, just the two of them, one last uninterrupted hour in which to convince her that she had married a man who was terribly wrong for her.

His fists were the only tools Max had to prevent this domestic sedition. He was six inches taller and forty pounds heavier than Alan. He had shoulders and biceps designed for dock work, and the outsized hands of a basketball star. However, he knew that split lips and broken teeth and a cracked jaw would silence Alan Tanner only temporarily. Short of killing him, there was no way to put an end to his meddling.

Anyway, Max no longer tried to solve his problems with his fists. He had promised Mary and himself that his violent days were gone forever.

Other than strength and the will to use it, Alan had all the weapons in this intensely personal war. Not the least of them was his appearance. He had black hair and blue eyes, like Mary. He was handsome, while Max was so rough-hewn that he barely avoided ugliness. Alan's powerfully sensuous features, highlighted by a look of boyish innocence, could affect even a sister.

*Especially* a sister.

Alan's voice was as sweet and persuasive as an actor's. He was able to create moods and build drama with his voice. He employed it subtly to gain Mary's sympathy and to cause her to look upon her new husband with mild, unconscious, but insidious displeasure.

Max knew his mind was better than average, but he also knew that Alan was his intellectual superior. It wasn't the voice alone that won arguments. There was wit behind those mellifluous tones.

And charm?

Whenever Alan needed it, charm oozed from him.

I'd like to roll him up tight like an empty tube of toothpaste, Max thought. Squeeze all the charm out of him and see if there's any truth behind it.

Most important of all, Alan and Mary had shared thirty years; he was thirty-three and, as an older brother, was welded to her by blood, common experience, more than a little tragedy, and three decades of day-to-day life.

As the crowd grew around him, Max watched yet another police car approach. He said, "You're right. She shouldn't be here any longer than necessary."

"Of course not."

"I'll take her to the hotel right away."

"You?" Alan asked, surprised. "You have to stay here."

"Why?"

"You know why."

"Tell me anyway."

Grudgingly, Alan said, "You're better at this than I am."

"Better at what?" Max asked.

"You know why you need to hear it? Because it's all you've got going for you. It's the only thing you can use to hold her."

"Better at what?"

"So insecure."

"Better at what!"

"You're better at getting the money. Does that satisfy you?"

Mary made a good living as the author of a syndicated newspaper column about psychic phenomena. She had also earned a lot of money with three best-selling books about her career, and she could have survived quite well on her speaking fees alone if she'd wanted.

Although she traveled extensively, aiding authorities with investigations of violent homicides whenever they asked her to do so, she didn't profit from any of that. She didn't charge for her visions. Once she helped a famous actress locate a hundred-thousand-dollar diamond necklace that was lost, and she took no fee. She never required more than expenses—airline tickets, car rentals, meals, and lodging—from those whom she assisted; and she refused even that much if she thought she'd been of little or no service.

When Max first came into her life, the collection of expense money was her brother's duty. But Alan had no talent or taste for quibbling with mayors, councilmen, and bureaucrats. As often as not, when Mary had done her work and the guilty man had been found, the local politicians who had summoned her tried to get rid of her without paying what they owed. Alan seldom pressured them. As a result, tens of thousands of dollars in expenses were lost each year; and although Mary earned considerable sums, she was slowly going broke.

Within two months following the wedding Max straightened out Mary's financial affairs. He renegotiated her contract with the lecture bureau and doubled her speaking fee. When her contract with the newspaper syndicate came due for renewal, he made a far more advantageous deal than she had thought possible. And he never failed to get a check for expenses.

"Well?" Alan said.

"All right. You take her back to the hotel. But remember what you said. I'm better at getting the money. And I always will be."

"Of course. You have a nose for it," Alan said. His smile had no warmth. "You sniffed out Mary's money pretty damned fast, didn't you?"

"Go," Max said.

"Too much truth in that for you?"

"Get out of here before you find yourself looking up your own ass for the rest of your life."

Alan blinked.

Max didn't.

Alan walked over to Harley Barnes.

Gradually Max became aware of a number of people in the crowd who were staring at him. He stared back at them, one at a time. Each grew self-conscious and turned away—but each looked at him again as soon as he moved his gaze.

None of them was close enough to have heard the argument. He realized that they were staring because his face was contorted by rage, because his shoulders were drawn up like those of a stalking panther, because his huge hands were in tight fists at his sides. He tried to relax, to let his shoulders fall. And he put his hands in the pockets of his raincoat so that no one could see he was too infuriated to uncurl them.

The hotel room had four ugly lamps with garishly patterned shades, but only one of them was on.

In a black vinyl armchair that stood on a swivel base, Alan folded his hands around a glass of Scotch that he wasn't drinking. The light fell over him from the left, carving his face with sharp shadows.

Mary was sitting up in bed, on top of the covers, well out of the light. She wished Max would get back so they could go out for a late

supper and a couple of drinks. She was hungry and tired and emotionally exhausted.

"Still have a headache?" Alan asked.

"The aspirin helped."

"You're drawn . . . so pale."

"There's nothing wrong that eight hours of sleep won't cure."

"I worry about you," he said.

She smiled affectionately. "You've always worried about me, dear.
Even when we were children."

"I care about you very much."

"I know that."

"You're my sister. I love you."

"I know, but—"

"He presses you too hard."

"Not this again, Alan."

"He does."

"I wish you and Max could get along."

"So do I. But we never will."

"But *why?*"

"Because I know what he is."

"And what's that?"

"For one thing, he's so different from you," Alan said. "He's not
as sensitive as you are. He's not as kind." He seemed to be pleading
with her. "You're gentle, and he's—"

"He can be gentle, too."

"Can he?"

"With me he can. He's sweet."

"You're entitled to your opinion."

"Oh, thank you very much," she said sarcastically. Anger flared
briefly in her but was quickly extinguished. She couldn't stay angry
with Alan for more than a minute. Even a minute was stretching it.

"Mary, I don't want to argue with you."

"Then don't."

"We never had cross words, not in thirty years . . . until he came
into the picture."

"I'm not up to this tonight."

"You're not up to anything because he presses you too hard and
too fast when he's guiding you through your visions."

"He does it well."

"Not as well as I did it."

"At first he was too insistent," she admitted. "Too anxious. But
not anymore."

Alan put down his Scotch, got up, turned his back on her. He went
to the window. Moody silence enveloped him.

She closed her eyes and wished Max would get back.

After a minute Alan walked away from the window. He stood at the foot of the bed, staring down at her. "I'm afraid to go away on vacation."

Without opening her eyes, she said, "Afraid of what?"

"I don't want to leave you alone."

"I won't be alone. I'll be with Max."

"That's what I mean—alone with Max."

"Alan, for Christ's sake!"

"I mean it."

She opened her eyes, sat up straighter. "You're being silly. Ridiculous. I won't listen to any more of this."

"If I didn't care what happens to you, I could walk out right now. Whether you want to hear it or not, I'm going to say what I think is true about him."

She sighed.

"He's an opportunist," Alan said.

"So what?"

"He likes money."

"So do I. So do you."

"He likes it too much."

She smiled indulgently. "I'm not sure you can ever like it too much, dear."

"Don't you understand?"

"Enlighten me."

Alan hesitated. There was sadness in his beautiful eyes. "Max likes *other people's* money too much."

She stared at him, surprised. "Look . . . if you're saying he married me for my money—"

"That's precisely what I'm saying."

"Then it's *you* who's pressing me too hard." There was steel in her voice now.

He changed his tone with her, spoke softly. "All I'm trying to do is make you face facts. I don't—"

She raised herself up, away from the headboard. "Am I so ugly that no one would want me if I were poor?"

"You're beautiful. You know that."

She wasn't satisfied. "Then am I some mindless little twit who bores men to death?"

"Don't shout," Alan said. "Calm down. Please." He seemed genuinely grieved that he had hurt her. But he didn't change the subject. "Plenty of men would give everything they own to marry you. And for all the right reasons. Why you ever picked Max—"

"He was the first decent prospect, the first full-fledged man who asked."

"That's not true. I know of four others who asked."

"The first two were spineless wonders," she said. "The third one was about as gentle and considerate in bed as a bull is in the ring. The other one was virtually impotent. Max wasn't any of that. He was different, interesting, exciting."

"You didn't marry him because he was exciting, or because he was intelligent or mysterious or romantic. You married him because he was big, strong, and gruff. A perfect father image."

"Since when have you practiced psychiatry?"

She knew Alan didn't want to pick at her like this. He continued only because he felt she needed to hear it. He was being a conscientious big brother. Even though he was misguided, his intentions were admirable. If she hadn't been certain of that, she would have asked him to leave.

"I don't have to be a psychiatrist to know that you need to lean on someone. You always have. From the day you realized what your clairvoyance was, what it meant, you've been frightened of it, unable to deal with it yourself. You leaned on me for a while. But I wasn't tall enough or broad-shouldered enough to fill the role for long."

"Alan, for the first time in my life I have the urge to slap your face."

He came around and sat down on the edge of the bed. He took her left hand in both of his. "Mary, he was a newspaper hack, a washed up reporter who hadn't covered a major story in ten years. You knew him just six weeks before you were married."

"That's all the longer I *needed* to know him." She relaxed, squeezed Alan's hand. "It's working out fine, dear. You should be happy for me."

"You've only been married four months."

"Long enough to like him even better than I did when he proposed."

"He's a dangerous man. You know his past."

"A few fights in barrooms . . . and he doesn't go to barrooms anymore."

"It's not as innocent as that. He nearly killed some people in those brawls."

"When they've had too much to drink and are feeling mean, some men will go after the biggest man in the room. Max was a natural target. He didn't start any of those fights."

"So he says."

"No one ever pressed charges."

"Maybe they were afraid to."

"He's changed. What he needed was someone who loved him, someone he could feel responsible for. He needed me."

Alan nodded forlornly. "Want a drink?"

"I'll wait for Max."

He drank his Scotch in three swallows. "You're absolutely sure about him?"

"About Max? Positive."

He went to the window again, studied the night sky for a moment. "I don't think I'll be returning to work with you after my vacation."

She got up, went to him, took hold of his shoulder and turned him around. "Say again?"

"I'm a fifth wheel now."

"Nonsense. You take care of so much of my business—"

"That's nothing a secretary couldn't handle," Alan said. "Before Max, I was vital. I was your guide through the visions. But there's nothing important for me to do anymore. And I don't need this constant friction with Max."

"But what will you do?"

"I'm not sure. I think I'll start by taking two months vacation instead of two weeks. I can afford it. You've been very generous to me and—"

"Not generous. You earned your share. Alan—"

"I've got enough money put away to keep me for years. Maybe I'll go back to the university . . . finish that degree in political science."

"Will you move out of the house in Bel Air?"

"That would be best. I can find an apartment."

"Will you live with Jennifer?"

"She dropped me," he said.

"What?"

"For another guy."

"I didn't know."

"I didn't want to talk about it."

"I'm sorry."

"Don't be. She wasn't my type."

"You two seemed happy."

"We were . . . briefly."

"What went wrong?"

"Everything."

"You won't move far away, will you?"

"Probably just to Westwood."

"Oh, then we'll practically be neighbors."

"That's right."

"We'll have lunch once a week."

"All right," he said.

"And dinner occasionally."

"Without Max?" he asked.

"Just you and me."

"Sounds lovely."

A childlike tear rolled out of the corner of her eye.

"No need for that," he said, wiping it away.

"I'll miss you."

"A brother and sister can't live in the same house forever. It's unnatural."

The sound of a key in the lock made them turn to the door.

Max came in and stripped off his raincoat.

Mary went to him, kissed him on the cheek.

Putting an arm around her, refusing to acknowledge Alan, Max asked, "Feeling better?"

"Just tired," she said.

"Everything went smoothly in spite of Oberlander," Max said. "I got the check for expenses."

"You always do," she said proudly.

During that exchange Alan went to the door and opened it. "I'll be going."

Only minutes ago she had hoped he would leave before Max returned in order to avoid one of those tiresome quarrels. Now she felt that Alan was drifting out of her life, and she was unwilling to let go of him so soon or so easily. "Can't you stay for another drink?"

He looked at Max and shook his head. "I don't think that would be wise."

Max said nothing. He didn't move, smile, or even blink. His arm at Mary's waist was like a stone bannister against which she rested.

She said, "We haven't talked about what happened tonight. There's so much to be discussed."

"Later," Alan said.

"You're still just going to spend your vacation driving up the coast?"

"Yeah. I'll spend some time in San Francisco. I know a girl there who's invited me for Christmas. Maybe after that I'll head for Seattle."

"You'll call me?"

"Sure."

"When?"

"A week or so."

"Christmas Day?"

"All right."

"I'll miss you, Alan."

"Watch out for yourself."

"I'll watch out for her," Max said.

Alan ignored him. To Mary he said, "Be careful, will you? And remember what I said."

He went out, closing the door behind him, leaving her alone with Max.

* * *

The small, downtown tavern was dimly lit, quite busy as late evening approached, but cozy in spite of the crowd. Max and Mary sat in a corner booth, and the bartender made two perfect vodka martinis. Later they ate roast beef sandwiches and split a bottle of red wine.

When she had finished half of her large sandwich, she pushed the rest of it aside, poured a third glass of wine for herself, and said, "I wonder if Dan Goldman's hospital bills will be covered."

"The town carries a comprehensive insurance policy on its cops," Max said. "Goldman got hurt in the line of duty, so he won't be stuck for a penny of it."

"How can you be so sure?"

"I knew you'd want me to be."

"I don't understand."

"I knew you'd wonder about Goldman's hospital bills, so I asked the mayor."

"Even if the bills are covered," she said, "I guess he'll lose some pay while he's off work."

"No," Max said. "I asked about that, too."

She was surprised. "What are you—a mind reader?"

"I just know you too well. You're the softest touch there ever was."

"I am not. I just think we should do something nice for him."

Max put down his sandwich. "We can buy him either a new electric range or maybe a microwave oven."

She blinked. "What?"

"I asked some of Goldman's buddies what he needs. Seems he's a serious amateur chef, but his kitchen leaves a lot to be desired."

She smiled. "We'll get him the range *and* the oven, and the best set of pots and pans—"

"Hold on a minute," Max said. "He's got an apartment kitchen, not a restaurant. Besides, why do you think you owe him *anything?*"

Staring into her wine, she said, "If I hadn't come to town, he wouldn't have been hurt."

"Mary Bergen, the female Atlas, carrying the world on her shoulders." He reached across the table and took her hand. "Do you remember the first conversation we ever had?"

"How could I forget? I thought you were weird."

The night they'd met he had been uncharacteristically shy. They'd been guests at the same party. He'd seemed at ease and self-confident with everyone but her. His approach had been so self-conscious and awkward that she felt sorry for him. He had begun with one of those analyze-yourself party games.

She smiled, remembering. "You asked me what machine I would choose to be if I could be any machine in the world. Weird."

"The last woman who answered that question said she'd be a Rolls Royce and go to all the best places. But you said you'd be some piece of medical equipment that saves lives."

"Was that a good answer?"

"At the time," Max said, "it sounded phony. But now I know what you are, and I realize you were serious."

"And what am I?"

"The kind of person who always asks for whom the bell tolls—and always cries buckets at even slightly sad movies."

She sipped her wine. "I played the game right back at you that night, asked you what machine you'd be. Remember?"

Max nodded. He pushed his unfinished sandwich aside, picked up his wine. "I said I'd be a computer dating service so I could hook you up with me."

She laughed girlishly. "I liked it then, and I like it now. It was a surprise finding a romantic under that big tough exterior."

Max leaned across the table, spoke softly. "Know what machine I'd be tonight?" He pointed to the colorfully lighted juke box at the far end of the bar. "I'd be that music machine. And no matter what buttons people pushed, I'd play love songs for you."

"Oh, Max, that's positively saccharine."

"But you like it."

"I love it. After all, I'm the lady who cries buckets at even slightly sad movies."

# 5
◆ ◆ ◆

The nightmare woke her, but the dream continued. For a minute after she rose up in fear from her pillows, colorful snatches of the nightmare swam in the air before her. Ethereal snapshots. Blood. Shattered bodies. Broken skulls. They were more vivid than any visions she'd ever known.

The shadows of the hotel room settled over her once more. When she grew accustomed enough to the darkness to see the outlines of the furniture, she got up.

The room was a carousel. She reached out for a brass pole that wasn't there, for something to steady her.

When she regained her balance, she went into the bathroom. She didn't close the door because she worried she might wake Max. For the same reason, she didn't use the main light. Instead, she turned on the much dimmer, orange-filtered heat lamp.

In that eerie light her mirror image disturbed her: dark rings around the eyes, skin slack and damp. She was used to a reflection that was the envy of most women: silky black hair, blue eyes, fine features, a flawless complexion. Now the person looking back at her seemed a stranger, an alien.

She felt personally threatened by what she had seen. The dead bodies in the nightmare were the first parts of a chain in which she might be the final link.

She drew a glass of cold water, drank it, then another. The tumbler rattled against her teeth. She had to use both hands to hold it.

Each time she shut her eyes, she saw the same remnant of the nightmare. A dark-haired girl with one blue eye gazing sightlessly at the ceiling. The other eye swollen in a macabre wink. Face torn, bruised, misshapen.

Worst of all, Mary felt that if the blood were swabbed from that face, and if its smashed features were restored, she would know it at once.

She put the glass down, leaned against the sink.

Who? she thought. Who was that girl?

The distorted face would not resolve itself.

As if she craved more fear than the dream had given her, she remembered the psychopath who had died that same night: his twisted features; his marble-chip teeth; his hands pressed to the squad car windows; his whispery voice, cool as cellar air when he spoke her name.

He had been an omen, a warning to her.

But an omen of what?

There might be nothing mysterious about his knowing her name. He could have heard she was in town, even though that information was limited to a select few. He might have recognized her from the photograph that accompanied her column, although the picture was not a good one and was six years old. That was Alan's explanation.

Although she had no good reason to disagree with Alan, she knew that his explanation was inadequate.

Maybe the madman had known her because he'd had his first (and necessarily last) telepathic experience in the instant that death seized him.

Or perhaps there was a meaning to the incident that couldn't be defined in rational terms. When she recalled the madman's demonic face, one thought circled through her mind: *He's a messenger from Hell, a messenger from Hell. . . .* She didn't know what that meant. But she didn't dismiss the thought simply because it had a supernatural ring to it.

Through her extensive travels, through her many conversations with clairvoyants like Peter Hurkos and Gerard Croiset, through her conversations and correspondence with other psychically gifted people, she had come to think anything was possible. She'd been in homes where poltergeists were active, where dishes and paintings and bric-a-brac and heavy furniture sailed through the air and exploded against walls when no one had touched them or been near them. She hadn't decided whether she'd seen ghosts at work or, instead, the unconscious telekinetic powers of someone in the house; but she did know that *something* was there. She had seen Ted Serios create his famous psychic photographs, which *Time* and *Popular Photography* and many other national publications had tried unsuccessfully to debunk. He projected his thoughts onto unexposed film, and he did so under the intense scrutiny of skeptical scientists. She had seen an Indian mystic— a fakir but not a faker—do the impossible. He planted a seed in a pot of earth, covered it with a light muslin sheet, then went into a deep trance. Within five hours, while Mary watched, the seed germinated, the plant grew, and fruit appeared—several tiny mangoes. As a result of two decades of contact with the extraordinary in life, she scoffed at nothing. Until someone proved beyond doubt that all psychic and supernatural phenomena were pieces of a hoax (which no one ever would), she would put as much faith in the unnatural, supernatural, and suprarational as she did in what more dogmatic people believed to be the one, true, natural, and only world.

*. . . messenger from Hell.*

Although she was half convinced that life existed after death, she didn't believe that it was accurately described by the Judeo-Christian myths. She didn't accept the reality of Heaven and Hell. That was too simplistic. Yet, if she didn't believe, why this unshakable certainty that the madman was a satanic omen? Why phrase the premonition in religious terms?

She shuddered. She was cold to her bones.

She returned to the bedroom but left on the bathroom light. She was uneasy in the dark. She put on her robe.

Max snored peacefully. She stroked his cheek with her fingertips.

He was instantly awake. "What's the matter?"

"I'm scared. I need to talk. I can't stand to be alone."

He closed his hand around her wrist. "I'm here."

"I saw something awful . . . horrible." She shuddered again.

He sat up, switched on the lamp, looked around the room.

"Visions," she said.

Still holding her wrist, he pulled her down to the bed.

"They started when I was asleep," she said, "and went on after I woke up."

"Started when you were sleeping? That's never happened before, has it?"

"Never."

"So maybe it was a dream."

"I know the difference."

He let go of her wrist, pushed his hair back from his forehead. "A vision of what?"

"Dead people."

"An accident?"

"Murder. Beaten and stabbed."

"Where?"

"Quite a distance from here."

"Name of the town?"

"It's south of us."

"That's all you've got?"

"I think it's in Orange County. Maybe Santa Ana. Or Newport Beach. Laguna Beach. Anaheim. Someplace like that."

"How many dead?"

"A lot. Four or five women. All in one place. And . . . "

"And what?"

"They're the first of many."

"You sense that?"

"Yes."

"Sense it psychically?"

"Yes."

"The first of how many?"

"I don't know."

"You saw the killer?"

"No."

"Pick up anything about him?"

"No."

"Not even the color of his hair?"

"Nothing, Max."

"Have these killings taken place yet?"

"I don't think so. But I can't be sure. I was so surprised by the visions that I didn't make any attempt to hold on to them. I didn't pursue them like I should have."

He got out of bed and slipped into his own robe. She stood up, moved against him. "You're shivering," he said.

She wanted to be loved and sheltered. "It was horrible."

"They always are."

"This was worse than usual."

"Well, it's over."

"No. Maybe it is over or shortly will be for those women. But not for us. We're going to get tangled up in this one. Oh, God, so many bodies, so much blood. And I think I knew one of the dead girls."

"Who was she?" he asked, holding her still closer.

"The face I saw was so badly disfigured. I couldn't tell who she was, but she seemed familiar."

"It had to be a dream," he said reassuringly. "The visions don't come to you out of the blue. You've always had to concentrate, focus your attention in order to pick them up. Like when you start tracking a killer, you have to handle something that belonged to his victim before you can receive images of him."

He was telling her what she already knew, soothing her in the manner of a father explaining to his still frightened young daughter that the ghosts she had seen in the dark bedroom were only the draft-stirred curtains she could now see with all the lights on.

Actually it didn't matter to her what he said. Just hearing him speak and feeling him close, Mary grew calm.

"Even when you're searching for a lost ring or necklace or brooch," Max said, "you have to see the box or drawer where it was kept. So what you saw tonight *had* to be a dream because you didn't seek it."

"I feel better."

"Good."

"But not because I believe it was a dream. I know it was a vision. Those women were real. They're either dead by now or they soon will be." She thought of the brutally beaten faces and she said, "God help them."

"Mary—"

"It was *real*," she insisted, letting go of his hand and sitting on the mattress. "And it's going to involve us."

"You mean the police will ask for your help?"

"More than that. It's going to affect us . . . intimately. It's the start of something that'll change our lives."

"How can you know that?"

"The same way I know everything else about it. I sense it psychically."

"Whether or not it's going to change our life," he said, "is there any way we can help those women?"

"We know so little. If we called the police, we couldn't tell them anything worthwhile."

"And since you don't know what town it will happen in, which police department would we call? Can you pick up the vision again?"

"No use trying. It's gone."

"Maybe it'll return spontaneously, just the way it came the first time."

"Maybe." The possibility chilled her. "I hope not. As it is, I've got too many nasty visions in my life. I don't want them to start flashing on me when I'm not prepared, when I'm not *asking* for them. If that became a regular thing, I'd end up in a madhouse."

"If there isn't anything we can do about what you saw," Max said, "then we have to forget about it for tonight. You need a drink."

"I had some water."

"Would *I* ever suggest water? I meant something with more bite."

She smiled. "At this hour of the morning?"

"It's not morning. We went to bed early, remember. And we've been asleep only half an hour or so."

She looked at the travel clock. Eleven-ten. "I thought I'd been conked out for hours."

"Minutes," he said. "Vodka and tonic?"

"Scotch, if you're having it."

He went to the small breakfast table by the window. The liquor bottles, glasses, and ice were there. In spite of his size, he was not awkward. He moved like a wild animal—fluidly, silently. Even the preparation of drinks was a study in grace when Max did it.

If everyone were like him, Mary thought, the word "clumsy" wouldn't exist.

He sat beside her on the edge of the bed. "Will you be able to get back to sleep?"

"I doubt it."

"Drink up."

She sipped the Scotch. It burned her throat.

"What are you worrying about?" he asked.

"Nothing."

"You're worrying about the vision."

"Not at all."

"Look, worry accomplishes nothing," he said. "And whatever you do, don't think about a blue giraffe standing in the center of a giant custard pie."

She stared at him, incredulous.

Grinning, he said, "What are you worrying about now?"

"What else? A blue giraffe in a custard pie."

"*See?* I stopped you from worrying about the vision."

She laughed. He had such a stern, forbidding face that his humor always came as a surprise.

"Speaking of blue," he said, "you look perfect in that robe."

"I've worn it before."

"And every time you wear it you're breathtaking. Perfect."

She kissed him. She explored his lips with her tongue, then teasingly drew back.

"You look perfect in it, but you'd look even better out of it." He put his drink beside hers on the nightstand and untied the sash that was knotted at her waist, opened the long blue robe.

A pleasant tremor passed through her. The cool air caressed her bare skin. She felt soft, vulnerable; she needed him.

With his heavy hands, now light as wings, he traced lazy circles on her breasts, cupped them, pressed them together, gently massaged them. He got on his knees before her, nuzzled her cleavage and kissed her nipples.

She took his head in her hands, pushed her fingers through his lush, shining hair.

Alan was wrong about him.

"My lovely Max," she said.

He moved his lips down her taut belly as she lay back, kissed her thighs, delicately licked the warm center of her. He slipped his hands under her buttocks, lifted slightly.

After many minutes during which her murmurs rose and fell, rose and fell again like the enigmatic susurration of the sea, he raised his head and said, "I love you."

"Then love me."

He took off his robe and joined her on the bed.

Agreeably exhausted, they separated at midnight, but the spell was not broken. Still enchanted, eyes closed, she drifted. In some ways she was more intensely aware of her body than she had been during intercourse.

Within minutes, however, memories of the vision returned to her: bloodied and crumpled faces. With her eyes closed, the backs of her lids were like twin projection screens on which she saw nothing but carnage.

She opened her eyes and the dark room appeared to crawl with strange shapes. Although she didn't want to disturb Max, she couldn't keep herself from tossing and turning.

Eventually he switched on the light. "You need a sedative." He swung his legs out of bed.

"I'll get it," she said.

"Stay put."

A minute later he came back from the bathroom with a glass of water and one of the capsules that she too frequently required.

"Maybe I shouldn't take it on top of liquor," she said.

"You drank only half of your Scotch."

"I had vodka before that."

"The vodka's through your system by now."

She took the sedative. It stuck in her throat. She choked it down with another swallow of water.

In bed again, he held her hand. He was still holding it when the chemically induced sleep finally began to creep over her.

As consciousness spun away from her like a child's ball rolling down a hillside, she thought about how wrong Alan was about Max, how terribly and completely wrong.

# TUESDAY, DECEMBER 22

◆ ◆ ◆

# 6
◆◆◆

"Anaheim police."

"Are you a police officer, Miss?"

"I'm the receptionist."

"Could I speak to an officer?"

"What's the nature of your complaint?"

"Oh, no complaint. I think you people do a wonderful job."

"I meant, are you reporting a crime?"

"I'm not sure. A very strange thing happened here."

"What is your name?"

"Alice. Alice Barnable."

"Your address?"

"Peregrine Apartments on Euclid Avenue. I'm in apartment B."

"I'll connect you with someone."

"Sergeant Erdman speaking."

"Are you really a sergeant?"

"Who's this?"

"Mrs. Alice Barnable."

"What can I do for you?"

"Are you really a sergeant? You sound too young."

"I've been a policeman for twenty years. If you—"

"I'm seventy-eight, but I'm not senile."

"I didn't say you were."

"So many people treat us senior citizens as if we're children."

"I don't, Mrs. Barnable. My mother's seventy-five, and she's sharper than I am."

"So you better believe what I've got to tell you."

"And what's that?"

"Four nurses share an apartment above mine, and I know they're in some sort of bad trouble. I called up there, but no one answers the phone."

"How do you know they're in trouble?"

"There's a puddle of blood in my spare bathroom."

"Whose blood? I'm afraid I don't follow you."

"You see, the water pipes that serve the apartment above mine are exposed, and they run up one corner of my spare bath. Now, I don't want you to think I live in a cheap place. The pipes are painted white, hardly noticeable. The building's old but elegant in its way. It's not cheap. It's quaint. My Charlie left me enough to let me live very comfortably."

"I'm sure he did, Mrs. Barnable. What about the blood?"

"Those pipes run through a hole in the ceiling. The hole's a tiny bit bigger than it needs to be. Just a quarter of an inch of space all the way around the pipe. During the night, blood dripped out of that hole. The pipes are streaked with it, and there's a large sticky spot on my floor."

"You're sure it's blood? It might be rusty water or—"

"Now you're treating me as if I'm a child, Sergeant Erdman."

"Sorry."

"I know blood when I see it. And what I wondered—I wondered if maybe your people should take a look upstairs."

Patrolmen Stambaugh and Pollini found the door to the apartment ajar. It was spotted with fingerprints that were cast in dried blood.

"Think he's still in there?" Stambaugh asked.

"Never can tell. Back me up."

Pollini went inside with his gun drawn and Stambaugh followed.

The living room was inexpensively but pleasantly furnished with wicker and rattan. On the white walls were colorful framed prints of palm trees and native villages and bare-breasted, nut-brown girls in striped sarongs.

The first body was in the kitchen. A young woman in black and green pajamas. On the floor. On her back. Long yellow hair streaked with clotted red bands spread around her like a fan. She had been stabbed—and kicked in the face more than once.

"Christ," Stambaugh said.

"Something, huh?"

"Don't you feel sick?"

"Seen it before."

Pollini pointed to several items on the counter by the sink—a paper plate, two slices of bread, a jar of mustard, a tomato, a package of cheese.

"Important?" Stambaugh asked.

"She woke up during the night. Maybe she was an insomniac. She was making a snack when he came in. Doesn't look like she put up a fight. He either surprised her, or she knew and trusted him."

"Should we be talking like this?"

"Why not?"

Stambaugh gestured toward the rooms that they hadn't yet investigated.

"The killer? He's long gone."

Stambaugh greatly admired his partner. He was eight years younger than Pollini. He'd been a cop only six months, while the older man had been on the force for seven years. In his view, Pollini had everything that a great lawman required—intelligence, courage, and street wisdom.

Most important of all, Pollini was able to do his job without letting it touch him. He didn't flinch at the sight of shattered bodies, not even when he encountered the most pathetic victim of all—the battered child. Pollini was nothing less than a rock.

Although he tried to imitate his mentor, Stambaugh usually got sick to his stomach in the midst of too much spilled blood.

"Come on," Pollini said.

He led Stambaugh back through the hall to the spare bath, where the harsh light glared on blood-splashed porcelain and on the hideously stained white vanity top.

"There was a struggle this time," Stambaugh said.

"But not much of one. It was over in seconds."

Another young woman, wearing only panties, was curled fetally in a corner of the bathroom. She had been stabbed repeatedly in the breasts and stomach, back and buttocks. There were between fifty and a hundred wounds.

Her blood had pooled around the pipes that came up from Alice Barnable's first-floor apartment.

"Funny," Pollini said.

*"Funny?"* Stambaugh had never seen such slaughter. He could not comprehend the violent mind behind it.

"Funny that he didn't rape either of them."

"Is that what he should have done?"

"His kind does, ninety percent of the time."

Across the hall the spare bedroom contained two unmade beds but no bodies.

In the master suite they found a nude redhead on the bed nearest the door. Her throat had been cut.

"No struggle at all," Pollini said. "He caught her while she was sleeping. Doesn't look like he raped this one either."

Stambaugh nodded. He was unable to speak.

Both women in the master bedroom appeared to be Catholics who were, if not devout, at least attentive to their faith. A number of religious objects were scattered on the floor.

A damaged crucifix lay beside the redhead's nightstand. The wooden cross had been broken into four pieces. The aluminum image of Christ was bent at the waist, so that its crown of thorns touched its bare feet; and its head was twisted around so that Christ was looking over his shoulder.

"This wasn't just broken in a scuffle," Pollini said, stooping over the remains of the icon. "The killer pulled this off the wall and spent a good bit of time demolishing it."

Two small religious statues had been on the redhead's dresser. These were also broken. Some of the pieces had been ground into chalky dust; there were a few white heel prints on the carpet.

"He sure has something against Catholics," Pollini said. "Or against religion in general."

Stambaugh reluctantly followed him to the last bed.

The fourth dead woman had been stabbed repeatedly and strangled with a rosary.

In life she had been beautiful. Even now, naked and cold, her hair matted with blood, nose broken, one eye swollen shut, face dark with bruises, there were still traces of beauty. Alive, her blue eyes would have been as clear as mountain lakes. Washed and combed, her hair would have been thick, lustrous. She had long shapely legs, a narrow waist, a flat belly and lovely breasts.

I've seen women like her, Stambaugh thought sadly. She would have walked with her shoulders back, with evident pride in herself, with joy apparent in every step.

"She was a nurse," Pollini said.

Stambaugh looked at the uniform and cap that were on a chair near the bed. His legs felt weak.

"What's the matter?" Pollini asked.

Stambaugh hesitated, cleared his throat. "Well, my sister's a nurse."

"This isn't your sister, is it?"

"No. But she's about my sister's age."

"You know her? She work with your sister?"

"Never saw her before," Stambaugh said.

"Then what's wrong?"

"This girl might have been my sister."

"You cracking up on me?"

"I'm okay. I'm fine."

"You'll get used to this stuff."

Stambaugh said nothing.

"This one was raped," Pollini said.

Stambaugh swallowed hard. He was dizzy.

"See that?" Pollini asked.

"What?"

"On the pubic hair. It's semen."

"Oh."

"I wonder if he had her before or after."

"Before or after what?"

"Before or after he killed her."

Stambaugh hurried into the master bath, dropped to his knees before the toilet, and threw up.

When his stomach spasms passed, he knew that in the past ten minutes he had learned something important about himself. In spite of what he'd thought this morning, he *never* wanted to be like Ted Pollini.

# 7
◆ ◆ ◆

Max came back to the room at eleven-thirty, just as she finished dressing. He kissed her lightly on the mouth. He smelled of soap, shaving lotion, and the cherry-scented pipe tobacco that he favored.

"Out for a walk?" Mary asked.

"When did you wake up?"

"Only an hour ago."

"I was up at eight-thirty."

"I slept *ten* hours. When I finally managed to throw myself out of bed, I felt dopey. I shouldn't have taken the sedative on top of liquor."

"You needed it."

"I didn't need to feel the way I felt this morning."

"You look wonderful now."

"Where have you been?"

"At the coffee shop downstairs. Had some toast and orange juice. Read the papers."

"Anything that's connected with what I saw last night?"

"The local paper has a nice story. You and Barnes catching The Slasher. They say Goldman is already off the critical list."

"That's not what I meant. The dead women in the vision. What about them?"

"Nothing in the papers."

"There will be this afternoon."

A worried look crossed his face. He put a hand on her shoulder. "You've got to relax once in a while. You've got to let your head clear out now and then. Don't run after this one, Mary. Forget about it. Please. For me?"

"I can't forget," she said unhappily. She wished desperately that she could.

Before leaving town, they stopped at an appliance store, chose and paid for an electric range and microwave oven for Dan Goldman.

Later they got off the freeway at Ventura to have lunch at a restaurant they knew. They ordered salads, manicotti, and a bottle of Cabernet Sauvignon by Robert Mondavi.

From their table they had a view of the ocean. The slate-gray water looked like a mirror reflecting the turbulent sky. The surf was high and fast. A few gulls swooped along the shoreline.

"It'll be good to get home," Max said. "We should be in Bel Air before two o'clock."

"The way you drive, we'll be there long before."

"We can go over to Beverly Hills for a few hours of Christmas shopping."

"Since we're going to get home in time, I'd rather see my analyst. I've got a four-thirty appointment. I've been missing too many of them lately. I'll do my shopping tomorrow. Besides, I haven't given any thought to Christmas gifts. I don't have any idea what to get you."

"I can see your problem," he said. "I *am* the man who has everything."

"Oh, are you?"

"Naturally. I have you."

"That's corny."

"But I mean it."

"You make me blush."

"That's never been difficult."

She put her right hand to her cheek. "I can feel it. I wish I could control it."

"I'm glad you can't," he said. "It's charming. It's a sign of your innocence."

"Me? Innocent?"

"As a baby," he said.

"Remember me in bed last night?"

"How could I forget?"

"Was that innocence?"

"That was heaven."

"So there."

"But you're still blushing."

"Oh, drink your wine and shut up."

"Still blushing," he said.

"I'm flushed from the wine."

"Still blushing."

"Damn you," she said affectionately.

"*Still* blushing."

She laughed.

Beyond the window thick curdled clouds continued to roll in from the ocean.

Over the spumoni and coffee Mary asked, "What do you think of adoption?"

He shook his head in mock despair. "We're too old to find parents now. Who would want kids as big as us?"

"Be serious," she said.

He stared at her for a long moment, then put down his spoon without eating the spumoni on it. "You really mean you and me . . . adopting a child?"

She was encouraged by the wonder in his voice. "We've talked about having a family," she said. "And since I'll never be able to have a baby of my own . . ."

"But maybe you will."

"No, no," she said. "The doctor made that very clear to me."

"Doctors have been known to be mistaken."

"Not this time," she said, almost too softly to be heard. "There's too much wrong . . . inside of me. I'll never have a baby, Max. Never."

"Adoption . . ." Max thought about it while he sipped his coffee. Gradually he began to grin. "Yeah. It would be nice. A cute little baby girl."

"I was thinking about a little boy."

"Well, sure as hell this is one thing we can't compromise on."

"We can," she said quickly. "We'll adopt a girl *and* a boy."

"You've thought of everything, haven't you?"

"Oh, Max, you really do like the idea. I can tell. We could talk to an adoption agency this week. And if—"

"Hold on," he said, his smile fading. "We've been married only four months. We should take our time, get to know each other and ourselves better than we do. Then we'll be *ready* for children."

She didn't hide her disappointment. "How long will that take?"

"It'll take as long as it takes. Six months . . . a year."

"Look, I know you. You know me. We love each other and we like each other. We've got intelligence, common sense, and loads of money. What else do we need to be good parents?"

"We need to be at peace with ourselves, in ourselves," he said.

"You don't fight anymore. You're at peace with yourself."

"I'm only halfway there," he said. "And you've got things to face, too."

Defiantly, although she knew the answer, she said, "Like what?"

"You've got to face up to what happened twenty-four years ago, remember what you've refused to remember . . . every detail of the beating you took . . . everything about what that man did to you when you were six years old. Until you come to terms with that, you'll continue to have the nightmares. You'll never know real peace of mind until those memories are confronted and exorcised."

She tossed her head, throwing her long hair over her shoulders. "I don't have to face what happened then to be a good parent now."

"I think you do," he said.

"But Max, there are so many kids without homes, without hope or a future. Right now we could give two of them—"

He squeezed her hand. "You're playing Atlas again. Mary, I understand you. There's more love in you than in anyone I've ever known. You want to share it; that's the meaning of you. And I promised you'll have the opportunity. But adoption is a big step. We'll take it only when we're ready."

She couldn't get angry. She smiled and said, "I'll wear you down. I promise."

He sighed. "You probably will."


Mary didn't like to drive fast. When she was nine years old her father died in an accident. She'd been in the car when it happened. To her, the automobile was a treacherous machine.

As a passenger, she endured high speeds only when Max was at the wheel. With him in command, she was able to relax and even to feel exhilarated as the scenery whipped past her window. Max was her guardian. He watched over her and protected her. It was inconceivable that anything bad could happen to her when she was with him.

He took great pleasure in handling the Mercedes at speeds that tested his skills and his ability to avoid police detection. He enjoyed the car as much as he did his gun collection; and when he drove, he was as single-minded as when he made love. On a long, uncrowded straight stretch of freeway, with all his attention riveted on the car beneath him and on the blurred pavement that succumbed to him, he rarely had patience for conversation. He looked like a bird of prey, flint-eyed, silent, hunched over the steering wheel.

When he drove like that, Mary could see the recklessness, the taste for excitement and violence that had gotten him into dozens of fights. Oddly, she wasn't frightened by that aspect of him; instead, she found him more attractive than ever.

They rocketed toward Los Angeles at ninety miles an hour.

The eighteen-room English Tudor house in Bel Air looked cool and elegant in the shade of thirty-foot trees. The two-acre estate had cost her virtually every dollar that she had earned from her first two best-sellers, but she had never regretted the cost.

When they parked in the circular drive, Emmet Churchill came out to greet them. He had gray hair and a neat mustache. He was sixty years old, but his face was unlined. A life in service had been re-markably agreeable to both Emmet and his wife. "Good trip, Mr. Bergen?"

"Fine," Max said. "Had it up to one-twenty for a few miles, and Mary didn't scream once."

"I would have," Emmet said.

Mary had expected to find another Mercedes in the driveway. "Isn't Alan home?"

"He stopped by for fresh clothes," Emmet said. "But he was anxious to be off on vacation."

She was disappointed. She'd hoped for another chance to convince him that he and Max *could* get along if they tried. "How's Anna?" she asked Emmet.

"Couldn't be better. When you called this morning to say that you'd be home, she started planning dinner right away. She's in the kitchen now."

"As soon as Max freshens up, he'll be going to Beverly Hills to do some shopping," Mary told Emmet. "You'll want to get our lug-gage out of the Mercedes before he leaves."

"Right away."

She started toward the front door. "And would you get my car out

of the garage? I've got a four-thirty appointment with Dr. Cauvel. I
want—''

*The man coming at her, relentless, power in the blow, a knife deep
in her stomach, blade twisting, flesh tearing, blood erupting, pain
erupting, blackness flowing, flowing . . .*

She regained consciousness as Max put her down on the bed in the
second-floor master suite. She clung to him. She couldn't stop shaking.

"Are you all right?"

"Hold me," she said.

He did. "Easy. Easy now."

She could feel the strong, unhurried beat of his heart. After a while
she said, "I'm thirsty."

"Is that all? Aren't you hurt? Should I call a doctor?"

"Just get me some water."

"You passed out."

"I'm fine now."

When he came back from the bathroom with the water, he helped
her sit up. He held the glass, tilted it as she drank, nursed her as if
she were a sick child. When she was finished, he said, "What
happened?"

Leaning against the headboard, she said, "Another vision that I
didn't ask for. Only . . . it's different from anything that's come
before."

She must have gone pale, for he said, "Calm down. It's over."

He looked good. Marvelous. So big and reliable.

She did calm down somewhat, merely because he told her she
should.

"I didn't just *see* the damned thing, Max. I *felt* it. A knife. I felt
a knife going into me, ripping me apart . . . "

She put one hand on her belly. There was no wound. No bruise.
The flesh wasn't even tender.

"Let me get this straight," he said. "You saw yourself being stabbed
to death?"

"No."

"What *did* you see?"

She got up, waved him away as he moved to support her. She went
to the window and looked out at the forty-foot pool behind the main
house, at the lush grounds and at the Churchills' little house at the far
end of the property. Ordinarily she would have been calmed further
by this evidence of prosperity; but now it had no effect on her. "I saw
another woman. Not me. But I felt her pain as if it were mine."

"That's never happened before."

"It did this time."

"Have you ever heard of another clairvoyant having the same experience? Hurkos? Croiset? Dykshoorn?"

"No." She turned from the window. "What's it mean? What's going to happen to me?"

"Nothing will happen to you." Convinced that she wasn't ill, he began the gentle interrogation that could guide her through a vision in progress or through the memory of a vision that had passed. "Has this thing you just saw happened yet?"

"No."

"This woman who will be stabbed . . . was she one of those you saw in the nightmare last evening?"

"No. A new one."

"Did you see her face clearly?"

"I did. But only briefly."

Mary sat in a wing-back chair by the window. Her hands, against the brown crushed-velvet upholstery, were pale, almost translucent. She felt lighter than air, as if her existence were tenuous, as if she were fading away.

"What did this woman look like?" Max asked.

"Pretty."

He paced before her. "Color of hair?"

"Brunette."

"Eyes?"

"Green or blue."

"Young?"

"Yes. About my age."

"Did you sense her name?"

"No. But I think I've seen her before."

"You thought the same of one of them last night."

She nodded.

"What gives you the idea you know her?"

"I can't say. It's just an impression."

"Was the scene of this crime the same as in last night's vision?"

"No. This woman will be murdered . . . in a beauty parlor."

"At a hairdresser's?"

"Yes. The beautician is a man."

"What will happen to him?"

"He'll be killed, too."

"Any other victims?"

"A third. Another woman."

She had sensed a great deal in the few seconds that the psychic images had coruscated through her mind. However, with each datum came the brutal recollection of that knife she had shared mystically with the dying woman.

"What's the name of the beauty shop?" Max asked.

"I don't know."

"Where's it located?"

"Not far from here."

"In Orange County again?"

"Yes."

"Which town?"

"I don't know."

He sighed, sat down in the armchair opposite hers. "Is the killer the same as the one you saw last night?"

"No doubt about it."

"So he's a repeater, a psychopath, a mass murderer. He's going to kill four or five people in one place and three in another."

"That may only be the start," she said softly.

"What does he look like?"

"I still don't know."

"Is he a big man or small?"

"I don't know."

"What's his name?"

"I wish I knew."

"Is he young or old?"

"I don't even know that."

The room was stuffy. The air was stale, almost rank. She got up and opened the window.

"If you can't get an image of him," Max said, "how can you tell it's the same killer in both visions?"

"I just *can,* that's all."

She sat down, face to the window.

She felt hollow, light. She could imagine being carried off by the breeze, slight as it was. The unbidden visions had sucked a lot of energy from her. She wouldn't be able to endure many more of them. Certainly not a life full of them.

Pretty soon, she thought, I won't need a tornado like Dorothy did. Just a puff of air will carry *me* off to Oz.

"What can we do to keep him from killing?" Max asked.

"Nothing."

"Then let's put him out of our minds for now."

She scowled. "Know when I feel worst? You know when I feel so awful I hardly want to live?"

He waited.

Her hands were in her lap, her fingers at war with one another. "It's when I know something horrible will happen—but I don't know enough to stop it from happening. If I must have this power, why wasn't I given it without strings attached? Why can't I turn it on and off like a television set? Why does it sometimes get all cloudy for me when I need it the most? Am I supposed to be tormented? Is it a nasty joke? A lot of people are going to die because I can't see clearly. Dammit, dammit, dammit!'' She jumped up, strode to the television. She turned the set on, off, on, off, on, off, with nearly enough force to break the switch.

"You can't feel responsible for what you see in your visions," he said.

"But I do."

"You've got to change."

"I won't. I can't."

He stood up, went to her, took her hand from the television controls. "Why don't you freshen up? We'll do some shopping."

"Not me," she said. "I have an appointment with Dr. Cauvel."

"That's two and a half hours from now."

"I'm not up to shopping," she said. "You go. I'll make the rounds tomorrow."

"I can't leave you here alone."

"I won't be alone. Anna and Emmet are here."

"You shouldn't drive."

"Why not?"

"What if you have another attack while you're behind the wheel?"

"Oh. Then Emmet can drive me."

"What'll you do until you see the analyst?"

"Write a column," she said.

"We sent a packet to the syndicate last week. We're already twenty columns ahead of schedule."

Although she didn't feel well, she managed a light tone. "We're twenty ahead because you wrote fifteen of them. It's time I did my share. Being twenty-one ahead won't hurt."

"There's some material on my desk about that woman in North Carolina who can predict the sex of unborn babies just by touching the mother. They're studying her at Duke University."

"Then that's what I'll write about."

"Well, if you're positive . . ."

"I am. Now scoot over to Gucci, Giorgio's, The French Corner, Juel Park, Courrèges, Van Cleef and Arpels—and buy me beautiful things for Christmas."

Trying to keep from smiling, he said, "But I already have something picked out at Woolworth's."

"Oh," she said, playing along with him, "then you won't mind that I'm only getting you a gift certificate for some McDonald's hamburgers."

He pretended to be disappointed. "Well, I might stop at Gucci and Edwards Lowell for a few things that'll go with the Woolworth's piece."

She grinned. "You do that. Then maybe I'll let you sleep in here tonight instead of on the couch."

He laughed and kissed her.

"Mmmm," she said. "Again."

She knew that she was loved, and that knowledge compensated somewhat for the horror of the past few days.

# 8
◆ ◆ ◆

The focal point of Dr. Cauvel's office was a collection of hundreds of glass dogs that were displayed on glass and chrome shelves to one side of his desk. No member of the menagerie was larger than Mary's hand, and most were a great deal smaller than that. There were blue dogs, brown dogs, red dogs, clear dogs, milky white dogs, black dogs, orange and yellow and purple and green dogs, transparent and opaque, striped and polka-dotted, hand-blown and solid glass dogs. Some of them were lying down, some sitting, standing, pointing, running. There were basset hounds, greyhounds, airedales, German shepherds, Pekingese, terriers, Saint Bernards, and a dozen other breeds. A bitch with a litter of fragile glass puppies stood near a comic scene of dogs playing tiny glass instruments, flutes and drums and bugles for beagles. Several curious figures shone darkly in the silent zoo: snarling hellhounds, demons with dog faces and forked tongues.

Glass was also the focal point of the doctor himself. He wore thick spectacles that made his eyes appear abnormally large. He was short, athletic looking, and compulsively neat about himself. The spectacles were never smudged; he polished them continually.

Mary and the doctor sat across from each other at a folding table in the middle of the room.

The psychiatrist shuffled a deck of playing cards. He dealt ten of them face-down in a single row.

She picked up a six-inch loop of wire that he had provided and held it over the cards. She moved it back and forth. Twice it dipped toward the table as if invisible fingers were tugging it out of her hands. After less than a minute of dowsing, she put down the loop and indicated two of the ten cards. "These are the highest values in the batch."

"What are they?" Cauvel asked.

"One might be an ace."

"Of which suit?"

"I don't know."

He turned them over. An ace of clubs. A queen of hearts.

She relaxed.

He revealed the other cards. The highest value was a jack.

"Incredible," he said. "This is one of the most difficult tests we've tried. But out of ten attempts, you've been ninety percent accurate. Ever think of going to Las Vegas?"

"To break the bank at the twenty-one tables?"

"Why not?" he asked.

"The only way I'd have a chance is if they spread out the cards and let me use a wire loop on them before they dealt."

Like all his movements and expressions, his smile was economical. "Not likely."

For the past two years her Tuesday and Friday appointments had begun at four-thirty and ended at six o'clock. On these days she was Cauvel's final patient. During the first three quarters of an hour she participated in some experiments in extrasensory perception for a series of articles he intended to publish in a professional journal. He devoted the second forty-five minutes to treating her in his capacity as a psychiatrist. In return for her cooperation he waived his fee.

She could afford to pay for treatment. She permitted the current arrangement because the experiments interested her.

"Brandy?" he asked.

"Please."

He poured Remy Martin for both of them.

They moved from the card table to a pair of armchairs that faced each other across a small round cocktail table.

Cauvel used no standard technique with his patients. His style was very much his own. She liked his quiet, friendly approach.

"Where would you like to begin?" he asked.

"I don't know."

"Take your time."

"I don't want to begin at all."

"You always say that, and you always begin."

"Not today. I'd just like to sit here."

He nodded, sipped his brandy.

"Why am I always so difficult for you?" she asked.

"I can't answer that. *You* can."

"Why don't I want to talk to you?"

"Oh, you do want to talk. Otherwise you wouldn't be here."

Frowning, she said, "Help me start."

"What were you thinking about on your way here?"

"That's no place to start."

"Try it."

"Well . . . I was thinking about what I am."

"And what's that?"

"A clairvoyant."

"What about it?"

"Why me? Why not someone else?"

"The top researchers in this field believe we all have the same paranormal talents."

"Maybe," she said. "But most people don't have it to the extent that I do."

"We just don't recognize our potential," he said. "Only a handful of people have found a way to use their ESP."

"So why did *I* find a way?"

"Haven't all of the best clairvoyants suffered head injuries at some time prior to the discovery of their psychic powers?"

"Peter Hurkos did," she said. "And a number of others. But not all of us."

"Did you?"

"Suffer a head injury? No."

"Yes, you did."

She sipped her brandy. "What a wonderful taste."

"You were injured when you were six years old. You've mentioned it a few times, but you've never wanted to pursue it."

"And I don't want to pursue it now."

"You should," Cauvel said. "Your reluctance to discuss it is proof that—"

"You're talking too much today." Her voice was hard, too loud. "I pay you to listen."

"You don't pay me at all." As always, he spoke gently.

"I could walk out of here right now."

He took off his glasses and polished them with his handkerchief.

"Without me," she said sharply, disliking his studied calm, "you wouldn't have the data to write those articles that make you a big man among the other shrinks."

"The articles aren't that important. If you want so much to walk out, do it. Shall we terminate our arrangement?"

She sagged back into her chair. "Sorry." She seldom raised her voice. It wasn't like her to shout at him. She was blushing.

"No need to apologize," he said. "But don't you see that this experience twenty-four years ago might be the root of your problem? It could be the underlying cause of your insomnia, of your periodic deep depressions, of your anxiety attacks."

She felt weak. She closed her eyes. "You want me to pursue it."

"That would be a good idea."

"Help me start."

"You were six years old."

"Six . . ."

"Your father had money then."

"Quite a lot of it."

"You lived on a small estate."

"Twenty acres," she said. "Most of it landscaped. There was a full-time . . . a full-time . . ."

"Gardener."

"Gardener," she said. She wasn't blushing anymore. Her cheeks were cold. Her hands were icy.

"What was his name?"

"I don't remember."

"Of course you do."

"Berton Mitchell."

"Did you like him?"

"At first I did."

"You said once that he teased you."

"In a fun way. And he had a special name for me."

"What did he call you?"

"Contrary. As if that were my real name."

"*Were* you contrary?"

"Not the least bit. He was teasing. He got it from the nursery rhyme. 'Mary, Mary, quite contrary' . . ."

"When did you stop liking Berton Mitchell?"

She wanted to be home with Max. She could almost feel his arms around her.

"When did you stop liking him, Mary?"

"That day in August."

"What happened?"

"You know."

"Yes, I do know."

"Well then."

"But we never seem to get further into this thing unless we start from the top each time."

"I don't *want* to get further into it."

But he was relentless. "What happened that day in August when you were six years old?"

"Have you gotten any new glass dogs recently?"

"What did Berton Mitchell do that day in August?"

"He tried to rape me."


Six P.M. Early winter night. The air was cool and fresh.

He left the car at the coffee shop and walked north along the highway, his back to the traffic.

He had a knife in one pocket, a revolver in the other. He kept his hands on both weapons.

His shoes crunched in the gravel.

The wind from the passing cars buffeted him, mussed his hair, pasted his overcoat to his legs.

The beauty shop, Hair Today, occupied a small detached building on Main Street, just north of the Santa Ana city limits. With its imitation thatched roof, leaded windows, plaster and exposed-beam exterior, the place resembled a cottage in the English countryside—except for the floodlights shining on the front of it, and except for the pink and green paint job.

The block was strictly commercial. Service stations, fast-food restaurants, real estate offices, dozens of small businesses, all of them nestled in neon and palm trees and jade-plant hedges, flourished like ugly flowers in the money-scented Orange County air. South of Hair Today was the sales lot of an imported automobile dealership. Row after row of sleek machines huddled in the night. Only the windshields and chrome gleamed malevolently under mercury-vapor lights. North, beyond the beauty shop, lay a three-screen motion picture theater, and beyond that a shopping center.

A dirty white Cadillac and a shiny Triumph stood on the macadam parking area in front of Hair Today.

He crossed the lot, walked between the cars, opened the cottage door, and went inside.

The narrow front room was a lounge where women marked time until their appointments. The carpet was purple and plush, the chairs bright yellow, the drapes white. There were end tables, ashtrays, and stacks of magazines, but at this late hour there were no customers waiting.

At the rear of the room was a purple and white counter. A cash register rested on it, and a woman with bleached blonde hair sat on a stool behind it.

In back of the woman a curtained archway led to the working part of the shop. The sound of a hand-held hair dryer penetrated the curtain like the buzz of angry bees.

"We're closed," the bleached blonde said.

He went to the counter.

"Are you looking for someone?" she said.

He took the revolver out of his pocket. It felt good in his hand. It felt like justice.

She stared at the gun, then into his eyes. She licked her lips. "What do you want?"

He didn't speak.

She said, "Now wait."

He pulled the trigger. The sound was masked somewhat by the noisy dryer.

She fell off the stool and didn't get up.

The hair dryer shut off. From the back room someone said, "Tina?"

He walked around the dead woman, parted the curtains and stepped through them.

Of the four salon chairs, three were empty. The last customer of the day sat in the fourth chair. She was young and pretty, with an impossibly creamy complexion. Her hair was straight and wet.

The hairdresser was a burly man, bald, with a bristling black mustache. He wore a purple uniform shirt with his first name, Kyle, embroidered in yellow on the breast pocket.

The woman drew a deep breath, but she couldn't find the courage to scream.

"Who are you?" Kyle asked.

He shot Kyle twice.


"My father wasn't at home that day," Mary said.

"And your mother?"

"She was up at the main house. Drunk as usual."

"And your brother?"

"Alan was in his room, working on his model airplanes."

"The gardener, Berton Mitchell?"

"His wife and son were away for the week. Mitchell . . . got me into his place, enticed me into it."

"Where was this?"

"Down at the far end of the estate, a little cottage with a green shingle roof. He often told me that elves lived with his family."

An awesome force pressed against her from all sides. She felt as if she was enfolded by leather wings, muscular wings that were draining the heat from her, squeezing the life out of her.

"Go on," Cauvel said.

Relentlessly the warmth dropped out of her like mercury falling in a thermometer. She was a cold, hollow reed of glass, brittle, breakable. "More brandy?"

"When you've finished telling me," Cauvel said.

"I need help with this."

"I'm here to help you, Mary."

"If I tell, he'll hurt me."

"Who? Mitchell? You don't believe that. You know he's dead. He was found guilty of child molestation, of assault with intent to kill. He hung himself in his cell. I'm the only one here, and I won't let anyone hurt you."

"I was alone with him."

"You're speaking so softly I can't hear you."

"I was alone with him," she said again. "He . . . touched . . . me . . . exposed himself."

"Were you frightened?"

"Yes."

The pressure was intense, unbearable, and getting worse.

Cauvel didn't speak, and she said, "I was frightened because he wanted me . . . to do things."

"What things?"

The air was foul. Although only she and the doctor were in the room, she felt that some creature had its lips to hers and was forcing its rank breath into her lungs.

"I need brandy," she said.

"What you need is to tell me all of this, to remember every last detail, to get it out in the open once and for all. What things did he want you to do?"

"Help me. You've got to guide me."

"He wanted to have intercourse, didn't he?"

"I'm not sure."

Her hands were numb. She could feel cords biting into them. But there were no cords.

"Oral intercourse?" Cauvel asked.

"But not only that."

Her ankles were sore. She could feel cords that were not there. She moved her feet. They were leaden.

"What else did he want to do?" Cauvel asked.

"I don't recall."

"You can remember if you want to."

"No. Honestly, I can't. I can't."

"What else did he want you to do?"

The embrace of the imaginary wings was so tight that she had difficulty breathing. She could hear them beating the air—*wicka-wicka-wicka* . . .

She stood up, walked away from the chair.

The wings held her.

"What else did he want you to do?" Cauvel asked.

"Something awful, unspeakable."

"A sex act of some sort?"

*Wicka-wicka-wicka* . . .

"Not just sex. More than that," she said.

"What was it?"

"Dirty. Filthy."

"In what way?"

"Eyes watching me."

"Mitchell's eyes?"

"Not his."

"Who then?"

"I can't remember."

"You can."

*Wicka-wicka* . . .

"Wings," she said.

"Rings? You're speaking too softly again?"

"Wings," she said. "Wings."

"What do you mean?"

She was shaking, vibrating. She was afraid her legs would fail her. She returned to the armchair. "Wings. I can hear them flapping. I can *feel* them."

"You mean Mitchell kept a bird in the house?"

"I don't know."

"A parrot perhaps?"

"I couldn't say."

"Work at remembering it, Mary. Don't let go of this thought. You've never mentioned wings before. It's important."

"They were everywhere."

"The wings?"

"All over me. Little wings."

"Think. What did he do to you?"

She was silent a long while. The pressure began to ease a bit. The sound of wings faded.

"Mary?"

Finally she said, "That's all. I can't recall anything else."

"There is a way to unlock those memories," he said.

"Hypnosis," she replied.

"It works."

"I'm afraid to remember."

"You should be afraid *not* to remember."

"If I remember, I'll die."

"That's ridiculous, and you know it."

She pushed her hair back from her face. For his benefit, she forced a smile. "I don't hear the wings now. I can't feel them. We don't need to talk about wings anymore."

"Of course we do."

"I *won't* talk about wings, dammit!" She shook her head violently. She was surprised and frightened by her own vehemence. "Not today anyway."

"All right," Cauvel said. "I'll accept that. That's not the same thing as saying you don't *need* to talk." He began to polish his glasses once more. "Let's go back to what you remember. Berton Mitchell beat you."

"I suppose he did."

"You were found in his place?"

"In his living room."

"And you were badly beaten?"

"Yes."

"And later you told them he did it."

"But I can't remember it happening. I recall the pain, terrible pain. But only for an instant."

"You could have lost consciousness with the first blow."

"That's what everyone said. He must have kept hitting me after I passed out. I couldn't have stood up to him for long. I was just a little girl."

"He used a knife, too?"

"I was cut all over."

"How long were you in the hospital?"

"More than two weeks."

"How many stitches for the wounds?"

"More than a hundred altogether."

The beauty shop smelled of shampoo, cream rinse, and cologne. He could also smell the woman's sweat.

The floor was littered with hair. It swirled around them as he moved onto her and into her.

She refused to respond to him. She neither welcomed him nor struggled against him. She lay still. Her eyes were like the eyes of the dead.

He didn't hate her for that. In the long run he'd never cared for passion in his women. For the first few months a new lover's aggression and delight in sex was tolerable. He could be tender for a short time.

But always, after a few months, he needed to see fear in them. That was what brought him to climax. The more they feared him, the better he liked them.

As he lay on her, he could feel this woman's heart thumping wildly, accelerated by terror. That excited him, and he began to move faster within her.

"You took a number of Mitchell's blows on your head," Cauvel said.

"My face was black and blue. My father called me his little patchwork doll."

"Did you suffer a concussion?"

"I see where all of this is leading," she said. "But no. No concussion. Absolutely not."

"When did your visions begin?"

"Later the same year."

"A few minutes ago you asked me why you'd been singled out to be a clairvoyant. Well, there's nothing mysterious about it really. As in the case of Peter Hurkos, your psychic talent came after a serious head injury."

"Not serious enough."

He stopped polishing his spectacles, put them on, and studied her with huge, magnified eyes. "Is it possible that a severe psychological shock could trigger psychic abilities in the same way that certain head injuries seem to do?"

She shrugged.

"If you didn't acquire your power as a result of a physical trauma, then maybe you acquired it because of a *psychological* trauma. Do you suppose that's possible?"

"It could be," she said.

"Either way," he said, thrusting a bony finger at her, as if repeatedly tapping a window between them, "either way, your clairvoyance probably goes back to Berton Mitchell, to what he did to you that you can't remember."

"Maybe."

"And your insomnia goes back to Berton Mitchell. Your periodic depressions go back to him. What he did to you is the underlying cause of your anxiety attacks. I tell you, Mary, the sooner you face up to this, the better. If you ever let me use hypnosis to regress you and guide you through the memories, then you'll never need my help again."

"I'll always need your help."

He scowled. His deeply tanned face was scored by lines like saber slashes. An ambitious portrait painter would have wanted to catch him with that expression, for it made him look fierce, yet fair and reliable. It was that expression that drew her to him at a party three years ago; and his distant but paternal manner caused her to seek his advice when her dependency on sleeping pills became absolute.

"If you'll always need my help," he said, "then I'm not helping you at all. As a psychiatrist, I must make you find all the strength you need inside yourself."

She went to the bar and picked up the decanter of brandy. "You said I could have another if I kept talking a while."

"I never break a promise." He joined her at the bar. "The day's nearly over. I'll have another, too."

As she poured for them, she said, "You're wrong about Mitchell."

"In what sense?"

"I don't think all of my problems date back to him. Some of them started the day my father died."

"I've heard you expound on that theory before."

"I was in the car with him when he was killed. I was in the back seat and he was driving. I saw him die. His blood sprayed all over me. I was only nine. And the years after he died weren't easy. In three years my mother lost all the money my father left us. We went from rich to poor between my ninth and twelfth birthdays. I think an experience like that would leave some scars, don't you?"

"It has," he said. He picked up his brandy glass. "But it's not responsible for the *worst* scars."

"How do you know?"

"You're able to talk about it."

"So?"

"But you aren't able to talk about what happened with Berton Mitchell."

When he finished with the woman, he stood, pulled up his pants, zipped his fly. He hadn't even taken off his coat.

He stepped back from her, looked at her.

Given the opportunity, she made no effort to cover herself. Her skirt was bunched around her hips. Her blouse was unbuttoned; one plump breast was visible. Her hands were fisted. Her fingernails had gouged her palms, and ribbons of blood were on her hands. Terrorized, reduced to little more than a cowering animal, she represented his ideal woman.

He took the knife out of his coat pocket.

He expected her to scream and scramble away from him, but as he moved in for the kill, she lay as if she were dead already. She was past fear now, past feeling anything.

Kneeling beside her, he placed the point of the blade at her throat. The flesh dimpled around it, but she didn't blink.

He raised the blade high, held it in her line of sight, over her breasts. No response.

He was disappointed. When time and circumstance allowed, he preferred to kill slowly. To get any thrill from that game, he required a lively woman for prey.

Angry with her for spoiling the moment, he rammed the knife down.

Mary Bergen gasped.

*The razor edge ripping her skin, opening muscle, opening the reservoir of blood, opening the dark place where pain was stored . . .*

She leaned into the corner formed by the wall and the side of the antique oak bar. She was only half aware that she knocked over an unopened bottle of Scotch.

"What's the matter?" Cauvel asked.

"It hurts."

He touched her shoulder. "Are you sick? Can I help?"

"Not sick. The vision. I feel it."

*The knife again, thrust deep . . .*

She put both hands to her stomach, trying to contain the eruption of pain. "I won't faint this time. I won't!"

"A vision of what?" Cauvel asked worriedly.

"The beauty shop. The same one I saw a few hours ago. Only it's happening now. The slaughter . . . God almighty . . . happening somewhere, happening right this minute." She put her hands to her face, but the images would not be shut out. "Oh, God. Sweet God. Help me."

"What do you see?"

"A dead man on the floor."

"The floor of the beauty shop?"

"He's bald . . . mustache . . . purple shirt."

"What is it you're feeling?"

*The knife . . .*

She was sweating. Crying.

"Mary? *Mary?*"

"I feel . . . the woman . . . being stabbed."

"What woman? There's a woman?"

"Mustn't black out."

She started to sag, and he held her by both shoulders.

She saw the knife gouging flesh again, but she felt no pain this time. The woman in the vision was dead; therefore, there was no more pain to share.

"Have to see his face, have to get his name," she said.

*The killer standing up from the body, standing in a cape, no, a long coat, an overcoat . . .*

"Can't lose the thread. Mustn't lose the vision. Have to hold it, have to find where he is, who he is, *what* he is, stop him from doing these awful things."

*The killer standing, standing with the butcher knife in one hand, standing in shadow, his face in shadow but turning now, turning very slowly and deliberately, turning so that she'll be able to see his face, turning as if he is looking for her—*

"He knows I'm with him," she said.

"Who knows?"

"He knows I'm watching."

She didn't understand how that could be true. Yet the killer knew about her. She was certain of that, and she was scared.

Suddenly half a dozen glass dogs leaped from the display shelves, flew through the air, and smashed with a great deal of force into the wall beside Mary.

She screamed.

Cauvel turned to see who had thrown them. "What the hell?"

As if they had come to life and had acquired wings, a dozen glass dogs swept off the top shelf. They spun, glittering like fragments of an exploded prism, to the high center of the room. They bounced off the ceiling, struck one another with the musical rattle of Chinese wind chimes.

Then they streaked toward Mary.

She raised her arms, covered her face.

The miniatures battered her harder than she had expected. They stung like bees.

"Stop them!" she said, not certain to whom she was speaking.

A hellhound with pointy horns struck the doctor in the forehead between the eyes and drew blood.

Cauvel turned away from the shelves, moved against her, tried to shield her with his body.

Another ten or fifteen dogs bulleted around the room. Two of them smashed through a stained glass panel in the bar. Others burst to pieces on the wall around Mary, icing her hair with chunks and slivers of colored glass.

"It's trying to kill me!" She was struggling unsuccessfully to avoid hysteria.

Cauvel pressed her into the corner.

More glass dogs whistled across the room, swooped over the psychiatrist's desk, scattered a sheaf of onionskin papers. The figurines clattered against the venetian blinds without shattering, rose up again, zigzagged crazily from one end of the chamber to the other, then pelted Cauvel's shoulders and back, rained fragments over Mary's bowed head.

Yet another squadron of dogs took flight. They danced in the air, swarmed ominously, fluttered against Mary, flew away, came back with greater determination, struck her with incredible force, stung, bruised, hung over her like locusts.

As suddenly as the macabre assault began, it ended. Almost a hundred glass miniatures remained on the display shelves, but they did not move.

Mary and Cauvel huddled together, not trusting the calm, waiting for another attack.

Silence prevailed.

Eventually he let go of her and stepped back.

She was unable to control the tremors that broke like waves within her.

"Are you all right?" he asked, oblivious to the blood on his own face.

"I wasn't meant to see him," she said.

Cauvel was dazed. He stared, uncomprehendingly.

"His face," she said. "I wasn't meant to see it."

"What are you talking about?"

"When I tried to see the killer in the vision," she said, "I was stopped. What stopped me?"

Cauvel gazed at the shards of glass on all sides of them. He began to pick splinters of glass from the shoulders and sleeves of his suit jacket. "Did you do this? Did you make the dogs fly?"

"Me?"

"Who else?"

"Oh, no. How could I?"

"Someone did."

"Some*thing.*"

He stared at her.

"It was a . . . spirit," she said.

"I don't believe in life after death."

"I wasn't sure about that myself. Until now."

"So we're haunted?"

"What else?"

"Many possibilities." He looked concerned about her.

"I'm not crazy," she said.

"Did I say you were?"

"We've seen a poltergeist in action."

"I don't believe in them either," he said.

"I do. I've seen them work before. I was never sure if they were spirits or not. But now I am."

"Mary—"

"A poltergeist. It came to stop me from seeing the killer's face."

Behind them the display shelves toppled and struck the floor with a thunderous crash.

# 9
◆ ◆ ◆

Max was not at home.

Without him Mary felt that the house was a mausoleum. Her footsteps on the hardwood floor seemed louder than usual, the echoes full of sinister voices.

"He called earlier," Anna Churchill said, as she wiped her hands on her apron. "He asked me to delay dinner half an hour."

"Why?"

"He said to tell you he wouldn't be back until eight o'clock because Woolworth's is open late for Christmas shopping."

She knew that Max had meant to make her laugh with that message, but she couldn't even smile. The only thing that would lift her spirits was the sight of him. She didn't want to be alone.

As she went through the parlor on her way to the mahogany staircase, she felt dwarfed by the heavy European furniture. With the memory of the poltergeist fresh in her mind, she expected each piece of furniture to come to life, and she didn't know how she would survive if the chairs and sofas and corner cabinets began to rush at her with murderous intent.

The furniture did not move.

Upstairs, in her bathroom, she took a bottle of valium from the medicine cabinet. She had been able to conceal her nervousness when she was with Emmet and Anna; but now her hands shook so badly that she needed almost a minute to get the safety cap off the container. She poured a glass of cold water, swallowed one of the capsules. One didn't seem like much. She felt she could use two. Maybe three. "God, no," she said, and she quickly replaced the cap before temptation got the better of good judgment.

As she was leaving the bathroom, the empty water glass fell to the floor, shattered. Startled, she whirled around. She was sure she hadn't set the tumbler on the edge of the sink. It had not fallen: something had knocked it off.

"Max, please come home," she said softly.

She waited for him in the second-floor den, his favorite room, a room crammed full of guns and books. Antique rifles expertly restored and mounted in wall display boxes. Matched sets of Hemingway, Stevenson, Poe, Shaw, Fitzgerald, Dickens. A pair of 1872 No. 3 Colt Derringers in a silk-lined, brass-bound carrying case. Novels by John D. MacDonald, Clavell, Bellow, Woolrich, Levin, Vidal; volumes of nonfiction by Gay Talese, Colin Wilson, Hellman, Toland, Shirer. Shotguns, rifles, revolvers, automatic pistols. Raymond Chandler, Dashiell Hammett, Ross MacDonald, Mary McCarthy, James M. Cain, Jessamyn West.

Guns and books were an odd combination, Mary thought. However, next to her, they were the two things that Max liked most.

She tried to read a current bestseller that she had been meaning to begin for weeks, but her mind wandered. She put the book aside, went to Max's desk, sat down. She took a pen and a writing tablet from the center drawer.

For a while she stared at the blank page. Finally she wrote:

*Page 1*
*Questions:*
*Why am I having these visions when I don't seek them out?*
*Why, suddenly, for the first time, am I able to feel the pain that the victims in the visions feel?*
*Why hasn't any other clairvoyant ever felt his visions?*
*How could the killer in the beauty shop possibly know I was watching?*
*Why would a poltergeist attempt to keep me from seeing this killer's face?*
*What does all of this mean?*

Ever since she was a child, through major and minor crises, she had felt that it helped to write down her problems. When they were before her, summarized in a few words, somehow more concrete in ink than in reality, they usually ceased to appear insoluble.

After she finished composing the list, she read each question carefully, first silently and then aloud.

On the next page of the tablet she wrote: *Answers.*

She thought for a few minutes. Then: *I don't have any answers.*

"Dammit!" she said.

She threw the pen across the room.


"Harley Barnes speaking."

"Chief Barnes, this is Mary Bergen."

"Why, hello. Are you still in town?"

"No. I'm calling from Bel Air."

"What can I do for you?"

"I'm writing a column about what happened last night, and I had some questions. The man we caught last night . . . what was his name?"

"Can't you get it with your clairvoyance?"

"I'm afraid not. I can't see everything I want."

"Name's Richard Lingard."

"A resident of your town, or an outsider?"

"Born and raised here. I knew his dad and mom. He owned a pharmacy."

"His age?"

"Early thirties, thereabouts."

"Is he . . . was he married?"

"Divorced years ago. No children, thank God."

"Are you sure . . ."

"Sure there aren't children? Oh, yes. Positive."

"No. I meant . . . is he . . . really dead?"

"Dead? Of course he's dead. Didn't you see him?"

"I just thought . . . Have you found anything unusual about him?"

"Unusual? In what way?"

"Did his neighbors think he was odd in any way?"

"They liked him. Everyone liked him."

"Was anything strange found in his home?"

"Nothing. He lived like anyone else. It's frightening how ordinary he was. If Dick Lingard could turn out to be a psychopathic killer, then who can you trust?"

"No one."

"Mrs. Bergen . . ." Barnes hesitated. "Did you take the knife?"

"What knife?"

"Lingard's knife."

"You can't find it?"

"It vanished from the scene."

"Vanished? Does that happen often?"

"Never before to me."

"I don't have it."

"Perhaps your brother picked it up."

"Alan wouldn't do that."

"Or your husband?"

"We've worked with the police many times, Chief. We know enough not to make souvenirs out of the evidence."

"We've searched Mrs. Harrington's place from top to bottom. The knife isn't there."

"Maybe Lingard dropped it on the front lawn."

"We've gone over every inch of that, too."

"He might have dropped it in the gutter when he collapsed against your squad car."

"Or on the sidewalk. We didn't search for the knife immediately, like we should have done, and there was a large crowd of spectators. Maybe one of them picked it up. We'll ask around. I imagine we'll come across the thing. At least we don't need it for any trial. Death solved that problem. There's no way a smart attorney can get Richard Lingard out on the streets again."

At seven-thirty the all-news radio station in Los Angeles carried a story about four young nurses who had been found beaten and stabbed to death in their Anaheim apartment.

Beverly Pulchaski.

Susan Haven.

Linda Proctor.

Marie Sanzini.

Mary didn't recognize even one of them.

Perplexed, she sat back from the edge of her chair. She recalled the battered face in last night's vision: the black-haired, blue-eyed woman. She was *certain* she knew that face.

8:00 P.M.

She met Max at the front door. When he came inside and closed the door, he put his arms around her. His clothes were cold, crisp with the night air, but the warmth of his body pressed through the fabric.

"Six hours of shopping," she said, "and no packages?"

"I left them to be gift-wrapped. I'll pick them up tomorrow."

Grinning, she said, "I didn't know Woolworth's did gift-wrapping."

He kissed her cheek. "Missed you."

She leaned back in his arms. "Hey, where's your overcoat? You'll catch the flu."

"It got splashed with mud," he said. "I dropped it off at the dry cleaner's."

"How'd it get muddy?"

"I had a flat tire."

"A Mercedes *wouldn't*."

"Ours did. The spot where I had to change it was muddy. I got splashed by a passing car."

"Did you get his license number? If you did, I'll—"

"Unfortunately I didn't," Max said. "At the time it happened I thought, 'If I could get the bastard's number, Mary would find out who he is and thrash him within an inch of his life.' "

"Nobody hurts my Max and gets away with it."

"I also cut my finger changing the tire," he said, holding up his right hand. The cuff of the shirt sleeve was soaked with blood, and one finger was bound in a bloody handkerchief. "There's a sharp metal edge on the jack," he said.

She took hold of his wrist. "So much blood! Let's see the cut."

"It's nothing." He pulled his hand away before she could remove the handkerchief. "It's stopped bleeding."

"Maybe it needs stitches."

"It needs pressure, that's all. It's a deep cut, but the area's too small to take stitches. And the sight will ruin your dinner."

"Let me look. I'm a big girl now. Besides, it has to be properly cleaned and bandaged."

"I'll take care of that," he said. "You go ahead to the table. I'll join you in a few minutes."

"You can't handle it yourself."

"Of course I can. I wasn't always married, you know. I lived alone for years." He kissed her forehead. "Let's not upset Mrs. Churchill. If we don't get to the table soon, she'll be in tears."

With his good hand he pushed Mary toward the dining room.

"If you bleed to death," she said, "I'll never forgive you."

Laughing, he hurried to the staircase and climbed the steps two at a time to the second floor.

Dinner was to Mary's taste, hearty yet not heavy. They had onion soup, salad, châteaubriand with bearnaise sauce, and strips of zucchini marinated in oil and garlic, then broiled briefly.

Over coffee in the library, drifting on a pool of serenity formed by a second valium taken just before Max arrived for dinner, she told him about her day: Cauvel, the pain-filled vision, the poltergeist that had kept her from probing the vision for the name and face of the killer. They discussed the radio report of the dead nurses in Anaheim, which he had also heard, and last of all she told him about her conversation with Harley Barnes.

"You're emphasizing the missing knife," Max said. "Isn't Barnes' explanation credible enough? A spectator *could* have taken it."

"Could have—but didn't."

"Then who did?"

She was beside him on the sofa. She kicked off her shoes, drew one leg under her, delaying until she could summon the right words. This was a delicate situation. If Max was unable to believe what she had to tell him, he would think her at least *slightly* mad.

"These visions are totally different from any I've ever known," she said at last. "Which means the killer, the source of the psychic emanations, is different from any killer I've ever tracked before. He isn't an ordinary man. I've been trying to find a theory that will make sense of what's happened to me since last night, and when I talked with Barnes I found the key. The missing knife is the key. Don't you see? Richard Lingard has the knife."

"Lingard? He's dead. Barnes shot him. Lingard couldn't have taken his knife anywhere but to a drawer in the morgue."

"He could have taken it wherever he wanted. Barnes killed Lingard's body. Lingard's spirit took the knife."

Max was amazed. "I don't believe in ghosts. And even if spirits *do* exist, they don't have substance, at least not as we think of it. So how could Lingard's spirit, a thing of no substance, carry off a very substantial knife?"

"A spirit has no substance, but it does have *power*," she said emphatically. "Two months ago, when you helped me cover that story in Connecticut, you saw a poltergeist in action."

"What of it?"

"Well, a poltergeist has no apparent substance, yet it tosses around solid objects, doesn't it?"

Reluctantly he said, "Yes. But I don't believe a poltergeist is the spirit of a dead person."

"What else could it be?" Before he responded she said, "Lingard's spirit carried away the butcher knife. I *know* it."

He drank his coffee in three long swallows. "Suppose that's true. Where's his spirit now?"

"In possession of someone living."

"*What?*"

"As soon as Lingard's body died, his spirit slipped out of it and into someone else."

Max got up, walked to the bookshelves. He looked at Mary with eyes that studied, weighed, and judged. "In every session with

Cauvel, you've come closer to remembering what Berton Mitchell did to you.''

"So you think that because I'm on the verge of knowing, I might be seeking escape from the truth, escape in madness.''

*"Can* you face up to what he did?''

"I've lived with it for years, even if I have suppressed it.''

"Living with it and accepting it are two different things.''

"If you think I'm a candidate for a padded room, you don't know me,'' she said, irritated in spite of the valium.

"I don't think that. But demonic possession?''

"Not demonic. I'm talking about something less grand than that. This is the possession of a living person by the spirit of someone dead.''

His square, almost ugly face was creased with worry. He spread his arms, his hands, palms up, a supplicant bear. "And who is this living person?''

"The man who killed those nurses in Anaheim. He's possessed by Lingard, and that's why the psychic emanations he puts out are so different.''

Max returned to the sofa. "I can't accept it.''

"That doesn't mean I'm wrong.''

"The poltergeist phenomena in Cauvel's office . . . You think—''

"That was Lingard,'' she said.

"There's a problem with that theory,'' he said.

She raised her eyebrows.

"How could Lingard's spirit be in two places at once?'' he asked. "How could Lingard be in possession of a man who he's forcing to commit murder—and at the same time be throwing glass dogs around Cauvel's office?''

"I don't know. Who's to say what a ghost can do?''

At ten o'clock, Max came to the master bedroom. He had gone downstairs to the library for a novel and had returned carrying a thick volume—not the book he'd been after. "I talked to Dr. Cauvel just now,'' he said.

Mary was sitting up in bed. She used a flap of the dust jacket to mark her place in the book she was reading. "What did the good doctor have to say?''

"He thinks *you* are the poltergeist.''

"Me?''

"He says you were under stress—''

"Aren't we all?''

"Especially you.''

"Was I?"

"Because you remembered about Berton Mitchell."

"I've remembered about him before."

"This time you recalled more than ever. Cauvel says you were under great psychological stress in his office, and that *you* caused the glass dogs to fly about."

She smiled. "A man your size looks just too cute in pajamas."

"Mary—"

"Especially yellow pajamas. You should wear just a robe."

"You're avoiding this." He came to the foot of the bed. "What about the glass dogs?"

"Cauvel just wants me to pay for them," she said airily.

"He didn't mention money."

"That's what he was angling for."

"He's not the type," Max said.

"I'll pay half the value of the dogs."

Exasperated, Max said, "Mary, that's not necessary."

"I know," she said lightly. "I didn't break them."

"I mean, Cauvel isn't asking to be paid. You're trying to avoid the main issue."

"Okay, okay. So *how* did I cause glass dogs to fly about?"

"Unconsciously. Cauvel says—"

"Psychiatrists always blame the unconscious."

"Who's to say they're wrong?"

"They're stupid."

"Mary—"

"And you're stupid for believing Cauvel."

She didn't want to argue, but she couldn't control herself. She was frightened by the direction the conversation was taking, although she didn't know why she should be. She was terrified of some knowledge that lay within her, but she couldn't understand what that might be.

Standing like a preacher, holding his book as if it were a Bible, Max said, "Will you listen?"

She shook her head to indicate she found him too irritating to bear. "If I'm responsible for his figurines getting busted up, am I also to blame for the bad weather in the East, for the war in Africa, for inflation, for poverty, for the recent crop failures?"

"Sarcasm."

"You encourage it."

The tranquilizer was doing her no good whatsoever. She was tense. Trembling. Like a shallow-water, feathery sea anemone quivering in the subtle currents that preceded a storm, she was nervously aware of unseen forces that could destroy her.

Suddenly she felt threatened by Max.

That doesn't make sense, she thought. Max isn't any danger to me. He's trying to help me find the truth, that's all.

Dizzy, confused, on the verge of anomie, she leaned back against her pillows.

Max opened his book and read in a quiet but urgent voice: " '*Telekinesis* is the ability to move objects or to cause changes within objects solely by the force of the mind. The phenomenon has most often and most reliably been reported in times of crises or in severe stress situations. For example, automobiles have been levitated from injured people, debris from the dying in fire-swept or collapsed buildings.' "

"I *know* what telekinesis is," she said.

Max ignored her, kept reading: " 'Telekinesis is often mistaken for the work of poltergeists, which are playful and occasionally malevolent spirits. The existence of poltergeists as astral beings is debatable and certainly unproven. It should be noted that in most houses where poltergeists have appeared, there resides an adolescent with serious identity problems, *or some other person under severe nervous strain.* A good argument could be made that the phenomena often attributed to poltergeists are usually the product of unconscious telekinesis.' "

"This is ridiculous," she said. "Why would I pitch those dogs around just when I was about to see the killer's face in the vision?"

"You really didn't want to see his face, so your subconscious threw those figurines to distract you from the vision."

"That's absurd! I *wanted* to see it. I want to stop this man before he kills again."

Max's hard gray eyes were like knives, dissecting her. "Are you sure you want to stop him?"

"What kind of question is that?"

He sighed. "Do you know what I think? I think you've sensed, through your clairvoyance, that this psychopath will kill you if you pursue him. You've seen a possible future, and you're trying like hell to avoid it."

Surprised, she said, "Nothing of the sort."

"The pain you felt—"

"Was the pain of the victims. It wasn't a foreshadowing of my own death."

"Maybe you haven't foreseen the danger consciously," Max said. "But subconsciously, perhaps, you've seen yourself as a victim if you pursue this case. That would explain why you're trying to mislead yourself with poltergeists and with talk about possession."

"I'm not going to die," she said sharply. "I'm not hiding from anything like that."

"Why are you afraid to even consider it?"

"I'm not afraid."

"I think you are."

"I'm not a coward. And I'm not a liar."

"Mary, I'm trying to help you."

"Then believe me!"

He looked at her quizzically. "You don't have to shout."

"You never hear me unless I shout!"

"Mary, why do you want to argue?"

I don't, she thought. Stop me. Hold me.

"*You* started this," she said.

"I only asked you to consider an alternative to this business about possession. You're overreacting."

I know, she thought. I know I am. And I don't know why. I don't want to hurt you. I need you.

But all she said was, "Listening to you, I'd think I was never right about anything. I'm always overreacting or mistaken or misled or confused. You treat me as if I'm a child."

"You're treating *yourself* with condescension."

"Just a silly little child."

Hug me, kiss me, love me, she thought. Please make me stop this. I don't want to argue. I'm scared.

He started toward the bedroom door. "This isn't the time to talk. You're not in the mood for constructive criticism."

"Because I'm behaving like a child?"

"Yes."

"Sometimes you fucking piss me off."

He stopped, turned back to her. "That's like a child," he said calmly. "Like a child who's trying to shock a grownup with a lot of dirty words."

She opened her book to the page she had marked and, refusing to acknowledge him, she pretended to read.

She would rather have suffered disabling pain than even temporary estrangement from Max. When they argued, which was rarely, she felt miserable. The two or three hours of silence that invariably followed a disagreement, and which were usually her fault, were unbearable.

She spent the remainder of the evening in bed with a copy of *The Occult* by Colin Wilson. As she began each page, she could not remember what had been on the page before it.

Max stayed on his side of the bed, reading a novel and smoking his pipe. He might as well have been a thousand miles away.

The eleven o'clock television news, which she switched on by remote control, headlined a grisly story about slaughter in a Santa Ana beauty salon. There was film of the blood-smeared shop and interviews with police officials who had nothing to say.

"You see?" Mary said. "I was right about the nurses. I was right about the beauty salon. And, by God, I'm right about Richard Lingard, too."

Even as she spoke, she regretted the words, and especially her tone of voice.

He looked at her but said nothing.

She looked away, down at her book. She hadn't meant to revive the argument. Quite the opposite. She wanted to get him talking once more. She wanted to hear his voice.

Although she often started arguments, she had never been able to initiate the conclusion of one. Psychologically, she wasn't capable of making the first gesture for peace. She left that move to the men. Always. She knew that wasn't fair, but she could not change.

She supposed that this inadequacy dated back to her father's violent death. He had left her so suddenly that she still sometimes felt abandoned. All of her adult life she had worried about men walking out on her before *she* was prepared to end the relationship.

And of course she wasn't ever going to be ready to end her marriage; that was for keeps. Therefore, whenever she and Max argued, whenever she had reason to worry about his leaving, she forced him to pick up the olive branch. It was a test which he could pass only if he would sacrifice more pride than she; and when he had done that, he would have proved that he loved her and that he would never leave her as her father had done.

The death of her father *was* more important than whatever Berton Mitchell had done to her.

Why couldn't Dr. Cauvel see that?

In the dark bedroom, when it became evident that neither of them could sleep, Max touched her. His hands affected her in the same way that the rapidly vibrating tines of a tuning fork would affect fine crystal. She trembled uncontrollably and shattered. She broke against him, weeping.

He didn't speak. Words no longer mattered.

He held her for a few minutes, and then he began to stroke her. He slid one hand over her silk pajamas, along her flank, across her buttocks. Slow, warm movement. And then he popped open two buttons on her blouse, slipped his hand inside, felt her warm breast, his fingers lingering on her nipple only for an instant. She put her open mouth to his neck, against the hard muscle. His strong pulse was transmitted to her through her tender lips. He undressed her and then himself. The bandage on his hand brushed her bare thigh.

"Your finger," she said.

"It'll be fine."

"The cut might come open," she said. "It might start to bleed again."

"*Sshhh,*" he said.

He was not in the mood to be patient, and although she hadn't said a word, he sensed she was equally anxious. He rose above her in the lightless air, as if taking flight, then settled over her. Although she had expected nothing more than the special joy of closeness, she climaxed within a minute. Not intensely. A gentle rush of pleasure. However, when she came a second time, moments before he finished far down inside of her, she cried out with delight.

For a while she lay at his side, holding his hand. Finally she said, "Don't ever leave me. Stay with me as long as I live."

"As long as you live," Max promised.


At five-thirty on Wednesday morning, in the middle of a nightmare vision of the killer's next crime, Mary was catapulted from sleep by the sound of gunfire. A single shot, ear-splitting, too close. Even as the *boom* was bouncing off the bedroom walls, she sat up, threw off the blanket and sheet, swung her legs out of bed. "Max! What's wrong? Max!"

Beside her, he switched on the lamp, jumped up from the bed. He stood, swaying, blinking.

The sudden light hurt her eyes. Although she was squinting, she could see there was no intruder in the room.

Max reached for the loaded handgun that he kept on the nightstand. It was not there.

"Where's the pistol?" he asked.

"I didn't touch it," she said.

Then, as her eyes adjusted to the light, she saw the gun. It was floating in the air near the foot of the bed, floating five feet above the floor, as if it were suspended from wires, except that there were no wires. The barrel was pointed at her.

The poltergeist.

"Jesus!" Max said.

Although no visible finger pulled the trigger, a second shot exploded. The bullet tore into the headboard inches from Mary's face.

She panicked. Gasping, whimpering, she ran across the room, hunched as if she were crippled. The gun traversed to the left, covering her. She came to a corner, stopped. Trapped. She realized she should have gone in the opposite direction, where she could have at least locked herself in the bathroom.

The third shot smashed into the floor beside her feet. Bits of a throw rug and splinters of wood sprayed up.

"Max!"

He grabbed at the gun, but it slid away from him, rose and fell and swung from side to side, bobbled and weaved, forced him into a clumsy ballet.

She looked for something to hide behind.

There was nothing.

The fourth shot passed over her head, piercing a framed, glass-covered watercolor of Newport Beach harbor.

Max connected with the pistol, clutched it. The barrel twisted in his hands until it was pointed at his chest. Sweating, cursing, he struggled to pull the weapon from a pair of hands that he couldn't see. Surprisingly, after a few seconds, the unseen contestant surrendered, and Max staggered backward with the prize.

She stood with her back to the wall, hands to her face. She couldn't take her eyes from the barrel of the gun.

"It's safe now," Max said. "It's over." He started toward her.

"For God's sake, unload it!" she said, pointing at the gun in his hand.

He stopped, stared at the pistol, and then took the magazine out of the handgrip.

"All of the bullets should be taken from the clip," she said.

"I doubt that's necessary if I—"

"*Do it!*"

His big hands were shaking as he took the bullets from the magazine. He placed all of the pieces on the bed: pistol, empty magazine, unspent ammunition. For a minute he studied the items, as she did, waiting for one of them to rise off the blanket.

Nothing moved.

"What was it?" he asked.

"Poltergeist."

"Whatever it was—is it still here?"

She closed her eyes, tried to relax, tried to *feel*. After a while she said, "No. It's gone."

# WEDNESDAY, DECEMBER 23

◆◆◆

# 10
### ◆ ◆ ◆

Percy Osterman, the Orange County sheriff, opened the door for Max and Mary, motioned for them to go ahead of him.

The room was gray. The paint was gray, the floor tile gray, the windowsills gray with dust. A set of gray metal storage shelves was bolted to one wall, and the wall opposite the shelves contained a lot of built-in file drawers with burnished steel fronts. The few pieces of furniture were fashioned of tubular steel and gray vinyl. The screens over the ceiling lights were gray, and the fuzzy fluorescent illumination transformed the scene into a chiaroscuro print.

The only spots of brightness in the room were the well scrubbed porcelain sinks and the slanted autopsy table, which was fiercely white with polished, gleaming stainless steel fixtures.

The sheriff was all hard lines and sharp angles. He was nearly as tall as Max, but forty pounds lighter and far less muscular. Yet he did not appear wasted or weak. His hands were large, bony, almost flesh-less, the fingers like talons. His shoulders sloped forward. His neck was thin with a prominent Adam's apple. In his pinched, sun-browned face, his eyes were quick, nervous, a curious pale shade of amber.

Osterman's frown was ominous, his smile easy and kind. He was not smiling when he opened one of the six large drawers and pulled the shroud from the face of the corpse.

Mary stepped away from Max, moved closer to the dead man.

"Kyle Nolan," Osterman said. "Owned the beauty shop. Worked there as a hair stylist."

Nolan was short, broad-shouldered, barrel-chested. Bald. A bushy mustache. Shave off the mustache, Mary thought, and he'd look like that actor, Edward Asner.

She put one hand on the drawer and waited for a rush of psychic impressions. Although she didn't understand how or why, she knew that, for a time after passing away, the dead maintained a bubble of energy around them, an invisible capsule that contained memories, vivid scenes of their lives and especially of their last minutes. Ordinarily, contact with the victim of a murder, or with the victim's belongings, would generate a torrent of clairvoyant images, sometimes clear as reality and sometimes hopelessly blurry and meaningless, most of them dealing with the moment of death and with the identity of the killer.

In this case, for the first time in her experience, she sensed absolutely nothing. Not even a shapeless flurry of movement or color.

She touched the dead man's cold face.

Still nothing.

Osterman closed the drawer, opened the one next to it. As he folded back the shroud, he said, "Tina Nolan. Kyle's wife."

Tina was an attractive but hard-faced woman with brittle, bleached hair that her husband should have found professionally embarrassing. Although they had been closed hours ago by the coroner, her eyes had come open again. She stared at Mary as if she were trying to impart some dreadfully important news; but in the end she provided nothing more than poor Kyle had done.

The woman in the third drawer was in her late twenties. She had once been beautiful.

"Rochelle Drake," Percy Osterman said. "Nolan's last customer for the day."

"Rochelle Drake?" Max said. He came closer, peered into the drawer. "Don't I know that name?"

"Recognize her?" Sheriff Osterman asked.

Max shook his head. "No. But . . . Mary? Does that name mean anything to you?"

"No," she said.

"When you foresaw these killings, you said you thought you knew one of the victims."

"I was wrong," she said. "These people are strangers."

"That's odd," Max said. "I'd swear . . . well, I don't know *what* I'd swear . . . except this one's name . . . Rochelle Drake . . . it's familiar."

Mary was not paying much attention to him, for she perceived a familiar electricity in the air, a stirring of psychic forces. The Drake woman was going to provide what the other bodies should have offered but didn't. Mary opened her mind to the psychic emanations, made herself as receptive as she could, and put her hand on the dead woman's forehead.

*Wicka-wicka-wicka!*

Wings.

Startled, Mary pulled her hand away from the corpse as if she had been bitten.

She felt wings, leathery wings, shuddering like the membranes of drums.

This isn't possible, she thought frantically. The wings have something to do with Berton Mitchell. Not with this dead woman. Not with the man who killed her. The wings have to do with the past, not the present. Berton Mitchell couldn't be involved in this. He hung himself in a jail cell nearly twenty-four years ago.

But now she could smell the wings as well as feel them, smell the wings and the creatures behind them—a dank, musty, musky odor that nauseated her.

What if the man who murdered Rochelle Drake and the others was not possessed by the spirit of Richard Lingard? What if, instead, he was possessed by the soul of another psychopath, by the spirit of Berton Mitchell? Wasn't it conceivable that Lingard himself had been possessed by Berton Mitchell? And when Barnes shot Lingard, perhaps Mitchell's spirit moved on to another host. Perhaps she had unknowingly crossed the path of an old nemesis. Perhaps she would spend the remainder of her life in pursuit of Berton Mitchell. Perhaps she would be compelled to follow him from one host to another until he finally found the opportunity to kill her.

No. That was madness. She was thinking like a lunatic.

Max asked, "Is something wrong?"

Wings brushed her face, her neck, shoulders and breasts and belly, fluttered against her ankles and up her calves and then against her inner thighs.

She was determined not to succumb to fear. But she was also half convinced that if she didn't stop thinking about the wings, they would carry her off into everlasting darkness. A ridiculous notion. Nevertheless, she turned away from the morgue drawer.

"Are you receiving something?" Max asked.

"Not now," she lied.

"But you were?"

"For an instant."

"What did you see?" he asked.

"Nothing important. Just meaningless movement."

"Can you pick it up again?" Max asked.

596 ◆ DEAN KOONTZ

"No."

She mustn't pursue it. If she did, she would see what lay behind those wings. She must never see what lay behind those wings.

Osterman closed the drawer.

Mary sighed with relief.

Sheriff Osterman went with them to the far corner of the municipal parking lot, where they'd left their car.

The December sky was like the morgue—shades of gray. The fast-moving clouds were reflected in the polished hood of the Mercedes.

Shivering, Mary put her hands in her coat pockets and hunched her shoulders against the wind.

"Heard good things about you," Osterman told Mary in his peculiarly economical way of speaking. "Often thought about working with you. Pleased when you called this morning. Hoped you'd come up with a lead."

"I hoped so, too," she said.

"Foresaw these murders, did you?"

"Yes," she said.

"Those nurses in Anaheim, too?"

"That's right."

"Same killer, you think?"

"Yes," she said.

Osterman nodded. "We think so, too. Have some evidence of it."

"What sort of evidence?" Max asked.

"When he killed the nurses," Osterman said, each word sharp and quick, "he busted up some stuff. Religious things. Two crucifixes. Statuette of the Virgin Mary. Even strangled one girl with a rosary. Found something similar in this beauty shop case."

"What?" Mary asked.

"Pretty ugly bit of business. Maybe you don't want to hear it."

"I'm used to hearing and seeing ugly things," she said.

He regarded her for a moment, amber eyes hooded. "Guess that's true." He leaned against the Mercedes. "This woman in the beauty shop. Rochelle Drake. She wore a necklace. A gold cross. He raped her, killed her. Tore the cross off her neck. Pushed it up . . . inside of her."

Mary felt ill. She hugged herself.

"Then he's a psychopath with some sort of religious hangup," Max said.

"Appears so," Osterman said. He looked at Mary and asked, "So where do you go from here?"

"Down to the shore," she said.

"King's Point," Max said.

"Why there?"

She hesitated, glanced at Max. "That's where the next murders will take place."

Osterman did not seem surprised. "Had another vision, did you?"

"Early this morning," she said.

"When will it happen?"

"Tomorrow night," she said.

"Christmas Eve?"

"Yes."

"Where in King's Point?"

"On the harbor," she said.

"Pretty good-sized harbor."

"It'll be near the shops and restaurants."

"How many will he kill?" Osterman asked.

"I'm not sure."

She was so *cold,* colder than could be accounted for by the California winter day and the wind, cold in the pit of her stomach, cold in her heart. She was wearing a stylish but thinly lined calfskin coat from North Beach Leather. She wished she'd chosen her heaviest fur.

"Maybe I'll be able to stop him before he kills anyone else," she said.

"You feel a responsibility to stop him?" Osterman asked.

"I won't have peace of mind until I do."

"Wouldn't want this talent you've got."

"I never asked for it," she said.

A truck rumbled by in the street. Osterman waited for the noise to die down.

"King's Point used to be in my jurisdiction," he said. "Two years ago they voted in their own police force. Now I can't poke my nose in unless they ask. Or unless a case that starts in the county ends up on their doorstep."

"I wish I could be working with you," Mary said.

"You'll be working with a jackass," Osterman said.

"Excuse me?"

"Chief of police at King's Point. Name's Patmore. John Patmore. A jackass. He gives you trouble, tell him to call me. He kind of respects me, but he's still a jackass."

"We'll use your name if we have to," Mary said. "But we aren't entirely without influence down there. We know the owner of the *King's Point Press.*"

Osterman smiled. "Lou Pasternak?"

"You know him?"

"Damned good newspaperman."

"Yes, he is."

"Quite a character, too."

"A little bit of one," she agreed.

The sheriff offered his hand to Mary, then to Max. "Hope you two do my job for me this time."

"Thanks for your help," Max said.

"Don't hesitate to ask for more if you need it. It's been my pleasure."

As Mary got into the Mercedes, a gust of wind sang in the power lines overhead.

They reached King's Point at two-thirty in the afternoon. Their first glimpse of it, as they topped a rise in the road, was from high above the harbor.

The sky was low. Thick gray clouds scudded inland. A mile offshore the ocean was shrouded in mist; and closer to the beach formidable waves churned beneath half a dozen scuba-suited surfers, fell frothily onto the sand, and exploded into spray against the stone breakwaters on both sides of the harbor entrance.

The town was on the Pacific Coast Highway, a few miles south of Laguna Beach, in a perpetually smogless pocket of sunshine and money. The sun was in hiding today, but the money was everywhere evident. Houses on the verdant hillsides were priced from $75,000 to $500,000, nearly all of them with well manicured decorative gardens and ocean views. Waterfront homes with docks were not as expensive as those in Newport Beach, but real estate brokers had no time for would-be customers who flinched at a base price of a quarter million dollars. In the flat land between harbor and hills the houses were cheaper—there were some apartment buildings, too—but even they were expensive by most standards.

The travel guides said that King's Point was "charming" and "quaint" and "picturesque," and for once they were telling the truth. The lawns were lush and green; the many small parks were filled with palms of all varieties, oleander, jade plants, magnolia trees, schefflera, dracaena, olive trees, and seasonal flowers. The houses were well cared for, freshly painted every year or two as protection against the corrosive sea air. Businessmen were required to forgo the most offensive neon signs and were forbidden by law to paint their stores in anything but soft natural tones.

The residents of King's Point appeared to think that with the proper local ordinances they could keep out everything that made the rest of the world a less desirable place to live. And they *did* keep out much that was tasteless, cheap, and gaudy.

But they can't keep out everything they don't want, Mary thought. A killer has come in from outside. He's walking among them now. They can't use local ordinances to keep out death.

From spring through early autumn the population of King's Point was sixty percent higher than in the winter. During these vacation months the motels were booked weeks in advance, the restaurants raised their prices except for locals who were recognized, the shops hired extra help, and the white beaches were crowded. Now, two days before Christmas, the town was quiet. When Max turned off the main highway onto a city street, they encountered very little traffic.

King's Point Police Headquarters was a single-story brick building of absolutely no architectural period, style, charm, integrity, or responsibility. It looked like an oversized, flat-roofed storage shed with windows. Even three blocks from the harbor, in the flats below the hills, in a limbo between the highest-value real estate parcels—waterfront and view—it was no credit to its neighborhood.

Inside, the public reception room was depressingly institutional: brown tile floor, muddy green walls, washed-out green ceiling, strictly utilitarian furniture. Tax money had purchased three desks, six-drawer filing cabinets, IBM typewriters, a copier, a small refrigerator, a United States flag, a glass-fronted case full of riot guns and pistols, a dispatcher's corner with radio—and a civilian secretary (Mrs. Vidette Yancy, according to the name plate on her desk) who was in her fifties, a woman with tightly curled white hair, pale skin, bright red lipstick, and an enormous bosom.

"I'd like to see Chief Patmore," Mary said.

Mrs. Yancy took a minute to correct a word she had just typed. "Him?" she said at last. "He's out."

"When will he be back?"

"The chief? Tomorrow morning."

"Could you give us his home address?" Max asked, leaning against the formica counter that separated the foyer from the work area.

"His home address?" Mrs. Yancy said. "Surely. I can give you that. But he isn't at home."

"Where is he?" Mary asked impatiently.

"Where is he? Why, he's up in Santa Barbara. He won't be back until ten tomorrow morning."

Mary turned to Max. "Maybe we should talk to a deputy."

"Deputy?" Mrs. Yancy said. "There are five officers under the chief. Of course, only two of them are on duty right now."

"If this guy's like we've heard," Max said, "it won't do any good to talk to subordinates. He'll expect to be dealt with directly."

"Time's running out," Mary said.

"Don't we have until seven o'clock tomorrow evening?" Max asked.

"If my vision's accurate, we do."

"Then if we see Patmore early tomorrow, that'll be soon enough."

"The officers on duty are out on patrol right now," Mrs. Yancy said. "Did you want to report a crime?"

"Not exactly," Mary said.

"Not exactly? Well, I have the forms right here, you know." She opened a desk drawer, began to rummage through it. "I can take down the information and have an officer get back to you."

"Never mind," Max said. "We'll be in tomorrow at ten o'clock."

At the bay end of the harbor, valuable shoreline was occupied by commercial enterprises—yacht clubs, yacht sales offices, dry docks, restaurants, and shops. Each of these businesses was as clean and attractive and well maintained as the many expensive homes that lined both sides of the harbor channel.

The Laughing Dolphin was a restaurant and cocktail lounge that fronted on the harbor. On the second level a narrow open-air deck was suspended over the water. In good weather patrons could get pleasantly drunk while the sun warmed their faces. This afternoon the deck was deserted. Max and Mary had it to themselves.

Holding a mug of coffee laced with brandy, Mary leaned against the wooden railing.

If you stepped out of the brisk sea breezes, the day was only chilly; but the wind from the ocean was downright cold. It nipped at her face and brought a healthy color to her cheeks.

When she looked up and to her right, she could see the Spanish Court, the hotel where she and Max had reserved a room. It stood on the north hill, high above the harbor. It was majestic, all white plaster and natural woods and red tile.

Closer to hand, eight dinghies were sailing in formation, snaking back and forth across the smooth slate-colored water. Against a backdrop of sixty-, eighty-, and hundred-foot sailing ships and motor yachts, the small vessels were lovely and amusing. Even today, without the sun upon them, their sails were dazzlingly white. Their graceful progress was a definition of serenity.

"Study the boats, the houses, the entire harbor," Max said. "Maybe something you see will trigger the vision."

"I don't think so," she said. "It was knocked out of my mind forever when I woke up and found I was being shot at."

"You've got to try."

"Do I?"

"Isn't that why you wanted to come?"

"If I don't go after this killer," she said, "he'll eventually come after me."

The wind gusted suddenly, flapped Mary's leather coat against her legs, rattled the large plate-glass windows of the cocktail lounge behind them.

She sipped her coffee. Tentacles of steam writhed across her face and dissolved in the wintry air.

Max said, "Maybe it'll help if you tell me again how it's going to happen." When she didn't answer, he coaxed her. "Tomorrow night at seven o'clock. Not too far from where we're standing right now."

"Within a couple of blocks," she said.

"You said he'll come with a butcher knife."

"Lingard's knife."

"Some knife, anyway."

"Lingard's," she insisted.

"You said he'll stab two people."

"Yes, two."

"Kill them?"

"Maybe one of them."

"But not the other."

"At least one will live. Maybe both."

"Who are these people he'll stab?"

"I don't know their names," she said.

"What do they look like?"

"I couldn't see their faces."

"Young women, like in Anaheim?"

"I really don't know."

"What about the high-powered rifle?"

"I saw it in the vision."

"He's got a butcher knife and a gun?"

"After he's stabbed those two people," she said, "he'll take the rifle up into a tower. He intends to shoot everyone."

"Everyone?"

"A lot of people, as many as he can."

At the far end of the harbor, a dozen sea gulls kited in from the ocean, riding very high on the wind, white feathers silhouetted dramatically against the stormy sky.

"How many will he kill?" Max asked.

"The vision ended before I could see."

"Which tower will he use?"

"I don't know."

"Look around," Max said. "Look at each one of them. Try to sense which it will be."

To her right, three hundred yards farther around the bend of the harbor's bay end and five hundred yards from the Laughing Dolphin, the Roman Catholic Church of the Holy Trinity lay one block from the waterfront. She had been inside it once. It was a brooding Gothic structure, an impressive fortress of weathered granite and darkly beautiful stained glass windows. The hundred-foot bell tower, which had a low-walled open deck directly beneath its peaked roof, was the highest point within two blocks of the harbor.

The sound of sea gulls distracted her for a moment. Above the formation of sailboats that were playing follow the leader, still soaring inland, the gulls began to squeal with excitement. Their sharp voices were like fingernails scraped across a blackboard.

She tried not to hear the birds, concentrated on Trinity. She received nothing. No images. No psychic vibrations. Not the vaguest premonition that the killer would strike out at King's Point from Trinity's bell tower.

St. Luke's Lutheran Church was between Mary and the Church of the Holy Trinity. It was two hundred yards north and half a block from the harbor. It was a Spanish-style building with massive carved oak doors, and a bell tower slightly more than half as high as the one at the Catholic church.

Nothing from St. Luke's either.

Just the ghostly wind and the cries of agitated sea gulls.

The third tower was to her left, two hundred yards away, at the edge of the water. It was only four stories high, part of Kimball's Games and Snacks, a clapboard and cedar-shingled pavilion that housed an amusement arcade. In the summer camera-laden tourists climbed to the top and took photographs of the harbor. Now the place was closed for the season, quiet, empty.

"Will it be Kimball's tower?" Max asked.

"I don't know," she said. "It could be any of them."

"You've got to try harder," he said.

She closed her eyes and concentrated.

Screeching angrily, a gull swooped down, flashed past their faces with only eight or ten inches to spare.

Mary jumped back in surprise, dropped her coffee mug.

"You okay?" Max asked.

"Startled. That's all."

"Did it touch you?"

"No."

"They don't dive that close unless you trespass on their nesting grounds. But there's nowhere around here they'd lay eggs. Besides, it's not the time of year for that.''

The dozen gulls that had entered the harbor a few minutes ago were circling overhead. They weren't taking advantage of the wind currents as gulls usually do; there was nothing lazy or graceful about their flight. Instead, they twisted and fluttered and soared and dived and darted frantically among one another within a tightly defined sphere of air. They seemed tortured. It was surprising that they didn't collide. Screeching at one another, they performed an unnatural, frenzied dance in midair.

''What's upset them?'' Max wondered.

''Me,'' she said.

''You? What did you do?''

She was trembling. ''I tried to use my clairvoyance to see which tower the killer will use.''

''So?''

''The gulls are here to stop me from doing that.''

Astounded, he said, ''Mary, that makes no sense. Trained gulls?''

''Not trained. Controlled.''

''Controlled by whom? Who sent them?''

She stared at the birds.

''Who?'' he asked again. ''Lingard's ghost?''

''Maybe,'' she said.

He touched her shoulder. ''Mary—''

''You saw the poltergeist that was after me, dammit!''

In a let's-calm-down-and-be-reasonable tone of voice that drove her mad, he said, ''Whatever causes poltergeist phenomena can lift and hurl inanimate objects—but not living animals.''

''Listen,'' she said, ''you don't know everything. You don't know—'' She looked away from him, looked up.

''What's wrong?'' he asked.

''The birds.''

The gulls still capered maniacally overhead, but they were silent. Perfectly silent.

''Strange,'' Max said.

''I'm going inside,'' she said.

She almost reached the mullioned door that connected the deck to the second-floor cocktail lounge when a sea gull struck her from behind, between the shoulders, like a hammer blow. She stumbled and instinctively put one arm across her face. The wings beat at her neck. Battered the back of her head. Thundered in her ears. These weren't like the wings that she associated with Berton Mitchell. Those wings had been leathery, membranous. These were feathered. But that didn't make the sea gulls any less frightening. She thought of the bird's wickedly sharp, hooked beak, thought of it pecking out her eyes, and she screamed.

Max shouted something that she couldn't hear.

She started to reach for the bird, realized it might tear her fingers, jerked her hand back.

Max knocked the gull away from her. It flopped on the deck, temporarily stunned.

Max opened the door, pushed her inside, went in after her, and pulled the door shut.

The bartender had seen the attack, and he was hurrying around the end of the counter, wiping his hands on a towel.

A heavyset, red-haired man at the bar swiveled around on his stool to see what was happening.

In one of the black vinyl booths by the windows a young couple—a pretty blonde in a green dress and a dark, intense man—looked up from their drinks.

Before the bartender had taken three steps, a sea gull struck the mullioned door behind Max. Two small panes broke inward. Glass tinkled musically on the floor.

The cocktail waitress dropped her tray and ran toward the stairs that led down to the restaurant foyer.

With a sound like a shotgun blast, another gull slammed into one of the five-foot by six-foot windows that overlooked the harbor. The glass cracked but held. The injured bird toppled backwards to the deck outside, leaving a smear of blackish blood to mark the collision.

"They'll kill me."

"No," Max said.

"That's what they want!"

He held her protectively, but for the first time since she had known him, his arms didn't seem big enough, his chest broad enough, his body strong enough to guarantee her safety.

A sea gull caromed off the window beside the young couple's table. The glass cracked in a jagged, lightning-bolt pattern. The pretty blonde shrieked and scrambled out of the booth.

An instant after her companion prudently followed her, another gull rammed the same window and shattered it. Large shards of glass collapsed onto the dark pine table, bounced up in many smaller pieces, and showered over the vinyl where the couple had been sitting.

The decapitated gull landed in the center of the table; and its bloody head plopped into the woman's martini.

Two more gulls flew in through the broken window.

"Don't let them!" Mary shouted hysterically. "Don't let them, don't, don't, oh don't, *please* don't!"

The young couple went to their knees, taking shelter behind and half beneath a table.

Max pushed Mary into the nearest corner. He shielded her as best he could with his body. One of the birds sailed straight at him. He threw up one arm to ward it off. The creature squealed in anger, shied away, circled through the room.

The other gull attempted to land on one of the round tables in the middle of the lounge. Its wings knocked over a centerpiece—a copper and stained-glass lantern with a candle inside—and the candle set fire to the tablecloth.

The bartender used his damp towel to extinguish the flame.

The gull swooped from the table to the shelves of liquor behind the bar. Two, three, four, half a dozen, eight bottles crashed to the floor. On his stool, a few feet from the crazed gull, the red-haired man was too bewildered to be frightened. He watched the bird with fascination as it flapped and kicked and sent more bottles to the floor. The fragrance of whiskey blossomed through the room.

The first gull flew at Max again. It came in above him, fluttered wildly in the corner, then with malign intelligence dropped behind his back, onto Mary's head.

Its feet tangled in her hair.

*"God, no! No!"*

She grabbed at the bird, not caring about its beak, not caring if it pecked her fingers. It was unclean. She had to get it off her. Max reached for it, too. Then it rose from her, up and away once more, circling into the room. In a second, however, it darted back and thumped into the wall beside her head. It dropped to the floor at her feet and twitched spasmodically.

Gasping for breath, her hands to her face and fingers spread, she backed away from it.

"It's terror-stricken," Max said.

"Kill it!" She hardly recognized her own voice; it was altered by fear and hatred.

He hesitated. "I don't think it's dangerous anymore."

"Kill it before it flies up!"

He kicked the bird into the corner, raised his foot, and with evident reluctance stepped on its head.

Gagging, Mary turned away.

The other gull flew away from the bar and left the room through the broken window.

Everything was quiet, still.

At last the intense, dark-skinned young man stood up, helped the blonde to her feet.

The heavyset, red-haired man at the bar tossed down his drink in one gulp.

"Christ, what a mess!" the bartender said. "What happened? Did anyone ever see gulls act like that before?"

Max touched her cheek. "Are you okay?"

She leaned on him and wept.

# 11
◆ ◆ ◆

6:30.

Lights speckled the nighttime King's Point hills like orange flame gleaming from within a jack-o'-lantern with a thousand eyes. To the west the ocean and sky melted into a single black shroud.

Max parked at the curb, switched off the headlights. He leaned over and kissed Mary. "You look lovely tonight."

She smiled. Surprisingly, in spite of what had happened to her today, she felt lovely, feminine, buoyant. "That makes six times you've told me."

"Seven's a lucky number. You look lovely tonight." He kissed her again. "Do you feel better? Are you relaxed?"

"The man who invented valium should be made a saint."

"*You* should be made a saint," he said. "Now don't move. I'm feeling terribly chivalrous. I'll come around and open your door."

The wind from the sea was no stronger than it had been during the day, although with nightfall it grew colder and seemed also to grow noisier. It shook badly fitted shutters until they clattered. It worried loosely hinged garage doors, made them groan and creak. It scraped tree branches against the side of the house, tipped over empty trash barrels, stirred brittle feathered-end palm fronds together in a chorus of snakelike hissing, and rolled a few discarded soda cans along the streets.

Sheltered from the worst of the wind by dense shrubs, pine trees and date palms, the small single-story house at 440 Ocean Hill Lane looked warm and cozy. Soft light radiated from the leaded windows. A carriage lamp glowed beside the front door.

Lou Pasternak—owner, publisher, and editor of the twice-a-week *King's Point Press*—answered the bell and hustled them inside. While they told each other how well they looked and how happy they were to see each other again, Pasternak kissed Mary on the cheek, shook hands with Max, and hung their coats in the closet.

Being in Lou's presence was, she thought, as relaxing as taking a tranquilizer. Except for Max and her own brother, Mary liked Lou more than any other man she'd ever met. He was intelligent, kind, too generous. He was also the worst cynic she had ever met, but the cynicism was tempered by humility and a marvelous sense of humor.

She worried about him because he drank too much. But he knew he did, and he was able to talk about his drinking dispassionately. He argued that if you understood how screwed up the world was, if you saw how like a paradise it *could* be, if you understood that what could be never *would* be because most people were hopeless jackasses— well, then you needed a crutch to get through life with your sanity intact. For some people, he said, it was money or drugs or any of a hundred other things. His crutch was Scotch. And damned good bourbon.

"My mother," Mary sometimes said to him, "led a miserable life as an alcoholic."

"Your mother," Lou always responded, "sounds like an alcoholic who didn't know how to hold her liquor. There's nothing worse than a sloppy drunk—unless it's a self-pitying drunk."

His drinking didn't appear to interfere with the full life he led. He had built and still operated an extremely successful business. His editorials and reportage had won several national awards. At forty-five, although he had never been married, he had more women friends than any man Mary knew. At the moment he lived alone, but that would not last.

Although she had seen him consume Herculean quantities of liquor, she had never seen him drunk. He did not stagger, slur his speech, become maudlin or loud or obnoxious. He not only could hold his liquor, he thrived on it.

"I don't drink to escape my responsibilities," he had once told her. "I drink to escape the consequences of other people's inability to meet *their* responsibilities."

"Alcohol killed my mother," she warned him. "I don't want to see you die."

"We all die, my dear. It's just as good to drop of a rotted liver as it is to be felled by cancer or a stroke. Actually, I think it's better."

She loved him as much as she loved Max, though in different ways.

He was a stocky man, a full foot shorter than Max's six-four, even slightly shorter than Mary. He was solidly constructed. His neck, shoulders, arms, and chest were thick with muscle, powerful. He was wearing a white shirt; the sleeves were rolled up; and his forearms were matted with hair.

His face was in stark contrast to his body. He had the fine features of an inbred aristocrat. He combed his brown hair straight back from his face. His brow was high; his lively brown eyes were deeply set and sensitive; his nose was narrow, the nostrils delicate; and his mouth was almost prim. He wore wire-rimmed spectacles that made him look as if he was a college professor.

"Bourbon and ice," he said, picking up a tall glass from the slate-topped foyer table. "My third since I got home from work. In case the wind blows down the power lines later on, I intend to be so lit up that I can do my bedtime reading by my own light."

Although there were armchairs and a comfortable sofa, the living room was primarily furnished with books, magazines, record albums, and paintings. Stacks of books stood beside and behind the couch; books filled the space under the coffee table; recent issues of magazines overflowed a rack meant to hold a hundred of them. The one wall that was free of records and books was covered with original oils, pastels, and watercolors by local painters. Dozens of pieces in every imaginable style had been squeezed so close that their beauty overlapped; they intruded upon one another; but Lou's taste was so good that even under these circumstances the eye was caught and held by each work at some point during a long evening. One of the armchairs was more tattered and lumpy than the other. That was where Lou sat, reading half a dozen books each week, drinking too much, and listening to opera, Benny Goodman, or Bach.

It was the friendliest room Mary had ever seen.

Lou brought their drinks. He put Bach, interpreted by Eugene Ormandy, on the stereo at low volume. "Now let's hear the whole story. Since you called this morning, I've been half crazy wondering what this is about. You were so mysterious."

Interrupted frequently by Lou's questions, digressing into discussions of poltergeists, Mary told him everything. She began with the tracking down of Richard Lingard and ended with the sea gull attack at the Laughing Dolphin.

When she finished, the house was abnormally quiet. A grandfather clock ticked solemnly in the dining room.

Thinking about what she had said, Lou poured himself more bourbon. When he returned to his armchair, he said, "So tomorrow night at seven o'clock this killer will stab two people, perhaps killing one of them. Then he'll climb a tower and start to shoot."

"You believe me?" she asked.

"Of course. I've followed your work for years, haven't I?"

"You believe about Lingard's spirit?"

"If you say I should, why wouldn't I?"

She glanced at Max.

"Will this man have anyone to shoot at tomorrow night?" Max asked. "Won't just about everyone be at home with their families on Christmas Eve?"

"Oh," Lou said, "he'll have plenty of targets around the harbor. There'll be Christmas Eve parties on dozens of boats. People on the decks. People on the docks. People everywhere."

"I don't think we can stop the stabbings from taking place," Mary said. "But maybe we can keep him from shooting anyone. Policemen can be stationed in all three towers."

"One problem," Lou said.

"What's that?"

"John Patmore."

"Your chief of police."

"Unfortunately, he is. It's not going to be easy to convince him that he should heed your visions."

"If he thinks there's even the slightest chance I might be right," Mary said, "why shouldn't he cooperate? After all, his job is to protect the people of King's Point."

Lou smiled crookedly. "My dear, you should know by now that many cops don't see their jobs quite the same way as taxpayers do. Some cops think that all they're required to do is wear fancy fascist uniforms, ride around in flashy patrol cars, collect envelopes of graft money, and retire at the public expense after twenty or thirty years of 'service.' "

"You're too cynical," she said.

"Percy Osterman told us Patmore's difficult," Max added.

"Difficult? He's stupid," Lou said. "Ignorant beyond description. The only reason you can't accuse him of being scatterbrained is because he doesn't have any brains to scatter. I'm sure he's never heard the word 'clairvoyant.' And when we are finally able to make him understand what it means, he won't believe it. If something's not within his personal experience, he doesn't accept its existence. I'm positive he'd argue against the reality of Europe simply because he's never been there."

"He can call some police chiefs I've worked with," Mary said. "They'll convince him I'm genuine."

"If he's never met them, he won't believe a word they say. I tell you, Mary, if ignorance is really bliss, then he's the happiest man in the world."

"Sheriff Osterman said we could tell Patmore to call him for an endorsement," Max said.

Lou nodded. "That might help. Patmore's impressed with Osterman. And I'll go with you to see him if you'd like. But I've got to warn you that I won't help your cause very much. Patmore hates me."

"I can't imagine why," Max said. "Except, you probably talk like this about him to his face."

Grinning, Lou said, "I've never been able to hide my true feelings, and that's a fact. You've met Mrs. Yancy, his flunky?"

"She was the only one in the office this afternoon," Max said.

"Isn't she a gem?"

"Is she?"

"A miracle worker," Lou said. "It's a miracle when she works."

"She *didn't* seem too efficient," Mary said.

Lou said, "She's a steady worker—and if she gets any steadier, she'll be motionless."

Mary laughed, sipped her dry sherry.

"Now, getting back to those sea gulls," Lou said. "Do—"

"No more about the gulls," Mary said. "No more about any of that. Tomorrow's soon enough. Tonight I want to forget about clairvoyance and talk about something else. Anything else."

Dinner was filet mignon, salad, baked potatoes, and cold asparagus spears.

As Max was opening the bottle of red wine they'd brought as a gift, Lou noticed the bandage. "Max, what happened to your finger?"

"Oh . . . I cut it changing a flat tire."

"Stitches?"

"It wasn't that serious."

"He should have seen a doctor," Mary said. "He wouldn't even let me look at it. There was so much blood—blood all over his shirt."

"I thought you might have been in a fight again," Lou said.

"I don't go to bars anymore," Max said. "I don't fight these days."

Lou looked at Mary, raised an eyebrow.

"It's true," she said.

"You worked two years for me," Lou said. "In all that time you never went more than a month or six weeks without getting in a bad fight. You went to the worst bars along the coast—biker bars and worse, to all the places where you were most likely to wind up in trouble. Sometimes I wondered if you went drinking more for the fighting than for the liquor."

"Maybe I did," Max said, frowning. "I had problems. What I needed was someone who needed me. Now I've got Mary, and I don't fight."

Although he had promised not to talk about clairvoyance anymore that night, Lou found himself unable to drop the subject during dinner. "Do you think the killer knows you're in town?"

"I don't know," Mary said.

"If he's possessed by a spirit, and if the same spirit possessed those gulls, then surely he knows."

"I guess he does."

"Won't he play it safe until after you leave town?"

"Maybe he will," she said. "But I doubt it."

"He wants to get caught?"

"Or he wants to catch me."

"What do you mean by that?"

"I don't know."

"If—"

"Can we change the subject?"

After she had finished eating, Mary excused herself from the table and went to the bathroom at the far end of the house.

When he was alone with Max, Lou asked, "What about this notion of hers?"

"That Lingard's come back from the dead?"

"Do you put any stock in that?"

"You're the student of the occult," Max said. "You're the one with hundreds of books on the subject. Besides, you've known her longer than I have. You're the one who introduced us. What do you think?"

"I've got an open mind," Lou said. "I gather you don't."

"Her analyst says *she* threw those glass dogs."

"Unconscious telekinesis?" Lou asked.

"That's right."

"Has she ever shown telekinetic ability before?"

"No," Max said.

"What about the revolver?"

"I think she was controlling that, too."

"Shooting at herself?"

"Yes," Max said.

"And she was guiding the sea gulls?"

"Yes."

"Controlling living animals . . . that's not telekinesis."

"It's telepathy of a sort," Max said.

Lou refilled his wine glass. "That's rare."

"It has to be telepathy. I can't believe those sea gulls were guided by a dead man's spirit."

"Why would she want to kill herself?"

"She doesn't," Max said.

"Well, if *she* is the poltergeist behind these phenomena, if *she* levitated that revolver, then it seems to me that she was trying to kill herself."

"If she was suicidal," Max said, "she wouldn't have missed. But she *did* miss with the glass dogs, with the revolver, and with the gulls."

"Then what's she doing?" Lou asked. "Why is she playing the part of a poltergeist?"

Max frowned. "I have a theory. I think there's something special about this case, something unusual. She's foreseen something about it that she refuses to face up to. Something devastating. Something that would completely unhinge her if she thought about it for long. So she pushed it out of her mind. Of course, she could only push it out of her *conscious* mind. The subconscious never forgets. Now, every time she attempts to pursue a vision that's connected to this case, her subconscious uses the poltergeist phenomena to distract her."

"Because her subconscious knows it will be harmful for her to pursue this man."

"That's right."

An icy tremor passed through Lou Pasternak. "What could she have foreseen?"

"Maybe this psychopath will kill her," Max said.

The thought of Mary dead hit Lou with surprising force. He had known her for more than a decade, had liked her from the moment he met her, and had grown to like her more each year. Liked her? Only that? No. He loved her, too. In a fatherly way. She was so gentle, good-natured. So vulnerable. But until this moment he had not realized how deeply he had come to love her. Mary dead and gone? He felt sick, feverish.

Max watched him with steady gray eyes that revealed nothing of his own emotions. He appeared unaffected, unmoved by the prospect of his wife's death.

He's had more time to consider it than I have, Lou thought. He's had time to become accustomed to the idea of Mary dead. He cares as much as I do, but his feelings have settled from the surface into darker, more affecting regions.

"Or maybe the psychopath will kill me," Max said.

"The two of you should give up on this one," Lou said. "Go home right now. Stay out of it."

"But if she *did* foresee something of that sort," Max said, "won't it happen regardless of what we do to avoid it?"

"I don't believe in predestination."

"Neither do I. Yet . . . what she foresees always seems to happen. So if we don't go after this killer, will he come after us?"

"Damn you," Lou said. "You've made me stone cold sober." He drank his wine, poured more.

"There's something else," Max said. "When she was six years old, a man apparently sexually molested her."

"Berton Mitchell," Lou said.

"How much has she told you about that?"

"Not much. The general outlines of it. I gather she can't remember most of it."

"Did she tell you what happened to Mitchell?"

"He was found guilty," Lou said. "He hung himself in his prison cell, didn't he?"

"Do you know that for a fact?"

"She told me."

"But do you know it for a fact?"

Lou was puzzled. "Why would she lie?"

"I'm not saying she lied. But what if no one ever told her the truth?"

"I don't follow you."

"Suppose," Max said, "that Berton Mitchell was never sentenced to a prison term. Suppose he had a good attorney who got him off scot-free even though he was guilty. It happens. If you were the father of a six-year-old girl who'd been molested and horribly traumatized, would you want to tell her that her assailant had walked away unpunished? Wouldn't you worry that she might suffer even more serious psychological damage if she knew that the monster who had abused her was on the streets, free to try for her again? If Berton Mitchell was acquitted, Mary's father might have decided the best thing was for her to believe that Mitchell was dead."

"Surely she would have discovered the truth when she got older," Lou said.

"Not necessarily. Not if she didn't want to discover it."

"Alan would have told her."

"Maybe Alan never knew the truth either," Max said. "He was only nine at the time. Their father would have lied to both of them. And if—"

Lou held up one hand for silence. "Let's say you're right. Let's say Berton Mitchell was acquitted. What's that have to do with this case?"

Max picked up his fork and poked at the rumpled pile of potato skin on his plate. "I told you I think Mary's foreseen something that terrifies her."

"That she'll be killed. Or you will."

"Perhaps that's it. But maybe she's also seen that the killer we're after is . . . Berton Mitchell."

"He'd be sixty years old if he was alive!"

"Is there some law that says all psychopathic killers have to be young?" Max asked.

In the bathroom Mary washed her hands, picked up the towel, looked in the mirror above the washbasin—and did not see her own face. Instead, she saw the face of a total stranger—a young woman with pale yellow hair and even paler skin and wide-set blue eyes, her features distorted by terror.

The mirror had become a window on another dimension, for it did not reflect anything in the bathroom. The blonde woman's face was disembodied, floating in misty shadows. Above and to the right of her, the only other object in the void beyond the mirror was a golden crucifix.

Mary dropped the towel, backed away from the sink until she bumped into the wall.

In the mirror a man's hand, also disembodied, appeared in the foreground of the surrealistic collage of psychic images. It was gripping a butcher knife.

Mary had never received a clairvoyant vision in this fashion. For a moment she didn't know what to expect. She didn't know what she should do; she was afraid both to move and to stay still.

The disembodied hand raised the knife. The blonde's face receded like a ball flying away, whirling and spinning and tumbling through endless space. The hand and the butcher knife receded, too, in pursuit of her.

Concentrate, Mary told herself. For God's sake, don't let the vision get away from you. Hold on to it at all costs. Hold it and expand upon it. Develop it until it provides the name of the man whose hand holds the knife.

The crucifix swelled until it filled the mirror. Then, in perfect, eerie silence, the icon exploded into a dozen jagged pieces and was gone.

Concentrate . . .

The woman's face reappeared. And the knife loomed large in the mirror. The blade gave off a fierce light of its own, as if it were made of neon tubing.

"Who are you?" Mary asked aloud. "You with the knife. Who in the hell are you?"

Suddenly the hand was no longer disembodied. The woman's face vanished, and the shoulder and the back of a man's head entered the scene, cloaked in shadow. The killer started to turn slowly, turned through laces of wan light and shifting shadows, turned so he would be facing out from the mirror, turned as if he knew Mary was now behind him, turned slowly and silently, turned as if in response to her request for his name . . .

Worried that she might lose the vision an instant before she had her answer, as had happened to her in Dr. Cauvel's office the day before, Mary said, "Who? Who are you? I demand to know!"

To her right, six feet away, the latch on the bathroom window opened with a sharp *click!*

Startled, Mary looked away from the image in the mirror.

The window slid up.

The wind threw aside the flimsy brown and black curtains and rushed into the room, making banshee noises as it came.

The night beyond the window was dark, far darker than she had ever seen.

Over the howling of the wind came another sound: *wicka-wicka-wicka!*

Wings. Leathery wings. Just beyond the window.

*Wicka-wicka-wicka!*

Perhaps it was a coincidental sound. The curtain rod vibrating in its fixtures? A branch or shrub rustling rhythmically against the side of the house?

Whatever the cause of it, she was certain she was not merely imagining the sound this time; nor was she receiving it as part of her psychic impressions. Some creature was actually close at hand, beyond that open window, some unimaginably bizarre creature with wings.

No. Insanity.

Well, go look, she told herself. Go see what it is that has these wings. See if it's anything at all. End this forever.

She couldn't move.

*Wicka-wicka-wicka!*

Max, help me, she said. But the words formed without sound.

To her left, beside the sink, the door of the medicine cabinet was wrenched open by invisible hands. Thrown shut. Wrenched open. Thrown shut. The next time it came open, it stayed that way. All of the contents of the cabinet—bottles of Anacin, aspirin, cold tablets, iodine, cough syrup, laxatives; tubes of toothpaste, skin cream, shampoo; boxes of throat lozenges, Band-Aids, gauze pads—leaped from the shelves to the floor.

The shower curtain was flung back by an invisible hand, and the shower rod sagged and bent as if someone quite heavy was hanging from it. The rod tore out of the wall and fell into the tub.

The commode seat began to bash itself up and down, faster and faster, making an incredible din.

She took one step toward the bathroom door.

It swung open as if urging her to leave—then a second later went shut with a crash like a thunderclap. It opened and closed itself repeatedly, almost in time with the clatter of the commode seat.

She put her back to the wall once more, afraid to move.

"Mary!"

Max and Lou were on the other side of the door, briefly visible as it swung open. They were staring, amazed.

The door closed with even greater power than it had before, flew open, shut, open, shut.

Max tried to come in as the door opened again, but it slammed in his face. The next time it opened he grabbed the doorknob and forced his way inside.

The door stopped moving.

The wind at the window decreased to a slight draft.

There were no wings beating now.

Stillness.

Silence.

Mary looked at the mirror above the washbasin and saw that, while the images in it had changed, it was still not an ordinary mirror and did not reflect the room in front of it. The pale blonde, the crucifix, and the man with the butcher knife were gone. The mirror was black— except for the very bottom of it, where blood appeared to seep through the glass and over the frame, where it dripped into the room, as if the world on the other side was nothing but a lake of gore with a surface that reached slightly above the lower edge of the mirror. The blood splashed on the faucets that were directly below the mirror, spattered the white porcelain sink.

Confused, Max said, "What the devil is this? What's happening here?" He looked from the mirror to Mary. "Are you hurt? Have you cut yourself?"

"No," she said. And only then did she realize that *he* saw the blood, too.

Max touched the rim of the mirror. Impossibly, incredibly, the blood came off on his fingers.

Lou squeezed into the small bathroom to have a better look.

Gradually the blood—on the mirror, faucets, porcelain, and on Max's finger—became less vivid, less brilliantly red, less substantial, faded until it was gone, as if it had never been.

Mary sat on the living room sofa and accepted a glass of brandy from Lou. When she brushed her hair back from her forehead, it felt greasy and cold. There was no color in her face. Her hands were clammy. The brandy burned her throat and brought a welcome warmth.

Standing in front of her, Max said, "What you saw in that mirror before we came after you—does that mean someone will die tonight?"

"Yes," Mary said. "The girl I saw. She'll die. She'll be stabbed before morning."

"What's her name?"

"I didn't see it."

"Where does she live?"

"Here in King's Point. But I didn't sense any address for her."

"Does she live on the hills, in the flats, or around the harbor?"

"It could be any place," Mary said.

"What does she look like?"

"She's got very light yellow hair, almost white. Kinky hair, worn long. Pale skin. Big blue eyes. She's young, in her twenties, very cute. Delicate. No, a better word . . . ethereal."

Max turned to Lou as the newspaperman finished a double shot of Wild Turkey. The way he tossed it back, he might as well have been drinking milk or cyanide. "This is your town, Lou. Do you know anyone who fits that description?"

"We've got ten thousand permanent residents," Lou said. "I don't know all of them. I don't *want* to know all of them. Nine tenths of them are hopeless jackasses, dullards, and bores. Besides, a lot of pretty young blondes are drawn to the Southern California beach life. Sun, sand, sea, sensitivity sessions, sex, and syphilis. In this town there must be at least two hundred tender, achingly ethereal blondes who could be the one Mary saw."

Unconsciously Max had picked up a copy of *The Nation* and had rolled it into a tight tube. He slapped it into the palm of his left hand. "If we don't locate the girl, she'll be killed tonight."

Mary's fear had metamorphosed into a depression like an endless plain of ashes; but beneath the ashes were scattered glowing coals of anger. She was not angry with Max or Lou or with herself, but with fate. Even as the anger built, she knew it was a luxury, that it had no effect or meaning; for the only weapon anyone had against fate was resignation.

"You forget what it means when I foresee something," she told Max. "It doesn't matter if we find this girl and warn her. Nothing matters. She'll die anyway. *I've seen it!* I can't see the names of the winning horses in tomorrow's races. I can't see what stocks will rise in price and which will fall next week. All I can see is people dying." She stood up. "Jesus, but I'm sick of the way I have to live. I'm sick of seeing violence and being unable to prevent it. I'm sick of seeing innocent people in trouble and being unable to help them. I'm tired of a life filled with corpses and violated women and battered children and blood and knives and guns."

"I know," Max said gently.

"I know." She went to the bar and jerked the stopper from the bottle of brandy. "I don't want to be a funnel for other people's misery! I want to be a mechanism for the destruction of that misery, for the amelioration of that misery, for the prevention of it." She poured herself a brandy. "If I'm going to have the all-seeing eye of a god, then dammit, I should have the power of a god, too. I should be able to reach out with that power right this minute and find the man we're after. I should be able to squeeze his heart in a vise of power until it bursts. But I'm not a god. I'm not even a complete mechanism. I'm like half a radio set. I can receive, but I can't transmit. I can be affected, but I can't cause an effect." She drank the brandy as quickly and smoothly as Lou might have done. "I hate it. Hate it. Why do *I* have to have this power? Why *me?*"

Later, at the front door, Lou said, "I wish you'd stay here tonight."

"We've seen your guest room," Max said. "Magazines and books, but no furniture. We appreciate your intellect and the size of your library, but we don't relish sleeping on stacks of old paperbacks."

"I could use the living room sofa tonight," Lou said. "You two could sleep in my room."

Mary kissed him on the cheek. "You're a darling man. But we'll be fine. Really we will. At least until tomorrow night."

# THURSDAY, DECEMBER 24

◆ ◆ ◆

# 12
### ◆ ◆ ◆

At one o'clock in the morning, rain slashed inland from the sea. It made the bare earth slick, flattened the dry grass, bounced off the macadam roadway.

He parked the Mercedes at the end of the paved lane, switched off the engine. Darkness wrapped the car. There was so little light that he could not even see his own hands on the steering wheel. The only sound was the incessant drumming of the rain on the hood and roof.

He decided to wait until the storm passed. The rainy season had come to Southern California; however, sudden cloudbursts like this one seldom lasted long.

The butcher knife was on the seat beside him. He felt for it, picked it up. He could barely see it in the poor light; but he was thrilled by the feel of it as much as by the sight of the well-honed blade. He pressed one finger to the cutting edge, not firmly enough to draw his own blood but hard enough to feel the energy of death lying inert but ready within the tempered steel.

At one-ten the rain slowed to a drizzle. Five minutes after that, it stopped altogether. He opened the car door and got out.

The air was clean and cool. The wind had died down.

Three quarters of a mile to his left and below him, the night around the harbor was strung with lights like Christmas decorations.

The only nearby light came from one of three cottages that stood two hundred yards to the west. These houses were lined up along the cliff, facing seaward, presenting their back doors to the dead-end macadam road. The northernmost cottage, which belonged to Erika

Larsson, was seventy yards from its neighbor and stood in a cluster of trees; lights shone from many of its windows.

As he had expected, Erika was awake. Probably working. One of her somber watercolors. Or a disquieting oil painting full of brooding faces rendered in blues and deep greens. She did most of her painting in the calm, early morning hours and went to bed at dawn.

He walked around the back of the Mercedes and opened the trunk. It was littered with guns—an Italian shotgun, two rifles, and seven handguns—and boxes of ammunition. He chose a .45 Auto Colt, a custom-made collector's piece, all the metalwork heavily engraved with wild animals fleeing from the muzzle back toward the handgrip. It was already loaded. All of the guns were loaded. He put the Colt in his jacket pocket and closed the trunk.

Holding the knife at his side, he walked down the dirt lane toward the lighted house. The night was so unrelievedly dark that he occasionally stumbled over the driveway ruts. His shoes squished in the mud.

Mary murmured in her sleep.

In her dream she was with her father. He looked as he had when she was nine years old; and she was a child again. They were sitting on a velvety green lawn. The sun was high; it came straight down on top of them; and they cast no shadows.

*"If I help people with my ESP, maybe they'll love me. I want people to love me, Daddy."*

*"Well, Sweetcakes, I love you."*

*"But you'll leave me."*

*"Leave my little girl? Nonsense."*

*"You'll die in the car. Die and leave me."*

*"You mustn't say things like that."*

*"But—"*

*"If I did die, you'd still have your mother."*

*"She's left me already. Left me for her whiskey."*

*"No, no. Your mother still loves you."*

*"She loves whiskey. She forgets my name."*

*"Your brother loves you."*

*"No, he doesn't."*

*"Mary, what a terrible thing to say!"*

*"I don't blame Alan for not loving me. All his pets die because of me."*

*"That's not your fault."*

*"You know it is. But even if Alan loves me, he'll leave me someday. Then I'll be alone."*

*"Someday you'll meet a man who'll marry you and love you."*

"*Maybe he'll love me for a little while. But then he'll leave, won't he? Like everyone leaves. I need protection against being left alone. I'm scared of being alone. I need lots of people who love me. If lots and lots of people love me, they won't all be able to go away at the same time.*"

"*Look at the time! I've got to be going.*"

"*Daddy, you can't leave me.*"

"*I don't have any choice.*"

"*I found Elmo this morning.*"

"*Alan's cat?*"

"*I found him all bloody.*"

"*Found him where?*"

"*At the playhouse.*"

"*Not another dead animal?*"

"*Someone cut him to pieces.*"

"*Does Alan know?*"

"*Not yet. Daddy, he'll cry.*"

"*Jesus, the poor kid.*"

"*He'll be awful mad at me.*"

"*Mary . . . you didn't . . .*"

"*No! Daddy, I wouldn't do something like that.*"

"*After what happened last week . . .*"

"*It wasn't me! It wasn't!*"

"*Okay, then it was the Mitchell boy again.*"

"*I wish Mrs. Mitchell would move out of town.*"

"*Berton Mitchell's boy cut up Elmo. Alan won't be mad at you.*"

"*But it's because I had his daddy sent away that he's coming here and killing all of Alan's pets.*"

"*Alan understands. He doesn't hold you responsible.*"

"*Alan's still mad because I threw his turtles in the creek last week.*"

"*You haven't explained why you did that.*"

"*Something told me to.*"

"*You deserved your punishment, you know. They were Alan's turtles, not yours.*"

"*Something told me to.*"

"*Who told you to?*"

"*Something. Something.*"

"*Mary, you're a strange child at times.*"

"*Stay here, and I'll be good.*"

"*Got to go.*"

"*I'll be alone if you go.*"

"*Got to go.*"

"*I'll be alone with the wings.*"

"*Good-bye.*"

"*Daddy, the wings!*"

Whimpering, weighted down in sleep by the sedative she'd taken, Mary turned over, unaware that she was alone in bed.

He pushed up the unlocked bedroom window and slipped inside without making a sound.

Toward the front of the cottage a stereo was playing one of Joan Baez' most soulful albums.

He crossed the bedroom and went down the narrow hall to the living room. Erika Larsson was sitting on a high wooden stool with her back to him. She was at a large easel, working on an oil painting.

The girl's black cat, Samantha, was curled up on an easy chair. It raised its head and stared at him with yellow eyes as he came out of the hallway.

There was a pleasant odor in the air. She had made herself some popcorn not long ago.

He was only ten feet from her when she sensed him and turned. "You," she said.

She was as beautiful as he remembered her. Thick, kinky blond hair. Pale, almost translucent skin. Huge blue eyes. She was wearing jeans and a T-shirt, and her dark nipples were prominent against the thin white material.

She got up from the stool. "What are you doing here?"

He didn't answer.

The black cat knew something was terribly wrong. It jumped down from the chair and ran into the kitchen.

He took another step toward Erika.

She edged around the easel. "Get out of here."

He knocked over the easel.

"What do you want?" she asked.

He held up the knife.

"No. Oh, no."

She backed up against the windows that looked out on the Pacific Ocean.

She held her hands in front of her, as if she would push him away when he tried to close the last few feet between them.

"Mary will know," Erika said.

He said nothing.

"Mary will see who did it," she said.

He reached for her.

"She'll turn you over to the cops. Mary will know!"

Near dawn.

The black cat named Samantha came out of the kitchen cabinet in which she had hidden and fallen asleep. She yawned and stretched. Then she stood for a minute with her head held high, listening.

The cottage was quiet. The wind soughed softly across the roof.

At last, Samantha padded into the living room. The Christmas tree had been knocked on its side. Ornaments were strewn across the floor; vand many of them had been stamped to slivers and dust. Samantha sniffed at a broken glass angel, pushed at its head with one paw. She tasted a crushed candy cane and investigated a broken crucifix that had once hung on the living room wall above the hall door. She nosed around a discarded pair of jeans and a rumpled white T-shirt.

Finally, warily, Samantha circled the body of Erika Larsson and tasted the blood as she had tasted the candy cane.

# 13
◆ ◆ ◆

Like scarecrows flapping on an empty snow-covered field, nightmares had studded her sleep. Most of them were based upon the worst moments of her childhood. This morning filthy rags of those dreams hung around her and made her uneasy, nervous.

Ordinarily, after she showered and before she dressed, she half dried her hair with a towel, then applied one hundred vigorous brush strokes. Now, curiously disturbed by her nakedness, she counted the twenty-eighth stroke and knew that she couldn't wait through seventy-two more before putting on her clothes.

She usually enjoyed performing this and other morning rituals in the nude. She admitted to being an exhibitionist. (See me, see my lovely breasts and ass and legs, see how unmarked, see how very pretty, like me, love me, love me.) But she was motivated by more than exhibitionism. She felt that by beginning the day unclothed, she acquired a sense of lightness and freedom that stayed with her through the afternoon. Dr. Cauvel said that perhaps by starting each day naked, she was trying to prove to herself that her nightly dreams had left no sign on her, that Berton Mitchell had left no sign on her; but she couldn't see the logic in that bit of analysis.

Sometimes Max would sit in perfect silence and watch as she brushed her hair and exercised in the nude. He could make her blush by referring to his voyeurism as "reading beautiful poetry."

But now Max was in the shower. There was no one in the motel room to read her poetry. Yet she felt that someone was staring at her.

Shivering, she put on a brassiere and panties.

When she opened the closet to get slacks and a blouse, she saw Max's muddy shoes and mud-streaked, blood-stained jacket. As she was examining the dark reddish blots on the jacket, Max came out of the bathroom. He was drying his hair with a towel, and another towel was wrapped around his waist.

"Did you hurt yourself?" she asked.

"All I did was take a shower."

She didn't smile. She held up the soiled jacket.

"Oh," he said. "The cut on my finger came open."

"How did that happen?"

"The bandage tore loose when I tripped and fell."

"Fell? When was this?"

"Last night," he said. "After you took your sedative you went right to sleep, but I couldn't keep my eyes closed. I went for a walk. I was three blocks from the hotel when it started to rain. It was a regular cloudburst. Surprised the hell out of me. I started to run back. Took a short cut through the vacant lot next door, tripped on a stone and fell. Pretty stupid of me. The bandage came off my finger and the cut popped open."

She winced. Looking down at the jacket in her hands, she said, "You bled a lot."

"Like a stuck pig." He held up his hand. The injured finger was swathed in clean gauze and adhesive tape. "It still aches."

He tossed aside the towel with which he'd been drying his hair, took the jacket from her, turned it over in his hands. "I don't think any dry cleaner is going to make this look like new." He took the jacket to the wastebasket and threw it away.

"You should have awakened me when you came in last night," Mary said.

"You were a mile under."

"You should have tried."

"What for? It wasn't anything serious. I applied pressure for fifteen minutes, until the bleeding completely stopped. Then I put on a new bandage. Nothing to worry about."

"You should see a doctor."

He shook his head. "No need."

"Well, it's apparently not healing."

"Give it time. It had just begun to heal when I fell and pulled it open," he said. "I'll be more careful."

"The next time you change bandages," she said, "I want to see the cut. If it isn't healing, you'll go to a doctor even if I have to drag you there."

He came to her and put his hands on her slender shoulders. "Yes, Mother." He had a charming smile which he reserved almost exclusively for her.

She sighed and leaned against his chest, where she could hear the slow, steady beat of his heart. "I worry about you."

"I know," he said.

"Because I love you."

"I know."

"Because I'd die if I lost you."

He unhooked her brassiere.

"But we don't have time," she said.

"We'll skip breakfast."

She moved her hands over him. He was solid, powerful. His size and strength had tremendous impact on her. She felt drugged and excited at the same time. Her eyes grew heavy, her legs weak; yet, in her breasts and belly and thighs, she felt an extraordinary heat and tension. The texture of his skin, the steeliness of his muscle and sinew and bone mesmerized her.

He stripped her, then took off the towel he had been wearing around his waist. He kissed her throat. She felt weightless. His hands slid down her back and cupped her buttocks.

"You could hold me so tight," she said, "squeeze me so tight that you'd cut off my breath. You're strong enough to break my neck."

"I don't want to break your neck," he murmured.

"But you could. So easily."

He took her ear lobe between his lips.

"If you . . . broke my neck . . . I don't think . . . I'd care."

He moved one hand between them and touched the moist center of her.

"You'd be so gentle," she said dreamily. "Even as you broke me, you'd be gentle. There wouldn't be pain. You wouldn't allow pain."

He took her to the bed.

As he entered her, as the piston of lovemaking grew slick with her clear oils, she thought about being crushed to death in his arms, and she thought how odd it was for her to consider such a thing, and how much stranger still to consider it without fear and with something very like desire, a melancholy longing, a curiously pleasant anticipation, not a death wish but a sweet resignation, and she knew that Dr. Cauvel would say this was a sign of her sickness, that now she was prepared to surrender even her ultimate responsibility (the fundamental responsibility for her own life, for deciding whether or not she was worthy of life), and he would say that she needed to rely more on herself and less on Max, but she didn't care, didn't care at all; she just felt the power, Max's power, and began to call his name, dug her fingers into his unyielding muscle and surrendered willingly.

"Roger Fullet speaking."

"Your name fits. Fullet, you're full of it."

"Lou? Is that you? Lou Pasternak?"

"I called and asked for Roger Fullet, the reporter, and was promptly told it's now Roger Fullet, the editor."

"It happened a month ago."

"The *Los Angeles Times* is degenerating swiftly."

"They finally recognized brilliance."

"Oh? You mean after just promoting you they're giving your job to someone else?"

"Very funny."

"Thank you."

"You're a funny man."

"Thank you."

"Plastic surgery might help."

"Watch it, Fullet. You're no match for me."

"Sorry. Lost my head."

"It wouldn't be the first time."

"Hey, Lou, I've got an office with this job that's almost as large as your whole shop."

"They gave you an office so they could lock you in it and keep you out from under foot."

"I dine with the brass."

"Because they don't trust you with the silver."

"Christ, it's good to hear your voice."

"How are Peggy and the kids?"

"Fine. Wonderful. Everyone's healthy."

"Give them my love and wish them a merry Christmas for me."

"I will. You'll have to come visit for a weekend soon. You know we haven't seen each other in six months? We live so close, only an hour or so apart. Lou, why don't we get together more often?"

"Maybe subconsciously we loathe each other."

"Nobody could possibly loathe me. I'm just a big Hershey Bar. My daughter says so."

"Well, Mr. Hershey Bar, I wonder if you could do me a favor."

"Name it, Lou."

"I'd like you to go back through the *Times'* morgue and get me all available background on a crime that interests me."

"What sort of crime?"

"Child molestation."

"Ugly."

"Also assault with intent to kill."

"Where did it happen?"

"Somewhere in West Los Angeles. A pretty good neighborhood. The girl lived on a twenty-acre estate that's probably since been subdivided."

"When was this?"

"Twenty-four, maybe twenty-five years ago."

"Who was the victim?"

"This gets touchy."

"How so?"

"Roger, she's a dear friend."

"I see."

"She's also a celebrity of sorts, very much in the public eye."

"I'm intrigued."

"I don't intend to write about this. And I don't want anyone else writing about it."

"If it's twenty-five years old, it's dead material for a newspaper."

"I know that. But someone might be able to use it in a magazine piece. It would hurt her badly if it were all dredged up again."

"If you aren't writing about it, why do you need to know?"

"She's in trouble. Bad trouble. I want to help her."

"Why can't you get the details of this thing from her?"

"She was only six years old when it happened."

"My God."

"She can't possibly remember it all—or remember it correctly."

"And what happened back then has some connection with the bad trouble she's in now?"

"I think it might."

"Okay. I won't send someone else to do the work. There'd be a leak if I did. I'll go down to the morgue and pick through the files myself."

"Thanks, Roger."

"And I'll go as your friend, not as a reporter."

"That's good enough for me."

"What's the victim's name?"

"Mary Bergen. No, wait . . . back then it was Mary Tanner."

"The clairvoyant?"

"That's right."

"We carry her column."

"So do I."

"Who was the assailant?"

"Berton Mitchell. B-E-R-T-O-N. M-I-T-C-H-E-L-L. He was the caretaker for the Tanner estate."

"I'll get the full background. Is there something about it that especially interests you?"

"I want to know if Mitchell ever stood trial. If he had his day in court, I want to know whether he was acquitted and set free, or found guilty."

"You said he was the assailant."

"That doesn't mean he was found guilty. You know what a good attorney can accomplish."

"Anything else?"

"Most of all, if Mitchell *was* found guilty, I want to know if he committed suicide."

"Is that what you've been told?"

"Yes. But I don't know if it's true."

"Lou, if he's still alive, and if he's not in prison, I doubt I could find him through our files."

"I'm not asking you to find him. If Mitchell's alive, then I think I know where he is."

"I'll get back to you this afternoon."

"I'll be at the office."

When he concluded his conversation with Roger Fullet, Lou placed a long-distance telephone call to the home of Dr. Oliver Railsbeck, an old friend who worked at Stanford University. They talked for fifteen minutes.

At nine-thirty, after he had learned what he could from Ollie Railsbeck, Lou walked down the hall to the guest bath. He had cleaned up the mess the previous night; the broken glass and spilled cough syrup were gone. He stood in the center of the small room and studied the mirror above the washbasin. There was no reflection but his own.

He touched the glass and the mirror frame, touched the faucets and the porcelain sink. The night before, all of these things had been splashed with blood that Mary had conjured up and briefly sustained with her psychic power. Thick wet blood that was real . . . yet not real. Blood that had substance, color, and texture (if only for a few seconds), but which was not of this world.

He wondered whose pain and suffering it had represented. It could be the symbolic blood of the blonde whose death Mary had predicted. Or perhaps it was Mary's blood that had vanished from Max's fingertips.

An omen of her death?

"God help her," Lou said aloud.

# 14
◆ ◆ ◆

Mary sat on an uncomfortable metal chair, her purse on her lap, her hands on the purse.

Max was on a chair at her left side. He knew she didn't like long conversations with policemen, and that the dreary, cold, atmosphere of police stations unnerved her. Several times during the past quarter hour he had reached out and touched her. Nothing obvious. Little pats and squeezes of affection and reassurance. As always, his presence buoyed her.

To her right Lou had turned another chair around so that he could sit with his arms crossed on the back of it.

The room smelled of stale cigar smoke. The overhead lights were too bright. The only decorations on the walls were photographs of the late J. Edgar Hoover, Chief Patmore's idol, and a military calendar that had a different battle scene for each month.

John Patmore, senior officer of the King's Point police force, hunched over his cluttered desk and spoke earnestly into the telephone to Percy Osterman. Apparently the sheriff was doling out a considerable amount of flattery in order to persuade Patmore to cooperate with Mary. A smile that was almost a smirk played at the corners of Patmore's weak mouth.

He was a surprisingly bland-looking man. Late forties. Round face. Mostly bald. Brown eyes. Plain features. Average height and average weight.

She worried that they hadn't made a strong case in their plea for Patmore's assistance. Lou had advised her not to discuss the more bizarre aspects of her story. She had said nothing about flying glass dogs, deadly sea gulls, or bathroom mirrors that brimmed with blood. All of that, Lou insisted, would confuse Patmore. After Lou explained the nature of Mary's psychic powers, she had told the policeman only that the mass murders of the last few days were the work of one man, that he had killed a young woman in King's Point last night (although the body had not yet been found), and that at seven o'clock this evening he would open fire with a high-powered rifle from one of the three towers that overlooked the harbor.

At last, Patmore said good-bye to Percy Osterman and put down the receiver. He leaned back in his chair. For almost a minute he stared off into space. He was smiling.

"Don't let the chief upset you. He doesn't *mean* to be insulting," Lou said to Max and Mary. "Every once in a while he stops to think and forgets to start again."

Ignoring the newsman, Patmore turned to Mary. "I don't like this— a lunatic killer in my town."

She said, "If we—"

Taking a cigar from the center drawer of his desk, Patmore said, "Not one bit do I like it. I run a very tight little town as chief of police."

"We can—"

"In each of those towers," Patmore said, "because Percy Osterman vouched for you, although I still have my doubts about this psychic stuff, at six o'clock, one hour ahead of schedule if you're right, I'll have the men."

Not certain that she had properly interpreted that convoluted sentence, Mary said, "Then you'll put men in the towers tonight?"

Patmore blinked. He had started to wet the end of his cigar. He took it out of his mouth. "Now, didn't I just say that?"

"You'll have to excuse the chief," Lou said. "He thinks that 'syntax' is the money the church collects from sinners."

Much to Mary's relief, the policeman studiously ignored Lou. He said, "Let's have the details again; your vision from start to finish."

She sighed and relaxed slightly.

She thought: this particular horror is drawing to an end.

Then: Is it? Or is it only just beginning?

"Are you feeling well?" Max asked.

"Yes," she lied.

On the sidewalk in front of police headquarters, Max turned to Lou and said, "Well, that was a lot easier than you said it would be."

Lou shrugged. "I'm surprised. Ordinarily it takes a surgical procedure to get a new idea into his head."

"Evidently," Mary said, "he's even more impressed by Percy Osterman than you thought."

Lou said, "That's definitely a part of it. But I guess it's also self-preservation. He knows that if he called you a charlatan and threw you out of his office, and then the killer *did* strike from one of those towers, I'd call for his resignation on the front page of my newspaper twice every week until he was out of a job.''

Max suggested they leave the cars parked and walk two blocks to the harbor. ''We can have drinks and lunch at The Sea Locker while we watch the boats.''

She walked between Max and Lou, and gradually her spirits lifted. The breeze scoured Patmore's cigar smoke from her; it sluiced away some of her tension and anxiety as well.

The weather had improved. Although the sky was still overcast, and although rain was forecast for tomorrow, this was one of those widely advertised Southern California winter days. The temperature had risen to seventy degrees. The air was so clean and fresh that it almost wasn't there. This was the kind of day that made all of the transplanted Easterners happy they had moved.

A block from the harbor they came to a pet shop where two spaniel puppies peered out from a window cage.

''Oh, aren't they cute!'' Mary said. She slipped from between Max and Lou, went to the window.

The puppies stood with their front paws on the glass and tried to sniff the hand she offered them. Their tails whipped frantically back and forth.

''Never cared for dogs,'' Lou said. ''They're too dependent.''

''They're sweet,'' she said.

''I don't like cats either.''

Max said, ''Why not?''

''They're too *in*dependent.''

''Lou, you're trying too hard,'' Max said.

Smiling, the newsman said, ''Well, in some quarters I'm known as a bitter curmudgeon. I've got to uphold my reputation, don't I?''

Mary spoke to the dogs through the window, and they wiggled and barked ecstatically.

''I know how much you love animals,'' Max said. ''I thought about getting you a dog for Christmas. Maybe I should have done it.''

''Oh, no,'' she said, still playing with the puppies. ''It would have died.''

Lou looked at her curiously. ''What an odd thing to say.''

Memories of mutilated cats and dogs and rabbits and other small creatures flickered in disgusting colors behind her eyes.

She turned away from the spaniels. ''Alan had a great many animals when he was a boy. I had a few myself. But all of them were tortured and killed.''

''Tortured and killed?'' Lou asked. ''What in the name of God are you talking about?''

"Berton Mitchell's boy did it," Mary said. "He thought I'd falsely accused his father. So he kept sneaking onto the estate and slaughtering our pets. One by one. Year after year. Until we finally stopped keeping animals."

With a tenderness that touched her, Max said, "So the nightmares didn't end when Mitchell hanged himself in that prison cell."

His gray eyes, so often flat and expressionless, were filled with sympathy and love.

Lou said, "I didn't know that Berton Mitchell had a family."

Mary nodded. "A wife and son. Of course, they moved off the estate after . . . after what happened. But they never left the city. They were always nearby."

She glanced at the spaniels, but they no longer appealed to her. When she looked at them now, she couldn't see anything but Alan's dogs: dead dogs with broken legs and dozens of knife wounds, gutted dogs, beheaded dogs, dogs with their eyes punched out . . .

Lou said, "This Mitchell boy—"

"No more about that," she said shakily. "Let's get to The Sea Locker. I can use a drink."

The men's room at the restaurant reeked of pine-scented disinfectant.

As they washed their hands at the twin sinks (Max being careful to keep his bandaged finger dry), Lou said, "Did I ever mention my friend, Ollie Railsbeck?"

"I don't recall the name," Max said.

"He's in charge of a relatively new research effort at Stanford University. They're investigating all kinds of paranormal things— clairvoyance, precognition, psychometry, telepathy, telekinesis, astral projection, *everything*."

"I think I *do* remember the name," Max said. He turned off the water and jerked a paper towel from the dispenser. "I think they've asked Mary to cooperate in some experiments, but she hasn't found the time yet."

Pulling a towel from the dispenser on the wall, Lou said, "Ever since we learned that the Russians are spending almost a billion dollars a year on research to find military applications for psychic phenomena, the Pentagon's been willing to part with a few bucks to fund general studies in the field. Ollie's department and the one that Dr. Rhine started years ago at Duke University are the best programs of their sort in the country."

"Mary's done some work at Duke."

"This morning I called Ollie Railsbeck and asked his opinion about what happened at the house last night, about the blood that came out of the mirror."

"What did he say?"

"He called it 'ectoplasm.' "

"I'm familiar with the word," Max said. He threw away his paper towel and turned toward the men's room door.

"Wait," Lou said. "I didn't want to bring this up in front of Mary."

Max leaned against the wall. "Go ahead."

"According to Ollie, that kind of experience isn't as unique as I thought it was. He says similar things occur at séances."

Max raised his eyebrows. "Your friend's spending our tax dollars to study séances? Those phony sessions the gypsies run, that dark-room-and-candles bit where people who want to talk to dead relatives get bilked out of their money?"

"There are some highly respected mediums who take their work seriously, who don't want money or notoriety, and who conduct some of the damnedest, scariest séances."

"They talk to ghosts?"

"Maybe. They think they do. They talk to *something* that seems to talk back. Anyway, Ollie says that every now and then the form of a spirit or an object will appear above the séance table or over the medium's head while she's in a trance."

"And it's not done with slide projectors focused on a plastic sheet or anything like that?"

"These apparitions have been seen and studied by researchers in a controlled laboratory environment," Lou said. "Sometimes blood will drip out of thin air. Or what appears to be tears. Whatever the nature of the manifestation, it has substance, just as if it's real."

"But only for a short time. Last night the blood that came out of that mirror faded quickly."

"Right. It usually lasts seconds. Sometimes a full minute. Ollie knows of a case where a child's face floated above the medium for twenty minutes, but that's rare. Temporarily solid apparitions like these are supposedly composed of ectoplasm, a supernatural material that, the mediums say, is able to pass between the dimensions of life and death."

Max said, "This friend of yours believes in ghosts?"

"No. He says most of the genuinely talented mediums have highly developed psychic abilities. They score well on card tests for telepathy. Most of them have well documented records of accurate predictions. Ollie thinks that somehow, by the use of a psychic ability we don't understand, they unconsciously create the ectoplasm."

"He doesn't believe it's material from another world?"

"No. And especially not from the afterlife."

Max thought about that for a moment. He said, "Then in Railsbeck's view ectoplasm is sort of the realized flesh of a psychic's subconscious thoughts."

"Exactly," Lou said.

"So Railsbeck supports what I've been saying."

"That's why I wanted to tell you when we were alone," Lou said. "I didn't want to upset Mary."

"There's no supernatural, demonic force operating here."

Lou sighed and shook his head. "I'm not absolutely convinced of that. You're probably right. But I'm keeping an open mind. However, you *are* convinced, and Ollie sides with you, so I'll keep my mouth shut."

Max made a fist of one hand and pounded it into the other. The sound was sharp; it startled Lou, and it echoed off the tile walls. "*Mary* created the blood that came out of the mirror, like she caused the poltergeist, but she doesn't realize it and refuses to believe it. She's seen something terrible, Lou. To keep from facing it, she's used psychic powers she never knew she had in order to construct a facade of 'supernatural' events to mislead herself. She's seen something she's had to force out of her mind, something she's buried in her subconscious. She's using poltergeists and other supernatural bunk to distract herself from the thing she most fears about this case."

Tense and depressed, Lou said, "We can't help her because we don't know what she's hiding from herself."

Max was grim. "We'll know at seven o'clock tonight." He looked at his watch. "A little more than seven hours to go."

The gray water looked cold and oily. It rolled against the docks; and the prows of boats cleaved it like knives slicing dark gelatin.

They had a window table at The Sea Locker. Initially, while Max and Lou talked politics, Mary sat in silence and studied the sky for sea gulls. But there were no birds today, and gradually she shifted her attention to the traffic on the harbor and to the conversation.

Although there were no gulls to worry her, she wasn't able to relax. She ate too little and drank too much; there were jokes about her trying to drink Lou under the table; but the whiskey didn't steady her hands.

At two o'clock, after Lou had gone to his office and they had returned to the motel, she stretched out on the bed, on her side, intending to take a nap. She would need to be rested and alert for the manhunt tonight.

She closed her eyes and tried to switch off her mind. The wine she had drunk at lunch was of some help. She felt she was drifting in lazy circles on a rubber raft in a gigantic swimming pool. She began some light meditation, repeating the word "one" to herself until it filled her and pushed out all other thoughts.

At the borderland of sleep she heard onrushing wings: *wicka-wicka-wicka!*

She opened her eyes.

Nothing there.

Imagination.

Max was behind her in an armchair, reading the *King's Point Press*. If there had been any unusual sound, he would have spoken.

She closed her eyes and began thinking the word "one" again.

*Wicka-wicka-wicka!*

She opened her eyes. Still nothing.

She knew the wings had something to do with Berton Mitchell. And they were also part of the case she was working on now. The killer she was stalking was somehow connected to Berton Mitchell. Impossible. Unthinkable. But . . .

She felt tormented. All she wanted was some peace. All she wanted was to be left alone. All she wanted was to *get through this case!*

She squeezed her eyes shut and tried to stop the tears, but they spilled down her cheeks anyway.

She was frightened. She wanted Max. She wanted him to get up and come to her. She started to roll toward him, was about to say his name, and then she thought: *No, by God! Be strong for once.*

Sooner or later she would have to learn to handle some of her own problems. She was increasingly aware of the fragility of life. She could feel her mortality—and not merely her own but Max's and Lou's and Alan's, too—feel it as surely as if it were fragments of ice melting through her fingers. Someday Max might be gone, and how would she survive if she couldn't deal with adversity on her own?

She would have to face up to what had happened twenty-four years ago. She would have to think, force herself back in time, find the meaning of the wings. She wouldn't be able to uncover the connection between Berton Mitchell and this killer until she remembered all about the wings and what had happened in the caretaker's cottage.

She waited until the tears had dried, then got up from the bed.

"Something wrong?" Max asked.

"Can't sleep."

"Do you want to talk?"

"Go ahead and read the paper. I just want to think."

She picked up the spiral-bound notebook and pen that were on the nightstand. She went to the small desk and sat down.

She would do what she always did when she had a problem that no one could solve for her: she would write about it. She would write dozens of questions, one on every sixth or seventh line, and search for answers to put on the lines between them. That process always relaxed her. Of course, she sought more than relaxation. She wanted answers. Sometimes she got them.

However, after all these years, she could no longer delude herself.

Knowing the solution and being able to act on it were two very different things. She had the wit but not the strength. Although she had performed this ritual with notebook and pen hundreds of times, she had never gotten from it what she most expected: she had yet to reach an important decision entirely on her own; she had yet to handle a serious problem without someone's help.

This time would be different. It *had* to be different. She sensed that if she failed to find a new strength within herself, she wouldn't survive much longer.

She opened the notebook which she had purchased the day before but had not yet used, and she saw writing on the first ruled page.

Mary! Run for your life!

It was written in ballpoint pen. The words appeared to have been put down in haste. And although it was definitely her own handwriting, she had no memory whatsoever of having scribbled it.

Roger Fullet called at four o'clock and gave Lou a detailed synopsis of the Berton Mitchell story as it had been reported by the *Los Angeles Times*. " . . . and after only twenty minutes of deliberation, the jury found him guilty of all charges. His lawyer immediately filed an appeal based on technicalities, but Mitchell must have realized there wasn't any chance of a new trial. His sentences on all counts were to be served consecutively and amounted to a minimum of twenty-five years."

"And he hanged himself?" Lou asked.

"Just like you've been told. He did it the day after the sentencing, before he was transferred from the county jail to prison."

"You mentioned his family."

"The wife and one son."

"What was the son's name?"

"Barry. Barry Mitchell."

"How old was he when this happened?"

"I didn't make a note of it. But I seem to remember he was sixteen."

"Was there anything more on him in your files?" Lou asked.

"He visited his father in jail every day. He was convinced Mitchell was innocent like he claimed."

"Anything else?"

"These days the press would badger the hell out of the wife and son. America's gotten more ghoulish in the past couple decades. Every day newspaper readers have a greater interest in peeking into personal tragedies than they had the day before. But twenty-four years ago

Americans still had some sense of privacy and propriety. The wife and son were left alone. There's nothing more in our files.''

Lou drummed a pencil on the top of his desk. ''I wonder what happened to the son.''

''Can't help you, I'm afraid.''

''You've done more than enough. Thanks, Roger.''

After they exchanged another round of holiday greetings, Lou hung up.

As he put down the receiver, his secretary came in to wish him a merry Christmas before going home. The office was quiet after she had gone.

He hadn't turned on any lights when he came back from lunch. Now, as the early darkness gradually descended, he sat alone in lengthening shadows, staring, thinking.

What was it that Mary feared?

What was so special about this case?

One pet theory had been demolished by what Roger Fullet had told him. The psychopathic killer loose in King's Point was not Berton Mitchell.

The son? Barry Mitchell? He would be forty, Max's age. Not much older than his father had been when he attacked Mary. Madness sometimes ran in families, didn't it? Like father, like son. Maybe it would be Barry Mitchell who would climb those tower stairs at seven o'clock tonight.

As the muddy evening light replaced the afternoon, the office grew chilly. Finally, for warmth, Lou got up and poured a double shot of bourbon.


Determined not to run to Max with the five-word warning in the front of her notebook, Mary wrote down fifty-four questions and half as many answers, seeking understanding and solutions in the only way she knew. As yet she had discovered nothing new about the tortures and outrages that had transpired in that cottage twenty-four years earlier, not the slightest clue to the meaning of the wings, but she was not ready to quit.

Although it interrupted her train of thought and made her increasingly nervous, she repeatedly turned back to the first page and read the two short sentences: *Mary! Run for your life!* She tried to convince herself that it was someone else's work, that some stranger had sneaked into the motel room and had written the warning while she and Max were out. Perhaps the killer had done it. But she knew that wasn't true. It made no sense. Besides, she recognized her penmanship. She must have gotten out of bed in the middle of the night without disturbing

Max and, while still sound asleep, scrawled an urgent message to herself. Asleep, she had foreseen great danger. But what knowledge had she possessed in sleep that eluded her now that she was awake?

Getting out of the armchair behind her, Max said, "Do you want to freshen up?"

She turned. "What?"

"It's five-thirty. We're to meet Lou at six. I thought you'd want to freshen up."

"Oh, sure." She closed the notebook. She stood.

"Are you okay?" he asked.

"Yes."

He stared at her, concerned.

"No," she said. "No, I'm not."

He came to her, kissed her cheek.

"I'm scared," she said.

"So am I," he said.

"What's going to happen to me?"

"Nothing bad," he said.

"I don't know."

"I *do* know," he said. "Stay close to me tonight, until they catch the bastard."

She asked, "What if they don't catch him?"

"You said they would."

"No. I just said he'd be in one of the towers."

"If they're waiting for him, they'll catch him," Max said soothingly.

"Maybe."

# 15
◆ ◆ ◆

6:00 P.M.

Officer Lyle Winterman parked the squad car out of sight in an alleyway and walked two blocks to St. Luke's Lutheran Church. Even with a streetlight every hundred feet Harbor Avenue seemed dark.

Winterman kept his right hand on the holstered revolver at his hip. The flap of the holster was unsnapped. His palm was on the gun butt.

He expected someone to leap out at him. After Patmore's talk at the station, the deputy was jumpy as hell.

Reverend Richard Erdman was waiting in the nave of the church. They shook hands and went to the door that opened on the bell tower stairs.

"What's this all about?" Erdman asked.

"We're working on a tip," Winterman said.

"A tip about what?"

"Chief Patmore would rather I didn't say."

"Is there going to be violence?"

"There might be."

"I don't want violence in my church."

"Neither do I, Reverend."

"This is God's house. It will remain a place of peace."

"I hope so. Just the same, you'd better go back to the rectory and lock your doors."

"I have a Christmas Eve service to prepare for."

"That doesn't start until later, does it?"

"Eleven," Erdman said. "But I begin preparing at ten."

"I'll be gone long before that," Winterman said.

The officer unhooked a flashlight that was clipped to his belt and switched it on. He directed its beam to the tower stairs, hesitated, then began to climb.

Erdman shut the door behind him.


6:05 P.M.

Officer Rudy Holtzman wasn't supposed to be working on Christmas Eve. It was his night off. All the way up the tower stairs he cursed John Patmore.

Psychics, premonitions, fortunetellers, extrasensory perception—it was all bullshit. The chief was making a fool of himself. Nothing new about that, of course. But a clairvoyant? Too much.

Holtzman reached the top of the tower at Kimball's Games and Snacks. Under him the deserted building was quiet.

He switched off his flashlight and looked out at the harbor for a moment. On a half dozen boats, parties had already gotten underway.

"Damn!" Holtzman said.

He sat down with his back to the waist-high wall around the observation deck. He put his revolver on the floor beside him.

He half hoped that some bastard with a rifle *did* try to come up those stairs. Maybe he would feel better if he could shoot someone.

\* \* \*

6:10 P.M.

A well lighted eighty-foot yacht cruised around the bay end of the harbor and started down the north channel toward the sea. Waves from its wake slapped rhythmically against the sea wall.

The wind from the ocean carried a vague odor of decay.

John Patmore and his assistant—a young, overweight officer named Rollins—used a corner of The Laughing Dolphin Restaurant's parking lot as a command post for the operation. From there they had a view of all three towers.

The Mercedes was parked beside the patrol car. Mary leaned against the fender. Max was at her left side, Lou at her right.

She was hoping for another vision. She still had time to foresee which tower the killer would try to use, time to help the police consolidate their efforts, perhaps even time enough to prevent the slaughter to come. Thus far, however, she had received no new images.

She was shivering uncontrollably, but not because of the cool night air.

At six-fifteen, Officer Teagarten, who was assigned to the Roman Catholic Church of the Holy Trinity, called Patmore on the walkie-talkie to say religious services were in progress. Furthermore, the Knights of Columbus were having a party in the church basement that would last until confessions began prior to midnight Mass. It was Teagarten's opinion that no killer, not even a psychopath, would attempt to use Trinity's bell tower if he had to walk through so many witnesses to get there. Teagarten wanted to go home.

"You," Patmore said over the walkie-talkie, "until I've told you different, stay right the hell where you are."

Officer Rollins divided his attention among the three towers, studying them through binoculars.

Patmore ignored Mary. He hadn't bothered to say hello when she arrived, and he still refused even to look her way.

"If this doesn't work out," Lou said, "the chief will swear he never met you."

6:30 P.M.

A dozen boat parties were in progress all along the harbor. Within an hour there would be a dozen more. Laughter, the squeals of young women, and music from several stereos drifted across the water.

Most of the craft, from the smallest sailboats to the largest motor yachts, were decorated for the season. Strings of colored lights wound around the deck railings and encircled the ports. A few of the biggest yachts, able to tap the power in their huge engines and banks of batteries, were swathed in layers of light, as if weighed down beneath scores of incandescent Hawaiian leis. There were boats with green lights arranged to form Christmas trees on their masts, boats that used golden lights to transform their masts into gigantic crosses, boats carrying life-size statues of Santa Claus, boats with cardboard and Styrofoam reindeer capering across cabin roofs, boats draped with paper chrysanthemums, evergreen boughs, holly, and fresh flowers. The ships blazed against the night.

In his own way Lou Pasternak was proud of King's Point. He could deliver an hour-long monologue dissecting its many faults, but he never failed to point out that it was, if nothing else, the loveliest beach town in California.

Pretty as it was, however, the harbor could not distract him for more than a few minutes tonight. He finally turned to Mary and said, "Can we talk about Barry Mitchell?"

She jerked as if he'd pinched her.

"Mary?" he said.

"You startled me."

"I'm sorry."

"What about Barry Mitchell?" she asked.

"He was what . . . ten years older than you?"

"About that, I think."

"Do you recall what he looked like?"

"He was tall, a big boy."

"What color was his hair?"

"Dark," she said. "Brown, I suppose."

"His eyes?"

"I don't remember."

"You said he killed Alan's pets."

"And the few I had as well."

"Was he caught at it?"

"Alan saw him killing a squirrel we owned."

"Was he apprehended in the act?"

"No. He was too big for Alan."

"Were charges ever brought?"

"We had no proof," she said.

"You had Alan's testimony."

"The word of one boy against another."

"So you stopped keeping pets," Lou said.

"Yes."

Max put his arm around Mary's shoulders.

"Nothing was done to Barry Mitchell?" Lou asked.

"My father's attorney had a talk with his mother."

"What did he accomplish?"

"Nothing. Barry Mitchell denied killing them."

Max asked, "Why all these questions, Lou?"

Lou hesitated, then decided there was no reason to keep his suspicions a secret. "You've told me there's something very unusual about the killer we're after tonight. Max has told me the same thing. The two of you disagree as to *what* is unusual about him. But suppose . . . what if the man we're tracking is Berton Mitchell's son?"

She shook her head. "No."

"Why not?" Lou asked.

"He's dead," she said.

Lou stared in surprise.

"You mean Barry Mitchell's dead?" Max asked.

"His mother, too," Mary said.

"What?"

"His mother died, too. The same night."

Lou asked, "When did this happen?"

"I was eleven at the time."

"Nineteen years ago."

"That's about right."

"They died together?"

"Yeah."

"How?"

"They were killed by an intruder."

"A burglar?" Lou asked.

"I suppose so. I don't remember."

"You don't know the killer's name?"

"Is that important?"

"Did they ever catch anyone?"

"I don't know," she said.

"Who told you about this?" Lou asked.

"Alan."

"Are you certain he knew what he was talking about?"

"Oh, yes," she said. "I think he might have showed me a newspaper clipping about it."

Lou sagged against the Mercedes, disappointed that yet another theory had been demolished.

But if the wife and son had been murdered just five years after Berton Mitchell committed suicide, why hadn't Roger Fullet found that information in the *Los Angeles Times'* files on the case?

Something exceedingly strange was happening. He was not a theatrical man given to bursts of melodrama. Nonetheless, he swore he could *feel* evil in the air that night.

A woman's laughter bounced across the rippled water, high and shrill.

\* \* \*

7:00 P.M.

Mary squeezed Max's hand and waited tensely. Any minute the walkie-talkie would crackle with a report from one of the deputies. Any second there would be news of a man sneaking up the stairs in one of those towers; and when it came, the chase would begin in earnest.

7:03.

Mary repeatedly glanced at her watch in the back glow of the police cruiser's headlights. She shifted restlessly from one foot to the other.

7:04.

For the first time in more than an hour, Chief Patmore looked at her, met her eyes. He wasn't happy.

7:06.

She was beginning to feel that she had been outmaneuvered, out-witted. For the first time in her career she had encountered an adversary who was a match for her. She was tracking a man against whom all of her psychic abilities provided no advantage.

7:09.

She was numb with fear. "Something's wrong," she said.

"What is it?" Max asked.

"The killer's not coming."

Lou said, "But you *saw* him do it."

"And what you see always happens," Max said.

"Not this time," she said. "This one's different. He knows I'm after him. He knows the cops are watching the towers."

Lou said, "If Patmore's men have been too obvious—"

"No," she said. "It's just that the killer's able to anticipate me. He isn't coming."

Lou said, "Don't tell Patmore. We've got to wait a little while. We can't give up yet."


When there was no sign of a suspect at any of the towers by 7:30, John Patmore began to stride back and forth in front of his patrol car, scowling. As the minutes passed, he paced faster.

At 7:45 he picked up the walkie-talkie from the hood of the car; for fifteen minutes he talked without pause to Winterman, Holtzman, and Teagarten. Twice he lost control and shouted at them.

Finally he put down the walkie-talkie and came to Mary.

"The man isn't coming," she said.

"Was he *ever* really expected?" Patmore asked.

"Yes, of course." She was miserable. She felt she'd hurt Lou by using his influence and then failing to deliver what she promised.

"What made him change his mind?" Patmore asked.

"He knows we're waiting for him," Max said.

"Yeah? Who told him?"

"No one," Mary said. "He senses it."

"Senses it? How?"

"He must . . . he probably . . . "

"Yeah?"

She sighed. "I don't know."

"In my office," Patmore said angrily, "you knew so much this morning. Everything you knew. Now you don't know anything all of a goddamned sudden. Obviously you also don't know that if I want, I can get nasty about someone coming to my office, this false crime report, a thing like that, wasting my time and the time of my men only to have some laughs, all for some sort of a lark!"

"Don't have a stroke," Lou said. "And don't try to give Mary a stroke."

Patmore turned away from her, faced Lou. "You'd share the blame if I pursued this."

"You don't have anything to pursue," Lou said patiently. "You know perfectly well that we didn't file a crime report—let alone one that was false. We simply came to your office to tell you that we had good reason to believe a crime would be committed."

Patmore glared at him. "You set me up."

"John, that is ridiculous."

"And Percy Osterman helped you. Why? Hell, no. You don't have to tell me. I see it, why he did. When people here voted, and Percy was against it from the start, for their own police, he was upset. He doesn't care for me much, does he? He never showed it, but he sure mustn't."

Lou said, "You're all wrong. Be reasonable, John. There's no conspiracy against you. Mary's sincere. Percy was sincere. We all are. We—"

"You want to make me look like a fool." Patmore wagged his finger in Lou's face. "You damned well better not print in your paper anything about this, about me falling for this psychic crap, because I'll sue you if you do for libel. I'll sue you for everything you've got." There was an uncharacteristic fire in his usually dull brown eyes.

Mary took hold of Lou's arm. "I'm wrung out, Lou. I don't want trouble for you or me."

"Yeah," Max said. "Let's drop it. Let's go."

Exasperated with the policeman, Lou said, "John, I'm not going to write about you. I haven't any desire to make you look like a fool in the *Press*. You've got to realize there's a psychopathic killer loose in this town and—"

Still seething, Patmore said, "You've written about me before."

Lou was getting angry. "I've always written tame 'loyal opposition' articles when I've disagreed with you. I've never been unfair to you. In fact, I think I've been too tolerant. It's not my style to do a hatchet job. God knows, if I'd wanted to make you look like an idiot, I could have done it.''

Mary squeezed Lou's arm, tugged at him.

Patmore said, ''You're a crummy reporter with a stinking two-bit newspaper, and you're a lousy drunk to boot.''

For an instant she thought Lou was going to hit him. But he only stared hard at Patmore and said, ''A drunk can always go on the wagon and sober up. But a stupid man who has a bottom-of-the-bucket IQ has to live with what he has forever.''

''Shit,'' Patmore said. He walked back to the front of the squad car, picked up the walkie-talkie, and called Winterman, Holtzman, and Teagarten out of the towers.

''I'm sorry,'' Mary said to Lou. ''I'm so sorry.''

''It's not your fault he's an idiot.''

Max opened the car door. ''Come on. Let's get out of here.''

When they were settled in Lou Pasternak's book-strewn living room once more, Max asked, ''What now?''

''We wait,'' Mary said.

''For what?'' Lou asked.

Wearily, she said, ''We wait for him to start killing people again.''

# FRIDAY,
# DECEMBER 25

◆◆◆

# 16
### ◆ ◆ ◆

The motel room was dark.

She was lying on her side. She turned onto her back.

She felt claustrophobic, as if the ceiling had begun to descend upon her.

"Can't shut off your mind?" Max asked.

"I thought you were asleep."

"I've been waiting for you to doze off first."

"You were so quiet," she said.

"Trying not to disturb you."

"What time is it?"

"Three o'clock."

"Go to sleep, darling. I'll be fine."

"I can't sleep if I know you're worried."

"I keep thinking I hear someone trying the door."

"No one's been at the door. I'd have heard it."

"And I keep thinking someone's at the window."

"Not that either. It's nerves."

"Screaming mimis," she said.

"Maybe you should take a sedative."

"I had a sleeping pill two hours ago."

"So take another."

"What is he, Max?"

"Who?"

"The killer."

"Just a man."

"No."

"Yes, Mary. Yes. Just a man."

Darkness pulsed around her.

"He's something more," she said.

"Take another sleeping pill."

"I guess I should. But I was beginning to cut down. I was beginning to break the habit."

"After this case you can go cold turkey. But right now the pills aren't an indulgence. You've got good reason to need them."

"Will you get one for me?"

He fetched a glass of water and the sedative, waited while she took it, switched off the light and returned to bed.

"Move close," she said.

Her back was against his chest. Her buttocks against his groin. Two spoons in a drawer.

Several minutes passed in warm silence.

At last she said, "I'm getting sleepy."

"Good." He stroked her hair.

Still later: "Max?"

"Hmmm?"

"Maybe he can't help being bad and doing awful things. Maybe he was born bad. Maybe evil isn't *always* learned. Maybe parents and environment aren't *always* to blame for an evil child. Sometimes maybe it's in the genes."

"Will you hush?"

"Max, am I going to die?"

"Eventually. We all do."

"But soon? Will I die soon?"

"Not soon. I'm here."

"Hold me."

"I'm holding you."

"I want to be strong."

"You are strong."

"I am?"

"You just don't realize it."

In ten minutes she was asleep.

He continued to stroke her hair.

He listened to her breathing.

He didn't want her to die. He hoped she didn't *have* to die. He wished with all of his heart and mind that she would give up on this case. Let the killing be done. She shouldn't feel responsible. Just let the killing be done. Did society feel responsible? No. Did the police feel responsible? They sometimes did their jobs, occasionally made an effort to find the killer, but they had as much contempt for victim as for victimizer; and none of them lost sleep over it. So let the killing be done. Forget it, Mary. Maybe she thought she was something special. Was that it? Unconsciously she might think that because of her psychic powers she couldn't die. Well, she could. Like all the rest of the tender, sweet young girls who thought they, too, would live forever. She would be as vulnerable, as soft against the knife as all the others had been. So she should stop. Go away from this. If she forced the issue, if she pursued the case, she might have to die. She was standing in front of a juggernaut. She was in the path of a force she didn't understand, a force that drew its greatest strength from the past, from an event that was twenty-four years old.

In the darkness, holding her as she slept, he wept at the thought of life without her.

Although sunrise was not far away, his flashlight was the only relief from inky blackness. His footsteps were the only sounds in the deserted arcade. He crossed the large main room. In summer it was filled with pinball machines and electronic games. Now the floor was bare, the main room empty. He entered the stairwell above which hung a large sign: THIS WAY TO OBSERVATION DECK.

The enclosed stairwell of the tower of Kimball's Games and Snacks was narrow, cold, and dirty. It had not yet been repainted for the next season. His flashlight played off yellow-white walls that bore a thousand stains: children's handprints, streaks of spilled soft drinks, names and messages scrawled in pencil and felt-tip markers.

The wooden steps creaked.

When he reached the walled platform at the top of the winding stairs, he switched off the flashlight. He doubted anyone would be watching at this hour; however, he didn't want to risk drawing attention to himself.

Dawn was nothing but a thin, lustrous purple line on the eastern horizon, as if a razor had been drawn lightly across the skin of the night.

He stared out at the harbor.

He waited.

In a few minutes, from the corner of his eye, he caught movement in the air. He heard the flutter of wings.

Something roosted in the crossbeams of the peaked roof, rustled for a moment, then was silent.

He stared into the crouching shadows above and trembled with pleasure.

Tonight, he thought. Tonight, the blood again.

He could feel death all around him, a thick and tangible current in the air.

To the east, the wound in the sky grew wider, deeper. Morning oozed into the world.

He yawned and wiped the back of one hand across his mouth. He would have to get back to the hotel soon, get some rest. He hadn't slept much in the past few days.

Three times within the next ten minutes, the sound of wings came again. On each occasion there was a temporary commotion in the rafters, and each time silence swiftly returned.

Eventually anemic light filtered through congealed masses of storm clouds and gradually painted the harbor, hills, and houses of King's Point.

He was filled with a deep sense of loss. With light came depression. He functioned best in the blackest hours. Always had. But recently that was increasingly true. He felt at home in the night.

Overhead the highest rafters remained shrouded in shadows. The inside of the roof—a hollow, inverted funnel—was fifteen feet high; and even at noon darkness clung to its upper regions.

Dim as it was, morning had arrived; and now his flashlight wouldn't be noticed by anyone below. He switched it on and pointed it up into the hollow roof.

This was what he had come to see: bats. A dozen bats or more. Clinging to the wooden rafters. Wings folded tightly around them. Some with eyes shut. Some with open eyes that gleamed iridescently in the beam of light.

The sight exhilarated him.

Tonight, the blood again.

At nine o'clock that morning Lou called Roger Fullet. "I'm sorry to have to bother you on Christmas."

"You're never a bother. Besides, you just saved me from a tedious little chore. The electric train went off the track and all the cars came uncoupled. If I talk to you for a few minutes, I'll get back to the layout after junior's got everything put back together."

"I've learned something very interesting about this Berton Mitchell case."

"Such as?"

"Apparently, Mitchell's wife and son were murdered."

"My God, when?"

"Five years after what he did to Mary."

"You've got to be wrong."

"Did you check to see if there were separate morgue files for the wife and son?"

"No. But even if there are, everything of importance should be duplicated in the Berton Mitchell file."

"Doesn't the *Times* make mistakes?"

"We're loath to admit it. But occasionally things don't get done right. Who killed the Mitchells?"

"Mary doesn't know."

"Nineteen years ago?"

"That's what she says."

"It happened here in L.A.?"

"I gather it did. Do me a favor?"

"I'm not working today, Lou."

"The *Times* doesn't shut down altogether on holidays. There are people working. Can't you call in and have someone check this out for me?"

"It's that important?"

"A matter of life and death."

"What all do you want to know?"

"Everything about the murders . . . if they took place."

"I'll call you back."

"How long will it take?"

"Maybe two hours."

Roger called back in an hour and a half. "There was a separate file on the murders of the wife and son. The story wasn't cross-filed as it should have been."

"It's nice to know even you big city slickers can be wrong."

"This is really a sick one, Lou."

"Tell me about it."

"After Berton Mitchell committed suicide, Virginia Mitchell and her son, Barry Francis Mitchell, rented a small house on the west side of Los Angeles. Judging from the address, I'd say it couldn't have been more than a mile from the Tanner estate. Nineteen years ago, on October 31, Halloween, at two o'clock in the morning, someone used gasoline to start a fire that nearly burned the place to the ground with the mother and son inside."

"Fire. That's the death I fear most."

"This has ruined my appetite for Christmas dinner."

"I'm sorry, Roger. I had to know."

"That's not the worst of it. Although the bodies were badly burned, the medical examiner was later able to deduce that mother and son were stabbed to death in their sleep before the blaze started."

"Stabbed . . ."

"Virginia had been stabbed so often in the throat that she'd been pretty much decapitated."

"Sweet Jesus."

"The son, Barry . . . was stabbed in the throat and chest. Then . . ."

"Then what?"

"His genitals were cut off."

"There goes my dinner, too."

"Before the fire burned it out, that place must have looked like a slaughterhouse. What kind of man could do all of that, Lou? What kind of maniac would be so gruesomely thorough?''

''Did they ever solve the case?''

''Never arrested anyone.''

''Did they at least have suspects?''

''Three of them.''

''What were their names?''

''I didn't bother jotting them down. Each of them had an alibi, and each alibi eventually checked out.''

''So their killer might still be alive and loose. Were the police sure of the bodies?''

''Sure of them in what sense?''

''Identities.''

''I guess they weren't burned beyond recognition. Besides, the house was occupied by Virginia and her son.''

''The woman's body was probably Virginia's. But isn't it conceivable that the dead man they found was her lover and not her son?''

''They were killed in different bedrooms. Lovers would have been found together. And if Barry was alive, he'd have come forward.''

''Not if he was the killer.''

*''What?''*

''It's not impossible.''

''Nothing's impossible, but—''

''Barry would have been twenty-one when the house burned that night. Maybe almost twenty-two. Roger, isn't that a bit old for a boy to be living with his mother?''

''Hell, no. Lou, we didn't all rush out to grab our piece of the action at sixteen, like you did. I lived with my folks until I was twenty-three. Why are you so anxious to believe Barry's alive?''

''It would make things easier to understand down here.''

''You're too good a newsman to try to reshape facts to fit some preconceived notion.''

''Yeah. You're right. I've run into another stone wall.''

''What's the story with this Mary Bergen? What are you involved in?''

''I'm afraid it's going to be very messy. I don't want to talk about it yet.''

''And maybe I don't want to hear about it either.''

''Go play with your train.''

''Somehow I'm no longer in the mood for play. Take care of yourself, Lou. Be careful. Be damned careful. And . . . Merry Christmas.''

# 17
### ◆ ◆ ◆

They sat in Lou's living room, listening to music—and waiting for something to happen. Mary couldn't imagine a grimmer Christmas. She and Max weren't even able to exchange gifts. The things he had gotten her were at the stores where he'd left them to be wrapped, and as she'd become preoccupied with this case, she'd had no opportunity to go shopping for him.

Her spirits lifted when Alan called at three o'clock to say he was in San Francisco at his friend's house. He'd tried the number in Bel Air, and the housekeeper had told him to call Lou. He was worried, but she understated the gravity of her situation and calmed him. No sense ruining *his* Christmas, too. When Alan finally hung up, her spirits sank again; she missed him so much.

Because no one had eaten breakfast or lunch, Lou served an early dinner at five o'clock. Chicken Kiev on a bed of rice. Cylinders of grilled zucchini filled with spinach paté. Tomatoes stuffed with hot cheese, bread crumbs, and peppers. There were baked apples for dessert.

No one was hungry. They picked at their food. Mary didn't even taste her wine. By six o'clock they were finished.

Over coffee Mary said, "Lou, do you have a Ouija board?"

He put down his cup. "I have one, but I haven't used it in years."

"Do you know where it is?"

"The spare bedroom closet, I think."

"Would you get it while Max and I clear the table?"

"Sure. What are we going to do with it?"

"I'm tired of waiting for the killer to make the next move," she said. "We're going to try to force the issue."

"I'm all for that. But how?"

Max said, "Sometimes, when Mary can't recall the fine details of a vision, she can prod her memory with a Ouija board. She doesn't get answers from the spirit world, mind you. The things she wants to know are things she's forgotten. They're buried in her subconscious. Not always, but often enough to make it worthwhile when nothing else works, the Ouija board provides her with a pipeline to her subconscious."

Lou nodded with understanding. "The answers the board gives actually come from Mary."

"Right," Max said.

"But I don't consciously guide the trivet," she said. "I let it go where it wants to go."

"Where your subconscious wants it to go," Max said. "You *do* influence the trivet with your fingers, but in a way that you're not aware of."

"I suppose," she said.

Lou put a few more drops of cream in his coffee and said, "So the Ouija board acts like a lens."

"Exactly," she said. "It focuses my attention, my memory, and my psychic abilities."

Lou drank his coffee in three long swallows and stood up. "It sure sounds interesting. Anything's better than sitting around waiting for the ax to fall. I'll be right back." He hurried out of the dining room and down the hall toward the spare bedroom.

Max and Mary stacked the dishes and silverware in the kitchen sink. She finished wiping off the glossy pine dining table just as Lou returned.

"One Ouija board, as requested," he said.

Mary went into the living room to fetch her notebook from the sofa where she'd left it with her purse.

Lou said, "Got to clean out that spare bedroom closet one of these days. The board was literally buried in crap."

"Literally?" Max said, amused.

"Well, it was under at least a hundred issues of *The New York Review of Books.*"

"Ouch," Max said. "You set me up for that one."

Lou took a note pad and pencil from the kitchen counter and sat down at the table. He was prepared to record each letter that the Ouija board gave them.

Mary opened the board on one corner of the table. She placed the felt-footed trivet on it.

Max sat down, laced his fingers, and cracked his knuckles.

She opened her spiral-bound notebook to a page filled with her handwriting.

"What's that?" Lou asked.

"Questions I want to ask it," Mary said.

She pulled up her chair and sat down at a ninety-degree angle to Max. She put the tips of her fingertips on one side of the plastic triangle. Max put his fingertips on another side of it; his hands were nearly too large for the game.

"Start easy," Max told her.

She was tense, and that was not good. The trivet wouldn't move an inch if her touch was too heavy. She took several deep breaths. She tried to make her arms limp. She wanted her fingers to feel independent of her—loose, soft, like rags.

Max wasn't as nervous as she was. He didn't appear to need any preparation.

Finally, when she had achieved a relatively relaxed state of mind and body, she stared at the board in front of her and said, "Are you ready to give us answers?"

The indicator didn't move.

"Are you ready to give us answers?"

Nothing.

"Are you ready to give us answers?"

Under their fingers, as if it were suddenly embodied with a life energy of its own, the indicator glided to that part of the board marked YES.

"Good," she said. "We are in pursuit of a man who has killed at least eight people in the last few days. Is he still here in King's Point?"

The indicator swept around the board, returned to YES.

She asked, "Is King's Point this man's hometown?"

NO.

"Where does he come from?"

ALL OUR YESTERDAYS.

"Make sense to anyone?" Lou asked.

Refining the question, trying to be more specific, Mary asked, "Where does the killer *live?*"

Letter by letter: BEAUTIFUL.

"Beautiful?" Lou asked. "Is that in answer to your question, Mary?"

"A town named beautiful?" she asked.

The trivet didn't move.

"Where does the killer live?" she asked again.

The trivet picked out seventeen letters.

Lou wrote them down as they were given, and when the indicator ceased to move, he said, "It says, 'THE AIR IS BEAUTIFUL.' What's that supposed to mean?"

The air at Mary's back seemed suddenly colder, as if an icy breath had been expelled against the nape of her neck. The answers the Ouija board gave were less direct and more perplexing than usual. Supposedly the Ouija messages came from her, from deep in her subconscious mind. Ordinarily she believed that was true. But not now. Tonight she felt another presence, an unseen presence looming over her.

"We're getting sidetracked," Max said impatiently. He looked at the trivet. "Where is the killer staying in King's Point?"

The indicator slid back and forth, then quickly moved from one letter to another.

Lou copied them down, but the word was so simple that Mary didn't need to ask what had been recorded: HOTEL.

"Which hotel?" Max asked.

The indicator didn't move.

"Which hotel?"

Again, it spelled HOTEL.

Lou said, "Try something else."

Mary said, "The man we're after has killed women with a knife. Where did he get that knife?"

"That's not important," Max said.

The trivet moved: LINGARD.

*"You* made it spell that," Max said.

"I don't believe I did."

"Then why did you ask it such a question? We don't really have to know where the knife came from."

"I wanted to see what it would say."

Max studied her with piercing gray eyes.

She looked away from him, consulted her notebook and addressed the board again. "Did I ever know a girl by the name of Beverly Pulchaski?"

SHE IS DEAD.

"Did I ever know her?"

SHE IS DEAD.

"Did I know a girl named Susan Haven?"

SHE IS DEAD.

Cold breath on the neck again.

She shuddered.

"Did I ever know Linda Proctor?"

SHE IS DEAD.

"Did I know Marie Sanzini?"

SHE IS DEAD.

Mary sighed. The muscles in her arms and shoulders flexed repeatedly, involuntarily. It was a struggle to stay sufficiently relaxed to allow the Ouija indicator to function. Already she was weary.

Lou said, "Who were those women?"

She said, "The nurses who were murdered in Anaheim. When I first foresaw their deaths, I had the notion that I knew or at least had met one of them. But if I ever did, I can't remember where or when it was."

"Probably because you don't *want* to remember," Max said.

"Why wouldn't I?"

"Because maybe if you remembered, we'd know who the killer was. And maybe you don't want to know that."

"Don't be absurd, Max. I want to know very much."

"Even if the killer's connected somehow to Berton Mitchell and the wings? Even if, by finding the killer, you're forced to remember what you've spent your life forgetting?"

She stared at him and licked her lips. "I'm feeling something right now that I never thought I'd feel."

"What's that?"

"I'm scared of you, Max."

There was an unearthly quiet in the house. The three of them seemed suspended in time.

Max spoke softly, but his voice filled the room. "You're scared of me because you think I'm going to force you to face up to what happened twenty-four years ago."

"Is that all it is?"

"What else?"

"I don't know," she said.

Max asked the board another question, but he did not take his wintry gray eyes from her. "Did Mary know Rochelle Drake?"

SHE IS DEAD.

"I know she's dead," Max said irritably, still watching Mary, suffocating her with his attention, pinning her with his gaze. "But did Mary ever know her?"

DEAD.

"Who's Rochelle Drake?" Lou asked.

Mary took the opportunity to look away from Max. Her mouth was dry. Her heart was beating much too fast.

To Lou, Max said, "Rochelle Drake was the girl who was killed in that Santa Ana beauty salon a few days ago. I swear I've heard the name before. Haven't you?"

"Can't say I have," Lou said.

"Well, I'm positive I heard the name before Percy Osterman used it in the morgue. I don't think I ever met the girl. But I heard the name. I can't imagine where."

Mary said, "Well, I *don't* remember her. I would have recognized her at the morgue if I'd ever seen her before."

Suddenly, beneath their hands, the trivet began to move in wide, aimless circles.

"What the hell?" Max said, surprised.

Lou said, "No one asked it a question."

Mary allowed her hands to float freely with the indicator as it moved less erratically and with increasing purpose. Her thoughts were too muddled at the moment, and she was too frightened to have the wit to decipher the chain of letters as it grew. Finally the trivet stopped. She took her hands from it at once; they ached with the strain of forced relaxation.

Lou said, "It's a name." He held up the note pad for them to see.

P-A-T-R-I-C-I-A-S-P-O-O-N-E-R.

*Patricia Spooner?* Mary thought. She stared at the name in disbelief.

She felt as if a snake of ice lay at the center of her, its crystalline tongue flicking rapidly, its sinuous body radiating cold like the coils of a freezer.

"Who's Patricia Spooner?" Max asked.

"Means nothing to me," Lou said.

"I . . . knew her," Mary said stiffly.

"When?" Max asked.

"Eleven . . . twelve years ago."

"You've never mentioned her."

"She was a good friend at UCLA."

"A college friend?"

"Yes. A very pretty girl."

"Why does her name come up now?"

"I don't have any idea."

"It came from your subconscious."

"No. I'm not controlling the trivet."

"Nonsense," Max said.

"There's someone . . . something here with us."

"Maybe the board just gave us the name of the next victim," Lou said, to avert a quarrel. "Have you kept in touch with this Patricia Spooner? Maybe we should call her and see if she's okay."

Max said, "Should we call Patricia Spooner? Mary?"

"She's dead," Mary said.

Lou said, "Oh, my God. Then the man we're after's already killed her?"

She had difficulty speaking. "Patty . . . Patty's been . . . dead . . . dead almost . . . eleven years."

Although the room was not warm, Lou was perspiring. He wiped his aristocratic face with his broad, thick-fingered, big-knuckled hand. He looked as pale as she felt. "How? Mary, how did Patty Spooner die?"

Mary shivered and closed her eyes. She opened them at once because the memories behind them were too ugly, too brutal. "She was . . . murdered."

The dead, Mary thought, don't stay dead. Not forever. Not even for long. They rise up from their graves. The ground doesn't hold them. Remorse doesn't hold them. Neither grief nor acceptance, neither fear nor forgetfulness holds them. Nothing holds them. They come back. Berton Mitchell. Barry Mitchell. Virginia Mitchell. My mother. My father. And now Patty Spooner. Oh, God, don't let them come back. I've been haunted by the dead most of my life. I've had enough!

"Murdered," Lou said quietly, almost as if in shock.

Mary said, "There was a church. Patty and I sometimes went to

Mass together. I was a practicing Catholic then. It was a lovely church. It had a very large, hand-carved wooden altar that was made in Poland and shipped over here in the early nineteen hundreds. The church was open all the time, night and day. Patty liked to go and sit in the front pew when no one else was there. Late at night. Her mother had died of a heart condition a few years before. She was always lighting candles for her mother. Patty was very devout. She . . . she died there.''

"In the church?" Lou asked.

Max was watching her intently. He put a hand on her shoulder; vibrations, more emotional than physical, neither good nor bad but powerful, exploded through her from the point of contact.

Max said, "Who killed her?"

"They never found him."

Lou leaned across the table. His eyebrows were drawn together, his face pinched. "She was your good friend. Didn't you use your psychic talent to see the killer's face, his name?"

"I tried," Mary said faintly. "I got a few things. Bits and pieces of images. But it was one of those cases when my power didn't help much. She was strangled with a priest's white silk stole. I got terrible emanations from it. Wicked, evil vibrations. No clear pictures. Just formless images. The church was filled with them. Like . . . invisible clouds of evil. The killer had damaged the altar . . . urinated on it.''

Lou got up so abruptly that he knocked over his chair, but he didn't appear to notice it. He stood with one hand on his head as if attempting to force back an unsettling idea. "It's madness. *What are we up against?* Is it possible that the man we're trying to find here in King's Point is the same man who killed your friend?"

"His style is the same, isn't it?" Max said.

"So damned brutal," Lou said. "And with the religious angle. The roots of these recent killings might go back at least eleven years. Perhaps a lot further than that."

Mary saw what he meant, though curiously, until this moment, she had never seen a connection between Patty's death and any other.

Sensing the effect Lou's revelation had upon her, Max squeezed her shoulder reassuringly. Sometimes he didn't seem to know his own strength; his grip was slightly painful.

Agitated as she had never seen him, moving quickly and jerkily, Lou went into the kitchen and got a twelve-ounce tumbler from the cabinet beside the refrigerator. He picked up a bottle of Wild Turkey that was on the counter by the sink, and he poured about four ounces for himself. Glass in hand, he came back and stood in the dining room archway. "It gets more complicated all the time. How many other people has this man killed that we don't even know about? Over the years, how many other unsolved murders was he responsible for?'' Lou swallowed some bourbon. ''This creature, whoever and whatever he is—and I'm increasingly disposed to think of him as a *thing*—has been prowling about, raping, killing, completely unchecked, unhindered for at least eleven years. It scares the hell out of me.''

A peal of thunder punctuated his last few words. It reverberated in the window glass. The Christmas night rainstorm was on the way, as forecast.

Max glanced at the plastic trivet. ''Let's ask the board how many victims there have been.''

She almost objected. My arms ache, she almost said. Too tired for more of that. Exhausted. Drained.

But she knew that fear was the real reason she didn't want to begin questioning the Ouija board again. She was afraid of what it might tell them.

If she surrendered to her fear so easily, she would never learn to rely on herself. And although she found the possibility disturbing, she had an ever-growing feeling that soon she would find herself in greater danger, against which Max could not or would not offer her protection.

She put her hands on the trivet, and so did Max.

Lou put his overturned chair on its feet. He sat down and picked up his pencil.

She spoke to the Ouija board. ''Are you prepared to answer more questions?''

YES.

Thunder rumbled over King's Point. The bulbs in the hanging lamp above the table flickered, nearly went out, then glowed brightly again.

''The man who killed Rochelle Drake has murdered other people, too. How many has he killed?''

35.

Lou said, ''My God! He's a regular Jack the Ripper.''

''Jack the Ripper didn't kill that many,'' Max said. ''The board's wrong. It has to be. Ask it again, Mary.''

Her voice wavered as she repeated the question.

35.

The hanging lamp flickered and went out.

''Power failure,'' Lou said.

Mary said, ''I don't want to sit in the dark.''

''If it lasts more than a minute,'' Lou said, ''I'll go get candles from the hall closet.''

An incredible barrage of lightning pulsed outside the windows. The sharp bursts of blue-white light created a series of choppy, stroboscopic images: Lou reaching in a half dozen seemingly disconnected movements for his glass of bourbon; Max turning his head toward her as if he were a character on a motion picture screen, with the film slipping and stuttering in the projector.

Then the lightning passed; the darkness was complete; the thunder receded to a distant growl. Rain should have followed that display, but it didn't; the sky held back the deluge.

Less than a minute after the lights went out, they fluttered dimly and came back on full strength.

She sighed with relief.

Max was eager to continue the questioning. "Ask the board when this man will strike again."

Mary repeated the question.

TONIGHT.

"What time tonight?"

7:30.

Lou said, "Little more than an hour from now."

"Where will he strike?" Mary asked the Ouija board.

THE HARBOR PARADE.

"You know what it means," Lou said to Max. He was grim. "For thirty years," he told Mary, "there's been a Christmas night parade of lighted boats on the harbor. Never heard of it?"

"Now that you mention it, yes."

"All those decorated boats you saw last night will be part of it. Plus some that don't use our harbor as home port. Maybe a hundred and fifty or more."

"They have parades like this at Long Beach and Newport Beach in the week before Christmas," Max told Mary. "But the King's Point shindig is more spectacular than any of the others."

Lou said, "There's pretty damned good prize money for the best decorated boats, thanks to a trust fund set up by one of our richer sailors who loved the parade. It's quite a sight. Most of the harbor restaurants open for it. They only serve a limited menu, but they're sold out a week or two in advance."

Mary looked at the Ouija board and asked, "Is the killer after anyone special in the boat parade?"

YES.

"Who?"

HE HAS A RIFLE.

"Who will he shoot?"

HE WANTS TO KILL THE QUEEN.

"The queen?" Mary asked.

"The queen of the parade," Lou said. "She'll make an easy target. She stands on the rear deck of the biggest boat in the lineup, usually midway in the procession. She's in the center of a spotlight. Literally."

"And," Max said, "she makes two complete circuits of the harbor along with the other boats. So if he isn't satisfied with the target he's got on the first circuit, he can wait to see if she presents herself any better the second time around.''

Although it had not been asked another question, the plastic trivet moved beneath their fingers, slid through a new series of letters.

KIMBALL'S GAMES AND SNACKS.

''Will he use the tower there?''

YES. KIMBALL'S TOWER.

''One hour to stop him,'' Max said.

Lou stood up. ''I'll call the police.''

''Patmore?'' Mary asked dubiously.

''He's the man with the authority.''

She said, ''But will he listen to you after the false alarm last night?''

''He's got to listen!''

Thunder again. And wind.

Mary took her hands from the trivet and hugged herself. She was still cold. ''But what if Patmore *does* agree to put a stakeout on the tower?''

''That's what we want, isn't it?''

''Don't you see?'' she said. ''Won't tonight be a repeat of last night? Last night the killer knew that we were waiting for him. Why won't he know this time, too?''

Lou hesitated, surprised by the question, worried, indecisive. Finally he picked up the tumbler and drank the last of his bourbon. ''Maybe he will anticipate us. Maybe we don't have a chance against him. If the Ouija board's right, if he's really killed thirty-five people and never been caught, then he's damned clever. Probably too clever for us. But we've got to try, don't we? We can't just sit here and talk about the weather and the latest books and the newest Paris fashions while he goes on killing!''

''You're right,'' Max said.

Lou put down his empty glass and went to use the telephone in the entrance foyer.

Mary began to exercise her cramped hands. She closed them into fists, opened them, closed them.

''You look exhausted,'' Max said.

''I am.''

''We'll get to bed early.''

''If we get to bed at all.''

''We will. Nothing's going to happen to us.''

''I've got awful feelings,'' she said.

''You've had a vision?''

''No. Just feelings.''

''Then forget it.''

''Tonight will be bloody.''

''Don't worry,'' he said soothingly.

She thought of Patty Spooner.

Rochelle Drake in the morgue drawer.

That feeling again: something behind her, chilly breath on the nape of her neck.

"I don't want to die," she said.

Max said, "You aren't going to. Not tonight."

"You sound so sure of that."

"I am. I won't let you die."

"Are you strong enough to stop it from happening, Max? Are you stronger than destiny?"

Lightning ripped open the sky again: the reflection of light from its blade shone through the windows; and for an instant it turned Max's eyes into icy blanks.

"King's Point Police."

"Missing persons, please."

"I can help you, sir."

"No. I want to talk to someone in the missing persons' bureau. Didn't you hear me?"

"We don't have a separate department for missing persons' reports."

"You don't?"

"We're a small police force. Can I help you?"

"What's your name?"

"Ms. Newhart."

"I'm Ralph Larsson. Let me talk to a policeman."

"We've only got two on duty tonight."

"One of them will be enough for me."

"They're both in cruisers right now."

"Dammit, my daughter's missing!"

"How old is your daughter, sir?"

"Twenty-six. She was—"

"How long has she been missing?"

"Look, Ms. Newhart, I'm in San Francisco. I live in San Francisco, and my daughter lives in King's Point. I just talked to her a week ago. She was fine then. But now that I think she may no longer be fine, I can't just jump in my car and drive several hundred miles to look in on her. This could be an emergency. She was supposed to call me on Christmas Eve, but she never did."

"Maybe she went to a party or something."

"I thought for sure she'd call sometime today, but she hasn't. I've tried calling her, but there's no answer. Now, dammit, it's not like her to do something like this! It's not like her to forget her family on Christmas."

"Have you tried calling her friends? They might know something."

"I don't know Erika's friends."

"Maybe her neighbors—"

"She hasn't got neighbors. She—"

"Everyone has neighbors."

"She lives in one of those three cottages on the South Bluff, at the end of the paved road. She's the only one who lives there year 'round."

"You know what? I'll bet your daughter's trying to call you right now. Why don't you hang up and see? If she doesn't call tonight, then ring us back tomorrow."

"Are you serious?"

"Well, we can't do anything anyway."

"What do you mean?"

"It is a policy of this department, and of most police departments, not to enter a missing person's case if the report involves an adult who's been gone less than forty-eight hours."

"She has to be missing more than two days before you're interested?"

"That's our policy."

"Well, how do I know she didn't disappear the day after she last called me, six days ago?"

"You said she was supposed to call last night."

"And didn't."

"So officially, she's only been missing since last night."

"Jesus!"

"I'm sorry. That's policy."

"If my daughter was ten years old instead of twenty-six—"

"That's different. Children are different. But your daughter isn't a child."

"So your officers can't become involved until tomorrow night?"

"That's right. But, sir, I'm certain your daughter will call you long before then."

"Ms. Newhart, my name is Ralph Larsson. I told you once before, but I want you to remember it. Ralph Larsson. I'm an attorney. A very successful attorney. I was also the governor's college roommate. Now, Ms. Newhart, if your officers don't take a drive out to my daughter's house to check on her right away, tonight, within the next half an hour, and if later we should discover that something happened to my daughter between this moment and tomorrow night, I will come down there to King's Point and find a reputable cooperating attorney. I will devote the next few years of my life to breaking you and your idiotic superiors. I will sue your fucking goddamned police department, and I will sue your chief for his stupid arbitrary policies. And by God, Ms. Newhart, I will also sue you for every nickel you now have or ever hope to earn. And even if I don't win the case, Ms. Newhart, you will go broke paying for your own lawyers. Do you read me clearly?''

Lou Pasternak was angry. Furious. The chief of police had hung up on him *twice!* The third time, his wife answered the phone and said he wasn't at home.

"A demitasse would fit Patmore's head like a sombrero!"

"I gather," Max said, "that he wouldn't put a stakeout on Kimball's tower."

Lou snatched his empty glass from the table, went into the kitchen, and picked up the bottle of Wild Turkey. "If the bastard had a little more sense, he'd be a half-wit."

From the dining room Mary asked, "Shouldn't we call the sheriff?"

"Remember, Percy Osterman can't step into King's Point police business unless Patmore asks him to."

"But when a man's killed people all over the country, isn't there an exception? Something called 'hot pursuit'?"

Lou said, "If a guy robs a bank that's in the county's jurisdiction, hops into a car, and flees into a city with its own cops, the sheriff's men can chase and arrest him. *That's* hot pursuit. This isn't."

Max said, "Maybe Osterman can persuade Patmore to cooperate again."

"Not a chance. Not after last night." Lou returned to the table with a fresh glass of bourbon.

"So what now?" Max asked.

Mary said, "We'll have to stop him ourselves. We'll have to go down to the tower."

Lou stared at her in amazement. "Are you serious?"

"It's absolutely out of the question," Max said.

She said, "What would you prefer to do? We can't just sit here and talk about the weather and the latest books and the newest Paris fashions while he goes on killing."

Lou recognized his own words, and he had no effective argument against them.

"If we just sit here," she said, "he'll kill the queen of the boat parade. And most likely a lot of other people, too."

"The rain might force the queen and her court inside, off the open deck," Max said. "Then she wouldn't be a target."

"It isn't raining," Mary said.

"It'll start soon."

"Do you want to bet their lives on that?" she asked. "Lou, we have to stop this man. We haven't any choice."

"I don't want him to kill again," Max said. "But he isn't our responsibility."

"If not ours, whose?" she asked.

Lou saw an uncommon determination in her lovely face. Unshakable resolve in those big blue eyes. He suspected that neither he nor Max could change her mind about this. Might as well argue with a post. He could see that. But he was frightened for her. And as her friend, he felt he should at least try to make her reconsider. "Mary, we're no match for this man."

"Why not?" she asked. "Isn't it just one of him against the three of us?"

"But he's a killer," Max said.

"And we're not killers," she said.

"Exactly."

"Knowing what he's done," she said, "and what he'd do to you if he had the chance, couldn't you shoot him if he came at you with a gun?"

Max said, "Of course, in self-defense—"

"That's just what this is," she said. "Self-defense."

"But this psychopath will have a rifle," Lou said. "And probably a knife. What would we have? Our hands?"

"There's a pistol in the dashboard of the Mercedes," Mary said. "Max is licensed to carry it."

He looked at Max and raised his eyebrows. "You're allowed to carry a concealed weapon?"

Getting up from his chair, heading toward the kitchen, Max said, "Yeah."

"How'd you manage to wrangle the permit? They usually reserve those for people in businesses where they've got to carry around diamonds or a lot of cash."

In the kitchen Max poured himself a double shot of Wild Turkey. "We worked on a couple of cases with the L.A. County sheriff's office. The sheriff saw what dangerous situations Mary can find herself in. He knew I collected guns. He knew I was a marksman, and he figured I wasn't the type to get excited and accidentally blow someone apart." Max drank his bourbon neat and quick: a nervous thirst that briefly exposed the tension that lay beneath his studied composure. "So the sheriff got me the permit." He rinsed out his glass under the kitchen faucet, came back to the dining room, and stood over Mary. "But I'm not going to load that pistol and go out hunting someone to shoot."

"You wouldn't be hunting just anyone," she said. "You'd be hunting a man who has—"

"Forget it," Max said. "I won't do it."

"Let's talk about it," she said.

"No use. It's decided."

Lou saw a spark of anger in her eyes. Max's resistance would do nothing but harden her resolve.

She said, "Okay, Max. Stay here. I'll take the gun and go by myself."

"Mary, for God's sake, you don't know how to handle a pistol!"

She stared up at him without blinking and said, "You take off the safeties and jack a bullet into the chamber, point, pull the trigger— and the son of a bitch falls down."

Lou knew how stubborn Max could be sometimes. He saw the set of the man's jaw, the drawing up of his shoulders, and he wanted to warn him off. Max was accustomed to playing father-lover to her, accustomed to saying what would be done and what wouldn't. But tonight she wasn't the easygoing Mary they both knew. Even now changes were occurring in her. Conflicting emotions played across her face, but the primary expression was always determination. She was going to make her own decision, and she wasn't going to heed anyone's advice. He had never seen such strength in her before, such purpose. It was exciting, attractive. He sat mute, wanting to advise Max against an authoritarian approach but unable to interfere.

"This is absurd," Max said. "Mary, I won't let you have the pistol."

"Then I'll go without it."

He glared down at her. "You aren't going anywhere."

She stood up, faced him. She met his eyes and held them, as if to prove, through the directness of her gaze, the depth of her commitment. She spoke with quiet intensity and with a foreboding tone that chilled Lou to the bone. "I'm up against something so big, so evil that I can only guess at the dimensions like a blind child feeling an elephant's leg. These past few days have been a living hell for me, Max."

"I know. And—"

"You can't know. No one can know."

"If you—"

"Don't interrupt," she said. "I want you to understand. So you've just got to listen. Max, I'm afraid to go to sleep, and I'm afraid to wake up in the morning. I'm afraid to open every door I come to, afraid to turn around. I'm afraid of the dark. I'm afraid of what might happen—and of what might *not* happen. Dammit, I'm even afraid to go to the bathroom alone! I cannot live like this. I refuse to live like this. There's something about this case that makes it different from all others, something that's working inside of me like acid, eating me alive. This case touched my life like nothing else I've worked on, but I don't know why. Max, I sense, I feel, I *know* that if I don't pursue this man with every ounce of energy I have and in every way I know how, then he'll come after me."

The trivet on the Ouija board moved, but Lou was the only one to see it. It slid to the spot marked YES, as if in agreement with Mary's prediction.

"If I don't take the initiative," she said, "I'll lose what little advantage I might now have. I can't walk away. If I try to run, I won't get far. I'll die."

Max said, "And if you pursue this man, if you insist on going down to that tower tonight, then you'll probably die sooner."

"I might," she said. "But if I do, at least I'll have taken responsibility for my own life and death. All my life, I've been scared of everything, and I've let someone else deal with my bogeymen for me. Not anymore. Because this time no one else *can* help me. The answer is inside of me, and if I don't find it soon, I'm finished. It's past time I stopped hiding behind strong men. I've got to take chances. When I risk something and fail, I've got to suffer the consequences like anybody else. If I'm always pampered, cuddled, and cushioned from shock, then my successes in life are meaningless. I've decided that no one—not Alan, not you, Max, and especially not that part of me that's still a dependent six-year-old—*no one* is going to stop me from living a full life."

They stood in silence for a while.

The grandfather clock chimed the quarter hour.

Lou said, "Forty-five minutes until he takes a shot at the queen of the boat parade."

Mary said, "Well, Max?"

Finally he nodded. "We better get moving."

Blood. Blood like ribbons tangled in her hair. Blood spotting her punctured breasts. Blood on her hands, her arms, her belly, her thighs. Blood on the sofa and chair. Blood on the draperies, on the wall. Bloody little footprints of a cat all across the light tan carpet.

Trying to hold down the taste of vomit, Officer Rudy Holtzman stepped carefully around the mutilated body of Erika Larsson, went into the dark kitchen, and turned on the lights. He used the wall phone to dial headquarters.

When the night girl, Wendy Newhart, answered, Holtzman said, "I'm out here at the Larsson place." His voice was strained and hoarse; it cracked on a couple of words. He cleared his throat. "The lights were on when I got here. Nobody answered the bell, but the door was ajar. She's dead."

"Oh, my *God!* Well, I'm not going to tell her father. That's out of the question. Someone else will have to tell him."

"Better get Charlie over here with the other squad car," Holtzman said. "Call the medical examiner right away. And Patmore, of course. Tell Charlie to move his ass; I don't like being here alone."

Wendy Newhart asked, "When was she killed?"

"How should I know? The medical examiner will know."

"I mean, did it just happen before you got there? Within the past half hour?"

"What's it matter?" Holtzman asked.

"Rudy, tell me! Did it just happen?"

"The blood's mostly caked and dry. I can't pinpoint the time of death, but it must surely have been a good many hours ago."

"Thank the Lord for small miracles," she said.

"What?"

She had hung up.

Holtzman put down the receiver and turned to see a black cat standing in the doorway between the kitchen and the front room, no more than five feet from him. Its fuzzy white muzzle had been tinted red-brown with blood. Holtzman took one step, kicked out at the cat, missed.

It squealed and ran.

They arrived at the harbor at five minutes past seven.

Max parked the Mercedes in a corner of the lot that, in season, served both a restaurant called Italian Villa and Kimball's Arcade. Tonight the restaurant's side of the lot was nearly full, while the other side was nearly empty.

The three of them got out of the car.

Lou drew up his shoulders against the cold. As the storm air had moved in from the Pacific, the temperature had dropped rapidly from a one o'clock high of seventy degrees to a current low of forty-four. The wind had increased, too; it whipped in from the harbor, lashed King's Point, made the night seem even cooler than it was.

Lou said, "I still think I should go with Max, and you should stay here, where it's safe."

"It's not safe anywhere for me," Mary said.

"At least if you stayed here in the car—"

She waved one hand impatiently, interrupted him. "We've got two weapons we can use against this man we're after: one is Max's handiness with guns, and the other is my psychic talent. The two of us shouldn't split up."

The sea wind lifted her long hair, made it flap like a banner behind her.

Max put one hand on Lou's shoulder. "I don't want her in the thick of the action any more than you do. But maybe she's right. She's probably not in any greater danger there than here. Besides, neither of us is going to change her mind.''

"I feel so useless," Lou said.

"We need someone here in the car," Max said. "You're our early-warning system."

"We're wasting time," Mary said.

Lou nodded glumly. He kissed her cheek and told Max to take good care of her.

They hurried into the wind, across the parking lot toward the huge, deserted barnlike building that housed the array of souvenir stands, trinket stores, amusements, and coffee shops known collectively as Kimball's Games and Snacks.

He got behind the wheel of the Mercedes and closed the door. Through the windshield he could barely see Max and Mary as they drew farther away and blended into the darkness around the clapboard and cedar-shingled pavilion.

A fierce gust of wind rocked the car. Forks of lightning stabbed through the sky, but still there was no rain.

Lou settled back, resigned to his role as a sentinel. If the killer didn't anticipate Mary tonight, as he had last night, he would probably approach Kimball's openly, brazenly. If Lou spotted a man moving toward the building, he would switch on the Mercedes' ignition and alert Max with two short blasts of the horn. The pavilion and tower stood only sixty yards farther along the boardwalk that connected seven or eight businesses on this section of the harbor. The sound of the horn would travel that far undiminished, but it wasn't likely the killer would recognize it as a signal. Even if Mary was able to foresee the exact time and direction of the man's approach, the horn would be a welcome confirmation of her vision.

Of course, the psychopath might have anticipated them again and already be at the pavilion.

Lou shifted uneasily behind the wheel.

He thought of Patty Spooner, strangled to death with a priest's stole. He thought of Barry Mitchell, hideously mutilated.

He looked left and right, peered into the rearview mirror. No one. He squinted at the deep shadows along the side of the pavilion. All was still.

The black cat crouched on the top of a seven-foot-high set of bookshelves, no more than eight or ten inches from the ceiling in the front room of the cottage. Its forepaws hung over the edge of the shelf; it was motionless, staring down at Rudy Holtzman with suspicion and contempt.

Filthy damned thing. He hated cats. Always had. And it gave him the creeps just to think about this one eagerly lapping up the murdered woman's blood.

It made a deep, throaty sound, as if daring him to approach it.

He didn't want to wait with the cat and the corpse, not even for the few minutes Charlie would need to get here in the other cruiser. He walked down the short hallway to inspect the part of the house he'd not yet seen.

In the bedroom he found an open window, where the wind played havoc with a pair of flimsy curtains and an oilcloth blind that was drawn down only halfway. The recent storms had soaked and badly stained the carpet.

Holtzman was suddenly excited. He studied the room, recreating in his mind those first few seconds when the sanctity of the house had been violated. He knew that more than rain had come in through that window. He was certain that he'd found the killer's entrance. And as his glance traveled over the floor, he could hardly believe what he saw. It was one of those lucky breaks you seldom get in police work. Apparently the pistol had fallen unnoticed from a coat pocket as the killer climbed through the window.

Holtzman knelt on the damp carpet to get a closer look at the weapon. He was careful not to spoil any fingerprints that might be on it. If this killer was the same man who had slaughtered those nurses and the people in that beauty salon—and the style sure seemed the same to Holtzman—then the Anaheim and Santa Ana police already had more than enough good prints. So far prints had been of no use in cracking the case because the killer evidently had never had his taken by any police organization in the country. Nevertheless, because he prided himself on being more professional than anyone with whom he worked, Holtzman didn't grasp the pistol and smear the evidence. He took a ball-point pen from his shirt pocket, slipped it through the trigger guard, lifted the gun off the floor, and held it in front of his eyes.

It was an unusual piece—a .45 Auto Colt. But nothing off the shelf. Something special. A collector's item. The metal was engraved with delicate leaves and vines. There were also a number of animals— rabbits, deer, pheasants, foxes—etched in positions of flight beginning at the forward sight on the barrel, all of them incredibly detailed, beautifully rendered, all racing toward the butt.

He saw what appeared to be printing on the steel, where it met the wooden handgrip. The bedroom light was poor. The letters were tiny, between a quarter and a half inch high, inscribed with a spidery flourish of the engraver's tool. Holtzman couldn't read them.

He stood up and, carrying the Colt on the pen, went to the nearest lamp.

*by W. Thorben*
*Seattle 1975*

A collector's piece like this one often passed through the hands of many owners who purchased and resold it at gun shows without bothering to register it with authorities. Nevertheless, with the engraver's name (and providing the gun had not been stolen from a collection), they should be able to find the man who had commissioned it from Thorben. From him they had a chance of tracing it to the man who'd dropped it while coming through the window.

Still manipulating the weapon with his ball-point pen, Holtzman looked at the opposite side. Again, where the steel met the wooden handgrip, there was writing. Not the same words. He squinted. He read it. Then read it again. "Well, I'll be damned."

A siren rose in the distance and grew rapidly nearer.

Holtzman went down the hall to the side of the house that faced the dead-end macadam road. He stood in the open doorway he'd first found ajar.

Another police car, emergency beacons blazing, roared up the long hill from town. Patmore's station wagon wasn't far behind it.

Beneath the hall light Holtzman held up the Colt and read the second legend again.

*commissioned by*
*Max Bergen*

# 18
◆◆◆

The darkness around the pavilion was lumpy, velvety, and deep. It offered dozens of hiding places.

Mary carried the flashlight, hooding it with one hand. Every time she made a sudden move in response to imagined noises, shadows danced.

She stayed close to Max as they circled the building, looking for a place where the killer might have gotten inside. Last night the police had entered with a key provided by the owners. That was a convenience denied both them and their quarry. The killer would have to break something to get in and reach the tower; he would have to leave a trail.

She was impatient. Twice she urged Max to hurry.

Already the parade of lighted boats had begun its first circuit of the harbor, entering from the staging area at sea, still far down the channel but approaching fast. By seven-thirty the queen of the parade might well have begun her first pass of the tower.

On the west side of the pavilion, which faced the harbor and was flanked with a railed boardwalk, they found a shattered pane of glass in one of the mullioned windows that looked in on the lightless, deserted coffee shop.

"Did the killer do this?" Max asked.

She directed the flashlight at the ground, and in the soft glow of its backwash, she studied the damaged window. With the fingertips of her left hand she traced the wooden ribs that framed the missing pane. The night was already chilly, but the air got suddenly colder as she concentrated on the psychic impressions that the window held for her.

*Wicka-wicka-wicka!*

She shuddered, squeezed the flashlight as hard as she could, gritted her teeth but refused to panic.

"Something?" Max asked.

"Yes. He did this."

"Is he inside now?"

"No. He was here . . . late yesterday . . . after the police left . . . I can see . . . many hours after the police left . . . early this morning . . . at dawn . . . up in the tower." She took her hand from the window, and an invisible connection snapped. "But he hasn't returned yet tonight."

"You're positive about that?"

"Absolutely."

"But he'll be here any minute?"

"Yes. So hurry."

*Wicka-wicka-wicka!*

Ignore it, she told herself. It's not real. Max doesn't hear it, does he? Only you hear it. Psychic impressions. Nothing is really overhead. No wings. No danger. No wings at all.

"We don't want to make this any more of a spectacle than we have to," Max said. "Some of these restaurants farther around the harbor might have a pretty good view of us. Better shut off the flashlight."

She did as he said.

The night closed around her.

Max put one hand through the missing pane, reached up, and fumbled for the latch on the vertical, metal center post. "Do you realize this is breaking and entering?"

"I suppose it is," she said.

"Doesn't that bother you?"

"Max, will you *hurry?*"

He swung the tall halves of the window outward without making a sound.

She climbed onto the sill, which was only three feet above the boardwalk, stepped down into the coffee shop. She glanced around the room, but she couldn't see anything.

Max looked both ways along the boardwalk, then followed her, closed and latched the window.

"It's even darker in here than it was out there," she said. "We'll be tripping over something every other step if I don't use the flash."

"Just be sure you don't point it at a window," he said. "Keep it hooded."

She switched on the light, shielding half the lens with her left hand.

The restaurant contained approximately thirty tables, all of them bolted to the floor. Apparently because the chairs couldn't be bolted down as well, they had been removed and put in storage until Kimball's reopened in the spring.

The only public entrance to the coffee shop—a pair of many-paned glass doors that matched the big mullioned windows—was from inside of the pavilion, of which this restaurant was but one small part. The killer had smashed the lock. When Max pushed open the doors, they moved stiffly and grated on their unlubricated hinges.

He stood still for a moment, listening to the settling sounds of the building. Finally he said, "You're really sure he's not here already?"

"Positive."

Although the psychic impressions were not always complete, they'd never deceived her. She hoped her talent hadn't failed this time; because if it had, if the killer *was* already here and waiting, she was as good as dead.

From the coffee shop they entered a corridor that curved out of sight in both directions. It was lined with small gift shops: Silly T-Shirts, The Ceramic Factory, The House of Glass Miniatures, and a dozen more, all empty and dark.

Max and Mary turned left and quickly discovered that the long corridor was a semicircle leading, at both ends, into the cavernous main hall of the arcade. That huge room was bare now, but in season it would be filled with a variety of pinball machines, shuffleboard bowling, shooting galleries, electronic games, and carnival booths where you could get your fortune told or where a boy could spend ten dollars in quarters to win a three-dollar toy animal for his best girl.

They walked to the center of the room. Their footsteps echoed hollowly from wall to wall and from curve to curve of the high domed ceiling.

Mary stopped and pointed the flashlight where Lou had said to look. She saw an archway at the rear of the room, steps beyond it. Above the arch was a sign: THIS WAY TO OBSERVATION DECK.

*Screams, the sound of wings, a body hurtling off the bottom steps and through the archway, wings, a body writhing on the wooden arcade floor, wings, strangled cries for help . . .*

She swayed under the impact of the psychic images.

"What's the matter?" Max asked.

"I see . . . " She tried to hold on to the vision, but it rapidly faded and would not be coaxed to return. "Someone's going to die tonight at the foot of those stairs."

"One of us?"

"I don't know."

"The killer?"

"I hope."

"It'll be him," Max said. "Not us. We'll live. We've got to. I know it."

Not as certain as he was, reluctant to think about it for fear her courage would vanish, she asked, "Where should we wait for him?"

"I'll wait at the bottom of the steps. You'll wait at the top of the tower."

"At the top of . . . oh, no!"

"Oh, yes."

"I'm staying with you," she said.

"Look, if Lou uses the car horn to warn us, we probably won't hear it in here. But you'd be certain to hear it if you were in the tower—"

"Forget it."

"—on the open deck."

"Max, I'm staying here."

"No, dammit!"

She took a step back from him.

His face was dark with anger. *"I'm* the one who's an expert with guns. If it comes down to a shooting match, you'll be in my way. If I have to move fast, I don't want to have to stop and worry whether you're in the line of fire."

"I'm not a hopeless idiot," she said. "I can stay out of your way."

He glared at her and said nothing.

She said, "But what if I have a vision while I'm up there, something important? How will I let you know what's going to happen?"

"I'll be here at the bottom of the steps—not more than sixty feet from you. You can reach me quickly if it's necessary."

"I don't know . . . "

"I'll put it more bluntly," Max said. "Either do what I say and go to the observation deck, or so help me God, I'm going to take a punch at you, lightly as I can, but hard enough to knock you out. Then I'll carry you back to the Mercedes and call this whole thing off."

"You wouldn't."

"Wouldn't I?"

She knew he wasn't making idle threats.

"I'll do it because I love you," he said. "I don't want you to get killed."

"And I don't want *you* killed," she said.

"Good. Then you'll listen to me. We've both got a better chance of living through this if you're not here to distract me when and if the shooting starts."

She was filled with conflicting emotions. "Will you kill him?"

"If he forces me to."

"Don't hesitate to do it," she said. "Don't give him a chance. He's too clever. Shoot him the second you see him."

"The police might have something to say about that."

"To hell with the police."

"Mary, *are* you going upstairs? There's not much time. Do we stay or do I carry you out of here? It's entirely your decision, but you've got to make your mind up fast."

Partly because she saw a glimmer of truth in his argument, but mainly because she had no choice, she said, "All right."

They walked quickly to the archway. At the foot of the stairs he put his hands on her shoulders, and she raised her face to him. They kissed.

"When you get to the top," he said, "don't stand around looking at the sights. Even at night someone on the ground might be able to see you. If the killer spots you, he might back off. You say we'll have to have a showdown with him sooner or later. So we may as well do what we can to end it tonight."

"Who gets the flashlight?" she asked.

"You keep it."

She was relieved, but she said, "You'll be in the dark down here . . . with him."

"If I switched on a flashlight when I heard him coming," Max said, "I'd only be making a target of myself. Besides, if he isn't aware I'm waiting for him, he's not going to enter a pitch-black building and try to navigate through it without a flash. I'll be able to see him by his own light."

She kissed him again, turned away, and climbed the eight flights of stairs alone.

At the top she doused the flashlight and stood for a moment in the fierce wind, looking out at the parade of lighted boats on the harbor.

Then she heeded Max's advice and sat down with her back to the waist-high wall that bordered the deck.

Darkness. Some light. Not much.

Alone now. All alone.

No. Not alone. Where did a thought like that come from? Max was nearby.

The wind raced through the belfry, moaned like a human voice.

She huddled in her leather coat and wished for a sweater.

It would rain soon. She could smell it in the air.

She pushed the read-out button on her digital wristwatch, and lighted numerals glowed blood-red in the dark.

*The eyes.*

She suddenly remembered the luminous, reddish eyes that she had seen in Berton Mitchell's cottage. She could not conjure up a face to go with them. Just the eyes . . . and the sound of wings . . . and the feel of wings all over her . . . and still the eyes, wild, inhuman.

She remembered something else, too; remembered it with a jolt—a small voice at the back of her mind, whispery but intense: *"I'm a demon and a vampire. I like the taste of blood."*

Someone had spoken those very words to her in Mitchell's cottage twenty-four years ago.

Who? Berton Mitchell himself? Who else could it have been?

Although she tried to use her psychic talent to transform the vivid memory into a clairvoyant vision, she was not able to bring much light to the gloomy, penumbral images that swam and pulsed malignantly. The mysterious face of the creature that spoke to her remained just out of sight.

But the inner voice grew louder. Somehow it swelled and thundered and overwhelmed her, yet remained a whisper. The harsh words came faster, even faster, and she was shaken by them. *"I'm a demon and a vampire. I like the taste of blood. I'm a demon and a vampire, I like the taste of blood, I'm a demon and a vampire—"*

"Stop it!" she said.

She put her hands to her ears and willed the voice from her mind. Gradually it faded. When it was gone, she slumped forward, dizzy.

"I'll be all right," she said softly, urgently. "It'll be all right. No one will die. It'll be all right. Tonight it ends. It'll be fine after tonight."

Slowly the realities of the night impressed themselves upon her once more: wind, cold, darkness.

Distracted by the memory of those luminous eyes, she hadn't noticed the time when she pressed the button on her watch. She pressed it again.

7:24.

Six minutes to go.

\* \* \*

Heavy ebony clouds, vaguely phosphorescent at their bearded edges, sailed soundlessly toward the east. The sky was silent for long minutes, a muffling blanket tented over the earth; but now it crashed and flared again.

The wind lifted a scrap of paper from the pavement, pasted it to the windshield of the Mercedes for a few seconds, then tore it away.

Lou shifted uneasily, leaned into the steering wheel, squinted at the purple-black shadows that flanked the pavilion. The longer he stared, the more the darkness seemed to shimmer as if it were alive. He kept seeing movement where there was none, his eyes played a hundred tricks on him. He didn't have the proper temperament for a sentinel. He had no patience.

He looked at his watch.

7:29.

Someone rapped three times, hard, on the window to his left, inches from his head.

He jerked around.

A familiar face peered in at him, smiled.

Confused and somewhat embarrassed by the terror that must have been visible on his face, Lou said, "Hey! You startled me." He felt for the latch, opened the door, and got out of the car. "What are you doing here?"

Too late, he saw the butcher knife.

Lights were on in most of the downstairs rooms at 440 Ocean Hill Lane, but when Rudy Holtzman rang the bell, no one answered.

Patmore tried the door and found it wasn't locked. He pushed it open. Wind rushed past him and swept a stack of unopened mail off the small table in the foyer.

Patmore couldn't see anyone in the entranceway or in the living room beyond. He leaned through the door and shouted, "Pasternak! You in there?"

No one answered.

"Maybe he's dead," Holtzman said.

Because he was wearing civilian clothes, Patmore took a silvery badge from the pocket of his overcoat and pinned it to his lapel. He drew his service revolver from the outer coat pocket, and, holding it with the barrel pointed at the ceiling, he stepped into the house.

Behind him, Holtzman cleared his throat and said, "We don't have a warrant."

Patmore stopped, looked back at him, and said, "Rudy, your ass, get it in here."

Syrupy darkness. A coppery odor. Barbed wire twisting inside him.

His tongue hurt. He'd bitten it. A coppery taste.

He was lying on his stomach. On the macadam parking lot. Near the Mercedes. His arms flung out in supplication. Head to one side. Ear against the ground as if listening for the approach of an enemy.

He opened his eyes but just barely. A pair of shoes were in front of his face. Inches from him. Gucci loafers. They turned and walked away. Toward the pavilion. In seconds they were out of sight, but he could still hear footsteps.

He tried to raise his head. Couldn't.

He tried to remember how many times he'd been stabbed in the stomach. Three, maybe four times. Could have been worse. But it was surely bad enough. He was dying. He had no strength at all; and now even his weakness was draining out of him.

I'm such an idiot, he thought bitterly. How could I have been so careless? A damned fool. The closest I'll ever come to a brainstorm is a light drizzle.

Should have known who the killer was. Should have known the moment the Ouija board said the target was the queen of the boat parade. She was one of his old girl friends. Seemed to get along with a woman for only a few months. So now he was going to kill one of his old girl friends. Probably had killed others. Why? No matter why. Should have known.

He felt as if thousands of insects were crawling inside of him, stinging and biting his guts.

He closed his eyes and thought, I don't want to die. I *won't!*

Then: You fool. Do you think you have a choice

A coppery odor. Syrupy darkness.

It didn't look bad.

Inviting, actually.

He floated in the inviting darkness. He sank down and down, away from the pain, away from everything.

Curious, John Patmore paged through the spiralbound notebook that lay open beside the Ouija board on the dining room table. The ruled pages were filled with neat, feminine handwriting that he supposed belonged to Mary Bergen.

Mostly she had recorded questions and answers that appeared to be connected with the case she claimed to be investigating. In the middle of the notebook, however, there was a page that contained only five hastily scrawled words: *Mary! Run for your life!*

The same message was repeated in the center of the following page. And then on a third.

Under the third warning there were more questions and answers:

*When did I write these warnings?*
*Don't know.*
*What do I mean by them?*
*Don't know.*
*Who am I afraid of?*
*Don't know, don't know, don't know!*
*Am I going crazy?*
*Maybe.*
*Where can I run to?*
*Nowhere.*

Strange.

It made him nervous.

There was a note pad at the other side of the Ouija board. Patmore began leafing through it.

> *A-L-L-O-U-R-Y-E-S-T-E-R-D-A-Y-S*
> *ALL OUR YESTERDAYS*
> *B-E-A-U-T-I-F-U-L*
> *BEAUTIFUL*
> *T-H-E-A-I-R-I-S-B-E-A-U-T-I-F-U-L*
> *THE AIR IS BEAUTIFUL*

He glanced at the Ouija board, at the trivet, then down at the note pad again. He remembered working a board with his mother when he was a boy. He began to read every other line of the transcript.

When he finished, he thought of Erika Larsson and realized she matched the description of the girl whose death Mary Bergen had predicted. Reluctantly, he admitted to himself that perhaps the clairvoyant was not a fake after all. "Holtzman!"

Rudy Holtzman returned from the far end of the house. "No one's here."

"Max Bergen intends to kill the queen of the boat parade."

Blinking in surprise, Holtzman said, *"What?* Jenny Canning?"

"Apparently Mary Bergen doesn't realize her husband's the man she's after." Patmore looked at his watch. "We might be too late." He ran through the cluttered living room, out the front door.

*Marie Sanzini.*

Unbidden, the name came to Mary.

*Marie Sanzini.*

Marie Sanzini was one of the nurses killed in Anaheim—and suddenly her name was familiar. Mary knew it, but she didn't know where she'd heard it before. Marie. Marie Sanzini. It teased her.

She closed her eyes, tried to see the woman's face, but it eluded her. She thumbed the button on her watch.

7:33.

No signal from Lou.

Was tonight just another wild-goose chase?

Standing in absolute blackness, Max began to feel that he was closed inside a coffin. Then he heard the coffee shop doors grating noisily on their hinges, and his claustrophobia was replaced by an even more elemental fear. Quietly, he stepped out of the archway into the arcade, the gun in his right hand.

A hundred feet away a man with a flashlight came out of the curved corridor that served the restaurant and gift shops. He kept the beam pointed at the floor ahead of him; behind it he, too, was in darkness.

Mustn't have come across the parking lot, Max thought. Lou hadn't blown the car horn. Must have sneaked between two buildings farther north along the harbor, and then down the boardwalk.

Max intended to wait until they were only fifty feet apart before ordering the killer to stop. Fifty feet would give him safety, room to maneuver. And if he's fifty feet from the corridor, Max thought, I'll have time to pull off a few good shots if the bastard tries to dodge out of sight.

Seventy feet now.

Sixty.

Fifty.

The killer spoke first, a hoarse, whispered: *"Max?"*

Shocked at being called by name, Max took one step into the darkness and asked, "Who's there?"

The man kept walking, hidden behind the light.

Forty feet.

"Who's there?" Max demanded.

Again, a forced whisper: *"It's me. Lou."*

Thirty feet.

Max lowered his gun. "Lou? For God's sake, it's only a few minutes past seven-thirty. We can't quit yet."

Lou said, still whispering, *"Trouble."*

Twenty feet.

"What trouble?" Max asked. "What do you mean?"

Ten feet.

Suddenly Max knew it wasn't Lou Pasternak.

The killer jerked the flashlight up, in the direction of Max's voice, temporarily blinding him.

Although for an instant he could see nothing, Max raised the gun and pulled the trigger. Once. Twice. The shots crashed like cannon fire in the huge, high-ceilinged room.

Simultaneous with the explosion, perhaps even a fraction of a second prior to it, the flashlight spun up and up, out to the right.

*I hit him!* Max thought.

Even before he completed the thought, the knife ripped into him, rammed out of the darkness and into him, felt like the blade of a shovel, enormous, devastating, so devastating that he dropped the gun, feeling pain like nothing he'd ever known, and he realized that the killer had pitched the flashlight aside as a diversion, hadn't really been hit at all, and the knife was withdrawn from him, and then shoved hard into him again, deep into his stomach, and he thought of Mary and his love for Mary and about how he was letting her down, and he grappled with the killer's head in the dark, got handfuls of short hair, but the bandage came off his finger and the cut was wrenched open again and he felt that pain separate from all the others, and he cursed the sharp edge on the car's jack, and the flashlight hit the floor ten feet away, spun around, cast lunatic shadows, and the knife ripped loose from him again, and he reached for the hand that held it, but he missed, and the blade got him a third time, explosive pain, and he staggered back, the man all over him, the blade plunging again, high this time, into his chest, and he realized that the only way he could hope to survive now was to play dead, so he fell, fell hard, and the man stumbled over him, and he heard the man's rapid breathing, and he lay very still, and the man went for the flashlight and came back and looked down at him, stood over him, kicked him in the ribs, and he wanted to cry out but didn't, didn't move and didn't breathe, even though he was screaming inside for breath, so the man turned away and went toward the arch, and then there were footsteps on the tower stairs, and, hearing them, he felt like such a useless ass, outsmarted, and he knew he wasn't going to be able to recover his gun and climb those stairs and rescue Mary because stuff like that was for the movies, pain was pulverizing him, he was leaking all over the floor, dripping like a squeezed fruit, but he told himself he had to try to help her and that he wasn't going to die, wasn't going to die, wasn't going to die, even though that was exactly what he seemed to be doing.

She stood up when the shots were fired. She went to the head of the tower stairs, and within a minute she heard footsteps.

"Max?"

No answer.

"Max?"

Just footsteps coming up.

She backed away from the stairs, across the observation deck, until her buttocks encountered the low wall.

*Wicka-wicka-wicka!*

Marie Sanzini.

She saw Marie's face, and she knew it.

Rochelle Drake. She knew Rochelle, too.

Erika Larsson. That was the name of the fuzzy-haired blonde—the delicate, ethereal woman who had been in the vision in the mirror at Lou's place.

Mary had known them all along, but she had forced the knowledge into her subconscious. If she cared to pursue it, the answer was there now, waiting. But she still didn't want to face the truth. *Couldn't* face it.

She reminded herself of her announced determination to find her own strength, her own solutions to the problems of life. Defeated already? But she couldn't shame herself; right now, she would accept perpetual weakness and dependence and continued ignorance of the past for a chance to get out of here.

From the stairwell: the slow ascent of footsteps.

"No," she said desperately. She pressed back against the low wall, eyes fixed on the entrance to the stairs. "I don't want to know." Her voice was high, tremulous. "Oh, God. No. Please!"

Lightning slashed the sky, sharp and bright. Thunder cracked. At last the storm broke: scattered pellets of rain testing the earth; then a sudden downpour; stinging, eroding sheets of water slanting in from the ocean.

The wind drove the rain under the overhang of the belfry roof. Fat droplets pummeled the back of her leather coat, soaking her long black hair. But she didn't care if she got wet. The only thing that worried her now was the past, for it kept coming back to her against her will:

*The living room of Berton Mitchell's cottage. Windows with paper blinds drawn almost to the sills. Lacy curtains. The only light, gray light, filtering in from a cloudy afternoon. Shadowy corners. Pale yellow walls. A dark brown davenport with a pair of matching, overstuffed chairs. Pine floor, rag-twist rugs.*

*A six-year-old girl lying on the floor. Long dark hair tied into two ponytails with orange ribbons. Beige dress with Kelly-green piping and buttons. Me. The little girl is me. On my back. Dazed. Confused. The side of my face hurts real bad. And the back of my head. What did he do to me? My legs are spread. I can't move them. Each of my ankles is tied securely to a different foot of a bulky armchair. My arms are stretched out behind me. My wrists are tied to the feet of another chair. Can't move. Try to raise my head to look around. Can't.*

*Maybe Mrs. Mitchell will come untie me. No. She's gone away. Visiting relatives with Barry. Mr. Mitchell is off someplace trimming hedges.*

*Scared. So scared.*

*Footsteps . . . Just him. Nothing frightening. Just him. But what's he want? What's he doing?*

*He kneels beside me. He has a pillow in his hands . . . big feather pillow . . . he shoves it . . . in my face . . . presses down on it. This isn't a good game . . . not good at all. This is wrong . . . scary. No light . . . no air . . . I scream . . . but the pillow muffles my voice. Try to breathe . . . can't draw in anything but linen. I thrash in my bonds. Daddy, help me! And then he pulls the pillow away. He's giggling. I gulp air and start to cry. He rams the pillow into my face again. I twist my head, can't get out from under. I bite and chew the pillow. Spinning. Dizzy. Weightless. Dying. Hollering in my mind for Daddy, thinking oh-so-hard of him, knowing he can't hear me. And then the pillow is taken away again; cool, delicious air rushes over my face, into my hot lungs. And the pillow is jammed onto me again. And in the final moment before I faint it's removed. Repeatedly reprieved on the verge of suffocation, I reach the thin red line between sanity and madness. And he's giggling as he tortures me. But finally he lifts the pillow and tosses it aside, finished with the game.*

*But there are worse games to come:*

*He takes my head in both hands . . . his fingers like iron claws. The ache at the back of my skull is getting infinitely worse . . . unbearable. He forces my head to one side . . . descends upon me . . . breathes across my face . . . hissing like a snake . . . moves toward my exposed neck . . . lips on my neck now . . . he takes a pinch of my skin between his teeth, bites hard, bites it off, swallows. I cry out at the sharp little pain . . . struggle . . . the cords bind. He puts his mouth to the tiny wound in my neck . . . sucks . . . draws blood. And when he finally raises his head and lets go of me . . . and I turn . . . I see him grinning, blood smeared around his mouth and streaks of blood on his teeth.*

*He is only nine years old, three years older than me, but his face is carved with a very adult hatred.*

*Weeping, choking, I say, "What are you doing?"*

*He leans even closer, inches from my face. His breath is fetid, corrupted by my own blood.*

*"I am a demon and a vampire," Alan says. There is a childish tone of make-believe in his voice. Yet he is also serious. "I like the taste of blood."*

Mary said, "Ahhhh," as if she had opened an enormous heavy door after many hours of strenuous effort.

And a flashlight beam swung back and forth at the head of the tower stairs.

And Alan walked onto the observation deck.

And he centered the light on her, but not in her eyes.

And they stared at each other.

And finally he grinned and said, "Hello, Sis."

* * *

*I am still spread-eagled on the floor.*

*Alan returns . . . wearing gloves . . . carrying a wooden box with a wire lid. He reaches through a spring trap in the lid . . . clutches something, withdraws it . . . a small dark creature, its head thrust out of the top of his fist . . . eyes luminous . . . a bat . . . a brown bat . . . one of those he found in the attic of the manor house. It doesn't appear to be scared of him . . . seems almost tame, not wild at all.*

*He isn't allowed to keep the bats as pets. They're dirty. Daddy told him to get rid of them.*

*He changes his grip on the beast, which flutters but is more docile than not . . . holds it with both hands . . . but lets the wings free.* Wicka-wicka-wicka! *He holds the bat above my head . . . six or eight inches from me . . . then slowly lowers it until the luminous eyes are staring directly into my eyes . . . until I beg to be released . . . beg him to take the bat away, put it in the box . . . until the membranous wings lightly brush me . . . until the wings strike my face with increasing force, with leathery flapping sounds,* Wicka-wicka-wicka!

When peals of thunder tolled over the harbor, Mary felt as if they were waves of some tangible substance passing through her; for deep within she shook sympathetically with each crash.

The past and present were two bottomless caverns of terror between which and above which she walked on a fine thread of self-control. She needed all of her attention and willpower to maintain her equilibrium as the memories swooped over her; she wasn't even able to speak to Alan; she couldn't find the strength to form words.

Without switching it off, Alan put his flashlight on the belfry floor, snug against the wall, where the rain hadn't dampened the boards. A rifle was slung from his left shoulder; he slipped the strap off his arm and put the gun down, too.

He still held the butcher knife.

He picked up the flashlight and pointed it toward the ceiling, into the hollow, cone-shaped roof. "Look, Mary. Look up. Go ahead. You should see this. Look!"

She looked—and tried to draw back from the sight. She was already pressed against the low wall; there was nowhere to run.

"They're not all here at the moment," Alan said. "Some have gone hunting, of course. But most of them stayed in tonight. They sensed the coming rain. See them, Mary? See the bats?"

*I am only six years old, and I am tied up, on the floor, my legs spread. Alan holds the bat with both hands. He moves it between my legs, under my dress. It squeals. I am sobbing, gasping for breath, pleading with him. Alan pushes my dress up immodestly. He's sweating. His face is pale. His lips quiver. He doesn't look like a nine-year-old boy; he is truly demonic.*

*The tips of the bat's wings tickle my bare thighs.*

*Tickle . . . then scratch painfully.*

*Although I am much too young to understand the more mysterious functions of my body, too young to imagine what pleasure and pain it will one day give me, I am engulfed by primal fear, overwhelmed by terror at the thought of the bat shoved against the exposed center of me. I find this much harder to bear than having the creature on my face, and I squirm and kick uselessly at Alan, and the wings beat in the cramped space between my spread legs, and then I feel what I most dread, for Alan has forced the bat against me, and the thing writhes and nips and claws and screeches shrilly against me, and Alan is trying to ram it inside of me, and I scream at the thought, spit, cry, and the bat is screeching, too, so Alan has great difficulty merely holding on to the thing, but he forces it against me with all of his strength, and suddenly a pain, a monstrous pain, shoots up through me—*

The memories were physical as well as mental agony. She had refused to face them for twenty-four years; and in that time they had acquired incredible power. They struck her as if they were a man's fists. She ached. She resisted the urge to vomit. Her legs were weak. She wept.

Alan put the flashlight on the floor again and shifted the knife from his left to his right hand.

Richard Lingard's knife.

Max had been right about that: no ghost had picked it up. She had refused to confront the truth, had been incapable of dealing with it; therefore, she'd convinced herself that the missing knife could be explained only as the work of supernatural forces.

"I killed Max," Alan said.

She knew that must be true, but she didn't want to consider it. The tears for that, the shattering grief would have to come later—if she lived long enough to grieve.

The observation deck was fifteen feet across. Less than three yards of wet pine flooring separated her from him.

He spoke softly, not much louder than the monotonous hiss of the rain. "I'm glad you came. It's time I finished what I started twenty-four years ago."

When asked where the killer was from, the Ouija board had said, THE AIR IS BEAUTIFUL. That wasn't a literal translation of "Bel Air," but it was close enough.

Why hadn't she seen that?

She hadn't wanted to see it.

At their feet the beam of the flashlight was diffused and cast back by the glossy paint on the deck wall, highlighting his chin and cheeks and nose. Because the rising light created odd shadows on his face, he was not handsome now; instead, he resembled one of the fright masks worn by a witch doctor in some savage ceremony. He held the knife in front of him, but he didn't come any closer.

"I *knew* you'd come tonight. We're so close, Mary. As close as two people can ever be. We share blood, but more than that, we share pain. I've dealt it out, and you've endured it. Pain binds us. Pain makes a far stronger cement than love does. Love is an abstract human concept, meaningless, nonexistent. But pain is real. I knew we were so close that I could communicate with you at a distance, without words. I knew I could make you come after me. Each day since Monday night I've meditated, put myself in a light trance. When my mind was clear, when I was relaxed, I tried to send thoughts to you, images of murders I intended to commit. I wanted to trigger your clairvoyant vision. And it worked, didn't it?"

He was a raving lunatic—and yet he had such a calm demeanor, spoke in such measured tones.

"Didn't it work, Mary?"

"Yes."

He was pleased. "I kept a watch on Lou's house, and when you showed up there, I knew you were after me."

An especially fierce gust of wind buffeted her, drove deafening blasts of torrential rain against the hollow roof.

He took one step toward her.

"Stop right there!" she said frantically.

He obeyed her. He hadn't decided suddenly to be merciful. And certainly he wasn't afraid of her. He stopped because he was willing, even eager, to see her cower before him and to kill her slowly.

If she played along with him, she would gain minutes of life, might even find a way to escape. "If you wanted to kill me, you could have done it Monday night at the motel, before Max returned."

"That was too easy. By making you pursue me, I had more fun."

"Fun? Killing is fun?"

"There's nothing like it."

"You're insane."

"No," he said serenely. "I'm just a hunter. And everybody else is a game animal. I was born to kill. It's my purpose. I've no doubt about that. I've been killing all my life. It started with the bugs."

She remembered: she was about four years old and Alan was seven; there was a praying mantis in a big glass jar; and Alan unscrewed the lid, squirted lighter fluid on the mantis, dropped a match into the jar.

For years he had gathered insects for the sole purpose of torturing them to death with chemicals, razor blades, pins, and fire.

She said, *"You* were the one who killed our cats and dogs."

"And all the other pets."

"Barry Mitchell had nothing to do with that."

He shrugged. "I got tired of the damned bugs."

He took a step toward her.

"Stop!"

He stopped, grinned.

That morning she had suggested to Max that evil was not always acquired, not always learned by example. Most educated people were convinced that, without exception, the motivations behind the anti-social acts of violent people had their roots in poverty, broken homes, childhood traumas, parental neglect or parental ineptitude. Sociologists insisted criminals were spawned primarily by social systems founded on injustice. Most psychologists appeared secure in the belief that any neurosis or psychosis could be explained in terms of Freudian or Jungian theory. But was it possible that some people were rotten from the start, hopelessly corrupt before environment had an opportunity to affect them? Was that a reactionary, medieval thought? She'd read a great deal about the XYY-man, the genetically ordained criminal type that had inspired so much scientific research over the past few years. Some people might be born less civilized than most—for chemical or genetic reasons that no one fully understood.

That was a dangerous theory. It could be misinterpreted. Every racist group would point to every hated minority as evidence of genetic inferiority. In fact, if there *were* people who were born to do evil, they were evenly distributed among all races, religions, sexes, and nationalities.

Born evil . . .

A bad seed . . .

She looked at Alan and knew that's what he was: a very special creature, both more and less than human.

A bat darted in from the rain, swooped into the hollow roof with a leathery flutter of wings that made her gasp and cringe.

*Wicka-wicka-wicka!*

"I wanted to meet you here at Kimball's," Alan said, "because neither of the other towers had bats in them. I thought they'd help you remember what happened twenty-four years ago."

*—and Alan takes the bat from between her legs, and it is dead, its neck is broken, soaked with her blood as well as its own, and she hurts so bad, and Alan tosses the dead bat into the box from which he got it, and he turns back to her, and she is unable to scream*

*anymore, unable to resist, drained of strength and will, and he begins
to pound her with his fists, blows landing on her stomach and chest
and neck and face, a flurry of small fists driving her down into darkness
. . . and when she comes to a short while later, he is standing over
her with a knife he's gotten from the Mitchells' kitchen, and he brings
it down, into her arm, then her side, the knife, Oh, God, the knife!*

Clean thrusts. In and right out again. Clean, quick thrusts. No
ripping. No tearing. No long, ugly gashes.

Max explored the dimensions of the bleeding holes with his hands
and figured there wasn't any danger of his intestines sliding out of him
through an enormous jagged rent in his flesh.

He supposed he should be thankful for that.

He was losing a lot of blood. His clothes were gluey, his hands
sticky, the floor stained with a warm and spreading puddle. But in the
dark it probably felt like a lot more blood than it really was. It felt
like *quarts!*

After resting only a few seconds, before the sound of footsteps
ascending the tower stairs faded away, he got up on his hands and
knees.

The four punctures in his chest and stomach throbbed wildly, incessantly. He choked on the pain. He felt as if a knife still protruded
from each wound.

There was no special agony when he drew his breath. Neither of
his lungs had been damaged.

Another small blessing.

He crawled to the left, then to the right, dripping on the floor,
groping in the perfect blackness for the gun he had dropped. He found
it sooner than he'd expected.

He located the nearest wall, pressed one hand against it to steady
himself, and got to his feet in spite of the pain that slammed through
him like an endless series of electric shocks.

He couldn't possibly climb the tower stairs. He was barely able to
walk on level ground; the steep stairs would kill him. And if by some
miracle he *did* reach the observation deck, he would make so much
noise in the ascent that the killer would be waiting for him; he'd be
blown away the instant he achieved the top step.

The only thing he could do was go for help. Back to the parking
lot. To the Mercedes. Fast as he could move. Let Lou know what had
happened.

Aware that every second wasted might count against Mary, he
pushed away from the wall. He staggered into the vast, dark room.
Although he was dizzy and slightly disoriented, he thought he knew
which way to go to find the corridor that served the coffee shop; but

in any event, he could do nothing but trust his instinct. Each step caused new bubbles of pain to burst in his guts. He felt as if he were walking miles, and he wondered if he were going in circles.

Just as despair began to grip him, he stumbled around a corner into a corridor that was less dark than the main hall of the arcade. Vague grayish light, the next thing to nonexistent, shimmered farther down the hall: light from the harbor boat parade, light shining through the coffee shop's exterior windows, bouncing around, then leaking thinly through the mullioned doors.

He walked down the corridor with his right hand on his stomach, as if trying to squeeze shut his wounds. He went through the coffee shop doors, between the tables, and fell to his knees at the window that looked out on the boardwalk and harbor. It was closed, and he didn't think he had the strength to lift it.

Love is strength, he told himself. Find strength in your love for Mary. What would you have or be without her? Nothing.

Outside, lightning ripped open the sky again. The reflections of light from its electric blade shone through the window; and for an instant it seemed to turn to ice the rain that streamed down the glass.

In the cold rain Chief John Patmore stooped beside Lou Pasternak and turned him onto his back, used the flashlight to study his face and then his blood-sodden clothes. "Bergen got to him. He's been stabbed."

Holtzman said, "Is he dead?"

The chief felt for a pulse in one of the cool, limp wrists. "I think he is. But you'd better call an ambulance anyway. There might be others."

Holtzman ran back to the patrol car.

Only seven or eight feet of rain-slicked planks separated her from Alan.

She had to keep him talking. The moment he lost interest in the conversation, he'd use the butcher knife. Besides, even if she were going to die, there were things she still had to know.

"So Berton Mitchell never touched me," she said.

"Not even once."

"I sent an innocent man to prison."

Alan nodded, smiled, as if she'd merely told him that he was wearing a pretty shirt.

"I caused him to commit suicide," she said.

"Wish I could have seen him swinging."

"I disgraced his family."

Alan laughed.

"Why would I do that?" she asked. "Why would I tell them that he attacked me when it was actually you?"

Alan said, "You were in the intensive care unit at the hospital for four days. When the crisis passed and you no longer needed the support machines, they transferred you to a private room."

"I remember."

"Father and I virtually lived there for two weeks. Even Mother crawled out of her bottle to visit every couple days. I played the concerned big brother, oh-so-attentive for a nine-year-old boy."

"The nurses thought you were cute," she said.

"There were lots of times when I was alone with you in that hospital room. Sometimes just for minutes, sometimes for as much as an hour."

Another bat flew in from the storm and settled in the rafters overhead.

Alan said, "Your lips and gums were so badly swollen and full of stitches that you couldn't talk for eight days—but you could *listen*. You were conscious most of the time. And when I was alone with you, I told you over and over again what I would do to you if you dared to expose me. I told you I'd come after you with the bats again . . . let them tear you apart." He was leering at her. "I told you I'd force you to eat the bats alive, that I'd make you bite off their heads and swallow if you told on me. I warned you that you'd better put all the blame on Berton Mitchell—or else."

She was shaking. She had to get control of herself, had to be prepared to move fast if she was given an opportunity to escape. However, the tremors continued, no matter how hard she tried to still them.

Alan said, "Then a funny thing happened. You told them it was Mitchell who did it to you—but you *believed* it. I'd achieved more than I thought. I'd gotten way down in you, way down where it counts, and I'd worked a little magic. You actually came to believe it *was* Berton Mitchell. You couldn't accept the truth, couldn't tolerate living in the same house with me after what I'd done to you, so you convinced yourself that I hadn't done anything at all, that I was your friend and that the bogeyman was someone else."

"Why?" she asked weakly. "Why did you hurt me?"

"I meant to kill you. I thought you were dead when I left the cottage."

"Why did you want to kill me?"

"It was fun."

"That's all? Just because it was 'fun'?"

"I hated you," he said.

"What had I done?"

"Nothing."

"Then why did you hate me?"

"I hate everyone."

696 ◆ DEAN KOONTZ

Lightning.

A gust of wind.

"You killed Mitchell's family."

"Seemed like a good idea, wiping out an entire family."

"Why? Was that 'fun,' too?"

"You should have seen the house burn."

"God Almighty, you were only fourteen then."

"That's old enough to kill," he said. "Don't forget, I tried to kill you five years before that. And when I thought you were dead . . . when I pulled the knife out of you for the last time . . . oh, Mary, you can't know how that felt! So natural. Like it wasn't my first kill at all. Like I'd stabbed people to death a thousand times before. And I was only nine!"

He stepped closer.

His shoes squished on the wet floor.

Desperately she said, "You killed Patty Spooner, too. Didn't you, Alan?"

"She was a bitch."

"No. She was sweet."

"A rotten bitch."

"Why did you defile the altar?"

The question clearly intrigued him. "Killing Patty in that church . . . was so different . . . so special. I knew that night that I truly *was* a demon and a vampire. I realized I was meant to destroy anything holy, anything good."

"You killed Marie Sanzini."

"And her three roommates."

"At one time, you loved Marie."

"No. I only dated her."

"Why would you want to kill her?"

"Why not?" he asked.

"You murdered Rochelle Drake."

"Don't tell me I loved her, too."

"You once said you did."

"I lied. I love no one."

"Why did you kill the beautician and his wife?"

"They were in my way."

A ship's horn blared across the water.

"You murdered Erika Larsson . . . and now you're going to kill the queen of the Christmas boat parade."

He glanced at the lighted vessels cruising slowly through the winter rain. "The storm will have driven her off the deck. I'll have to take her some other time."

"But what is she to you?"

"Don't you know who's queen? Jenny Canning."

"Ah, not her. She's good. So gentle. She mustn't die."

"She's just the most recent of my bitches. She's game like all the others." He was getting weary; he looked at the blade in his hand and licked his lips.

"Your women always leave you," Mary said.

"Or I leave them."

"Why can't you hold one?"

"Sex," he said. "Tenderness is a bore. They all want me to be tender. I can only manage it for a few weeks or months."

"What do you mean?"

"I like sex rough," he said, his voice almost a growl. "The rougher the better. After a while, when the novelty of a new body . . . a new girl . . . wears off, then the only way I can come is when I hurt them. And that turns them off . . . that and the other thing."

"What other thing?" she asked.

"They won't let me drink their blood."

She stared, shocked.

He said, "Now and then I like to have sex . . . and drink their blood."

"You cut them?"

"No, no. Menstrual blood."

Shocked, she closed her eyes.

Heard him move.

Opened her eyes!

He took two quick steps and was less than the length of the knife from her.

Max rolled from the yard-high windowsill onto the boardwalk, and the short fall seemed like twenty miles. In his mind, at least, he tumbled over and over. For a long moment after he fell, floating in a sea of pain, he considered the appealing, beckoning emptiness that welled up inside of him. Then he thought about Mary and about transforming love into physical strength. Somehow he smothered the pain and clambered to his feet.

The pistol was still in his left hand. It felt impossibly heavy. He tried to drop it, but he wasn't able to let go. His paralytic fingers were hooked tightly, immovably around the butt.

He swayed and looked at the line of decorated boats gliding through the rain and thought how pretty they were—and suddenly realized that he wasn't here to watch the parade. Silently cursing himself, he lumbered along the boardwalk. Each shaky step he took was an adventure ten times greater than the one before it; and each yard of ground he covered was a triumph.

On all sides of him, the night pumped in and out, in and out like the muscles of a heart.

He turned the corner of the pavilion and saw that no more than a hundred feet away two men were coming behind flashlights.

Lou and who else?

He tried to shout.

He had no voice.

Alan's eyes seemed to have light *behind* them. They were blue eyes like hers, but a peculiar and piercing blue. Eyes like the blade of the knife in his hand—sharp, cold, deadly.

"How many people have you killed?"

He didn't answer.

He raised his left hand. He put his icy fingertips against her temple, felt the pulse thumping there. He slid his fingers down, traced the delicate line of her jaw, then raised them and touched her lips.

Trembling, she said, "You've killed more than thirty-five, haven't you?"

"How'd you know that?"

"If you killed so many over the years," she said, "why didn't I go after you before this?"

"You were asked to work on some of the murders I committed," Alan said, "but you refused. I advised you to turn down all of those cases, and you listened to me. I think you suspected the truth, but you hid it from yourself."

"You tried to murder me when I was six years old. So why have you waited twenty-four years to try again?"

"Oh, I originally intended to get you a few months after you were released from the hospital. I figured I'd have to wait that long to allay suspicions. But then I was going to knock you off in a carefully planned accident."

His fingertips gently stroked her brows.

He said, "I thought of throwing you down a long flight of stairs and then saying you tripped and fell. But I finally settled on drowning you in the swimming pool."

"Why didn't you?"

"By the time I could safely go after you again, you'd begun to exhibit psychic powers. You fascinated me. I wanted to see what would happen to you next."

She said, "If Max is dead, I'll need your help again. I'll need you to guide me through the visions."

He laughed. "Darling, I'm not naïve."

"Do you think I'd turn you in to the police? I haven't told them about you for twenty-four years. Why would I now?"

"Then, you didn't know," he said. "But now you do."

He put his hand on her breast.

She flinched.

"My lovely little sister," he said.

"Don't."

Carrying a flashlight in his left hand and a revolver in his right, his shoulders drawn up in an unsuccessful attempt to keep the cold rain off the back of his neck, Rudy Holtzman accompanied the chief along the side of the pavilion.

Patmore stopped suddenly.

"What's the matter?" Holtzman asked nervously. He was very keyed up.

"There's a man ahead."

Holtzman raised his flashlight.

A man was approaching them, no more than fifty feet away.

"It's Bergen," Patmore said.

Bergen was staggering like a drunk.

"He's got a gun!" Patmore said.

Remembering Erika Larsson's viciously mutilated body, remembering the blood splashed everywhere inside her house, remembering Lou Pasternak on the macadam parking lot, Holtzman raised his service revolver and fired.

Max Bergen was flung backward by the impact of the bullet.

Alan pressed against her. He put his left hand around her throat.

She told herself to resist, to fight back. She was strong, not weak. A weak person would have sought escape in madness twenty-four years ago. But she was strong; she had hung on to her sanity and had developed psychic abilities as a way to keep herself alive. She should be able to find the will to fight him now.

He held the blade to her cheek as if branding her, the point below her right eye.

"I wonder," he said, "if you were blind, could you still see your clairvoyant visions?"

She snapped. Abruptly, violently, her fear vanished in an explosion of anger and hatred far more intense than any emotion she'd ever known. Twenty-four years of hidden, festering hatred went off like a bomb in her subconscious. She despised him. Loathed him. He wasn't fit to live. Never had been. Never would be. All she wanted was a chance to hurt him as badly as he had hurt her. She didn't even care any longer whether she lived or died. She wanted only to get him down, tie him down, torture him, hurt him, cut him, choke him, beat him, see him cry. She wanted most of all to put the bats on him, to rub them in his face, make them claw and bite, force them into his mouth while they were squirming and still alive—

Overhead two dozen bats began to scream in the darkness: a shrill chorus of tiny voices.

Startled, Alan looked up.

A single bat swept down, hooked its claws into Alan's coat collar. It fluttered wildly at his neck.

She couldn't believe what she had done.

Alan let go of her, reached behind him, grabbed the animal. He struggled with it, finally tore it loose and pitched it away from him.

His hand was bleeding.

In the past few days, every time she'd had a vision in which the killer's face began to be revealed as Alan's, she had chased away the truth by distracting herself with poltergeists. She had been responsible for the glass dogs careening around Dr. Cauvel's office; the pistol floating in air; the sea gulls at The Laughing Dolphin Restaurant; inanimate objects flying this way and that in Lou's bathroom. Max had been right.

Now she would use the bats.

Another one flew down and clung to Alan's face.

He screamed. Ripped it away. Dropped the knife.

Blood streamed from his forehead into his eyes.

Chittering, beating the air furiously with their wings, three more bats attacked him. One tangled in his hair. The other two fixed themselves to his throat.

"Kill him," she said.

Flailing at himself, Alan turned away from her. He weaved across the platform toward the stairs.

Every bat in the rafters descended upon him. They tore at his head and face and neck, clawed his hands, bit his fingers and hung on and wouldn't be shaken loose. When he screamed, one of them got into his mouth.

He stumbled down the tower stairs, bouncing from wall to wall.

She picked up the flashlight and followed him.

The bats stayed with Alan. If anything, their cries grew louder, angrier.

Five steps down he fell, rolled to the next landing, got up, went on, plucked a bat from his nose, tried to shield his eyes with one arm, fell again, couldn't keep from screaming, had to bite another bat that crawled from his chin into his mouth, had to spit out part of it, gagged, choked, stumbled, leaped from the final flight of stairs into the dark arcade and collapsed.

She walked out of the archway and stood over him.

He was very still.

One by one the bats rose from the body, circled, and flew back up the stairwell to the belfry.

# AFTER...

◆ ◆ ◆